ROSIE'S WAR

Rosie Gardiner is ashamed of the vain and cocky girl she used to be – it brought her nothing but trouble. Now she's a single mum, raising her daughter, Hope, while trying to give the gossips a wide berth – they'd give their ration books to know who fathered the child. Meanwhile the Blitz may be over and Hitler on the run, but that hasn't stopped him launching his secret weapon on London's jaded citizens. Rosie's father wants to take Hope away from danger, but little does Rosie know he has his own reasons for clearing off. For Rosie, trouble never seems very far away...

ROSIE'S WAR

ROSIE'S WAR

by

Kay Brellend

Magna Large Print Books
Long Preston, North Yorkshire,
BD23 4ND, England.

British Library Cataloguing in Publication Data.

A catalogue record of this book is
available from the British Library

ISBN   978-0-7505-4334-7

First published in Great Britain in 2016 by Harper,
an imprint of HarperCollins*Publishers*

Cover illustration © Elisabeth Ansley by arrangement with
Arcangel Images Ltd.

Kay Brellend asserts the moral right to be identified as the author of
this work.

Published in Large Print 2017 by arrangement with
HarperCollins Publishers Ltd.

Magna Large Print is an imprint of Library Magna Books Ltd.

Printed and bound in Great Britain by
T.J. (International) Ltd., Cornwall, PL28 8RW

ACKNOWLEDGEMENTS

Angela Raby for her absorbing book
The Forgotten Service, detailing the wartime work
of the London Auxiliary Ambulance Service,
1939–1945.

This book is dedicated to all the unsung heroes who served in the London Auxiliary Ambulance Service (LAAS) during the Second World War.

Equally for the volunteers who served in other cities during the conflict.

Not forgotten.

Also, for Mum and Dad.

PROLOGUE

Doctor's Surgery, Shoreditch, October 1941

'My mum died young so I'm a bit worried … in case I've got the same disease.' The young woman sat down on the edge of the hard-backed chair. 'Mum was only thirty-three when she passed away.'

'You look a lot younger than that and as fit as a fiddle, my dear.' The doctor raised his wiry grey eyebrows, peering over his spectacles at the exceptionally pretty young woman settling a handbag on her lap. Her platinum hair was in crisp waves and her sea-blue eyes were bright with nervousness. She was nicely dressed and he guessed she had a good job keeping her in such style. He was more used to seeing women with careworn faces, and toddlers on their scruffy skirts, perching nervously at the other side of his desk.

Rosie Gardiner wasn't sure whether Dr Vernon's casual dismissal of her concerns had cheered her or left her feeling more anxious. She'd not yet turned twenty and had a healthy glow from a brisk walk on a blustery autumn day. Or the flush could be a fever. In Rosie's opinion the least he could do was stick a thermometer in her mouth to check her temperature instead of just sitting there tapping his pen on a blotter. Feeling exasperated by his silence she added, 'It's hard dragging myself

13

out of bed some mornings. Then I spend an hour bending over the privy out back being sick. It's not like me to feel too rough to go to work 'cos I like my job at the Windmill Theatre.'

'Mmm...' Dr Vernon cast a glance at the young woman's bare fingers. In wartime women sometimes pawned their jewellery to buy essentials. An absence of an engagement ring didn't necessarily mean that the lass hadn't given her fiancé a passionate send-off to the front line, getting herself into trouble in the process.

'Putting on weight?' Dr Vernon asked.

'Not really ... no appetite ... so I don't eat much.'

'Monthlies on time?'

Rosie blushed, wondering why he was asking personal questions like that when she was frantically worried she had the cancer that had put her mother in an early grave. Prudence Gardiner had seemed to be recovering from an operation to remove a tumour but then pleurisy had finished her off. But Rosie had only spotted a little bit of blood instead of proper monthlies.

'You look to be blooming, my dear ... might you be pregnant?'

'No ... I might not!' Rosie spluttered. 'I'm not married or even got a sweetheart. I've never even wanted to...'

'Right... I'd better examine you then if there have been no intimate relations to cause trouble.' Dr Vernon got up from his chair, gesturing for Rosie to stand also; 'Abdominal fullness, you say, with sickness...' The muttered comment emerged as he got into position to prod at her with his fingers.

Rosie stayed in her chair, the colour in her complexion fading away. *Intimate relations...* The phrase hammered in her head and she felt stupid for not having made the connection herself about why her body seemed horribly different. But there had been nothing intimate about that one brutal encounter with a man she'd despised. Rosie's mind wanted to flinch from the memory but she forced herself to concentrate on the man who'd attacked her all those months ago. Lenny and his father had been her dad's associates. They'd worked together churning out bottles of rotgut, much to Rosie's disgust. But what had disgusted her even more was Lenny's attention. She'd made it plain she'd no intention of going out with him but he wouldn't take no for an answer. They'd attended the same school, their fathers were friends and Lenny thought that gave him the right to pester her for dates and then call her names when she turned him down. Rosie had hated her father getting involved in crime and had nagged him to break up his illegal booze racket but she hadn't let on that his association with Lenny was a prime reason for her wanting him to go straight. At that time, she'd been a proud independent woman: a Windmill Girl, and Windmill Girls were able to look after themselves, whether fending off catty theatre colleagues, or randy servicemen lying in wait at the stage door. With youthful arrogance she'd believed she could deal with Lenny herself.

Then one night Rosie had met him by chance in the East End when she was feeling a bit the worse for wear. She'd discovered in just a few vicious minutes that she wasn't as sassy as she'd thought; she certainly hadn't been as strong as

15

Lenny, though she'd fought like a maniac to try and stop him.

'Ah...' Dr Vernon had seen her stricken look and turned back towards his desk. 'You've remembered an incident, have you, and think there might be reason to count the months after all?'

'Yes...' she whispered. 'But I'm praying you're wrong, Doctor.'

He smiled kindly. 'I understand. But better to incubate a life than an illness, my dear.'

Rosie thought about that one. The odd weight she'd sensed in her belly was not a nasty growth in the way she'd thought; but it could destroy her life. 'If you're right – and I pray to God you're not – I think I'd sooner be dead than have his baby,' she whispered.

CHAPTER ONE

February 1942

'Well done, dear ... good girl ... just one more big push. Come on, you can do it...'

Rosie knew that the midwife was being kind and helpful but she just wanted to bawl at her to go away and leave her alone. She had no energy left to whisper a word let alone shout a torrent of abuse. She didn't want to push, she didn't want the horrible creature fighting for life in her hips but she knew the agony wouldn't stop unless she did something... She raised her forehead from the sweat-soaked pillow, dragging her shoulders off the rubber sheeting to grip Nurse Johnson's outstretched hands. Rosie clung on to the two sturdy palms as tightly as she might have to a piece of driftwood in a raging sea, and gritting her teeth she bore down.

'What're you planning on calling her?'

The whispered question emerged tentatively as though the man anticipated a tongue-lashing. And he got it.

'Calling her?' Rosie dredged up a weak laugh from her aching abdomen. 'How about bastard ... that should suit. Now go away and leave me alone.' Rosie turned her pale face to the wall and groaned, drawing up her knees beneath a thin blood-streaked sheet.

The fellow hesitated, then tiptoed about the bed. He knew the poor cow had been driven mad with pain because he'd heard her shrieking even above the din of the wireless. When things had quietened down overhead he'd guessed the worst was over. Then he'd spied the dragon barging down the hall, uniform crackling. As soon as she had disappeared into the front room with a bucket of stuff to burn he'd crept upstairs while the coast was clear.

'What do you think you're doing?' Trudy Johnson burst into the back bedroom and glared at the intruder; childbirth was nothing to do with men, in her opinion. They might put the bun in the oven but should stay well out of the way at the business end of things. The midwife had been disposing of soiled wadding in the parlour fire while waiting for her patient to enter the final

17

stage of labour. But she'd heard voices and speeded up the stairs to see what was going on.

'I've every right to be here.' John Gardiner sounded huffy. 'She's me daughter and that there's me granddaughter.' He pointed at the swaddled bundle at the foot of the bed. The infant was emitting mewling squeaks while punching feet and fists into her straitjacket. He almost smiled. The poor little mite was unwanted but she was a fighter. John moved to pick up the newborn but the midwife advanced on him threateningly, fists on starched hips. He backed away, muttering, his hands plunged into his pockets.

'I think your daughter deserves some privacy, Mr Gardiner. I'll let you know when she's ready for a visit.'

Chastened, John trudged meekly onto the landing, then peeped around the bedroom door. 'Put the kettle on, shall I? Bet you'd like a cuppa, now it's all over, wouldn't you, dear?' He addressed the remark to his exhausted daughter but gave Nurse Johnson a wink when she raised an eyebrow at him.

'I'd be obliged if you'd make yourself scarce till it is over. But you can put the kettle on. I need some more hot water. Leave a full pot outside the door for me, please.'

Trudy looked at her patient as the door closed. The girl was fidgeting on the protective rubber sheet, making it squeak. The afterbirth was about to be expelled. After that it would be time to set about tidying up the new mum; Trudy hoped having a wash and a brush through her hair might give the poor thing a boost.

Rosie Deane didn't look more than nineteen and was as slender as a reed. She had battled to get the baby through her narrow hips and finally succeeded after a lengthy labour.

'Here ... have a cuddle ... she's fair like you...' The midwife placed the baby against Rosie's shoulder, hoping to distract the young woman from dwelling on her sore nether regions.

'Take her away from me. I don't want her.' Rosie's hands remained clenched beneath the sheets and she turned her face away from her first-born.

''Course you do; just got a bit of the blues, haven't you, love? Only natural after what you've been through. All new mums say never no more, then quickly forget about the rough side of it.' Trudy knew that to be true, but not from personal experience. She had no children, but she'd delivered hundreds of babies over more than a decade in midwifery. Some of the women on her rounds in Shoreditch seemed to knock out a kid a year, even into their forties. Mrs Riley, Irish and no stranger to her old man's fists, had borne fifteen children, twelve of them still alive, and eight of them still at home with her.

Trudy was about to say that the pelvis opened up more easily after a good stretching in a first labour in the hope of cheering up this new mum. Then she realised the remark would be insensitive. The girl's father had told her that Rosie's husband had been killed fighting overseas only months ago, so Trudy kept her lip buttoned. In time Rosie would probably remarry and go on to have a brood round her ankles. She was plainly an attractive girl, despite now looking limp and bedraggled after her ordeal.

'You've got a wonderful part of your husband here to cherish.' Trudy glanced at the child her patient was ignoring. She pushed lank fair hair from Rosie's eyes so she could get a better view of her baby. 'See, she's got her eyes open and is looking at you. She knows you're her mum all right...'

'I said take her away from me.' Rosie levered herself up on an elbow, grabbing at the child as though she might hurl her daughter to the newspaper-strewn floorboards. Instead she held the bundle out on rigidly extended arms. 'Take her ... give her away ... do what you like with her...' she sobbed, sinking down and turning her face into the pillow to dry her cheeks on the cotton.

'Come on, love; don't get tearful.' Trudy placed the baby back by the bed's wooden footboard then gave her hiccuping patient a brisk, soothing rub on the back. 'Just a few minutes more and we can give you a nice hot wash down. You're almost done now, you know.'

'Almost done?' Rosie echoed bitterly. 'I wish I was. It's all just starting for me, Nurse Johnson...'

CHAPTER TWO

'You don't mean that!'

'If the girl says that's what she wants to do, then that's what she wants to do,' Doris Bellamy stated bluntly. 'A mother knows what's best for her own child...'

'I'll deal with this,' John Gardiner rudely interrupted. Doris was his fiancée, and a decent woman. But she wasn't his daughter's mother, or his grandkids' nan, so he reckoned she could mind her own business and leave him to argue with Rosie over the nipper's future.

'You won't change my mind, Dad. I've already spoken to Nurse Johnson and she says there are plenty of people ready to give a baby a good home.'

'Does she now!' John exploded. 'Well, I know where that particular baby'll get a good home 'n' all. And it's right here!' He punched a forefinger at the ceiling. 'The little mite won't have to go nowhere. She's our own flesh and blood and I ain't treating her like she's rubbish to be dumped!'

'She's not just *our* flesh and blood, though, is she, Dad?' Rosie's voice quavered but she cleared her throat and soldiered determinedly on. 'She's tainted by *him*. I can't even bear to look at her in case I see his likeness in her.'

'Forget about him; he's long gone and can't hurt you no more.' John flicked some contemptuous fingers.

'It's all right for you!' Rosie was incensed at her father's attitude. 'You just want a pretty toy to show off for a few years till you're bored of teething and tantrums. You certainly won't want her around if she turns out anything like that swine.' Rosie forked agitated fingers into her blonde hair.

'I think you'd better take that remark back, miss!' John had leaped up, flinging off Doris's

21

restraining hand as she tried to drag him back down beside her on the sofa. 'How dare you accuse me of play-acting? It's you keeps chopping 'n' changing yer ideas, my gel.' John advanced on his daughter, finger wagging in emphasis. 'I offered at the time to put things right. Soon as we found out about your condition I said I'd stump up to sort it out. Wouldn't have it, though, would yer? Insisted you was having the baby and was prepared for all the gossip and hardship facing you as an unmarried mother.' He barked a laugh. 'Now you want to duck out without even giving it a try.'

'I said I'd have the kid, not that I'd give it a permanent home,' Rosie shouted. 'I've got to act before it's too late: once she gets to know us as her family it wouldn't be fair to send her away.'

'It ain't fair *anytime,* that's the point!' John roared.

'But ... I might never love her. I might even grow to hate her,' Rosie choked. 'That'd be wicked because she could have somebody doting on her. She's not got a clue who we are!' Rosie surged to her feet at the parlour table, knocking over her mug of tea in the process. Automatically she set about mopping up the spillage with her apron.

She couldn't deny that some of what her father had said was true. She'd not wanted an abortion; the talk of having something dug out of her had made her retch. The idea of enduring horrible pain and mess had been intolerable; now she knew that the natural way of things was pretty awful too.

Yet Nurse Johnson had been right when she'd

said the memory of the ordeal would fade; her daughter was only four weeks old yet already Rosie felt too harassed to dwell on the birth. She guessed every other new mum must feel the same way. But she doubted many of those women were as bitter as she was, and her father, much as he wanted to help, was just making things worse.

'Cat got yer tongue, has it?' John was prowling to and fro in front of the unlit fireplace. 'You should be ashamed. And I ain't talking about what happened with Lenny. I know that weren't your fault.' After a dramatic pause he pointed at the pram. 'But if you abandon the little 'un you should hang your head, 'cos it should never have come to this.'

'I'm not a murderer,' Rosie muttered. 'I'm not a hypocrite either. Don't expect me to play happy families.' Attuned to her daughter's tiny snickers and snuffles Rosie glanced at the pram. It was an ancient Silver Cross model that her father had got off the rag-and-bone man for a couple of shillings.

He'd brought it home a month before the date of her confinement. The sight of it had shocked and frightened Rosie because up until then she'd shoved to the back of her mind how close she was to having Lenny's child. John had ignored his daughter's announcement that he'd wasted his time and money on the pram because the Welfare was getting the kid.

The creaking contraption had been bumped down the cellar stairs and John had toiled on it in his little workshop, as he called the underground room that doubled as their air-raid shelter. Screws had been tightened and springs oiled, then he'd

23

buffed the scratched coachwork and pitted chrome until they gleamed. At present John's labour of love was wedged behind the settee, with the hood up to give the baby a bit more protection from the chilly March air in the fireless room.

'She's gonna be as pretty as you, y'know.' Taking his daughter's silence as an encouraging sign, John tried a bit of flattery.

'Good looks don't make you happy,' Rosie stated bluntly. 'If you force me to keep her, none of us'll be content.' She didn't hate the child: the poor little thing was an innocent caught up in a vile web of violence and deceit.

'We'll make sure this is a happy place, dear.' John sensed his daughter was softening. 'No point in suffering like you did, then having nothing good to show for it in the end, is there?'

With a sigh, Rosie gathered up their tea things, loading them onto the tray ready to be carried into the kitchenette. She knew it was pointless trying to win over her father. It was always his way or nothing at all. But not this time. She had one final duty to perform before she slipped free of the yoke the poor little nameless mite had fastened around her neck.

She avoided her future stepmother's eye. Rosie knew that Doris had been watching her, pursed lipped, throughout the shouting match between father and daughter. The woman had resented being told to shut up and had sat in stony silence ever since.

'Nurse Johnson's due soon. She said after today it's time to sign us off home visits.' Rosie was halfway to the door with the tea tray before adding, 'I'm going to tell her to start things moving on the adoption.'

'If you ain't got the guts to look after her, I'll do it meself,' John sounded adamant. 'No granddaughter of mine's ending up with strangers, and that's the end of it.'

Doris leaped to her feet. 'Now just you hang on a minute there. Reckon I might have something to say about getting landed with kids at my age.' They'd recently spoken about getting married in the summer so Doris thought she'd every right to have a say.

'If you don't like it, you know where the door is.' John snapped his head at the exit.

Doris gawped at him, her expression indignant. 'Right then. Couldn't have made that plainer, could yer?' She snatched up her handbag, then marched over the threshold and into the hallway.

'Well, that was bloody daft.' A moment after the front door was slammed shut, Rosie sighed loudly. 'If Doris never speaks to you again it'll be your own fault, Dad.'

'Don't care.' John shrugged. 'There's only one person I'm interested in right now.' He kneeled on the sofa and peered over its threadbare back into the pram. The little girl was sleeping soundly, long fawn lashes curled against translucent pearl-spotted skin. A soft fringe of fluffy fair hair framed her forehead and her tiny upturned nose and rosebud mouth looked as perfectly delicate as painted porcelain.

John stretched out a finger to stroke a silky pink cheek before pulling the blanket up to the infant's pointed chin. 'Don't know you're born, do you, little angel? But I won't let you down,' he promised his granddaughter in a voice wobbling with emotion.

'You're just feeling guilty,' Rosie accused, although she felt quite moved by her father's melodramatic performance. But what she'd said about him feeling guilty had hit the spot. And they both knew it. A moment later John flung himself past her and the cellar door was crashed shut as he sought sanctuary in his underground den.

Rosie placed the tea tray back on the table. For a moment she stood there, leaning against the wood, the knuckles of her gripping fingers turning white. The baby started to whimper and she automatically went to her. Seated on the sofa she reached a hand backwards to the handle, rocking the pram and avoiding looking at the infant, her chin cupped in a palm. Within a few minutes the room was again quiet. Rosie stood up, drawing her cardigan sleeves down her goose-pimpled arms. She took off her pinafore and folded it, then looked in the coal scuttle, unnecessarily as she knew it would be empty.

It was a cold unwelcoming house for a visitor but it didn't matter that her father was too thrifty to light the fire till the evening. When Nurse Johnson turned up Rosie intended to say quickly what she had to, then get rid of her so she might start planning her future.

She wandered to the window, peering through the nets for a sighting of the midwife pedalling down the road. It had been many months since she'd hurried from Dr Vernon's surgery to huddle, crying, in a nearby alleyway. She'd been terrified that day of going home and telling her father the dreadful news that she was almost certainly pregnant, yet he'd taken it better than she had herself. But now, at last, Rosie felt almost content because the prospect of returning to something akin to her old life seemed within her grasp.

Under a year ago she'd been working as a show-girl at the Windmill Theatre. Virtually every waking hour had been crammed with glamour and excitement. She'd enjoyed her job and the companionship of her colleagues, despite the rivalry, but she couldn't go back there. Her body was different now. Her breasts had lost their pert youthfulness and her belly and hips were flabby. Besides, Rosie felt that chapter of her life had closed and a new one was opening up. Whether she'd wanted to or not, she'd grown up. The teenage vamp who'd revelled in having lavish compliments while flirting with the servicemen who flocked to the shows, no longer existed. Wistfully Rosie acknowledged that she'd not had a chance to kiss goodbye to that sunny side of her character. That choice, and her virginity, had been brutally stolen from her by Lenny, damn the bastard to hell...

But once her daughter was adopted Rosie knew she'd find work again, and she wanted her own place. Her father's future wife resented her being around and Rosie knew she'd probably feel the same if she were in Doris's shoes.

Suddenly she snapped out of her daydream, having spotted Nurse Johnson's dark cap at the end of the Street. Rosie let the curtain fall and pulled the pram out from behind the sofa so the midwife could examine the baby. Although she was expecting it, the ratatat startled her. Rosie brushed herself down then quickly went to open the door, praying that her father wouldn't re-appear to embarrass her by making snide comments.

Half an hour later the examinations were over and Rosie was sitting comfortably in the front parlour with the midwife.

'She's a beautiful child but would benefit from breast milk rather than a bottle, Mrs Deane. She might put on a bit more weight.'

Rosie smiled weakly; she hated people calling her by the wrong name. Her father and Doris had persuaded her to pass herself off as a war widow to stop tongues wagging. But that hadn't worked: the old biddies were still having a field day at her expense. Rosie had chosen to use her mother's maiden name as her pretend married name. She cleared her throat. 'What we spoke about last time, Nurse Johnson...'

Trudy Johnson put down her pen on the chart she'd been filling in. 'You still want to have her adopted?' she prompted when Rosie seemed stuck for words.

'I do ... yes...'

'Why? You seem to be coping well, and you have your father's support.'

'I'm not married,' Rosie blurted, although she was sure the midwife had already guessed the truth. 'That is ... I'm not widowed either... I've never had a husband.'

Trudy sat back in the chair. It wasn't surprising news, but Rosie's honesty had taken her aback.

Families who were frightened of ostracism often came up with non-existent husbands to prevent a daughter's shame tainting them all. And now it was clearer why the baby still hadn't been named. Much of the falsehood surrounding illegitimate births unravelled when awkward questions were asked at the registry office.

'I guessed perhaps that might be the case.'

'You don't know the ins and outs of it all.' Rosie bristled at the older woman's tone. 'Nobody does except me and Dad.'

Trudy Johnson could have barked a laugh at that. Instead she put away her notes in the satchel at her feet. At least this young woman had had the guts to go through with it, whereas lots of desperate girls allowed a backstreet butcher to rip at their insides. She had been approached herself over the years by more than one distraught family to terminate a 'problem' for them. Trudy had always refused to abort a woman's baby but it didn't stop them going elsewhere. And, to Trudy's knowledge, at least two of those youngsters had ended up in the cemetery because of it.

'Your situation's more common than you think.' Again Trudy's tone was brisk. 'Unlike you, though, I've seen some poor souls turfed out onto the streets with their babies. Your father is keeping a roof over your heads.'

'It's the least he can do, considering...' Rosie bit her lip; she'd said enough. Besides, she didn't want to get sidetracked from the important task of finding her daughter a new home.

Trudy stood up, buckling her mac, and gazed into the pram. The baby was awake. She'd been

29

just five pounds at birth and was struggling to put on weight. Arms and legs barely bigger than Trudy's thumbs were quivering and jerking, and just a hint of a smile was lifting a corner of the little girl's mouth. It was probably wind but Trudy tickled the adorable infant under the chin.

'I want her adopted,' Rosie stated firmly. 'And I want it done soon, before she gets attached to us.'

'If you're sure that's what you want to do, then I'll have her. I've never been married but I've always wanted a child.' Trudy sent Rosie a sideways smile. 'I almost got married when I was seventeen but...' She shrugged. Her memories of Tony were too precious to share. She even avoided talking about her dead lover with her elderly parents. They'd liked him, and had mourned his passing almost as much as she had herself.

'I see ... sorry...' Rosie finally murmured, recovering from her shock. On reflection she realised that the child would probably get no better care than from someone with Nurse Johnson's skills. 'Will having a baby interfere with your work?' Rosie didn't think that the midwife would leave a tiny baby for long periods of time, yet neither did she expect the woman would pack in her vocation just like that.

'I share shifts with other nurses and know a good nursery,' Nurse Johnson explained.

'I'm not sure...' Rosie felt awkward. She didn't want to upset Nurse Johnson but her intention had always been that her baby be taken into a family where she could be mothered properly. Then in the evenings the woman's doting husband would come home from work to coo over his new daughter. 'I'll think about it and I'd better let Dad know, too,' Rosie said slowly, avoiding the older woman's eye.

'Of course...' Trudy withdrew her hand from the pram. It wasn't the first time that she'd attempted to foster a child only to be shunned because of her age and spinster status.

'Did your sweetheart ever get married?' Rosie blurted, keen to change the subject.

'He lost his life in the Great War. He was too young to join up, but he went anyway. Lots did. He was killed at Ypres, still eighteen. I've grown old without him.'

'You met nobody else?' Rosie asked, saddened but still inquisitive.

'I'd have liked to find somebody, but so many young fellows of my generation are still in Flanders, aren't they?' Nurse Johnson's expression turned rather severe, as though she regretted betraying her feelings. 'Does your father agree with your plan for adoption?'

'It's up to me to decide what's best for her,' Rosie blurted. 'He doesn't like the gossip going round, in any case.'

'Neighbours chinwagging?' Nurse Johnson asked with a slight smile.

'They've been told I'm Mrs Deane, too, but they're not green. I did go away and live with my aunt in Walthamstow for a few months, so I could say I'd had a whirlwind wedding before he bought it overseas.' She smiled. 'I've already had a run-in with Mrs Price; I don't suppose it'll be the last time.' She frowned. 'I'm going to find work that

31

takes me away somewhere. Then I can start afresh and Dad'll marry his fiancée...' Rosie glanced at the midwife. She was not a bad sort. She'd not turned sniffy on knowing the baby was illegitimate. Neither had she gone off in a huff when her offer to take the baby hadn't been snapped up. 'I think you'd make a good mum,' Rosie said kindly. 'Good enough for me, anyhow,' she added on impulse.

'You mean ... shall I start to make arrangements for myself then?' Trudy's eyes had lit up, her voice shrill with emotion.

'I'm glad it's you.' Rosie sounded more enthusiastic than she felt. 'I only want the best for her, you know.'

'I know you do, dear.' Nurse Johnson stood up and Rosie did too. They took a step towards one another though they might embrace but instead shook hands just as the baby started to cry.

'She takes her bottle without any trouble,' Rosie informed the midwife quickly. She'd never wanted to feel a soft pink cheek against her naked breast and the baby gazing up at her with steady, inquisitive eyes.

Rosie glanced down and noticed that her clothing was wet.

'You'll need to bind yourself up, dear.' Trudy nodded at the damp patches on Rosie's bodice.

'I know ... it's a right nuisance.' Rosie frowned, grabbed the pinafore and put it on again, hiding the stains on her blouse. 'How long will it all take ... the adoption?'

'You're sure you don't want to think about it for longer?' Trudy felt conscience-bound to ask although she prayed Rosie wouldn't back out now when she was considering Angela as a lovely name for such a blonde cherub.

Rosie nodded vigorously. 'I'd offer you tea, but I've a pile of ironing to do.' There were only two of her father's shirts and one of her blouses in the basket, but Rosie wanted the woman gone. She felt a strange raging emotion within that was making her want to sink to her knees and scream. She guessed her conscience was troubling her but she mustn't let it. Her father might accuse her of being selfish and heartless, but she truly wanted the best for her daughter.

'It's all right ... I've got to get on too.' Trudy realised that the young woman wanted to be on her own now. With a surreptitious look of longing at the baby, she gathered up her things and followed Rosie towards the front door.

CHAPTER THREE

'Gone has she, the interfering old bag?'

Her father must have been waiting for the midwife to leave. He'd emerged from the cellar almost before Rosie had shut the front door, having seen the woman out,

'Yes, she has ... but you've no need to speak about her like that. She's all right, is Nurse Johnson.' Rosie knew that crossed-armed, jaw-jutting stance of her father's meant another row was in the offing. He was likely to hit the roof when he found out what arrangements she'd made, and spit out a few more choice names for the nice nurse.

'Go and see if little 'un's all right, shall I?'

'She's fast asleep; I've only just come out of the bloody front room and you know it,' Rosie retorted in response to his cantankerous sarcasm.

'How long are we going to keep calling the poor little mite "she"? Getting a name, is she, before her first birthday?' John continued sourly.

His barbs were starting to get on Rosie's nerves but she reined in her temper. They had a serious conversation in front of them and she'd as soon get it over with. 'Come and sit down in the kitchen, Dad. There's something I've got to tell you.'

Rosie took her father's elbow and, surprisingly, he allowed her to steer him along the passage.

'Let's wet our whistles.' Rosie began filling the kettle, hoping to keep things calm if not harmonious between them.

John pulled out a stick-back chair at the kitchen table and was about to sit down when he hesitated and glanced up at the ceiling. Rosie had heard it too: the unmistakable sound of aeroplane engines moving closer.

'Must be some of ours,' Rosie said, putting the kettle on the gas stove and sticking a lit match beneath it.

There'd been no warning siren and the afternoon was late but still light. The Luftwaffe mostly came over under cover of darkness. Since the Blitz petered out last May, German bombing had thankfully become sporadic and Londoners – especially East Enders who'd borne the brunt of the pounding – had been able to relax a bit.

John peered out of the window, then, frowning, he opened the back door and stepped out, head tipped up as he sauntered along the garden path. His mouth suddenly fell agape in a mixture of shock and fear and he pelted back towards the house, shouting.

But the sirens had belatedly begun to wail, cutting off his warning of an air raid.

Rosie let the crockery crash back to the draining board on hearing the eerie sound and sprang to the back door to hurry her father inside. Before John could reach the house a short whistle preceded an explosion in a neighbour's garden, sending him to the ground, crucified on the concrete at the side of the privy.

Crouching on the threshold, arms covering her head in instinctive protection, Rosie could hear her father groaning just yards away. She'd begun to unfold to rush to him when debilitating terror hit her. She sank back, shaking and whimpering, biting down ferociously on her lower lip to try to still her chattering teeth. Tasting and smelling the metallic coppery blood on her tongue increased the horrific images spinning inside her head. She rammed her fists against her eyes but she couldn't shut out the carnage she'd witnessed in the Café de Paris a year ago. Her nostrils were again filled with the sickly stench of blood, and her mind seemed to echo with the sounds of wretched people battling for their final moments of life. Some had called in vain for loved ones ... or the release of death. Limbless bodies and staring sightless eyes had been everywhere, tripping her up as she'd fled to the street, smothered in choking dust. For months afterwards she'd felt dreadfully ashamed that she'd instinctively charged to safety rather than staying to comfort some of those poor souls.

'Rosie... can you hear me...?'

Her father's croaking finally penetrated Rosie's torment and she scrambled forward, uncaring of glass and wood splinters tearing into her hands and knees. She raked her eyes over him for injuries, noting his bloodied shin, although something else was nagging at her that refused to be dragged to the forefront of her mind.

'Think me leg's had it,' John cried as his daughter bent over him.

Rosie was darting fearful looks at the sky in case a second attack was imminent. The bomber had disappeared from view, but another could follow at any moment and drop its lethal load. Obliquely Rosie was aware of neighbours shouting hysterically in the street as they ran for the shelters, but she had to focus on her father and how she could get him to safety in their cellar.

'Take my arm, Dad ... you must!' she cried as he tried to curl into a protective ball on hearing another engine. Thank goodness this aeroplane, now overhead, was a British Spitfire on the tail of the Dornier. 'Come on ... we can make it ... one of ours is after that damned Kraut.' Rosie felt boosted by the fighter avenging them and murmured a little prayer for the pilot's safety as well as their own. But then her attention was fully occupied in getting her father to cooperate in standing up. He was slowly conquering his fear and

36

squirming to a seated position with her assistance.

Regaining her strength, she half-lifted him, her arm and leg muscles in agony and feeling as though they were tearing from their anchoring bones. Gritting her teeth, she managed to get both herself and her father upright. With her arm about his waist she dragged him, limping, into the kitchen. John Gardiner wasn't a big man; he was short and wiry but heavy for a girl weighing under eight stone to manhandle.

Slowly and awkwardly they descended the stairs to the cellar, crashing onto the musky floor two steps from the bottom when Rosie's strength gave out. John gave a shriek of pain as he landed awkwardly, attempting to break his daughter's fall while protecting his injured limb.

Rosie scrambled up in the dark, dank space and lit the lamp, then crouched down in front of her father to inspect him. The explosion had left his clothes in rags. Gingerly she lifted the ribbons of his trouser leg to expose the damage beneath. His shin was grazed and bloody and without a doubt broken. The bump beneath the flesh showed the bone was close to penetrating the skin's surface.

Her father's ashen features were screwed up in agony and Rosie noticed tears squeezing between his stubby lashes. She soothed him as he suddenly bellowed in pain.

'Soon as it's over I'll go and get you help,'she vowed. 'We'll be all right, Dad, we always are, aren't we?' She desperately wanted to believe what she was saying.

Rosie thumped the heel of her hand on her forehead to beat out the tormenting memories of the Café de Paris bombing. It seemed a very long while ago that she'd gone out with two of her friends from the Windmill Theatre for a jolly time drinking and dancing to 'Snakehip' Johnson's band, and the night had ended in a tragedy. Three of them had entered the Café de Paris in high spirits but only two of them had got out alive.

Rosie forced the memories out of her mind. She sprang up and dragged one of the mattresses, kept there for use in the night-time air raids, closer to her father, then helped him roll off the floor and on to it to make him more comfortable. There was some bedding, too, and she unfolded a blanket and settled it over him, then placed a pillow beneath his head.

Sinking down beside her father, Rosie pressed her quaking torso against her knees, her arms over her head as the house rocked on its foundations. Another bomber must have evaded the Spitfire to shed its deadly cargo.

'We've taken a belting ... that's this place finished ... we'll need a new place to live,' John wheezed out between gasps of pain, his voice almost drowned out by the crashing of collapsing timbers and shattering glass. 'Come here, Rosie.' He held out his arms. 'If we're gonners I want to give you a last cuddle. Be brave, dear... I love you, y'know.'

They clung together, terrified, the smell of John's blood and sweaty fear mingling in Rosie's nostrils. After what seemed like an hour but was probably no more than a few minutes the dreadful sounds of destruction faded and the tension went out of John. Pulling free of his daughter's embrace he flopped back on the mattress, breathing hard.

'That's it over then, if we're lucky. Everything seemed all right while we still had this place.'

Rosie knew what her father meant. This had been the house her parents had lived in from when they were married, and it was Rosie's childhood home. Wincing as she picked a shard of glass from her knee, Rosie mentally reviewed their options. Doris lived in Hackney and she might let them stay with her until the housing department found them something. Then Rosie remembered the woman had stomped out, making it dear she wasn't getting landed with kids...

As though the memory drifted back through a fog in her mind Rosie realised that it wasn't just her and Dad any more. Her baby was upstairs. She'd saved her own skin and her father's, oblivious to the fact that there were three of them now. Her little girl was all alone and defenceless in the front room and she'd not even remembered her, let alone made an effort to protect her from the bombing.

Rosie pushed herself to her, feet. She stood for less than a second garnering energy and breath, then launched herself up the cellar steps, her hands and knees bloodied in the steep scramble as she lost her footing on the bricks in her insane haste. The door was open a few inches and she flew into it to run out but something had fallen at the other side, jamming it ajar. With a feral cry of fury Rosie barged her arm again and again into the door until it moved slightly and she could squeeze through the aperture. Frenziedly she kicked at the obstacles blocking her way.

Masonry from the shattered kitchen wall was

piled in the hallway but she bounded over it, falling to her knees as the debris underfoot shifted, then jumping back up immediately. She'd no need to fight her way into the front room. The door had fallen flat and taken the surround and some of the plaster with it.

Rosie burst in, her chest heaving. The top of the pram was covered in rubble and a part of the window frame, jagged with glass, lay on the hood.

Flinging off the broken timbers, she swept away debris with hands and forearms, uncaring of the glass fragments ripping into her flesh. Oozing blood became caked with dust, forming thick calluses on her palms.

Hot tears streamed wide tracks down her mucky face as finally she gazed into the pram. Very carefully she put down the hood, and removed the rain cover. She was alive! Rosie picked up her daughter, wrapped in her white shawl, and breathed in the baby's milky scent, burying her stained face against soft warm skin until the infant whimpered in protest at the vice-like embrace.

'Thank you, God ... oh, thank you...' Rosie keened over and over again as the white shawl turned pink in her cut hands. She bent over the tiny baby as though she would again absorb her daughter into herself to keep her safe. Her quaking fingers raced up and down the little limbs, checking for damage, but the infant's gurgling didn't seem to be prompted by pain.

'Let's go and find Granddad, shall we?' Rosie softly hiccuped against her daughter's downy head. 'Come on then, my darling. I'm so sorry; I swear I'll never ever leave you again.'

When she pushed open the cellar door Rosie found her father had crawled to the bottom step and was in the process of pulling himself up it. He choked on a sob as he saw them, flopping back down against the wall.

'I forgot about her, too,' he gasped through his tears. 'What sort of people are we to do something like that?' He shook his head in despair, wailing louder. 'It's my fault. I was too concerned about meself to even think about saving me granddaughter.'

'It's all right, Dad. She's fine, look...' Rosie anchored the baby against her shoulder in a firm grip, then descended as quickly as she could, hanging onto the handrail. 'Look, Dad!' she comforted her howling father. Gently she unwrapped the child to show her father that the baby was unharmed. 'We're not used to having her around yet ... that's all it is. No harm done. She's in better shape than us,' Rosie croaked. She felt a fraud for trying to make light of it when her heart was still thudding crazily with guilt and shame.

John blew his nose. For a long moment he simply stared at his granddaughter, then he turned his head. 'Can see now that you're right, Rosie,' he started gruffly. 'She'd be better off elsewhere. Let somebody else care for her, 'cos we ain't up to it, that's for sure.'

Somewhere in the distance was a muffled explosion, but neither John nor Rosie heeded it, both lost in their own thoughts. Rosie settled down on the mattress. Her lips traced her daughter's hairline, soothing the baby as she became restless. She placed the tiny bundle down beside

41

her and covered her in a blanket, tucking the sides in carefully.

John studied his wristwatch. 'Time for her bottle. I'll watch her if you want to go and get it.' Muffling moans of pain, he wriggled closer to peer at the baby's dust-smudged face. He took out from a pocket his screwed-up hanky.

'No! Don't use that, Dad. It's filthy; I'll wash her properly later ... when we go upstairs.' Rosie smiled to show her father she appreciated his concern. But she wasn't having him wiping her precious daughter's face with his snot rag.

'She's hungry,' John said, affronted by his daughter's telling off.

Rosie made to get up, then sank back down to the mattress again. 'Kitchen's blown to smith-ereens. Won't find the bottles or the milk powder; won't be able to wash her either, if the water's off.' She began unbuttoning her bodice. 'I'll feed her,' she said. Turning a shoulder to her father so as not to embarrass him, she helped the child to latch onto a nipple. Her breasts were rock hard with milk, hot and swollen, but she put up with the discomfort, biting her lip against the pain. She encouraged the baby to feed with tiny caresses until finally she stopped suckling and seemed to fall asleep with, a sated sigh.

'What you gonna call her?' John whispered. He had rolled over onto his side, away from mother and child to give them some privacy. His voice sounded different: high-pitched with pain still, but there was an underlying satisfaction in his tone.

Rosie smiled to herself, wondering how her

father knew she'd been thinking about names for her daughter. 'Hope...' she said on a hysterical giggle. 'Seems right so that's what I'm choosing. Hope this bloody war ends soon ... hope we get a place to live ... hope ... hope ... hope...'

'Hope the doctors sort me bloody leg out for us, I know that.' John joined in gruffly with the joke.

'You'll be right as rain with a peg leg... Long John Silver,' Rosie teased.

They both chuckled although John's laughter ended in a groan and he shifted position to ease his damaged limb.

In her mind Rosie knew she'd chosen her daughter's name for a different reason entirely from those she'd given. Her greatest hope was that her daughter would forgive her if she ever discovered that she'd abandoned her like that. The poor little mite could have suffocated to death if she'd not been uncovered in time. Or the weight of the shattered window frame on top of the pram might eventually have crushed the hood and her daughter's delicate skull. The idea that Hope might have suffered a painful death made bile rise in Rosie's throat. She closed her eyes and forced her thoughts to her other hope.

She hoped that Nurse Johnson would forgive her. The woman desperately wanted to be a mother, and Rosie had promised her that her dream would be real. Rosie sank back on the mattress beside Hope and curved a protective arm over her daughter as she slept, a trace of milk circling her mouth.

But Rosie had no intention of allowing anybody

to take her Hope away now. She'd do anything to keep her.

'Hear that Dad?'

'What ... love?' John's voice was barely audible.

'Bells ... ambulance or fire engine is on its way. You'll be in hospital soon,' she promised him. While she'd been cuddling her little girl she'd heard her father's groans although he'd been attempting to muffle the distressing sounds.

'Ain't going to hospital; they can patch me up here,' he wheezed.

'Don't be daft!' Rosie said but there was a levity in her tone that had been absent before. She couldn't be sure which of the services was racing to their aid and she didn't care. She was simply glad that somebody might turn up and know what to do if her father passed out from the pain that was making him gasp, because she hadn't got a clue,

'Anybody home?'

The shouted greeting sounded cheery and Rosie jumped up, clutching Hope to her chest. This time she emerged carefully into their wrecked hallway rather than plunging out as she had when in a mad scramble to rescue her daughter. A uniformed woman of about Doris's age was picking her way over the rubble in Rosie's direction.

'Well, you look right as ninepence,' the auxiliary said with a grin. 'So does the little 'un.' The woman nodded at Hope, now asleep in Rosie's arms. 'Can't say the same for the house though, looks like a bomb's hit it.' She snorted a chuckle.

Rosie found herself joining in, quite hysterically,

for a few seconds. 'Dad's in the cellar ... broken leg. He caught the blast in the back garden.'

'Righto ... let's take a shufti.' The woman's attitude had changed to one of brisk efficiency and she quickened her pace over the rubble.

Even when she heard her father protesting about being manhandled, Rosie left them to it downstairs. She had instinctively liked the ambulance auxiliary and she trusted the woman to know what she was doing. A moment later when she heard her father grunt an approximation of one of his chuckles Rosie relaxed, knowing the auxiliary had managed to find a joke to amuse him too. Stepping carefully over debris towards the splintered doorway she stopped short, not wanting to abandon her father completely by going outside even though the all clear was droning. She found a sound piece of wall and leaned back on it, rocking side to side, eyes closed and crooning a lullaby to Hope, who slept contentedly on, undisturbed by the pandemonium in the street.

CHAPTER FOUR

'My, oh my, look how she's grown. Only seems like yesterday little Hope was born.' Peg Price stepped away from the knot of women congregated by the kerb. They were all wearing a uniform of crossover apron in floral print with their hair bundled inside scarves knotted atop their heads. Peg ruffled the child's flaxen curls. 'She'll be on her feet soon, won't she, love?'

To a casual observer the meeting might have seemed friendly, but Rosie knew differently and wasn't having any of it. She attempted to barge past the weedy-looking woman blocking her way. But Peg Price was no pushover and stood her ground.

'Some of 'em are late starters,' another woman chipped in, eyeing the toddler sitting in her pram. 'Don't you worry, gel, kids do everything in their own sweet time.'

'I'm not worried about a thing, thanks.' Rosie gave a grim smile, attempting to manoeuvre around the trio of neighbours stationed in front of her. They were all aware that her daughter was walking because they spied over the fences and watched Hope playing in the back garden.

Even, after two years the local gossips hadn't given up on probing for a bit of muck to rake over. Rosie knew what really irked them was that she had so far managed to remain unbowed by their malice. She'd never crept about, embarrassed. She'd brazened out their snide remarks about her daughter's birth. And her father and Doris had done likewise.

After the Gardiners' home had been destroyed at the bottom end of the street the council had rehoused them in the same road, so they were still neighbours with the Price family.

'Coming up to her second birthday, by my reckoning.' Peg stepped into the road to foil Rosie's next attempt to evade her.

'She's turned two.' Rosie glared into a pair of spiteful eyes.

'Shame about yer 'usband, ain't it? Proud as punch, he'd be, of that little gel.' May Reed chucked the child under her rosy chin. ''Course, she'll ask about her daddy, so you'll be ready with some answers for the kid, eh, love?'

'Yeah, I've already thought of that, thanks all the same for your concern.' Rosie's sarcasm breezed over her shoulder as she moved on, ignoring May's yelp as the pram clouted her hip.

'Looks like you, don't she, Rosie? Just as well, ain't it?'

It wasn't the sly comment but Peg Price's tittering that brought Rosie swinging about. 'Yeah, she's just like me: blonde and pretty. Lucky, aren't I, to have a daughter like that? Jealous?' Rosie's jaunty taunt floated in her wake as she marched on.

It wasn't in Rosie's nature to be vindictive, but she was happy to give as good as she got where those three old cows were concerned. Over two years Peg and her cronies had done their best to browbeat her into admitting her baby was a bastard and she was ashamed of Hope. But she'd never been ashamed of Hope, even in those early days when she'd considered giving her away.

Everybody knew how to shut Peg Price up: rub the woman's nose in the fact that her only child was an ugly brat. If anybody was ashamed of their own flesh and blood it was Peg. Not only was Irene a spotty, sullen teenager, she had a reputation for chasing after boys.

'Conceited bleedin' madam, ain't yer?' Peg had caught up with Rosie and grabbed her arm. All pretence at geniality had vanished.

'Well, that's 'cos I've got something to be conceited about.' Rosie wrenched herself free of the woman's chapped fingers. 'Bet you wish your Irene could say the same, don't you?'

'What d'yer mean by that?' Peg snarled, shoving her cardigan sleeves up to her elbows in a threatening way. 'Come on, spit it out, so I can ram it back down yer throat.'

Rosie gave her a quizzical look. Peg's pals were enjoying the idea of a fight starting. May Reed had poked her tongue into the side of her cheek, her eyes alight with amusement as she waited expectantly for the first punch to be thrown.

'You don't want to let the likes of her talk to you like that, Peg.' May prodded her friend's shoulder when a tense silence lengthened and it seemed hostilities might flounder.

'At least your Irene's decent, unlike some I could mention.' Lou Rawlings snorted her two penn'orth. 'Widow, my eye! I reckon that's a bleedin' brass curtain ring.' She pointed a grimy fingernail at Rosie's hand, resting on the pram handle.

'Decent, is she, your Irene?' Rosie echoed, feigning surprise and ostentatiously twisting her late mother's thin gold band on her finger. 'Go ask Bobby West about that then ... 'cos I heard different, just yesterday.'

Rosie carried on up the road with abuse hurled after her. She already felt bad about opening her mouth and repeating what Doris had told her. Peg's daughter had been spotted behind the hut in the local rec with Bobby West.

Although they'd lived close for many years the gap in their ages meant Rosie and Irene had never

48

been friends. Previously they'd just exchanged a hello or a casual wave; once Irene found out who'd dropped her in it Rosie reckoned she'd get ignored ... or thumped by Irene. In a way she felt sorry for Peg's daughter. The poor girl had every reason to stomp about with her chops on her boots with that old dragon for a mother.

Lost in thought, Rosie almost walked straight past her house. They'd been rehoused for ages but the Dorniers had kept coming although their street had so far avoided further damage. She still headed automatically to her childhood home, further along. She found it upsetting to see the place in ruins so usually took a detour to avoid the bomb site it now was. She unlatched the wooden gate, fumbling in her handbag for her street door key. Glancing over a shoulder, Rosie noticed that trouble was on its way: Peg was marching in her direction with fat Lou and May flanking her. The unholy trinity, as her father called the local harridans, looked about to attack again before Rosie could make good her escape.

Rosie stuck her bag back under the cover of the pram then wheeled it about and set off along the road again. She was feeling so infuriated that, out-numbered or not, she felt she might just give Peg Price the scrap she was spoiling for. She wasn't running scared of them; but Rosie was keen to avoid upsetting her little girl.

Hope was sensitive to raised voices and a bad atmosphere. Just yesterday her daughter had whimpered when Rosie had given Doris a mouth-ful. Rosie didn't mind helping out with all the household chores, but she was damned if she was going to act as an unpaid skivvy for her new step-mother.

Since she'd moved in as Mrs Gardiner, Doris had made it clear she thought her husband's daughter had outstayed her welcome and she'd only tolerate Rosie's presence if she gained some benefit from it.

Rosie didn't see herself as a rival for John's affections, but Doris seemed to resent her nevertheless. Naturally, her father's second wife wanted to be the most important person in her husband's life. Unfortunately, John still acted as though his daughter and granddaughter had first claim on him. John and Doris weren't exactly newlyweds, having got married six months ago, but Rosie thought that the couple were entitled to some privacy.

'And so do I want some bloody privacy,' she muttered to herself now. She dearly wished to be able to afford a room for herself and Hope, but the cheapest furnished room she'd found was ten shillings a week, too dear for her pocket. So for now, they'd all have to try to muddle along as best they could. On fine days like today Rosie often walked for miles because the balmy June air was far nicer than the icy atmosphere she was likely to encounter indoors.

Now that her daughter was potty-trained Rosie felt ready to find Hope a place at a day nursery so she could get a job. Her father had never fully recovered his fitness after they'd been bombed out and Rosie wasn't sure he was up to the job of caring for a lively toddler, although he'd offered. Rosie didn't want to be beholden to her stepmother. Doris had a job serving in a bakery and was always complaining about feeling tired after being on her feet all day.

Rosie turned the corner towards Holborn, tilting her face up to the sun's golden warmth. It was late afternoon, but at this time of the year the heat and light lingered well into the evening. If John had prepared her tea he'd put the meal on the warming shelf for her to eat on her return.

'Hey ... is that you, Rosie Gardiner? Is it really you?'

Rosie was idly window-shopping by Gamages department store when she heard her name called. Pivoting about, she frowned at a brunette hurrying towards her bouncing a pram in front of her. She didn't recognise the woman, and assumed she'd been spotted by a forgotten face from schooldays.

'Don't remember me, do you? Bleedin' hell, Rosie! It's only been a few years!' The newcomer grinned, wobbling Rosie's arm to jolt an answer from her. 'I can't have changed that much.'

It was the young woman's rough dialect and unforgettably infectious smile that provided a due. The poor soul *had* changed; in a short space of time her acquaintance from the Windmill Theatre looked as though she'd aged ten years. If Rosie had relied on looks alone to jog her memory, she'd never have identified her. 'Oh ... of course I re-member you. It's Gertie... Gertie Grimes, isn't it?'

Gertie nodded, still smiling. Then she gave a grimace. 'It's all right, nobody from the old days recognises me. Look a state, don't I?' She sighed in resignation.

'No...' Rosie blurted, then bit her lip. There was

51

no point in lying. Gertie Grimes was nobody's fool, Rosie remembered, and wouldn't appreciate being treated as one. 'Been a bloody long war, Gertie, hasn't it?' she said sympathetically.

'Oh, yeah...' Gertie drawled wearily. 'And it ain't done yet.'

'There's an end in sight, though, now the troops have landed in Normandy.' Rosie gave the woman's arm a rub, sensing much had happened in Gertie's life since they'd last spoken to make her sound so bitter.

'Perhaps we'll be having a victory knees-up soon.' Gertie brightened. 'Come on, tell me all about it.' She nodded at the little girl spinning the beads threaded on elastic strung between the pram hood fixings. 'Beauty, she is; what's her name?' Gertie lifted Rosie's hand and saw the wedding ring. 'I suppose you married an army general to make me really jealous. I remember the top brass were always fighting over you at the Windmill. Could've had yer pick, couldn't you; all the girls envied you.'

'I was a bit of a show-off, wasn't I?' Rosie replied with a rueful smile. 'Her name's Hope; but you go first. I remember you had boys, but this isn't a boy.' Rosie tickled the cheek of the little girl with dark brown hair and her mother's eyes. The child looked to be a few months older than Hope and the two little girls were now leaning towards each other sideways, giggling, to clasp hands.

'Never got a chance to tell you I was pregnant, did I, 'cos I left soon as I found out?' It was a fib; Gertie had concealed her pregnancy for quite some time from everyone at work, and from her cuckolded husband. 'She's called Victoria and she's gone two and a half now.'

'Crikey, you've got your hands full, Gertie. I know you've got four sons, so a girl must've been a lovely surprise for you and your husband.'

Gertie frowned into the distance. None of what Rosie assumed was true. Gertie now had just two children alive and, far from being delighted about another baby, her husband had knocked her out cold when he found out he'd not fathered the child she was carrying. 'Got just the one boy now. Three of them was lost in a raid during the Blitz. Direct hit … happened before Vicky was born.'

'Oh … I'm so sorry,' Rosie gasped. The memory of almost losing Hope when their house was destroyed still tormented her. Her remorse over that day was a constant companion and she could see in Gertie's eyes that the woman was battling similar demons.

'Don't blame yourself,' Rosie said softly. 'I can't know how you feel, not really, so I won't say I do. But I nearly lost Hope so I know what it is to feel guilty.' She paused. 'She was nearly crushed to death in her pram on the day we got bombed out in Shoreditch. It was my fault, no getting away from it.' Rosie cleared the huskiness from her voice with a small cough. 'My dad had been injured in the back garden, you see, and I was so concerned about getting him indoors that I forgot all about my baby in the front room.' It was the first time Rosie had admitted to anybody what she'd done. Not even Doris knew what had

53

occurred that terrible afternoon.

'I still wake up at nights howling about the night my boys were killed. I feel so ashamed,' Gertie croaked. 'Least you was close enough to put things right before it was too late.' She sunk her chin to her chest. 'I wasn't there for them ... nor was me husband ... or me eldest boy. All out, we was, and Simon and Adam and Harry perished all alone in the house. Harry was just about the age Vicky is now. But it's the other two that I ache most for. Being older, they might've understood and been so frightened, the poor little loves.' Gertie swiped the heel of a hand over her cheeks. 'Please God they didn't suffer too much.'

Rosie put an arm about Gertie's shoulders and hugged her tight. 'They're at peace now, Gertie,' she soothed. 'You've done it so far, you can carry on a bit longer ... then a bit longer after that. That's what I told myself, when I felt like beating my head against the wall to punish myself.'

'The ambulance girls ... they fought like demons to keep my Harry alive. He was protected a bit by being in his pram, you see.' Gertie gulped back the lump in her throat. 'But they couldn't save him. One of the poor lasses was bawling almost as loud as me when they put the three bodies in the back of the ambulance.'

'Oh, Gertie, I'm so sorry...'

Gertie sniffed and blew her nose. 'Wanted to join the ambulance auxiliaries after that. Rufus wouldn't hear of it. But I went along for the interview anyhow.' Gertie looked crestfallen. 'Didn't pass the test, though. Best if you've got no young kids, they said, 'cos of the dangerous nature of the job.' Gertie grimaced. 'I told 'em about the dangerous nature of living in the East End. Didn't go down too well with the snooty cows.'

Rosie was impressed that Gertie had tried to join the auxiliaries. It seemed such a fitting thing to do in the circumstances. She remembered how efficiently the ambulance teams had got on with things when they'd been bombed out at home. At the time Rosie had been wrapped up in caring for her daughter and had happily allowed the auxiliaries to take over tending to her father. The middle-aged woman who'd patched him up, along with a younger female colleague, had almost carried him up the cellar stairs. Though the two of them looked like butter wouldn't melt, they'd come out with a few risque jokes to distract John while loading him into the back of a makeshift ambulance.

With bad grace Doris had offered Rosie and Hope a roof over their heads with her in Hackney until John came out of hospital and the Council re-housed them. None of the trouble they'd suffered though could compare with Gertie's suffering.

'What's your oldest lad's name?' Rosie asked 'Bet he's quite the young man now, isn't he?'

'Oh, Joey's cock of the walk, all right. Thirteen, he is, and giving me plenty of lip.' Gertie managed a tiny smile. 'Mind you, that one always did have too much to say for himself. Gets that off his dad.'

'I bet your husband dotes on his princess.' Rosie nodded at Victoria. 'My dad calls Hope his princess.' She gave her friend a smile. 'Best be getting off, I suppose ... be late for tea. Dad'll wonder where we are.' Rosie regretted drawing attention to her own circumstances; Gertie would wonder why she was referring to her father so much rather than to a husband.

'Fine reunion this has turned out to be,' Gertie's mumble held a hint of wry humour.

'Glad I bumped into you, Gertie,' Rosie said, glancing at her daughter, clapping hands with Victoria.

'Shall we meet up again?' Gertie looked at Rosie quite shyly as though anticipating a rebuff. 'The little 'uns seem to be getting along. We could take them for a stroll round a park another day. Perhaps have a picnic ... if you like.'

'I'd like that very much,' Rosie said enthusiastically. 'We can reminisce about old times. What a to-do that was about Olive Roberts. Who'd have thought it?'

'Never liked that woman,' Gertie's eyes narrowed as she reflected on the kiosk attendant at the Windmill Theatre who'd been unmasked as a dangerous Nazi sympathiser.

'Quite hair-raising, wasn't it?' A gleam of nostalgia lit Rosie's eyes. 'We saw some times there, didn't we? Good and bad.'

Gertie grunted agreement. 'I miss the old place,' she said. 'Funny thing is, when I was at work, I couldn't wait to finish a shift and get home to me boys, though they drove me up the wall. Now I'm home all the time I wish I'd got a job.'

'Now Hope's turned two I'm after a nursery place for her so I can get back to work.' Rosie tidied her daughter's fair hair with her fingers. 'I want to help bring this damned war to an end.'

'Not going back on stage?' Gertie asked.

'No fear.'

'Before you disappear, you must tell me about your other half.' Gertie teasingly prodded Rosie's arm.

'Tell you more when I see you next week,' Rosie replied, turning the pram about, ready to head back towards Shoreditch. 'How about Thursday afternoon at about three o'clock? We could meet right here outside Gamages...'

'Suits me; Rufus goes to a neighbour's to play cards on Thursdays.'

'Your husband back on leave, is he?' Rosie asked.

'Oh ... 'course, you wouldn't know that either. He's been invalided home from the army,' Gertie said briskly to conceal the wobble in her voice.

Rosie read from Gertie's fierce expression that the woman felt she'd suffered enough condolences for one day. 'See you Thursday then.' Rosie let off the brake on the pram.

The two women headed off in opposite directions, then both turned at the same time to wave before settling into their strides.

Rosie walked quickly, aware her dad would be wondering where she'd got to, but at the back of her mind was the conversation she'd had with Gertie about the ambulance auxiliaries. Rosie wanted to do a job that was vital to the war effort and in her book there was nothing more important than saving lives. So she reckoned she knew what employment she'd apply for. All she had to do was break it to her dad that she was going to volunteer for a position with the ambulance auxiliaries.

CHAPTER FIVE

'Long time no see, mate.'

John Gardiner almost dropped the mug of tea he'd been cradling in his palm. He'd opened the front door while carrying it, expecting to see his daughter on the step. He'd been about to say, 'What, forgot your key again, dear?' because Rosie had earlier in the week knocked him up when he'd been snoozing on the settee.

Instead his welcoming smile vanished and he half closed the door in the wonky-eyed fellow's face. It'd been a year since he'd caught sight of Frank Purves, and then they'd only nodded at one another from opposite pavements. On that occasion John had been tempted to hare across the road to throttle the man for having spawned a fiend. But, of course, he hadn't because that would have given the game away. And John would sooner die than cause his daughter any more trouble. He kept his welcome to a snarled, 'What the hell d'you want?'

'Well, that ain't a very nice greeting, is it?' Frank stuck his boot over the threshold to prevent John shutting him out. He stared at his old business partner although just one of his eyes was on the man's face and the other appeared to be studying the doorjamb. Popeye, as Frank was nicknamed, had never let his severe squint hold him back. 'Just come to see how you're doing, and tell you about a bit of easy money heading your way, John.'

'I told you years back that I ain't in that game no more, and I haven't changed me mind,' John craned his neck to spit, 'I've got a wife and family, and I don't want no trouble.'

'Yeah, heard you got married to Doris Bellamy. Remember her. All used to hang about together as kids, didn't we?' Frank cocked his head. 'Gonna ask me in fer a cuppa, then?' He nodded at the tea in John's unsteady hand. 'Any left in the pot, is there, mate? I'm spitting feathers 'ere...'

'No, there ain't.' John glanced to left and right as though fearing somebody might have spotted his visitor. 'Look ... I'm straight now and all settled down. Don't need no work.' As a last resort he waggled his bad leg at Frank. 'See ... got a gammy leg since we got bombed out up the other end of the road.'

'Yeah, heard about that, too.' Frank gave the injury a cursory glance. 'Thing is, John, that bad leg ain't gonna hold you back in your line of work, is it?' He shifted his weight forward. 'You owe me, as I recall, and I'm here to collect that favour.'

'Owe you?' John frowned, the colour fleeing from his complexion. Even so, he was confident that what he was thinking wasn't what Frank Purves was hinting at. John reckoned that Popeye couldn't know anything about that, 'cos if he did the vengeful bastard wouldn't be talking to him,

59

he'd be sticking a knife in his guts. Lenny's actions had started a feud between the Gardiners and the Purveses that Popeye knew nothing about. But one day he would and when that day came John wanted to get in first.

'When you chucked it all in you left me high 'n' dry with a pile of labels I'd run off. Never paid me for 'em, did yer? Plus I had a fair few irate customers waiting on that batch of gin.'

John's sigh of relief whistled through his teeth. He ferreted in a pocket and drew out some banknotes, thrusting them at Frank. 'There! Go on, piss off!'

Frank looked contemptuously at the two pounds before pocketing them. 'I'm in with some different people now. They're interested in you, John. I been singing your praises and telling 'em you're the best distiller in London. They ain't gonna like your attitude when they've stumped up handsomely to sample your wares.'

John's jaw dropped and he suddenly reddened in fury. 'You had no right to tell a fucking soul about me. I don't go blabbing me mouth off about you doing a bit of counterfeiting.'

'Yeah, well, needs must when the devil drives, eh?' Frank leaned in again. 'Lost me son, lost me little bomb lark business 'cos me employees crippled themselves. A one-armed short-arse and a fat bloke wot got nobbled in France. Ain't saying they aren't keen but, bleedin' hell, they're a fuckin' liability.' Frank finished his complaint on a tobacco-stained smile. 'Got nuthin' but me printing press to fall back on.' He glanced over a shoulder. 'Need a few extra clothing coupons, do you, mate?' He gave John a friendly dig in the ribs. 'That'll put you in the missus's good books. Get herself a new frock, can't she? Get herself two if she likes.'

'You forging coupons now?' John whispered, aghast.

'I'm forging all right, just like I was when I run off all them dodgy spirit labels for your hooch.' Frank's lips thinned over his brown teeth. 'We need to talk, mate ... seriously...'

John knew he'd never get rid of Popeye until he'd let him have his say. And he didn't want the neighbours seeing too much. Popeye lived the other side of Shoreditch but he had a certain notoriety due to his ducking and diving. Not that you'd think it to look at him: Popeye had the appearance, and the aroma, of a tramp. 'Just a couple of minutes; they'll all be in soon fer tea. Don't want no awkward questions being asked,' John snarled in frustration.

'Right y'are...' Frank said brightly and stepped into the hall.

John pointed at a chair under the parlour table by way of an invitation. He limped into the kitchen and quickly poured a cup of lukewarm tea with a shaking hand. 'There, get that down yer and say what you've got to.' John glanced nervously at the clock, dreading hearing his wife's or his daughter's key in the lock.

'Look at us,' Frank chirped, watching John fidgeting to ease his position. He pointed at his left eye. 'There's me with me squint and you with yer gammy leg.' He guffawed. 'Don't hold yer back, though, John, do it, if you don't let it?' He grinned wolfishly. 'Bet you still manage to show Doris yer love her, don't you? Bit of a knee trembler, is it, balancing on one leg on the mattress?' He winked. 'Gotta get yer weight on yer elbows.' Popeye leaned onto the tabletop to demonstrate, rocking back and forth on his seat. 'I've got meself a nice young lady works in the King and Tinker, name of Shirley.' He paused. 'Your daughter's called Rosemary, if I remember right. Heard you'd got a grandkid; so young Rosie's given up the stage, has she, and got married now?' Popeye paused to slurp tea.

'Fuck's sake, you got something to say, or not?' Agitatedly, John snatched Popeye's cup of tea off him. He'd been about to throw it down the sink but knew if he disappeared into another room, Popeye might decide to follow him. And he was desperate to get him out of the house, not further into it.

'So what's the nipper's name? Rosie call her after her mum, did she? Prudence, God rest her, would have liked that, wouldn't she, John?'

'Me granddaughter's name's Hope,' John ejected through his teeth. 'She's a lovely little darlin' and I don't want her coming back home and having you scare the bleedin' life out of her with yer ugly mug.' John grimaced at Popeye's dirty clothes and the greying stubble on his face.

Frank ran a hand around his chin, understanding John's look of disgust. 'My Shirley's always telling me to smarten up. Perhaps I should.'

'Sling yer hook before they all come in!' John had almost jumped out of his skin at the sound of next door's dustbin lid clattering home.

'Right, here's the deal.' Suddenly Popeye was deadly serious, mean eyes narrowed to slits. 'I know this outfit what's deep in with anything you like: dog tracks, bootlegging; pimps 'n' spivs, they are. Based over the docks–'

'I get the picture,' John interrupted, having heard enough. 'You're out of your league and you've promised 'em stuff you can't deliver. Ain't nuthin' to do with me, Popeye. I've paid you up. That's us quits.'

'It ain't me who's got to deliver on this occasion, it's you, mate. I've run 'em off a nice line of girly mags in the past and I've been doing their booze labels. Trouble is they've got no bottles of Scotch to stick 'em on. Their distiller got his still broken up by the revenue men a while back.'

'Well, let yer big mates buy him another one.' John hobbled to the door and held it open.

Popeye ignored the invitation to leave and sat back comfortably in his chair. ''Spect they would do that, but trouble is the fellow what knows how to use it's doing a five stretch. So I told 'em I knew how to help them out.'

'Right ... thanks for the offer of the work. But I ain't interested. Ain't even got me still now.'

'Now, I know you ain't destroyed it, John.' Popeye pulled an old-fashioned face, crooning, 'Don't you tell me no lies, now. Might not be down in the cellar ... where is it?' He jerked his head back, gazing at the ceiling. 'Attic? I reckon since you moved here you've stashed it away all neat and tidy, ain't yer?'

'I got rid of it when we was bombed out of the other place.'

'Don't believe you for one minute. It's here all right … somewhere…' Popeye glanced around thoughtfully as though he might set off in search of it.

'Get going; we're done here.' John yanked at Popeye's sleeve to shift him.

'Don't think so, mate.' Frank ripped his arm out of John's grasp. 'If you don't sing along they're gonna want their cash back, ain't they?'

'What?' John tottered back a step, apprehension stabbing at his guts. 'What fucking cash?'

'The cash they give me, to give to you.' Popeye shrugged. 'I told them you'd need an advance to buy stuff to get going so they give us a monkey up front.'

John licked his lips. Five hundred! That was a serious sum of money. 'Well, you'll just have to give it back, won't yer?'

'Can't … do … that…' Popeye warbled. 'Make me look like a right prat. Anyhow, I ain't got it.' He sniffed. 'Needed some readies meself so I had to use it to keep someone sweet. You know the old saying: rob Peter to pay Paul, but John's getting it in the end.' He gave a wink. 'You know I'm always good for my word. Never once not paid you up, have I?'

John swallowed noisily. 'Sounds like you've got some explaining to do then when they come looking for you.'

'Not me … you.' Popeye nodded slowly. 'This is where they'll head. You don't cross people like that, John. You should know that.'

'They come here looking fer me I'll call the Old Bill and tell 'em everything, especially that you've just tried to blackmail me to get involved in counterfeiting.'

Popeye came to his feet in quite a sprightly fashion considering he was over sixty and over-weight. 'Now, that ain't wise, talking like that, John. I'll pretend I never heard it.' Popeye walked up to the smaller man and eyeballed him as best he could, before strolling out into the hallway. 'Right ... be seeing you then. You come to me next time; only fair ... my turn to make the tea. Say, end of the week and we can make arrangements to put the still up in my basement if it's likely to cause ructions with your Doris. Give the missus my regards now, won't you?'

'Fuck off.' John slammed the door after Popeye and ground his teeth when he heard the faint laughter coming from the other side of the panels. He paced to and fro then went upstairs as quickly as his limp allowed. He found the steps in the airing cupboard and positioned them beneath the loft hatch. A few minutes later he poked his head into the cool, dark roof void, his heart thumping so hard he thought it might burst from his chest.

He'd promised Rosie on his life that he'd never make another drop of moonshine. Doris had no idea that he ever had run an illegal still. Nobody had known, other than his daughter and his business associates. Now Popeye had blabbed his business about, God only knew how many people were aware he'd once risked a spot of hard labour.

John hauled himself into the loft, wincing from the effort, and approached the dismantled still covered in tarpaulin. He crouched down and peered at the tubes and funnels and receptacles. Suddenly he smiled wryly. The contraption had survived the bombing, having been wedged in the corner of the cellar with a cover over it. Now he was wishing that the bloody thing had been in the loft of his old house, and been smashed to smithereens with the roof. But the hundred pounds in his Post Office book had come courtesy of this little beauty. And that money was being saved up for another little beauty, and one day she'd thank her granddad for buying her presents. John felt his eyes fill with tears as he put the hatch back in place. He'd do anything for his little Hope, and protect her with his life, if need be.

CHAPTER SIX

'Insult my Irene again, you bitch, and I'll wipe the floor with yer.'

Rosie spun about to see that Peg Price had sprinted down her front path to yell and jab a finger at her. The woman must have been loitering behind the curtains, waiting for her to return, Rosie realised. On the walk home her surprise meeting with Gertie, and everything they'd talked about, had been occupying her mind and she'd not given her run-in with her rotten neighbours another thought.

Rosie contemptuously flicked two fingers at the woman's pinched expression before pushing the pram over the threshold and closing the door behind her.

A savoury, aroma was wafting down the hall from the kitchen, making Rosie's stomach grumble.

'That you, Rosie?'

'Yeah. Sorry I'm late.' Rosie carried on unfastening Hope's reins, thinking her father had sounded odd. But she gave his mood little thought; she was too wrapped up in counting her blessings. And she was determined to work for the London Auxiliary Ambulance Service. If she got turned down, as Gertie had, she'd try again and again until she was accepted.

Rosie cast her mind back to the time when the female ambulance auxiliary had entered their bombed-out house and with a simple joke made her laugh, then tended to her father with brisk professionalism. Rosie had been impressed by the service, and the people in it. But her baby daughter had taken up all her time and energy then. Now Hope was older, toddling and talking, and Rosie had the time to be useful. She wanted her daughter to grow up in peacetime with plentiful food to eat and a bright future in front of her. Wishing for victory wasn't enough; she needed to pitch in and help bring it about, as other mothers had throughout the long years of the conflict.

From the moment Gertie had recounted how the ambulance crew had battled to save her baby's life, Rosie knew that's what she wanted to do ... just in case at some time the baby dug from beneath bomb rubble was her own.

John appeared in the parlour doorway wiping

his floury hands on a tea towel.

Lifting her daughter out of the pram, Rosie set Hope on her feet. The child toddled a few steps to be swept up into her granddad's arms.

'How's my princess?' John planted a kiss on the infant's soft warm cheek.

In answer Hope thrust her lower lip and nodded her fair head.

'See what Granddad's got in the biscuit tin, shall we, darlin'?'

Again Hope nodded solemnly.

'Don't feed her up or she won't eat her tea,' Rosie mildly protested, straightening the pram cover. She watched her father slowly hobbling away from her with Hope in his arms. Lots of times she'd been tempted to tell him not to carry her daughter in case he overbalanced and dropped her. But she never did. Hope was her father's pride and joy, and his salvation.

In the aftermath of the bombing raid, it had seemed that John's badly injured leg might have to be amputated. Sunk in self-pity, he'd talked of wanting to end it all, until his little grand-daughter had been taken to see him in hospital and had given him a gummy smile. At the time, Rosie had felt pity and exasperation for her father. In one breath she'd comforted him and in the next she'd reminded him he was luckier than those young servicemen who would never return home.

John carefully set Hope down by her toy box and started stacking washing-up in the bowl.

'You stewing on something, Dad?' Rosie asked. Her father was frowning into the sink and he would usually have made more of a fuss of Hope than that.

'Nah, just me leg giving me gyp, love.' John turned round, smiling. 'Talking of stew, that's what we've got. Not a lot in it other than some boiled bacon scraps and veg from the garden but I've made a few dumplings to fill us up.'

'Smells good, Dad,' Rosie praised. 'Sorry I didn't get home in time to give you a hand. We had a nice walk, though.'

''S'all right, love. Enjoy yerself?' John enquired, running a spoon, sticky with suet, under the tap. 'Anyhow, you can help now you're back. There's a few spuds in the colander under the sink. Peel 'em, will you?'

Having filled a pot with water, Rosie sat down at the scrubbed parlour table and began preparing potatoes while filling her dad in on where she'd been. 'First I went to the chemist and got your Beecham's Powders.' She pulled a small box from the pocket of her cardigan and put it on the table. Her dad relied on them for every ailment. 'Then I took a walk to Cheapside and bumped into an old friend from the Windmill Theatre—'

'You're not going back there to work!' John interrupted. 'If you want a job you can get yourself a respectable one now you're a mother.' He had spun round at the sink and cantankerously crossed his wet forearms over his chest.

'I don't even want to go back there to work, Dad,' Rosie protested. 'Gertie doesn't work there now either. She's got a little girl a bit older than Hope. The two kids had a go at having a chat.' Rosie smiled fondly at her daughter. 'Made a friend, didn't you, darling?'

'Gertie? Don't recall that name,' John muttered, and turned back to the washing-up.

Rosie frowned at his back, wondering what had got his goat while she'd been out. But she decided not to ask because she'd yet to break the news to him about the employment she was after and she wasn't sure how he'd take it.

'Gertie was one of the theatre's cleaners. She left the Windmill months before me.'

'Mmm ... well, that's all right then,' John mumbled, flicking suds from his hands. He felt rather ashamed that Popeye's visit had left him on edge, making him snappy.

'I am getting a job, though, Dad.'

'Ain't the work I'm objecting to, just the nature of it,' John muttered.

'You didn't mind the money I earned at the Windmill Theatre, though, did you?' Rosie reminded him drily, dropping potatoes in the pot.

'If you'd not been working at that place you'd never have got in with a bad crowd and got yourself in trouble,' John bawled. He pursed his lips in regret; the last thing he wanted to do was overreact and arouse his daughter's suspicions that something was wrong.

'I got into trouble because of the company *you* kept, not the company *I* kept,' Rosie stormed before she could stop herself. It was infuriating that her father still tried to ease his conscience by finding scapegoats. In Rosie's opinion it was time to leave the horrible episode behind now. They both adored Hope so something good *had* come out of bad in the end.

The slamming of the front door had John turning, tightlipped, back to the sink and Rosie lighting the gas under the potatoes.

'What's going on?' Sensing an atmosphere, Doris looked suspiciously from father to daughter.

'I was just telling Dad that I saw an old friend from the Windmill Theatre. The poor woman has had dreadful bad luck. A couple of years ago their house got hit and she lost three of her young sons.'

Doris crossed herself, muttering a prayer beneath her breath. 'She was lucky to get out herself then...'

'She was very lucky, and so was her husband and eldest boy,' Rosie said after a pause. She knew Doris could act pious, so she wasn't going to mention that the three children had died alone. Her stepmother would have something to say about neglect despite the fact that her own daughter-in-law and grandson rarely came to visit her because they were never invited

'Didn't realise it was bad news you got from your friend,' John said gruffly by way of apology. That terrible tale had momentarily edged his own worries from his mind.

Doris's sympathy was short-lived, however, and she was quick to change the subject. 'Just got caught outside by Peg Price; sounding off about you, she was.' Doris wagged an accusing finger.

Rosie shrugged, refusing to take the bait. Doris would always make it plain she felt burdened by the duty of sticking up for her.

'Saw somebody else with a long face.' Doris gazed at her reflection in the mantel mirror and started pushing the waves back in place in her faded brown hair. 'Nurse Johnson was in civvies down Petticoat Lane.' Doris looked at the little girl crouching on the floor. 'You'd think she'd pop in once in a while to see how Hope's getting on.'

'I expect she's too busy,' Rosie said succinctly. Doris enjoyed bringing to her attention that she'd caused enmity on several fronts.

Rosie hadn't spoken to her midwife since the day she'd broken the news about withdrawing from the adoption. At the time Rosie had thought that the woman seemed to take it quite well. Trudy had listened to her explanation, then said the sort of things that Rosie had been expecting to hear about being surprised and disappointed. Ever since, if they met out walking a brief nod was the most Rosie got from the woman. Rosie couldn't blame Trudy Johnson if she had felt bitter about what had happened.

'Going upstairs to put a brush through me hair before we have tea.'

Once his wife had gone out of the room John said, 'Didn't mean to snap earlier, Rosie; just that I worry about you, y'know, grown up though you are.' He pulled out a chair at the table and sank onto the seat. 'God knows we've had to cope with some troubles these past few years.'

'Not as much as some people, Dad,' Rosie said pointedly, to remind him of Gertie's catastrophe.

'I know ... I know ... but you're still my little girl, however old you are. And I won't never stop worrying about you and Hope s'long as I'm drawing breath.'

'You've no need to worry, Dad, I'm able to look after myself and Hope now.' After a short silence Rosie saw her father seemed to have gone into a trance, staring into space. 'What is it, Dad?' She sat down opposite him and rested her elbows on the tabletop. 'You seem odd … thoughtful. Something up?'

'Nah, just this leg getting me down,' John lied. He forced a smile. 'Wish you could meet a nice young man, dear.' He took Rosie's hands, in his. 'You need somebody to care for you, 'cos I ain't always going to be around. Robbie likes you, y'know, and he's not short of a bob or two … or a couple of pork chops.'

Rosie tutted in mock exasperation at her father's quip. Robbie Raynham was the local butcher, and at least fifteen years her senior. He was pleasant enough and not bad-looking but Rosie didn't like him in that way. She didn't like any man in that way. Rosie knew Doris often sent her to get their meat ration in the hope the smitten butcher might slip a little bit extra in for them in return for the promise of a date.

But Rosie didn't have any interest in marriage or men. Since she'd been dragged into an alleyway then thrown to the ground and raped, a cold dread had replaced any longing she'd once had for an exciting romance and a husband. Love and affection were saved for her daughter; all she wanted to do was keep Hope safe and make plans for her future.

Rosie took a deep breath and blurted, 'I'm going to apply to join the London Auxiliary Ambulance Service.'

John gawped at his daughter as though she were mad. 'Why?' he eventually asked.

'Because it's an important job needs doing.'

'Being a mother to that little girl's an important job needs doing,' John replied pithily. 'Ambulance work's too dangerous. You'll be covered in blood and muck.'

'I was covered in blood and muck when the Café de Paris got bombed and again on the afternoon our house was wrecked. I'm used to it now.'

John had the grace to blush as he recalled how she'd nursed him and dressed his wounds till they could get help on that dreadful afternoon.

'Dad, d'you remember how that auxiliary helped you that day?'

''Course...' John muttered. 'And I was grateful to her, but that don't mean I want you taking them sort of risks.' He pointed a finger. 'She were a lot older than you, for a start...'

'Her colleague who helped you up the stairs wasn't. And she was driving the ambulance, if you remember. She looked to be in her twenties, like me...'

'Don't want you doing it, Rosie...' John began shirtily.

'I'm going to apply,' Rosie said firmly. 'Hope'll be fine in a nursery. I'm going to the WVS tomorrow to see if they can sort out a place for her.'

'If you're determined, me 'n' Doris can see to the little 'un between us.' John sounded affronted.

'I'd like her to make some more friends,' Rosie answered diplomatically. 'She had a lovely time playing with Gertie's little girl.'

'Time enough fer that when she's older. I'll

mind her.' John sounded stubborn. He'd always been very protective of his granddaughter but suddenly after Popeye's visit it seemed more important than ever to keep a close watch on Hope.

'It's time for me to get my own place, too, Dad. Now you and Doris are married you deserve some privacy. Besides, I need to learn to stand on my own two feet. So as soon as I'm earning I'll be able to pay rent.' Rosie had been planning on saving that blow for another day. But as her father had seemed to accept her work, albeit reluctantly, she had decided that 'in for a penny, in for a pound' might be the best approach.

'Leaving home and standing on your own two feet backfired on you once before.' John pressed his lips into a thin line. He'd not wanted to hark back to that episode. 'Anyhow, people my age don't need a lot of fuss. Ain't as if me and Doris are starry-eyed. Known each other too long for any of that.' John coughed, recalling Popeye's dirty talk.

'Still, it'd be nice for you both to have some peace and quiet.' Rosie understood her father's unease about discussing intimate things.

'I know kids have tantrums, so that don't bother me one bit. I brought you up, remember,' he added darkly.

Rosie smiled faintly. Her stepmother wasn't happy about losing her sleep. The woman had let Rosie know she'd been kept awake by Hope crying as she'd barged out of the bathroom that morning.

Suddenly Rosie was missing her mum with such strong sadness that she felt momentarily unable to speak. Prudence Gardiner had passed away when she was in junior school but Rosie could recall her vividly. She could also remember that her mother's affair hadn't lasted, but the bitterness between John and Prudence had. He'd taken her back ... *for the girl's sake* ... the words stuck in Rosie's mind as the reason he'd bawled at his wife when she'd shown up again, suitcase in hand. Rosie knew that Prudence would have adored her beautiful granddaughter. Had her mother still been alive perhaps Hope might have succeeded in doing what Rosie had yearned to do but had failed at: bring her parents some shared happiness.

She glanced, at her father's lined face, feeling a rush of pity that his second wife was unlikely to bring him any more contentment than his first had. 'I'm grateful that you've taken care of me and Hope till now. But I'll cope on my own, Dad.'

'You won't!' John's anxiety had manifested itself in anger. 'You're staying right here where I can keep an eye on you both.'

'Might be that yer daughter's got a point about being independent and paying her own way,' Doris said, entering the kitchen. 'And as your wife, you might like to ask me my opinion on things that concern me.'

Rosie knew that Doris was thoroughly in favour of her moving out, and the sooner the better.

'Stew's done.' John turned his back on his wife, stooping to open the oven door. With a teacloth protecting his hands he drew out a sizzling-hot clay pot.

'That's yer answer, is it?' Doris snorted in disgust. 'Dinner's ready!'

'Let's eat, then talk about it later.' Rosie gave

her stepmother a smile, signalling a truce. It seemed there was something eating away at her father and she'd no idea what it might be. But she was quite sure it had little to do with her wanting a job and some independence.

CHAPTER SEVEN

'So you can hear it 'n' all, can you, Rosie love? I thought me ears were playing tricks on me.'

John was crunching along the cinder path in the back garden dressed in his pyjamas and bedroom slippers. His palms batted against his ears at intervals as though to unblock them.

At the sound of her father's voice Rosie turned and gave him a quick nod before fixing her eyes again on the moonless sky.

It was a humid June night and Rosie had been restlessly dozing, when the wail of an air-raid siren had brought her swiftly to her feet. She'd glanced at Hope, sound asleep, then padded to the window to stare out. It was just a week away from midsummer and, though not yet dawn, the sky hadn't fully darkened. She'd been able to see for some distance. She'd heard the ack-ack guns start up and seen bullets tracing the heavens, but a weird noise had made her snatch up her dressing gown and investigate further.

A few months ago the first warning wail would have had Rosie grabbing her daughter and flying downstairs to the safety of the cellar, but there had been a lot of false alarms recently; German reconnaissance planes had skimmed over the capital but there hadn't been a bombardment since the winter. The Normandy landings had been such a success that nobody was expecting one while the Luftwaffe had their hands full elsewhere. But something was surely closing on London, or why were the defence batteries blasting away?

The drone of approaching bombers was terrifyingly familiar to East Enders, whereas whatever was up there tonight was making an odd roaring noise as though a mechanic's giant blowtorch had taken flight. The searchlights were in full swing yet Rosie hadn't had a glimpse of a plane's silhouette. She rubbed the back of her stretched neck, wondering if the eerie throb was coming not from above but from some new-fangled machinery down on the Pool of London, where supply ships heading for Normandy were being loaded up.

Suddenly the sky directly overhead was striped by a searchlight, making Rosie anxiously blurt out, 'Not taking any chances, Dad. I'm getting Hope and going to the cellar. Come on ... don't care if it is another false alarm. Never heard anything like that before and it can't be one of ours or the guns would have stopped.'

'What the bloody hell is that?' John yelled, pointing towards the south. ''S'all right, love. Look, it's not a bomber. It's much smaller ... a fighter plane, I reckon, and the Jerry bugger's taken a hit. Look!' He wagged his finger at the sky.

Rosie halted by the back door, again gazing heavenwards.

There, caught in a crosshair of searchlights, was

the outline of a plane; and it did, indeed, have a plume of brilliant fire spurting from its tail.

'It'll crash, Dad,' Rosie shouted. 'Get inside.'

'It's gonna crash all right,' John said in awe, watching the fast-moving object. 'Blimey! Wonder if the pilot's ejected. Keep an eye out for a parachute, love. Don't want no Kraut landing on me roof.' Suddenly he went quiet, as did the V1 rocket, but the weapon glided on silently before its nose dipped...

'Come on, Dad!' Rosie was already inside the back door, holding it ajar for him. 'Quick! Let's get in the cellar!'

'What in God's name's going on?' Doris had shuffled into view, belting her dressing gown. 'We got a proper raid?'

'Is that Jerry? Taken a hit, has he?' a fellow bawled across fences. 'Bailed out, has he? See anything, did yer, John?'

'Dunno what the hell it is, mate,' John yelled back at Dick Price. Peg's husband was yawning and scratching his pot-belly beneath a grimy vest. John had noticed that the trail of flames had disappeared at about the same time that the aircraft's engine cut out. He didn't reckon that the pilot would've managed to extinguish that fire. As the thing had got closer he'd also noticed that it had the Luftwaffe cross on it but it wasn't even big enough to be a Messerschmitt.

'Reckon it might be wise to get under cover.' Finally John's fear overtook his amazement. He waved his arms in warning at his neighbour before limping into the house and following Doris down the cellar stairs. Rosie joined them seconds later with Hope clinging sleepily around her neck.

When the explosion came a few minutes later Rosie instinctively curled her body protectively over her small daughter until the mortar that had been loosened from the bare brick walls had finished coating them in fine dust.

'Reckon that was over Bethnal Green,' John said after a short silence. 'Bet Jerry sent over some sort of Kamikaze pilot in a toy plane. I ain't never seen the like of that before.'

'If you're right, I hope there's just the one of them.' Rosie cradled Hope, soothing her whimpering daughter with gentle murmurs.

'Don't reckon Hitler'll get many volunteers. Jerry ain't like the Nips when it comes to that sort of thing.' Doris picked up the knitting she kept in the cellar to while away the time during air raids. 'If this is a sign the Blitz is starting all over again then I'm getting out of London. I was living on me nerves last time, never knowing which way to run to the nearest shelter.' Doris threw down the needles, unable to concentrate on counting stitches. 'D'you reckon there'll be more of those blighters tonight?' She gazed at her husband for a response but John was still shaking his head to himself in disbelief at what he'd seen and heard out in the garden. 'Well, I ain't having it,' Doris said shrilly. 'I'm off to me son's place in Kent for some peace and quiet. Already been invited to stay so I'm taking me daughter-in-law up on it.' Still John sat rubbing his bad leg and gazing at the ceiling. With an agitated tut, Doris picked up the cardigan sleeve and started knitting a row of purl.

As soon as Rosie's father had shouted out that there was a letter for her it had been a relief to give up the pretence of rest and hurry down-stairs. They'd all trooped up to bed when the all clear sounded but Rosie had found it impossible to get back to sleep. The sinister chugging that had first woken her had continued to pound through her brain. She'd buried her head in the pillow to try to block it out but by then the sun had been filtering through the curtains.

Her father was obviously not in the mood to share any news about her forthcoming job inter-view so with a sigh Rosie returned to her bed-room with her letter. Within half an hour she had got dressed, neatly filled in the Form of Appli-cation for National Service, and put on her mac as it was drizzling outside.

'Just off to the post box. Will you mind Hope for a few minutes?' Rosie poked her head round the kitchen door to ask her dad. 'She's still asleep so shouldn't be any trouble.'

'What name you going under then?' John asked, pointing at the envelope in his daughter's hand.

'My real name. I'm Rosemary Gardiner, aged twenty-two, spinster, born and bred in Shore-ditch.'

'So your daughter doesn't exist then?'

'Oh, she does!' Rosie vehemently declared. 'But Hope's my private business and there's no reason to bring her into it.'

'Well I say there is!' John retorted. 'Round here you're Mrs Deane now and that's the way it should be. Using two different names'll brew up trouble.'

'Answering questions about my poor dead "husband" will brew up trouble,' Rosie replied flatly. 'I don't want to start off in a new job telling a pack of lies about myself; they always trip you up in the end.'

John muttered beneath his breath but he couldn't deny the truth in what his daughter had said. He wished in a way that he'd agreed to brazen out Rosie's pregnancy. It had been what his daughter had wanted rather than stooping to deceit. At the time he'd sided with Doris and insisted his daughter protect the family name by inventing a story. It hadn't stopped the gossip; in fact he could see now that it had just provided more grist for the mill. But they couldn't back-pedal on it now or it would make matters worse.

Rosie felt frustrated with her father's attitude but she didn't want an argument with him so tried a different tack: 'Look, I've been shirking conscription for years, pretending I'm a married woman.'

'Ain't shirking. Women with kids – legitimate or not – ain't breaking the rules in staying home and caring for them,' John returned. 'Anyhow, you've been fire watching plenty of times.'

Rosie gave up trying to put her point across and headed for the front door.

'It'll come out you're an unmarried mother,' John called out after her. 'Then when they're all talking about you behind yer back you'll wish you'd done things differently.'

The deputy station officer of Robley Road Auxiliary Ambulance Station in Hackney – or Station

97 as it was better known – was seated behind a battered wooden desk. Having studied the notes in front of her she inspected the young woman perched on a chair opposite.

Rosie neatly crossed her ankles, nervously clasping her hands in her lap. She was wearing a smart blue two-piece suit purchased years ago when she was flush from working at the Windmill Theatre. It was a bit loose because she'd lost a few pounds running round after her toddling daughter, but was still in pristine condition. And the colour suited her. Her pale blonde hair had been styled into a sleek chin-length bob rather than jazzy waves, and she'd applied her make-up sparingly: just a slick of coral lipstick and some powder to cool the colour of her peachy complexion.

'Your references are very good.'

Since leaving her job at the Windmill Theatre Rosie hadn't had much to deposit in her bank account but the elderly manager of the Barclays Bank in the High Street had agreed to give her a character. And so had the retired draper who'd employed Rosie as a youngster, winding wool for pocket money on Saturdays. Rosie had carefully chosen her referees from people who were unaware she was a mother and had always known her as Miss Gardiner. She might be withholding personal information, but it wasn't the same as lying in Rosie's opinion.

'Do you consider yourself to be strong and healthy?'

'Oh, yes, I'm fit as a fiddle,' Rosie immediately returned.

'You'll need to be,' Stella Phipps emphasised. 'It's surprising what a severed limb weighs. Then there are the stretchers to lug about. Lifting those to the upper position in an ambulance can put a person's back out.' Stella cocked her head, examining Rosie's figure dubiously. She looked soft and petite, whereas most of the female recruits were strapping individuals.

'Oh, I'm used to lifting...' Rosie's voice tailed off. She'd been on the point of adding that she'd got a chubby two-year-old who liked to be carried about but stopped herself in time. She was Rosemary Gardiner, spinster, no dependants. 'My dad's got a bad leg injury so I've lugged him up and down the cellar steps in the past, amongst other things.'

'That's the sort of stuff that comes in useful, but you do seem a bit weedy, dear, if you don't mind me saying so.' Stella took off her glasses to polish them. 'Of course, you're very attractive so no offence meant.'

'I'm very capable,' Rosie returned stoutly. 'And I'll prove it.'

'I'm sure you'll do your best, Miss Gardiner. It's just that I feel obliged to impress on you that the work is arduous ... and gruelling.' Stella sighed. 'Apart from physical sturdiness you need to be prepared for some harrowing sights. Have you had any medical training?'

'No, but I'd quickly learn,' Rosie said eagerly. 'And the sight of a bit of blood doesn't bother me. I tended to my dad when he got badly injured.'

'The sight of "a bit of blood" is what you might encounter here when the sanitary bin in the ladies'

84

convenience overflows.' Stella replaced her spectacles and gazed grimly at her interviewee, ignoring the girl's blushing. If Miss Gardiner were serious about getting a job with the London Auxiliary Ambulance Service she'd better be prepared for some plain speaking. 'If you're accepted and your experience follows mine you'll encounter rat-eaten bodies and scraps of terry towelling nappies containing burned flesh ... all that remains of what was once a human baby.' In the silence that followed Stella stabbed her pen nib repeatedly on the blotter, eyes lowered. 'I'd been in the job just a fortnight when I observed a parachute descending and in the dark I thought it might be a German who'd bailed out. It was something far deadlier ... a landmine. It exploded in Brick Lane about a hundred yards from where we'd just been called to another incident. That was during the winter of 1940 at the height of the Blitz.' Stella paused. 'We lost two of our ambulance crew that night.'

Rosie swallowed, hoping she didn't look too green about the gills. She knew the deputy station officer wasn't being deliberately cruel. In fact, she was being very kind. 'I understand... I'm prepared for the worst,' Rosie vowed in a quavering yet resolute tone.

'You're a better person than I then, Miss Gardiner,' Stella replied. 'I wasn't up to it at all; I brought my heart up the first time I had to deliver a man's leg to the fridge at Billingsgate Market.' She saw Rosie shoot her a horrified glance from beneath her thick lashes. 'Oh, that's sometimes the first stop for odds and ends before they make it to the mortuary, you see. We're not cannibals in England ... not yet, anyhow, despite the paltry rations.'

Rosie smothered a giggle. Stella Phipps might be a fierce-looking dragon but she had a sense of humour. Rosie realised that it was probably an essential requirement for working in the LAAS, the London Auxiliary Ambulance Service. Having heard those stomach-churning anecdotes, she relaxed and decided she liked the woman who might soon be her boss.

'I can book you on a first-aid course with the St John Ambulance if you pass the interview.' Stella closed the manila folder in front of her. 'Any driving experience? We could do with drivers.' She sighed. 'Most of the men we had in the service have gone off on active duty, you see.'

'I used to drive my dad's car,' Rosie burst out. She was determined to be taken on; and if that meant embellishing the truth a little, she'd do it. The only driving she'd ever done had been at the age of fifteen when her father had taken her for a day trip to Clacton and after much badgering had allowed her to get behind the wheel in a country lane. It was the first and last time, though; Rosie had scraped the paintwork of John's pride and joy after swerving into a hawthorn hedge while fighting with the stiff gears.

'Do you still drive a car?' Stella asked optimistically.

'Um... no,' Rosie owned up. 'Since Dad got injured he's sold the Austin. And I never actually passed a test.'

'At least you've a head start, dear. An RAC

course might be all that's required to bring you up to scratch.'

Rosie nodded, feeling a fraud. None the less she added stoutly, 'I'm sure I'll do fine so long as I can remember where the brake is.'

Stella chuckled, then looked thoughtfully at the new recruit. The volunteers were usually keen, eager to be of service. Some lasted just a few weeks before they took fright. Others, like herself and her friend Thora Norris, had been serving since the start of the Blitz. In those days they'd turned up for work dressed in their civilian clothes without even a pair of sensible shoes between them. As the war dragged on the service had become a lot more organised and efficient.

'Following the landings in Normandy it seemed as though we might wind down when victory seemed finally within reach,' Stella said. 'The routine here had become quite mundane. Oh, we still got called out, but on the whole we were dealing with domestic incidents or road accidents.' She shook her head in despair. 'You'd be surprised at how many dreadful injuries have been caused by the blackout. It's as lethal as any Jerry bomb.'

'But if the damage done by that bloody rocket coming over and causing havoc is anything to go by, you might need more volunteers...' Rosie had anticipated what Stella Phipps was about to say and blurted it out, rather bluntly. She blushed, mumbled, 'Sorry ... language...'

Stella smiled. 'You'll hear worse ... say worse ... than that, dear, if you join our little team at Station 97. Letting off steam is essential in this line of work. So no apology required.'

Rosie smiled sheepishly.

The recent explosion in Bethnal Green had everybody talking fearfully about a fiendish new weapon, although Whitehall was doing its best to keep the details under wraps to avoid a panic. But rumours were already spreading that the blazing plane Rosie and her father had watched speeding across the sky was a bomb shaped like a rocket and there had been whispers of others falling across London.

'I saw that first one come over; the noise it made was deafening and very eerie,' Rosie said. When she noted Stella's interest she rushed on, 'Dad and I watched it from the garden. Dad thought it was a miniature Messerschmitt and wondered whether the pilot might bale out and land on our roof because it seemed to be on fire.'

'Let's hope the rumours are just that,' Stella said. 'We don't want a return to the Blitz.'

Stella's concern reminded Rosie of her step-mother fretting about London being heavily bombarded again. Doris had moaned constantly whilst they'd waited for the all clear to sound that night.

'I'll get one of my colleagues to show you around our station, though you might be posted to another one. Have you any preference where you'd like to be sent?'

'As close to home as possible,' Rosie answered quickly, following the older woman out into the corridor. 'Here at Station 97 would be just fine.'

'Righto…' Stella said, striding along at quite a pace. 'Of course when we get called out it's not always to local incidents. If a Deptford crew for example are engaged on a major incident we might be required to cover for them on their patch.'

'I understand,' Rosie said, trotting to keep up with the older woman.

'Have you seen Thora Norris?'

Stella's question was directed at a brunette who was propped on an elbow against the wall, smoking. She turned about, flicking her dog end out through an open door into the courtyard. 'I think she's gone shopping with the new mess manager, ma'am. We're low in the cupboards, by all accounts.'

'I'm hoping there are no petrol cans stored out there, Scott.' Stella Phipps angrily eyed the stub smouldering on concrete.

'Sorry ... didn't think.' The young woman trotted outside to grind the butt out with a toe, looking apologetic.

'Mmm ... and not the first time, is it?'

The young auxiliary was dressed in a uniform of navy-blue safari-style jacket and matching trousers. The letters 'LAAS' were picked out in gold embroidery at the top of a sleeve. She turned to look Rosie up and down. 'How do? You mad enough to want to join us, then?' She stuck out a hand and gave Rosie's small fingers a thorough pump.

'Nice to meet you, and yes, hope I've got the job.' Rosie sent a peeking glance at the deputy station manager.

'I think you'll fit in,' Stella said with a severe smile. 'I'll leave you in Hazel Scott's capable hands.' Her eyebrows hiked dubiously. 'She'll show you round the place and even if you're not

89

posted here, you'll get a feel for things, Miss Gardiner. The auxiliary ambulance stations are all much of a muchness.'

'Only ours is best.' Hazel said sweetly, earning a smile from her superior.

'Don't mind her,' Hazel hissed as Stella's rigid back disappeared round a corner. 'Bark's worse than her bite and all that. I've worked in three different stations now and some of the DSOs – that's deputy station officers to the uninitiated – well, they're worse than the top dog.' Hazel stuck her hands in her jacket pockets and chuckled. 'Got something to prove, I suppose.'

'She seemed very nice, I thought.' Rosie managed to get a word in edgeways. She was glad to have any information about ambulance station life. She realised that there had been no need to turn up looking so demure: Hazel's eyelashes were laden with mascara and crimson lipstick outlined her wide mouth.

'Nice? Really?' Hazel rolled her eyes in a show of surprise. She drew out her pack of Players and offered it to Rosie. 'Don't smoke?' she snorted when Rosie declined with a shake of the head.

'Used to ... gave it up.'

'Not for long in this place, you won't. Couldn't get by without a fag an hour, me.' Hazel's cockney accent seemed to have become more pronounced. She took a long drag on the cigarette then pointed with it. 'Fancy a cuppa? Canteen's just down this way.'

'I'm Rosemary Gardiner, by the way. Rosie, friends call me.'

Hazel slanted a smile over a shoulder. 'I'll call

90

you Rosie then, and I'm Hazel to my friends. Most of the others here address us by our surnames. But I don't go for being formal with people I like.'

It was a typical canteen set with uncomfortable-looking chairs pushed under Spartan rectangular tables. Hazel led the way into the kitchen at the back and filled the kettle at a deep china sink. Having rummaged in a cupboard for some cups and saucers she turned to give Rosie a searching stare.

'Got a man in your life?'

Rosie shook her head, having noticed that Hazel was glancing at her fingers, probably searching for a ring of some sort. Her mother's wedding ring was wrapped in tissue in her handbag. 'You got a boyfriend?' Rosie always turned a leading question on its head. Her home life wasn't up for discussion.

'Mmm ... he's a sailor. Chuck's due back on leave soon.'

'Lucky you,' Rosie said with a friendly smile.

'Lucky him ... if you know what I mean,' Hazel winked a weighty eyelid, lewdly puckering up her scarlet lips. She cocked her head. 'Can't believe you've not got a feller.' She tutted. 'Sorry, that was a bloody stupid thing to say, all things considered. There've been so many casualties in this damned war.'

'No, it's all right; I've not lost anybody over there or here. Just not got anybody special in my life ... a man that is...'

Rosie's private smile as she thought of Hope went unnoticed by Hazel.

Hazel spooned tea into a small enamel pot.

'Best get this down us before the hordes descend. Teatime at four thirty.' She glanced at her watch. 'Oh, got half an hour to spare.' She poured boiling water onto the leaves and stirred. 'Come on, while that brews I'll show you a bit more of the set-up.'

Hazel was tall and solidly built. From the young woman's forthrightness Rosie reckoned Hazel was no shrinking violet when it came to cleaning up the human wreckage left behind after Hitler had dropped his calling cards.

'This is the common room.' Hazel waved at a young fellow who was filling some hurricane lamps ranged in front of him on a table. In response he called out a cheery hello.

'New recruit, Tom,' Hazel informed. 'Tell Miss Rosie Gardiner she's barmy; go on, she won't believe me.'

'Listen to Hazel,' Tom called with a rather effeminate wave. 'Scarper while you still can.' He then turned his attention to the funnel he was using to drip oil into the lamps.

'Tom Anderson is a conchie,' Hazel said quietly. On seeing Rosie's bemusement she explained, 'Conscientious objector. We've had a few of those sent here. He might not want to fight but he's a bloody godsend with the ambulances. He's a driver and knows a thing or two about mechanics. He used to drive a tractor on his dad's farm.'

Rosie hoped Tom was unaware that Hazel had been gossiping about him. His boiler-suit-style uniform made him look more like a plumber than an ambulance driver.

'Table tennis...' Rosie had spotted the net shoved

into a corner, bats and balls scattered on the top. 'I used to be pretty good at table tennis.'

'I'll give you a game if we end up on the same shifts,' Hazel offered. 'What did you do before this damned war buggered us all up?'

'Worked in a theatre a few years back.'

'Me, too!' Hazel burst out, delighted. 'Which theatre?'

'The Windmill...' Rosie started examining the table tennis bats. She never volunteered the information that she'd worked as one of the theatre's famous nudes. But neither did she deny what she'd done, if asked directly.

The Windmill Theatre had stayed open throughout the war. But Rosie had never felt any inclination to go back for old times' sake and see a show, or look for the few old colleagues who might remain working there.

'I worked as a magician's assistant,' Hazel informed her. 'He was always trying to have a fiddle down the front of me costume so I dropped him and went out on my own. I could do a bit of singing and dancing but never made much of a name for myself.' Hazel click-clacked a few steps with toes and heels, hands jigging up and down at her sides. 'I was in the chorus at the Palladium once when one of the girls went sick at the last minute.' She sniffed. 'Never got asked back, though. They said I was too tall for the chorus line.' She gazed at Rosie admiringly. 'The Windmill! Now why didn't I try there!' She grinned. 'What's the place like? Bit racy, ain't it, by all accounts? All the servicemen flocked there. Chuck and his navy pals used to race to get a seat at the front. Bet you had a few followers, being as you're so pretty.'

'Take a look at an ambulance, can I?' Rosie asked brightly. 'I'd better see what it's all about just in case I'm lucky enough to get to drive one.'

'You think that's lucky? Oh, come on, the tea'll be stewed.' Hazel led the way back towards the canteen. 'Getting behind the wheel of a meat wagon is no picnic, I can tell you. Gully Crump had held a motor licence for years yet she drove an ambulance straight into a wall in the blackout. Knocked herself sparko and ended up in the back of the blighter on a stretcher.' Hazel chuckled. 'Gave in her notice shortly after when she got out of hospital. You'll need to do a few practice runs under instruction before they'll let you loose on your tod with an assistant.'

'You won't put me off, you know.'

Hazel poured the tea then held out a cup, grinning. 'You look like the sort of girl that does all right whatever she turns her hand to. Some people just have that sort of luck. Whereas me... I bugger up everything.'

'I bet you don't!' Rosie returned, thinking ruefully that if Hazel knew her better she'd be revising her opinion.

Rosie rather liked her new colleague's droll manner. She knew already that she'd chosen well in applying to the service; it didn't feel like home yet, but it did feel right being here with Stella Phipps and Tom Anderson and Hazel Scott. In fact, she was itching to get started.

CHAPTER EIGHT

'Didn't know if you'd still come over for a picnic after what's gone on,' Gertie called out as soon as she saw Rosie rounding the corner.

''Course I'd come for a picnic. Been looking forward to it. Take more than a load of flying bombs to keep me away from our day out.' Rosie grinned although she wasn't feeling quite as chipper as she sounded. While heading to their rendezvous spot Rosie had also wondered if she was making a fruitless journey. She wouldn't blame Gertie for wanting to stay day and night right by an underground shelter after losing three children in the Blitz.

'Head off towards the park, shall we?'

Gertie nodded. 'We had a couple of close shaves in our street. Get any blasts your way from those damned rockets?'

'Where I live they're always coming too close for comfort,' Rosie replied with feeling. 'Thankfully, no hits in the street. I saw the first one come over, though.' She shook her head as she recalled that night. 'Couldn't believe my ears ... or eyes.'

That first doodlebug had come down in Bethnal Green, blowing to smithereens the railway line and several houses. Unfortunately, Stella Phipps' hopes that the rumours weren't true had been dashed. Hundreds more of the missiles had whizzed overhead since in a relentless German onslaught. The sight of a fiery tail approaching, coupled with a sinister roaring, was dreadful enough, yet when the rocket's engine died and it carried on silently for several seconds, the uncertainty of where it might drop was even more terrifying.

They turned in through the iron gates of a small square recreation area. A couple of urchins in plimsolls and short trousers raced past, almost colliding with them. Having mumbled an apology they hared off again. The local school had turned out and the park was crowded with mothers and children making the most of the afternoon sun. But Rosie noticed that a lot of women looked anxious and were keeping an eye on the open skies. The missiles hadn't only been arriving after dark and there was a tension in the air despite the children's joyful voices.

'Here'll do.' Gertie swiped away a crust of bird droppings on a bench's slats. Having sat down she delved into her shopping bag, pegged on the pram handle. 'Brought a flask.' Gertie held out the Thermos. 'Not much in the way of a picnic, though. Sorry, me rations are low.'

'I've got some Spam sandwiches.' Rosie dug into her bag and found a small packet. She unwrapped it and offered the sandwiches to Gertie. 'Would have been corned beef but Dad wanted to keep that to fry up for our teas tonight.'

'Blimey! They're fit for a queen!' Gertie looked admiringly at the tiny neatly cut triangles, unlike the doorsteps of bread and jam encased in greaseproof paper that she'd brought along. 'Thanks.' She took a bite before unscrewing the Thermos and pouring two weak brews into plastic cups.

'Bread's a bit dry; only had a scraping of Stork left in the pack,' Rosie apologised.

'Tastes fine to me,' Gertie said truthfully, taking another hungry bite. At home she never had sandwiches with butter or marge. Those rations were saved for her husband and kids.

'Your little 'un's good.' Gertie nodded at Hope, sitting quietly in her pram. Victoria, on the other hand, was rocking herself on her bottom and banging her heels against the thin mattress to get her mother's attention.

'She's too big for the pram now,' Gertie said, giving her daughter's nose a wipe. 'Like to get out and walk, don't you, Vicky?' Gertie lifted her daughter out of the pram and let her sit beside her on the seat. 'Behave yourself,' she warned. 'Be a good girl like Hope.'

'You wouldn't have said that if you'd heard the little madam last night,' Rosie responded ruefully. 'Thought Doris was going to have a fit...'

'Doris?' Gertie asked, holding out Rosie's tea to her. She noticed Rosie's expression change. ''S'all right ... not prying, honest.' Gertie rummaged for a jam sandwich. She broke off a piece for her daughter and Victoria stopped fidgeting and tucked in. 'Can Hope have a bit?'

'Yeah ... I've got her bib somewhere.' As Rosie fastened the terry towelling about her daughter's neck she said, 'Doris is my stepmother. Dad got married again recently.'

'Take it things ain't always easy between you two.' Gertie followed up with a knowing laugh. 'I had some of that with me mother-in-law. Mustn't

97

speak ill of the dead, though, so enough said.' She handed a morsel of bread oozing thick dark jam to Hope who promptly took a bite then threw the remainder overboard.

'She's not very hungry,' Rosie apologised. 'Dad gave her a few biscuits about an hour ago. He spoils her.' She glanced at Gertie. 'You've probably guessed that I've not got a home of my own and live with Dad.'

'Me 'n' Rufus started off married life at my mum's,' Gertie replied flatly. 'Couldn't wait to get out and into me own place.'

'Drive you mad, did they?' Rosie asked.

'Wasn't them; they did what they could for us. But couldn't take living with me younger brother.' Gertie clammed up. She never spoke about Michael. She didn't want to see or hear from him ever again. In fact she hoped that the nasty bastard was six feet under. He'd been a thorn in her side for decades; even as kids they'd not got on. Then he'd plunged a dagger in her heart when her little boys died; she blamed him for the children having been left alone in the house that night.

In Gertie's experience most of life's troubles revolved around the men in her life. And she reckoned that Rosie was reluctant to talk about Hope's father because she held the same opinion.

'Army, is he, your husband?' Gertie asked sympathetically. 'Rufus ain't the easiest man to live with yet when he was in France I fretted no end about him. Almost came as a relief when he got invalided home; I know that's a wicked thing to say.' She wiped her jammy fingers on a hanky. 'Sometimes I'd not have the wireless on in case of any bad news about the Middlesex Regiment. Didn't want Joey to hear it; it didn't seem fair landing that on him as well after he'd lost his brothers. 'Course, now his dad's back we don't have that bother.' Gertie gave a bashful smile. 'Sorry, going on a bit, ain't I?'

'I like to hear about your family, Gertie. You must miss your sons so much,' Rosie said quietly.

Gertie nodded. 'Joey took it badly. Thought at one point he'd need a dose of something from the doctor to calm him down. But we got through it ... the two of us. After Rufus enlisted it was just me and him for a while, before Vicky was born.' She sniffed, glanced at Rosie. 'I understand if you don't want to talk about your husband, though...'

'I said I'd tell you more about myself today, didn't I?'

''S'all right; you don't have to say a thing if you don't want to. Plenty of stuff in my past I never talk about.' Gertie grinned. 'Bet that's come as a surprise to you after listening to me rabbiting nineteen to the dozen.'

Rosie sat back sipping her tea. 'I don't have a husband,' she suddenly blurted. 'My name's still Rosie Gardiner and never been any different although some people think I'm a widow called Mrs Deane.'

'Stops 'em yakking, don't it, if they see a ring on your finger?' There had been a long silence before Gertie's reply, but when it came it sounded matter-of-fact. 'Wrong 'un who ran off, was he, the father?'

'He was a wrong 'un all right,' Rosie said bitterly. 'But he didn't run off. He never knew, thank God.'

'Didn't want no help off him?' Gertie asked, surprised.

Rosie shook her head vigorously. 'Never wanted to see him again. And I got my way. I never did. He died before I even found out I was expecting.'

'Killed in action?'

'He got discharged as unfit before he'd ever held a rifle. Didn't do him much good, though; he perished in a nightclub fire. The day I found out I could have jumped for joy. Some people might think that wicked.'

'Not me. He raped you.' Gertie's quiet statement was husky with sorrow.

'I didn't say so,' Rosie rattled off. Suddenly she regretted revealing too much about her past. Her dearest wish was to protect Hope, and hearing gossip that your father had raped your mother was a dreadful thing for any child to deal with. Having a chat and a picnic couldn't alter the fact that she and Gertie still didn't know one another well enough to share secrets.

'You don't need to worry,' Gertie reassured. 'Like I said, there's plenty of stuff in my past I don't talk about. So I'd never talk about your'n, promise.'

'Thanks,' Rosie mumbled. 'Hark at us! Right pair of miserable cows, aren't we? Thought I was getting out of the house to cheer myself up.' She got to her feet, brushing sandwich crumbs from her skirt. 'Let's have a quick stroll round the grass before the heavens open.' A cliff of dark cloud was menacing the horizon. People were gathering up their belongings and hurrying towards the park gates as they noticed the air changing.

'Don't fancy getting drenched.' Gertie put the flask back in her bag and they headed off side by side, pulling the hoods up on the prams in preparation for a downpour.

'I volunteered to work as an ambulance auxiliary. I've been talking about making myself useful for ages, so I finally did something about it.'

Gertie looked surprised, then smiled. 'Glad to hear it! They'll take you on, no trouble, especially if a fellow interviews you.' She glanced sideways at Rosie's stylish skirt and blouse, so much prettier than the faded cotton frock she was wearing herself.

'A woman interviewed me. And I got a letter this morning offering me a job.'

'Good for you!' Gertie glanced at Hope. 'Yer stepmother going to mind the little 'un for you?'

'Dad'll help out as Doris is working.'

'I'll give a hand babysitting, if you like,' Gertie volunteered. 'She's such a cutie it'd be a pleasure to have her round to play with Vicky.'

'Dad got moody when I spoke about getting Hope a nursery place. He's determined to mind her,' Rosie quickly rattled off. She liked Gertie but the woman was a rough-and-ready sort and she didn't know enough about the Grimes family to let Hope stay there.

Rosie felt bad for thinking she was a better mother than Gertie. Considering what life had thrown at the poor woman she deserved praise for coping so well.

At the park gates Rosie turned to give Gertie a spontaneous hug. 'Thanks ... for everything.'

'Ain't done nothing,' Gertie replied bashfully.

'Yeah you have, and I'm so glad we bumped into each other that day. Don't know what my shifts are going to be yet but I hope we can keep on meeting up.'

Gertie took a scrap of paper from her bag. 'Shopping list,' she explained the spidery scrawl filling half of one side. Turning it over she printed her address on it with a stub of pencil found in a pocket. 'There. When you get a day off, come and see me, if you like. I'm usually about.'

With a wave the two women quickly set off in opposite directions as fat raindrops were spotting the hoods of the children's prams.

It had been clear skies when Rosie had set out for a picnic so she hadn't bothered to stuff a scarf in her pocket, fearing the weather might turn. By the time she trotted up to her front door her stylish fair locks were glued to her cheeks in sleek rat's-tails.

'Crikey, you did get caught in it, didn't you?' John clucked his tongue while inspecting his daughter's bedraggled figure.

Rosie gave her head a shake and quickly un-buttoned her cardigan and took it off, hanging the sodden wool over a chair back.

'How's yer friend? Have a nice time, did you, dear, despite getting a soaking?' John seemed in jovial mood, fetching her a towel from the kitchen and draping it over her scalp. Doris followed him out and between them they managed to get Hope out of the pram without tipping on the floor the water that had pooled on the gabardine cover.

Rosie was surprised to see her stepmother. She stopped drying her hair to remark, 'Thought you were on shift this afternoon, Doris.'

'Got some time off. Anyhow; I'm handing me notice in tomorrow as we're moving to Kent,' Doris called over a shoulder as she set off, gingerly holding the cover, to tip the rainwater down the sink. Rosie thought she must have misheard but when Doris reappeared she added, 'It's time to start packing things up.'

Rosie suddenly glanced at a box in the corner of the room that she'd not paid much attention to before. 'Moving to Kent?' she echoed.

'Now don't make out you didn't hear us talking the other night.' Doris sounded prickly as she hooked the cover over the fireguard to drip dry on the hearth.

'I heard you say your daughter-in-law offered to put you up for a break if there's no let-up with the doodlebugs. I didn't think it was a permanent arrangement.'

'I'm going for as long as she'll have me. Can't stand this a moment longer.' Doris whirled an agitated hand over her head. 'This war ain't coming to an end! Hitler's got his second wind and I'm done with living on me nerves! I saw me old neighbour in Commercial Road earlier. She said three bodies got dug out of my old house. One of 'em could've been mine. Always the Londoners what suffer.' Doris ceased ranting to draw breath. 'I'm off where it's safer and yer father's coming with me.' Doris gave her husband a glare, daring him to defy her. 'You can too, if you want, Rosie.'

Rosie knew her stepmother wasn't exaggerating

the effect the V1s were having on her. And Doris wasn't alone in feeling wretchedly despondent. Rosie had been queuing in the butcher's the other day when a woman behind had gone into hysterics because she'd thought she could hear a rocket on its way. The alarming noise had turned out to be a steamroller lumbering towards the rail yard. But nobody had made a joke of it in the way they might have done a couple of years back. During the Blitz a natural belligerence and optimism had seen people through. But now the mood had changed; the euphoria following the D-Day landings was fast evaporating and Doris was by no means alone in wanting to throw in the towel and flee to a safer place.

'All settled then, is it? You're definitely going to Gravesend?' Rosie looked at her father. He avoided her eye when she added drily, 'Thanks for keeping me in on it.'

'While Charlie's away on his frigate...' Doris referred to her son's active service. 'Me daughter-in-law says there's room for all of us. Her boy, Toby, can kip in with her. We'll have the spare bedroom, and you and Hope can have Toby's small bedroom, if you want. But ain't forcing you to do nothing you don't want to do.'

''Course Rosie wants to come,' John snapped. 'She ain't daft enough to want to stay here with the little 'un now we all know what's in store for us. It's far too dangerous.' He glared at his wife. 'I told you to let me bring this subject up. Shouldn't have flung it at her like that. Look, she's not even had a chance to dry herself off yet.'

'Sorry, I'm sure,' Doris said sarcastically. She

went into the kitchen and returned with crockery to stack in the box, ignoring the tense silence between father and daughter.

'And you can give that a rest for a while; it ain't urgent,' John testily addressed his wife. 'Time for Hope to have her tea. It's gone five o'clock.'

'It's all right, Dad.' Seeing Doris's boiling expression, Rosie tried to smooth things over. She didn't want the couple to row on her account. She felt a fool for not having realised her stepmother had been dropping serious hints when mentioning staying with her family in Kent. 'Hope's not hungry anyhow; we had a picnic in the park.' Rosie's conciliatory smile for Doris wasn't returned.

'Sorry about that, love,' John mumbled after his wife had clattered the crockery into the box and stomped off upstairs. 'She means well and she ain't exaggerating how it's affecting her. She hardly gets a wink of sleep for fretting we'll be next to get our roof blown off.' John hung his head. 'Think I'm in danger of losing me marbles too, way things are going.'

John wasn't just thinking of Gravesend being a safe haven from the bombardment; he wanted to get away from Popeye. He'd had another visit from the man but had managed to avoid any discussion. John had been outside on the pavement, talking to Dick Price at the time. Popeye had loitered by the lamppost on the opposite pavement trying to catch John's eye, but John had walked off up the pub with Dick. By the time he got back Popeye had disappeared.

'I'm sorry I snapped, Dad, but it came as a

105

shock about you going to Gravesend.'

'You're not thinking of staying behind?'

'I am,' Rosie replied quietly. She'd not had time to give the upheaval much thought but realised her spontaneous answer was the right one.

'That's bloody selfish!' John erupted. He peered suspiciously at Rosie. 'What is it? Found a boyfriend? Thinking of him rather than Hope, are you?'

Rosie limited her exasperation to a long weary sigh and a pithy, 'Thought you realised I've got no time for men in my life.'

Hope was becoming upset by the hostility between her mum and granddad. The child trotted from the kitchen into the parlour, lower lip thrust out, and threw to the floor the muddy potato she'd been playing with. Rosie sat down at the table with her daughter on her lap, her chin resting on a small crown of silky fair hair. 'A week on Monday I'm starting work at Station 97 in Robley Road. I know you're worried about me staying behind, but I'll do all right and I'll take good care of myself when on duty.'

'I reckon you should take good care of the little 'un first by getting her out of harm's way.'

Rosie used an edge of the tablecloth to rub potato mould from her daughter's fingers. 'Hope's going to have a future; I want to do whatever I can to make sure of it.' She gazed at her father with fierce eyes. 'She'll go to school and get a good job and meet a nice man when her time comes. And live in peace.' She smiled ruefully. 'Until she has kids of her own to drive her up the wall. But by then I'll have done my bit.'

'Give her here!' John tried to wrestle his grand-daughter from Rosie, making the child whimper. 'Someone's got to look after her properly.'

'Leave her alone, Dad. You're frightening her.' Rosie took a deep breath before blurting, 'When you go to Kent I want you to take her with you.'

That took the wind out of John's sails. He sank down into the chair opposite Rosie at the table.

Rosie stroked the side of her daughter's face. The idea of being separated from Hope had put a thick wedge of emotion in her throat. But she quashed it. Thousands of Londoners had known the heart-ache of sending their children away to be cared for by strangers. At least she had the comfort of knowing that Hope had her doting granddad watching over her during her evacuation.

''Course I'll take her with me,' John finally croaked out. He glanced at his wife who'd just entered the room. 'Love to have her, won't we?'

Doris chewed her lower lip. 'Yeah,' she muttered before going into the kitchen. 'As nobody else's made a start I'll get a pot of potatoes on the go, shall I?'

Rosie went to help her stony-faced stepmother prepare their teas. Her eyes were so teary that she misjudged what she was doing and cracked the enamel pan on the side of the sink when she tried to fill it with water. She gritted her teeth against an urge to blurt out that she'd changed her mind and Hope must stay with her. Rosie became aware that her daughter had appeared at her side and was gazing at her with huge blue eyes.

Swiftly Rosie crouched down and gently re-moved the thumb from Hope's mouth. 'Guess what? Granddad's going to take you on a lovely holiday in the countryside soon. Like that, won't you, sweetheart?'

Hope nodded solemnly. 'You come?' she whispered.

'When I can,' Rosie replied softly. 'And I'll speak to you on the telephone now you're getting a big girl, promise I will.'

'Reckon we'll see about that, won't we?' Doris sniffed. 'Could be you'll find you're too busy having a good time to remember your little kiddie out in the countryside.'

Rosie stood up slowly, realising how strongly she disliked her stepmother. 'When I had my interview, my station officer told me to prepare myself for some awful sights on a call-out. If you reckon that collecting body parts is having a good time then I'm not sure you're the sort of person I want around my daughter.'

'She don't mean nuthin' by it, Rosie.' John had come out into the kitchen and given his wife a glare. 'Doris is talkin' out of her backside because all this bombing's got to her.'

'Charming, I'm sure!' Doris, boiling with anger, barged past and stamped up the stairs.

John swooped on his little granddaughter and lifted her up, making her squeal in delight as he threw her a few inches into the air. 'Going on holiday with Granddad, aren't you, you lucky gel.'

Hope gave his bristly cheek a soft kiss, making her mother's strained expression soften.

'She'll be right as rain with us, Rosie,' John vowed solemnly. 'You just make sure you're all right too.'

CHAPTER NINE

'Just come to say I'm moving away so don't come looking for me 'cos you'll be wasting your time.' John was turning away when he heard the sound of a striking match. He darted his eyes back past his old business associate glimpsing, behind the tobacco smoke snaking his way, a dark silhouette in Popeye's gloomy hallway. If he'd known Frank had company he'd have given him a wide berth this evening. A sunset-streaked black saloon was parked at the kerb and John silently cussed at having ignored an obvious clue that Popeye wasn't indoors alone.

'Can't stop; said what I had to.' John hurried down the path as fast as his limp would allow, his mouth dry. Although he'd not got a clear view of Popeye's visitor, he had a bad feeling about him.

In a few days' time John was taking his wife and granddaughter to Kent. But there'd been something he had felt duty-bound to do before he caught that train. He distrusted and feared Frank Purves but had forced himself to come here. The last thing John wanted after he'd gone was this man turning up on his doorstep looking for him and frightening the life out of Rosie.

'This is a nice surprise, John, and right on cue. Don't rush off now, mate. There's somebody here I know'd like to meet you.' John had reached the gate but, before he managed to unlatch it, Popeye had snatched his elbow. 'You'd best not upset him; he'll have yer guts fer garters,' Popeye snarled, jerking his head at his front door. ''Ere ... come on inside, don't be shy.' Popeye's voice was now loud and jolly for the benefit of his acquaintance.

Popeye's banter didn't fool John. But he knew if he didn't sort things out between them before he went to Gravesend, his fears for Rosie's safety would eat him alive every day he was away.

'Just a few minutes then; me wife's waiting on me to help her pack.' John's trepidation mounted as Popeye suddenly stuffed some cash into his pocket.

'That's a bit up front to buy goods. Don't go telling him I've tried to stitch you up, 'cos I ain't, see,' Popeye hissed in his ear.

John tried to free his hand to return the money but Popeye propelled him into his house and shut the door, trapping the three of them in a dark narrow corridor.

'So where you off to then, mate? Somewhere nice?' Popeye asked amiably.

John wasn't falling for that one. If Popeye found out where he was heading he wouldn't put it past the bastard to come after him.

'The missus has got family over in Wales,' John lied, hoping to flummox him.

'Doris a Taffy? Well, I never!' Popeye drawled ironically. 'Glad you stopped by, 'cos I was going to pay you a visit tomorrow. Just saying to Mr Flint here that it was time to prod you over that order.' He rolled his wonky eyes and emphasised his warning by baring two rows of brown teeth. 'Told him your missus is cutting up rough over it

110

all and delaying things,' Popeye again muttered close to John's ear.

'Ain't a story!' John spluttered. 'Doris'll go berserk.'

Sweat slipped down his spine as he glanced at the fellow who was standing sideways on to them, hands dug in his pockets and cigarette drooping from his lips. Far from seeming bothered, he looked bored stiff with proceedings.

John's eyes were adjusting to the dimness inside the house and he could see the bloke looked to be fit and strong. And young. He put his age at about thirty and his snug-fitting suit jacket was moulded on biceps any man would envy.

'Now I promised you a cuppa, when you come to see me, didn't I, mate? Sit yerself down and I'll stick the kettle on.' Popeye sounded hospitable but the shove that accompanied the offer of tea sent John stumbling down the corridor.

It seemed the other fellow wasn't having tea. He wasn't having a seat either. He'd stationed himself by the empty hearth in Popeye's back parlour and upended against his lips a silver flask, taken from an inside pocket.

John watched him screwing the top back on the flask then flinched when a steady gaze bored into him.

'Frank's forgotten his manners,' the stranger said. 'Seems he's not making formal introductions.'

At least he wasn't stranded in the company of one of Frank's Brummie associates, John thought hysterically. He had met a few of those when he'd been distilling, and thought them mad as a box of

111

frogs. Of course, the, East End had its fair share of dangerous lunatics too, so a London accent wasn't necessarily a relief.

John sidled closer to the door, wondering whether his quaking legs would be up to him making a dash for it. He sensed he was under observation again and flinched beneath Flint's quiet amusement.

'Look, dunno what Frank's told you, but I ain't agreed to do no distilling...'

The young man held out a hand, ignoring John's breathless excuse. 'I'm Conor Flint, and you must be John Gardiner. Right?'

John backed away a pace as though fearing those long dark fingers might suddenly leap to squeeze his throat. He quickly shook hands, pulling free as soon as possible.

'You were saying about the distilling?' Conor prompted, levelling a navy-blue stare on John's blanching face.

'Dunno for sure what Pop's game is ... well, I do 'cos he told me...' John cleared his throat. 'But he's wrong, see. I don't get involved in that no more. Got married again ... got a daughter and a grandkid now...' He suddenly clammed up, features frozen in regret. Belatedly he realised that the last thing he should have advertised to this stranger was that he had vulnerable dependants.

'Right...' Conor propped a hand on the mantelpiece again. 'That's disappointing, 'cos I was expecting to take a sample of the stuff out of here with me.'

'Ain't been in touch with Popeye fer years,' John stressed. 'Then he turns up outta the blue

112

and starts going on about setting up me still again. I told him straight–'

'Told me straight you was up for it, didn't yer?' Popeye ambled into the room, giving John a poisonous look. But he thrust a cup of tea at him, slopping some over the rim to wet the solitary Rich Tea biscuit balanced on the saucer.

John dropped the crockery on the table. 'Don't want no fuckin' tea,' he exploded. 'Tell him I said I wasn't getting involved. Go on!' He pulled the wad of cash out of his pocket and threw five ten-pound notes on the table. 'And you can have that back.'

John sensed Flint believed him until the man laughed, soft and chilling, and swung a look between him and Frank.

'Which of you's trying to stiff me? Popeye?' It was a mild query but Conor began drumming his fingers on the mantelshelf in strong, irritated rhythm. 'That's not all I handed over, is it?'

'No, it ain't, Mr Flint.' Popeye turned to John, all indignation. 'If you're trying to weasel out of this deal, you'd better divvy up the rest.'

'What rest? That's all you've given me!'

'I ain't playing games, John. You come up with all the cash now, or you get started on the distilling.'

John licked his lips, reading in Popeye's triumphant expression that he thought he had him backed into a corner. An uncontrollable urge to throttle the deceitful bastard made John lunge forward but his quarry dodged aside.

'Now, now, John. That ain't any way fer a man of your age to behave. We can do this civil–'

113

John stabbed a finger at Popeye's chest. 'I'm off out of town and you'd better leave me and mine alone, y'hear?'

'Just give us a few days to get started, Mr Flint.' Popeye sounded all concerned now. 'John's daughter, Rosie's, been widowed, see, and her with a little 'un ... he ain't hisself at the moment.'

'Don't you go spreading my business!' John roared, outraged.

'No harm meant, mate, y'know that.' Popeye sounded sincere. He turned to Flint. 'I bet if you ask nicely, John'll find you a couple of good vintages from way back when. Got some ain't yer, John? Can't save it all fer Christmas.'

Conor suddenly pushed off the mantelpiece and walked to the door. 'Way I see it, between you, you'd better come up with my monkey, plus twenty-five percent interest, plus another hundred for wasting my time.' He glanced between the two middle-aged men. 'Reckon you can do that, 'cos I'm out of patience.'

'Yeah, 'course...' Popeye flicked idle fingers but his receding hairline was shiny with sweat. 'Give us a couple of weeks, we'll sort this out.'

'You've got a few days.' Conor glanced at his watch and smiled. 'One of 'em's nearly over.' He walked up to John and gazed down at the man's ashen, lined face before turning to Popeye. 'So just to be clear, that's seven hundred and twenty-five quid.'

'Mental arithmetic,' Popeye chortled nervously. 'My boy used to be a dab hand at adding up, God rest him.' He tapped his forehead.

As Flint strolled out into the hallway Popeye

was right behind him, still making promises.

John glanced at the tenners abandoned on the table. On impulse he picked them up, pocketing them. He knew Popeye would come back into the room itching to have a scrap. Now all John wanted to do was get home and get packed. He barged past Popeye and out of the house on the crook's heels, then loitered by the hedge. The moment the Humber drove off he hopped outside the gate, employing it as a barrier between him and Popeye.

Popeye came bursting out of the house, snarling, 'Give us that back, you thieving bastard, or get that still up 'n' running.'

John looked at the Humber turning the corner. Flint had seen him throw that cash on the table. So if the crook believed what he'd said about that being all Popeye had given him, he was in the clear. John knew he should give it back to Popeye but he could do with a bit extra while he was away from home. But that wasn't the main reason for him being unable to pull the notes out of his pocket. Popeye had tried to pin it all on him. He'd made out he'd handed over five hundred quid when in fact John hadn't seen a penny piece before today. He wouldn't have had five tenners slid into his pocket if it hadn't suited Popeye's devious purpose. Popeye deserved getting turned over for fifty quid for trying to turn him over for ten times as much.

'Don't come looking fer me 'cos I ain't coming back to Shoreditch for a while. And you ever pull a stunt like that again and I'll...' John let his threat tail off. A couple were strolling across the road.

115

'You'll do what?' Popeye scoffed.

'You've dropped yerself in shit dealing with the likes of him, and you can pull yerself out.' John saw his chance to get going. He nodded politely at the young couple and hobbled off up the road directly behind them.

He took a quick peek over a shoulder and saw a pair of crossed eyes on him. When Popeye jabbed a finger threateningly John swallowed noisily. He'd let revenge and temper get the better of him and might have just made things worse for Rosie, not better.

'What you doing up?'

'Hope's been a misery; I brought her downstairs for a breath of air. It's so close tonight.'

John limped slowly towards his daughter, who'd been pacing up and down in their small front garden with the child in her arms.

Rosie glanced at Hope, thumb in mouth, drowsing on her shoulder. She guessed it to be about nine o'clock from the faint shine on the horizon. She had on her dressing gown and slippers and she squatted down on the front doorstep with her daughter on her lap. John closed the gate and Rosie could see from his furrowed features that he was fretting on something.

'What's up, Dad?' she asked. 'Where've you been?'

'What is this? Spanish Inquisition?' John barked, before sighing regret. 'Sorry, love.' He stooped to ruffle his granddaughter's fair hair. 'Sleepy head...' he crooned softly.

'I'm not checking up on you ... just worried,'

Rosie explained.

'I know, love. It's just there's a lot of sorting out to do before we go. Had a couple of people to see and bills to pay; posted 'em in the box now, though, so I can tick that off the list.' He sighed wearily. 'Where's Doris?'

'She was packing up stuff in the bedroom. I expect she's turned in now.' Rosie angled her head to read his expression. 'What needs sorting out? Is it something I can help with?' She smiled. 'I know you think I haven't got a clue, but I can write a cheque for the electricity and post a letter. I'll make sure the rent's paid too, while you're away.'

John gazed at his daughter's lovely face turned up to his. 'Sometimes, dear, I know you've got more sense in your little finger than I've got in me whole body.'

Again Rosie sensed something more than household accounts was behind her father's moping. She was about to dig further into it and ask him again where he'd been when the air-raid siren started wailing. She scrambled up, putting her daughter unsteadily on her feet. 'Oh, here we go!' She pointed up to a depressingly familiar object in the sky.

'That blighter's heading west.' John breathed in relief.

'What about those?' Rosie cried, squinting at the horizon. 'Oh good God, there are dozens of them.' She felt her stomach curdling in fear.

The dusky sky was becoming scarred with fire and the humming sound grew louder as a host of V1 rockets, scattered across the heavens, speeded in their direction.

'Come on, Dad, quickly ... cellar.' Rosie again scooped her daughter into her arms. 'We could be down there for hours before the all clear. I wanted a good night's sleep, too.' Sensing her father wasn't right behind her Rosie glanced over a shoulder. He was by the gate staring at a car, its shaded headlights dying, parked at the opposite kerb. She had been half aware of a vehicle stopping but hadn't taken much notice of it.

Now she did; she couldn't clearly see the driver, but the glowing end of a cigarette was visible in the gloomy space above the steering wheel. 'Who's that? D'you know him, Dad?' The sudden tension in Rosie's chest was caused as much by her father's hunted expression as the imminent danger from the German attack.

'Get inside, Rosie,' John croaked. 'Go now!' he thundered when she hesitated.

She did as she was told, colliding with Doris in the hallway as the woman scurried down the stairs.

'Let's get that front door shut. Is yer father home?' Doris demanded, agitated.

'He's just outside. He won't be a tick.' For some reason Rosie kept to herself her suspicion that John had gone to speak to the car driver. She thrust her daughter into Doris's arms. 'You take Hope to the cellar; I'll help Dad down the stairs.' She knew Doris didn't mind her taking the brunt of the heavy work where John was concerned.

Rosie rushed into the front room. A tremor from a bomb a few days earlier had put a diagonal crack in a windowpane. The glass had been crisscrossed with tape to prevent lethal flying shards in an explosion. She gingerly lifted an edge of blackout curtain to peer into the street. Rosie watched her father steady himself against the vehicle then duck down to speak to the driver. Fascinated, she saw the stranger lower the window and she caught a glimpse of a strong male profile. Rosie certainly didn't recognise him. He appeared younger than any friend of her father's she'd known. A moment later John was hurrying in an uneven gait back towards the house and Rosie rushed to meet him in the hallway.

'Who was that, Dad?' She took her father's arm, supporting his weight as they started to descend to the cellar.

'Nobody important ... just somebody come to say goodbye.'

'At this time of the night?'

John held back as Rosie tried to shift him down to the next step. He turned, gazing at his daughter's frowning face. 'I want you to come with us on Friday, Rosie,' he burst out. 'It ain't safe here; you're acting daft staying, and you know it.' He sounded angry and frustrated yet spoke in a voice that was pitched to prevent his wife's hearing.

'We've already spoken about my job. I thought you'd accepted I need to stay in London and do my bit.' When he avoided her eyes Rosie asked quietly, 'Are you worried about that bloke in the car, Dad?' As far as Rosie was aware there was only one sort of dodgy business her father had ever been in: distilling. He'd been lucky not to have ended up in gaol considering the amount of moonshine he'd dispatched from their cellar, but he'd sworn on her life he was finished with all that.

'What did he want with you, Dad?'

'Don't question me. Just listen to me,' John hissed.

Rosie remained quiet, chewing her lower lip, but though her father's mouth worked he seemed to be finding it difficult to spit out what he wanted to say.

'Frank Purves came round here one day when you was out and tried to force me into starting up me still again,' he eventually burst out. 'Told him to go to hell.' He winced at his daughter's appalled expression. 'That's why I want you to come with me. Just want you out of his way, dear, in case he calls by looking for me again. He thinks I'm going to Wales; I told him that to throw him off the scent, but he could turn up to check that I've not spun him a yarn about scarpering.'

'That wasn't Frank Purves outside in the car,' Rosie ventured, finally conquering her shock. 'That fellow looked far younger.'

'Business associate of Frank's, he is, name of Conor Flint. You know the sorts Popeye knocks about with, so 'nuff said on that score.'

'What you two doing up there? Want a hand, Rosie, getting him down the steps?' Doris called out. 'Hang on, I'll put Hope down on the mattress and be with you.'

'No, it's all right,' father and daughter chorused.

'I'm not bothered by either of them, Dad, honestly,' Rosie whispered. 'If anybody comes looking for you I'll soon tell them to sling their hooks. And if they don't get the message, I'll get the Coppers on them–'

'No!' John interrupted, vehemently shaking his head. 'Whatever you do, don't go involving the police. Ain't done, Rosie!' he stressed. 'No, I'll stay with you.' He suddenly swiped a hand about his quivering mouth. 'Ain't leaving you behind on yer own 'cos it's too risky. I'll have a word with Doris about taking the little 'un with her on Friday. 'Least that'll get Hope somewhere safe, then I'll join them later on when this is sorted out.'

'You'll do no such thing!' Rosie shook her father's arm. 'I've said I can look after myself. I'm not a child, you know. I'm a parent myself.' She gave a grim smile. 'I'm no use to Purves or his pals 'cos I don't know the first thing about distilling, and even if I did I'd refuse to give 'em the time of day. They won't waste their time with me. So you're going, and that's that.'

John started to protest but an explosion close by made him quickly resume descending the cellar steps, leaning heavily on his daughter's shoulder. 'I hope you're right, Rosie. But if you're not, don't say I didn't warn you.' He sank his bony fingers into her soft flesh, reinforcing the seriousness of his concern.

John lay down on the mattress, pulling the blanket over himself and his wife. He turned sideways, watching his daughter and granddaughter. Rosie was cuddling Hope, softly singing a nursery rhyme and tickling her under the chin to distract the child from the lethal commotion that ebbed and flowed above their heads.

He closed his eyes, playing over in his mind the one-sided conversation he'd just had with Flint.

121

He'd told him again, truthfully, about Popeye stitching them both up. Flint hadn't commented, he'd just sat, smoking, in that eerily thoughtful way of his, while the rockets roared closer.

John had burbled out everything he could remember about the day Popeye had turned up Out of the blue, and at the end of it the fellow had given a nod as though in acceptance. But John couldn't bring himself to pull the fifty pounds out of his pocket and hand it over to its rightful owner. If Flint knew he'd taken back the cash off Popeye's table he'd smell a rat. As it was, Flint seemed to believe Popeye was the culprit.

But as John had limped towards his front door he'd glanced back and seen Flint staring at the house in a way that had made the blood in his veins run cold. But it'd been too late then to run back and beg the fellow to take the fifty pounds and never come back.

CHAPTER TEN

'Tea should be brewed by now. Pour yer dad his cuppa, will you, Joey, while I see to Vicky?'

Joey Grimes raised his chin from his palms. He'd been sitting reading at the table but he folded his *Dandy* comic, then lifted the woolly-clad pot by his elbow. With a private wink for Rufus he snaffled a Bourbon out of the tin and put it on the saucer by the custard cream Gertie had placed there earlier.

'Good lad,' Rufus praised his son, eagerly taking a swig from the deep brown brew. He fidgeted, making himself comfortable and his injured hand, braced on the chair arm, buckled and he upset the tea with a yelp.

'No better'n a bleedin' baby, am I!' he bawled in frustration, hurling his soggy biscuits to the floor. 'Can't even get tea to me mouth without wetting meself.' He gazed forlornly at the dark stain down the front of his trousers. 'Burned me balls 'n' all ... not that that matters much,' he muttered, throwing his wife a sour look. 'They're out of action...'

'Fer Gawd's sake! What now?' Gertie spat, getting up from where she'd been crouching by her daughter. She lifted Victoria off her potty and wiped the child's bottom.

'Pull her knickers up, Joey, while I see to your father,' Gertie called over her shoulder, halfway to the kitchen for a towel to dry off Rufus.

Obediently Joey jumped up again and helped his little sister get dressed before settling her on the couch. He perched beside Victoria, solemnly watching his parents battling their irritation. But Joey knew that things had turned bad for them as a family long before his father had been shipped home on a stretcher. His mum and dad had started arguing before Vicky had been born, worsening after his little brothers had been killed in an air raid. And Joey knew it was his fault that Adam, Simon and Harry had been left alone in the house that night. If he'd stayed at home with them he'd have woken them up and got them to the safety of an air-raid shelter. But instead he'd

123

chased after his mum who'd hared out to stop his dad battering another bloke. Up until then his mum had made sure to keep all her kids close by, especially after dark when an attack was likely, in case they needed to dive into an underground shelter.

'Here, use that while I clear up this bloody mess you've made.' Gertie lobbed a cloth her husband's way.

Rufus dabbed his trousers, glancing sullenly at his wife. 'Need me other pair to put on.'

'Well you can't have 'em, 'cos I only did the washing this morning and none of it's quite dry yet.' Gertie carried on crawling around on her hands and knees by his feet, using a rag on the rug to soak up the spilled tea and mashed biscuits.

'Get chaps, I will, sitting about in wet stuff,' Rufus grumbled.

'You want to try dunking sheets out in that bleedin' washhouse; that'll give you something to complain about,' Gertie came back at him. She snatched the towel he was flicking aimlessly at his lap and took over mopping him with vigour.

As far as Rufus was concerned he was still master in his own home, even if he was a war cripple. He looked in disgust at his withered right arm that terminated in a hand with just three digits. The thumb and index finger were rotting somewhere in France, or more likely had been eaten by rats by now. His right leg had also taken some shrapnel and was weaker than the left, making him slow getting about.

'For heaven's sake!' Gertie exploded as she heard somebody rattling the handle on the kitchen

124

door. 'If that's the milkman, Joey, tell him I ain't in and I'll settle up with him next week.'

'Ain't interruptin' anything, I hope?' a lewd voice asked a moment later. The new arrival had entered the parlour to find Gertie on her knees fiddling with her husband's trousers.

'Fuck's sake, look who's here,' Rufus breathed in shock.

Gertie scrambled up and gawped at her brother. Slowly her eyes filled with loathing. Joey fidgeted by the door, shamefaced; he was very aware of the feud between his parents and their visitor. He had recognised his fugitive uncle straight off although none of them had spoken to him for years.

'Don't blame him,' Michael Williams said, as his sister's reproachful gaze fixed on her son. 'He tried to block me way but I thought it was time we all had a little get-together. Lucky Joey did let me in or I'd've clumped the little bastard.' Michael glowered at the nephew he'd grown to resent, then at the niece he'd never met. 'Oh hang on ... wrong one. That's the bastard, ain't it?' He nodded at Victoria, gazing up at him with limpid brown eyes.

It was her daughter's shy smile for the uncle who'd insulted her that made Gertie's control snap. 'You mind your mouth around my kids!' she hollered, slapping out. But even with his disability her brother managed to swipe her aside so, she bounced down beside Victoria on the couch.

'What d'you think yer doin' to my wife?' Rufus snarled, manfully struggling up from his chair. His arm and leg wobbled and he fell back, screwing up his fade in frustration.

125

'Ain't so easy, mate, is it, throwing yer weight around when you've got a useless mitt?' Michael sauntered closer, raising the stump that had once been his right arm. He sniggered at Rufus's humiliation, grabbing him and holding their maimed limbs together, comparing them. 'Almost snap. You're still better off 'n me. Got a piece of paw left, ain't yer, Roof?'

'Fer what bleedin' use it is.' Rufus wrenched himself free of his brother-in-law.

Gertie had watched the two men with mounting disbelief as they swapped self-pity. 'You gonna let him speak to me and Vicky like that?' She sprang to her feet, rage shaping her features as she advanced on her husband.

Rufus coloured up, aware of his cowardice but inwardly making excuses for it. He knew he could have another go at staying upright and swinging a left hook. But Midge – as his short-arsed brother-in-law was nicknamed – was no pushover despite his size; the weasel would play dirty and knee him in the nuts before he could nip aside.

A few years back Rufus had been a fine figure of a man: broad and strong. He could have taken Midge on with one hand tied behind his back. But he was fat and unfit now from sitting day in day out in an armchair. He regretted not having heeded his wife when she'd nagged him to stop wallowing and get out of the house for a walk after he'd been discharged from hospital.

Rufus knew he'd never live down his pint-sized brother-in-law flooring him ... not when over the years he'd often put Midge on his back with no more effort than was needed swatting a fly. To his son he was still a hero, if a bit battered around the edges, but he wouldn't be for long if he acted on the message blazing at him from his wife's despising eyes.

'He's just having a lark, ain't yer, Midge?' Rufus mumbled. 'Not funny, though; tell yer that fer nothing.'

'I see. Lost yer bottle!' Gertie snapped in disgust. 'I'll deal with him then.' She surged at Michael, fists on hips. 'You're not welcome here. On yer way, or I'll call the police.' Gertie pointed at the door. 'Don't think I won't. The law's still after you. Couple of plain clothes come round not so long ago asking after your whereabouts.'

It was a lie; it had been years since the police had bothered her with questions about her brother because he was wanted for murder and desertion from the navy. Gertie had known where he'd been hiding, too, and had later regretted not having grassed him up when she'd had the chance.

'Don't take it to heart, Gert; just a bad joke, like Rufus said,' Midge scoffed, brushing past to sit down next to his niece. 'Beauty, ain't she, like her mum? Looks like you. That's handy, ain't it?' He tickled the little girl under her chin, making Victoria giggle. Slyly his eyes slanted up, tormenting Gertie. 'Any more tea in that pot?' He nodded at the table.

Gertie swung Victoria up in her arms, out of Midge's reach, not deigning to answer him. She darted glances between the room's occupants. She didn't want to create a bad scene in front of her children, but she couldn't trust herself to remain in her hateful brother's company without ending up ripping his eyes out.

'You're taking a risk, ain't yer, showing yer face round here?' Rufus knew his wife was boiling up and tried to defuse things by changing the subject. Besides, he was very curious to know what had brought Midge back to his old stamping ground where he might get recognised and arrested. If he was taken to court on a murder charge, Rufus reckoned that Midge'd swing because he knew his brother-in-law had killed a fellow seaman before deserting. Oddly, Rufus was glad Midge had resurfaced; if the law caught up with him it'd do what he was itching to do, but couldn't: put the swine six foot under.

'Old Adolf's done me a favour sending over them rockets.' Midge grinned. 'Coppers are too busy helping to shovel up bricks and bodies to bother coming after us duckers 'n' divers.' He chuckled then began to sing 'Happy Days Are Here Again' in a tuneless croak.

'Could be you'll be one of them bodies getting shovelled up if you stick around these parts.' Gertie gave a sour laugh. 'If there's any justice in this world, that is.'

'Got the luck o' the devil, me.' Midge sniffed cockily. 'But when me number's up, I'll go quietly. So I'll kip on the couch tonight, shall I?' he tacked innocently onto the end.

'You certainly won't!' Gertie stormed. 'I'll turn you in meself if I have to, to get you outta my house.'

'Don't think you will, sis. I know things ... remember...' Midge eyed Joey, sitting tensely on

128

the couch, listening to every word.

Gertie glanced at her son, too. At thirteen Joey was old enough to pick up on a lot of the hidden meaning in adults' talk. And she didn't ever want him knowing that his little sister had a different dad from him. Her brother was hinting at letting that cat out of the bag if he couldn't get his own way. It would kill Rufus, too, if word got round that his wife had got knocked up with another man's child and was rearing it as his own. All her husband had left was his pride; he spent every day in the same clothes, in the same chair, smiling vacantly into space, sheltering in the memories of the confident active fellow he'd once been.

But they still held the ace in the pack: nobody, other than her and Rufus, knew for sure who had fathered Vicky. So her brother could threaten all he liked but he was spitting in the wind, and she told him so.

Midge ignored his sister's triumphal hiss. 'I got some news about a pal of ours. Want to hear it?' He grinned at Rufus, banking on his brother-in-law not being able to turn down a gossip about old times.

Gertie watched Rufus's features lift and felt her spirits sink. He'd told her once that if he ever crossed paths again with her brother he'd kill Midge after what he'd done to their family. Now it looked like he wasn't going to make good on that promise any time soon.

'You've got ten minutes,' Gertie snapped close to her brother's ear before she marched towards the door, carrying Victoria in one hand and the sloshing potty in the other. 'Don't make me come back and repeat meself, 'cos I meant what I said about calling the Old Bill if you don't leave.'

'I meant what I said 'n' all,' Midge purred through a set of dirty uneven teeth, giving his nephew a significant nod. He couldn't prove that his niece was a cuckoo in Rufus's nest, but Midge strongly suspected Victoria was the sprog of a fellow that Gertie used to char for a few years back. Midge had caught them at it on one occasion. The repercussions of him spying on his sister and her lover, then recounting what he'd seen to Rufus, had been the reason the couple had been out, arguing and fighting in the street, on the night their home was demolished with three of their sons in it. Before the tragedy they'd barely tolerated him; now he knew they hated him even though in his opinion he'd done nothing wrong. The way Midge saw it, he'd done Rufus a favour telling him his missus was cheating on him, even if he had done it out of spite.

'Joey! Come on, I need a bit of shopping fetched in.' Gertie narrowed her eyes at her husband on quitting the parlour. As soon as her brother had gone, she'd have something to say to Rufus.

Once Joey had been sent up the road for tea and milk, Gertie stopped slamming around in the kitchen and tiptoed to hover outside the closed parlour door, listening to the conversation going on inside.

'Seen Popeye a few times lately,' Midge said. 'He was asking after you.'

'Yeah? What d'you tell him?' Rufus replied. He was well aware that his wife was irate, and the longer Midge stayed put, to rub it in that he'd leave when he was ready and not before, the more inadequate and guilty Rufus felt at not being able to protect his family from this man.

Midge shrugged, fishing out of a pocket his pouch of Old Holborn. With great deliberation he opened it, pulling out papers and tobacco to have a smoke. 'Nothing much *to* tell Popeye, being as I ain't spoken to you in so long.' Midge rolled the cigarette one-handed on his knee. 'He knew you'd been invalided home, so that weren't news to him.'

'How d'you find out what happened to me?'

Midge's tongue swiped an edge of a Rizla, then he stuck the limp cylinder in his mouth and struck a match against the box wedged between his knees. 'Make it me business to know about me family, don't I?' he said from behind the wagging cigarette. 'I ain't been far away, never fear.'

Rufus could believe that. If anybody could slither out of sight when required, it was this man. He wouldn't be surprised to discover that Midge had been spying on them for some time, picking the right moment to make his presence known.

At one time they'd been partners in crime, and done pretty well at it, too, hoisting goods in Popeye's gang, until Midge injured his hand on a job and the wound turned gangrenous, resulting in an amputation. Then, like a row of dominoes they'd all slowly toppled. Even Popeye had suffered. Rufus blamed his brother-in-law for his little sons' deaths. In the aftermath of that terrible night, crazy with grief and fired up with revenge, Rufus had sworn he'd get even. He'd gone looking for Midge to batter him, but his brother-in-law had already disappeared, something he was a dab hand at doing.

Midge winked, as though reading his brother-in-law's thoughts about their past antics. 'We had some larks in the old days. Remember that time we nearly got caught with a barrow-load of army boots, right outside Popeye's warehouse?' Midge snorted back a guffaw. 'You told those two rozzers that we was taking 'em down to the docks to get shipped out to the artillery. *And* they believed you.' Midge dragged on his wonky roll-up and started coughing. 'Hand it to you, mate, you had the gift of the gab that night,' he croaked. 'If, they'd've opened up that warehouse and taken a gander inside, we'd all have been for it.' Midge merrily shook his head. 'Popeye owes you a good drink 'cos he'd still be serving time over that one.'

'So would we be,' Rufus pointed out sourly. A moment later he was reflecting that he'd sooner have done a bit of hard labour than volunteered: at least he'd still have his health and his little sons. If he'd been in prison, then Midge wouldn't have been able to wind him up over Gertie's affair. Left alone, he and his wife would've worked things out between themselves, but Midge hadn't wanted that. Midge was only happy when he was making everybody else as miserable as he was.

Midge struck another match and relit his dying cigarette. He puffed away on it while thinking along similar lines to Rufus that he'd've been better off doing a stretch inside. If he'd got arrested, instead of returning to his ship, he'd not have heard Jack Chivers calling him a little runt. Midge was sensitive about his size and the rating had always delighted in belittling him. So Midge knifed him, but he'd not expected the stupid bastard to die ... just lick his wounds a bit and keep his gob shut in future.

Rufus stared into space, torn between pride and regret as he recalled how after his road-sweeping shifts for the council he'd go bomb chasing at night in Popeye's gang. When an explosion took out a shop front, he and his cronies would be waiting to dive in and pinch everything they could reach. Domestic houses had also yielded rich pickings. People would return home from the underground shelters to find they'd been cleaned out during a raid. When he thought about it now, Rufus felt guilty about having thieved from ordinary folk. The affluent shopkeepers he couldn't give a toss about. He might have damaged his arm but the chip on his shoulder was still in place.

After the spoils were divided Rufus would have his pockets full of cash to spend. He'd have a different tart every night when Gertie gave him the cold shoulder and he'd live it up in Soho dives till the early hours. But after his sons had perished Rufus had put all his bad ways behind him, sure he was being punished for his sins. He'd gone to fight the Boche and avenge his dead boys to make amends. And look where that had landed him: back at home, no use to anybody.

'Popeye's got some stuff needs doing; asked me to find out if you was interested in coming out of retirement.' Midge sat back comfortably on the couch, crossing what was left of his arms over his chest.

'Sod me!' Rufus chortled. 'He's hit rock bottom

if two cripples are all he can afford.' He was starting to enjoy his chat with his brother-in-law and that made him feel guilty. Midge had caused bad trouble for him and Gertie and Rufus knew the last thing he should be doing was having a laugh and a joke with him. He grimaced to show his lack of interest in the work, adopting a bored expression and staring out of the window.

Midge sensed that Rufus was going cold on him so decided a bit of flannel wouldn't go amiss to bring him round. Midge had always been able to manipulate his brother-in-law. It was one of the reasons why his sister hated him. But this time he'd need to tread carefully or Gertie would burst in on them. He knew the nosey cow was just out-side the door with her ear pressed to the keyhole. 'You 'n' Gertie done well to hold it all together after what the Germans did to yer.' Midge eyed his brother-in-law from under his brows, nodding solemnly, 'Them little boys didn't deserve to go like that.'

'Seem to recall you had a hand in it,' Rufus snarled.

'Weren't my fault, mate, you know that. We might've had our fallings out over the years but Jerry bombed yer house, not me.'

Rufus flicked a hand as though he couldn't be bothered arguing with Midge. In fact he would've loved to be able to jump up and smack the smug smile off his brother-in-law's chops.

'You might have taken a few knocks in France, getting back at 'em for what they done to yer, but I bet you took a few of them Krauts down first, didn't you?'

Rufus gave a sulky nod, his mouth tilting in the start of a smile.

Midge tapped his skull, 'Can see you've stayed strong up here, where it counts, ain't yer Roof?'

'Had to ... family relying on me, ain't they?' Rufus sat straighter in the chair, chest puffing out. He turned to face his brother-in-law. 'So, what sort of pony work has Popeye got that suits a couple of cripples like us, then?'

'Might be that cripples are just what he needs.' Midge squinted craftily through a haze of tobacco smoke.

'Ain't going out begging, and that's final,' Rufus stated. 'If I wanted to use a crutch and rattle a tin, could do it on me own. Don't need him.'

'Ain't begging,' Midge replied scornfully.

Rufus frowned. 'Gonna explain then?'

'Popeye's still doing his printing...' Midge offered up the titbit then got up with a comfortable stretch and placed his open pack of rolling tobacco on Rufus's lap.

Rufus had watched how his brother-in-law made himself a smoke with one hand and fierce concentration. He knew that Midge's lazy gaze was on him, challenging him to match his skill. And Rufus would like a fag. He'd felt jittery having this man turn up on him out of the blue, and he hadn't yet fully calmed down.

Midge and Popeye were ghosts from Rufus's past and just hours ago he'd have said he didn't want memories of them haunting him. But Midge was hinting some cash might be in the offing, and Rufus definitely liked the sound of that. He pushed his good hand into the tobacco. 'Well, spit it out, if you've got something to say.'

'Pop's counterfeiting ration books and wants our help with it 'cos he knows he can trust us. That's what he said.'

Rufus slowly withdrew his empty fingers from the tobacco pouch. 'Eh?' He screwed up his features as his hopes died. He knew nothing about working a printing press but guessed he'd never manage it one-handed.

'Pop's sidekick's had his collar felt delivering ration books to clients. The bloke didn't grass Pop up, though. Bad news for Pop was that he had to shell out to keep the geezer's missus sweet. She went berserk when her husband went inside and started threatening calling the police unless she got a payout.' Midge sat down again on the couch as he got further into his tale. 'Pop's lost a lot of stock, 'cos the ration books the bloke had on him when he was nicked got confiscated. Pop needs to get going again quick 'cos he borrowed the hush money off a docker, name of Flint. And Flint's not happy 'cos he was expecting a nice big consignment of rotgut off Popeye's contact in return for his cash. Now he wants his money back and Popeye ain't got it.'

'Sounds like a right mess to me,' Rufus said.

'And me,' Midge chirruped. 'Thing is, s'long as I get paid I don't give a toss how Popeye sorts the rest out.'

Rufus grimaced agreement to that. 'So ... we're supposed to take over from Popeye's pal who's in prison?'

Midge gave a nod.

Rufus threw back his head and thudded softly.

'I like old Pop's sense of humour. He wants two blokes who ain't got a full set of hands between 'em to do deliveries.'

'We'd be inconspicuous ... left alone, Pop said. 'Nobody's gonna suspect two poor old soldiers are up to no good now, are they?'

Rufus was listening intently. 'How we supposed to be getting about delivering these here fake ration books? Takes me ten minutes to get to the corner shop.'

'He's got a car we can use.'

This time Rufus exploded in laughter, his fat belly wobbling and tears of mirth running down his cheeks.

Midge chuckled too but he carried on explaining: 'Left-hand drive, it is; Pop got it shipped in cheap, just before the war started 'cos he fancied a French coupé to show off to the tart he likes down the pub.'

Midge got up from the sofa, settled his backside on the chair arm next to his brother-in-law and demonstrated steering with his left hand. He nudged Rufus. 'Now you change gear.' He nudged Rufus again, harder, when he refused to play along.

Rufus mimed wrenching on a gear stick and handbrake with his left hand.

'See, easy as pie.' He winked at Rufus. 'Let you drive once in a while, if yer like, and I'll do the gears.'

'Sounds daft to me,' Rufus said, but there was a smile in his tone.

Outside in the hallway, Gertie had almost danced on the spot in rage when she heard her husband laughing with the brother-in-law he was supposed to detest. When she'd heard Midge talking, about her dead sons she'd almost burst in to batter him for daring to mention them. But she'd not done so because she'd wanted to learn more. And the rest of what she'd overheard had shocked and worried her.

Of course she'd known Rufus had been a member of Frank Purves' little gang of looters, so hearing the two men reminiscing about that hadn't come as a surprise. Years ago she'd been pleased to share the benefits of her husband's illegal profits. He'd brought her in clothes and household goods that had been filched from top stores, although he always kept for himself the cash he earned from Pop. But that had all occurred during the height of the Blitz, when things had seemed delightfully carefree compared to the dogged unhappiness of their lives since.

Now she'd lost three of her beloved children, and her husband. Oh, Rufus might be a physical presence in her life, but he wasn't the man she'd fallen in love with and married. That strapping attractive fellow no longer existed. When she thought hard about it, she realised Rufus might just as well have been buried along with Adam, Simon and Harry. He'd not withered in France, but on the night he'd unearthed three small bodies from the rubble of their home.

Much as Gertie wished her husband could get himself out of the house to work, becoming involved again with Midge and Popeye seemed like trouble they could all do without. Suddenly her mounting fury and anxiety were no longer controllable. She burst into the room and swung a glare between her husband and brother.

'Time's up ... get going.' Gertie jerked her head at the door.

Midge got to his feet without comment. He removed his pack of Old Holborn from Rufus's lap and rammed it into a pocket.

'Be seeing you then,' Midge said cheerily.

Rufus mumbled a reply, regretting that he'd not managed to get a smoke out of Midge. A fag was one of the few pleasures left to him and Gertie was always grumbling about the cost of tobacco. But he was thinking about the carrot his brother-in-law had dangled. It sounded a ridiculous scheme, but he'd thought that when Midge had first tempted him with the bomb lark. And how he'd love a return to those days.

'Don't ever show yer face here again.' Gertie followed her brother out into the kitchen to the back door, shoving the bolt home after him the moment he was outside.

She heard his laugh, triumphant and low. Midge was letting her know that he'd got what he came for: Rufus was his for the taking and she, and the kids, didn't matter.

CHAPTER ELEVEN

'Doing Mummy's shopping again, are yer, Grime-sie?'

Joey's response to being taunted was to thrust two fingers up at the sniggering boys. They used to be his friends although they were in the year below at school. Joey didn't spend much time with any of his school pals now and couldn't wait to leave at the end of term and find work. Sticking close to his mum for the past few years had made him a joke figure amongst the lads he used to knock about with, but he didn't care. Joey had grown up since tragedy struck his family.

After his brothers' funeral his dad had made him promise to look after his mum when he went off to fight. His mum had been expecting Vicky then, and after she was born, staying at home had stopped being a chore for Joey. From the first peep at his tiny sister, he'd adored Victoria, and had gladly lent a hand with nappies and bottles. Now that she was older, toddling and causing mischief, Vicky still had him wrapped around her little finger. Joey regretted now having made excuses to skive off when his mum had asked him to mind his younger brothers. He'd give anything to have them back, sitting on the hearthrug with him, playing a game of cards. They'd been useless at it, too: too young to understand even a game of Snap. But he'd enjoyed teaching them as they'd gazed up at him with wide, admiring eyes, while their mum worked out in the wash-house.

One of the taunting boys made a lunge for the bag of shopping Joey was swinging in a hand. Instinctively Joey jabbed with a fist in the way his father had taught him, when Rufus had still been capable of giving him boxing lessons.

'I saw that, Joey Grimes,' a lecturing voice said.

A mousy-haired girl had been sitting on her front step, watching the boys while shelling peas into a colander. Wiping her hands on her pinafore, Becky Pugh got up and joined Joey as he carried on down the street, leaving the boys bawling abuse.

'You'll get into trouble,' Becky warned, crossing her thin arms over her middle. 'He'll go crying to his dad.'

'So what?' Joey shrugged. 'He started it.' A few years back no man in the neighbourhood would have come to their house to complain to Rufus Grimes about his son in case he got a thick ear. But things were different now. Much as his dad might want to defend him, Joey knew he couldn't.

He looked up, noticing in the distance somebody else capable of causing trouble for them. His uncle had just left their house and was bowling towards him in that cocky way he had. Deliberately, Joey crossed the road to avoid Michael.

'Who's that?' Becky nodded her head in Midge's direction, trotting after Joey. She'd also seen the short fellow swaggering out of the Grimeses' back gate.

'Nobody ... he ain't nobody.' Joey muttered contemptuously. He slung Becky a frown as though

141

annoyed at her tagging along when he was brooding on important stuff.

His uncle was too far away for Joey to read his expression, but Midge was sure to have a smirk on his ferret-like features. His turning up out of the blue seemed a very bad omen to Joey. He would never forget his brothers, but for all of their sakes he didn't want his uncle's spite breathing new life into a tragedy that had occurred years ago.

Becky huffed, trying to gain Joey's attention as he strode on down the street. She ignored the hint to get lost when she received another irritated look from him.

She liked Joey, and was sure that under his gruff exterior he liked her too. They'd both turned thirteen and Becky was ready for her first proper boyfriend. She glanced at Joey's stocky body and wiry auburn hair as they strolled side by side. His jaw and upper lip had a fuzz of gingery whiskers that made him resemble his father as he'd once been. Now Becky hardly recognised the big, strong neighbour who'd once kept the local men in awe of him.

'Oi, Joey, see you again soon, mate.'

Joey ignored his uncle's cheery shout because he knew Michael was trying to wind him up. Joey wouldn't take his bait in the way his mum and dad did. He stared straight ahead, swallowing the urge to spit in the gutter as they passed on opposite pavements.

Midge hated him, and Joey knew why that was: when his uncle had injured his hand on a looting spree the others hadn't wanted him along any more, slowing them down. Joey had taken Midge's place in the gang before he'd turned ten years old and had been the one nipping in and out of small spaces, gathering up the merchandise, in the way Midge used to do. He'd enjoyed the work, and the tanners he'd earned in wages. But Midge had let him know in snide remarks that he resented losing his job to a kid.

'He been visiting yer dad?' Becky asked. 'Looks like he's been in the wars too,' she remarked sympathetically. 'Old army mates, are they?'

'He ain't done nothing to be proud of, take it from me,' Joey said sourly, and let himself in the back gate.

'You should come to the station to see us off.'

Rosie shook her head, blinking back her tears. 'I can't, Dad.' She forced the words out past an enormous lump in her throat. She knew that if she went with them she might break down on the station platform and refuse to let go of her daughter. 'We'll say our goodbyes now, won't we, sweetheart?' she whispered, swaying her body to and fro with the little girl clasped tightly to her.

'There's no need fer goodbyes.' John gripped Rosie's shoulder. 'You can still come with us. We'll catch a later train,' he urged. 'I can see you're eaten up, love, at the thought of being without her. Get a suitcase packed on the quick and I'll get the taxi to come back in an hour...'

'Fer Gawd's sake! How many times does the girl have to say she's staying behind?' Doris interrupted. She was pulling on her white cotton gloves. She'd dressed in her Sunday best for the train trip to Kent, and was ready and raring to

143

go. And nobody would have begrudged Doris her eagerness to get out of London. In the past few days the doodlebugs had hardly let up, and the damage to property and the loss of life was shattering the morale of even the sturdiest folk.

Rosie buried her face into her daughter's sweet-smelling hair. Last night she'd given Hope a bath and let the little girl choose which outfit she wanted to wear the following day for her big adventure. Even as Rosie had folded small clothes and packed them in a trunk it hadn't fully sunk in that Hope was going away from her ... and, if fate decreed, they might never see one another again. Constantly Rosie impressed on herself that her sacrifice wasn't unique; every day mothers stood weeping on station platforms waving off their children to safety. Then they turned round and went to work, braving the dangers of driving buses or mobile canteens, never knowing if they'd survive another night of the Luftwaffe's bombardment.

Rosie avoided looking at her father; she knew if he begged her again to go with them, her resolve might yet waver despite her good intentions.

'Give her here...' Doris firmly removed the child from her mother's possessive clutch. 'Come on, that's the taxi driver getting impatient.'

A car hooter had blasted twice outside in quick succession.

''Bye, Dad.' Rosie hugged her father before cupping his face and brushing away the tears on his cheeks with her thumbs. Picking up his suitcase in one hand and Doris's in the other, she set off down the hallway, knowing that if she kept

144

occupied she'd be less likely to break down as well. The little party filed out into strong summer sunshine. The moment he'd seen them emerge from the house the cabby had jumped out to open the back door of his vehicle.

The practicalities of getting the cases stashed away safely took Rosie away from her daughter. By the time the boot was slammed shut her little girl was sitting between John and Doris on the back seat.

John immediately wound down the window and put his hand out to take Rosie's. She kissed its clasped knuckles but her hand was soon weaving past to stroke her daughter's soft, smiling cheek. With a pang she realised that Hope was excited to be going on holiday without her.

'What did I tell you?' Rosie whispered.

'Be good girl...' Hope murmured with a grin for her mum.

'And what else?'

Hope shook her head to indicate she'd forgotten.

'Love you lots and lots.'

Hope repeated the mantra, blinking solemnly.

'She will be good ... you're always good, aren't you, poppet?' Doris gave Rosie an encouraging smile as her stepdaughter pulled a handkerchief from a sleeve to wipe her eyes. An uneasy truce had formed between the two women following their bad argument on the day Rosie learned about the planned move to Gravesend.

'Take care of yourself, Rosie,' John called as the driver put the cab into gear. 'Remember, we're just a phone call away, any time of the day or night.

Where's that number I gave you?' he demanded agitatedly, turning on the seat as the car started to move. 'Have you put it somewhere safe?' He poked his head out of the window to shout out.

Rosie pulled the scrap of paper from her pocket and shook it to reassure him.

As the cab picked up speed she saw that her dad had helped Hope to her feet so the child could wave to her from the back window. Frantically, with both hands, Rosie waved until her shoulders ached but her daughter's face soon blurred to an indistinct pink oval as Rosie's eyes were awash with tears.

Hazel Scott dropped her crochet and jumped up from her armchair. 'You remember me, don't you?'

Rosie juggled the folded uniform in her arms to shake hands with her new colleague. 'Of course I remember you.' Rosie was pleased to see the young woman again.

'I'll let Scott introduce you to everybody,' Stella Phipps said, hands on her hips, creasing the three stripes on her navy-blue sleeve. There was a proprietary tilt to her chin as she glanced about the room scented with burned toast from the canteen. People were reading or doing handicrafts while waiting to go on duty at nine o'clock. 'Let's hope the peace and quiet continues for your first day, Gardiner. It might look like we're all skiving, but when the tide *does* come in ... by God, we all know it.' She sighed. 'I'm going to be in my office for an hour or two, writing up the week's timetables with Norris. When Lawson turns up, she'll give you your instructions.' The deputy station officer strode off, wafting lavender water in her wake.

'You've not yet met Thora Norris, have you?' Hazel said. 'She's a shift leader, going off duty soon. Her and Stella are *good friends,* so they shut themselves in the office when they can, if you get my drift.'

Rosie didn't, and she frowned enquiringly.

'Pair of lesies, but nobody here turns a hair at that. A couple of the conchies have a smooch when they think nobody's about. We're very broad-minded at Robley Road.' Hazel's mascaraed lashes drooped in a subtle wink.

Rosie bit her lip, suppressing a smile and hoping she wasn't blushing too obviously. She didn't think Hazel was joking but her candid account of some of her associates' love lives was startling and rather bizarre. It was also quite terrifying to Rosie. She liked Hazel, and hoped they'd become friends, but the brunette obviously enjoyed a gossip and that made Rosie determined to guard her tongue over her personal circumstances.

A woman who appeared to be knitting a length of scarf raised a hand to welcome Rosie.

'That's Clarice. She's all right, is Clarice. Office orderly; answers the phone and dishes out the dockets for incidents and so on. She'll be going on shift with us at nine o'clock. What time is it?' Hazel glanced at the clock on the wall. 'Oh, shame: no time for another cuppa. Have you eaten breakfast?'

'Had a chunk of bread and jam before I left home.' Rosie realised that the people who were due on shift with her were packing away their things. She'd reported for duty in Stella Phipps's office at eight fifteen that morning, but it seemed she wasn't the only one to have arrived early for work.

'Damn! I overslept again!' a newcomer announced, hurrying into the room, clipboard and pencil poised theatrically.

'Should've kicked him out of bed sooner,' Hazel muttered dirtily.

'Oh, really, Scott! You are crude.' The young woman approached them, smiling amiably. 'The DSO said somebody was starting today.'

'I'm Rosie Gardiner. Pleased to meet you.'

'I'm Janet Lawson, shift leader.' Two manicured fingers tapped briskly at a pair of stripes on her upper arm. She looked at her watch. 'I'd better go and start the inspection so we don't get lumbered cleaning up the previous lot's shoddy work. I found an upturned bucket of pigswill by the shed yesterday; I know there's a water shortage, but they could've put a bit of elbow grease behind a broom.'

Rosie watched the pretty redhead disappear, admiring her outfit. 'She looks very smart.' Rosie had noticed that Janet's uniform was of far better quality than the safari-style serge jacket and plain navy-blue skirt and trousers that she and Hazel had been issued with. A gabardine cap with ear-flaps and a tin hat rested on the top of the clothing she was carrying, as did her auxiliary's badge.

'Her father's something big in the city so she's got plenty of money to splash. Janet gets her uniform specially tailored ... unlike the rest of us, who have to make do with regular kit.' Hazel hitched her thick navy skirt to display that her black stockings had an obvious darn in them. 'All sorts volunteer to be auxiliaries, you know,' she added. 'We've got posh ones and intellectual ones...' Hazel nodded at a grey-haired fellow who was stuffing a novel into a pocket of his navy-blue fatigues. 'Jim Warwick's a university professor. He reads poems aloud to us sometimes. He mucks in as a driver in between his lectures. No airs and graces ... unlike some.'

Having heard his name mentioned, Jim gave a polite nod and Hazel made proper introductions.

'Right, come on then, Rookie,' she said. 'You'd better get dressed for action. I know I've got to clean the inside of our ambulance so no point putting it off. They do get in a right state.' She grimaced revulsion. 'As you can imagine. You can lend a hand, if you like.' Hazel led the way to the door. 'I work as Tom Anderson's assistant. You remember Tom, don't you, from the day of your interview?' Hazel indicated her partner, who was boxing some dominoes. 'Tom's a bloody good driver as well as being our mechanic. Perhaps when you pass your driving test I can pair up in a wagon with you instead.' Hazel giggled. 'It'd be a hoot, the two of us!'

Rosie hoped she didn't look too surprised, or disappointed. She'd imagined that ambulance auxiliaries tended the sick and wounded rather than the equipment. While waiting for an emergency call-out she'd visions of the staff winding bandages and fastening them neatly with safety pins, or making themselves useful in other lady-like ways.

'It's bloody hard work,' Hazel snorted, reading Rosie's mind. 'And not all guts and glory, or doctor-and-nurse romance, as you'll find out.' She nudged Rosie. 'Mind you, there is a particularly nice young GP who pops in and out at the Sparrow Road first-aid post.' She gave Rosie a knowing glance. 'You're in the market for a boyfriend, aren't you? I'll introduce you to Richard Clark!' she declared.

Rosie chuckled, but kept to herself her aversion to a romantic entanglement. It seemed there'd never be a dull moment with Hazel Scott about.

By lunchtime Rosie felt shattered even though she'd not lifted a single heavy stretcher. She could certainly understand why Stella Phipps had asked her if she considered herself to be physically fit. Regular housework was nothing compared to this.

Hazel hadn't been joking when she said the vehicles needed to be gleaming to pass muster. And they weren't even proper ambulances but motors that had been converted by adding a box van body and fittings for four stretchers. Makeshift or not, the inside had to be scrubbed from top to bottom and finished off with furniture wax, especially the stretcher runners to help them slide easily. The blankets had to be inspected and aired or replaced with clean ones. All the internal fittings had to be checked. While she and Hazel had beavered side by side, jostling and bumping in the confined space, Tom had washed and polished the Studebaker's coachwork before opening the bonnet. He'd topped up the tanks, then tinkered about with nuts and bolts. Tom had told Rosie that the basic engine checks would be her responsibility if she were successful in passing through as an ambulance driver, so she'd watched carefully as he dipped the oil and wrote his findings and the mileage in a logbook.

'So, what did you think?' Hazel asked when they sat down in the canteen at one o'clock to have lunch. 'Not what you signed up for?'

Rosie sank her weary spine against the chair back. 'Give me a while to recover and I'll let you know.' She took a hungry bite from a cheese sandwich. Never had anything tasted so good.

'So, what's next on the agenda?' she asked eventually, feeling energised by the two strong cups of tea she'd downed.

'You could tackle a bit of sewing, if you like. The spare set of blackout curtains are on the mending shelf. Any good with a needle and cotton?' Seeing Rosie's expression hovering between disappointment and disbelief, Hazel slapped the table in glee. 'I promise you, in a few weeks' time, when you're out on a call, soaked to the skin from fire hoses, you'll be crying out for a day like this.'

Rosie smiled; Hazel was no doubt right. But the thought of being doused with water was preferable to that of tending to the injured and dying. She'd briskly patched her dad up when the blast had torn open his leg and ever since she'd rescued Hope from her rubble-strewn pram she had managed to quash the debilitating fear that had been with her since the Café de Paris blast. What frightened Rosie now was that she'd be found wanting when her help was essential. Gertie's tale

151

of begging the ambulance auxiliaries to save her sons' lives on the night they'd perished haunted Rosie's mind. Those women hadn't been able to grant Gertie her greatest wish, and Rosie sensed such inadequacy would be hard for her to bear when thoughts of her own daughter were never far from her mind.

CHAPTER TWELVE

'My dad's gone away.'

'Yeah, I know.'

His lazy answer threw Rosie, as did his unexpectedly casual attitude. When she'd first opened the door she'd been stunned into gawping idiotically. Previously she'd only caught a glimpse of his profile in the twilight, yet she'd immediately recognised him.

During their hushed conversation on the cellar steps as doodlebugs roared overhead her father had mentioned his name but now she couldn't bring it to mind. He was Frank Purves' friend, she remembered that, and Popeye was a person Rosie wanted nothing to do with, ever.

Suddenly she realised that her unwanted visitor might try to barge past to check if her dad was home, so she jerkily repositioned in readiness to shut him out. She prickled beneath the assessment of a pair of deep-blue eyes. 'If you know my dad's not here, why d'you bother coming round?'

'To see you.'

'To see me?' Rosie demanded hoarsely, unwittingly pulling the door open again.

'Last time I saw you, you were in your nightie.' He settled back comfortably against the porch wall. 'Can't blame a bloke for coming back for another look.' He cast a jaundiced eye over her navy-blue uniform. 'No such luck...' he muttered wryly.

Unable to conjure up a quick riposte, Rosie slammed the door in his face, her cheeks burning.

Nervously she yanked it open again. She didn't want him to know he scared her. He hadn't moved; he was still leaning against the rose trellis, hands in pockets, as though he'd known she'd succumb to curiosity about him. She was glad he hadn't started hammering on the door and brought the likes of Peg Price out to find out what was going on. The nosy old cow would enjoy gossiping about her having gentlemen callers in her father's absence.

'I know you're friends with Frank Purves, my dad told me,' Rosie challenged. 'He said one or other of you might come round asking after him. He's gone to Wales and he's not coming back.'

'Wales, eh?' The comment was heavily ironic. 'Taking the scenic route via Kent, is he?'

Rosie licked her dry lips. So his air of boredom was fake He'd been checking up on them. 'Don't know what you're talking about. Now get lost or I'll...' Her voice tailed away. Her father had impressed on her not to use the police as a threat against him.

'Or you'll do what?' he prompted.

'Just get fucking lost,' Rosie choked and again

153

made to close the door. But this time his hand stayed it, sending her stumbling back into the hall. She saw then that he had a perfect opportunity to come in if he wanted to. He turned on the step, his height and breadth filling the open doorway. He'd only to put a foot over the threshold and close the door behind him.

'Phoning up your dad later, are you?'

Rosie bit her lip.

'Easy question: are you speaking to John later?'

Rosie clamped her lips together and gave a curt nod.

'Tell him I'd like my money back. He can put a cheque in the post.' A corner of his mouth quirked. 'Pick it up from here, shall I?'

'My dad doesn't owe you any money, he told me so. Go and bother Frank Purves about it.'

'Yeah, I would, but he's in hospital.'

Rosie's eyes widened in alarm, her heart drumming beneath her ribs.

'Nothing to do with me, honest.' He put his hands up in mock defence. 'Cross-eyed git got his finger trapped in his printing press and it gave him a nasty turn.'

Rosie frowned, wondering if the man was joking.

'Straight up. Tell you what, Mrs...?' He paused. 'What is your name, by the way?'

'What's yours?' Rosie threw back at him.

'Conor Flint. Call you Rosemary then, shall I? Frank Purves said your name was Rosemary although he didn't know your married name.'

Rosie darted to the door to slam it but he had stepped over the threshold and past her without so much as brushing her slender figure with a smartly suited elbow.

'Get out!' she ordered. 'If you don't, I'll call the police.'

Within seconds she regretted letting him panic her into saying that when he sent the open door into its frame by a flick of his fingers, cutting off the mellow evening sun. Then he frowned at the ceiling. 'Not a good start, this, is it?'

Rosie remained silent and still for a few seconds, gathering her courage. Then she pointed at the door. 'Go away. I've got to go on late duty.' It was a lie; she had just finished work at Station 97 and had got home only about fifteen minutes ago. She'd been on the point of going to the phone box on the corner to have a chat with her dad before settling down for the evening. She wondered if Conor Flint knew she was lying and had watched her come in.

'Ambulance Auxiliary, are you?' He glanced at the badge pinned on her lapel.

'Very astute,' Rosie mocked.

'Where's your daughter?'

'Daughter?' Rosie echoed.

'You had a little blonde girl with you last time I saw you. Reasoned it must be the granddaughter your dad spoke about.'

'My dad spoke about her?'

'You going to repeat everything I say?'

'No, I'm going to repeat what I said. Clear off and don't come back.'

'I take it John didn't ask you to give me something?'

'Like what?' Rosie demanded after an uneasy pause.

'An envelope stuffed with cash?'

'The only thing I'll give you is a warning not to harass me or there'll be trouble.' Rosie knew that her empty threat hadn't worried him in the least, but for some reason he allowed her the victory.

'All right, I'm going. But when you speak to your dad tell him I said hello and that I want my five hundred quid.'

'Five hundred quid?' Rosie choked.

'You're doing it again.'

Rosie's fretting was interrupted by a ratatat on the door. Her heart leaped to her throat and she cursed beneath her breath that somebody else had turned up at such an embarrassing moment. She watched Conor Flint raise an enquiring eyebrow then, when she stayed put, he reached out a hand and turned the latch.

'Collecting for the Turners, Mrs Deane.' Peg Price thrust out a cup with a few coins in it. 'Spare something, can yer, for the poor souls?' The woman's sly eyes swung towards Conor. 'You can chip in, too, if yer like, Mr...?'

'Flint,' Conor said, digging in a pocket.

'Ooh, you're a gentleman, Mr Flint; come back again, you can,' Peg simpered as he folded a crisp ten-shilling note and placed it on top of the copper and silver.

Rosie was aware of his smile deepening as she smothered a snort at Peg's praise. Then her neighbour whipped the cup gleefully in her direction.

'Oh ... right ... I'll just get my purse,' Rosie said although tempted to tell them both to sling their hooks.

The Turners had lived a few streets away until

a rocket destroyed their home and possessions and killed their eldest son. Rosie was pleased that the local community was rallying round for the family. But she wasn't glad that she'd been wrong in thinking Peg might be oblivious to a stranger in the vicinity. The woman made it her business to keep her eyes peeled. The old muck-spreader must have been hovering behind her nets to have arrived so promptly.

'Saw you come in from work, dear, and thought I'd pop along before you went to bed.' Again Peg's crafty eyes veered between the couple. 'Won't keep yer long. Don't mean to interrupt nuthin'.'

'You're not,' Rosie ejected between her teeth.

'Oh, forgotten yer wedding ring, have yer?' Peg nodded at Rosie's bare fingers, her expression amused.

'No, I haven't; I don't wear it to work, 'case it gets lost, if you must know.' It was a lame excuse and Rosie felt blood flood her cheeks. Most married women never took off their gold bands, whatever they were doing. She turned away quickly to go to rummage for a few shillings, then realised it would be best not to leave her un-wanted visitors alone together. Flint had already learned more about her because of the woman's big mouth. Peg would take a delight in telling him everything she knew ... or suspected ... about the widow *Mrs Deane*.

'I'll come up to yours with some money in a moment.' Rosie nodded at her front gate in a significant way.

''S'all right, I've got to be off.' Conor gave Peg a smile then glanced at Rosie. ''Bye, Mrs Deane.

Be in touch...'

Rosie was sure he'd used her fictional name sarcastically, as though he also believed she'd never been anybody's wife.

'Don't run off on my account,' Peg called after him cheerily.

He didn't reply as he closed the gate after him.

'Sorry, love, didn't mean to scare him off like that. Charmer, ain't he?' Peg cocked her head at Rosie, challenging her to say what was on her mind. She didn't have to wait long to get a response from the younger woman.

'I bet you put those coppers in yourself, didn't you, just so you could make out you was collecting and come round and spy on me? Well, you're wasting your time thinking you've found something to chew over with your cronies. He knows my dad, that's all there is to it.' Rosie was about to slam the door in Peg's face but she wanted to contribute something to the Turners' whip-round. She didn't like Peg Price but she did trust the woman to hand over what she'd collected. Rosie was halfway down the hall to fetch her money when Peg's remark drifted after her.

'So the mice are at play while the cat's away, eh?'

'Sorry ... don't get you?' Rosie said, although she knew very well what Peg meant. The old witch still wasn't satisfied that she'd stirred the pot thoroughly enough.

'Good-looking feller ... generous, too.' Peg shook the cup, smirking. 'Bet you get lonely don't yer, dear, now the family's gone down Kent?' She jerked her head after Conor. 'He asked me if John was in; told him he'd gone to Gravesend. Still come 'n' knocked, though, didn't he?' She leaned to pat Rosie's sleeve. 'Nobody would blame a pretty young widder wanting a bit of company, 'specially once the kiddie was out of the way.'

'You've got a dirty mind, Mrs Price.' Rosie marched back towards the door. 'And I'll thank you to keep your nose out of my family's business.' She dug in her uniform pocket for a bit of change to get rid of the woman quickly. Dropping a florin and a thrupenny bit in the cup, she shut the door in Peg's livid face. 'I told you he's a friend of my dad's!' she yelled through the panels, unable to stop herself again justifying Flint's presence in her house. Immediately, though, she felt irritated at herself for having done it.

'So now he knows yer dad's not about, he won't be back, I suppose,' Peg crowed. 'I'd put ten bob on it that he will.'

Rosie heard the woman stomp off and slam the gate. Peg reckoned Flint would be back and, with a feeling that was part dread, part thrill, Rosie feared the old cow might be right.

Rosie unbuttoned her jacket. She was going to telephone her father later from the box on the corner, but she wouldn't mention Flint's visit. Her father would panic and want to come home and protect her. Rosie knew they had all settled in well at Doris's daughter-in-law's because John had told her so when they'd spoken on the phone at the beginning of the week. He'd put Hope on the line that evening. There'd been no tears from her daughter; her little girl had chattered on about cows in a field and her pink eiderdown. But Rosie had sobbed all the way back to her front door. She was missing her daughter dreadfully but it was the knowledge that Hope was content without her that really made her feel melancholy.

CHAPTER THIRTEEN

'What you so happy about?'

Gertie had lugged a bag of shopping into the kitchen to find Rufus whistling while making himself a pot of tea.

'Oh, just feeling in a good mood.' Rufus set another cup and saucer for his wife then hobbled jauntily to the pantry to fetch a bottle of milk. He splashed some into china then spooned in a generous amount of sugar.

''Ere! Steady! That's all we've got left.' Gertie snatched the bowl away, then dumped the shopping bag on the table to unload it. The few pounds of potatoes were stowed under the sink, together with a cabbage; the loaf and bag of broken biscuits she left out, ready for teatime. She wasn't feeling as chirpy as her husband, having just spent over an hour queuing at the bakery so they could have jam sandwiches later.

'There y'are ... get that down yer, Gert.' Rufus pushed his wife's tea towards her on the wooden draining board. 'I'll put the wireless on, shall I? Just catch the end of *Worker's Playtime*. I know it's your favourite.'

Gertie mumbled thanks and watched Rufus as

he disappeared into the parlour. She only half listened to the programme being tuned in because she was brooding on the remarkable change in her husband.

Rufus was brighter and moving about faster than she'd have thought possible after he'd been invalided home. Gertie knew who she had to thank for that, and it wasn't his doctor. It was her detestable brother. Midge was the one who'd got Rufus to buck his ideas up with talk of wages and old times. A couple of weeks had passed since Midge put in a surprise appearance but ever since his visit her husband had been in training for something.

Not so long ago Rufus would lie in bed till noon and not bother bathing till his wife told him he stank. Now he got up before she did and boiled a kettle every morning for a wash and shave. Rufus would never have offered to bring in the groceries; now he made a point of asking Gertie if he could go shopping to stretch his legs. He'd have done the trip today if he'd not been up to his elbows in soil. He was slowly digging them a vegetable patch ... and that was a first in all their years of marriage. Previously, even cutting the hedge had been too much of a chore and Joey had been given the task as soon as he was old enough to handle the shears. Now Rufus only sat in his armchair during the day to take a breather from his hectic activities.

Midge hadn't been back – leastways, not while Gertie had been home. But she suspected that the swine had been in the house. She knew how her brother's mind worked; he'd loiter out of sight till he was sure that Rufus was on his own, then sneak round to the back door and persuade his brother-in-law to let him in. What annoyed Gertie was that Rufus had been denying any secret meetings had taken place when she confronted him.

Gertie had returned home once to a smell of tobacco smoke in the parlour. Rufus had said he'd rolled himself a smoke, but Gertie knew he was lying. He'd not had any tobacco or any cash to nip out and buy some. Sooner or later she'd catch the two of them cosying up and all hell would break loose.

'Off out later this evening, Gertie,' Rufus blurted in a way that was, at the same time, appealing and assertive.

Gertie put down the slab of margarine she'd been about slide onto the butter dish. 'Oh … where you off to then?' she demanded.

'Now don't go getting all narky, but me 'n' Midge got a job on. You're always saying we need proper money coming in, love,' he added persuasively.

'So owning up at last, are you?' Gertie snapped, ramming her fists on her hips. 'He's been in here with you while I was out. I knew it!'

Rufus opened his mouth on a lie, then let the truth roll off his tongue instead. 'Yeah, Midge called in and I'm feeling strong enough to go off to work this evening with him. We're doing some deliveries for Popeye.'

'Are yer now?' Gertie stormed. 'Forgot all about your little boys already, have you, 'cos your brother-in-law's waved a quid in yer face?'

'Ain't just a quid,' Rufus exploded excitedly.

'Got the chance to pull in more'n that, Gertie.' He saw the subtle change in his wife as she considered that information, so pressed home his advantage. 'I've told Midge to piss off a couple of times, love, but I know I'm just cutting me nose off to spite me face.' He shrugged. 'I hate him, he knows that...' He hesitated, darted a nervous look Gertie's way. 'But weren't all his fault, what happened. We left the boys in on their own that night the house got hit.'

'Only 'cos of the trouble he'd started!' Gertie yelled, infuriated that Rufus seemed to be defending Midge. 'I wouldn't never have chased after you in the blackout if it hadn't been for him stirring things up between us in the first place!'

'I know ... I know...' Rufus soothed her with clumsy pats. 'But I can use your brother to get what we need.' He gripped Gertie's shoulder with his good hand. 'Ain't only gonna have wages coming in, but lots more of this 'n' all.' He pointed at the bread and marge on the table. 'Be able to get you all the coupons you want, courtesy of Popeye's printing press. Meat, clothes, sugar...' With his three remaining fingers he spun the glass sugar bowl that she'd taken off him earlier. 'You name it, I'll get it for you.' He winked. 'Be able to get Vicky kitted out like a princess, won't we?' Rufus knew which buttons to push where his wife was concerned; her little daughter was the apple of her eye.

'So Popeye's gone into counterfeiting, I take it?' Gertie narrowed her gaze on her husband but she didn't push him away. She'd overheard snippets of that first conversation between Midge and

Rufus. As the weeks had passed and nothing changed Gertie'd thought she'd listened to two invalids spouting hot air about rejoining Popeye's gang.

'I'm feeling chipper; don't spoil it for me, love.' Rufus massaged her shoulder. 'I ain't forgiving Midge, ever, just calling a truce. He's a nasty piece of work but he ain't a Kraut, is he? They're the *real* enemy. Don't mean I wouldn't like to see your brother punished. But the law could yet catch up with him.' He chucked his wife under the chin. 'Ain't gonna be asking him round fer tea, if that's what's eating at you.'

Gertie pondered on Rufus's tempting offer of extra rations and realised she'd have to trek further afield for them. If she regularly went to the same places she'd be asking for trouble. But she could certainly use more coupons: Joey was always hungry because Rufus expected the lion's share of every meal she prepared before she or the kids got a look in. But equally important to Gertie was the thought that she might have been handed on a plate a little income of her own: if Rufus gave her the coupons she'd have a chance to sell on any that were surplus to requirements.

'How good are these fake ration books? Ain't turning up at stores and getting me collar felt.'

'Better than the Real McCoy, Midge said.' Rufus gave his wife a spontaneous smacker on the lips and, unusually, Gertie let him.

A moment later, when Rufus tried to get his fingers inside her blouse, she elbowed him away, having heard her daughter whimpering. Vicky had been snoozing on the trip home from the shops and Gertie had parked the pram in the hallway.

'Go upstairs for ten minutes, shall we?' Rufus breathed against his wife's cheek. 'This is feeling stronger 'n' all...' he growled, thrusting her hand to a hardening bump at his groin.

'That's Joey back.' Gertie sprang away from her husband as she heard the key, hanging on string on the front door, clattering through the letter-box. Joey never knocked these days: ever since his father had gone away to fight he'd got used to letting himself in. He was searching for work now he'd finished at school at the end of term.

'Had a good day?' Rufus greeted his son jovially despite his wife's rebuff.

Joey mumbled something indistinct. He had his little sister in his arms. He'd picked Vicky up from the pram where she'd been grizzling and straining against her reins to get out. 'Starving. Tea ready?' He gazed eagerly at the uncut loaf, standing Vicky on her feet.

'I'll do you a sandwich, if you want. You get your sister on the potty for me before she wets herself.' Gertie started sawing at the loaf. 'Any luck with a job?'

'Can start at Higgins, if I want; only seven shillings to begin with, though,' Joey muttered un-enthusiastically. The butcher had told him he could have a week's trial as a delivery boy.

Rufus gave his son a playful punch in the shoulder. 'Saw you and young Becky Pugh out walking the other day. Taking her to the flicks Saturday, are you, mate, now you've got a job?'

Before Joey could deny everything his mother

165

jumped to his defence, pointing the bread knife at Rufus. 'No, he ain't; he's got better things to do than spend his money on girls.' She glanced at Joey. 'Mrs Smith wants you to cut her hedge at the weekend. That'll boost your wages and keep you out of trouble.'

'Right...' Joey mumbled gruffly. He didn't mind doing odd jobs for neighbours and putting a bit of cash in his pocket. He got nothing off his mum and dad for all the chores he did, though he was willing to help out, especially with Vicky. He'd go to the moon and back for stardust for his little sister if she asked him to.

'Definitely be able to take the girl out if you're flush, won't yer?' Rufus's teasing sent Joey scuttling out of the room to find the potty.

'Our luck's turning, Gertie, I know it. Things'll be back to how they were for us.'

Gertie gave a wan smile, spreading marge. 'Most of them old days weren't nothing to romanticise about, y'know.' She'd sounded wistful. The times her husband was fondly speaking of had seen her working at the Windmill during the day and charring most evenings as well while he was out either robbing or whoring till the early hours.

Yet when she'd had an affair with one of the clients she cleaned for, Rufus had gone berserk. He would never have found out about it, and would have believed Vicky his own daughter, but for her bastard of a brother telling Rufus from pure spite.

But in those early Windmill days she'd had all her boys. And that alone made Gertie yearn to put back the clock.

'Are you all right, Gardiner? Not about to keel over, dear, are you?'

'I'm cold, that's all.' Rosie had been supporting a hip against the ambulance to keep herself upright when Jim Warwick came over to see how she was bearing up. Briskly Rosie began banging together her rubber-gloved palms to warm her fingers and stir herself into action. Despite it being a summer night she was chilled to the bone.

Hazel Scott had warned her that she'd likely get soaked by fire hoses when on an incident, but it was the sight of the headless corpse that had put ice in her veins, not the mist from water jets. The woman's body had been strung in the remnants of her nightgown. It had been impossible for Rosie to look for more than a few seconds at the mutilated flesh wearing ribbons of cotton. Jim, describing himself as an old hand hardened to such sights, had guessed the deceased was about Rosie's age. The other three dead bodies were, it seemed, a family: husband, wife and teenage daughter had been unearthed sheltering together under what remained of their dining table.

The brigade was still dousing the ruins although the flames were almost extinguished and sizzling steam bathed the black atmosphere. Firemen were sloshing in and out of craters in their gumboots as they shifted position to redirect the hoses. Rivulets eddied and flowed off the toppled masonry, carrying debris that tumbled over Rosie's galoshes.

She stooped, picking up a soggy rag doll that had bumped against her foot.

'You'll get used to it,' Jim said kindly as he removed the toy from her fingers. He put it on top of a pile of rubble. 'If they heeded the siren and got to safety she might come back with her mum looking for it tomorrow,' he explained.

Rosie gazed at the dome of jumbled wreckage off to her right. Once it had been a corner shop and three terraced houses. She wished she'd not spotted the doll because it had brought bile back to her throat.

She'd believed that she'd cope with stomach-churning sights, but now she knew her arrogance had been foolish. Passing her St John Ambulance first-aid test with flying colours had boosted her confidence no end, but hadn't prepared her for what she'd been confronted with that evening. Beneath her rubber gloves, Rosie knew her hands were sticky with blood from the wadding she'd pressed on injuries while working at Jim's side. Like a true gent, he'd taken the brunt of the grisly work, leaving her to fetch and carry, and attempt to soothe the traumatised victims on this, her first major incident.

'Have they brought out any children?'

'Not as far as I know. People round here should've had the sense to evacuate their kids when the doodlebugs started arriving. I'm praying we've no more to load up.'

Rosie gazed up at the benevolent-looking heavens, twinkling with pretty stars, from which a couple of hours ago a V1 rocket had dropped, killing at least four people and maiming others. She thought of her beautiful little daughter, sleeping soundly in Kent, and silently echoed her partner's plea that there'd be no more bodies.

Jim's eyes crinkled at Rosie from beneath the brim of his tin helmet. 'My boy's too old to be evacuated: flies bombers – Wellingtons, to be precise.'

'Just the one boy?' Rosie asked, glad of something – anything – to talk about to distract her eyes and mind from the row of blanketed cadavers yet to be loaded into the ambulance.

Jim nodded. 'The wife wanted more children, but it didn't happen. Now she works as my secretary at the college and goes fire watching three times a week. She grumbles because I spend so much time at Station 97. But Bob's home on leave soon; that'll keep her occupied. She spoils him rotten. Time he got himself wed.' Jim cast an amused eye Rosie's way. 'Like an introduction, Miss Gardiner? He's an accountant by trade and takes after his dad so he's a good sort.'

'Hazel's already got me engaged to her doctor friend down at the first-aid post. Not that I've met him either.' Rosie finally felt able to smile; she was grateful to Jim for creating a normal little interlude amidst the horror. 'If the road was clear the others should've reached the hospital by now,' she said.

Hazel and Tom had sped off ten minutes ago to take the casualties to the infirmary. For Rosie and Jim there was no rush: the mortuary was their destination. And now she was feeling strong and ready to finish the job and she told Jim so. He patted her arm and led the way to the first stretcher.

It seemed unbelievable that just a few hours ago she'd been sitting in the common room with

169

Hazel, knitting scarves for the crew of her boy-friend's ship; Rosie kept her mind whirring although her teeth were gritted and her shoulders protested at the weight they were bearing. Finally the bars of the stretcher were in the runners and with an almighty shove from her and Jim it slid into position on the top rung.

As she jumped down from the back of the vehicle to help Jim with the next body she esti-mated that the time had been about nine o'clock when a call had come through for crews from Station 97 to assist at an incident at Marylebone. Clarke had shouted through the message hatch that local crews were already out dealing with another blast on their patch. While Tom and Jim had run outside to start up the ambulance en-gines, Stella had rounded up the attendants. As Jim's usual partner hadn't turned in on her shift, Rosie had been allocated to him although she wasn't yet fully fledged. Now she was glad that her baptism of fire had been with Jim Warwick at her side. His quiet calm manner had been just what she'd needed.

They'd set off, with sinister fire from the rockets pluming overhead, Rosie feeling light-headed with dread. Now she felt anaesthetised with mental fatigue; even the burn in her muscles as she lifted dead weights didn't trouble her as much as it should. But she'd know about it tomorrow ... and after that she'd be stronger, in every way, she'd make sure of it.

The last stretcher had been loaded and Jim handed her a towel from the back of their ambu-lance and took another to mop his brow. 'Once you get the first call over, it's all downhill,' he said wryly, attuned to her thoughts.

Rosie nodded, sniffing. She took off her tin helmet, rubbing vigorously at her perspiring face with the cloth, till her cheeks fizzed with blood. She felt glad of the sensation, glad to be alive. Perhaps next time she might help to save a life rather than transport the corpses.

CHAPTER FOURTEEN

'That blonde, bitch is making a play for your Conor.' Ethel Ford poked her daughter in the arm.

'Ain't my Conor, Mum, he's made that plain enough.' Patricia took a gulp of port and lemon, then plonked the glass down on the table.

The two women shifted on their chairs, craning their necks to get a dear view across the crowded pub. Conor Flint had an elbow resting on the bar. A woman who looked to be about the same age as he had draped herself on his shoulder. As though irritated by his sister-in-law's unwanted weight he straightened, dislodging her.

'She's got some brass neck with her husband not yet cold.' Ethel rummaged in her bag for a pack of Capstan. Having lit up, she pursed her lips and eyed her daughter through a swirl of smoke. She whipped the cigarette out of her mouth and pointed it at Patricia. 'You gonna let him slip through yer fingers just like that, then?' Ethel banged a length of ash into the ashtray at the centre of the stained table.

Patricia helped herself to the cigarettes when Ethel made no move to offer her one, brooding on her mother's comment.

'Ain't no wonder you're still single with that attitude,' Ethel muttered. While her daughter struck a match she gave Patricia the once-over. Ethel had been married at seventeen and as soon as Patricia turned that age she had nagged at the girl to get engaged and out from under her feet. Seven years on, Ethel still had Pat living at home with her. But Patricia was a good looker with hair that was thick and black and eyes of deep hazel. She suited make-up: bright red lips and powdered cheeks enhanced her dusky beauty. Several of the dockers who frequented the Red Lion had been sending her appreciative looks.

But when Conor had arrived a short while ago he had barely acknowledged the girl he'd thrown over a few weeks back. Not that it had been any lengthy romance. They'd started walking out when he came home on leave from the army at Christmas. But Ethel had had hopes of it leading somewhere. The Flints were important people round these parts. Or they had been until Hilda Flint's eldest boy, Saul, got killed in an air raid. Saul had been the guvnor. Now all anyone knew was that Conor was back from France, recuperating from a bullet wound in the shoulder, and running the show.

'If you ain't gonna make an effort to talk to him, I'm off.' Ethel opened her bag, perched on the table, and lobbed her Capstan inside. 'Ain't missing me programme on the wireless for no reason and I ain't shellin' out fer no more drinks fer you, neither.'

Pat eyed her mother from beneath heavy eyelids. 'Righto! I'll go and speak to him.' She almost got to her feet, then the port kicked in and she slid back to the seat. 'And don't blame me if I take a swing at that smug cow.' Pat made out she'd sat down on purpose because she'd thought of something to say.

With an effort she shoved back her chair and successfully stood up. On her way towards the bar she slapped away a calloused hand that fondled her behind, making her stumble.

'On yer own, love? Want some company?' Beery breath fanned Patricia's cheek.

She tossed back her dark wavy hair from her face to snarl, 'Piss off. I'm with him...' She nodded at Conor, then slid into position at his side.

'Been waiting for you to come over and buy me 'n' Mum a drink, Conor.' She swayed, putting a hand on the bar to steady herself.

Conor jerked his head, ordering two port and lemons from the barman without losing place in the conversation he was having with his younger brother.

Patricia bit her lip; she was tipsy but not so far gone as not to feel humiliated. She glared a challenge at Angie Flint, but the woman looked to be equally unhappy with the treatment she'd been getting from her brother-in-law. 'Angie...' The single word from Patricia was all the greeting Saul's widow got.

The blonde gave a brittle smile, crossing her

arms over her ample bosom. 'You can fill that up 'n' all if you're getting a round in.' Angie tapped her empty glass by Conor's elbow. She'd be damned if she'd let him buy the drunken slut a drink without offering her one as well.

'Charmer, ain't he?' Patricia said loudly. 'Can't even be bothered to have a little chat with the women he knocks about with.'

Conor turned his head then, cold blue eyes travelling over her. 'Reckon you've had one too many bevvies, Pat. Why don't you go home and sleep it off?' He picked up the drink he'd just ordered her and knocked it back in one swallow, making Angie snort gleefully.

'Find that funny, do you?' Patricia spat through gritted teeth. She pushed off the bar where she'd propped herself and tottered the few steps needed to yank at Angie's peroxide locks.

Ethel had been waiting for a catfight to erupt. With a gleam of satisfaction in her eyes she surged through the stevedores who were hooting and slow clapping as Angie in turn grabbed at Pat's dark waves.

'You ought to be ashamed of yourself,' Ethel hissed, poking Conor's bicep but making no attempt to free her daughter's hair from Angie's fist.

Finally Conor successfully separated the women. He held them apart at the end of his rigid arms while they kicked savagely at each other and mouthed obscenities. Unable to take the cigarette from his lips he spat it on the floor, growling an angry curse.

'Your brother ain't been gone a few weeks and you're carrying on with the likes of her?' Ethel's pinched features were contemptuous as she pointed at Angie. 'Bet she's throwing herself at him when you're not about.' She jerked her chin at Steven Flint.

Conor glanced at his younger brother. Steven seemed to be having trouble knowing whether to speak up or get going: In the end he chose to do both.

'Fucking hell, I'd shoot meself if she did! I'm off down the Railway fer a drink where the company's better. Coming?' He pushed off the bar and wove through the crowd towards the exit.

Conor grabbed his sister-in-law's elbow, ignoring the twinge in his shoulder at the sudden movement, pushing her in front of him to the door in Steven's wake.

'Come back here and buy me a drink, you bastard!' Patricia yelled after him.

The nearest docker saw his chance. Hitching his trousers up neatly around his spare tyre, he slapped some coins down on the counter. 'Get the lady a drink.'

Billy Morris wearily did as he was told and slid another port and lemon in front of Patricia, wishing that Conor had done him a favour and taken her with him as well. The Ford women were a handful and he reckoned that Ethel's old man preferred kipping at the bottom of the sea to sleeping next to the old dragon every night. Roland Ford had perished at the Battle of the River Plate, soon after the war started, but the loss hadn't tempered Ethel's moods, and Patricia seemed to be following in her mother's footsteps.

Pat looked at her drink, aware of her mother

175

fuming at her side. She was in two minds whether to down it or chuck it in the bloke's ugly mug. She smiled sweetly and upended the glass against her mouth before handing it to the barman. 'You can get me another, if yer like, and one for me mum 'n' all.'

'And what do I get?' the docker whispered in her ear, but not as quietly as he might.

Billy Morris's expression turned yet more cynical as he shuffled off on his slippers to fill two glasses.

'A big thank you, that's what you get,' Patricia said as soon as the drinks had arrived and she'd downed half of hers.

The docker sat down amidst his pals' jeering laughter.

'You'll go too far one of these days, my gel,' Ethel said. 'You don't tease the likes o' them in front of their mates.' Picking up her port and lemon, she stomped back to the table to sit down.

'Get indoors.'

'Coming in with me then?'

'Get the fuck inside.' Conor spun his sister-in-law away from him as she tried to slide her arms up around his neck and gave her a shove towards her front door.

'You going back to her?' Angie had flounced about and jerked her head at the Red Lion on the corner. 'She's a bleedin' drunk. Don't know what you ever saw in someone like that. She's got no self-respect.'

'And you do?' Conor, replied drily. 'Saul deserved better than you as a wife.'

'And I deserved better than him,' Angie returned. She gazed at Conor. 'I *had* better than him... I had you.'

'Long, long while ago.'

'Could go back to that now,' Angie whispered. 'We're both free and it was always you I wanted, Con. Only married him 'cos you went off to fight in the bloody war.' She again tried to draw his dark head down to hers so she could kiss him.

He yanked her hands from his lapels and stepped backwards, swearing in irritation. 'You're a right bitch, aren't you? Saul thought the sun shone out of your backside and you can't even make a show of grieving for him.'

Angie shrugged. 'I ain't a hypocrite. Anyhow, you can't pick who you fall in love with; if you could I wouldn't want you, would I, when you treat me like dirt?'

'You can pick who you fucking marry! You should have left him alone and let him find someone else if that's how you felt.'

Angie started chewing the inside of her cheek, eyeing him from beneath her lashes. 'Don't make out you didn't have feelings for me, 'cos I know you did.'

'My feelings for you were basic and temporary, and I never made out otherwise. Saul saw you differently.'

'I'll take what we had, fer now,' Angie said persuasively, sliding his hand inside her jacket to press against her large round breast. 'Basic enough for you? Just give it another go, Con ... eh?'

Conor withdrew his fingers, shaking his head in disgust. 'You should've pissed off when we broke

177

up, Angie, and let my brother settle down with somebody decent.'

'He didn't want anyone decent!' she snorted. 'He loved what I did to him, and so did you.' Angie was incensed at being rejected when she'd have let him take her in the alley against the wall. 'Ain't *so* long ago that I was your girl; I can remember what we used to do in the back of your Humber down by the canal...'

'Get indoors,' Conor said quietly, unwilling to argue with her. He knew she'd love to provoke a commotion in the street just so she could kid herself she had the upper hand and he was dangling off it. 'Stevie's waiting for me up the road.' Conor started walking towards the corner. 'And don't wake Mum up when you go in.'

Conor heard the door slam and knew the cow had made a noise on purpose, because he'd asked her not to. He searched in a pocket for cigarettes and looked up at the sky, wondering if there'd be a raid. But for the ache at the top of his arm where twenty stitches were holding a bullet wound together he'd still be dug in around Sword Beach and he was beginning to think it'd be preferable to what he was doing now. Separating the two warring women in the Red Lion had set off a slow throb in his shoulder and he gave the sore area a massage as he strolled along smoking and thinking.

His brother Saul had been one of the first victims of the V1 rockets. His mum couldn't get over her eldest son's loss, but Saul's wife had managed to ... in record time. But then, as Angie readily admitted, she'd never really wanted Saul in the first

place. Sometimes she'd made that so embarrass-
ingly apparent that Conor had avoided visiting his
family when on leave in case she threw herself at
him. He had taken up with Patricia in the hope
that Angie would accept he'd moved on to
someone else and there was no going back to the
summer of 1939. He was a different person now.
That lairy chancer had disintegrated in the army,
finally dying at Dunkirk, along with half his regiment.

In a way Conor resented Saul for getting himself
blown up and forcing him to sort out his mess. He
didn't want to deal with people he didn't like ...
such as Frank Purves and his pals. His thoughts
transferred to the distiller's daughter, a rueful
laugh scratching his throat. He could come to like
Rosemary Deane ... more than he should.

'Didn't think you'd be coming,' Steven said as
Conor joined him at the bar in the Railway Inn.
'Thought one or other of 'em would dig their
claws in.'

Steven had been about thirteen when Conor
joined up. He could recall the fight that'd broken
out between his brothers when Conor came back
on his first home leave and discovered Angie
married to Saul. Then things calmed down and
Conor returned to his regiment, having made it
clear he wished the couple well and no hard feelings. Saul and Angie had moved into the house
next door and everything seemed back to normal,
except that Conor didn't turn up on leave very
much after that.

'Which one you going for then?' Steven was
mildly curious as to whether Conor would choose

his sister-in-law or the younger and prettier of the two women.

'Neither of 'em,' Conor smiled, and ordered a light and bitter. 'You still thinking of enlisting?'

'Yep, so don't try and stop me.'

Conor struck a match, dipping his head to the flame. 'Mum won't be happy.' He blew smoke out of the side of his mouth, shoving the pack of Weights over the bar in his brother's direction.

'Ain't coming as a surprise to her. I told her I'd go when I was eighteen.'

'You're not eighteen till October.'

'Only a few months to go ... close enough fer me.' Steven got comfortable on his bar stool. 'Time to get this war won or none of us are gonna have anything left. Poor bastards over there'll have fuck all to come back to. Won't be a London street standing, way them rockets are raining down every night.' He glanced at Conor. 'You going back soon as you get signed off by the army doc?'

Conor gave a brief nod. 'That's why I reckon you should stay fer as long as you can. You'll get your enlistment papers soon enough but right now Mum needs you.'

'She's got her daughter-in-law to look out for her.'

'Yeah...' Connor sounded sarcastic. 'Already thought of that ... so I reckon you should stay and take care of Mum 'cos Angie'll only ever look out for herself.'

'Get that monkey back off the distiller over Shoreditch?' Steven changed the subject. He didn't want a row but he wasn't about to alter his plans and babysit his old mum. Saul had always taken care of business and family problems.

His eldest brother had got an exemption from call up by blackmailing a quack with a gambling habit into giving him a lung condition. Saul used to say it was more important to keep the home fires burning and the businesses chugging for the family than join the fighting. Steven had reckoned that for a bloke with a lung condition Saul could come out with a lot of hot air. Saul had chosen to stop at home from cowardice rather than a duty to the rest of the Flints. It was ironic that he might have survived a stint overseas in the army whereas ducking and diving at home had proved fatal for him.

'So Popeye's mate's coming up with the booze after all, then, is he?' Steven's thoughts had returned to the Shoreditch deal and he prodded his brother to gain his attention and get an answer about it.

Conor puffed on his cigarette, looking preoccupied. 'Nope...' he finally said.

'Not writing off five hundred quid, are yer?' Steven sounded shocked. 'Saul wouldn't have let anybody get away with it. You can't let the bastard make us a bleedin' laughing stock.'

'Didn't say anybody'd got away with it, did I?'

'Saul reckoned that consignment of rotgut would make us thousands. He knew a bloke worked down Harringay dog track who could shift it under the bar, no trouble.'

'Perhaps it would've shown a good profit if the bloke with the still had come in on the deal. Five hundred quid's worth of Popeye's whisky labels stuck on empty bottles ain't much to shout

181

about.' Conor took a swallow of beer. 'Saul jumped in with both feet on it without doing his homework.'

'You've been turned over 'cos you ain't got Saul's clout with these geezers.' Steven slammed his tankard on the bar. 'I'll come with you and pay the distiller a visit. He needs a lesson.'

'He's left London.'

'He's done a fuckin' runner? And you've let him? I knew that cross-eyed sod couldn't be trusted to set up the deal. Only met Purves the once when he ran us off some girly mags. Never liked him. Go after him instead, then, shall we, Con?' Steven hopped off his bar stool, spoiling for, a fight.

'Calm down,' Conor said. His younger brother was too hot-headed. His older brother had been the reverse. If Saul hadn't been so easily led by a well-spun yarn, he'd never have got hooked up with Angie Rook, and he might still be alive.

The night the first V1 came over Saul had driven to East London to meet Frank Purves and pay for some boxes of stolen silk stockings. Purves had heard the sirens and got himself to safety rather than risk the rendezvous. But Saul, driving on through the blackout in Bethnal Green to buy his wife the luxuries she wanted, had ended up in the wrong place at the wrong time.

Angie had definitely mourned the loss of those stockings, if not the husband who'd lost his life trying to get them for her. And much as Conor disliked Angie's attitude, he hated his dead brother too. He wished Saul were still around just so he could shake the life out of him for getting himself killed and putting a spoke in things.

When they were growing up Conor had given his brothers plenty of space to do what they wanted, so that he could too. But now he couldn't escape; his mother expected him to be the engine of the family. Her husband and her eldest son had died and her attention had finally turned to him to keep the money rolling in. And he wasn't sure why he felt duty-bound to please her when she'd never bothered with him.

His father had always run a small-time racket alongside his shifts down the docks. All Harry Flint's sons had followed in his footsteps to the Pool of London as stevedores. When Harry died of a heart attack in 1926 Steven had just been born and Saul had just started work. Conor had always been the boy in the middle and he occupied himself while his mother fussed over the son who was now the man of the house, and the baby in her arms.

'We gonna do something about this, then, or not?' Steven was pacing to and fro in agitation. 'If you ain't got the balls to get that monkey back I'll go meself and take Mickey with me.'

Mickey Rook was Angie's brother, a few years older than Steven, and mad as a box of frogs.

'Perhaps you're right,' Conor said coolly. 'You should get yourself joined up. Dodging bullets might knock some sense into that thick head of yours.'

Steven shoved his snarling face close to his brother's. 'Getting yourself promoted to sergeant don't mean a fuck round here.'

'Don't mean a fuck over there either. You're as pissed as Patricia. Go home.'

'When I'm ready.' Steven sounded belligerent but glanced warily about. He was drawing attention to himself and he knew if he carried on his brother would chin him. It wouldn't be the first time Conor had slapped him down. And over in the corner, with her dad, was a girl Steven had liked since he'd sat behind her at school.

'Ain't drunk ... just bleedin' angry,' Steven muttered, by way of apology. He thumped his elbows on the bar. 'That cash would have paid for Saul's wake a hundred times over.'

Their brother's send-off had gone on for two days and close to a hundred people had attended. Billy Morris had run out of rum to serve their late dad's old navy pals. With a snort of amusement, Steven reminded Conor about that. 'Could've sold the miserable old fucker some rotgut ... if we'd had it earlier.' Steven started to guffaw and after a moment Conor's smile turned to laughter. So infectious was their hilarity that half the people in the pub started chuckling, though they'd no idea why.

'I'll get more out of this deal with Purves than crates of booze,' Conor finally said, wiping mirthful tears from his eyes. 'What I've got in mind won't require a still, just a printing press.'

Steven sniffed himself into seriousness, then frowned in curiosity.

'Purves has taken to counterfeiting in a big way. He's good, too. While he was out of action with his dodgy ticker I let myself into his warehouse. Stacked high with fake ration books, it is.'

'We gonna nick 'em?' Steven suggested brightly.

'No need to steal what we own. He can't come

up with the moonshine, or the money, we'll have the coupons instead... Extra petrol's always handy, I reckon, 'specially since the allowance got cut.'

'So we forget about John Gardiner and concentrate on Popeye to come up with the goods?'

Conor swigged from his glass, eyes half closed. He wasn't thinking about a couple of old timers at all. He still had the image of Rosemary Deane in her nightdress stuck in his head. And the obsession to go back again and see her was driving him mad.

Something about her seemed familiar. He'd racked his brain over what it might be, or where he could have bumped into her before. The silvery shade of her natural blonde hair and the turquoise of her eyes were memorable, and he reasoned he should know why that was. He knew he'd go back and see her if for no other reason than to ease his curiosity about that ... and this time he'd be the one asking her why she didn't wear a wedding ring although the answer was pretty damned obvious. Rosemary Deane led a double life: one at home and another at work at the LAAS.

The spiteful old biddy up the road might call her Mrs Deane but she'd guessed too that Rosemary hadn't ever had a husband.

The idea that John Gardiner's daughter had got herself in trouble should have boosted Conor's hopes of an easy conquest; instead he felt strangely angry that a bloke might have run out on her. Sorry, too, that the bastard might have turned her off getting involved with other men. She'd cer-

185

tainly not responded to him in the way most women did when he gave them a look and a line. Nevertheless the desire he felt for her was still niggling at him, putting a cramp low in his belly.

He knew he was acting like an idiot wanting to chase after a woman with a kid when he had two willing women wanting to sleep with him.

'You listening to me?'

Steven's words penetrated the fog in Conor's mind.

'Yeah. What?' Conor finished his beer.

'Just forget it...' Steven muttered moodily, aware his question didn't need an answer.

'Better get back and check on Mum.' Conor pushed his empty glass away. Hilda Flint had always been a problem but since Saul got killed she'd used his death as an excuse to be an even greater pain in the arse.

'Good luck,' Steven muttered, ordering himself another drink with a whisky chaser.

CHAPTER FIFTEEN

'Slam your foot on the brake!'

'Me foot is on the bleeding brake.'

The Citroën shuddered to a stop, scraping the kerb, and Rufus breathed a sigh of relief. 'This ain't a good idea, Midge. Shanks's pony's safer than us driving this contraption.' Rufus sank back in his seat. He'd thought they'd been about to career into a lamppost at the edge of the pavement. 'You probably can't steer it 'cos it's French.'

'Ain't me, or it! It's you!' Midge exploded. 'You're putting me off, barking in me ear 'ole like a bleedin' old woman. "Right! Left! Brake!"' he mimicked. 'I know what I'm doing, so stop interfering.' He let go of the steering wheel and reached across, slapping Rufus's fingers off the handbrake. Then he jerked his chin repeatedly at the gears. 'That's your job fer now and I'll tell you when I want otherwise. Now shove that stick in first, and away we go.'

With a mutter Rufus did as he was told and they pulled off smoothly, continuing for about a hundred yards in sulky silence.

'Shit! Coppers at two o'clock,' Rufus hissed, making Midge lose concentration and tug the steering wheel to the left though he corrected the swerve quickly.

Midge darted a glance at the Black Maria coming to a halt at the junction ahead. 'Just act natural. They aren't on to us.' Despite his boast Midge again let go of the steering wheel to adjust the brim of his hat so it obscured more of his face. He was still a wanted man, but enough years had elapsed since he first went on the run to make him confident even his mother would have difficulty recognising him. He'd aged ten years in four: his face was haggard and his hair already turning grey although he had only just turned thirty. 'If you stop staring at 'em we'll breeze past,' Midge snarled.

They did; and fifteen minutes later they'd pulled up at a builder's yard in King's Cross and were making their first delivery of petrol coupons in

Popeye's foreign motor.

'We collecting payment as well?' Rufus asked when they'd done the deal and were back by the Citroën.

'Pop won't let us handle the cash ... only these...' Midge pulled a few stray vouchers from a pocket. 'He's sorting the rest out himself.'

'So, no chance of a bit of hey diddle then?' Rufus said forlornly. In the past when working for Popeye he'd often use his guvnor's money on a dead cert at the race track and to top up his wages. Then after collecting his winnings he'd go and divvy up with Popeye.

'Well, that depends on how you see it...' Midge opened the car door with his good arm, sliding onto the driver's seat.

Rufus got in beside him. 'How do you see it?' he enquired. He knew that his crafty brother-in-law always had an eye to the main chance so was all ears when Midge spouted his pearls of wisdom.

'This *is* as good as money.' Again Midge pulled the coupons in his pocket into sight.

'Pop's got every one of them logged up here,' Rufus scoffed, tapping his forehead. 'You won't get one over on him like that.'

'Pop might do his sums, but those blokes in that yard aren't gonna notice straight off that a number are missing from a batch of hundreds. When they do I'm guessing they'll either think it's one of their own got sticky fingers, or Popeye's short-changed them. So they'll either feel too stupid to bring it up, or they'll swallow it in case the forger gets the hump and won't deliver no more.' Midge looked back at the yard where an open-back truck was being loaded up with ladders and lengths of timber. 'Petrol coupons are manna from heaven where these blokes are concerned. No fuel, no work...'

'You reckon they'll swallow it, do you?' Rufus's warning was laced with sarcasm. He jerked his head at a fellow in overalls lumbering towards him with an associate in tow.

'Shit!' Midge moaned. 'I only had six out of all that lot.'

A bang on the car window made him regret that they'd not driven off the moment they'd got in the Citroën.

'All right, mate? What can I do fer you?' Midge said cheerily, winding down the window with an effort.

'Me pal 'n' me would like some clothing coupons,' the bloke whispered. 'Got any spare on yer today so we can keep the missus sweet?'

'Nah, sorry, all allocated. Tell Popeye, shall I, and bring yer some next time?'

''Spose so,' the man answered grumpily, and ambled back to work.

'Like taking candy from a baby,' Midge chortled beneath his breath, putting up the glass.

Rufus stretched out his hand, palm up. 'By my reckoning six nicked coupons divided by two means three's mine. I'll take 'em now 'cos I can walk home from here.'

'Not coming fer a pint?' Midge sounded disappointed.

'Nah, Gertie's a bit under the weather ... gotta look after the nipper.' It was a lie. Gertie was fine, but she'd bust a gut if she found out that he was supping in a pub with the brother she hated.

'Pick me up tomorrow, same time, top of Commercial. Road?' Rufus asked, pocketing the three coupons Midge reluctantly handed over.

They had agreed to have their rendevouz point somewhere busy where nobody would take much notice of another vehicle stopping and picking up a passenger. A meeting under Gertie's nose was out of the question; she tended to spit fire at any sight of her brother. Also Midge didn't want any of the Grimeses' neighbours taking notice of the flash car. Some of them had been around long enough to remember Gertie had a half-pint brother who'd deserted. Midge had stayed away from his sister's place not simply because he knew he'd not be welcome but because he ran the risk of being recognised.

'Dunno what's happening tomorrow. Popeye said he might want the motor to take his girl out now he's feeling better.'

'What?' Rufus frowned. 'Ain't he well?'

'Silly old sod had a bad turn after he trapped his hand in the machinery.'

'This caper's going down the pan before it's properly started, is it?' Rufus huffed in disappointment.

'Nah, far from it.' Midge leered at Rufus. 'If he's had a heart attack it's 'cos he's exerting hisself more than he should. That bird he's knocking around with's built fer speed, just like this jalopy, and poor old Pop can't handle either at his age.' Midge's dirty laugh filled the car. 'But he's feeling good as new, so he said.'

190

'How you doing, Nurse Johnson? Not seen you in quite a while, gel.'

Trudy swung about to see a fellow propping an elbow on the doorjamb of the pub she'd just passed. She'd not recognised him at first because his appearance had altered in the few years since she'd last clapped eyes on him. She'd heard the rumours that Frank Purves did all right from a thriving printing business, and had some dodgy sidelines going on, too. His squint hadn't improved but she knew his grin was aimed at her so she approached him for a chat, pushing her bike at her side. Other people might think this man a villain but she'd always felt rather sorry for him losing his wife in childbirth.

'I've been nursing at St Thomas's for almost three years,' Trudy said, explaining why she'd not been seen around. 'Can't train the girls up quick enough at the hospitals, what with the war dragging on and casualties on the rise again at home. But I'm back on the beat as a district nurse a few days a week.' She swivelled the handlebars of the ancient pushbike. 'Just hope this old thing holds out so I can get to my new mums quick as I need to when their husbands bash on me door in the middle of the night.'

'Still a midwife as well then, are you?' Popeye sounded impressed.

'Oh, yes. The babies keep coming, no matter what.'

'More than ever since the Yanks arrived with their fags and nylons, I expect...' Frank coughed. He'd forgotten for a moment that he wasn't exchanging banter with a bloke at the bar. 'Sorry, love, didn't think...'

Trudy shrugged. She was too long in the tooth and too jaded by her job to be offended by a salty quip. 'Been in the wars, have you, Mr Purves?' Frank had removed his hand from his pocket and she'd noticed a bandage wound about it.

'Ah... that's nothing!' Frank indolently waggled his fingers. 'Me own fault, that was; got a thumb caught in me printing press fer being careless.'

'Ooh, bet that hurt.'

'Cor, not 'alf!' Frank sucked his teeth, wincing at the memory of it. 'Gave me a nasty turn but I managed to get meself home before I passed out cold. Me neighbour sent for an ambulance 'cos he couldn't wake me. But I'm all right now. Shock set me angina off or something, so the quack said.'

'Want me to take a look at that dressing? I'm off up to number sixty-one to do a leg ulcer but I'll pop in on the way, back, if you like.'

'If it ain't no trouble, dear. I was heading home anyhow once I finish this.' He raised the tankard in his healthy hand.

With a wave Trudy continued on her way up the road and Frank finished off his pint of mild. He was looking forward to having the nurse visit. As a young probationer she'd delivered his only child. Trudy Johnson was sure to remember that day because he'd lost his wife giving birth to Lenny. Not that Frank blamed Nurse Johnson for his wife dying. He could remember the poor cow, probably not more than twenty-five at the time, sobbing her heart out while fighting to stanch the haemorrhage. If anybody had been to

192

blame it'd been Lenny, tearing his mother's insides to shreds. But his son was dead now, too, so reluctantly Popeye knew there was nobody left to accuse but himself. He'd got her pregnant, after all, when she'd told him she didn't want kids spoiling her figure.

Just as he was about to set off home, Frank hesitated, thinking he recognised a sailor who'd just ordered a pint at the bar. Keen to jog his memory, he put down his empty tankard and slid onto the stool next to the young fellow.

'On leave, son, are yer?'

'Yeah, just a weekend pass. Gonna make sure I enjoy it 'n' all. Deserve a break from over there.'

'Ain't no picnic over here, neither,' Popeye said drily. 'Feel I should reckernise you; don't know why. From round here, are you?'

'Used to be. Grew up in Shoredi'tch.'

'Might know your folks, then. What's your name?' Popeye asked.

'Charles Bellamy.'

Popeye slapped his thigh. 'Doris's son! Now I know you. If you've come on a visit, you'll be out of luck. Yer mum 'n' stepdad's gone off out of town. Didn't they write 'n' let yer know?'

'I've just come from Gravesend,' Charles said with a sour smile. 'Can't swing a cat in my place with everybody there. Me missus is run off her feet. I'm stopping in London with a pal for a night or two before heading back to Portsmouth. Some leave this has turned out to be.'

'That's it, Gravesend,' Popeye said with a smile. 'I remember now where John said he was off to. Said I might pop down and see him sometime, being as we go way back. Got his address, have you, mate?'

Bellamy wrote it down and Popeye pocketed the scrap of paper and plonked down his glass.

'Fancy a drink?' Bellamy said.

'Can't, mate. Got a woman waiting on me,' Popeye winked, thinking about Nurse Johnson.

Bellamy downed his pint. 'Hoping the same,' he muttered, and ordered another.

Twenty minutes later Frank was at home and had set the cups ready to receive his visitor. The moment he heard the knock on the door he put the kettle to boil.

'Want a cuppa, love?' Frank helped Trudy park her bike against his front wall then followed her into the back parlour.

'Best not. Got to get back and write up my notes.'

'Oh ... right y'are...' Frank said, disappointed. He went into the kitchen and turned the gas off under the hissing kettle.

'Remember the day you brought my Lenny into the world, do you, Nurse?' he called out.

Trudy nodded and gave a sigh. Even after more than twenty-four years the memory of that tragedy remained in her mind. Mrs Purves had been the first patient to die on her. Since then many more women had succumbed to the ravages of childbirth during her career spanning more than a quarter of a century. 'Dreadful shame about your wife–'

'All in the past, love,' Popeye interrupted. 'No need to mention it now. I've found meself a young lady, y'know. Shirley works in the pub and we keep each other company since her husband passed on. She's almost young enough to be me daughter, but we rub along all right.'

'And how's Lenny?' Trudy asked. Taking Frank's hand, she began unwinding the bandage.

'Oh, course you wouldn't know,' Frank said. 'Lost Lenny 'n' all, three years back now.'

Trudy stopped what she was doing and sighed sadly. 'Oh, so sorry to hear that, Mr Purves. Was he home or abroad when it happened?'

'Oh, he weren't serving. Bad eyes ... like me.' Popeye knew there'd been nothing wrong with his son's vision. Lenny had swung the lead to avoid conscription because he was a coward. But Frank couldn't let Nurse Johnson know what a useless specimen his son had turned out to be. His late wife wouldn't have liked him being disloyal to the child that had sent her to her grave.

'Got caught in a fire in a nightclub,' Popeye briefly explained, turning his face away in a pretence of grieving. He didn't want any more questions on the subject.

'There've been some dreadful tragedies.' Trudy patted his arm in comfort. 'Please God we'll see an end to it all soon. A lot of people have had enough and upped sticks to escape the blasted rockets.'

'Family I know did that,' Popeye volunteered. 'My old pal John Gardiner's gone to the country and taken his wife Doris and their grandkid with him.'

Trudy stopped removing the dressing and glanced at Popeye. She remembered the family, of course, although she didn't know Mr Gardiner had finally married his fiancée. Neither did she know that they'd left Shoreditch. She'd never forget how close she'd come to adopting Rosemary Gardiner's beautiful little girl. Then Rosemary had changed her mind and broken her heart. Even now Trudy felt a twinge of pain in her chest at the thought of what she'd lost. It seemed daft to imagine she could have loved the child from the short contact she'd had with her. She'd delivered many infants since, but none had stuck in her memory in the way that blonde angel had.

'I know John Gardiner's family. I delivered his granddaughter. Do you know what they named her?'

Frank racked his brain, screwing up his grizzled features. 'Hope! Sure that's what John said. Bet she's pretty if she's like her mum. Good looker, that Rosemary Gardiner, as she was, of course. Don't know what name she goes by now.' He paused, perhaps hoping that Trudy might supply it but the nurse continued dabbing his scab with antiseptic.

'Rosemary and my Lenny went to the same school. I know he liked her,' Frank continued. 'I reckon he'd've taken things further with the gel, given a chance, but...' Popeye shook his head, a grimace on his face describing Lenny's rejection better than words could've. 'Old John never speaks about his son-in-law – never speaks about his daughter neither – but you can tell he's proud as punch of the nipper,' Popeye chuckled.

'She was a beauty,' Trudy said, blinking back a prickling heat in her eyes.

196

'I'd've liked grandkids,' Popeye reflected. 'Too late now, though.'

'You just told me you've got a lady friend,' Trudy ribbed him. 'Make an honest woman of her and never say never.'

Frank roared a laugh. 'You're right, Nurse. There's life in this old dog yet, but I reckon Shirley's childbearing days are behind her. When I said she was younger'n me didn't mean she was no spring chicken. She's forty-nine next birthday and I'm sixty-four.' He winked his good eye.

'And you're looking very good on it, too, if I may say so,' Trudy said stoutly. Having finished patching him up, she collected her things together. 'Best be off; take care of that hand and your ticker.' She nodded at his chest. 'When I'm back this way I'll call in and see you, if you're about.'

Frank walked Trudy to the door, feeling he should offer the woman something for her trouble. 'Need anything, love?'

'No, not at all. I was passing this way anyhow,' she said, guessing he was offering to pay her for her time.

'How about a few clothing coupons? Got a few going spare.'

Trudy hesitated. She did need some summer blouses now it'd turned very warm and she'd no coupons left. 'Well ... I...'

Frank tapped his nose to indicate it was a secret. 'You just ask me for whatever you want in the way of rations and I'll get it for yer.' He trundled into his front parlour and pulled open a drawer. 'Keep a little stash at home for me good friends, y'see.' He returned with some clothing coupons.

Trudy stared at them, realisation dawning over what the man had been printing on his press when he injured his hand. But they were good; she'd never have spotted anything amiss in their colour or design.

'Take 'em up town ... Oxford Street ... get yerself a nice frock.' Popeye closed her hand on the coupons on her palm. 'If you want more just ask.'

'Thanks,' Trudy said faintly and pocketed them.

'Take care of yourself, love,' Popeye called out as the nurse wheeled her bike out of his front gate. He watched her go, thinking that for a woman of her age – which he put at coming up fifty, same as Shirley – she wasn't a bad looker. And unlike his girlfriend, who was hard to please, Trudy seemed easy-going and kind with it.

CHAPTER SIXTEEN

'I told you not to come back here.'

'Yeah, I remember.'

'So are you too thick-skinned or too thick-headed to do as you're told?' Rosie demanded.

She was pleased she'd covered her shock and managed to sound confident. As days had passed with no sign of Conor Flint she'd relaxed, believing he'd accepted that her dad had told him the truth. Yet niggling at the back of her mind had been, an idea he would return, if only to see her. The tension between them that day had been as much to do with attraction as aggression. For the first time in many years she'd talked with a man while her wandering mind wondered how his mouth felt. There was no point in denying that she found him handsome, or that she knew he was exercising self-control for her sake rather than her father's. The grievance he had was real, even if John Gardiner had been wrongly implicated in it because of past misdemeanours.

'I told you I'd be back, Mrs Deane; and I reckon you've been expecting me so don't bother with the outraged-innocent act. It doesn't suit you, does it?'

His smile seemed rather sinister to Rosie and her face grew hot as his eyes drifted to her bare fingers. He was letting her know that he'd understood Peg Price's hint about her absent wedding ring.

'If you've got something, to say, don't be shy, spit it out,' Rosie snapped. Good-looking he may be, but she didn't care what a common criminal thought of her. But then her father had been one too so she curbed an urge to throw that barb at him.

'I've been trying to work out where I've seen you before.' Conor flexed the bruised knuckles on his right hand. 'Last night I got into a scrap and suddenly it came to me.'

'If we'd had a fight I'm sure I'd remember it,' Rosie returned flippantly,'

'Oh, I'd remember that tussle, too,' he said silkily. 'I fought *over* you, not *with* you.'

Rosie looked startled; he wasn't joking, or even smiling any more.

'It happened when you were working at the

Windmill Theatre. You did work at that place a few years back, didn't you?'

A silent intake of breath abraded Rosie's throat. If he'd recognised her from that time then he must have watched her posing on stage. The idea that he'd seen her nude was mortifying, flaming her cheeks again.

'What if I did?' she finally blurted.

'Just thought you might like to apologise as I once took a punch in the mouth on your account.'

Rosie darted a searching glance at him. She couldn't recall him from those days but that wasn't surprising. During her time as a nude statue in the theatre's living tableaux she'd been pestered by hundreds of servicemen lying in wait at the stage door. And there had been occasions when men had fought to get her attention. Winning permission to take a fêted Windmill Girl for a drink was quite something to a fellow, and probably still was, Rosie realised.

'You don't remember me, do you?'

'Sorry. It was a long time ago.'

'February 1941,' he said.

'Did you write it in your diary?' Rosie mocked. 'I must have made quite an impression.'

'Oh, you did ... on every man who watched you up there, but that's something else you know, isn't it?'

Rosie did remember him then. A corporal and a sergeant had come to blows over her and although the younger man had won the fight, she'd chosen to go for a drink with the senior of the two. The incident had sparked a bitter argument with some of the Windmill's chorus girls. They'd called her a show-off and a tease, dragging the theatre's name through the mud.

Rosie knew that at eighteen she'd been silly and vain, but she wasn't owning up to it to Conor Flint. The fracas was brought further into focus the more she dwelled on it. The sergeant had been stocky and fair-haired, and she'd gladly escaped his company after a single drink at the Starlight Rooms when he started taking disgusting liberties.

Rosie knew that had been her trouble: as the theatre's new recruit she'd loved rivalling the experienced girls for compliments, but she'd been too trusting and naïve with men to know how to handle the attention when she got it. Flaunting herself had always been different from giving herself, but her admirers had never seen it that way. Her rapist certainly hadn't...

'Remember me now?' Conor watched the play of emotion on her face. He'd embarrassed her by bringing up her racy past more than he'd intended. The ebullient little flirt he remembered was nowhere in sight. If he pushed her further she might either slap him or burst into tears.

'I ... I met lots of people then,' Rosie stammered. 'All the men were the same to me ... just drooling punters.'

'Yeah ... that was me.' Conor grunted a sour laugh, stuffing his hands in his pockets. 'But I'm different now,' he said coolly.

'Me, too,' Rosie avowed with the bleakest of humour.

Three and a bit years had passed since that night yet there was no hint of the fresh-faced soldier she'd rejected in favour of his older colleague. Conor Flint's features had hardened and seemed permanently set in lines of cynicism that slanted his narrow mouth and creased the edges of his deep-blue eyes. Only his hair, thick and very dark, looked the same.

'If you're here to reminisce, I'm too busy. But I will say sorry you got in a fight over me and that I went out with your pal instead of you. Satisfied?'

'What do you think?' He was pinning her gaze down while he produced a pack of cigarettes from his pocket and offered her one.

Rosie shook her head, closing the door until just a few inches remained between it and the jamb. 'I'm expecting somebody at any minute. It's not a good time for you to be hanging around.'

'It is for me.' Conor's lazy gaze travelled over the silky pink wrap she was wearing and trying to shield from his view. 'You could apologise properly and agree to a night out with me. Perhaps at the end of it I might be satisfied.'

'I wouldn't go out with you if you were the last—' Rosie bit her lip, knowing insults weren't wise. 'I'm getting ready to go to a dance with some friends.'

Rosie still had a lipstick clutched in her hand. She'd only outlined her top lip when she'd heard the ratatat on the door. A party of people from Station 97 was going to a shindig at the town hall. Tom lived in Hackney and had said he'd give her a lift as he had to pass her door. She'd whizzed downstairs to invite her colleague to wait in the parlour for her while she put on her dress and shoes. Now she was regretting not having peered out of her bedroom window before opening the door so readily.

'Is your dad coming back on a visit? I'd like a chat with him.' Conor shifted off the step as though preparing to go away.

'No,' Rosie retorted.

'Doesn't matter; I'll go to Gravesend and have a word with him.' He sauntered off down the garden path, feeling a bastard for resorting to that.

'You bloody won't!' Spontaneously Rosie nipped after him, before glancing towards Peg Price's house, hoping the woman hadn't spotted her cavorting in her dressing gown with Mr Flint, 'the gentleman'.

A wail from an air-raid siren made Rosie automatically turn her face up and mutter a curse beneath her breath.

'You'd best get to a shelter.' Conor's tone had turned serious and he began scouring the murky twilight. The whole day had been overcast with rumbles of thunder threatening a storm. There was no sight yet of approaching aircraft but the terrifying throb of engines was growing louder with every passing second.

'I've a cellar; I stay in that.'

'Well, get down there quickly.' He pointed as the first black shape broke through the cloud at high speed.

'What about you?' Rosie was back-stepping towards her front door, her glance veering between the doodlebug and him.

'Is that an invitation?'

'Oh, come inside!' Rosie ordered, her conscience getting the better of her good sense. She speeded into the hallway as a deafening roar drowned out further conversation. 'I hope Tom's safe. He might be close by and hammering to be let in soon.' Quickly she led the way to the cellar, flicking the light switch on the wall at the top of the stairs before descending them. A single bare bulb on the limewashed cellar ceiling gave little light but threw large, eerie shadows onto the rough masonry walls.

'It's always cold down here, even in summer,' she said to break the ice.

Conor sat down on the hard-backed dining chair her father sometimes used when his bad leg ached from lying down for too long. Rosie paced to and fro, then perched on the mattress and draped the blanket around her shoulders, as much to hide her state of undress as for warmth.

'Usually, if there's time, I make us a flask of tea,' Rosie chattered on to cover her uneasiness. 'That helps.'

'D'you want my jacket?'

'No, I'm fine, thanks...' A moment later she nearly jumped out of her skin as the first rocket exploded and showered them with brick dust loosened from the ceiling. 'That sounded close.'

'Where were you going?'

'Going?'

'You said you were going out with Tom to a dance.'

'Oh... the town hall. The local Church arranged it for convalescing servicemen.'

'Tom's your boyfriend?'

'Tom's an ambulance driver who's on the same

shift as me. We're on again bright and early in the morning.'

'So he's not your boyfriend?'

'No, he's not. Are you on leave from the army?'

'Sort of. I'm convalescing... Perhaps I'll invite myself along to your dance,' he suggested drily.

'You've been injured?' She raked him over with her eyes. He looked healthy enough to her.

Conor waggled his left shoulder. 'It's on the mend now.'

'When are you going back?'

Conor grunted a laugh. 'Not as soon as you'd like me to, Rosemary Deane, of that I'm sure.'

Rosie shuffled backwards on the mattress till her spine was pressed against the gritty wall. She drew her knees up to her chin and hugged them. He had a rough yet quiet voice, and she found the tone oddly soothing.

'I couldn't have timed it better to get injured,' he added when she continued staring wide-eyed at him. 'If I'd not taken a bullet, I'd've probably asked for a bit of compassionate leave.' He paused. 'My elder brother was killed in a blast and my mum took it bad.'

'Sorry about that,' Rosie said with genuine sympathy. 'Did his house get destroyed?'

'He was miles away from home when it happened.'

'I see... Did he leave children?' Rosie had been nine when her mum had died. She still missed her and thought about her every day. She knew it must be much worse for little ones to cope with losing a parent in an air raid. It was so sudden ... so brutal a loss. People went about their daily

205

lives knowing the worst might happen yet expecting to survive. She'd gone to the Café de Paris with her friends with no thought that they might not all return to work the next day. One moment they'd all been dancing and drinking; the next, one of them was dead.

'Saul didn't have children, just a wife. He looked after business and family matters so things are a mess at the moment.'

'I can imagine...' Rosie was aware of his eyes burning her profile and burrowed further into the blanket, pulling it closer about her shoulders Eighteen-year-old Rosie would have thrown it off, let him have a good look at her figure, then run a mile when he acted on the temptation. She hated the person she'd once been.

'Why did you get into that fight?' Her clasped hands were on her knees and she rested her chin on them.

'I wanted to take you out for a drink.'

'No, not *that* fight.' Rosie tutted. 'You said you'd been in a scrap last night.' She nodded at his bruised knuckles.

'It was nothing much.'

'It was either money or a girl,' Rosie guessed, trying to lighten an atmosphere that seemed to be filling with sultry heat despite the cold cellar walls.

'It always is.'

'So which was it?'

'Both, and neither worth the effort.'

'Very gallant,' Rosie muttered. 'I'm sure she'd be pleased to know it.'

'She does know it; I told her. Doesn't make a

blind bit of difference, though; she'll carry on giving strangers the come-on to spend money on her then slap the bloke down when he expects payment in kind.'

Rosie flinched beneath the brutal truth. He could be talking about her, and he knew it. But he didn't know that she now despised that type of girl as much as he seemed to.

'Were you protecting your sister from somebody?' she asked after a long pause.

Conor lit a cigarette, brooding that he regretted flooring the docker for Patricia's sake in the Red Lion last night. At one point his past girlfriend had perched on the fellow's lap, no doubt to make him jealous. 'She's not my sister, she's just somebody I know,' he said. He knew he'd have no regrets fighting again for the blonde he was with now.

'It was good of you to step in and help her then.' Rosie guessed he was talking about his sweetheart although he seemed reluctant to call her such. And it was hypocritical of him to run the woman down. Conor Flint was no model of fidelity; he'd need no more than a certain smile to join her on the mattress. Oddly, she trusted he would wait for a signal before making his move.

'D'you miss your daughter?'

Rosie threw back her head, frowning at the vibrating ceiling. 'Of course I miss her; I speak to her on the telephone sometimes and feel like my heart's breaking.' Vaguely she was aware of a bell clattering. It sounded like an ambulance and there was a rumbling in the distance as a building collapsed.

'And what about her father?' Conor asked quietly.

'What about him?' Rosie got up and paced to and fro, the blanket trailing on the floor in her wake. His suspicions about her marital status had been made clear in the way he'd asked about the child's father rather than her husband. Suddenly she went to the bottom of the cellar steps, listening. 'I thought I heard a knock on the door.'

'I'll go.' Conor got up and disappeared up the cellar steps two at a time.

A few minutes later Tom descended into the cellar with Conor following behind.

The newcomer collapsed on the vacant chair, fanning his grimy face and breathing heavily. 'I thought I was a goner. I couldn't drive through so I left the car and dashed here on foot. I had to clamber over a mountain of rubble.' He brushed down his dusty trousers. 'Hope we don't miss the dance.' Pulling a handkerchief from his pocket Tom started scrubbing dirt from his face.

Rosie was glad to see that her colleague looked bright as a lark despite his ordeal. She quickly made introductions, noticing Tom glancing curiously at her visitor as the men shook hands. 'Mr Flint came to see my dad.'

A moment later, she realised that Conor might resume their conversation about her daughter and her heart jumped to her throat. None of her colleagues – not even her friend Hazel – knew that Miss Gardiner masqueraded under a different name. And that was the way it had to stay.

She darted a frantic look at Conor and gave a subtle shake of the head, hoping he understood her signal. His calculating smile told her he understood very well. But there was no reassurance in his eyes that he'd comply with her wordless plea.

'So you didn't know that Rosie's dad's had the good sense to skedaddle to Kent then?' Tom glanced at Conor, who'd propped an elbow on the cellar wall rather than perch on the mattress beside Rosie.

'Thought he might be back here on a visit. When *is* he coming back on a visit?' he asked Rosie, laughter in his voice. He dragged on his cigarette stub.

Tom swung a glance between them, sensing the electricity. He gave Rosie a wink, which she realised meant that he thought Conor attractive too.

'He won't be back for ages; he's got too much sense to return here.' Rosie's sniping made Conor smile as he looked down, grinding out the cigarette butt beneath his foot.

The all clear sounded and Tom started brushing himself down with renewed vigour. 'If we get going we'll not be too late. Everybody else has probably been delayed, in any case.'

'I'll get dressed. It won't take me long.' Rosie noticed her colleague's startled glance; Tom had obviously thought her fully clothed under the enveloping blanket. 'I was getting ready when the siren went off,' she blurted in explanation and started for the steps.

It took Rosie less than five minutes to put on her dress and shoes and drag a comb through her hair. Having finished colouring her mouth with crimson lipstick she stood back, surveying her reflection in the dressing-table mirror. Her silvery hair seemed waywardly wavy, but she'd no time to sleek it. Her complexion was still rosy from constant blushing; opening her compact, she toned it down with a few pats of powder, giving her nose a final dab. Picking up her handbag, she went downstairs to find Conor and Tom chatting in the hallway.

'Suppose we'll have to walk. Won't get back to my car and the buses'll be overflowing, if they're running at all,' Tom said.

Rosie was aware of Conor's appreciative glance but he didn't compliment her on her appearance as she collected her jacket from the hall cupboard.

'I'll give you a lift if you like. My car's outside.'

'Would you? You're a dear.' Tom put a hand on Conor's arm.

If Conor hadn't realised straight off that Tom had no romantic interest in women, Rosie reckoned he must've guessed by now.

'Enjoy yourselves,' Conor said as Rosie and Tom alighted from his car a few minutes later. He got out and stood on the pavement with them.

'You can be my chauffeur any time.' Tom pumped Conor's hand in thanks for the ride. He crooked an elbow at Rosie to escort her into the dance.

'Go on in. I'll join you in a mo,' she told him. When Tom was out of earshot she turned rather bashfully to Conor. 'Thanks for the lift, and for not saying anything.'

'Saying anything about what?'

'You know what.'

'Yeah, but I want you to tell me.'

'Well, you'll wait for ever then.' Rosie didn't sound shy now.

He caught her arm as she would have walked away, tightening his fingers when she stiffened. For a moment Rosie held her breath, thinking he was either going to kiss her or coerce an answer out of her. He did neither.

'You look beautiful,' was all he said, and let her go.

'That colour suits you very well, Gardiner.'

'Oh ... thanks.' Rosie smiled at Stella, glancing down at her turquoise summer dress. It was a shade of blue she favoured as it matched her eyes. They were standing together on the edge of the function room watching some of their colleagues Jitterbugging.

Rosie became aware of Stella giving her another appreciative look and she blushed.

'It's all right, I'm not going to ask you to dance, dear,' Stella said in her wry, weary way.

'I know...' Rosie couldn't help but give a nervous giggle at the unspoken message that she could relax because Stella didn't fancy her. The woman the DSO did fancy was attempting to waltz with Tom while being jostled by couples capering energetically to the jazz band.

'Norris should let her partner teach her a few steps of the Jitterbug,' Stella said, watching her girlfriend's sedate progress round the dance floor. 'He offered to but she said a waltz was more her mark. I wouldn't mind learning how to do it.' Stella attempted to copy a few of the frantic steps, hands waving at her side and stout knees jerking

211

up and down.

Rosie had never seen her boss acting so carefree and she wondered if Stella had had more to drink than the two gins she'd seen her down. On impulse Rosie said, 'I'll teach you...' and grabbed at Stella's fingers. 'I learned how to dance when I worked at the Windmill Theatre.' She pulled her Senior Officer forward then began, with little pushes and shoves, to get Stella to spin about on the fringe of the Jitterbuggers.

'I didn't know you were a Windmill Girl, Gardiner,' Stella said as, laughing, they came face to face.

'I was a nude in the living tableaux, but don't broadcast it; I was just a kid in those days.' That she'd been immature in more than just years back then ran through Rosie's mind as she whipped Stella to arm's length while demonstrating how to jiggle the hips. She felt quite joyous and un-inhibited without knowing why. She'd had two brandy and sodas but had certainly not sunk enough to be sozzled. She and Stella met quite often on the same shifts but they'd never been so informal with one another before, although Rosie had liked her DSO since the day of her interview.

'A nude, were you indeed?' Stella puffed breathlessly and gave a wink. 'I won't tell a soul; we've all got our racy little secrets.' She glanced at Thora.

The music stopped and laughing people started strolling from the dance floor. Suddenly Stella pressed Rosie's fingers. 'I'm here if you want to have a chat at any time, you know.'

Rosie darted her a glance. 'A chat?' she asked brightly but felt a pang of apprehension in case

Stella was hinting at something specific.

'You haven't danced as much as the others this evening, and not from a lack of willing partners.'

Rosie smiled. 'I haven't said no to them all!' she protested mildly. 'I did the Foxtrot with that poor chap over there.' She nodded at a private with an arm in a sling. 'And I danced with him too,' she indicated a corporal who had a walking stick. 'I trod on his foot,' Rosie ruefully related, although the mishap hadn't been her fault. When Corporal Smith had asked her to dance she'd immediately agreed, thinking of the time she'd rebuffed another Corporal, called Flint, and she'd come to the surprising conclusion that she regretted it. Having discarded his stick Smith had tried to keep his balance by hanging on to her but had almost pulled them both over, much to his embarrassment.

'You're a very pretty girl and bound to attract the chaps.' Stella paused, pondering on something. 'Despite the crowds and hubbub everywhere in London there are a lot of lonely people wanting to snatch a little happiness, perhaps for the last time. And who can blame them?'

Stella raised Rosie's hands in her own. 'Thank you for that dancing lesson, Gardiner. I very much enjoyed it.' She sighed, glancing about at the happy faces of their colleagues. 'It's good to have a break every so often.' Stella nodded at somebody over Rosie's shoulder just as the band struck up again. 'Your corporal is on his way back. You can't have bruised his toes too badly, dear.'

After a waltz in which they both stayed upright Rosie let the soldier return her to her friends but refused the drink he offered to buy her. After he'd left to rejoin his pals Hazel slipped onto the seat next to Rosie.

'He's quite a dish. Seeing him again?'

'No...' Rosie tutted. 'He's got a sweetheart. She's serving with the NAAFI in Scotland.'

'Never mind; plenty more fish in the sea,' Hazel said. 'I've still got Dr Clark in reserve for you anyway.'

'Wonder how they're coping over at Station 97? They must've got a call out after that awful raid this evening.' Rosie frowned. A good many of her colleagues who weren't on shift had struggled through the debris to attend the dance at the Town Hall. A core of defiance still existed in those determined not to let the Germans batter their morale as well as their city.

Rosie was aware of Hazel chattering about the billet-doux she'd received from Chuck but she was only half-listening. She finished her drink, while watching Stella and Thora dancing together. Stella was attempting to teach her partner the few steps of Jitterbug Rosie had demonstrated.

From what Stella had said to her Rosie guessed her boss suspected she was lonely. Did she also suspect she lived a double life? If her DSO had found out something about her, Rosie trusted Stella would keep the knowledge to herself. The woman had hinted that she could be told something in confidence, but still Rosie was determined to guard her privacy carefully. They all worked together ... ate together ... some had died together, according to Stella's account of two crew members who'd perished on a call-out back in the

Winter of 1940. But what did any of them really know about each other? Hazel happily volunteered personal information about herself. But Rosie had only sketchy details about others' backgrounds, just as they knew little about her. Since her attendance at her first major incident, when Jim Warwick had told her about his wife and son to calm her down, he'd not mentioned his family again. Really, they were all just strangers drawn together in a common aim to help save the lives of people caught up in a hateful conflict.

'Raffle!'

Hazel nudged Rosie to gain her attention. 'Got your tickets ready? They're drawing the numbers.'

Rosie drew some small pink papers from her dress pocket. 'I never win these things.'

'Me neither,' Hazel moaned. 'Could murder those peaches 'n' all. If I win I'll end up with the boot polish.'

'Very useful too.' Rosie couldn't remember the last time she'd tasted tinned fruit. A few minutes later there was just the tin of peaches left on the raffle table.

The number was called and Rosie and Hazel groaned, simultaneously screwing their tickets up.

'Fix!' Hazel called good-naturedly as Stella waved the winning ticket then collected her prize.

'We could do with that tin of fruit in the canteen to liven up the rice pudding,' Tom called out, making the others laugh.

'No fear!' Stella said. 'These are being put away for Christmas.'

Corporal Smith caught Rosie's eye, raising, his beer glass in salute and farewell now the evening was coming to an end. She smiled back, gave him a wave on standing up, but thoughts of another man were niggling at her mind again as she collected her handbag and jacket, ready to leave. Conor Flint hadn't been the only fellow to compliment her that evening though it was the memory of *his* words and voice that was now stuck in her head.

CHAPTER SEVENTEEN

'Ah, nice to see you,' Popeye lied. 'Come on in.'

As Conor Flint crossed his threshold, Popeye caught a glimpse of the two fellows lounging against the Humber parked outside. His heart plummeted to his boots; he'd hoped the man would turn up alone, as last time.

Flint had telephoned him and told him plainly of his intention to take his stock of petrol coupons in compensation for John Gardiner's booze. Popeye's protestation that he'd no idea what coupons the other man was talking about had been quickly silenced. Conor had also admitted breaking into his warehouse and could list everything inside it that Popeye had hoarded over decades. As most of it had been stolen or counterfeited Popeye knew Flint had him over a barrel. He'd need to tread carefully or the bastard might grass him up to the coppers ... anonymously, of course.

Popeye had considered attempting a swindle

but that'd gone out of the window now. Conor was nobody's fool, unlike his brothers, and if the scam went, wrong the two gorillas loitering outside would enter the fray and maul him.

He'd recognised Steven Flint from the day he'd turned up with his brother Saul to collect an order of pornography. Popeye hadn't liked him from the off; the youngest Flint boy reminded him of his Lenny, all gob and swagger.

As for Mickey Rook, he was a well-known thug who'd hired out his fists to several East End outfits. But it seemed his loyalty was now reserved for the Flints because his sister had married into the clan.

Shuffling down the hallway after the younger man, Popeye realised his own back-up was far too weak to be of any bloody use whatsoever if things turned nasty.

'This them, here?' Conor lifted the lid of a cardboard box on the table.

'That's it,' Popeye said in a defeated sigh. As a last resort he was willing to give plan B a go. 'Can hire you out a couple of blokes to shift that lot round the streets, if you like. Cheap rates and they've even got the use of me motor.' Popeye jokily elbowed Conor in the ribs. 'Ain't as if you'll be short of petrol for me Citroën, is it?'

'Got my own people for deliveries, thanks.' Conor cast a look at Frank Purves' sidekicks. If he'd been in a better mood he'd have had a chuckle at being offered their services.

As it was he simply braced a hand on Popeye's table and began examining the counterfeits. They were top quality but still he wondered whether his brother Saul had lost his marbles, getting himself involved with the likes of Popeye. Judging by the clowns the printer used as henchmen, Purves was fit for retirement. Yet Conor was glad Saul had come over to Shoreditch on business or he wouldn't have crossed paths again with Rosemary.

He knew the unlikely lads were watching him; the short, grizzled one had lost a hand but definitely looked to be the fitter and more able of the two. The fat fellow with the limp was unhealthily sallow and unattractively surly.

'I know they don't look up to much but they've been doing the business fer me and even pulled in a few new customers out on the rounds.' Popeye inclined closer, pouring his visitor a whisky. 'Thing is ... we go way back, and I like to see 'em all right. They need the wages and they're honest as the day's long.' Frank added that straight-faced despite knowing that Midge Williams and Rufus Grimes were as bent as nine-bob notes. 'See now you've taken all me stock of coupons, Mr Flint, it'll be some while before I can get up and running again and give me crippled lads a day's work.'

'I'm gonna hear violins in a minute, am I?' Conor said sourly, still counting coupons.

In fact Popeye couldn't give a toss about Midge and Rufus, but he did want Conor to employ them. It was the only way he was likely to get some of his coupons back. Midge was a dab hand at playing both sides to the middle. Popeye was confident the little man could work his magic on a fair amount of the coupons just till things

218

started rolling again. As it was, Popeye was out of paper and ink to run off more, and almost out of money too, what with Shirley always wanting this and that. The idea of having to break into his investment savings was almost choking him.

Midge and Rufus were fiddling off him, Popeye knew, but he was prepared to turn a blind eye because his old cronies were cute enough to make sure the customers rather than their boss suffered.

'So now you've taken all me petrol rations off me,' Popeye repeated forlornly, hoping for a more sympathetic response this time.

'I've not taken them off you,' Conor corrected, straightening from his lounging position. 'I've purchased them with my five hundred quid plus all the interest you owe me. This is business and, all things considered, I reckon I've been generous and patient.'

'Without a doubt you have,' Popeye grovelled, nodding gravely. He realised Conor's civility didn't make him a pushover. And he didn't reckon the bloke's generosity and patience were on his account either, but he'd racked his brains over why he'd not been back sooner with his demands and couldn't come up with an answer.

Conor knocked back his whisky and Popeye was disappointed to see him already preparing to leave. In a matter of seconds his visitor had loaded the coupons back into the cardboard box and handed him the empty glass.

'Tell you what, you can have Midge 'n' Rufus on a trial, if you like,' Popeye blurted. 'Then if they do all right you can settle up with me later. I wouldn't let 'em out in me car, would I, if they was no good?'

'Ain't interested in them or your sob stories.' Conor lifted the box and within a few minutes Popeye was wrathfully watching the Humber pulling away from outside his house.

'What did he say?' Midge and Rufus chorused as soon as Popeye came back into the room.

'You heard what he bloody said,' Popeye snarled. 'You ain't deaf as well as the rest, are yer?' He began pacing to and fro in his back parlour. 'Fucking bastard! Took the lot! That was worth much more'n five hundred quid!'

'You should have kept some hid,' Rufus muttered.

Popeye turned on him. 'That's what I should've done, should I?' he mimicked sarcastically. 'Flint knew exactly what I'd got in Houndsditch down to the last packet of fags. Surprised he didn't ask fer them 'n' all.'

Popeye hadn't mentioned the break-in at the warehouse to his cohorts until now, fearing he'd be thought a fool for allowing it to happen. He'd known for some time that the padlocks on his warehouse wouldn't keep out a skilful picklock but he'd been too tight-fisted to shell out for new ones. Conor Flint had had the decency just to take a look around and close up on his way out, Popeye had to give the man that.

'Bleedin' hell! You can get out of shtoock by printing off some more coupons, can't yer?' Midge sounded outraged by his boss's carelessness.

'What with? No paper, no ink, no nothing.'

Rufus's shoulders sagged. He'd got to go home and break it to Gertie that the work had dried up.

Since he'd been bringing in a nice few bob and handing over his knocked-off coupons, she'd been cosying up in bed again instead of turning her back every night. 'No point hanging about here, is there? I'm getting off now.' Rufus stomped to the door. 'If things straighten out and you need me you know where to find me.'

Once Rufus had gone Midge slumped down uninvited into Popeye's armchair and helped himself to the whisky. 'Can't you get nothing on credit at the wholesaler?'

'What, and lose me discount for cash? That'll eat into profits.' The idea of being overcharged was something else that stuck in Popeye's craw.

Midge slanted his boss an old-fashioned look but knew better than to criticise. Popeye was still his port in a storm. 'I blame that John Gardiner fer this.' Midge downed a shot of Scotch and wiped his mouth with the back of his hand. 'He's loused it up for all of us and brought them Flints down on our backs.' Midge peered at Popeye for his reaction. He knew he'd have to stir his guvnor into some sort of action or his income would dry up and he'd be back rummaging in dustbins. For years Midge had had to lay low and earn what he could, when he could. If he showed his face at the Labour Exchange for a handout he'd be done for as soon as they asked for his name and checked his background. Even the people at a couple of the soup kitchens he'd frequented had started asking awkward questions so he'd stopped going.

'Them Flints'll be back. Now they know what you've got stashed they'll clean you out, Pop, mark my words.'

Popeye was already brooding on the possibility that his new padlocks might not keep Flint out any better than the old ones. It took a thief to catch a thief, so they said, and he reckoned he might be finished because Conor Flint, and not the Old Bill, pulled the rug on him.

'Can't you get Gardiner to change his mind?' Midge burst out in desperation. 'If he sets up his still again me 'n' Roof can deliver bottles instead of coupons.' Midge jumped to his feet, flailing his good arm, annoyed at Popeye's inertia. 'There's gotta be a way of persuading the fucker to play along! You'll be done for, else.' He jabbed a cautioning finger.

'Shut up! I'm thinking!' Popeye roared.

There was nothing likely to change John Gardiner's mind, in Frank's opinion. He'd got no scandal to blackmail the man with. Gardiner lived a pretty clean life now, and Doris wouldn't be that bothered to learn her old man had dabbled on the wrong side of the law before they'd got together. That avenue would lead nowhere and just give John the hump that his missus had been dragged into things. Grassing the distiller up to the police was also pointless as John would return the favour and Popeye had far more to lose than he.

Gardiner's weak points were his womenfolk. Him and Doris were no great romance, that was plain to see. But Rosie and his little granddaughter were another kettle of fish; he adored them both. John had let on once that Rosie had gone berserk when she'd found out Lenny was delivering to him labels for counterfeit booze brewed up in the cellar. From what Popeye knew of John

Gardiner's daughter, she was an independent and opinionated sort who'd holler blue murder if she thought she was under threat.

So that left only the nipper as a bargaining tool. Popeye reckoned that if he managed to do John Gardiner a good turn on account of his little Hope, then tit for tat was on the cards and Popeye could name his own price.

'Not seen you in a while, Gertie. How've you been?' Rosie called out.

Grabbing her change from the stallholder, Gertie elbowed her way towards Rosie, who was also dodging marketgoers to meet her.

'Well, this is a nice surprise,' Gertie said when they were face to face. 'I wondered if I'd ever again run into you out shopping now you're up to your armpits in bandages.' She grinned, giving Rosie a spontaneous hug.

'I've wanted to see you, too,' Rosie said, returning the embrace. 'I'd've called round on my day off but I lost your address. Let's find a spot over there.' Rosie indicated a break between the stalls in Petticoat Lane where they might chat without being jostled.

'I'll write me address down for you again before I forget.' Gertie delved into her bag to tear off a scrap of envelope, then scribbled on it with a pencil got from the same place. Having handed it over she shook the paper bag she was holding. 'Just bought some thread to sew up me husband's shirts. He's bust the buttons off on a couple, the podgy sod.'

'I've bought Hope some hair ribbon. I couldn't

223

resist it; it's such a lovely colour and matches her eyes.' Rosie pulled out of her bag a twist of tissue paper containing a small coil of turquoise silk.

'Matches your eyes too,' Gertie said. 'Lucky thing, you are, having such lovely looks.'

Rosie smiled her thanks for the compliment but was thinking that for all Gertie's chirpiness the woman looked tired and worried.

'No Victoria today?' She'd been surprised to see Gertie without her daughter.

'Rufus is minding Vicky for me. She's getting too big for the pram and the little madam plays up if she's on her reins for too long.' Gertie shielded her eyes from the late August sun, feeling hot and bothered. She gave Rosie an envious glance; the younger woman looked as poised and pretty as ever despite the sultry heat. 'Life seems to be treating you well as an ambulance auxiliary. Enjoying it, are you, if that's the right word?'

'I'm glad I joined,' Rosie replied. 'But I'll admit there've been times when I've felt overwhelmed by it all.'

'I know you must see some terrible sights.' Gertie sounded solemn and there was a deep sadness lurking at the backs of her eyes.

'The others have been taking the worst of it for me up till now.' Rosie didn't elaborate; this woman of all people needed no description of the carnage facing an ambulance crew following a bombardment. 'I've got my driving test soon.' Rosie was both buoyed and terrified by the forthcoming event.

Tom had told her to expect the examiner to be rigorous. On his test he'd been required to drive with a full pail of water on the floor of a makeshift ambulance. Tom had sloshed some water over the sides of the bucket due to the double declutching needed in the boneshaker, but the RAC official had passed him anyway saying that on the whole his gear changes had been acceptable.

'You'll pass with flying colours,' Gertie encouraged.

'My colleagues are nice,' Rosie volunteered. 'I've found a good friend in a girl called Hazel Scott. We all go out sometimes to a dance or the pictures on days off.'

'Must be nice...' Gertie sounded rather wistful. 'Your dad's looking after Hope, is he, when you're working? Don't forget I can lend a hand if you're stuck at any time.'

'Thanks for the offer, but Hope's gone to Gravesend with her granddad,' Rosie explained. 'They're staying with my stepmother's family. It was agony waving Hope off but...' Rosie didn't want to sound pious and say that she'd bear any heartache to keep her daughter safe. Back in the days when they worked at the Windmill Theatre Gertie used to boast she'd never let strangers care for her kids. How the poor woman must regret that decision now. 'I speak to Hope on the telephone most days. I race home from work for that treat and it keeps my spirits up.'

'Sensible of you to send her away like that,' Gertie said quietly. 'If I'd done the same with my boys instead of being selfish...'

'I doubt I'd've let Hope out of my sight if she wasn't with somebody who loves her.' Rosie squeezed Gertie's hands.

'Joey and Vicky and me spend more time down the bloody air-raid shelter than ever we did during the Blitz. First peep from the siren and we're off like greyhounds from a trap. Rufus comes too when he's about. And he's home most of the time since he lost his job.'

'So he got some employment?' Rosie was glad to change the subject; Gertie's eyes were glistening from speaking about her lost boys.

'He had a delivery job, but the work's dried up now.' Gertie left it at that. She didn't want a nice person like Rosie Gardiner to know her husband – or she, for that matter – handled fake ration books. Ashamed or not, Gertie missed having the independence her earnings from the coupons had given her. She also missed having Rufus out from under her feet for the best part of the day. Her husband was again sitting scowling in his chair for hours on end.

'Any nice fellows been chatting you up in the Ambulance Service?' Gertie asked, determined to stop brooding and enjoy this chance meeting with Rosie.

'No such luck!' Rosie matched Gertie's bantering tone but at the back of her mind she wished that Conor Flint hadn't immediately entered her head at Gertie's mention of nice men. From what she knew of him, he was anything but nice, and whether he'd chatted her up or intimidated her was debatable too. But she couldn't forget the look he'd given her when he'd told her she looked beautiful. He wanted her, that was plain, but there'd been gentleness as well as desire in his eyes.

'I'm at work this evening so'd better get cracking.' Rosie pocketed Gertie's scrap of paper. 'If we don't bump into each other I'll pop round and see you as soon as I get a mo.'

The two friends said their farewells then wove paths through the crowds, heading in different directions.

On getting back from her shopping trip Rosie quickly undressed and started putting on her uniform. She'd made herself late by idling with Gertie in the market. She was buttoning up her crisp white blouse when she heard the ratatat. Past experience had taught her to have a scout out of the window before answering the door. With a frown she went downstairs to open up, shrugging on her uniform jacket.

'Hello, locked yourself out, have you, Irene?' A year or so ago Peg's daughter had accidentally left her key at home and Rosie had invited the girl in for a cup of tea while Irene waited for her mum to return. At the time Hope had been toddling and Irene had made quite a fuss of her, treating her like an amusing little toy.

'Not locked out, Mrs Deane,' Irene mumbled, shifting uneasily. 'Just wanted to talk to you, if that's all right?'

'Oh ... d'you want to come in then?' Rosie issued the invitation when the girl didn't immediately say what was on her mind.

Rosie was curious to know what might have brought Peg's daughter calling; usually if they spotted one another in the street they'd exchange a hello or a wave but that was about it. Peg had no doubt warned her daughter to steer clear of the brazen hussy up the road. But whatever Irene wanted to say Rosie hoped she'd be quick about it so she could get on.

'I'm sorry about me mum being such a cow to you,' Irene blurted before Rosie had got the door properly closed behind her.

'That's all right, don't worry about it.' Rosie smiled neutrally, wondering why on earth the girl had felt it necessary to come and tell her that. 'I'd make a pot of tea, Irene, but haven't the time as I'm off to work.'

'Sorry ... didn't realise ... I'll go...' Irene turned back to the door, shoulders slumped and greasy head bowed.

Poor Irene seemed even spottier and fatter than Rosie remembered her. She felt guilty for having insulted the girl to her mother months ago. Irene took after her dad, both in build and in character. Rosie reckoned that inheriting Peg's sour moods would've been far more of a handicap than Irene's stolid homeliness.

'I've got a few minutes yet before I set off,' Rosie said, trying to make amends with kindness. 'Come and take a seat in the parlour.'

Irene suddenly snorted back a sob. Then, unable to control herself, began weeping noisily, her forearms raised over her face to hide her distress.

'What's wrong?' Rosie demanded in alarm, prising Irene's arms off her face to hear what the girl was mumbling. She got a handkerchief from her pocket when Irene started scrubbing her wet face with her cardigan sleeves.

'Don't know what to do, Mrs Deane,' Irene gasped.

'About what?' Rosie guided her hiccuping visitor towards a chair in the parlour.

'I've been seeing a boy,' Irene choked out. 'Mum's gonna kill me when she finds out.'

Some months ago Doris had told her about Peg's daughter and Bobby West getting friendly behind the park shed. But Rosie hadn't a clue why Irene would choose to confide in her about romance problems.

'Bobby West's your sweetheart, isn't he?' Rosie wanted to get to the heart of the matter, conscious of the clock ticking on the wall. She was due on shift in five minutes.

Irene nodded. 'How d'you know about us? Is everybody yakking about me already?' She scrubbed her eyes again, sniffing loudly.

'My stepmother heard that you'd been seen together, that's all.' Rosie patted the girl's arm in reassurance. 'Why don't you tell your mum you like Bobby? If he's polite she might let you walk out together, y'know. Sometimes parents get funny if they think you're going behind their backs.' Rosie hoped that was sound advice. It struck her that she'd need to practise what she preached when Hope got to be Irene's age. Her beautiful little daughter would attract a lot of admirers. At present the idea of any randy fellow laying a finger on Hope filled Rosie with fury and dread. 'Have a sit down and a breather, then you'll feel better about going home and facing your mum.' Rosie pulled out a chair at the parlour table. As Irene perched on the edge of it Rosie noticed a bump beneath her dress that hadn't been obvious when the girl had been standing up.

It didn't look like puppy fat.

Irene blushed, pulling her cardigan's edges over her belly. 'Mum won't let me 'n' Bobby walk out ... and she'll never let me have me baby neither,' she blurted.

Rosie bit her lip, wishing she were still in blissful ignorance of that explosive news. Irene was expecting her to come out with something helpful but whatever she said Peg would be livid with her for interfering, and mortified to know her daughter had spread such a private matter before the family could hush it up.

'Your mum's not guessed yet?' Rosie asked, surprised to see Peg's daughter shake her head. The woman seemed to be an expert at spotting a scandal yet had missed one right under her nose.

'Me mum's always saying I'm too fat ... never looks no further than that,' Irene said resentfully. 'She's always going on about you being an unmarried mother, too.' Irene peeped at Rosie from behind a curtain of lank, mousy hair. 'Me dad gives you credit for the way you conduct yourself and bring up your little gel.' Irene picked at her ragged fingernails. 'I think me mum don't like you just 'cos me dad does. Anyhow, I think me dad's right about you, Mrs Deane.' She slid an admiring glance at Rosie. 'I've always wanted to be like you, even when you used to work at the Windmill Theatre. You was so glamorous and pretty.' Irene hung her head again. 'I've come to see you 'cos I want to conduct meself properly, and I want to keep the baby. If me mum gets her way she'll make me give it up, or get rid of it before anybody knows and starts gossiping. What shall I do?'

Rosie speared agitated fingers through her hair. Again she glanced at the clock on the wall as it gained fifteen minutes past the hour. She knew it would be callous to usher Irene out of the house at such a critical time. 'Does Bobby know he's got you pregnant?'

'He's told me to get rid of it, 'cos he's too young to be tied down. Don't know how to get rid of it and neither does he.' Irene's expression turned angry. 'He's only sixteen but he reckons he'll join up if me dad finds out and sets about him.' Irene raised her bloodshot eyes, pleading wordlessly for assistance. 'Don't want you to think I'm being rude or nosy, but there's nobody to talk to who understands how I feel. You kept your little gel ... and your dad's been nice about it ... so I might be lucky, eh?'

'Hush...' Rosie crouched down at the side of Irene's chair as she started weeping again. Rosie knew she could act indignant but Irene had come to see her from desperation, not malice, and she'd not the heart to have a go at her.

'Did the fellow run out on you?' Irene's watery eyes were fixed on Rosie's face. 'My dad says he must've been mad if he did.'

'It was different for me,' Rosie said quietly. 'I didn't want him to stay.'

'But you always wanted your little girl?'

Rosie nodded although she remembered how determined she'd been to have her precious daughter adopted in those weeks after the birth. Nurse Johnson had nearly been Hope's mother.

'You need to tell your mum or your dad,' Rosie gently persuaded. 'I won't let on that you've said a

231

word to me, promise.' She sighed, as Irene's crying got louder and she began shaking her head. 'You must, Irene, because they'll know eventually, and then it'll be worse for you.'

Irene nodded dejectedly.

'Come on, off you go now.' Rosie helped the girl to her feet. At the front door she said softly, 'My dad did go mad, and I did think that things would never come right for me just after Hope was born. But they did. I'm happy now. And you will be, too.'

Rosie watched Irene close the gate, wishing she'd managed to come up with a better solution for the girl's predicament. But what was there? Irene, young as she was, had already worked out for herself the options that were open to her: an abortion, or a scandal. Most parents wanted to avoid the disgrace and shove the baby out of sight. Her own father had, but from the moment he'd seen the small angelic face peeping from swaddling he'd changed his mind. Rosie hoped with all her heart that the Prices would feel the same way, because judging by Irene's waistline she might already be too far gone to take the dangerous backstreet route.

CHAPTER EIGHTEEN

'You look just the ticket: short and skinny.'

Rosie had been bandaging a gashed forehead when she received that backhanded compliment. She was jerked away from her patient and marched off, leaving the poor woman collapsed on the pavement next to her dead husband and robustly cursing all Germans to perdition.

'There's a little chap trapped down there. That hole isn't big enough for any of us men to clamber through, but you might measure up.'

Rosie pushed back her tin helmet to stare at the stocky chap, grinning amiably at her. He still had hold of her elbow and was studying her figure with scientific approval as though inspecting a thoroughbred racehorse. His meaning suddenly became clear and made Rosie's insides lurch. Confined spaces terrified her.

'Rosie Gardiner, meet Dr Richard Clark.' Hazel Scott had trotted over to them, and made a quick introduction. She even managed a knowing wink for Rosie to indicate he was the heart-throb from the first-aid post. Hazel's gas mask was hanging about her neck and she shoved it aside, looking over her shoulder. 'We've got a girl with a broken arm on a stretcher over there. She's told us her younger brother's in the basement; bad news is that his leg's wedged beneath some fallen concrete. He was howling, she said. But it's gone quiet in there now.' Hazel nodded at the jagged opening that led into the murky bowels of the ruined house. 'The lad's sister managed to crawl out through here.' Hazel gave Rosie's slender frame the once-over in much the same way Dr Clark had. 'She's fourteen but not that much different in size from you.'

'Would you have a go at rescuing the poor little blighter?' Richard Clark hunkered down, pulling away debris to widen the entrance and show Rosie what she was up against. The rocky passage seemed to dip down at a perilous angle before disappearing from view. He leaned in, shouting, then they all kept quiet, straining to hear any sound that might indicate human life endured beneath the tons of rubble. 'I'd go in myself and investigate,' he said, frowning at Rosie, 'but I'd not manage more than a yard or two before getting stuck and being a bloody hindrance to everyone.'

Hazel eyed her own buxom figure with a grimace that made words superfluous.

Rosie licked her lips. Two pairs of eyes were on her, demanding an answer. She knew there was no time for dithering. A yes or a no was all that was required.

''Course I'll give it a go,' she croaked.

Hazel gave her shoulder a hearty pat. 'Well done. Knew you would, Rosie.'

'If the lad's got any broken bones, you'll have to use your own judgement about whether to manhandle him. If he seems willing to move he's probably fit enough to do so,' the doctor quickly instructed. 'Guide him back so we can see to his injuries out here. Don't hang about patching him up.' His voice became harsh. 'If you can't help him and things look hopeless, report back at once, Miss Gardiner ... no unnecessary heroics.' He looked up at some groaning joists that had collapsed to form a charred apex. Roof tiles were being shivered downwards to pile up in what remained of the guttering.

'Dr Clark means no use you croaking in there too,' Hazel interpreted bluntly.

'You can give him a jab of this if he's in distress.' Richard snatched a syringe from his medical case. 'It should stop the worst of it for the poor little chap.'

Rosie stretched out shaking fingers for the capped needle and put it in a pocket. With an intake of breath that seemed interminable she dropped to her knees. Immediately she drove herself forward on her elbows, allowing nothing into her mind other than the thought that she was relieved she was wearing her twill trousers rather than her regulation skirt. But she'd not got far into the blackness before the demons attacked. The choking dust mingling with the fear-induced nausea at the back of her throat made her chest heave and her cheeks billow. Lowering her face to her forearms she dug in for a moment, taking a breather, counting out ten seconds slowly. Again she pulled herself onwards, covering ground, inch by inch. She looked up at the uneven stones above her head, blinking grit from her lashes. By touch she made out the iron legs of a bedstead to her left, realising that it had probably crashed down through ceilings and floors to land in the base-ment. She wriggled under it and gave silent thanks as the access widened into a low cave; she still couldn't stand but at least she no longer had entombing brick scratching her sides.

Rosie heard a faint cough, then another. She took the torch from her breast pocket, bouncing the light this way and that until she saw the little boy up ahead, about thirty feet away.

'Try and keep still, there's a good lad, till I can take a look at you.' She had forced cheerfulness into her hoarse voice.

'It hurts ... my head hurts...'

'I know; but you're doing well, aren't you? I reckon the soldiers out fighting Jerry would like to be as brave as you.' Rosie scuttled on as carefully as she could. She was terrified of dislodging masonry that might fall and block her path. She halted to adjust the chinstrap on her tin helmet. The perspiration on her forehead was running into her eyes and she flicked her head to dislodge it before dropping to knees and elbows, crawling onwards as the tunnel tightened. Broken glass was beneath her gloved palms and she tried to swipe it aside, knowing she'd meet it again on the way back.

'What's your name?' Rosie called out. The boy had gone quiet and that was more unnerving to her than hearing any yelps of pain. 'Mine's Rosie and I know where you are, y'know.' She came to a halt, flopping down to rest her chin on a filthy fist. Taking the pencil torch out of her breast pocket again she waved the beam to and fro to soothe him with the light. Then she steadied it on his face, making him flinch from the glare. Her heart leaped to her mouth as she realised he was probably only six or seven. She turned the beam on her own face so he could see her. 'I'm very close by and about to get you out of here. Will you tell me your name?' she asked again.

'Herbert... Herbie, me mum calls me,' came a faint response followed by a dry cough.

'Right then, Herbie,' Rosie was enormously relieved that he'd not lost consciousness. 'Bet you're ready for a nice hot cup of char, aren't you? I know I am.'

She just caught his murmured yes and realised he'd started crying. 'The ladies from the WVS have set up their canteen outside. The kettles are singing away ... can you hear them? So, we'd best get you on your feet and in the queue in case they run out of Bourbons.' With a final frantic effort Rosie hauled herself to his side, panting heavily by the time she reached him. She allowed her pumping chest to relax against her hands for a few seconds. Then she shoved the helmet back on her head and assessed him. But it was hard to tell the dirt from the caked blood on Herbie's small face.

She gave him a grin. 'Well done. Is it just your head that aches?'

'And my leg.' He pointed solemnly at the leg trapped under rock.

Putting the torch between her teeth, Rosie examined him by running her hands over his arms and shoulders while trying to keep the torch steady. He had a deep cut on his cheek and another on his scalp but he kept turning his head to protect his eyes from the torchlight, preventing a proper examination. Rosie studied the large slab of concrete imprisoning the boy. It looked far too heavy for her to lift on her own. She felt cold sweat dripping down her spine because she knew she couldn't go away and leave him. Not now.

'If I have a go at shifting this big boulder d'you reckon you could scoot backwards, Herbie?'

He nodded, tears of pain and fright beading his lashes in the torchlight. 'Will my leg ache more if you move it?' he gulped.

'Don't think so...' Rosie said honestly. She had no idea what sort of mess his shin might be in. With any luck the bone could be intact.

'Want to get out... I'm hungry ... missed me tea 'cos I was playing football.'

'Can't have that, can we?' Rosie said. 'Bet you play in a team with your pals, don't you?'

'I play at the back.'

'Crikey, your pals'll need you up and running again then, won't they? Who's going to stop the other teams shooting at goal if you're laid up?' While talking Rosie had been using the torch to try to find something nearby to use as a lever. There was a length of timber just within reach but she knew if it was wormy it might splinter and break. If the slab were to crash back on little Herbie's legs it would shatter them.

She leaned sideways, her fingers spread wide, stretching until she felt she'd rip her arm from its socket. Eventually her nails made contact with splintery wood and slowly she worked her hand, along its length till she could grip it. By hauling back on one elbow she managed to drag it towards her, then slowly manoeuvre it into position underneath the slab. With a foot she guided the plank into place, slowly shifting it to and fro until she was satisfied with her engineering. Then she rammed it home with two savage stamps until it was stuck fast.

'We ready then, Herbie?' Rosie panted, a wedge of fearful emotion thickening her throat. 'Can you move backwards for me now as fast as you would if the other team were on a run for goal?'

She watched for his nod, accompanied by a faint smile, the first she'd seen him give.

'Righto ... when I say "Now!" you scoot. The opposition's coming and off you go... Now! After them, they're past you, you can't let them win, Herbie,' Rosie panted in desperation, feeling that her arms and neck muscles would explode from the load they were bearing.

The timber cracked and the rock fell with a thud that lifted Rosie inches off the floor and filled her mouth with dust.

Rosie's head dropped to her crossed forearms. 'Can you hear me, Herbie?' she called. 'Please say you can...'

'Have they really got Bourbons?'

Rosie gasped a sob of utter relief into the grimy material of her sleeves. 'Oh, yes ... and I'll get you two, I promise, Herbie.'

Rosie emerged into the humid night, Herbie clinging on to her left foot with two determined hands. Obliquely she heard applause and cheering. Exhaustion hit her like a physical blow and much as she wanted to help Herbie out into the air she couldn't. But there were strong hands lifting the boy onto a stretcher and raising her to stand on unsteady feet.

'Bloody marvellous job!' Hazel thumped Rosie's back then took the cigarette from between her lips and stuck it in Rosie's mouth. 'No arguments! Have a good drag; you need it.'

Though she hadn't smoked in years, Rosie did as she was told, finishing off the cigarette with relish. She drew the smoke deep into her dusty lungs, coughing all the while.

'Cup of tea?' Hazel suggested, opening a new pack of cigarettes.

'She deserves a double Scotch…'

'And a medal…'

Rosie heard the disembodied praise and was aware of a succession of uniformed people – firemen, policemen, the women from the WVS canteen – snatching a moment to trot over and pat her on the back. But she was too concerned about keeping her promise to Herbie to acknowledge them properly.

'Get two teas, Hazel, one for Herbie. And make sure you get him a couple of Bourbons to go with it, won't you?'

'Anybody home?'

'Come in, love. Got time for a drink today?'

'Oh, thanks, Mr Purves. Don't mind if I do have a brew. I'm parched.'

'Can open a bottle of brown ale, if you prefer.' Popeye emerged from the back parlour and gave Nurse Johnson a wink.

'I'm on duty! You trying to get me sacked, Mr Purves?' she complained, parking her bike then stepping over the threshold. Trudy had been pedalling past and seen his front door open. A lot of the houses also had their windows flung wide to let in a breath of air on what was a sticky Indian summer afternoon.

'I will rat on you, love, if you don't stop calling me Mr Purves. Me name's Frank to me friends.' Popeye pulled out a chair at the table. 'Now sit down and I'll put the kettle on.'

Frank had kept the dressing on his thumb although the wound had healed up. He'd liked the idea of Trudy popping in to see him and laying her soothing hands on him. Since his counterfeiting business had hit the buffers, affecting his cash flow, Shirley had become a constant nag and was driving him up the wall.

'You look smart, Frank,' Trudy said, cocking her head to assess his appearance. He had on a pristine shirt and a tie, despite the heat.

'In your honour, love.' He did a little jig. 'Thought you might pop by, seeing as it's a Wednesday,' he added jokily, making his visitor tut at him. In fact what he'd said was the truth. For the past two Wednesdays Frank had spruced himself up and left his door open, hoping to tempt the nurse to come in if she was on her rounds in the district.

'Let's have a gander at that hand, then, while the tea's brewing,' Trudy said as Frank emerged from the kitchen and put the milk and sugar bowl on the table.

Frank sat opposite her and stretched his fingers out on the tablecloth.

'Almost good as new, it is. Just let the air get to it,' Trudy gave her verdict, having examined the pink flesh. 'Can't do any more for you.'

'You can...' Before the nurse could drop his hand to the cloth Frank turned his fingers, clasping hers. He coughed and loosened his tight collar from his flushing neck. 'If you want to say no, just say no ... but I wondered if you'd like to come to the pictures Saturday night?' The surprise on the woman's face made him quickly set her free. 'Sorry, love... Forget about it. I'm just a silly old sod.'

'What about your friend Shirley?'

Popeye glanced at her. So Trudy must have been thinking about their conversations or she wouldn't have remembered his girlfriend's name. He shook his head regretfully. 'Me 'n' Shirley ain't been getting on. I reckon it's time to call a halt to that.'

'When?' Trudy asked pointedly, sitting back and crossing her arms over her chest. She didn't fancy Frank but he did make her laugh, and she had precious little fun in her life. Besides, she was lonely and a casual companion would be nice to have. But she wasn't getting involved in any rivalry with another woman who might have deeper feelings for him.

'When?' Frank pretended to be mystified while he mulled that one over.

'When are you telling Shirley you're not seeing her again?'

'Whenever you say, love.' Frank had made his decision and suddenly felt quite light-hearted.

'And how will Shirley feel about it all?'

Popeye shrugged. 'Reckon she'll soon realise it's for the best, if she don't already. Ain't seen her in more'n a week.'

That was good enough for Trudy. She gave him a smile. 'I wouldn't mind seeing the picture on at the Odeon, if that's all right with you, Frank?'

'Even treat you to a penn'orth of chips on the way home, if yer good.'

He winked his good eye, making Trudy guffaw.

CHAPTER NINETEEN

'There's a man over there staring at you.' Hazel nodded at the bar then took another sip of her gin and orange. 'Wouldn't mind having that dream-boat's attention myself. Only joking … my Chuck's the man for me.' She sunk her chin into a cupped palm, gazing whimsically into space. 'He's taking me to meet his folks soon.' Hazel waggled her ring finger. 'Sparkler'll be on that in a few weeks. Can't wait to get married and have kids. Don't care if it's a poor do. My cousin had registry office, in her work costume and laddered nylons, then a cheese sandwich in a pub afterwards.' Hazel blew a sigh through her pouting lips. 'Got to grab at it, I reckon, 'cos we might be blown to kingdom come tomorrow.'

Rosie understood her friend's philosophy on life, sad though it was she often wondered if her father had married Doris with the same depressing attitude. The couple argued so much that it seemed weird they'd bothered tying the knot when they could have jogged along as they were. But Rosie was surprised to hear that Hazel hadn't met Chuck's parents when her friend considered herself practically engaged.

'I thought Chuck had been your boyfriend for ages.'

''Bout seven months now. Chuck told me his parents are miserable sods who've frightened off his past girl-friends. That's why he's still single at twenty-nine. But he's determined they won't send me packing, so he wants to pick the right time.' Hazel thumped the table with a fist, causing Tom and Jim, sitting opposite, to stop talking about football and start listening to the girls' conversation. 'They won't shift me so easily! Chuck's getting the ring first, then taking me along to make the announcement. I'm twenty-six soon and want my man, so if they don't like me ... tough!'

'Does your mum like him?' Rosie knew that her friend's parents were estranged; Hazel never saw her father or the older sister he'd taken with him when he set up home with another woman.

'Oh, she thinks Chuck's nice enough. They've only met the once but Mum don't care what I get up to, anyhow. She's got religion since the new vicar moved into the village. Reckon she's got her eye on him.' Hazel snorted amusement. 'Speaking of people having an eye on someone, I reckon that fellow might come over and speak to you.' Hazel craned her neck to look past Rosie at the people at the bar. 'Go on, give him a smile, he's gorgeous. Oh, hang on, he's with a girl, though.' Hazel had spied the blonde seated on a barstool.

'What man?' Rosie glanced casually over a shoulder. She was used to her friend's matchmaking. Hazel couldn't understand why any single girl wouldn't want to chase a romance and an engagement ring.

'D'you know him?' Hazel had noticed her friend's expression change.

'Sort of ... through my dad,' Rosie said, gulping her drink. The idea that Conor Flint might come over and greet her as Mrs Deane had made her mouth dry. The pub's smoky atmosphere hadn't concealed the mocking intensity in his eyes as they'd met hers over the rim of his glass.

Rosie reminded herself that they'd got over their initial hostility. Last time they'd met they'd parted on reasonable terms. He'd given her and Tom a lift to the dance and told her she looked beautiful. He'd been perfectly charming. But he was an unpredictable man ... unfathomable ... and she knew she'd be wise to err on the side of caution with him.

'That's your dad's friend Mr Flint, isn't it?' Tom grinned. 'He did us a good turn, didn't he, Rosie, getting us to the ball on time.' He struck a theatrical pose. 'I felt like Cinderella even though Prince Charming was driving a Humber rather than a pumpkin,' he quipped. 'Shall we go over to say hello?'

'I'll just have a quick word with him on my way out,' Rosie said, knocking back what remained of her brandy and soda and standing up. 'It's time I got going anyway; I promised Dad a phone call before bedtime.'

Quickly Rosie said goodbye to her friends, wishing she'd gone straight home when she'd clocked off instead of having one for the road with her colleagues in their local. Then it struck her that, in her absence, Tom might have had the opportunity for a good chinwag with Conor; he seemed keen to get reacquainted.

Rosie edged a path through some rowdy work-men, avoiding their coarse compliments and sour smell as best she could. Glancing at the bar, she noted that Conor was on his way to meet her.

'Nice surprise, bumping into you, Mrs Deane.' Conor drew her away from the press of oily-overalled men.

'Don't call me that!' Rosie hissed quietly.

'Why not?'

'You know why not,' she muttered, flicking a glance up at him.

'True, but I'm still waiting for you to confirm some details.'

Rosie glanced past him, sensing that they were under observation. An attractive woman with bright blonde hair and crimson lips was watching them while talking to a younger man.

'Never seen you in here before,' Rosie said, hoping to find some neutral ground.

'I'm over this way on business. Come in here often, do you?'

'We sometimes have a quick drink before heading home. I'm with colleagues.'

'Yeah ... the uniform sort of gave it away.'

'You don't live round here then?'

'Live Wapping way. Been to the solicitor's this afternoon to tie up some matters about my late brother's estate.'

'Is that your brother? He looks like you.'

'Yep.'

'What's his name?'

'Steven.'

'Is that the woman you had a fight over?'

'Nope.'

'Oh ... who is she then?'

'My sister-in-law.'

'Man of few words, aren't you?' Rosie muttered. She was reluctant to give him the upper hand but before she set off home she had to ask him not to betray her. 'I'm catching my bus; would you step outside with me so I can say something?' Rosie set off without waiting for a reply, trusting he'd follow.

As soon as the pub door swung shut on them she blurted, 'The people at work know me as Miss Gardiner, so if we meet by chance when I'm in their company–'

'Fine by me,' he smoothly interrupted.

'And they don't know about my daughter.'

'Didn't think so.'

'Glad you understand.'

'Not sure I do... Like I said, I'm waiting for you to explain a few things.'

'I don't have to explain a damned thing to you!' Rosie exploded, feeling cornered. 'And I think you've got a fucking nerve expecting me to.'

He grunted a laugh, moving past her as though going back inside.

Quickly Rosie yanked on his sleeve, halting him. 'Where are you going? I'm not finished yet. D'you promise to keep quiet, then?'

'What's it worth?'

Rosie let go of him and furiously dug in her handbag. Whipping a pound note from her purse she thrust it at him in deliberate insult. She knew very well the reward he was after wasn't money. 'That's all you understand, isn't it? Oh, not enough for you?' she taunted when he didn't even look at the cash. His eyes were holding hers easily, unpleasant amusement in their depths. Rosie turned her head, feeling ashamed of her behaviour.

'Sorry,' she eventually said. 'Shouldn't have sworn at you ... don't know why I let you rile me.'

'Know what I think?' Conor said quietly. 'I think there's more to your temper than you having an illegitimate daughter to hide away.'

'I don't hide her away!' Rosie cried, then bit her lip. 'I don't! She's gone away with her granddad so he can keep her safe from all this.' Rosie gestured at broken buildings on the opposite side of the road.

'You could have gone with her.'

Rosie shook her head. 'No, I want this war over with so she'll be free. There are enough people shirking doing their bit and making grubby money out of the chaos.'

'You mean me?'

'If the cap fits...' Rosie muttered.

'I'm going back to my regiment as soon as I'm signed off fit. And the "grubby money" your father got out of his still ... spend any of it for him, did you?'

'No, I did not!' Rosie burst out before remembering that Hope's layette, together with the cot and pram, had been paid for out of her father's savings. John had also been prepared to meet the cost of her abortion out of his nest egg. She knew

248

very well that counterfeit booze had built his bank balance.

'You're no different from me, Rosie. We're caught up in a mess other people made, and now we have to do things we don't like, and associate with people we don't like, because of it.'

Rosie gazed at him; it was as if he knew that her father was partly to blame for her having a secret to keep.

'I certainly don't like you, or what you do. And you don't have to explain yourself to me, 'cos I'm not about to return the favour.' Rosie snapped her face away from his.

'I want to explain things to you, 'cos I've gone beyond pretence now, even if you haven't.'

Rosie felt indignant at the inference she was play-acting. 'I'm not pretending anything!'

'You're doing it now: pretending you don't like me and that you don't know I want you.'

Rosie swallowed, avoiding his eyes and hating him for being so blatant about it. She'd prefer it to remain as it was between them ... just hint and innuendo that would allow her to think about him in private, lying in bed in her empty house with nothing else to do through sleepless nights but reflect on the people occupying her mind.

'D'you promise to be careful what you say when my colleagues are around?' she asked stiltedly.

'Yes.'

'Thanks,' Rosie said. 'Your brother and sister-in-law are probably wondering where you've gone.'

On cue the door swung open and the blonde sauntered out. Conor blasphemed beneath his breath.

'Oh, there you are, Conor. Thought you'd gone off and left us.' Angie linked arms with him. 'Gonna introduce us, then?' She tilted her head to one side, assessing Rosie's appearance. 'What's that get-up?' Angie crinkled her nose at Rosie's uniform as though it gave off a bad smell. 'Auxiliary Fire Service, are you?'

'Ambulance Auxiliary,' Rosie returned, taking an instant dislike to the older woman. But she held out a hand. 'I'm Rosie Gardiner.'

'Angie Flint.' Having limply shaken hands, Angie asked, 'How d'you two know each other then?'

'Through my dad.' Rosie was tempted to tell the woman to mind her own business but she didn't want it to seem that she'd been having more than a casual chat with Conor.

'Go back inside.' Conor disentangled himself from Angie's possessive clutch, battling his irritation.

'It's all right, I'm off now ... got a bus to catch.' Rosie turned away and started walking briskly towards the corner.

'Toodle-oo,' Angie called mockingly.

'Want a lift?'

'No, thanks all the same, I'll wait.'

Conor wound up the car window then got out and came to stand next to Rosie in the bus queue.

'Go away. You're making people stare at us.' She darted a look to and fro.

'Get in the car then.' He took out his cigarettes and offered her the pack.

Rosie took one and drew on it before his match had extinguished. She'd taken up smoking again after the night she'd rescued little Herbie.

The bus pulled up and people surged forward to get on board, Rosie included, but when it set off, she wasn't on it. She turned to Conor, a look of confusion on her face. He put out a hand, beckoning, and she went to him.

He straightened her lapels, his eyes travelling over her drab uniform. 'Pink suits you better,' he said, cigarette wagging between his lips.

Rosie ignored the reference to her dressing gown. When he'd pulled up moments ago she'd been reflecting on the identity of Angie Flint's husband. Steven looked too young to be married to a woman in her thirties. 'Was your sister-in-law married to your late brother?'

'Yeah, she was Saul's wife. Angie's taking it hard ... as you can see,' he said with biting irony.

Rosie didn't protest when he took her arm and steered her towards the car.

'Pick a subject, shall I?' Conor said after they'd driven about half a mile in silence.

'I think I'd sooner start a conversation.' Rosie avoided his challenge.

'Off you go then.'

'Your sister-in-law fancies you.'

'I'll pick a subject,' Conor said drily.

Rosie turned her head and stared at him. She'd spoken half in jest, but it seemed it was no joke. 'It's true, isn't it?'

Conor shrugged.

'She's your brother's widow yet she's already chasing after you?' Rosie sounded disgusted.

251

'She gets no encouragement from me, whatever she might say.'

'What does she say?'

'Nothing worth listening to these days.'

'Did your brother know about ... things?' Rosie gestured the rest of her meaning.

'Yeah, Saul knew. He knew it was over, too.'

'Over?' Rosie shot him a blameful glance. So any affair was partly his fault, she guessed.

'Me and Angie knocked about together before Saul was daft enough to marry her. After that it was finished between us. Now he's gone she thinks she can pick up where we left off. I'm not interested.'

'But she is?'

'That's about it.'

'It's as well they didn't have children then.'

'Amen to that,' Conor drawled solemnly.

Rosie was intrigued – and oddly piqued – by his romantic entanglement with his brother's wife. But she didn't want him to think his affair with his sister-in-law, interested her so she changed the subject.

'Your brother Steven looks young.'

'He's eighteen in the autumn but says he's joining up before then. I want him to stay and take care of things at home. He reckons it's my turn to do that. Perhaps he's expecting me to desert.' Conor gave a half-smile. 'My little brother wants a taste of adventure. I think he's under the impression we've been having a bit of a lark in France.'

Rosie understood the bitterness in his voice. 'Were you there for the D-Day landings? Is that when you got injured?'

'Yeah, I took a bullet in the shoulder on Sword Beach.'

'You look to be recovering well. I imagine it was dreadful over there.'

'Dunkirk was worse.' He turned his head. 'Let's talk about something cheerful.'

'Did you get your money back off Frank Purves?'

'I took payment in lieu.'

'You needed some printing done?'

Conor turned towards her, laughing. 'He's good at what he does. So, yeah, I had some printing off him.' He pulled up outside Rosie's house and turned off the engine. 'Nightcap would be nice.'

'Haven't got any booze.'

'Doesn't have to be kosher. I trust your old man's skilled enough not to poison me.'

'Haven't got any of that either,' Rosie said hoarsely.

'Cup of tea, then.'

'All out of tea ... used up the rations.'

'I might be able to help you there,' Conor said drolly, thinking of the coupons he'd seen in Pop-eye's warehouse. 'Glass of water?' he suggested sardonically. 'Or is the tap out of action?'

Rosie glanced at him. 'Got work in the morning ... up bright and early.'

'Me, too. Have you got a boyfriend?'

Rosie looked startled. 'Me? No!'

'Why d'you say it like that?'

'Like what?'

'As though having a man in your life's out of the question. You're a beautiful girl, as you know; you must get asked out.'

'I'm a mother now.'

'You're a woman, too.'

'That's all finished with.'

'What's all finished with?'

'Look, I worked at the Windmill Theatre when I was eighteen, and didn't have a clue about things,' Rosie stormed, feeling again that he'd cornered her. 'I don't want constant reminders of what my life used to be rammed, down my throat.'

'Wasn't thinking of ramming that down your throat,' Conor said.

'Oh, well, if we're being clever, what were you going to ram down my throat?' Rosie demanded, through gritted teeth. 'Come on, why don't you say it? You think I'm a tart. I've got an illegitimate child because I've no morals and I used to strip off and flirt so it serves me right I got in trouble. Especially as I turned you down.' She swiped spontaneous tears off her lashes. 'That's it, isn't it? You can't get over that I rejected you. Well, if it makes you feel any better, Corporal Flint, your sergeant made me feel sick. Most of them did … all of them…'

Rosie jumped out of the car and flung off his hand when he stopped her by her door.

'Was it a serviceman got you pregnant?'

Rosie shook her head. 'No…' she said hoarsely, remembering the coward who'd raped her. 'He'd no stomach for that sort of fighting.'

Conor dropped her hand and stepped back, staring at her with dark unsettling intensity. 'I see…' His voice was barely audible. He rubbed a hand across his mouth, fingers travelling on to pinch the bridge of his nose. He prowled along the pavement for some yards before returning to her side. Slowly he dipped his head and kissed her cheek.

"Night, Rosie,' he murmured.

Without another word he turned and got in his car, pulling away immediately.

Rosie shrunk back against the front gate. From wanting him gone, she suddenly wanted him with her. But he wouldn't be back. Men like Conor Flint, who were attractive to the opposite sex, were repulsed by women like her, who couldn't respond to them.

But she wanted to be able to.

Rosie watched the car turn the corner with tears soaking her cheeks. She didn't want to flinch from a man's touch but she did. Lenny Purves might be dead but she couldn't escape him. He'd left her his legacy: an adorable child and a frigid body.

Rosie went indoors and found her dad's rotgut whisky in the sideboard. She poured herself a drink and took it with her upstairs to bed. It wasn't until after midnight that she remembered she should have phoned her dad and spoken to Hope.

CHAPTER TWENTY

'Thought it was high time I came to introduce myself; I bet you don't remember me, do you?'

Rosie had been cutting the dead heads off roses in the front garden when the sailor appeared, leaning on the gate and startling her.

She shielded her eyes from the evening sun with her fingers to get a better view of him.

'I'm Charles Bellamy ... Doris's son. Charlie to me family.' He extended a hand. 'And I reckon we are family now, ain't we, Rosie?'

Quickly Rosie wiped her fingers, sticky with sap, on her skirt and shook his hand. 'Oh ... right ... nice to meet you.' She felt awkward, unsure what to say. She vaguely remembered Charlie Bellamy from when she was a youngster. Doris and her only child had lived a few roads away. In one of their rare friendly chats Doris had told her that within the space of one month her husband had got her pregnant and got himself shot in Flanders.

'Shall I put the kettle on, or are you pushed for time?' Rosie felt uncharitable for hoping that he would go away but she sensed she wouldn't like her new stepbrother. There was a mite too much familiarity in his eyes, despite the way he'd courteously tucked his naval cap under an arm when speaking to her.

'I'd love a cuppa. Got a forty-eight-hour pass.'

Rosie led the way indoors, noting that Peg Price was making a show of sweeping her front path while keeping a beady eye on her. She gave the woman an ironic salute, letting her neighbour know she was well aware of being spied on.

Fleetingly, Rosie wondered how young Irene was coping. She'd not heard any commotion coming from the Prices' house, and Peg's daughter still ambled up and down the road, looking fat and miserable. There'd been no opportunity for Rosie to have a chat with Irene and ask how things were going. Probably, unable to face her mother, the poor girl had decided to let things ride.

'So ... you still a Windmill girl then, are you, Rosemary?' Charlie studied Rosie from beneath his eyebrows as he sat down in the parlour.

'No, not been working there for years,' Rosie called, disappearing into the kitchen. Her instinct to get rid of him quickly heightened at his remark and the look that had accompanied it. She filled the kettle and set the cups, aware that he'd come up behind her.

'Your wife'll be pleased you're back on leave,' Rosie said over a shoulder, feeling suffocated because he was standing too close to her. 'You'll be catching the train to Gravesend soon, won't you?'

Charlie shrugged. 'Now me mum and your dad have set up camp in our house with your kiddie it's got too crowded for my liking.' He gave Rosie a direct stare. 'Bet you've got plenty of room here, ain't yer?' He raised his eyes to the ceiling. 'Any chance of kipping here while I'm staying over in London?'

'Sorry ... my boyfriend wouldn't like that arrangement,' Rosie lied fluently.

'Who's that, then? Yer dad said you weren't settled with anyone new.' Charlie sounded rather indignant.

'Don't tell my dad everything, do I?' Rosie snapped, fed up with his personal questions.

'Your little gel's a beauty, just like her mum, ain't she?' Charlie's gaze wandered over Rosie's rear view.

'I'm very proud of her.' Rosie stirred the teapot.

257

She felt her insides tighten, resenting his breath on her neck. She wished she knew what this man had been told about her past. Doris tended to stick to the story of her stepdaughter being Mrs Deane, a widow, but Rosie suspected the woman's close family might know better.

'Pity about yer husband, Rosemary. Where did he cop it? Artillery, wasn't he, so I heard?'

His sly tone of voice confirmed Rosie's suspicions. When she felt a heavy hand massaging her shoulder in a show of comfort, she immediately shrugged him off but kept up the sham. 'His body wasn't recovered ... sorry, I don't like to talk about it. Sit in the parlour and drink this, shall we?' She carried two cups of tea into the room, placing them on the table.

'Your Toby's a fine lad. Saw him and your wife at the wedding ... shame you missed it. Only a small quiet affair but nice all the same.' Rosie was determined to change the subject and to remain civil, despite a growing urge to show him the door.

'Yeah ... couldn't make it being as I was sailing past Gibraltar at the time.' Charlie gulped his tea. 'Wasn't expecting 'em to up and get leg-shackled. Don't know why they did at their age, if I'm honest.'

Rosie knew her view matched his but she said, 'Wartime, isn't it? People do funny things.'

''Spose...'

He sat back in his chair and stared boldly, making Rosie feel uneasy again.

'Remember seeing you on stage at the Windmill; used to say to me pals: that blonde up there,

I know her ... used to be neighbours, we did, when she was just a flat-chested kid. Ain't a kid now, though, are yer, Rosie?'

'Don't hardly remember you at all. 'Course, you're a lot older than me, aren't you? You were married when I was in junior school.' Rosie got up and opened the sash window, feeling hot.

'Bet you miss the work ... all that glitz 'n' glamour,' Charlie purred.

Rosie darted a glance at him. She could see he'd finished his tea and she wished he'd get going. 'Prefer what I'm doing now.' She picked up his empty cup and her own and took them to the kitchen, hoping he'd take the hint.

'So ... what *are* you doing now, Rosie? Must still be in showbiz. Crying shame else, with that figure...' Charlie had stationed himself in the kitchen doorway, a shoulder propped on the jamb with his arms crossed over his chest. 'Built for attention, you are, gel.'

Rosie knew he'd got her trapped and she'd either have to ask him to move or push past him to get out.

'Better get that; I'm expecting somebody.' The knock on the door had greatly relieved Rosie. She'd spoken the truth, too; she was certain she'd open up and find Peg on her step, ready to cross-examine her about her gentleman caller.

Charlie sauntered away into the parlour and Rosie went to open the door, cursing below her breath because he'd made himself comfortable again.

She went pale as she looked up at Conor.

He glanced past her as Charlie gave a loud

cough, on purpose Rosie reckoned, so her visitor would know she already had company.

'Bad time?'

'No...' Rosie breathed, feeling strangely euphoric once the shock of seeing him had worn off. 'Not at all. Come in.'

When they entered the back parlour Charlie was on his feet and immediately swinging a glance between the couple.

'This is my stepbrother, Charlie Bellamy. And this is Conor Flint, friend of my – friend of mine.' Rosie had previously introduced Conor as her father's acquaintance, but just now she knew she'd far sooner be stranded in his company than Charlie's. 'My stepbrother's off to visit his wife in Gravesend. My dad's been staying with Charlie's family ... as you know.'

Conor shook hands with the sailor. 'Won't hold you up as you've got a journey in front of you.' The words seemed inoffensive but at odds with the expression in his deep-blue eyes.

'Say hello to them all for me, won't you?' Rosie said as she walked into the hall with her step-brother.

He gave a terse nod. 'So that's yer boyfriend, is it?'

Rosie gave an almost imperceptible nod, hoping Conor hadn't heard what Charlie had said.

'So what d'you do now you're not a Windmill girl?' Again an unpleasant glint was in his eyes.

'I'm an ambulance auxiliary.'

Charlie looked as though she'd shocked him. He licked his lips. 'Stationed round here, are yer?'

'Mmm ... Robley Road. Station 97.'

'Best be off. Thanks for the tea.'

Rosie waved to Charlie as he closed the gate, then she shut the door and with a deep breath went back to the parlour.

'How are you?'

They spoke the question simultaneously. Rosie gestured for Conor to continue and thought he would say something but instead he frowned through the open sash window. The net curtain billowed gently in the summer breeze but he seemed oblivious to the lacy veil brushing his face.

Rosie felt a poignant sadness as she watched him battling to find the right words to speak to her. Previously his confidence had been unstoppable, his arrogance overwhelming. But he was different now.

'I know you want to apologise for having got me wrong, but there's no need,' she said softly. 'There you were, thinking I was up for a good time, and I don't blame you. It's what most men think when they recognise me.' She could have added that even her married stepbrother classed her as a slag. But she kept her thoughts about Charlie to herself. 'When men discover I've got a daughter and no husband ... well, it just confirms their suspicions about me and my past.'

'Are you hoping I'll deny it, Rosie?' Conor grimaced wryly. ''Course I thought I was in with a chance of getting you into bed. It's why I've kept coming back. It's why I've not bothered seeing the girl I used to knock around with. Pat's her name. She was the one I got into a fight for.'

He plunged his hands into his pockets. 'No great romance, but she was all right till I saw you.'

Rosie nodded, blinking heat from her eyes, angry at herself for feeling like weeping when she'd nothing to cry about.

'Well ... perhaps she'll take you back, or you'll find someone else...'

He grunted a mirthless laugh. 'Won't help. Can't stop thinking about you, that's the problem.'

Rosie examined her hands, picking at the thorn nicks from the pruning she'd done. 'Been cutting back in the garden. Better go and tidy up ... left the shears and the secateurs out there. The kids round here'll pinch anything, soon as your back's turned.' She glanced at Conor; he was watching her with a look in his eyes she'd never seen before. She hoped it wasn't pity. The idea that it might be straightened her shoulders and strengthened her voice. 'Anyhow, I know my dad was an idiot ever getting involved with Frank Purves again. I know you could have made life miserable for him, so thanks.' Rosie abruptly went into the kitchen and started washing up the teacups, straining to hear the telltale sound of her front door closing. He'd salved his conscience and her pride by coming to see her and she thought it fair to give him a chance to slip away.

She upended the washing-up bowl into the butler sink, then turned about to see him stationed in the doorway, just like her stocky, sandy-haired stepbrother had been earlier. But Conor Flint, with his lean frame and dangerous dark looks, didn't intimidate her; quite the reverse. She was tempted to rush at him and hug him for comfort.

But of course she wouldn't because he'd get the wrong idea.

'Who was it?'

'It doesn't matter now.'

'Tell me.'

'He's dead, so it doesn't matter now.'

'Who killed him?'

Rosie stopped drying the saucers and looked at him. 'What makes you think somebody killed him?'

He grimaced. 'I would've.'

Rosie knew he meant it.

'Did your dad go after him?'

Rosie resumed drying the crockery. 'Dad didn't need to. He died in a nightclub. Drank some moonshine and passed out, then set fire to the mattress with a cigarette.' A darting glance caught him frowning so she explained, 'The club was a brothel, too. He was in bed with a prostitute. They both died.' Suddenly she flung down the cloth and gripped the edge of the sink until her knuckles showed bone. 'Can we not talk about this?' She spun about. 'Is your mum feeling better?'

'Want to come and see her?'

Rosie gazed at him, wondering if he was joking. 'Why? I don't think I can help.' She gave a smile. 'My forte is crawling about in bombed-out buildings tending to small boys trapped in the rubble.'

'Really?'

Briefly Rosie told him about Herbie, glad to lighten the atmosphere between them, even if it was at poor Herbie's expense.

When they'd got him to hospital they'd discovered that the lad had a fractured skull, whereas his trapped shin had suffered just cuts and bruises. Rosie had heard her patient was making a slow recovery and she was planning on visiting him when the doctors said he was ready. At present only his family were allowed in.

'Quite the heroine, aren't you?'

He sounded genuinely impressed rather than patronising; nevertheless Rosie's smile faded. 'Just doing what anybody would do. If it was my child in there, hurt and frightened, I'd want somebody to do that for her.' She paused. 'Herbie's mum had gone to the shelter with her other kids. Herbie's only six but she had three younger than that; he was out playing football with his pals and naturally rushed home to find his mum when the sirens sounded. Do-gooders say she should have waited for him to return rather than leave her eldest daughter behind to wait for him. But who do you save? All of them? One of them? Just a wrong decision … that's all it takes to lose them. A friend of mine lost three of her little sons because she and her husband weren't home when the bombs dropped.' Rosie knew she'd never fully comprehend Gertie's pain and suffering. 'But Herbie's doing all right – that's the main thing – and nobody to blame if he wasn't, 'cos we're all careless at times.' The thought of the day her baby daughter had only by luck escaped injury in the bombing haunted her mind and she knew it would continue to do so till the day she died. Hope might have suffocated in her pram because she'd forgotten the infant existed.

'You're a good girl, Rosie, know that?'

'Sorry ... went on a bit, didn't I?' Rosie replied bashfully. 'Wasn't angling for praise.'

'I know,' he said softly. 'Fancy going to the flicks later?'

Rosie shrugged, avoiding his eyes. 'I should get on with the ironing.'

'See the film ... have a bite to eat ... bring you back ... won't even try to kiss you... Scout's honour.'

The gentle humour in his voice made her smile and raise an eyebrow at him. 'You have to make the sign or it's not a proper promise.'

Solemnly he raised his fingers to his forehead.

'Do I know you? What've you done with that scoundrel Conor Flint?' she teased.

He laughed, throwing back his head and Rosie joined in, laughing till she cried.

'Come here.' He held out his arms.

Without hesitation Rosie went to him, nestling into his shoulder and letting him hold her and stroke her hair because the good tears had turned to bad before subsiding.

'Pick you up at seven?'

Rosie sniffed. 'Thanks.'

'What for?'

Rosie shrugged, again feeling shy. 'Understanding,' she said, and went back to the kitchen, smiling to herself when she heard her front door quietly being closed.

CHAPTER TWENTY-ONE

'Don't think I took to your stepbrother,' Conor said.

'Join the club!' Rosie replied with feeling.

'D'you know him well?'

'No, I hardly know him at all; he turned up to introduce himself this afternoon. My stepmother has always lived round our way but I was a school-kid when her Charlie got married and moved off.' Rosie paused. 'Don't remember ever having had a conversation with him before today. He's a lot older than me.'

'I'd say he's about my age,' Conor said ruefully.

'Really? You seem younger. Perhaps you're immature,' Rosie teased, earning herself a heavy hand planted on the scruff of her neck.

She hunched her shoulders to her ears. 'Only joking,' she squeaked, laughing. His fingers stroked tenderly on her nape before sliding away to plunge back into his trouser pocket.

'Did Charlie say or do something to make you dislike him?'

Rosie shook her head. 'Just found his manner a bit unpleasant.' With hindsight she was prepared to give her stepbrother's crafty remarks the benefit of the doubt. It might have been Charlie's clumsy way of being complimentary.

They were strolling side by side, having just emerged from the Odeon. There had been vivid sunshine when they'd gone in but they'd exited into twilight an hour and three-quarters later. Rosie glanced up at the starry heavens, arms crossed over her middle.

Softly, she murmured a prayer that there wouldn't be an air raid. 'Please don't come tonight.'

'Think you're hoping in vain, Rosie,' Conor said flatly. 'They'll be over before dawn.' He casually ruffled her blonde hair. 'If there can be a good side to these doodlebugs it's that they're a sign Adolf's been badly rattled by the D-Day landings. He'll run out of rockets and launching sites along the French coast if we can keep pushing the Krauts back inland. Sooner or later those damned V1s won't make it past the Channel.'

'Please God you're right.' Rosie suddenly squeezed Conor's arm. 'Oh, no, look who's coming! Crikey! That's a turn-up!' she gasped. 'Never imagined I'd see those two walking arm in arm!'

From the expressions on the faces of the approaching couple they were also surprised at this unexpected meeting.

'Is it too late to cross over the road?' Rosie whispered.

''Fraid so. Who's the woman with Frank Purves?' Conor asked.

'She's a midwife. Nurse Johnson delivered Hope, and...' Rosie tailed off. She'd almost blurted out that after Hope was born she'd nearly let the woman adopt her daughter.

'Frank...' Conor said in terse greeting.

'Taking a stroll then, are yer, Mr Flint?' Frank's wonky vision settled on Rosie. 'Didn't know you and John's daughter were acquainted.'

'No reason why you should,' Conor returned coolly.

'How've you been keeping, young Rosie? A mum now, ain't yer, so I heard?' Popeye sounded amiable. 'Seen your dad recently, or is he still out of town?' he asked, sliding a subtle look at Conor.

'Dad's still away,' Rosie answered quickly.

'Got a bit of unfinished business, have me 'n' John, so when you speak to him, love, remember me to him, won't yer now?' Popeye was boiling up, and feeling a worse mug than before for letting Flint take his petrol coupons. The randy sod hadn't pursued John Gardiner for his booze or his money because he was knocking off the man's daughter! The lucky bastard had got a leg over with a Windmill Girl for no extra charge.

Popeye knew that John's daughter had been on the stage, posing starkers. His Lenny had told him all about that, not that it had been any secret. Most of the folk roundabouts had known that the good-looking Gardiner girl had got a part in the theatre's famous performances. John would never be drawn on discussing his Rosie's job, and anybody who brought it up, hoping for a bit of smut, was disappointed.

Popeye was bent on getting his revenge on John. There had always been an amount of rivalry between them but Popeye liked to think he was top dog. Popeye hadn't intended taking John for a ride on the distilling deal; he'd have paid him up fair and square once the profits started rolling in. But Gardiner had done him up like a kipper, when he was least expecting it. John might only have got away with fifty quid out of five hundred but to Popeye the humiliation and betrayal was as strong as it would have been had he been cheated out of the lot.

'Nice to bump into you,' Rosie lied, desperate to get going in case Popeye mentioned his late son. She could feel the nurse's eyes on her and she gave Trudy a brief nod, stepping away.

'And how's your daughter?' Trudy asked. 'Must be two now; Hope's her name, isn't it?'

Rosie had never told the nurse her daughter's name and it annoyed her that Trudy had made it her business to find it out. 'She's very well, thanks. She's staying with her granddad.'

'Lost yer husband, didn't you, dear?' Popeye sounded sympathetic but if the girl was knocking about with Flint he reckoned he knew what sort she was. He wondered if her kid was her husband's or a punter's, or whether she'd ever even had a trip down the aisle.

Rosie nodded, making brief eye contact with Trudy. The midwife hadn't forgotten their conversation about her using an alias because the neighbours were gossiping.

'Be seeing you...' Conor put an arm about Rosie's shoulders to lead her on.

'Reckon you will be,' Popeye replied through his teeth.

'You've gone very quiet since we bumped into those two.' Conor tickled Rosie's cheek with a knuckle to gain her attention. 'Not worried about Popeye, are you? He won't bother your dad. He knows he got what he deserved. I was never going to go after John for any cash. I used that as an excuse to come round and get to know you.'

They were parked outside Rosie's house and she glanced through the dim interior of the car at Conor. 'You make it sound as though you're still at loggerheads with Frank Purves. I thought you had some printing off him to square things up.'

Conor stretched out his legs under the steering wheel, easing back in the car seat and pillowing his head on his clasped hands. 'I did get some printing off him. Didn't say he wanted to give it to me, though.'

'You didn't hit him, did you? He's just an old man.'

Rosie hadn't been able to escape an unpalatable truth this evening. Frank Purves was Hope's grandfather. In the past she'd banished that fact from her mind. Popeye had been just somebody who used to know her dad years ago. But things had changed. Purves had turned up like a bad penny, worming his way into John's life again. And this evening she'd come face to face with him, and he'd mentioned her daughter. Nurse Johnson's presence had only served to heighten Rosie's uneasiness.

Just after Hope's birth she'd been at a low ebb and had confided in her midwife, something she now bitterly regretted. She had a niggling fear that the sheltered little world she'd built for herself and her daughter could be under threat. Trudy might tell Purves that she'd never had a husband, and that Rosie had once almost let her adopt the child.

The thought of Popeye discovering Hope had his blood running in her veins terrified Rosie. She glanced at Conor. She didn't want him to know either. She liked him, and was starting to trust him. He'd guessed she'd been raped, but he'd had the decency not to ask her to confirm what had happened. But she couldn't predict how he'd react to knowing that Popeye's son had been her attacker.

'Did you hear what I said?'

Rosie started to attention, shaking her head, and looking apologetic.

'I said of course I didn't hit him, what d'you take me for?' Conor smiled at the memory of Popeye offering him the services of his two crippled henchmen. 'Frank's just an over-the-hill racketeer. He's got a couple of youngish blokes as his back-up. First glance you'd take 'em for middle-aged but they're likely to be no more than early thirties. Both of 'em seen better days. Felt sorry for them 'cos they're probably war cripples.'

'I'd better go in. I'm on early shift.' Rosie had just noticed Peg's blackout curtain twitching. The woman was a tireless nosy parker.

'Right...' Conor nodded slowly, without looking at her.

'Neighbours are spying on us,' Rosie explained.

'Right...' he said again.

Rosie anticipated him saying, 'Well, let's go inside then.' He didn't, but the words filled the space between them. She sat tensely, wondering if he'd give her a peck on the cheek as he had before. She'd liked the feel of his mouth on her skin. When he sat unmoving she leaned in quickly and kissed him on the cheek instead, uncaring if Peg Price had seen her. 'Thanks for taking me out.'

'Do it again?'

'Mmm, I'd like to.'

'Forget about Frank Purves.'

'Yes … I will,' Rosie said stoutly. But it was a lie. She couldn't forget about Hope's other grandfather now or in the future. She felt as though the Sword of Damocles was hanging over her. The meeting between the four of them had been an omen of bad things to come.

Rufus twiddled the knobs on the wireless to tune in a news broadcast as it was coming up to one o'clock.

'I need some wages. The tight-fist should pay us a retainer while he's sorting things out.' Midge was pacing restlessly to and fro in front of his seated brother-in-law.

The idea of Popeye shelling out so freely made Rufus guffaw in disbelief. 'We talking about the same person?' he asked. 'You got more chance of one of us passing a medical and enlisting than him doing that.'

'Don't fuckin' want to enlist,' Midge snorted. 'Just want to get back earning. We was doing all right, you 'n' me, driving Pop's motor and delivering counterfeits.'

'Yeah, we was,' Rufus agreed nostalgically. Once he'd got the hang of driving the Citroën, he'd enjoyed those trips out with Midge, haring along narrow country lanes close to Edgware, whooping like a couple of kids on a seaside outing. And the cash had been good to have, too.

Midge flopped down on the couch in Rufus's parlour, restlessly tapping his feet on the bare

272

wooden boards. He'd just been round to Pop-eye's place to try to persuade his boss to give him a sub against future work. Popeye wasn't having any of it, and had been like a bear with a sore head still moaning about Flint getting his petrol coupons and John Gardiner stitching him up. But he'd boasted about his new lady friend and how he liked taking her out for a ride in his flash motor. Midge had slunk out without even getting a tot of Scotch out of the miser.

A few moments after sitting down Midge was again on his feet, peering out of the window for a sign of his sister returning home. He knew he'd have to shift a bit lively if Gertie showed up. She'd not softened towards him. He still had to creep in and have a cuppa and a chinwag with Rufus when the coast was clear.

'Stick the kettle on, Midge, will yer?' Rufus leaned his ear close to the gramophone, listening to the lunchtime bulletin through crackling inter-ference.

Midge cast a jaundiced eye on his brother-in-law. 'I'm not yer servant; you've got me sister to fetch 'n' carry for you.' But he got up and stomped into the kitchen, rattling crockery about and miss-ing the moment when Gertie let herself in.

'Can yer lend us a few bob, Roof, before I go?' Midge called plaintively, pouring boiling water on tea. 'I ain't had a hot meal in an age and as fer getting me end away...'

'Shame about that ... and no, he bleedin' can't,' Gertie snapped, standing in the open kitchen doorway with her hands on her hips. She knew her brother had been coming round in her ab-

273

sence and she'd turned a blind eye to it because, much as she detested Michael, Rufus was content to have his company. And Gertie had come to the conclusion that no price was too great to pay to shut her husband's moaning up.

Today she couldn't pretend ignorance of her brother's clandestine visits. Joey was due in soon, too, and she didn't want the two of them clashing. Joey despised his uncle, and Gertie knew her son was starting to dislike his father for allowing Midge houseroom.

'Where's me little Vicky?' Rufus asked genially, trying to lighten the atmosphere.

'Becky's playing with her out the front.' Gertie turned her attention back to Michael. 'You can drink that, then get going.' She nodded at the cup of tea in Midge's hand. 'Get it down yer.'

'He's been round Pop's and only come here to let me know there might be some work coming up soon.' Rufus stuck up for his brother-in-law with a white lie.

Gertie pretended to be unimpressed when in fact the idea of Rufus getting back out earning was music to her ears. 'When's that then? This week?'

'Not sure yet... Pop's gonna let us know,' Midge said, gulping at his tea.

'In other words, sometime never,' Gertie said sourly.

'Ain't our fault this all come about.' Rufus felt affronted. He knew his wife was itching to get him out from under her feet.

'Gardiner deserves a right spanking for putting a spoke in the works,' Midge snarled. 'I remember a few years back him 'n' Pop and Lenny was doing a roaring trade with bottling up and labelling the rotgut. Then all of a sudden, right about the time that Lenny croaked, Gardiner packed up his still.' Midge took another slurp of tea. 'I thought it was Popeye wanted out as he was cut up over Lenny, but he reckons no. John called a halt and never would say why.'

'Probably about the time his grandkid was born.'

'According to Pop, it were long before that.' Midge smirked. 'Pop reckons John's daughter's a part-time tart who used to be on the stage and got herself in the family way. Pop's theory is that Gardiner withdrew into his shell because he didn't want questions asked about his grandkid's father. Seems they made up some tale about the girl's husband dying in action when they'd only been married a few months.'

Gertie had been half listening to their conversation from the kitchen while pulling some shopping out of her bag. She'd been thinking about finding work now Rufus was back at home and able to babysit. But the groceries and the jobs were abruptly forgotten as the bits and pieces she'd heard lined up in her brain. She went back into the parlour and asked, 'What's this girl's name?'

Midge and Rufus turned to stare at Gertie.

'Dunno ... why d'you ask?' Rufus said.

Gertie shrugged. 'Used to char up in the West End theatres, didn't I? Thought I might know her.'

'Rosie ... that's it,' Midge burst out, pleased at having brought the name to mind.

'Sound familiar, does she?' Rufus asked his wife, pleased she'd joined in the conversation and seemed to have calmed down.

Gertie shook her head. Turning away she went back to the kitchen. 'Finished that bleedin' tea, have yer?' she called over a shoulder. 'Come on, get going before Joey gets home.'

The moment she heard the back door closing Gertie locked it, then went in to the back parlour. She sat down on the couch, picking over in her mind what she'd heard and finding it did make shocking sense to her.

'If I tell you something, d'you promise to keep it to yourself?' she asked her husband.

Rufus was trying to tune the wireless to a variety programme now the news had finished. The ear-splitting whining noise filled the room, making Gertie shout at him to turn the bloody thing off.

'Was that *him* in here again?' Joey bawled over the tuneless racket. He'd just passed Midge out in the street and had spat in the gutter as he did so. He'd let himself in and now stood glowering at Rufus. 'Don't want him in here. I hate him and you!'

'Who d'you think you're talking to?' Rufus roared, struggling up out of his chair again, puce in the face. 'You bleedin' cheeky little git. You'll feel the back of my hand ... telling me what to do in me own home.'

Joey turned and stamped up the stairs.

'What was you saying, love?' Rufus asked his stony-faced wife. He got out his handkerchief and patted his red face.

Gertie had jumped up when Joey stormed in,

ready to lunge between father, and son if necessary. Joey seemed to be finding his feet now that he was out at work. He was finding his voice, too, and Gertie didn't like kids back-chatting their parents any more than Rufus did. But she knew her son had a point.

'Weren't saying nothing at all. Will say this, though, and you'd better listen: Joey's right about Midge. Tell him to stay away.'

CHAPTER TWENTY-TWO

'Ssh ... here she comes! We'd better pick the right time to tell her.'

Rosie guessed she'd been the subject of, the men's cautious whispering. 'Tell me what?' she asked.

Tom and Jim were standing in the common room, uniformed and ready to go on shift. Rosie glanced around.

'Hazel not turned up yet?' The wall clock showed just after nine o'clock; it was unusual for her friend to be late.

'Probably on her way,' Tom said, prowling to and fro and feeling awkward that Rosie had overheard his comment.

'Come on, out with it!' Rosie's smile transformed to a frown. 'Has my driving test been rebooked after all?'

Rosie had almost failed her driving test for braking too sharply and filling the examiner's turn-ups with water from the bucket on the floor. The fellow hadn't taken the soaking too well but had given her a pass as he'd said he believed her nerves had got the better of her. She was now a relief driver and still doing a bit of night-time practice with Jim by her side giving sound advice. The blackouts could be cripplingly hazardous, what with the broken glass, and the civilians popping out of the dark when least expected.

'Crikey! Hazel looks upset.' Tom stopped pacing, having spotted his partner. 'Something must've happened and that's why she's late.'

Rosie noticed her friend had halted by the door. Hazel was puffing furiously on her cigarette as though building up her courage to come and join them.

'What's the matter?' Rosie kept her voice soft as she approached Hazel and noticed her eyes were bloodshot.

Hazel burst into fresh tears so Rosie ushered her along the corridor and out into the fresh air of the courtyard to talk privately. Hazel was a stoic character who usually took upsets in her stride.

Hazel dropped her cigarette butt and stamped on it, indicating her distress held an edge of temper. 'He's thrown me over. The rat! He's thrown me over when we were supposed to be getting engaged.' Hazel pulled a note from her pocket, glancing at a paragraph of pencilled scrawl before crumpling it in a fist. 'Didn't even have the decency to tell me to my face. Just sent this!'

Rosie hugged her friend. 'He's a bloody fool, then, and you were far too good for him,' she declared.

A sob burst from Hazel. 'He reckons his folks have found out about us and we'd best cool things in case they cut up rough. I know he means it's finished. He didn't have the guts to say so, though.'

'D'you want him back, if he's scared of his parents at his age?' Rosie enquired.

Hazel yanked a packet of Capstan from her pocket. Clumsily she tried to light up but dropped the Vestas on the concrete. Rosie scooped up the box and a couple of matches then lit two cigarettes. For a few minutes the two young women smoked silently.

'I've already written back to him and told him he's a pathetic specimen, tied to his mummy's apron strings,' Hazel spat, snorting smoke from her nostrils.

'Hear, hear!' Rosie exclaimed. 'That's the spirit!'

Hazel scrubbed at her face with a handkerchief. 'Bloody mascara's run all over the place, I suppose,' she sniffed, looking at the sooty stains on the hanky.

Rosie took the sodden cloth and wiped the make-up off her friend's cheeks. 'There ... scrub up well, don't you?'

'Might just as well look a fright now I've no man to call me own.' Hazel gave a wan smile.

Rosie was pleased to see that Hazel seemed to have calmed down. 'If Dr Clark finds out you're fancy-free, he might ask you out.' Rosie had noticed the doctor watching Hazel when they bumped into one another out on calls. Rosie was full of admiration for the way her friend capably strode about attending to vomit or gore without a hint of squeamishness. Richard Clark often watched Hazel too, smiling in a special way that went beyond admiration of her professional competence.

'I'm off men after this,' Hazel muttered, but managed a wry grimace. She dug in her handbag for her purse and pulled out a photograph, which she thrust at Rosie. 'Tear that up for me; can't bring myself to do it.'

Hazel had shown her the small square snap before. Chuck looked clean cut in his naval uniform with his cap and sunglasses warding off the Mediterranean glare. Rosie tore the photo into four pieces.

'Thanks. And this one.' Hazel pulled another picture from her bag's inner pocket and handed it over.

Rosie's fingers were gripping the top, ready to rip, when she glanced at it. She brought the image closer to examine it, then burst out, 'What's Chuck's full name?'

'Why d'you want to know?' Hazel said, rummaging in her bag.

'Tell me his name,' Rosie demanded quite brusquely.

'Charles Bellamy, but all his navy pals call him Chuck,' Hazel answered with a frown. 'He doesn't like being called Charlie. Says that's what his folks call him.'

'They do,' Rosie confirmed, shocked. There was no doubt: she was staring at the photograph of her stepbrother in civvies. Then she remembered how Charlie had seemed odd when she'd told him that she worked at Ambulance Station

97. And no wonder! Hazel had believed him her fiancé, but the swine had dropped her like a hot potato now he realised his adultery might be uncovered.

'You know him, don't you?' Hazel took the photo back, gawping at it.

Rosie was reluctant to make her friend cry again, yet Charlie Bellamy deserved to be exposed as a liar and a cheat, as much for his wife's benefit as for Hazel's.

'He's married, isn't he?' Hazel burst out in sudden enlightenment. 'His "folks" are a wife and kids!'

Rosie was relieved that she'd only to confirm her friend's suspicions rather than grass Charlie up, though he deserved it. 'I'm so sorry, Hazel. My dad married Doris Bellamy, Charlie's mother.' Rosie frowned. 'We're sort of related although I've only spoken to him once. He's got a wife and son, and if I'd realised Chuck and Charlie were one and the same, I'd've told you sooner.'

'What a *bastard!* No wonder he said his family wouldn't like me! Well, the poor cow's welcome to him!'

Jim and Tom approached cautiously, giving warning coughs as they stepped outside.

'Everything all right?' they chorused.

'Everything's just fine,' Hazel said, sniffing fiercely. She tilted up her chin. 'Cleaning out the jalopy, I suppose, are we, first thing? Might as well get started.' She and Tom set off in the direction of the parked ambulances, Tom throwing a bewildered look over a shoulder as Hazel marched ahead.

'Her boyfriend's thrown her over and, believe me, she's better off without him,' Rosie briefly answered Jim's unspoken question.

He raised his eyebrows and shook his head, about to follow their friends when Rosie caught his sleeve and looked into his kindly eyes.

'Why were you talking about me earlier, Jim? What don't you want me to know?'

Jim looked sad, and sheepish. 'We thought it best not to say anything just yet...' he sighed. 'I don't know why because it'll be just as upsetting to know later as it is right now.'

'It's not about my driving test, is it?' Rosie asked.

Jim wearily shook his grey head. At that moment Rosie thought he looked more than his fifty-seven years.

'Young Herbie didn't make it, after all, Rosie.'

'What d'you mean?' Rosie demanded, feeling ice enclose her heart. 'I'm going to visit him on Friday when he's not so sleepy,' she announced. 'I phoned the hospital and they said his family didn't mind me going in to see him...'

'His concussion proved to be worse than they thought. He had a brain haemorrhage. He died in the early hours of this morning. Stella Phipps got a call from Richard Clark. He knew our two crews would want to know the little lad's fate. Stella passed on the news before she went off duty this morning.'

Rosie felt her lower lip starting to tremble and her eyes swim with tears. She tipped back her head blinking at the blurry blue sky, screaming inside at the injustice of it.

Jim put a comforting hand on her shoulder, then let it fall to his side. Quietly he stood with her, listening to her sobs before he said huskily, 'Don't ever think it wasn't worth it, and you'll quit and knit socks instead. If the service loses the likes of girls like you, Rosie Gardiner, we're all buggered.'

'What did you say your name was?'

'I'm Rosie – Rosie Gardiner – and I'm pleased to meet you, Mrs Flint.' Rosie peered through the gloom at a small wizened face with a coil of plaited hair pinned either side of it.

'Likewise.' The elderly woman cocked her head, studying Rosie as though still making up her mind about her, whatever she'd said.

Conor slanted Rosie a private smile while showing her to an armchair by the hearth.

'Open the curtains, shall I, Mum? Let some light and fresh air in for a while before it gets proper dark.'

'No, you don't!' Hilda Flint's tiny figure was struggling up from the chair. 'Y'know Saul don't like people spying in on 'im. Keep 'em drawn.'

'Saul's gone, Mum.' Conor left the curtains as they were and sat down in the armchair opposite his mother, planting his elbows on his knees.

'He's off doing deals, ain't he? Him 'n' yer father's always out earning.' Hilda rubbed together arthritic fingers. 'Bringing in this, ain't they, so I can have me fags 'n' milk stouts in the evening?' Slyly she added, 'Look after me, those two do...'

'Dad's gone 'n' all, Mum ... long time ago. They're both dead.'

'Dead! That's a fuckin' wicked thing to say

283

about yer own.' Hilda sent a poisonous look at her son while he continued to regard her with mild interest.

Conor had brought a few milk stouts and a pack of cigarettes in with him. He rose and put a bottle by his mother's chair and a packet of Capstan on her lap, to no response.

'It's too warm in here, Mum; open the door, shall I?' Conor took off his jacket and loosened his tie.

There was a fire burning in the grate and the small room felt stifling and reeked of stale beer and tobacco smoke.

'Leave the door alone. I'm cold ... could do with a bit more coal on that,' Hilda snapped.

Rosie exchanged a glance with Conor, biting her lip to stop a slightly outraged chuckle. The fug was almost unbearable, but she kept her cardigan on although perspiration beaded her top lip.

'Get the girl a cup of tea then.' Hilda smiled at Rosie. 'What's yer name, dear?' She opened a bottle of stout and poured it into the dirty glass wedged by her hip on a cushion.

'Her name's Rosie; she's told you that already.'

Rosie had listened, fascinated, to the exchange between mother and son. She admired Conor for not humouring her, as she obviously wanted him to, but Mrs Flint seemed cantankerous rather than upset, and that made Rosie wonder how much of her confusion was put on for effect.

'Want tea, Rosie?' Conor asked.

''Course she wants a cup of Rosie Lee, don't you, Rosie?' Hilda slapped her thigh and chortled at her little joke.

Conor shook his head in a resigned way. He got up and went through to the kitchen.

As soon as he'd disappeared, the woman shot her frail figure forward on her seat, craning her neck. The rainbow-hued crocheted shawl draping her shoulders dropped onto the chair back. 'Only fair to warn you, love, he's a sod around the women. Worse'n me other two boys put together. Saul's got a wife, and Steven – he's me other lad – he's only ever had one girl at a time.' She jerked her head at the kitchen door. 'Him!' she spat. 'Too randy by 'alf. Come a cropper, he will, and get a dose of the clap.' Hilda sat back in her chair and folded her hands, assessing the effect she'd had.

Rosie was stunned but she was determined not to show it because she knew that's what the woman wanted. In an odd way she was glad to have this glimpse into Conor's upbringing. She didn't like his mum and she guessed the woman didn't like her. More tellingly, Hilda Flint didn't seem to like Conor either, and that saddened Rosie, making her want to champion him. Perhaps he *was* a womaniser but so far he'd been good to her, and that was enough.

'Don't say much, do you?' Hilda sounded irritated as she dragged the shawl back up about her bony shoulders.

'Sorry, had a tiring day at work.'

'Doing what?' Another impolite question.

'I'm an ambulance auxiliary.'

'Are yer now?' Hilda harrumphed. 'Could've done with one of your lot showing up when my Saul got bombed. Bled to death, he did. Now me life's ruined without him. Best son in the world, he was.'

'I'm very sorry about that,' Rosie said, and she was. She knew from distressing experience that casualties who might have survived didn't when crews were unable to get through because of fires and debris blocking the roads.

'Left behind a wife, did my Saul ... she's no good.' Hilda grimaced disgust. 'Weren't never right for him. Angie's *his* cast off.' Again Hilda jerked her head at the kitchen where the kettle had started to sing.

By now Rosie was wishing Conor hadn't left the room. She felt increasingly awkward, and convinced that he was aware of the horrible way his mother was talking about him. Yet he was a loyal son and had not bad-mouthed his mother to Rosie.

'You're pretty but Pat's his girlfriend now, so I've been told, not that he brings her in. Perhaps he'll swap yer if you're better in bed.'

Rosie fidgeted, wondering whether to try to distract the old woman by offering condolences about Saul's death. She decided to avoid mentioning the subject. 'I'm only just getting to know Conor, Mrs Flint–'

Hilda snorted. 'You watch him then 'cos he'll be inside yer knickers 'fore yer know it, then leave yer high 'n' dry with yer belly swole.'

'Want another milk stout, Mum?'

Conor was in the doorway holding two cups of tea. He put them on the table.

'Ain't started on this one yet,' Hilda said, making a show of taking a swig from her glass.

'Talking too much, were you?' Conor said.

He beckoned Rosie and she immediately stood up and went to him.

'Right ... we're off down the road for a drink.'

'Well, put them bottles where I can reach 'em, if yer going already,' Hilda ordered testily. 'Waste of me tea 'n' milk, that was,' she tutted, pointing at the untouched cups on the table. 'If the girl didn't want none, she should've said.'

''Bye, Mrs Flint.' Rosie gave a small wave as Conor took her hand and pulled her out of the door.

''Bye, Pat ... nice to see yer. Pop in again ... I get lonely, y'know...'

'You can see why Steven wants to escape abroad, can't you?'

'I can see why *you'd* want to,' Rosie replied, aware Conor was still holding her hand though they were outside on the pavement.

'I did warn you.'

'Not quite enough, though.' Rosie's amusement held a hint of reprimand. In the car on the way to his mother's he'd said the woman could be difficult. Rosie classed her father as *difficult;* Mrs Flint was something else entirely.

Conor let go of Rosie's hand to shrug into his jacket, then they began strolling along the street towards the Red Lion.

'Why d'you bring me to see her?' Rosie shot him a glance. 'You know what she said about you, don't you?'

'Yep.'

'So why?'

'Has she scared you off?'

'No, but I don't have to live with her.'

'Neither do I.'

Rosie accepted the cigarette he was offering, glancing at him. 'Oh ... where d'you live then?'

'Round the corner. Got my own place. Steven wants to move in with me.'

'But you won't let him,' Rosie guessed, dipping her head to the flame cupped in his palm.

Conor smiled an affirmative. 'Somebody has to keep an eye on her. She'll drop a fag down the side of her chair when she's drunk and set light to herself. Wouldn't be the first time.' He suddenly threw back his head. 'Sorry ... stupid thing to say. Didn't mean to remind you of–'

'You didn't. I never think about him,' Rosie quickly interrupted.

'Who? Tell me who you never think about.'

Rosie avoided his eyes. 'Why? You don't know him.'

'You did.'

'Not from choice,' Rosie blurted. 'Never liked him even when...' She suddenly clammed up. He had a knack of making her say more than she wanted to.

'Even when you were kids?' he guessed.

'That's enough!' Rosie pulled away from him, cigarette clenched between two quivering fingers. She dropped it, ground it out with a toe. 'I'd better go home. Work in the morning...'

'Yeah, work in the morning,' he mimicked, softly sarcastic, but he caught her by the elbows, jerking her forward when she tried to walk off.

Rosie kept her head lowered, knowing he was staring down at her, brooding.

'D'you believe any of what she told you about me?'

'Some of it,' Rosie answered. 'Well, you told me about your sister-in-law and girlfriend so that didn't come as a surprise.'

'She wanted it to.'

'I guessed as much,' Rosie said. 'That's why I kept quiet and didn't encourage her.'

'What about the rest?'

'You've been fair to me up till now,' Rosie said with a shrug.

'In other words, you're not sure about the rest.'

'Does Pat get on with her?'

'Pat hardly knows her. My sister-in-law told Mum I was seeing Pat. I never take girls in there.'

'I'm not surprised,' Rosie said wryly.

'It's not that. I've never bothered before showing anybody what I'm made of.'

Rosie raised her face to meet his eyes. 'And your father?'

'He was worse. A bully and a womaniser. He turned her into what she is.'

'Are you like him?'

'No. I look like him ... so people say. Handsome, he was, obviously.' He smiled as he took her hand, pulling her on. 'That's why Mum's set against me. I remind her of him.'

'Thought she missed him. She spoke as though she did.'

'Just keeping up appearances; every old girl round here has nursed her black eye and pretended her husband's a diamond. Didn't see her shed a tear when he was put in the ground. Since then it's been rose-tinted spectacles all the way.'

He pushed open the door to the pub and with an arm about Rosie's shoulders, ushered her in.

Rosie hadn't expected the whole saloon bar to go quiet while everybody turned and stared at them and then greeted Conor with coarse shouts.

''S'all right,' Conor murmured, gently urging her forward. 'Come on. I want Steven to meet you.'

CHAPTER TWENTY-THREE

'What you drinking then, Rosie?' Steven asked after Conor had introduced them. 'Reckon you're a gin 'n' orange type of gel.'

'Yes, thanks ... that'd be fine,' Rosie said, feeling so overwhelmed by unwanted attention that she'd have agreed to a pint of hemlock.

Angie Flint was perched on a barstool. As soon as she made eye contact with Rosie she hopped down and sauntered over.

'I remember you: Rosie from the ambulance service.' Angie had wedged herself between Conor and Rosie, separating them. She combed her coral-tipped fingers through her hair, and a glimpse of chunky gold pinned to an earlobe flashed through the silver strands. 'Don't know how you can bear to deck yerself out in that horrible dark suit.' Rosie's stylish summer dress and cardigan got a thorough appraisal, but there was no compliment.

'No choice in the matter,' Rosie said. 'Comes

with the job.'

Conor seemed occupied talking to his brother but Angie knew he was keeping tabs on everything they were saying. And she knew why. He'd found a girl he really liked this time.

'Conor might be your dad's pal; but I reckon you're keen to know him better yourself, aren't you?'

'Perhaps I am.' Rosie was determined not to feel intimidated. She sipped her drink and glanced about. A sulky brunette with large red lips straightened in her chair, a challenge in her eyes as they met Rosie's.

'Better warn you about him then, 'cos I reckon you're out of your depth,' Angie purred.

'Don't bother,' Rosie replied. 'His mother's already given me a talking-to.'

'So he's taken you to see the old girl,' Angie snickered in surprise. 'That's a first.'

Rosie gazed at Conor's profile, wondering why he'd abandoned her to his old flame's jealousy. But she wasn't about to seek his protection. She should be able to look after herself and give as good as she got. She'd been a Windmill Girl and back in those days rivalry and catfights had been par for the course.

'Told you about *her*, has he?' Angie jerked her head at the brunette watching them. 'That's Pat Ford and the old dragon with her is her mum, Ethel; he's finished with Pat ... so he says.' Angie clucked her tongue. 'Bloody typical of him to try and rub her nose in it by bringing you in here. He's a bastard like that, playing one of us off against the other.'

'She's got nothing to worry about from me,' Rosie returned, draining her glass. 'And neither have you.' She realised she preferred the company of Conor's obnoxious mother to this crowd of raucous men and gaudy women. Steven Flint seemed nice, but as for the rest of them...

Rosie's gaze flitted over labourers standing cheek by jowl with men in flash suits, pulling luxuries from their pockets and hawking them around. She watched money change hands for a watch and a silver lighter. A group of soldiers was stationed at the far end of the bar, buying cigarettes and vodka from another spiv. And they all knew Conor. He'd received bawled greetings from every corner of the pub.

It was easy to believe there wasn't a war on in this part of town. Mrs Flint squandered fuel on a warm evening when most people struggled to keep their bunkers stocked in wintertime. Rosie knew she wouldn't bother asking him why he indulged his mother, buying her black-market coal to keep her house ridiculously hot. He'd put a ten-shilling note in Peg Price's collecting bowl, exactly the sum she couldn't afford to pay for a week's rent on a small furnished room for her and Hope. At the time she'd thought him acting flash. Now she realised he'd done it because he could ... in the same way he could afford to sound mildly put out at being owed five hundred pounds.

The Flints and people like them were different from the working-class East Enders she'd been bred amongst. In this pub the atmosphere was seedy yet sweetly perfumed by women in heavy jewellery, and bank notes littered the slop-covered bar. Her father used to count out coins to take when he treated himself to a trip to the local. And John Gardiner had always had the decency to be ashamed rather than brash about his criminal activities.

Rosie guessed that for Conor ducking and diving wasn't a necessary evil but a way of having everything he wanted.

And he'd told her he wanted her.

'Ladies' convenience in here somewhere?' Rosie asked, sliding her empty glass onto the bar.

'Show you if yer like,' Angie said, nodding to a corner.

'I'll find it, thanks.' Rosie didn't want Angie Flint dripping any more poison in her ear. Besides, she didn't need the ladies' room.

'That door leads to the street ... just in case you want to use that as well,' Angie informed her mockingly. 'Don't fit in round here, do you, Ambulance Rosie?'

'But you do,' Rosie returned before slipping into the crowd. She was annoyed that Angie had guessed she'd no intention of powdering her nose. Neither did she want Conor's sister-in-law thinking she'd gained a victory in sending her packing. But primitive intuition was telling Rosie to leave, and gratefully she let the pub door swing shut behind her.

She knew he'd come after her as soon as he realised she'd fled. And she wanted to be somewhere out of sight when he did.

An alleyway or a tube station she could dash into would serve as shelter and as she hurried along, peering over a shoulder, it seemed as though she'd been sucked into a dark sinister place and she was trying to outrun Lenny through Soho. She'd bumped into him outside a nightclub and been unable to make him take no for an answer. Then a pal of his had side-tracked him, allowing her some precious minutes to make her escape. But he'd caught up with her, grabbed her by the throat and forced her to the ground with him...

'Whoa ... where you off to?'

Rosie lashed out blindly, till Conor let her go and backed off, hands slightly elevated in surrender. She stumbled back against the wall, her chest heaving with gasped inhalations.

'Sorry ... didn't know it was you.' She could see she'd scratched his cheek.

'Who d'you think it was?'

'You don't have to see me home.' Rosie composed herself and thrust her shaking hands into her pockets. 'You can stay and have a drink with your friends.'

'I thought *we* were friends.'

'I don't like them.'

'D'you like me?'

Rosie glanced at him, standing in front of her, blocking her in.

'Do you like me, Rosie?'

'I ... I don't know,' she said. 'Will you move so I can get past?'

'I'll take you home.'

'No...' She pulled a hand from a pocket to gesture. 'You don't have to babysit me. I can find my own way home.'

'Yeah, but you don't have to 'cos I'll take you.'

'I don't want you to!' Rosie cried. 'Just go away.

I can find my own way home.' Still he didn't move and Rosie lacked the courage to shove him aside.

'I know you can; you found your way underground through a bombed-out building so getting to Shoreditch should be a piece of cake.' He came closer, hands moving to hold her, but they dropped back and he rested against the wall by her side. 'Have a cigarette. Take one!' he insisted, pulling a cigarette out of the pack for her, and lighting it before turning it and placing it between her lips.

Rosie dragged on it deeply. 'Sorry I scratched you. You startled me, that's all.'

'Don't be frightened of me, Rosie.'

'I'm not.'

He smiled sideways at her, cigarette drooping in his lips. 'Perhaps you should be. Scare myself sometimes, stupid way I act.'

'Why did you take me in there, with those people?'

'Because I'm an idiot.' He took her hand and eased her away from the wall.

'Take you home.'

'No ... it's all right...'

'Don't say it's all right, Rosie, 'cos it fucking ain't.' The words emerged in slow staccato bursts.

Rosie knew then his mild manner was a sham but she let him lead her back to his car, parked outside his mother's house, rather than carry on resisting.

'Did you visit that lad in hospital?' Conor asked as he pulled away from the kerb.

A look of intense sadness had flitted over

Rosie's features at that reminder. She hadn't told him about little Herbie's death.

'No ... no, I didn't.' Rosie clammed up, knowing if she started to explain she'd end up crying, she felt so jittery. She could already sense her nose stinging and sniffed.

Rosie kept her eyes on the skies as they sped through London. The streets seemed unusually quiet, as though others knew what they did not and an attack was imminent. But no siren sounded and they pulled up outside her house in what seemed like just a few minutes.

'I want you to know who I am, that's why I took you there,' Conor said. 'Those are the people I grew up with, work down the docks with, sleep with.'

Rosie moistened her lips. 'I didn't know you were a docker.'

'That's why I took you there. I want you to know. That's who I am. Nothing to hide.' He turned fierce eyes on her. 'Thing is, Rosie, I'm still not sure who you are 'cos you're still hiding ... and that's the way you want it to stay, isn't it?'

Rosie nodded, looking quickly away.

He stretched out a hand to turn her face back to his but instinctively Rosie shrank from his strong masculine fingers.

He grunted a hoarse, fatalistic laugh. 'Yeah ... and then there's that.' He punched his fist against the steering wheel, then immediately got out of the car and came round to open her door.

'I'm sorry about the kid dying. I know it must be a choker after what you went through to save him.'

'How did you know?' Rosie gasped.

'I can work most things out for myself. But I shouldn't have to, and there's a lot you should just tell me.'

Rosie knew he'd left his car door open because he was going to drive off straight away. And, oddly, she didn't want him to. Now she'd calmed down she wanted them to finish the evening on good terms.

'Go in, it's late. Take care of yourself.'

She suddenly realised he was saying goodbye, not good night, and her stomach lurched. She wanted to know for sure so blurted out, 'Are we going out again?'

'Have you decided if you like me?' His gaze was boring into her profile.

Rosie nodded.

'You like me?'

She nodded.

'And trust me?'

Rosie moistened her lips, then nodded.

'Enough to let me touch you?'

'I don't know...' she murmured.

'Well, when you do, come and find me. I've showed you where.'

Rosie watched the car's dim rear lights till they were just faint needle pricks before she went inside.

She went to the sideboard and poured herself a large glass of moonshine. She sat in bed smoking and drinking and staring out into the darkness. A vivid trail of fire was arcing the heavens, and she sat and watched it. The siren sounded late yet still she stayed where she was, wondering if he'd gone back to the pub to find brassy Angie or sullen Pat, and sleep with them. If what his mother said about him was true, perhaps he'd bedded them both ... at the same time...

Rosie drew shakily on the cigarette and thumbed tears off her lashes. She might think herself a cut above those women but at least they were women, not empty shells. The ground shook, jolting her out of her stupor and into thoughts of her daughter. Jumping out of bed she raced down two sets of stairs into the relative safety of the cellar.

'You've seemed a bit browned off lately, gel.' Popeye glanced at Trudy as they strolled along the path in the park. 'Fancy a trip down Kent way to buck you up? I'll show you where me and Lenny used to go hopping, if yer like. Yalding, it was. Nice place. Took him fer a week in August most years when he was at school. Us grown-ups had some larks after dark when the work was done and kids were akip.' In fact, Popeye's intention in heading in that direction was to find John Gardiner rather than have a holiday. Frank wanted his fifty pounds back off the man, with interest, or John would get the treatment.

Popeye was confident that Midge and Rufus, between them, should manage to swing a bit of lead pipe at a man to teach him a lesson. In their heydays, both his henchmen had been a force to be reckoned with. Rufus had had the brawn and Midge the sly speed to make an impact.

'What I'd like's a trip down Memory Lane, and take a different turning this time,' Trudy sighed. 'Been looking back on my life just lately and wishing...'

'You wish you'd got married, you mean?' Frank had guessed before from things his girlfriend had said that she regretted devoting her youth to other people's children rather than her own.

'I do,' Trudy owned up. 'I might not have loved any man the way I loved my childhood sweetheart, but I might have rubbed along all right with somebody else. A family's what I miss. Would've liked kids ... nearly had one a few years back.'

Frank cast a startled eye on his girlfriend. She looked a bit too long in the tooth to be producing sprogs. 'What, you had a miscarriage you mean?' he asked carefully.

Trudy burst out laughing. Pulling Frank by the hand she led him to a bench so they could sit and talk. 'No, I did not have a miscarriage. I've never even got engaged. What d'you take me for?' But she sounded amused rather than angry as she watched a trio of boys playing cricket. 'I had a chance to adopt an unmarried mother's child but then the girl went and changed her mind on me.'

Frank tutted. 'Weren't bloody fair after you'd set your heart on it. I suppose she was a bit of a good-time gel, was she?'

'She was a showgirl in the West End but she seemed nice enough. Never found out who the father was but got the impression he was a wrong 'un and she didn't want reminders of him. Then she went back on her word and kept the baby.'

Trudy wondered if she'd disclosed too much and he might guess who it was she'd been talking about. Frank knew the Gardiners and she didn't want to cause the family any trouble. But since they'd bumped into Rosie out walking with her boyfriend, Trudy couldn't put little Hope Gardiner from her mind. She wanted to unburden herself and then, with Frank's blunt perspective on things, banish the longing for a family from her head because at forty-nine it was too late to get pregnant but not too late to rear children.

Frank had an agile mind and almost immediately he'd pounced on the probable identity of the unmarried mother. Ever since the day they'd bumped into Conor Flint and Rosie, Trudy had been a bit melancholy. But Frank remained sitting, arms crossed over his chest and face screwed up thoughtfully as though chewing things over.

'Reckon I've hit on who you mean, Trudy. Only know one showgirl round these parts and I've always had me doubts about her kid's father copping it before anybody had met him.'

'I was just telling you something in confidence; it wasn't a problem to solve, Frank,' Trudy said quickly.

'You were going to adopt Rosie Gardiner's baby, were you?' Frank patted at Trudy's hand in comfort.

'I never said that, Frank! Don't you go saying I did.' Trudy jumped to her feet. Something in his expression made her wish she'd not confided in him.

'Don't fret, love; soul of discretion, me,' Frank soothed. He gave a sprightly little leap to his feet and, pulling Trudy's arm through his, he led her back towards the path.

The smile on Popeye's face stretched from ear to ear as they strolled. So, now he'd no need to get rough with John Gardiner to get even. He had a much better way of persuading the man to see sense, hand over his fifty quid and set up his still.

The apple of John's eye was a bastard and the man wouldn't want that bandied about. And not only that, his daughter was likely to get knocked up again if she carried on seeing Conor Flint.

'Stop off for a few bevies on the way back, shall we, Trudy?' Popeye suggested jovially. He felt he had something to celebrate.

CHAPTER TWENTY-FOUR

'I feel rough ... think I'm going to throw up again.' Hazel clapped a hand to her ballooning mouth.

'I ordered you home, Scott.' Stella Phipps had emerged from her office in time to see Hazel making a dash for the ladies' convenience. 'How are you Gardiner? Any symptoms to worry about?'

'Not so far, Ma'am,' Rosie replied with a sigh of grim relief.

A bout of food poisoning had spread like wild-fire through Station 97, depleting numbers. Blue-bottles were thought to have spread the infection from the pigswill out in the yard to the canteen and both shift leaders had blamed each other for failing to impose rigorous cleaning regimes.

The senior staff members that hadn't been affected were now out on active duty with the rank and file volunteers. Janet Lawson, Rosie's shift leader, had got such a bad dose of sickness and diarrhoea that she'd ended up in hospital for a few days and hadn't yet returned to work.

Those who had escaped the infection were doing double hours and sleeping on mattresses on the floor to keep the station open for business.

Hazel reappeared, groaning and clutching her tender belly.

'Home! Now!' Stella pointed at the exit.

'But the all clear's not sounded yet. We might get a call out,' Hazel protested. 'We're already short staffed.'

'You ought to go and get some rest, Hazel,' Rosie said kindly. Her friend's complexion was ashen and although Rosie admired Hazel's conscientiousness she anticipated the young woman being more of a hindrance than a help if they were sent out on an emergency.

'God, you look terrible,' Tom announced bluntly as he came up beside the trio of women in the corridor.

'Thanks,' Hazel said, suppressing a burp.

'Where's Warwick? Has he clocked in yet?'

'He's just 'phoned in to say he's got the runs.' Tom pulled a face.

'There's enough of us here to make up a couple of crews. That'll have to do,' Stella said. 'I can drive, Norris can be my assistant, and Gardiner can pair up with you,' she told Tom.

'I'll man the 'phones then if we get a call out,' Hazel insisted. 'I can nip to the toilet when I need to. Clarice can't do all the dockets and 'phones by herself.'

Stella jerked a nod of acceptance.

'I'll see you in my office, Gardiner.' Stella turned away and opened the door just behind her.

Rosie's heart increased tempo. She'd not forgotten the talk she'd had with Stella at the dance and wondered if the woman had something more specific to say this time rather than dropping hints about secrets. Rosie's apprehension increased when Hazel gave her a mystified look before walking off along the corridor with Tom.

When Rosie entered Stella's office the older woman was rummaging in a cupboard where stationery was kept. Stella produced her raffle prize of a tin of peaches and held it out.

'I wanted to give you this in private. Not enough for us all to have a taste so I thought you might like to take it home.'

Rosie blinked in surprise but didn't immediately take the gift. 'Well... It's awfully kind of you... Are you sure you'd rather not save it for Christmas?'

'Christmas is a long way off. Anyway, I expect I'll be on my own. Shame not to share it with someone.'

Rosie could think of nothing to say other than, 'Oh ... sorry to hear that...'

'Norris's husband will be back home, she expects. He's top brass in the army.' Stella cleared her throat then thrust the peaches at Rosie. 'Do take it; children love fruit... My nephews do anyway... Nice treat...' She put the tin on the edge of the desk. 'Now, off you go, I've got to get these timetables sorted out; never know if that damned telephone might ring and scramble us any second.'

'Thank you.' Rosie picked up the peaches and turned for the door, feeling in a daze. She'd no idea that Thora Norris was married, or that Stella Phipps had nephews. But she no longer wondered if Stella knew her secret; it seemed she did, and the gift for Hope was Stella's way of saying it made no difference to her that her newest recruit was an unmarried mother.

Tom took far greater risks driving in the black-out than Jim did, Rosie thought while hanging onto the door handle for support as they swerved around a corner in the Studebaker. By the time they reached the address of the incident in Stepney Rosie's heart was in her mouth. Twice they'd almost collided with other vehicles as Tom raced through the dark streets with just infernos lighting the way as he careered around obstructions.

She breathed a sigh of relief as the vehicle braked sharply some distance from a burning building. She jumped from the ambulance carrying her gas mask and her medical bag then hared, stumbling, over bomb wreckage towards what looked to have been a church hall about a hundred yards away.

'Harvest Festival was taking place in there. Quite a few kids and their parents trapped inside,' Stella shouted.

Stella and Thora had set off first when the call came through and had arrived a few minutes before Rosie and Tom turned up. Tom sprinted up with an armful of blankets ready to be used to wrap the casualties.

The roar of the fire was drowned out by the chug of another rocket overhead. But they knew they were safe from that one, even if some other poor souls were not; the murderous weapon would glide on for a distance once the engine cut out before diving on a target.

'There's kids down here, you fucking bastards,' a fireman shouted, tears dripping from his sooty eyes, as the screaming in the church hall reached a crescendo. He shook a furious fist at the sky while the other held the hose steady on the burning building.

'It's the ones you can't bloody hear that's the problem,' Tom said, giving the fellow a sympathetic pat on the back.

Rosie bit her trembling lip against the howl of anguish pulsing in her throat. The feeling of uselessness was hard to endure. But until the fire was contained there was nothing much they could do.

'Let's get the stretchers ready,' Tom bawled at Rosie, grabbing her elbow and shaking her.

Like an automaton Rosie darted after him, blocking the horrible mental images that were torturing her mind. She knew the sight of burned and broken bodies would soon be a filthy reality ... but not yet. She widened her eyes on the debris-strewn ground she was covering, scouring it for anything likely to trip her up as she bounded towards the ambulance. Once there, they worked together with ferocious efficiency, wordlessly yanking the stretchers from their runners and stacking them ready to be carried back.

And then the darkness exploded in white light. Rosie was lifted off her feet and against the open door of the ambulance, banging her back and scalp with some force. Instinctively she twisted sideways, gripping an edge of metal as a blast of violently hot air hit her, threatening to suck her from her life support and carry her away. She screwed up her face, trying to fight against the pain in her ears and the incandescence in her skull. As the vortex of blast pressure decreased, Rosie let go of the door and fell to her knees on the ground, her arms cradling her head.

She panted, fighting to keep the blackness at bay. She wanted to yell out to Tom but though her mouth opened and closed no sound could be forced from her throat. Finally she struggled to her feet, swaying against the ambulance door that had saved her, as Tom lifted himself upright beside her, batting at his ears.

'Are you all right?' Rosie gasped out, staring at Tom's dirt-streaked features. He was grimacing at her and she realised he'd not heard what she'd said. She shouted her question again, shaking his arm.

He nodded. 'Gone deaf,' he mouthed, poking at his ears again.

Rosie gasped in a breath, then another, her body heaving with the effort. She turned to gaze back to the spot where minutes ago she and Tom had been waiting with Thora and Stella for an opportunity to tend to the blaze victims.

An inferno now marked where their colleagues and the church hall had once stood. In shock she stared for almost a minute then looked at Tom to see he was crying, his shoulders quaking; nothing could have survived that.

'Ready to go?' Rosie croaked out after a couple of false starts, her face running with a mixture of brine and blood from the cut on her scalp.

Tom nodded. In unison they stooped to pick up the stretchers and set off back the way they'd come.

CHAPTER TWENTY-FIVE

'Dad! What are you doing here?'

Rosie had been pegging out washing in the back garden when she'd thought she'd heard a noise in the house. She'd hurtled inside, scared somebody had broken in, and got the best surprise of her life.

'Oh, my darling!' Rosie swooped on her daughter, cuddling her in her arms so tightly that Hope squealed. But the feel of her little girl's arms about her neck was heavenly. Rosie kissed a hot pink cheek. 'Miss your mummy, did you?'

Hope nodded solemnly, tightening her grip on Rosie's neck.

'Why've you come home, Dad? Why didn't you write and warn me? Where's Doris?' Having rattled off her breathless questions Rosie spun round with her daughter. 'Oh, I'm so pleased to see you,' she murmured into Hope's silky fair hair.

'Get that kettle on, Rosie. I'm parched.' John sounded weary, in body and in mind.

Rosie put her daughter on her feet and gave him a searching look. Already her euphoria was fading; her father had yet to explain his sudden return and she sensed it wasn't going to be good news. But she'd draw her happiness out for a while and delve deeper after the new arrivals had had something to eat and drink.

'She's fasto ... the journey must have exhausted the poor love,' Rosie said as she came back into the parlour. She'd tucked Hope up in bed as soon as the child had finished her milky tea and jam sandwich. Halfway through 'Baa Baa Black Sheep', Hope had curled on her side, thumb in mouth, and fallen deeply asleep.

'Put the kettle on again, Rosie. I'll have another brew before unpacking. I left the case in the hallway.'

'Why d'you come back, Dad?' Rosie sat opposite John at the table once the kettle was filled and on the gas stove. She took his hands in hers. 'Have you and Doris had a bust-up?'

'Sort of,' he said, withdrawing his bent leathery fingers from his daughter's smooth palms. 'Weren't really her fault; it's that bloody son of hers. Charlie's back home on convalescence.' John grimaced disgust. 'Not much wrong with him, if you ask me. Just scratches on his legs from shrapnel, but he's managed to swing it. Anyhow, he made it clear we'd outstayed our welcome. I ain't stopping where I'm not wanted, and I told 'em so.' John's lips tightened. 'Doris tried to make light of it you know ... saying her boy was just having a snap 'n' snarl 'cos he's in pain.' John shook his head. 'Didn't fall fer that 'cos it ain't the first time Charlie's come out with snide remarks about us being in the way. So I got our stuff together. Doris said she was staying and weren't ever coming back here to get blown up. So I told her, do what you like.' John clasped his hands together on the table. 'She said Hope could stay. But I weren't leaving my princess there with them. Doris don't love her like we do, and she makes no bones about showing it. So here we are, back home again.'

'I wouldn't have wanted you to leave her, Dad. But it's wonderful to have you home. I've been lonely here on my own.'

John gave his daughter a penetrating stare. 'That's another reason I had to come back. In the middle of our barney Charlie come out with something else made me want to knock his teeth down his throat. He said you was entertaining Conor Flint in my house. True is it?' John's lower lip started to tremble as he read his daughter's embarrassed reaction. 'Have you ... has he made you do things, Rosie, 'cos he says I owe him money and you've been trying to protect me from him?'

Rosie jumped to her feet. 'No! He's not like that. He's nice.'

'*Nice!*' John was also on his feet. 'He ain't *nice*, and if you think he is it's 'cos he's better at handling women than Lenny was! Have you been to bed with him, Rosie? Tell me! He's after his fifty quid's worth off you, 'cos I got away with it. I'll kill him, I will!'

'Hush...' Rosie had turned white with strain, but she embraced her distressed father. 'Nothing like that's gone on, Dad, honestly.' She hadn't seen Conor for some weeks and the more time went on the more she wanted to. She'd not contacted him because they both knew what that would signal. She wasn't ready for intimacy; she didn't know if she ever would be. So her father had nothing to fear.

John pulled himself from his daughter's arms and flopped down in the chair. 'I did have some of Flint's money, Rosie: fifty pounds I took off Popeye and didn't give it back when I should've.' He blew his nose. 'Charlie said that you called Flint your boyfriend.' John shook his head. 'He ain't your boyfriend, love, whatever sweet talk he comes out with. Him and his brothers are all spivs 'n' pimps, Pop told me that. Reckon it's one of the few truths to come out of that bastard's mouth.'

Rosie swallowed a painful lump in her throat. 'Perhaps he is those things, but he's treated me well. Anyway, he won't be back now so no need to worry. And I only told Charlie that Conor was my boyfriend to get rid of him.'

John was up on his feet again. 'Charlie done something, has he?'

'No!' Rosie could tell her father's guilt was making him panicky. 'He called to say hello and asked if he could stop here instead of travelling to Gravesend. I said my boyfriend wouldn't like it, but really I was worried Mrs Price would spot him coming out of the house in the morning. Luckily, Conor turned up and Charlie put two and two together and I just went along with it to hurry him on his way.'

'You think it was lucky Flint turned up here?' John gave a sorrowful sigh. 'You do like him, don't you? Oh, Rosie ... I wish I'd never gone to Gravesend. You've not fallen for him, dear, have you?'

''Course not!' Rosie blurted but her heart had leaped to her throat in the way it always did when she lied to her father. 'I can understand why you wanted to avoid Charlie. I don't like him either.'

She decided to keep quiet about Charlie being an adulterous rat. Heaven only knew how Doris would react if she discovered that her son had been romancing an ambulance auxiliary as though he were a carefree bachelor.

'Have you still got that fifty pounds, Dad?' she asked, inwardly praying her father hadn't spent it and was intending to return it.

John nodded. 'Don't worry, love, it's going straight back to Popeye tomorrow, then my hands are clean.' He sat down again with a faint smile. 'Another cup of tea'd be nice.'

Rosie filled the kettle and lit the gas stove, glad her father seemed to have calmed down and that he had promised to return the money to Popeye. She trusted he would.

'So ... how's it all been going at work?' John called out.

Rosie set the cups and sniffed back spontaneous tears at the memory of the colleagues who'd been blown to smithereens in Stepney. So had the fireman, and the people trapped inside the building. But Rosie couldn't tell her dad about any of it; he would again be on his feet, frantic with worry that she might be next to cop it. And terrified as Rosie was, as her remaining colleagues were, about the risks they were running, they were all determined to carry on.

'I'm being kept busy, as you can imagine,' Rosie said, sounding quite jolly. 'I've made some friends and been out dancing with them.'

John came up behind his daughter and laid a hand on her shoulder. 'I'm proud of you, y'know; should have told you that sooner.'

Rosie turned about and gave him a watery smile. 'I know you are,' she croaked.

'What is it, love?' John crooned, taking his daughter in his arms and stroking her soft silver hair.

'So pleased to see you and Hope... Such a lovely surprise,' Rosie mumbled, the words muffled by his shoulder as the tears flowed.

'Come on, buck up,' John said gently. 'We're back for good.' He gave Rosie's back a rub. 'What's this?' John had turned his attention on the tin of peaches in the cupboard and picked it up.

'A friend gave it to me.' Rosie wiped her eyes with her hanky. 'She won it in a raffle but gave it to me. She said children love fruit.'

'You told somebody about Hope then?'

'She guessed,' Rosie said. 'But she'll keep it to herself and... She's gone away now anyhow.'

'Well, that's mighty nice of her.' John turned the peaches in his hand. 'Good sort was she? You'll miss her, I'll bet.'

'One of the best, she was,' Rosie said, handing her dad his cup of tea. 'And yes, I'll miss her dreadfully.'

'Fancy going greyhound racing on Saturday?' Patricia was sitting on the edge of Conor's bed in her petticoat, reapplying her smeared lipstick. 'Mickey's going with some pals; we could get a big party of us up.'

'You go. I'll be busy this weekend.'

Pat put down the hand mirror she'd been using and pouted, watching him shrug into his shirt. She'd been dressed already this morning then she'd teased Conor into taking her back to bed for a quick romp.

'Go for a drive today, shall we? How about Southend? I'm bored.'

'Get a job then.'

'What ... ambulance auxiliary?' Pat taunted, and got a hard glance before Conor quit the bedroom, buttoning up his cuffs. She flung herself back on the mattress. He might have responded to her seduction and started sleeping with her again, but she knew his heart wasn't in it, and never would be. When they'd first got together, months ago, she'd made the running and eventually caught him. She'd been optimistic that she could make Conor buy her an engagement ring, despite Angie hanging around like a bad smell. Now Pat knew she was just being used, and, if she told him she wasn't having it and he could show her some respect and affection, he'd shrug and show her the door.

And it was all the fault of that prissy bitch he'd brought to the pub. Angie had told her the girl's name was Rosie and she worked for the LAAS. And it seemed she'd given Conor the elbow. Pat knew that must have surprised him when he was so popular with women. She was hoping it was his pride that was hurting but something told her it wasn't. He seemed different ... frustrated ... even when he was on top of her.

Conor found a pint of milk in the kitchen and took a swig from the bottle. He sat down at the table and started to read the paper, then folded it with a curse when he spotted a report of an ambulance bursting into flames in Hammersmith.

The phone started to ring and he answered it to hear his mother's screeching voice on the other end of the line.

'The little bleeder's gawn down the recruiting office, I know he has,' Hilda whined. 'I'm gonna lose another one of me sons, and if I do I'll blame you.'

'He's down at the docks, Mum.' Conor looked at the clock on the wall and knew if his brother had been on late shift he would have been home by now.

'No, he ain't; he didn't come home last night. Ain't seen him in nearly two days.'

'I'll come round in a bit.' Conor put the receiver down.

'Who's that?' Patricia had got dressed and entered the kitchen. 'Angie, is it, checking up on you?'

'Seen anything of Steven lately?' Conor asked.

Pat shook her head, but she avoided his eye. She knew Steven had enlisted because Mickey Rook had told her. Her and Mickey went way back. They'd been sweethearts at school, then Pat had outgrown him and found herself more sophisticated lovers. But she'd had a fling with Mickey recently while Conor had remained unresponsive to her.

'Mickey know where Steve is?' Conor asked sardonically.

Pat flushed, knowing he was on to her, on both counts. 'Can't be a surprise to you to find out your brother's gone and joined up; he's been saying he would fer months. And I'm glad.' She coiled her arms about Conor's neck, rubbing

314

together their groins. 'If you stop around here a while longer ... I'll make sure and thank you,' she purred.

Taking Pat by the elbow, Conor led her to the door.

''Ere, what you doing?' she said indignantly. 'Ain't even had a cup of tea for me breakfast yet 'cos you took me back to bed. You can't just throw me out when you've had what you wanted, you know.'

'It was what you wanted. If you don't like it, don't turn up on me doorstep every fucking evening.'

'You're a right bastard, aren't you!' Pat stormed.

'Yeah ... I am.' Conor closed the door behind her, then went back to pick up the receiver that had been ringing ever since he'd put it down.

'Ain't stopping; just come to give you this.' John thrust an envelope at Popeye; the man was looking at him as though he'd seen a ghost.

'Well, this is a bleedin' surprise, I must say!' Popeye recovered quickly. 'Thought you was miles away in Kent, mate, and I was gonna fetch up down there and say hello. Looks like you've saved me the trip.'

'Make sure that gets back to Flint. I'll find out if it don't.' John jerked the envelope containing fifty pounds, wanting Popeye to take it off him.

'Come in ... let's have a chat and a cuppa. Tell you what, I'll find us summat a bit stronger.'

Popeye flung the door wide and after a moment's hesitation John stepped over the threshold. He didn't want anything more to do with Popeye but he did want to find out what had gone on in his absence.

His daughter might think the docker was all right but John knew differently. Conor Flint was a businessman with a reputation to preserve and he wouldn't have walked away from a sour deal smiling. There would've been a price to pay ... there always was.

Popeye poured two whiskies and then opened the envelope, taking a cursory peer inside. He lobbed it on the table and took a sip of his drink. The last thing he wanted off John Gardiner now was five tenners and a handshake. He wanted John to resurrect his still and make them all some *real* money. He'd suffered because of the man, and he was after compensation.

'Sorry about going off with that; needed it to settle us in Kent,' John explained gruffly. 'But sorted things out now.'

'Back home then, are yer?'

'I am. Doris ain't.'

'How about the nipper?'

'She's back with her mum, where she should be,' John snapped at the impertinence.

'Yeah ... need their mums, don't they?'

John thought Popeye sounded sarcastic but he let it ride. He wanted to ask his question and get going. 'Flint's off your back then, is he?'

'Oh, yeah; I got him off me back ... at a cost.'

John licked his lips, knowing he was about to hear something bad.

'Took all me stock of petrol coupons, didn't he? Worth thousands, they were. Left me and Midge 'n' Rufus high 'n' dry. Been scratching around fer cash, and me with a lovely new girlfriend to impress. How does that look?' Popeye narrowed his good eye on John. 'You ain't been popular, pal, causing all that trouble when all you had to do was set up yer still and give the man what he wanted.' Popeye laid a heavy hand on John's shoulder. ''Course, now Doris ain't about you'll be able to get to work again, won't yer?'

John shrugged him off. 'Already told you I ain't ever getting back into that.'

'Reckon you are, mate, 'cos if you don't you'll cause yourself and your lovely little family a mighty lot of trouble.'

'I ain't frightened of you and yer threats. As fer Flint, him and Rosie are on good terms.'

'Yeah ... saw that, John, with me own eyes.' Popeye leered. 'That girl of your'n knows how to put it about, don't she?'

'What did you say?' John snarled, fists tightening at his sides. 'You insulting my daughter?'

'I wouldn't do that, John. But other people would when they find out that kid of hers is a bastard and she's lying about having been married.'

John turned the colour of parchment and his mouth worked like a beached fish.

'I know what it is to have bad blood in the family, mate,' Popeye crooned, all sympathy. 'Be the first to admit my Lenny was no good, so I ain't calling your gel a slag 'cos she got herself in trouble...'

John lunged at him, pummelling at Popeye's face and body with his fists. 'She didn't get herself in trouble!' He roared through foam-flecked lips. 'Your fucking Lenny did! He was a monster and if the bastard was still here I'd kill him all over again. He raped my daughter ... he *raped* her, left her covered in blood 'n' bruises in some stinking alley...'

The red mist in John's eyes faded and he suddenly realised what he'd done. He tottered back from Popeye as though he'd accidentally touched something venomous. But the horror shaping his features wasn't the result of recalling his daughter's dreadful ordeal; fear for the future was churning his guts now the terrible secret was out.

Popeye had been about to swing a right hook at his assailant's head when snippets of John's ranting had started penetrating his brain and he'd been stunned into paralysis.

Now he stood massaging his battered chin, blinking at John. His hand became still as he finished slotting the pieces of puzzle in place.

'You stay away from me and mine,' John spat, darting for the door.

Popeye leaped into action, dragging John back by the collar. 'Sounds to me like you've a bit more explaining to do 'fore you get off.' Popeye's lips flattened on his stumpy brown teeth. 'You telling me we share an interest in that little kid?'

With a sob of anguish John tried to nut him and break free but Popeye was ready for him. Neither man was fit but Frank was heftier and he knocked John to his knees with a crafty blow to his windpipe.

Popeye crouched down so his face was level with John's purple complexion. 'My Lenny was poisoned to death with a bottle of bad rotgut. Know anything about it, do you?'

'Fuck off,' John croaked. 'He set fire to his-self…'

'Yeah … 'cos he dropped his fag after he passed out drinking rotgut. Yours, weren't it? You fuckin' murdered my son!'

'You can't prove a thing,' John wheezed through his damaged throat.

Popeye stood up, gazing at the wall with his jaw dropped open. Then he looked down at the man gasping for air and he gave him a savage kick in the head. He bent down again. 'That kid's Lenny's, ain't it?'

John tried to anchor himself on Popeye's shoulder to drag himself to his feet. His only focus now was to get out of the house before Popeye beat all the truth out of him, or killed him trying.

Popeye shoved John off so he sprawled on the floor again. He started to pace to and fro, gurning in disbelief at the mad thoughts circulating in his brain.

With a monumental effort John forced himself to get up, swaying unsteadily, and stumbling to-wards the door. His vision was blurred with the blood trickling from the wound on his scalp. Even so, he could see enough of Popeye's expres-sion to know the man wasn't finished with him yet. John changed direction, stumbling to the table as though for support, but he grabbed the whisky bottle, smashing it against the wooden edge then lunging towards Popeye's face with the jagged glass.

John staggered to the front gate, whimpering with the excruciating pain in his skull. He'd managed to take his enemy by surprise, slashing at him then kicking him in the balls. The tactic had given him just enough time to haul himself out of the house. But, looking back, he could see Popeye moving behind the door, his hand cupped over his gaping cheek.

'You're done for now, mate!' Popeye bellowed as John limped away into the dusk.

'It's nothing ... don't fuss, Rosie.'

John had collapsed in the hall. He'd dragged himself home, swaying like a drunk, glad of the darkness and of the air-raid siren that had sent people scuttling for shelter, allowing him to pad through the empty streets unobserved.

Rosie fell to her knees by her father. 'What on earth ... oh, Dad!' She dapped a hand to her mouth, her eyes filling with tears. 'Where have you been? Who did this to you?' She sank back, recalling what her father had said about Conor being owed fifty pounds and that he'd take his money's worth out of her. He hadn't got any more out of her than holding hands and a peck on the cheek.

'Did Conor do this to you?' Rosie whispered, dreading hearing the answer.

John carefully shook his aching head. 'Popeye. The bastard still wants me to make moonshine. Told him no, and he didn't like it.' John couldn't bring himself to tell his daughter the whole truth. Not yet. His eyes smarted with tears of guilt and remorse as he realised the extent of what he'd done. He'd gone to see his old associate with the best of intentions and had been hijacked by his own stupidity. On the interminable trek home he'd tried to work out how Popeye had found out about Rosie's secret; the man hadn't been pissing in the wind. Popeye had known Hope was illegitimate.

With Rosie's help John managed to get into the back parlour. As soon as she'd got him lolling in an armchair she scooted to get him a glass of water.

'Get us a Beecham's Powder, love. Me head's thumping fit to burst,' John panted.

Again Rosie disappeared into the kitchen and came back with the medicine, stirring the milky water briskly with a spoon. She handed it over and John threw it back as though it were Scotch.

Rosie thrust her fingers into her hair. 'Will he leave us alone now you've had a fight over it?' Her little daughter was asleep downstairs in the cellar, and she thanked God that Hope hadn't been up and about to see her granddad in such an awful state.

John nodded, keeping his face low so his daughter wouldn't see the despair in his face. He knew it wasn't over with Popeye; it was just beginning. 'Soon as I'm well enough we'll take Hope away again. We'll get out of London, and you'll come too this time.'

'But my job—'

'Never mind your fucking job!' John's fingers, supporting his bowed head, crabbed into talons. 'We go away ... fresh start for all of us. Please, Rosie, do as I say.' He began to weep softly into his palms.

'It's all right, Dad ... hush...' Rosie soothed him by stroking his hand, her fingers staining with his blood. 'I'll get hot water and a flannel and clean you up...' They both instinctively ducked as a loud explosion sounded close by, rattling every door and window in the house.

Rosie had been fretting down in the cellar about her father still being out during an air raid. She'd loitered at the top of the stairs with the cellar door ajar, straining to hear his key striking the lock. The moment it had she'd burst out to help him down the stairs. The sight that had met her eyes had winded her like a punch in the guts, making her nauseated.

'You'll have to try and get into the cellar, Dad. Quickly! They're dropping very close.'

The slow descent to their musky shelter was marked by John's gasps of agony. Rosie tried to soothe him with murmured encouragement but by then she was crying too as his blood dripped down over her arms and clothes onto the cellar steps. She was finding it hard to block out the memories of that other time when her father had been dreadfully injured during a raid. But no Luftwaffe bomb had inflicted his wounds this time. Rosie knew she now feared the enemy close to home far more than she did the Germans.

She listened to her father's laboured breathing. He lay on the mattress, eyes closed, twitching in pain, and Rosie prayed that he wasn't concussed because he might lose consciousness. She'd cleaned him up as best she could with a towel found on the mattress and had been relieved to find that the wound on his scalp had started to form a sticky crust beneath matted hair. Rosie wiped her hands on a less sodden edge of linen, then threw the stained cloth aside. She settled down next to Hope, gently smoothing her daughter's hair as she lay sleeping. She sensed there was more to her father's distress than having taken a bad beating. He'd started to cry and insisted they get away, and she knew that's what they must do because there was evil lurking; she could feel it.

'Rosie! You there, Rosie? We've got to go now.'

Rosie stretched across to reassure her father with a touch on his arm. He sounded delirious, as though he'd started from a terrifying dream. 'I'm here. Go back to sleep. I will come with you. Soon as you're well enough we'll go away somewhere safe. I'll give my station boss a week's notice, promise.'

CHAPTER TWENTY-SIX

Gertie was still being a miserable cow to him so Midge hadn't visited Rufus this morning, knowing it was washday and his sister would be around. Instead he'd headed in Popeye's direction in the hope of a handout. Just as he'd turned the corner Midge had seen Frank's lady friend go into the house, so he was loitering, waiting for her to leave. Bored of peering from behind the hedge, he'd decided to mosey off to the British Legion to cadge a fag when the door opened and out she came. The nurse set off up the road at quite a speed with her face on her boots. As Midge nipped through Popeye's front gate he was praying the couple hadn't had a row or he'd have more chance of getting blood out of a stone than a cup of char out of his boss.

'How you doing, Pop?' Midge rattled off, squeezing himself into the hallway before Frank could shut him out. It was a dingy passage, painted sepia brown, and it took Midge a moment to notice that Popeye had a large dressing on his cheek. 'Bleedin' hell! What you done to yerself?'

Popeye didn't answer; he shuffled back down the passage, Midge following dejectedly behind him.

'What's gone on then?' Midge asked cautiously. He sensed that Popeye was festering on something seriously bad. 'Saw the nurse leaving a moment ago; been in to patch you up, has she?'

Popeye fingered the lint. He refilled the whisky glass on the table and poured another shot for Midge. 'Glad you come by; got something for you to do.'

Midge brightened up. 'Yeah? Back swinging on the deliveries, are we?'

'You and Rufus can use me car to collect the stuff I need to get going. Me account's open again at the wholesaler's.'

Midge knocked back his drink, feeling happy as Larry. 'How d'you come a cropper?'

'John Gardiner did it just after he give me back the fifty quid he nicked.' Popeye loosened the dressing and winced as he peeled it off, showing Midge the deep damage to his cheek. Trudy had agreed to stitch him up but apart from that she'd made it clear it was over between them. She'd been disgusted when he'd told her what had happened. She'd blamed him for betraying her trust and using private information, told in confidence, against the Gardiners. Much as he was fond of Trudy, Popeye was prepared to sacrifice her for the chance of getting to know his grandchild. Besides, he reckoned once he was in touch with the little girl, Trudy would come round. She'd told him she would've loved to have mothered Rosie's kid. At the time Popeye hadn't taken a lot of notice of what she'd said, but he knew things now that he hadn't known then. As far as he was concerned, Trudy was still his girlfriend and he'd no objection to her spending time with his little granddaughter.

Having taken a good look at the puckered flesh on his boss's cheek Midge whistled through his teeth. 'Gardiner deserved a right good kickin' fer doing that to yer.'

'He got a kicking, all right. But weren't about the money; was personal. So there's another job I've got for you, if you're up for it.'

Midge put his empty glass back down on the table. 'Go on,' he said. 'I'm listening.'

'Keep this just between you 'n' me. Don't tell Rufus 'cos if he blabs to his missus the world'll know.'

Midge sensed big money was in the offing now, and he didn't mind what he did to get it. As far as Midge was concerned he was a dead man, and had been for some time, it was just a question of when his luck would run out. Before it did, he'd do anything in a bid to outrun the grim reaper.

'You still got a blade and prepared to use it?'

Midge jerked a nod, fingering the weight in his

coat pocket. He never went anywhere without a knife. Owing to his size Midge had been vulnerable to bullies; from an early age he'd been vigilant about having help at hand. At one time he'd had a gun too, but he'd lost that along the way.

'Right, sit down then and I'll tell you all about it,' Popeye said, pouring them both another drink.

'Hello, stranger! This is a lovely surprise. Come in, I'll make us a pot of tea.'

Having put the brake on the pram Rosie unbuckled Hope, lifted her out, then followed Gertie inside her home.

'Excuse the mess,' Gertie said, stepping over a pile of newspapers that Rufus had left scattered round the base of his armchair. 'He's an untidy sod, me 'usband. He's out delivering, thank heavens, so we can have a natter in peace.'

With a clap of her small hands Vicky jumped off the couch and trotted to greet her friend.

'Look at that,' Gertie said. 'Not seen each other in ages yet they remember one another.' She led Rosie through to the kitchen and filled the kettle. 'So your dad's home on a visit from Kent, I take it?'

'He is back,' Rosie said, putting Hope down so the children could play chase. 'But he's not at all well at the moment.'

'Lot of it about. My Rufus had bellyache fer days last week. Probably down to the amount of ale he sinks, though.' Gertie clucked her tongue.

'I've no time for tea actually, Gertie. I've come to ask a favour, and I'm sorry it's such short notice,' Rosie said awkwardly. 'I wouldn't burden you but Dad's too ill to look after Hope just now and I was wondering if you'd have her while I go to work.'

Her father was brighter than he'd been a few days ago following his beating, but Rosie knew that her lively little daughter was beyond his control. And he'd realised it too; John hadn't protested when she'd said she'd ask a friend to have Hope while he recovered.

'You want me to babysit?' Gertie sounded delighted.

Rosie nodded. 'Just for this afternoon, if you would. I tried to get leave so I could nurse Dad but we're short-staffed and I'm the only relief driver available today. I feel I should turn in as I stayed home with him yesterday. And what with these bloody rockets coming thick and fast, we're getting calls day and night.'

'You passed your test, then?'

Rosie nodded.

Gertie bent down to talk to her daughter. 'Lucky girl. You've got a little friend to play with this afternoon.'

'Are you sure you don't mind? I'll be back and pick her up before seven o'clock.' Rosie delved into her bag and brought forth some milk and fish-paste sandwiches.

'Didn't need to do that!' Gertie protested. 'I'd've given her her tea.'

'No, I must; rations are tight and it's only fair.' Rosie looked again at Gertie. She liked the woman, and their daughters got on well, but she felt uneasy about leaving Hope with anybody other than her dad. But she also felt a fierce loyalty to the LAAS and the colleagues and friends she had there, and soon would lose. She'd given in her notice and felt terribly sad and empty to be leaving Robley Road. 'Are you sure you don't mind?' she again asked.

'Don't mind one bit!' Gertie exclaimed. 'Be a pleasure – and you drive carefully.'

Once Rosie had left, Gertie found all of Vicky's toys and put them on the couch, then she picked up the children and placed one either side of the few rag dolls and wooden bricks. She made her cup of tea, then settled down opposite the little girls with a contented smile on her face, watching them play.

'In here,' Gertie called when she heard the front door being opened.

'Who's that?' Joey had come into the parlour and grinned at Hope.

'She's me friend's little gel; Hope's her name. Little blonde angel, ain't she, Joey? Vicky loves to see her. Me and Hope's mum used to work together at the Windmill, way back.'

Joey liked little 'uns, and he sank to his knees in front of the couch and started building bricks with the children, using the cushion as a base. 'Can I show her to Becky? She's a dope fer kids.' Joey sounded gruff. He and Becky often took Vicky for walks, one either side of her, holding her hands, swinging her between them.

He was getting to like Becky more and more; all through the summer they'd been sitting on her front step, talking for hours about getting better jobs and better money, then saving enough to run off to live in a cottage in the countryside. Joey knew it'd never happen, even if Becky didn't, but pipe dream or not, it put a smile on his face while he rode the butcher's bike and took round the orders to the big houses.

Gertie peered out of the window. 'Where is Becky? Bring her in, can't you?'

'She won't come in here case *he* turns up,' Joey said bluntly.

His father teased him and Becky non-stop when he was about, calling them lovebirds and making twittering noises. Now Becky refused to enter the house just in case he rolled up unexpectedly and embarrassed her.

Joey picked up the rag dolls and danced them together in front of the little girls' laughing faces. Hope made to snatch one of them and Joey jigged it out of reach, making her chuckle and try again.

'Well, all right, you can show her to Becky for a few minutes then bring her back in,' Gertie said, smiling at Joey.

She felt for him. Although her remaining son was growing up, working and walking out with a girl, in his heart he'd always be a grieving boy yearning for his little brothers to play with.

'Well, this has been a bloody uneventful four hours so far.' Hazel was speaking while furiously polishing the common-room windows with her screwed-up newspaper. 'Not even an expectant mum to deal with.'

Rosie, beside her, wrung out her cloth in the bucket of water, then continued washing. 'Wonder if poor Jim's feeling better?' she said. Jim had taken a tumble off the kerb in the blackout and sprained his ankle. He'd hobbled in on crutches to show them he wasn't malingering. He'd moaned that it was typical he'd done himself a damage while off duty rather than on.

While Rosie worked alongside her friend, she was only half contributing to their conversation. Hazel's chatter had flowed over her because serious worries were cramming Rosie's head. She was fretting about Hope and whether her daughter was behaving herself. Worse, the poor little thing might be crying because she was missing her mum and granddad. Her daughter didn't know Gertie well, and didn't know the woman's husband at all. Rosie hoped that the fellow wouldn't be angry to discover a stranger's child beneath his roof.

Then Rosie had the anxiety of her father maybe taking a turn for the worse, or being in need of anything while she was out. He'd promised not to answer the door to a soul and to stay in the basement in case a siren sounded. He'd never be able to descend to the cellar under his own steam, so had agreed to remain down there all day. Before she'd left that morning Rosie had made him comfortable with extra blankets and put sandwiches and a flask of tea next to his bed.

Her greatest fear had been that Popeye would come round after her vulnerable father, but John had reassured her on that score. Frank Purves hadn't got away scot-free during their fight; her father reckoned his opponent would also be licking his wounds for a while yet.

Rosie dropped her cloth into the bucket and

buffed the smears from the glass with newspaper. She stood back staring at the gleaming pane. 'Right, that'll do,' she announced. 'Let's start up the ambulance.'

Following the tragic deaths of Stella and Thora at Stepney, Janet Lawson had been promoted to DSO. Tom had taken on the additional role of Shift Leader as well as being an ambulance driver until some new people were taken on. In the immediate aftermath of the tragedy the atmosphere at Station 97 had veered between shock and disbelief. But a defiant war cry had gone up in the common room the following day led by a battle-weary Tom and Rosie. Amidst the tears, everybody had vowed to defy the Germans to their last breath and increase their efforts to save as many lives as possible. But it was inevitable that volunteers would be slow in applying once they were aware of the reason for Station 97 being depleted in numbers.

Jim had taught Rosie to check the vehicle's engine from time to time during the day. It was no good sprinting out on an emergency to find at the last moment that the blighter was playing up, he'd told her. Rosie glanced at the clock; she'd be relieved when her shift was over and she could collect Hope.

'I shall miss you when you leave, you know,' Hazel said as they walked outside. 'Jim reckons he'll never get another assistant as good as you.'

'I shall miss you lot, too,' Rosie returned stoutly. 'Never know, perhaps I'll be back at some time when Dad's feeling more the ticket.' Rosie had told her colleagues she'd got to quit and care for her crippled father for a while. She was glad she'd not lied and had got away with being merely economical with the truth.

'I'll pair up with you today if we get an incident.' Hazel winked. 'I've already had a word with Tom. He doesn't mind me abandoning him 'cos his friend's swapped shifts and can jump in my seat if need be.'

'Nights are drawing in already.' Rosie glanced up at the sky where a low autumn sun was streaking orange into blue. She realised it would be getting dark by the time she got to Gertie's to pick up Hope.

'Spoke too soon.' Hazel stared upwards as the air-raid siren wailed.

Rosie searched the skies too, but nothing was yet visible. She trotted on across the yard to the ambulance and turned the ignition. The engine jumped into life and throbbed noisily. But she was hoping Station 97 wouldn't get a call and she wouldn't be driving it later. She'd reassured herself that Hope would be safe during a raid: Gertie had told her she hared to the shelter with her kids every single time an alarm sounded. But Rosie just wanted to bring Hope home to reassure herself she was safe.

Joey and Becky were swinging the little girls between them, making them giggle, when they heard the warning. Joey let his sister's feet touch the ground. Hope, thinking it was her turn, put out her arms to him.

Becky picked her up, balancing her on her jutting hip like a seasoned mum. 'You're so pretty,' she said, kissing Hope's forehead. 'Wish you was mine.'

'Come on, better get home. Mum'll be worrying.' Joey glanced back and saw Gertie by their gate, waving frantically at him.

They had moved towards the end of the street in their game of lifting the little girls off their feet and swishing them to and fro, higher and higher till they whooped with delight. Gertie had come out several times to check that everything was all right with the children, bringing them some biscuits and a flask of tea so they could all carry on enjoying being outside on such a glorious afternoon.

Joey picked up Vicky, and with an arm about Becky he hurried her along with him.

When they were almost halfway home a car pulled up, crawling at the kerb beside them.

'Get back home, son, and help yer mum to get all of yous down the shelter,' Rufus had bawled through the Citroën's open window.

He frowned at Becky carrying a little girl. He knew the Pugh family didn't have any youngsters and he didn't recognise the toddler as belonging to any of the neighbours.

'Who's that?' He smiled at the beautiful child and she shyly averted her face.

Joey could see his uncle in the car beside his father, steering one-handed and looking pleased with himself with his homburg pulled down low over his eyes like a gangster.

'Her name's Hope. Mum's babysitting for a friend who used to work at the Windmill with her.' Joey put on a sprint as the siren continued to wail but he could tell that Becky was struggling to keep up.

The car stopped and Midge hopped out. 'Here y'are, love, let's take her for you. Bit of a weight, ain't she? Chubby little thing...'

Midge relieved Becky of the child and Rufus also took Vicky and put her on the back seat of the car. 'You two big 'uns run on. We'll bring these two. Go on, get going,' Rufus bawled at his son.

The bigger kids did as they were told, and Rufus was soon scouring the skies for a sight of the threat. 'There it is, the Kraut bugger.' He pointed towards the sunset. 'Too bleedin' close fer comfort. Shoreditch, that'll land, I reckon.'

Midge didn't answer. He was laughing silently, but he wasn't sharing the joke with Rufus. Popeye had told him not to.

The Citroën pulled up outside Gertie's home at the same time as Joey and Becky did. Gertie pushed Joey towards the house.

'Get yer coat, Joey; it'll turn cold overnight. Bet yer life we'll be stuck down there for hours.'

Joey did as he was told, waving to Becky as she pelted on up to her own gate.

'Bring those two little 'uns in,' Gertie yelled at Rufus, before turning and going to find the belongings she always took with her to the shelter.

Rufus entered the house, carrying his daughter. 'I'll come with you. Finished fer the day now, love.'

'Where's little Hope?'

'Midge is just bringing her in, then he's off down the British Legion, he said.'

After a few seconds Gertie felt a twinge of panic. She dropped her bag and raced to the front door. The car had gone and there was no sign of Midge or Hope.

CHAPTER TWENTY-SEVEN

Rosie felt as though she might explode with anxiety as she swerved the ambulance around obstacles. The clatter of the bell sang in her skull but she hardly registered it. Every time she'd speeded up in her race through the streets she'd had to brake, then coax the vehicle over debris strewn in the road. She'd backed up, gears screaming, and taken a run at an impassable hillock and was now fretting that the front tyres had punctured. But as they'd bounced back to earth and jolted onwards she'd again stamped on the accelerator.

'Doing great...' Hazel encouraged her. 'Chin up, Rosie! The explosion is right up the other end of your street. I can feel it in me bones. We can do this, we always do!'

'I know,' Rosie croaked. 'Please God,' she whispered, 'let my dad be all right...'

The vile images of the Stepney disaster wouldn't stop circulating in her mind. Nothing had remained of Stella and Thora, or of the fireman who'd cursed the Hun. The rocket had landed just a yard or two from them and in a way Rosie had been glad of small mercies. The prospect of having to gather up and identify bits of those two particular victims had made her feel bilious. She'd never really come to know Thora as their shifts had rarely coincided and she had been a reserved woman. But Stella, Rosie had liked and admired ... and taught to dance...

They'd done what they could for the people in the Church Hall. None had survived but nevertheless Rosie and Tom had worked on alongside the firemen throughout the night, recovering remains out of a sense of respect for the deceased and their families.

Tom had suffered days of deafness, and a deep cut to his left arm, but he'd refused to stay away from Robley Road to recover. Similarly, Rosie's gashed scalp and the painful bruises that had covered her back had not kept her at home. Now the scars were fading from her body, if not her mind. Rosie knew she'd been luckier than Tom who might suffer a permanent loss of hearing in one ear. She'd gained better protection than he from the ambulance doors and she nightly whispered a prayer of thanks, sure her mum had been her guardian angel, just as she was sure Prudence Gardiner had watched over her when the Café de Paris was hit years ago.

Tom and Rosie had returned to the station, speechless with shock. Hazel had then patched them up and, unusually, left them alone once she understood the enormity of what had happened. The following day, having snatched less than four hours' rest on mattresses at the station, Rosie and Tom were both back at their posts, hollow-eyed from grief and exhaustion. Thankfully, the food poisoning that had been responsible for Stella and Thora being on active duty was now forgotten and nobody had the energy, or the will, to say any more about where the blame might lie for that episode.

'Move, damn you!' Rosie shouted at a motorist having an animated discussion with a policeman. He was hanging out of his car window and gesturing at the flames that Rosie knew were from fires in her neighbourhood. It had been about twenty minutes after they'd heard the siren that afternoon that they'd got a call-out to an incident in Shoreditch. Rosie had nearly swooned on hearing the name of the street they were being sent to, but she'd raced outside to start the engine while. Hazel collected the docket from Clarice.

The policeman waved the motorist aside, and Rosie on, and she rammed her foot on the accelerator.

'It's the Prices' house that's taken the worst of it, and those to the left,' Rosie gasped, bringing the ambulance to a shuddering stop. 'And it looks like May Reed's lost part of her roof.'

Her father's house, many yards away in the opposite direction, appeared untouched, and momentarily Rosie was rooted to her seat in relief.

'Your place safe, is it?' Hazel demanded briskly. She'd had her door open before the ambulance came to a halt and had already jumped down.

'Thank God ... yes, it is,' Rosie gasped. Feeling guilty and selfish at her reaction, she pulled her mind back to the job in hand and scrambled out of the vehicle. Her training kicked in and she sprinted to open the back of the ambulance and get the equipment ready.

'You're needed over here!' A fireman beckoned to them and pointed to a huddled figure with a hand clapped over her eye.

'Let's have a look at you then, Mrs Reed,' Rosie said, recognising her neighbour at once as she gently removed the woman's fingers from her head. The eye was dreadfully mangled but Rosie managed to say cheerily, 'Right ... let's get a dressing on that, then get you into the ambulance, and you'll be right as ninepence.'

'Rosie Deane, ain't it?' May panted, trying to blink at the young woman through sticky hair.

'Just Rose'll do,' Rosie said, glad that Hazel was out of earshot dealing with another casualty.

'Lost me eye, ain't I?' May snorted a sob.

'You'll be winking again next week. Hold still, almost finished.' Rosie continued winding the bandage as gently as she could about the woman's head.

'Peg all right, is she?' May asked, wincing with the effort of speaking. 'Lucky mine are all out at work. Just me home. Peg's husband, Dick, was out, but I think her 'n' Irene were indoors.'

Rosie was squinting through the wavering heat mist at the firemen directing hoses at the top windows of the Prices' house. The ground floor seemed to have escaped the blaze so far.

'They could've made it down to the cellar.' Rosie adopted an optimistic tone but she'd seen enough as an ambulance auxiliary to know that people were often just moments too late seeking shelter.

'God help us! What's happened to my gel?'

Rosie had just settled May in the back of the

ambulance when she saw Peg Price had barged through firemen to the front of a group of neighbours; some were assisting the walking wounded who'd been peppered by flying glass.

'I was visiting me sister in Hackney.' Peg gaped in horror at her house. 'Where's my Irene?' she screamed. As a fireman made to restrain her rushing towards the blazing house, Rosie hurried over.

'Where's me daughter?' Peg begged Rosie. 'Seen her, have you? She's been in all day, not feeling well with dreadful bellyache; she was up in her bedroom.' The woman's appalled eyes widened on the shattered top-floor windows.

'Not seen her yet, Mrs Price.' Rosie glanced at the fireman, who was shaking his head, dashing her hopes that a survivor had been pulled from the wreckage.

'Someone's in there!' A shout went up from the front and Peg beat the fireman off with her fists, surging forward to clamber over jagged timbers towards what remained of her home.

The fireman grabbed Peg again just as Hazel trotted over, calling, 'Young woman name of Irene's in there; she says she can't come out. She sounded hysterical.'

'Fire ain't properly out.' The fireman sucked his teeth. 'Wait a bit, if I was you, before attending to her.'

'What, wait till it's too late, you mean?' Hazel returned drily. 'I'll go in this time,' she firmly told Rosie. 'You've done more'n enough just lately.'

Rosie knew that Hazel felt guilty for having been off sick on the evening of the Stepney incident. All the staff who'd been too ill to work now knew fate had smiled on them even if they hadn't seen it that way at the time.

'I'll talk to Irene: I might be able to calm her down, as I know her,' Rosie said, as the two young women climbed over wreckage towards the house.

'Let it cool down a bit; you might set fire to your clothes,' a younger firemen advised as Hazel tested the uneven ground that led into the fumy hall.

'Put the hose on me,' Hazel said bluntly, hoisting her medical bag. 'Ain't had a bath this week.'

'Daft cow,' the fireman said, but his crinkle-cornered eyes were full of admiration. 'I'll come with you then; summat might need lifting. Can't do that on yer own, young lady like you.'

'You'd be surprised what we can do on our own, chum,' Hazel challenged.

'Can you hear me, Irene? It's Rosie from down the road; you'll soon be out.'

'Mrs Deane? Is it you?' A note of utter relief shrilled in Irene's voice. 'Come and help me. Don't want nobody else. Is me mum there?'

'She's here, Irene, and don't worry, she's fine. Are you trapped? Are you in pain?'

'Who's she talking to?' Hazel asked, looking around. 'Who's Mrs Deane?'

'I am,' Rosie admitted.

'Right...' Hazel said, masking her surprise. This was no time for personal questions.

'Someone's coming to help you. Her name's Hazel. Where are you, Irene?'

'Only want you!' Irene screeched. 'Tell 'em to leave me alone. I ain't coming out.'

The fireman shoved back his helmet and gawped at Hazel, who in turn stared at Rosie.

'She's gone into bad hysterics. Ain't that unusual. Better give her a shot of something,' the fireman said. 'Last one like that fought like a demon to stay under the stairs.'

A terrible thought had occurred to Rosie. In all the commotion she'd forgotten that Peg's daughter was pregnant, and probably nearing her time. A shock such as this might have induced a miscarriage. Peg obviously had no idea her daughter was pregnant or in her panic she'd have blurted it out. But she had said that Irene had been laid up with bellyache ... and Rosie remembered such cramps.

She couldn't broadcast her fears; if she were wrong, and Peg *had* found out and had made her daughter have an abortion weeks ago, Rosie knew she'd do Irene untold damage by mentioning the matter in front of the neighbours. The girl's reputation would be ruined for no reason.

'I'm coming in to see you, Irene,' Rosie yelled. She felt Hazel's strong grip on her shoulder, squeezing in a show of support and admiration.

'Give us a shout if you need assistance, Mrs Deane,' the fireman said.

'She's crawled underground through rubble; walking in there's a doddle for her,' Rosie heard her friend proudly tell him.

As Rosie squirmed her way under and over wreckage, water dripped on her from the hoses directed at the top floor, soaking her head and shoulders. She knew she should be worried about her false identity having got out, but it seemed a triviality at a time like this. Stella would never have probed for details about her other life; Hazel was bound to. And Rosie would offer up answers because she no longer cared who knew that she had a beautiful little girl and was raising her on her own. 'Where are you, Irene? Guide me,' she shouted, shaking the water from her head and keeping her medical bag secured beneath an arm.

'Back parlour...' Irene started to cough.

Inside, the room was a maze of mangled timbers and the unbearably humid atmosphere made Rosie gasp.

She caught sight of Irene crouching in the furthest corner and scrambled towards her.

'Can you move? Where are you hurt?'

Irene stared at her lap and Rosie saw the pool of blood soaking her skirt.

'Have you miscarried?' she croaked.

'Don't know. Don't tell Mum. She still don't know,' Irene whimpered, grabbing at Rosie's leg as though to prevent her leaving. 'Don't tell my mum ... please, don't.'

Rosie hunkered down and pinched Irene's fleshy chin in her slender fingers. 'Hush! It'll be all right. Let's have a look at you.'

'Don't tell...' Irene keened.

'Shush now!' Rosie ordered harshly, feeling her heart drumming beneath her ribs. Rosie lifted back Irene's filthy skirt and saw the gore. Her shaking hand plunged forward to investigate then almost recoiled on encountering a small smooth head, but it raced on over a tiny sleek body, with a beating heart.

'You'll have to help me, Irene, 'cos I'm no great

342

shakes at this. Hold back your clothes so I can see what's what.'

Irene did as she was told and gently Rosie drew the tiny infant towards her into view, staring at its minuscule limbs in wonder. It was far smaller than she recalled her daughter had been at birth and Hope had been just five pounds. Cradling it in the crook of an arm, she opened her bag and cleaned mucus from the baby's face with lint.

'What is it?' Irene whispered, aghast at the sight of the purple creature. 'Is it a baby? It hurt something awful. I was in bed with bellyache but managed to get downstairs when the siren went off.'

Rosie cleaned the tot's nether regions of blood and vernix. 'You've a little boy. I think he's weeks early, though. We need to get going and get you both to hospital.'

'I'm staying here. You take him. Mum'll kill me. She don't know.' Irene shuffled back on her posterior towards the wall, jerking the umbilical cord.

'Keep still!' Rosie commanded. 'I'll have to cut this and separate you.'

Suddenly the baby gave a wail and so did Irene.

'Make it be quiet! They'll all hear,' Irene choked. She lunged forward as though to silence the infant.

'I said keep still!' Rosie found herself snarling. She knew that Irene was frightened, but so was she and it was making her impatient.

'Can't we just leave it here?' Irene garbled in a whisper. 'Please ... hide it over there where nobody'll see it. I don't want it. I can say I fell and cut meself badly but I'm all right now. Then

343

nobody'll know...'

Rosie forced up the girl's chin with her hand. 'Now you listen to me, Irene, you'll do nothing of the sort. Your mum'll be upset at first but she'll get over it. She'll have to ... like my dad had to.' Rosie waggled the girl's face as Irene started to snivel. 'And you'll cope ... like I had to. And you'll be a good mum ... like I'm a good mum. And in a year's time you'll wonder how you came to feel such love for something you didn't want and wanted to hide because she's beautiful and your heart wants to burst with pride every time she wakes up in the morning...'

Rosie blinked the mist from her eyes, realising she'd been talking about her daughter, and saw that Irene was silently howling. Quickly Rosie fumbled scissors from her bag and cut the cord, then clumsily knotted it after a few tries with her nervous fingers. She took off her jacket and carefully wrapped the baby, then stood up, cradling him against her shoulder. She held out a hand to Irene but the girl screwed her face up, shaking her head.

'You said you wanted to be like me, didn't you?'

Irene nodded, snuffling and smearing mess from her face.

'Well, bloody well be like me then. Get up! Let's go!'

Irene extended her trembling fingers and Rosie grasped them, jerking her to her feet. She put an arm about Irene's shoulders, hugging her fiercely in praise and encouragement. 'Well done,' she said then began guiding the new mother back over the rubble.

'Christ Almighty! You'll need a stiff drink after that, then, love.'

Rosie had just recounted to her father what had happened out in the street and shocked him to the core. He'd heard the blast close by, but it was the news about Peg's daughter that had made him offer his own girl a livener.

'Can't have a drink, Dad, I'm still on duty.' Rosie gave a tired smile. 'We've dropped the patients off at the hospital and I only popped in to see how you are. Hazel's waiting for me outside; I've got to get the ambulance back to the station, then I'm going to fetch Hope home.'

'Your friend Gertie'll keep her till morning, won't she, love? 'Spect she's guessed you've been held up with the raid.' John shifted on the mattress. He was still in considerable pain but the tale he'd just heard had taken his mind off his own problems. 'Gertie won't expect you to turn up at this time of the night. Must be almost nine o'clock by now.'

'I want Hope home with me,' Rosie said quietly. She'd been kneeling by the side of the mattress to talk to her dad, and now she stood up wearily. Her uniform felt stiff with muck and blood from the newborn, and her hair, though dried, had plastered to her scalp. But she knew she'd not rest till she was wheeling Hope home in her pram through the black and damaged streets of Shoreditch.

CHAPTER TWENTY-EIGHT

'Me husband's out looking for me brother now,' Gertie sobbed. 'He's been searching for hours. He's been back once. He went first to the British Legion to find out if they'd seen him. That's where Michael reckoned he was heading when the siren went off. Rufus is in a terrible rage; he'll kill Midge if he finds him, and good riddance, I say.' She shook her head into her hands. 'I'm so sorry, Rosie; don't know what to do... Please don't hate me, or Joey; it 'specially ain't his fault.'

Joey was sitting on the couch with his little sister; he bowed his head on hearing his name mentioned. Vicky, too, was unusually quiet; young as she was, she'd sensed the sad atmosphere.

'Where's your husband gone now?' Rosie's shock on learning Hope was missing had robbed her of the will to cast blame on anybody. Something inside was screaming but she felt too numb to cry.

'Don't know; he's been gone ages. Might've gone to his boss to find out if he knows where Midge is. Frank Purves is his name and he lives–'

'Frank Purves?' Rosie echoed in a hoarse whisper.

'Popeye, they call him, and he lives–'

'I know where he lives.' Rosie rushed past Hope's empty pram by Gertie's front door, bursting out into the night.

She charged in the direction of Popeye's house,

stumbling and pulling herself along in the black-out against walls and hedges to find junctions and crossroads. Her breath was burning her throat and her chest heaving so badly that when she finally dragged herself to his gate she stood leaning on it, panting and retching.

She banged on the door, calling out Purves' name but the house remained silent and dark.

'You're making a bleedin' racket, love. You after Frank?' A man next door had opened up to make his complaint through a narrow crack.

Rosie nodded.

'Saw him go out in his car earlier. With another fellow, he was.'

'Did you see a little girl with them?' Rosie demanded.

'In his car, he was,' the man repeated, shaking his head, then closed his door.

Rosie collapsed to sit on the front step, her head in her hands. Her forearms slid up to cover her scalp and she rocked to and fro, sobbing till her eyes were arid and reason edged back into her brain. She wiped her nose with her knuckles and got up.

'I'm going to the police. I don't care if you get locked up – it's your fault!' Rosie shouted.

'I know it's my fault, Rosie,' John choked, using his sodden hanky on his face. 'But please don't involve the police. Let me try and reason with Popeye. I'll give him every penny of me savings... I'll do anything he wants to get her back. Just wish I'd known who your friend Gertie was earlier.'

Rosie turned white. 'What do you mean?'

'Your Gertie's husband's a petty criminal and her brother is a navy deserter who stabbed his mate. Oh, Rosie, you stupid gel! You should never have left Hope with such wrong 'uns.'

'I've never met those men... I like Gertie...' Rosie whispered. She sat down on the edge of the chair in the cellar, wrapping her arms about herself. 'I'm going to the police!'

'Popeye knows that he's Hope's grandfather. He guessed too that...' John wiped a hand over his mouth, unable to finish the confession.

'He can't know Hope's Lenny's! How could he?' Rosie dismissed angrily. Her eyes widened as she read her father's expression. 'You told him?' She pushed to her feet, her heart vaulting to her mouth.

'I didn't mean to!' John whined. 'He was calling you vile names, saying people would think you a slag when they found out you was an unmarried mother. He said he saw you putting it about with Conor Flint. I just exploded and it all come out. I told him Lenny was a monster, and he was!' John raged.

As if in a trance, Rosie sank back to the chair. 'He'll think he has a right to Hope. He'll say to the police he's Hope's family.' She gazed in horror at her distressed father. 'What have you done, Dad?'

'Well, *I* didn't tell him you weren't a widow! How'd he know that?' John burst out. 'That's why it all come about: him finding out that was a lie! And you never told me he'd seen you 'n' Flint out together.'

'It wasn't important; Popeye was out walking

with Nurse Johnson...' Awful enlightenment made Rosie screw up her eyes in anguish. 'He found out from her! Trudy must have told him she was going to adopt Hope.'

'That midwife believed you was a widow. I remember telling her myself your husband had died in action,' John argued.

'I ... I told her the truth, when we were discussing the adoption.' Rosie owned up in a whisper. 'We'll have to go to the police, Dad.' Rosie's shoulders started to quake. 'Oh, please ... I can't stand it ... I want her back.'

John limped to his daughter and enclosed her in an unsteady embrace. 'I'll go and see Frank ... talk sense into him...'

Rosie shook her head, unable to speak at all because of sobs racking her. She calmed herself to hiccup, 'We'll get the police.'

'There's something else Rosie...' John sniffed, and a long pause followed. 'Popeye's guessed I gave Lenny the rotgut that killed him. He can't prove it, but he might turn me in, and if they investigate and things go bad for me ... it's a murder charge.'

Rosie was staring at her father through gritty, uncomprehending eyes, as though he'd spoken in a foreign language. 'What d'you mean, you killed him? He died in a fire in a nightclub.'

'After I found out what he'd done to you, I pretended to him I didn't know 'cos you'd kept it a secret. I pretended to him we was still mates. I gave him a bad bottle of moonshine, made it 'specially for him, I said ... like it was a present instead of poison. He took it, pleased as punch,

349

and a few days later he was dead.'

Rosie was so shocked she couldn't blink. 'He got the bad drink in a nightclub ... that's where he got it.'

John shook his head. 'Don't reckon he did. He was always too tight to pay bar prices.' He stared defiantly at Rosie. 'Not sorry fer what I did. I'd do it again, for you. That animal left you there on the ground, bleeding...' He paused. 'The police might still have the bottle as evidence. What if they get prints off it after Popeye grasses me up? We'll get her back, Rosie. Just me 'n' you'll do it on our own, I swear we will.'

Rosie sat motionless for several seconds, then she said hoarsely, 'No we won't, Dad. We haven't got a chance.'

Rosie stood by the pub and listened to the clamour inside. Somebody was playing a piano and a woman was belting out 'Roll Out the Barrel'. She looked down at her crumpled uniform, realising she looked dirty and unattractive. She'd not wasted time in changing her clothes before hailing a taxi to take her to Wapping. She slipped off her jacket and straightened her blouse over her breasts although the white cotton was stained with Irene's baby's blood. Her shaking fingers raked through her fair hair, trying to press some style into it. With a deep breath she tilted up her face and walked in.

This time her appearance didn't cause a break in the hubbub; it was almost closing time and the patrons of the Red Lion had better things to do than bother eyeing a bedraggled ambulance auxiliary. Only one person immediately noticed her, as though he'd been watching the door for her arrival, just as her frantic gaze had searched for and located him.

Conor put down his glass and Rosie whimpered with relief as he weaved through the crowd towards her.

She'd wondered what to say ... how to plead with him to help and how she'd offer him anything he wanted just as long as he brought Hope back. But when he was so close that she could feel his warmth and smell his scent, all she could do was stand before him, quaking, not hearing a word he was saying because her grief was shrieking again in her head, deafening her. And then they were outside and she was clinging to him, grinding her forehead against his shoulder and howling soundlessly.

She wasn't sure how she got to his home – whether she fainted and he carried her there, or she walked – but she surfaced again, shivering on his chair, just as he came out of the kitchen carrying a glass of brandy. Rosie took it with an unsteady snatch and gulped it immediately in case she dropped it.

'My daughter's gone,' she whispered, hearing his question this time.

Conor came down beside her, his face level with her own and she could see the hunger in his eyes.

'What d'you mean, she's gone?' he demanded in a strangely calm and quiet voice.

'A man called Midge kidnapped her.' Rosie pressed her fingers to her mouth to try to contain the nausea fomented by the hideous fact.

'Popeye's sidekick? Do you know why he's taken her?'

Rosie nodded and started to recount what had happened, jerkily at first, but as Conor remained still and silent her concentration strengthened. She told him about her father going to return the fifty pounds to Purves; about them ending up fighting, and John being too badly beaten to babysit; and the dreadful conclusion when she'd found out that her father had probably deliberately killed Lenny for raping her. Then she stumbled, and retraced her way over every vile fact. As she finished Conor was shrugging into his jacket and holding out a hand to her.

She shook her head. 'I'll stay.'

He turned and looked at her.

'I'll stay where I am,' she whispered. 'Bring her back here.'

'I don't need to; I know where you live.'

Rosie shook her head. 'I can't go back there. I blame him, you see. I've always blamed him for what happened to me. If he hadn't started making moonshine and getting into business with the Purveses...' She swallowed, blinked at the ceiling. 'What will you do?'

'Whatever I need to.'

'So will I,' Rosie said, and she went out into the hallway and climbed the stairs.

'I had the fucking locks changed so you wouldn't break in again. Ain't come at a good time, though, have yer, son, being as I'm in here?'

'Time's all right for me, Frank. Been in the wars, have you?' Conor nodded at the wound on the older man's cheek.

Frank ignored the taunt. 'You must've seen the Citroën outside.' He narrowed suspicious eyes on Conor.

'Quick on the uptake ... I like that.' Conor nodded at Midge. 'He gonna use that knife or play with it?'

Midge had sprung up from his chair and had pulled the blade from his pocket on seeing Flint emerge from the shadows in Popeye's warehouse. Midge had also thought the chump had broken in to burgle and picked the wrong time, but he was starting to feel uneasy. He noticed that Frank was edging a hand towards his desk drawer, as though he might jerk it open. Midge knew his boss kept an old army revolver in there because he'd seen it and a few stray bullets rattling around.

'Well ... Midge might stab yer, and I might say he had to in self-defence when you come in here to rob me tonight.'

'Could've robbed you months ago.'

'So what you here for then?' Frank asked genially, although his busy mind had already pounced on the answer.

Flint was sleeping with Rosie Gardiner and she'd persuaded him to help bring her daughter back. But Frank wasn't having that; the man was an outsider and could mind his own business.

Popeye had accepted he'd no family left, and previously it hadn't bothered him that much. His wife had died so long ago that sometimes he couldn't recall her face; his son had been a nasty piece of work, and Popeye believed John Gardiner about Lenny raping Rosie. But Lenny had done something right after all in leaving him a grandkid who looked like she could've been a model for those china dolls lined up in Gamages. As far as Frank was concerned the Gardiners didn't deserve to keep little Hope. Her mother hadn't even wanted her and had tried to give her away, whereas he'd cherish the gift of her every day of his life.

Midge kept pace with Conor as he strolled to and fro in the aisle between stacked boxes, his knife pointing at the man's guts.

'Looking for someone, are yer?' Frank taunted. 'She ain't here; *my* grandkid's somewhere safe. I've just come along to me warehouse to pay Midge his wages.'

'Well, you'd better tell me where my daughter is, 'cos if you don't I'll use that knife on your throat before I remove his other arm.'

Popeye slowly got to his feet. 'What you fucking talking about? What shit's that whore got you talking?' Popeye snarled. 'She's *my* granddaughter ... my Lenny's kid...'

Conor laughed. 'Who told you that? Gardiner? Not saying he's lying 'cos that is what he believes. Seemed easier at the time to let him think a dead man'd knocked up his daughter than a live one had run out on her. But I'm back now and I want what's mine.'

'You're fucking lying!' Popeye dragged the gun out of the drawer and aimed at Conor's chest. 'You didn't even know Rosie back then.'

'Yes I did. I knew her when she worked at the Windmill; I got into a fight for her with my old sergeant and a lot of people remember it, especially him, being as I beat the shit out of him. Spring 1941, it was ... I remember it well. I remember her well. You never asked yourself why I'd bother sending my brother over here to get involved in a two-bob outfit who knows a distiller name of Gardiner? Weren't you I was interested in, you prat, it was them. Soon as I found out about my daughter I was after getting me foot in the door.'

Midge glanced at Popeye, wondering where this was going. It seemed to him that there was more sense in what Flint was saying than what Popeye had told him. Lenny raping John Gardiner's daughter and getting her pregnant, then getting poisoned for it, seemed too far-fetched. Midge had worked with Lenny for years back in the old days, and got to know him. He remembered that Lenny had always used prostitutes. He didn't recall Popeye's son bothering women out of his league, and Rosie Gardiner was definitely that. Midge had seen her a few times and had been very impressed by the stylish blonde showgirl.

'Get going and make sure Hope's all right; she might have woken up. I'll take care of this.' Popeye lobbed a key at his cohort. He'd left Hope at a hotel, fast asleep. She'd been crying for her mum so Frank had given her a dose of laudanum to knock her out for a few hours while he paid Midge off and decided what to do. But he reckoned she might be waking about now and start hollering. He was planning on taking the child round to Trudy's in the hope of winning his girl-friend over with the news that he was going to fight for custody of the little angel. He was sure that once he told the courts John Gardiner was a murderer and the child's mother was a whore who'd tried to give away her baby, he'd have a real chance of success.

Once Frank had got over the shock of meeting his only surviving flesh and blood, and the little darling had given him a smile, he'd been smitten. Frank had told Midge the kid was staying with him, and Midge had shrugged because he knew he could add a nought to the sum he was expecting in payment. Midge was easy to control; if the price was right he'd do whatever he was told.

Frank had known that Gardiner would be after him, although he was confident that John wouldn't involve the police. He hadn't reckoned on Flint being so involved with Rosie, but he was lying about the kid being his, Popeye knew it.

Once Midge had gone Frank cocked the pistol at Conor's head. 'Nice try, son, but you'll have to go back and tell her it won't wash. Tell the Gardiners 'n' all that we can work things out between us. Ain't saying they can't see the kid – we're all family – but I can give her more than they can. I can certainly afford a better lawyer if it turns nasty. I know that John Gardiner murdered my son ... don't forget that...'

'Yeah, and don't you forget that if I'd got to the bastard first, you'd have been burying him in bits.' Conor seemed as though he was ready to start strolling again but he suddenly launched himself across the desk, punching the gun upwards with one hand, while his other smashed open the wound on Frank's cheek. As Popeye fought to

control the pistol his finger tightened on the trigger, sending a bullet thudding into the ceiling.
Connor grabbed the older man by the nape, ramming his face down into the desk with a sickening
crunch. He jammed his knee on Popeye's back,
pinning him there while wrenching the gun from
Frank's rigid fingers.

'Hope ain't yours, is she?' Popeye gasped
through the blood bubbling off his split lips.
'Admit it! You're fucking lying!'

Conor dragged him by the collar towards the
exit, gritting his teeth as pain shot through his
damaged shoulder. 'Don't even want to hear you
say her name again. Where's Midge gone?'

Once by the doorway Popeye tried to break free
but he was savagely punched down close to a tall
stack of cartons filled with printing paper. Conor
lit a cigarette and held it over an open box. He
knew that sticking it on the man's good eye would
have less effect than threatening his money.
'Where's he off to?'

'You ain't gonna do that.' Popeye struggled to a
sitting position, blinking in horror at red-hot ash
dropping onto the paper. 'There's ten grand's
worth of merchandise in here. You could have
half of it if you piss off and leave me in peace with
me granddaughter.'

Conor dropped the cigarette, then deliberately
felt in an inside pocket and took out a pewter
flask. He upended the lot on top of the paper;
even when the flames soared up to the warehouse
ceiling he kept shaking whisky out of the metal
flask.

Popeye tried to scramble up as the heat from

357

the fire became unbearable but Conor ground his heel harder into his chest.

'The Mermaid Hotel,' Popeye shrieked. 'That's where Midge has gone to get her. Now help me put this out 'fore everything goes up.'

Conor removed his foot. 'Put it out? I was thinking of locking you in and letting you burn.'

Midge drove along glancing every so often over his shoulder at the child on the back seat. He knew that Popeye was expecting him to take the girl to the warehouse. But Midge had a bad feeling about things. He was sure he didn't have a conscience to be bothering him, and he knew he didn't like kids, but the little 'un was an innocent in all of this. Besides, he didn't want Flint after him, and Midge reckoned the man had more claim on the kid than Popeye did. So unless Popeye killed Flint the Wapping boy would be a thorn in everybody's side. Midge didn't reckon Popeye had that sort of bottle. When he got back to the warehouse, he reckoned his boss would probably hand him the gun and expect him to pull the trigger after he'd scarpered with the kid. Midge had been provoked into stabbing Jack Chivers; he wasn't sure he could kill in cold blood.

In Midge's opinion the feud with John Gardiner over the distilling business had made Popeye lose his marbles. On impulse, Midge did a U-turn in the middle of the quiet street; he'd picked up the kid at his sister's place and that's where he was dropping her off. After that they could fight it out amongst themselves. He'd got his wages in his pocket and he knew Popeye wouldn't shell out any more now things had turned sour. So Midge was ready to disappear.

Midge took his hand off the steering wheel to change gear and saw the black Humber speeding towards him. Though he ducked his head he knew Flint would recognise Popeye's flash Citroën. Midge stamped on the accelerator, roaring along the dark streets, but he had his eyes in the rear-view mirror and saw the Humber wheeling around to start a pursuit.

Midge made the top of Gertie's road and knew if he went into it he'd have to reverse out. By that time Flint would be on him. Midge braked, shooting the child off the seat and making her cry in alarm. He nipped to the back door, dragging the little girl out by an arm. 'Go on, clear off,' he snarled, giving Hope a push. Seconds later he was crashing the gears and the cabriolet leaped forward.

Conor saw the Citroën's tail-lights and he knew he'd not been that close earlier; the vehicle had stopped for some reason. He slowed down, wondering if his eyes were playing tricks on him or if he'd actually seen a flash of fair hair in the blackness. He swerved and braked, then jumped out. He sprang round to the nearside of the car, crouching and searching but finding nothing. He got a torch from the glove box.

'Hope?' he called, sensing she might be close but too terrified to answer.

He walked slowly along the street, swinging the torch on and off the doorsteps and found nothing but empty milk bottles. Then he saw her crouching down by a low brick wall as though she'd made an effort to hide.

Conor closed his eyes and offered up a prayer as he walked over and sat down on the kerb close to her. He was at a loss to know what to say so he didn't frighten her any more than she was already. Her huge eyes were dry but the expression in them was heartbreaking. He kept the torch low, shining it between them on the pavement.

'Wanna go and see your mum? She's waiting for you,' he said gruffly, feeling choked with emotion. He lifted the torch slightly to illuminate her reaction.

Hope pulled a trunk with her tiny lips, darting glances at him.

'Know who I am?'

She slowly moved her head from side to side.

'I'm your mum's friend, called Conor. You got friends?'

She nodded.

'Yeah? What's their names, then?'

'Vicky 'n' Joey 'n' Becky.'

'You got more friends than me.'

Hope nodded, almost smiled but pouted instead.

'Mummy know your friends, does she?'

'No ... she's at work...'

'She's home now. Go and tell her about them, shall we?'

'All right.'

Conor held out his hand and shone the torch on it so she could see it.

As soon as she touched him he lifted her up in his arms and carried her to the car.

CHAPTER TWENTY-NINE

Midge saw flames shooting into the night sky and wondered if he'd missed a lightning German raid. He'd not heard the siren again. He'd intended to park up Popeye's Citroën outside his house, then get going to the train station. He knew his boss would be gunning for him – properly gunning for him with his pistol – once he discovered he'd let the child go. Midge knew he'd no option but to get away till things calmed down. He'd turn up again at some time – perhaps when the war was won or lost – and he understood what he needed to do to survive. But for now he had enough cash in his pocket to keep him on the move.

Midge had seen the Humber stop in Gertie's road and reckoned Flint had found the kid wandering about. Midge hoped he had. She was the prettiest little thing he'd seen in a while and it was right she go back home to her mum.

Popeye was no good for a child like that. He'd never been any good for anybody, even his own kid. Lenny had turned out to be a useless tosser. If Frank kept Gardiner's granddaughter he'd just ruin the girl's life, not improve it.

Midge started slowing down as he realised the fire in the distance was coming from the area where Popeye's warehouse was. An omen of what he might find if he turned in that direction got the better of his instinct to flee and he spun the wheel.

'Where the fuck have you been?' Popeye roared through his puffy bleeding lips the moment Midge jumped from the motor outside his warehouse.

Midge gawped at the inferno, slowly digesting all that it signified.

'Been waiting for you to turn up,' Popeye snarled. 'Where's me granddaughter?'

Midge slowly approached his boss, half collapsed against the wall on the opposite pavement to the blaze.

'Flint do this to yer?' Midge shouted over the roar of the fire. 'Phoned the brigade, have yer, Pop?'

'Too bleedin' late for that!' Popeye cried, tears in his eyes. 'That's a lifetime's collar in there.' He pointed a shaking finger at the burning doors. 'Everything I own gone up in smoke. I'm gonna have him for this! I swear on me granddaughter's life I'll have him or die trying.' Popeye staggered over to the Citroën and peered inside. 'Where is she?' He swung about. 'What you done with her?'

'He took her,' Midge said evasively. He was wishing now he'd not come round to take a look at what was going on but had kept going.

With difficulty Popeye yanked open the passenger seat door and fell in. 'You drive, mate,' he told Midge. 'Get going over Wapping way.' With an effort he pulled the gun from his inside pocket and started to push bullets into the revolver.

On hearing a bell getting louder, Midge reversed the car at speed out of the hot alley.

'Get going before the bleedin' fire brigade turn up,' Popeye yelled. 'Ain't answering no questions.'

'Got insurance?' Midge asked brightly.

'Fuckin' insurance!' Popeye spat. 'Ain't worth the paper it's written on.'

Midge reckoned no further answer was needed then. Popeye was skint. But as he fought with the gears, he bucked up, interested to know what Popeye thought he was going to do to Flint to get even. Whatever it was, Midge had already decided to watch from afar. There was nothing in it for him.

'Me friend'll never forgive me fer this. Only time she asks me to mind her little Hope and I mess it up... Rosie hates me now, I know she does.'

Rufus patted his wife's quaking shoulder. 'Calm down, love. She must have found the little girl. That's why she ain't been back. Bet yer life her family's got the police involved and serve Midge right if that's his number up at last. Ain't before time.'

'You'll have to go out looking again, Rufus. Go back and try Popeye's place again. Someone might be in now.' Gertie glared at her husband as he remained seated.

'Me feet are killing me, love; you know I can't get about like I used to with this damned injury.' Rufus waggled his trouser leg. 'Anyhow, the old bloke next door said they'd driven off and no sign of a kid. Midge wouldn't take her there. What would old Pop want with a kid? If it ain't gonna turn him a profit, he ain't interested.'

'He wouldn't stoop to...' Gertie swallowed. She knew she should have spoken up sooner about her suspicions that Rosie Gardiner was John Gardiner's daughter, the fellow Popeye had a feud with about distilling. She'd wanted to keep the confidence that Rosie had placed in her when she'd told her she was an unmarried mother who hated being gossiped about. Rosie had naturally wanted to protect Hope from spiteful people, and Gertie could understand that. She knew her neighbours would have a field day if they knew that her Vicky wasn't Rufus's.

'What was you going to say, love?'

'Popeye wouldn't stoop so low as to kidnap John Gardiner's granddaughter to make him start up his still, would he?'

Rufus looked gormless for a moment while that sunk in. 'You ain't saying yer friend's related to the distiller?'

'I think she is,' Gertie owned up.

'But Midge don't know that.' Rufus struggled to his feet. 'Well, reckon Midge might know that, actually. There's been something making that brother of your'n smirk lately.' Rufus's mouth tightened into a hard line. For days Rufus had suspected that his brother-in-law thought he had one over on him. 'I'll go back round Popeye's place. Might try the warehouse too, just in case...' he said grimly as he shrugged into his jacket.

'It could've been Vicky as well. That scumbag could've driven off with 'em both,' Joey said, his narrowed eyes fixed on his lap. He had been sitting on the settee listening to his parents arguing for hours. His father had come back several times to report he'd had no luck turning up hide or hair of Midge or the child. Now Rufus had gone back out and Joey and his mother had been sitting in silence, lost in their own troubled thoughts.

Gertie shook her head, although she knew her son had spoken the truth. 'He wouldn't harm his niece. He knows I'd kill him if he did.'

Joey had earlier put his little sister to bed while his parents were going at it hammer and tongs. As he'd kissed her on the forehead he'd thanked God Vicky was safe. But he was crying inside for the little girl who was missing. Hope was sweet and Becky had loved playing mum to her.

'Going up the road to see Becky,' Joey said, getting up.

'It's too late to be paying visits,' Gertie protested. 'Must be close to midnight.'

'Don't care; Becky'll be waiting for news. Said I'd tell her if we had no luck finding out anything.'

'Come straight back if the siren goes,' Gertie called after her son.

Joey hurried past Becky's house and straight to the telephone box on the corner. He ferreted in his pocket for change, looking over his shoulder as he dialled the number. Round these parts nobody grassed family up, however evil they were. But as far as Joey was concerned, Michael Williams wasn't his family. And he wanted him dead.

'Take another route,' Popeye shouted when Midge slowed down, then stopped to allow an oncoming army truck and several cars to file around the pile of bomb damage blocking the road.

'Ain't doing a three-point turn 'less I have to,' Midge snapped back. 'Ain't exactly the world's best driver, am I?' He ruefully displayed what remained of his right arm.

365

'Well, let me drive,' Popeye barked, blinking blood from his good eye.

'You can't see nuthin' at the best of times,' Midge chortled. 'Look, we're moving again. Shut up and sit back.' Midge shoved the gear stick forward and pulled off with a lurch.

He motored on, putting his foot down as the road became deserted.

'Slow down!' Popeye hissed.

'You just told me to get going,' Midge protested.

'Old Bill...' Popeye had glimpsed through his blurry vision a police car parked up.

Midge immediately braked, then when the vehicle pulled out after him, he jammed his foot down on the accelerator. He licked his lips. 'They was bleedin' waiting for us.' He glanced agitatedly at Popeye. 'The law's on us; Flint or Gardiner have grassed you up. Kidnapping a kid's a serious offence.'

'You don't know that; could be they clocked you speeding.' Popeye glanced over a shoulder. He knew if they were stopped he'd have some explaining to do, not least about why a man with one arm was driving his car, and he was looking badly beaten.

'Pull round a corner and we'll swap places on the quick so I can say I was driving.' Popeye started scrubbing at his bloodied face with his hanky in an attempt to look more presentable.

'Ain't stopping fer nobody,' Midge growled. He knew as soon as the police started asking questions he'd be arrested, and after that he'd face a hangman's noose for Jack Chivers' murder.

'Slow down!' Popeye bawled as the Citroën's engine roared.

The bell on the police car started to clatter and he turned to gawp through the back window at the police gaining on them.

'Go down by the docks; lose 'em easy down there,' Popeye panted. 'Lots of alleys 'n' sheds. Might find one open we can pull into and hide.'

Popeye's heart was thudding, making him feel faint. If the police stopped them and searched them he'd be arrested as well as Midge. He had a gun and bullets on him. And he knew Midge had his blade in a pocket. Midge was a goner if he was caught – they both knew that – but Popeye reckoned he might still be able to talk himself out of things...

'They're gaining on us,' Midge said quite calmly, eyes in the rear-view mirror. 'Apart from that, Pop, we're almost out of juice.' He glanced at the dial, the needle pointing at empty.

'Find somewhere quick then ... here ... down here!'

Popeye pointed desperately at a long narrow lane leading off into blackness.

Midge took it, tyres screaming and shoved his foot to the floor. If Popeye had been able to see, Midge inwardly laughed, he'd've known that this road didn't lead anywhere other than the water.

But it was good enough for him. He'd sooner drown than swing, in any case. As for Pop ... well, he'd got nothing left so he'd probably thank him in the long run ... if he could...

CHAPTER THIRTY

Rosie had sat watching the closed door, her hands locked on her opposite shoulders, for what seemed like hours. She had been sure she'd spring from the seat the moment she heard the sound of a key in the lock. Instead when it opened she remained statue-like, gazing at her daughter. Slowly she wobbled to her feet, holding onto the arm of the chair. Her hands fluttered to her face, up over her hair, then the sob broke and she rushed forward and took Hope from him, smearing her tears against the child's neck. 'Thank you,' she whispered over and over again.

Conor went into the kitchen and filled the kettle, then put it on the gas stove even though he didn't want tea. He guessed she didn't either. But he reckoned it was probably what people did at such a time. He turned and stood in the doorway, hands braced on either jamb and watched as Rosie sat her daughter on the chair then removed the tot's shoes, talking to and touching Hope in a way he remembered his mother had done with Steven as a kid. But he couldn't remember her ever fussing over him.

Rosie looked up, smiling shyly, but he went back into the kitchen. She joined him in there with Hope in her arms. 'She told me she's got more friends than you,' Rosie said with a sweet attempt at a normal conversation.

Conor raised an eyebrow at Hope and set two cups.

'Does she want a biscuit?' He smiled as Hope nodded before her mother could answer.

'You'll spoil her,' Rosie said as he handed her daughter an open packet of custard creams. She took one out and gave it to Hope, then put the rest back in the cupboard.

'Can I have a drop of hot from that kettle and give her a wash?'

''Course...' He poured steaming water into the tin bowl and mixed it with some from the tap till it was lukewarm.

Rosie sat Hope on the kitchen table and started taking off her clothes. 'Have you got something to dry her with?'

'Somewhere...'

He went out and she heard him on the stairs, then he came in with a bar of soap and a flannel and towel.

'Lucky girl ... nice soap ... Pears. We have the cheap stuff.'

Conor poured the tea, then left them both cups and went to sit down on an armchair with a newspaper open on his knees.

'Can I put her to bed in the spare room?' Rosie asked. Her daughter was pink and fragrant from a thorough washing, dressed in just her vest and knickers and ready to be tucked up.

Conor closed the paper and sat back in the chair regarding her steadily. 'Gonna tell me why you're doing this?' He made an exasperated gesture and stood up. 'It doesn't matter... I already know. It's time for you both to go home.'

'I don't want to go home.'

He gave a soft bitter laugh. 'Oh, yes you do.' He pulled his car keys from a trouser pocket. 'What's more, I want you to go home.'

Rosie hugged her daughter to her, rocking the child who was already drifting off. 'D'you want to get rid of me because you're expecting someone?'

'Why d'you ask?'

'The phone went. I answered it because I thought it might be you.'

'Who was it?'

'She said her name was Patricia. She was rude so I put the phone down on her.'

'Right ... definitely time for you to go home, then. She'll be on her way round.'

Rosie knew he was being deliberately cruel to keep her at arm's length. 'Let her come; if you won't tell her to go away I will. She can have you tomorrow. This is my night,' Rosie said with a poise she was far from feeling. 'You told me to come and find you when I trusted you enough. Here I am.'

'Why tonight?' He turned, deep-blue eyes boring into her profile. 'What am I, a mercenary to be paid off? A dog to be rewarded for good behaviour? Or did you think I'd let that maniac have her unless you agreed to stay with me? Which is it? All of it? What about last night ... and the night before that ... when I wanted you? You didn't come over then and tell me you trusted me enough.'

Rosie flinched, wondering if he was hurt more than angry. She hadn't expected more than a token rejection from him, to preserve his pride, before he took her to bed. 'I thought you'd be pleased. What d'you want me to do, beg you to take me upstairs? All right I will...'

Conor laughed, swung narrowed eyes her way. 'Don't push me too far, Rosie. Take her home. You've got what you want.'

'I want you to have what you want, too.'

'You don't know what I want.' He looked at her. 'Do you?'

'And Patricia does, is that what you mean?' Rosie said. 'You think I'm not up to the job?'

She thought he'd laugh and drawl an answer but he walked away and struck a fist on the wall, leaning into it.

Rosie went into the hallway with Hope hugged tight to her chest and climbed the stairs to the smaller room. She'd gone into the big bedroom earlier. Just after he'd left she'd curled on her side on his mattress, staring sightlessly at the wall, with the tobacco musk of him beneath her cheek. But the sweeter smell of Jicky perfume on the other pillow had driven her back to the living room to continue her vigil in the armchair.

She tucked Hope in, smoothing her soft hair back from her brow in long slow strokes till her daughter's eyes fluttered closed. Still she sat with her, watching her sleep until she was drowsing herself and her chin was sagging towards her chest. She jerked awake and went back downstairs. Conor was lounging in the armchair, legs stretched in front of him, in the way her father would do on a Sunday afternoon after a roast dinner, in those old, glorious days when such things had existed for her family.

'Are you angry with me?' Rosie asked softly, unsure if he'd dozed off.

'No.'

So he wasn't asleep. 'I ... I didn't mean to insult you, if that's what you think I did. It's just ... I don't think you appreciate how much it meant to me, what you did. I'd've done anything to get her back.'

'What if I'd not managed to bring her back? What if I couldn't find her?'

'I knew you would. It never crossed my mind otherwise,' Rosie said simply and truthfully.

'Would you have done anything for Midge to barter for her?'

Rosie licked her lips. 'Yes ... I'd do anything for anyone – even Lenny, if he was still alive – to have Hope safe at home.' She jerked up her face. 'I suppose that disgusts you.'

'No, it's as it should be between a mother and her kids. But you don't need to get into that with me.'

'Why not? I thought you liked me.'

'Yeah?' he said, sounding sarcastic. 'What makes you think that?'

'I'm not frightened of you now. I might've been once but not now.' Rosie tilted her head to read his lowered expression. 'I know you'll be kind and gentle...'

He jerked forward, sank his head into his hands, spearing fingers through his long dark hair. 'D'you know how French women feed their kids when they've been bombed out or their husbands have been carted off by the Gestapo?' He looked up, his eyes fierce and narrowed.

Rosie shook her head, although she knew the answer, and she hadn't fooled him by pretending otherwise.

'They say they're not frightened and they like you. The week before it might have been a Nazi they'd stripped off for ... the uniform doesn't matter, so long as food or francs or cigarettes change hands at some point.' He sat back, but his eyes never left her face. 'They're lying too; they detest all of us. But they keep on coming.'

Rosie swallowed, feeling chastened and anxious. 'Are you talking about somebody in particular ... a woman you really liked?'

'Never met any woman I *really* liked over there or over here. Then I came home with a bullet in the shoulder and everything changed.'

'I don't blame those women... I don't blame you; you must get lonely...' Rosie blurted, feeling relieved that he hadn't fallen in love with a French girl. 'Why're you telling me what you do over there? I don't want to know.' She spun away from him, feeling suddenly angry.

'I don't do anything, that's the point, but there are lots who do, and brag about it afterwards, especially if they've copped off without paying.'

'I told my dad I was coming here to ask you to help, and the only thing that frightened me – frightened me to death – on the journey was that I'd turn up and find you'd gone back to your regiment.'

'Next week you would've.'

'You're going back?' Rosie asked forlornly, turning back to face him.

He nodded.

'I'll miss you. I have missed you ... that's the truth.'

'I've missed you, too.'

'Good, that's a good start, isn't it?'

Rosie saw him smile to himself, shake his head in mock despair. She heard the low fluid swearing beneath his breath. Aloud he said, 'She's nodded off?'

'Mmm...'

Rosie sank down by the side of his chair, curling her feet under her, feeling nervous. She wanted to get closer to him, yet knew he'd move away if she said or did something wrong.

'I don't want to talk about how you got her back for me. I don't care what it took anyway,' Rosie said. Her hand slid over his, idle on the chair arm. She thought for a moment he was going to slip free but he didn't.

'You asked me if I liked you ... and trusted you. I do. I like you and trust you a lot and I know you think I'm just saying that because...' She glanced up at him to gauge his reaction to her amateur seduction, but he had his eyes on the opposite wall. 'You think I'm saying it because of what you've done for me tonight, but it's not that. It's honestly not that.'

'How many others were there?'

'What?'

'Before he raped you, how many men had you slept with?'

Rosie knew her blush had betrayed her. 'It doesn't matter now.'

'How many men had you kissed then?'

'Lots,' she said defiantly. 'Lots of them. I kissed

374

that sergeant of yours, for a start.'

'You said he made you feel sick.'

'He did. But it was my own fault; he got the wrong idea. They all got the wrong idea. They thought I was a sophisticated vamp. I expect you did too. I was stupid and naïve.' She sank her teeth into her lower lip; she'd not told anybody other than her father how bitterly she regretted her behaviour. She moved her hand on Conor's, almost a caress. 'It should've been you; it would all have been different then. I wish it had been you,' Rosie told him with quiet vehemence, realising she'd never meant anything more. *If only* ... whispered through her mind. If she'd spent the evening with him she'd have been a Windmill Girl with a boyfriend to write to overseas. She would have welcomed him home, waiting in a fever of anticipation, as Hazel used to when she knew Chuck was due back on leave but for her and Conor it would have been no half-hearted affair, it would have been real. She believed that as much as she understood he was waiting for a sign from her that he could trust. He wanted to be sure that gratitude and debt played no part in what might happen between them tonight. But such honesty required some answers.

'My dad said you Flints are pimps and spivs.'

'Remind me to thank him,' Conor said drily.

'Are you?'

'A spiv, perhaps; a pimp, no. Nor was Saul. By all accounts, my father ran a few brasses down by the docks for the sailors during the war. Last war, that is. He's been dead about eighteen years.' He tilted his head against the chair back, gazing at the ceiling. 'I'm no saint but I don't reckon I'm a proper villain either. I've always had regular work. Other than that, I do what I have to when I want more.'

'What more do you want?'

'It's in my blood ... who I am. I showed you that,' he said tonelessly.

'What more is there to want?' she persevered. 'A house, a job and a family to love – that's all there is, really.'

'Is that why you worked at the Windmill Theatre? For just a job and a family to love?'

Rosie felt heat flood her cheeks at his cool irony. She'd wanted the glamour and the excitement, and the adulation. She couldn't deny it.

'There's always a price to pay for thrills,' Rosie said stiffly. 'I paid it and it wasn't worth it.' She withdrew her hand from his, folded it into the other on her lap. 'He thought me a whore. He saw me come out of the Palm House with a bruise on my face and my dress torn and said I must've short-changed a punter. He said I wouldn't short-change him.' Rosie paused. 'It was the second time that night a man wanted to rip my clothes off. First time was inside the place. An army major, he was. He went off in a rage when I told him no. But first he whacked me and tore off some buttons.'

Conor sat forward with a jerk and sank his forehead into a hand. 'What were you doing at that dive, for God's sake?'

'A workmate from the Windmill and her boyfriend took me along. I was paying rent on a room in their house. They told me it was just a nightclub; I found out later it was a brothel. Turned out he was a pimp and she was working for him as well as at the theatre. They'd set me up with a client ... oh, it doesn't matter.' Rosie frowned at her fingers. 'I just ran out when I realised what was expected, and straight into...' She couldn't utter Lenny's name. She glanced at him, wondering if she'd repelled him with her pathetic conduct. She changed position, kneeling then sinking back more comfortably on her heels. 'Would you have still wanted to take me for that drink if you'd known I was just a silly little girl?'

'I was counting on it.' Conor smiled crookedly.

'No, you just told me you're different. You didn't need to though. I *know* you're different ... not like them.' Rosie cocked her head, realising he was making a joke of it because she'd moved him with that story. 'You're not like your family either,' she said. 'You're certainly not like your mum.'

'That'll please her.'

After a pause Rosie asked gently, 'Why doesn't she like you?'

'Because I'm not like the others. I never needed her in the way they did. She never needed me either ... till now.' He shrugged. 'I was always the kid in the middle, stuck between the baby and the big boy taking over from his dad.'

'I was stuck in the middle,' Rosie said.

'Thought you were an only child.'

'I was. I got stuck in the middle of my mum and dad. She left him, you see, when I was little. Went off with another man. Then she came back for a while, before she passed away. I wanted them to get on and be happy, but it seemed it was only me that did.' Rosie shook her head. 'Think it was a relief for Mum to die and get away from all the long, cold silences.'

'Got anything cheerful to talk about?' Conor asked in that dry way he had.

Rosie looked thoughtful. 'Persuaded a girl to come out from a bombed-out house today, if that counts.'

Conor tenderly traced a finger down her cheek, touched the dirty collar of her shirt with a finger flick. 'You look as though you've been coal mining again.'

'My road got bombed. Oh, our house is standing and Dad's all right,' she reassured him, seeing his concerned frown. 'It was further up,' she chattered on, glad of a neutral subject. 'Do you remember Mrs Price? You gave her ten shillings. Her house was hit and her daughter went into labour. Well, Irene might already have been in labour before the explosion. But the shock must have brought the baby shooting out. Poor girl. She's only fifteen. Baby's premature … I pray he survives.' Rosie raised her eyes, finding Conor watching her steadily. 'Mrs Price won't be able to have a go at me any more, not now her daughter's an unmarried mother, too.'

'Had a rough time of it, haven't you?' he said gruffly.

'Didn't bother me,' Rosie said, immediately defiant.

'You wanted to give Hope away.'

'She wasn't Hope then … just *his* baby,' Rosie retorted hoarsely. 'Popeye told you?'

Conor nodded.

'It's true,' Rosie admitted huskily. 'I didn't want any reminder of him. I thought I'd never be able to look at her and not hate her because of him.'

'I told Frank she's mine and the rest's a pack of lies. I'll keep telling him that, and anybody else for that matter, for as long as you want me to.'

Rosie was momentarily speechless with astonishment. 'Why did you do that?'

'Why not? Could've been true, if you'd come for that drink with me. Dates almost work out.'

'Yes...' Rosie murmured, her eyes engulfed by his. 'If it gets out ... what you've said ... will it cause trouble for you with people like...'

'Like?'

'Like Patricia,' Rosie blurted, suddenly feeling possessive. 'Your girlfriend'll be hopping mad if she finds out you've done that, and I can't say I'd blame her.'

Conor smiled; an old smile, the sort he used to give her when he knew he had the upper hand and was pleased about it. 'You're jealous.'

'No, I'm not,' Rosie said, bristling. 'I've always known about your women. You told me, remember, about her and Angie.' She scrambled up at the same time as he got to his feet.

They stood facing one another and Rosie felt suddenly awkward and annoyed without knowing why. 'Sorry ... it's none of my business what you tell any of them, especially your girlfriend.'

'You know she's not my girlfriend. That's why she's not come round. She knows I'll throw her out. I told you I'd finished with her.'

'So you did,' Rosie said brittly. 'But she phones you up and your bed smells of perfume.'

'The sheets need changing.'

'You don't have to explain to me!'

'Yeah, you really believe that, don't you, Rosie?' he taunted. "Course I have to explain to you. Whatever you want I do, because you're what I want. All right, I'll admit I slept with her last week. She phones me up, comes round and sometimes I'm tempted to let her stay.' He closed his eyes. 'I thought there was no chance you'd ever feel for me what I felt for you, so I drink too much and sleep with other women.' He shoved a hand through his hair. 'I'm signed off fit and getting shipped out to France next week and fuck the lot of them here' He drew her closer. 'Trouble is, now you're here with me and I don't want to leave you ... don't want to leave my daughter either.'

'Oh, Conor,' Rosie choked, and flung her arms up about his neck, pressing herself against him and fiercely kissing his cheek.

He crushed her to him, his hands gently caressing. 'Kiss me properly ... please, Rosie.'

Rosie hadn't kissed a man for years and even then she'd received rather than given, and hadn't liked much of it at all. She placed her mouth on his, moving it softly to and fro till she felt his lips tilt into a smile.

'You even kiss like a virgin,' he said, drawing her head back to his when she would have indignantly reared away. 'It's not a complaint, Rosie,' he said gently. 'God knows, it's a compliment, knowing what you've been through. How did you manage to stay so sweet and decent after what he did to you?'

'I wouldn't let somebody like him ruin my life,'

Rosie said. 'Not when I had you waiting for me.'

He swung her up in his arms, nuzzling her cheek with soft wooing kisses. 'You know I love you, don't you?'

'I do now ... and ... I...'

He put a finger on her lips. 'Tell me tomorrow, if you still want to.'

'I will,' she said. 'Over and over again.'

'I don't reckon I've ever made love either ... not really ... not like I want to now with you. My first time, you might have to show me how.'

Rosie cupped his unshaven chin in a hand. 'I might enjoy that, Corporal Flint.'

'Sergeant. I got promoted.'

'Must be a quick learner, then. Are you?'

'Nope ... could take all night...' he said, and closed the door with his foot on the way up the stairs.

CHAPTER THIRTY-ONE

'Come back to bed.'

Rosie was standing by the window in her petticoat, peering out. 'Somebody's knocking on the door,' she said.

'Forget it ... it's probably the milkman. Come back to bed.'

Rosie dropped the curtain on the morning sun peeping over the rooftops. She kneeled on the mattress, leaning over Conor to kiss him. His fingers immediately slid to the back of her head, holding her close while she tasted his lips, like a hungry child about to devour an exciting new treat.

'You all right?' he asked, smoothing a curtain of silky fair hair back from her face.

'I will be after we've done it all again so I can make up my mind if I like it,' she said provocatively then squealed when he rolled her onto her back. She wriggled in delight as his sweetly seductive mouth slipped over her lips then travelled on to her throat and earlobes.

'Like that?' he teased.

She nodded, coiling her arms about his neck. A moment later, attuned to the sound, she slipped free and sat up, clutching the eiderdown to her chest.

'Come here, sweetheart ... you're up early,' Rosie said breathlessly. Her daughter was hovering just inside the door, rubbing her eyes. Hope had never seen her undressed with a man before. In fact the only man the child really knew was her granddad.

Conor slid to the opposite side of the mattress and came upright, buttoning up his trousers before turning to the little girl, slipping a vest over his head. 'Have a nice kip in my house, did you?' he asked Hope and came round the bed to pick her up.

She nodded her fair head, giving him a shy half-smile.

'D'you remember my name?'

'Conor.'

'Clever girl,' he praised and ruffled her hair. 'Hungry are you? Find some bread and jam, shall we, and a nice cup of tea?'

Hope's reply to an offer of breakfast was drowned out by some hollering from outside.

Rosie's eyes widened on Conor. 'That's your mum's voice,' she hissed in a horrified whisper.

Conor elevated his eyebrows but seemed no more than mildly surprised, or put out, by his mother visiting him at the crack of dawn. He went to the sash window and shoved it up, one-handed, still holding Hope.

'What in Gawd's name's that you've got there?' Hilda yelled up at her son, jerking her wizened face at the child.

'Her name's Hope,' Rosie said, coming to stand at Conor's side, annoyed at the way the woman had referred to her precious daughter. Apart from that she felt she should support him against the harridan.

Hilda planted her hands on her bony hips, mouth pursed. 'Hah ... so it's you then is it?' she spat. 'Turned out to be better in bed than the other one, did yer, or is she up there 'n' all?' Hilda barked a nasty laugh. 'Just getting to know him, Mrs Flint...' she mimicked what Rosie had told her. 'Didn't take yer long to know him pretty damned well, did it? Well you can take yerself and yer kid off now he's done with yer. I've got im-portant things to talk about with me son...'

'What d'you want Mum?' Conor cut across Hilda's rant.

'I want my Steven back, that's what I want. You go 'n' fetch him from Surrey 'fore he finishes his training and gets shipped out.' She pointed at the child. 'And don't want no bastards in the family. The kid's father can have the cost of shelling out on that one.'

'Yeah, he can and I'll give my daughter whatever she wants.' Conor started pulling down the
sash. 'Now go home. I'm not getting Steven, he's
made his choice.'

'Just you wait a fuckin' minute!' Hilda roared.
'I ain't finished...'

'I'm busy.'

'Yeah, can see that,' Hilda snorted, but the rest
of her coarse observation was cut off as the sash
was rammed home and the curtain fell in place.

'You meant what you said then?' Rosie was
gazing up at him, eyes glowing. She'd not really
believed until now that he'd announce to his kith
and kin that he was Hope's father.

'I meant it.' He glanced at the beautiful child in
his arms with a rueful smile. 'She'll need her dad
when the boys start coming round after her.'

Rosie nodded, waiting, hoping he'd ask her immediately before a proposal burst from her
instead. She knew now how Hazel had felt being
in love and yearning to be married.

A stone hit the window, making Conor curse
beneath his breath. Putting Hope down, he used
both hands on the sash this time to shove it up.

'Me mum's just seen Hilda in the corner shop;
she told her you've got a girl in there and a kid.
What the fuck's going on?' Ethel Ford had
nipped out to get a paper and a pint of milk a few
minutes ago and met Hilda in Wainwrights. As
soon as she'd got the gist of what the woman was
saying Ethel had hurried back home to drag her
daughter out of bed and recount that Conor had
knocked a girl up years back and had now moved

her and her kid into his house. Pat had needed no second telling and had raced round to confront them in her dressing gown.

'Nothing's going on that you need to know about,' Conor said. 'Clear off.'

'You had *me* in that bed not so long ago,' Pat screeched. 'And what's this about a kid? Your old girl gone senile, or something?'

'No ... she's not,' Rosie said, whipping into view next to Conor. 'She's a pain in the backside, without a doubt, but his mum's not mad.'

'Might've known it was you answering his 'phone last night,' Pat stormed. 'Ain't he turfed you out yet? Come down 'ere, then, you cow; I'll soon send you packing.'

Conor tried to pull Rosie away as though to shield her from any more unpleasantness. But she whipped free of him and leaned on the windowsill staring down into the sulky brunette's face. Without make-up Pat looked washed out. 'We're getting married, so it's you slinging your hook. Don't come back here, or you'll be sorry.' She pulled the sash down and turned, pink-checked, to Conor.

'Sorry ... overdid it, didn't I? D'you think she'll take any notice of me?'

'I wouldn't mess with you...' he said, laughing.

Rosie went to sit on the edge of the bed, feeling silly for having jumped the gun when he'd not asked her to be his wife.

Conor put Hope on the mattress beside Rosie then crouched down in front of her.

'So ... did *you* mean it?'

'What?'

'Are we getting married?'

'You haven't asked me,' Rosie replied, the colour in her cheeks deepening.

'Only 'cos I haven't got you a ring yet, or asked your father for his permission.' He sat down beside her. 'You deserve everything done properly, Rosie,' he said, cupping her blushing face in a hand.

'Just say it,' Rosie pleaded, drawing her daughter to her side with an arm about her. Barely had the age-old question passed his lips when Rosie breathed, 'Yes ... oh, yes, please.' She pulled him down on to the bed, giggling, and Hope, wanting to join in the game, jumped on top of them.

'Rosie. Hold up!'

The raucous shout stopped Rosie in her tracks. She swung about and saw Peg Price waving and hurrying in her direction. Rosie handed her door key to her new fiancé, saying, 'I'd better have a word with her. I want to find out how Irene and the baby are, in any case. Would you take Hope inside? Dad'll be frantic with worry about us.' She gave Conor a grateful smile as he led her daughter towards her front door.

Rosie had just lifted Hope off the back seat of the Humber when Peg, who'd been salvaging in the wreckage of her home, called to her. Rosie squared her shoulders wondering whether she was about to get a mouthful, or a pat on the back.

'I'm so sorry about you getting bombed out, Mrs Price.' Rosie hoped the less explosive subject of her neighbour's property being blown to bits might be a good place to start this conversation. She could see the woman had been crying: her eyes were bloodshot and her lashes wet.

386

'Least of me troubles … just glad we're all still breathing,' Peg croaked. She wiped her sooty palms on her pinafore. 'Poor May has lost her eye. Popped in to see her in the hospital last night. She won't be out for a good while, the poor cow. Not that she's got a home to go to now.'

Rosie gave a sorrowful sigh, although she'd guessed that May Reed had been badly injured when she'd patched her up. 'Have you been re-housed yet?' Rosie asked, glancing past at the Prices' obliterated home.

'Moved in with Dick's sister round the corner. She said we can stop with her till the council find us something.' Peg pushed straggly wisps of hair into the scarf knotted on top of her head, giving Rosie humble peeps all the while. Suddenly she lunged at the younger woman's hands, clasping them to her bony chest. 'Gotta thank you for saving my Irene. You was terribly brave going in there when it could've all collapsed around yer ears.' Peg fiddled again with her headscarf. 'Irene said that she confided in you about the baby and you told her months ago to speak up about it.' Peg shook her head. 'Silly gel! Wish she had told us so me 'n' Dick could have…' Peg sniffed, blinked in consideration. 'Don't know what we would have done; anyhow too late to worry over it, just got to make the best of things. Better to be angry than grievin'.'

Rosie smiled agreement to Peg's philosophy, glad the woman seemed to have mellowed. 'The baby's doing all right?' she asked, hoping to hear that he was. 'And Irene too?'

'Irene's right as rain, as for the baby … tiny little

scrap, he is, but the doctor said he's a fighter. Ain't quite four pounds in weight but they're planning on letting him and Irene come home in a couple of weeks. Dunno how we'll all cope, or what we're gonna say to people...' Her voice wobbled.

Rosie gave Peg's hands a comforting squeeze before gently removing herself from the woman's grip. 'You'll all just get on with it. And you'll tell the gossips to mind their own business, same as we had to,' Rosie said simply.

'I know I deserved that,' Peg mumbled. She blew her nose and bucked herself up. 'Dick won't leave the little lad alone. The matron had to throw him out of the maternity ward last night for outstaying his welcome.' She almost smiled then cleared her throat instead. 'Sorry for being a spiteful cow to you. Even if you hadn't done so much for my Irene I should still be ashamed of meself, and I am.' On impulse, Peg shook Rosie by the hand. 'I know yer dad's proud of you and I ain't surprised. Lucky man, he is; so's that nice Mr Flint I just seen go in yer house with little Hope.' Peg sounded more like her old self. She managed a wink before her shoulders slumped and she returned to rummage with her husband in the charred wreckage of their home

'Don't cry, Dad, it's all turned out right in the end.'

'I know...' John blubbed, mopping his face with his hanky. 'But I've caused you more problems than I ever should've and me little granddaughter too. I'm so ashamed of meself. And I'm so sorry, Rosie, for everything. Don't hate me...'

'Of course I don't hate you, Dad.' Rosie put her arms around her father. 'Can't say I've not felt like throttling you at times ... but I know I've done my fair share of stupid things in my time to make you mad. Forgive and forget now, eh?'

John looked bleakly at the man standing a diplomatic distance away so father and daughter could have a private reunion.

'Come on, cheer up, it's a day for celebrations,' Rosie patted her father's back. 'Hope's safe and...' Rosie's words tailed off. She glanced at Conor as he squatted down to stack bricks with Hope on the parlour floor. She'd let him bring up the subject of their wedding, as he'd said he wanted to formally approach her father.

When she'd entered the house following her talk with Peg, Conor had been in the process of helping her father up the cellar steps so they could make themselves comfortable in the parlour. It seemed that Conor had only briefly answered John's questions about Hope's ordeal and Rosie was thankful for that. Her father seemed too emotional to be told more than the bare bones at the moment.

'You'd better make an honest woman of my daughter after keeping her out all night,' John suddenly burst out, only half-joking. He stuffed his hanky in his pocket and puffed out his chest as he limped to confront Conor in his role as protective father.

Conor came slowly upright, his amusement subdued. 'Take it you'll not object then if I ask her to marry me, Mr Gardiner?'

'Well ... had high hopes for her, of course.

Accountant ... solicitor ... with her looks she could have her pick of eligible fellows.'

'Dad!' Rosie exclaimed, shaking her head at Conor in apology.

'I'll do my best to be worthy of her, Mr Gardiner,' Conor solemnly promised.

'Make sure you do,' was all John said but he gave his daughter a subtle smile as he limped to the settee and sank down. 'Come and tell grand-dad what you've been up to.' He held out his hands to his granddaughter.

'Don't question her, Dad,' Rosie said quickly. 'I want her to forget about it.'

'I know,' John answered gruffly. 'Just gonna talk about her little friend, that's all.'

Rosie pulled Conor by the hand into the kitchen, then rested back against the sink.

'Sorry about him, he can be so rude.'

Conor smiled. 'I reckon my mum can trump him,' was all he said before putting a hand either side of her and leaning close. 'I want us to get married before I go back overseas. Then you can call yourself Mrs Flint, can't you, Mrs Deane.'

'That'll be nice...' Rosie murmured against his mouth.

'Is that Peg come knocking, d'you think?' John called out following a bang on the door. 'Conor said you was talking to her outside. That old cow better not turn up here with a begging bowl, the trouble she's tried to stir us up.'

'She's got bad luck of her own to keep her occupied now, Dad, so a little sympathy wouldn't go amiss,' Rosie called over Conor's shoulder.

'I'll get the door,' Conor offered.

The sound of children's chatter brought Rosie out of the kitchen just as Hope trotted to greet Vicky who'd arrived with her mum.

'Please let me stay just long enough to say what I have to. That's all I want,' Gertie burst out. She put a hand to her chest, breathing heavily. Her eyes were fixed on Hope, devouring the child. 'I'm so glad she's all right. I've been beside meself with worry. Not had a wink of sleep; nor's Rufus...' She started to cry, wiping her eyes with a hanky.

'You 'n' me both,' John snapped belligerently. He'd guessed he was talking to Midge's sister and struggled to his feet to have a dingdong.

Rosie put a restraining hand on her father's shoulder. 'Gertie's not to blame for any of this trouble. She was doing me a favour babysitting because you were laid up after that run-in you had.'

The pointed remark reminded John that he'd started the ball rolling on this particular calamity many years back when he'd got involved with his own, and Frank Purves', illegal enterprises. Chastened, he sat down.

'We got Hope back yesterday and she's fine, Gertie.' When her comforting words seemed to have no calming effect on her friend Rosie added, 'I know you and your husband had nothing to do with it, Gertie. It's just a case of bad luck and bad company.'

'Does your husband know where Midge is?' Conor asked bluntly.

Gertie nodded, looking apprehensive as the handsome stranger moved closer as though to interrogate her.

'It's all right, Gertie, this is Conor ... we're getting married.' Rosie slipped her hand through her fiancé's arm while making proper introductions, between the two. 'Conor found Hope and brought her back last night. He's dealt with Frank Purves before so knows what sort of devil he is.'

Gertie's moist eyes darted back to Conor. 'I expect you already know what happened to my brother then, if you were there.'

'He drove off in Frank's Citroen; that's the last I saw of Midge.'

'You don't know he's dead then?' Gertie whispered so the laughing children wouldn't hear what was being said.

'Dead?' John chirruped, looking joyfully shocked. 'Well, that's a turn up.'

Conor frowned, wondering if Midge's sister was lying to throw him off the scent. From the moment he'd set fire to the warehouse he had known that before he returned overseas he'd need to take steps to protect Rosie and her family from Popeye's malice. But he didn't regret what he'd done. Frank Purves wasn't simply a racketeer, he was an evil monster who would have taken a little girl from the people who loved her while claiming the moral high ground. But without his little empire, housed in that warehouse, Popeye was impotent. Eventually though he'd rebuild his stock. Conor knew the man would have cash stashed somewhere to start him off ducking and diving again.

'Rufus went out looking for Popeye and Midge again this morning,' Gertie explained, shoving her hanky up her sleeve. 'He banged on Frank's door and a neighbour came out and told him Popeye wouldn't ever be coming back. The police had been round, the fellow said, and asked questions because Frank Purves' car had gone into the river by Wapping with two men inside.'

Rosie and Conor exchanged a look as they guessed the identity of those in the car, and why they'd been in the vicinity. Popeye and Midge had driven to Wapping because they'd been on their way to get even and snatch Hope back.

'Me 'n' Rufus was worried that little Hope might have been in the car as well but the police didn't know about it.' Gertie started to weep again. 'That's why I had to come round and find out if she was all right. Been torturing us, it has.' Gertie pulled her hanky back out to scrub at her eyes. 'They've just recovered one body so far ... it was a man of about sixty, so it wasn't Midge, must've been Popeye.'

'Good riddance to bad rubbish,' John piped up, still sounding cheery.

'Sorry to come 'n' bother you like this, but needed to put my mind at rest.' Gertie took a deep breath and with a final wipe of her eyes, picked up her daughter. Vicky began to wriggle and squeal to get down so she could continue playing.

Gertie knew guilt played a part in her distress. She couldn't blame it all on Rufus, and earlier he'd told her so in no uncertain terms. Her husband might have got embroiled again with Midge and Popeye, but once she'd got her hands on the fake ration books, and the extra money they brought in for her, she hadn't wanted Rufus to give up working for a counterfeiter.

'Let's meet up again in a few weeks, when this has blown over and we feel calmer.' Rosie followed Gertie into the hallway, wanting to let her friend know that she bore no grudges. 'I'll be a married woman by then,' she added, feeling quite excited.

Gertie gave Rosie a spontaneous hug that was fully returned. 'I'm pleased for you, Rosie. He's a good looker and I can tell he makes you happy. 'S'pect you're wondering where I got your address from. Rufus knew where John Gardiner lived. He knows of your dad in a roundabout way ... through Popeye.'

Rosie grimaced understanding; Gertie had discovered her father had been a criminal too, in his time.

'Men!' Gertie snorted. 'They're a pain in the backside.'

'I can't say that I'm sorry about what's happened to Frank Purves or your brother without being a hypocrite. I expect Popeye knew that Conor lives in Wapping and he and Midge were coming after him for Hope.'

'I'm not sorry they're gone either,' Gertie returned hoarsely. 'But for me mum 'n' dad's sake I expect I'll put up a pretence when we come to bury Michael. He was never no good and I'm relieved he went like this rather than breaking me parents' hearts by swinging on a gib.'

Back in the parlour, John was gazing at his future son-in-law's broad back as Conor stared out of the window into the autumn afternoon. 'If that were any of your doing, you've got my eternal thanks, son.' John kept his voice low and his eye on the door for his daughter's return.

'Nothing to do with me.' Conor pivoted about, hands in pockets and assessed his future father-in-law. 'Popeye and Midge were alive last time I saw 'em.'

John shrugged. 'Nevertheless you brought back me granddaughter and for that alone you've got me deepest respect.'

'I'd like to be able to return you that sentiment, at some time John,' Conor said.

CHAPTER THIRTY-TWO

'I'm going to carry on working at the LAAS. I've put my notice in but I don't need to quit now so I'll withdraw it. As soon as Dad's fit to mind Hope, I'll start my shifts again.'

'Keep you out of trouble, I suppose, won't it,' Conor said. 'But you stay safe and no more tunnelling underground.'

'Just want this damned war over with,' Rosie sighed, laying her head on his shoulder. 'When you're posted, you'd better write to me every day, you know.'

'I will.'

Rosie's head was crammed with ideas about what life together might bring them but first a victory was needed to allow her to realise her dreams. The delay was frustrating yet she still felt happier than she could ever recall being in her twenty-two years. They'd left Hope with her granddad for half an hour and gone out for a short drive to get some privacy before Conor returned home to Wapping. He had parked in a quiet turning so they could chat about the future while blackbirds welcomed the twilight with a haunting evensong.

'I know I said last night that I didn't want to know how you got Hope back from Midge and Frank Purves, but please tell me you didn't...'

'I didn't...' Conor answered. 'Not to say I wouldn't have, if I'd needed to.'

Rosie snuggled against him. 'I'm glad, for your sake, not theirs. Wouldn't want you in court over those two wrong 'uns. Perhaps it was just an accident. Anyhow, they deserved what was coming to them. Poor Gertie; disaster seems to follow her around.'

The air-raid siren made Rosie jerk upright, wailing, 'No, not now!'

Conor had already turned the ignition and put the car in gear. The darkening horizon was streaked with orange fire from the tails of a dozen or more V1 rockets speeding in their direction.

They were home in a few minutes and Conor helped John safely into the cellar while Rosie hurried behind with a sleepy Hope in her arms. A moment later an explosion made them duck.

'That was close,' Conor muttered.

'Lightning don't strike twice in two days. Jerry hit here yesterday. Give us a break will yer?' John shouted at the ceiling then gave a nervous laugh.

Within a short while of them making themselves comfortable on the chairs and mattresses, ambulance and fire-engine bells were audible.

Suddenly Rosie groaned as the noise reminded her where she should be. With all the recent drama she'd completely overlooked the fact that she was an ambulance auxiliary who should have been on shift at Station 97. 'I forgot to go to work. And I didn't ring in either with an excuse. I hope they managed to cover for me.'

'Well, you had a bleedin' good excuse to miss yer shift, didn't you, seeing as your daughter was kidnapped,' John retorted a second before the wall exploded.

Rosie instinctively grabbed her daughter and spun away from the flying shrapnel, curving her body protectively about Hope. She felt her back being peppered with debris and cowered close to the ground. The impact of the rocks stung but she knew she'd sustained no more than cuts and bruises. Hope was screaming but a quick examination reassured Rosie that her daughter was unharmed, just terrified. She put the child down by the cellar steps away from the worst of it then scrambled back through the choking dust filling the cellar, feeling her way. Her father was groaning on the mattress.

'That's not done me legs no good,' he moaned, sounding dazed, while heaving plaster off his shins.

'Conor?' Rosie tried to rub the grit from her eyes but made the smarting worse. She saw where he was then. A huge slab of bricks and mortar had detached in one chunk, locking him, crouching, in a corner. She weaved her hand through a gap till she could touch him, her fingers racing to and fro till they found one of his hands to squeeze. 'Can you hear me? Are you all right?'

'Think so.' His warm fingers stroked her palm. 'Get yourself and Hope out of here, Rosie. Get help for me and John.'

'I'm not leaving you 'n' Dad...' she choked.

'You are! Get out now!' He coughed. 'We might take another hit. Get out of here, damn you! You rescue other people's kids ... now save your own.'

Rosie knew he wanted to antagonise her to spur her into action because his concern was for her rather than himself. But his spirit and the strength of his voice gave Rosie hope that he wasn't too badly hurt. Filtering through her shock was the knowledge that Conor was right. Hope was her first priority and always would be. And he'd applaud her view. *It's as it should be between a mother and her kids*, he'd said when she'd admitted she'd prostitute herself to keep her daughter safe.

Rosie became aware of Hope tugging on her skirt and glanced down at a small dirty face smudged with tears. 'Come on, poppet,' Rosie croaked, scooping her up.

'I'll be back soon, Dad,' she reassured her father before quickly making for the cellar steps.

Outside Rosie could see that at least three houses were ablaze on their side of the road. The bomb that had wrecked their cellar seemed to have exploded in the house next door. It had been partially obliterated during the Blitz and had stood empty ever since.

Further along the street Rosie spotted the fireman who'd attended the scene yesterday during Irene's rescue, unwinding a fire hose. She jogged clumsily towards him, panting in anguish because she couldn't move faster, weighted down with Hope. Her daughter was still howling, frightened by the commotion. Rosie murmured soothingly to her, sensing her own distress was upsetting the child.

'Mrs Deane, isn't it?' The fireman tipped up the brim of his helmet and looked at Rosie as she came to a breathless halt by his side. The flames he was dousing were putting an orange sheen on his perspiring profile. 'Off duty then? What's up?' He'd blinked sweat from his eyes and read her agitation.

'My family are trapped just along the road.' Rosie retreated from the searing heat of the inferno, pointing back the way she'd come

'What happened to you?' Hazel had just jumped from the Studebaker that had screeched to a halt at the kerb and was racing across the pavement. 'Knew something was up when you didn't turn up for work. Then a call for Shoreditch came in.'

'We've been hit, this time, Hazel.' Rosie tasted the tears, salty in her mouth, although she'd not realised she was crying. 'Our cellar wall's been blown in and my dad and my fiancé are still down there. Please help me get them out.'

'Badly injured?' Tom barked. He'd sprinted after Hazel and heard what had been said.

'Don't think so, hope not,' Rosie rattled off. 'But Conor's trapped behind a block of masonry. Please hurry ... if the fires spread that way...' Rosie was unable to voice her horrific fears, or block from her mind the people in the church hall at Stepney who'd burned to death.

'Let's go then,' the fireman commanded and

immediately handed his hose to a colleague. He pelted after Rosie who, trusting them to follow, had set off.

Hazel put on a sprint and caught up with Rosie. She eyed Hope while trotting at Rosie's side. 'Dead ringer for you, she is,' she puffed.

'My daughter,' Rosie said and even her distracted state couldn't erase the pride from her voice.

Lou Rawlings was outside her house gawping at the devastation all around. 'First Peg and May. Now you. Be my place next, know it will,' the woman said morosely.

'Mind Hope for me, will you, Mrs Rawlings?' Rosie gasped, handing her daughter over.

Lou willingly obliged. It was already going round the neighbourhood that the Gardiner girl was a heroine in the LAAS. She'd saved Peg's daughter's life, and Irene's baby, that nobody had known a thing about. And if people asked about it in the wrong way Peg gave them a choice mouthful.

Rosie raced to her door, blocking the tormenting thoughts of little Herbie from her mind. He'd been trapped and had seemed to have minor injuries ... but they'd killed him all the same.

She vaulted over debris in the hallway and led the team down into the cellar. Obliquely she was aware of the all clear sounding and swore aloud at the irony of it.

'I reckon you must be Mr Gardiner. I'm Hazel come to fix you up,' Hazel said, sitting beside the grizzled man on the mattress. 'Let's have a gander then. Blimey! Couple of stitches needed in that.' Hazel opened her medical bag and drew out lint to dab at John's torn shin.

'Same bleedin' leg as last time,' he grumbled.

'Best way; at least you've got one good 'un then,' Hazel ribbed him.

Rosie yanked the fireman by the elbow over to where Conor was trapped in the corner and Tom followed.

'All right mate?' the fireman said genially, bending and assessing the boulder from all angles.

'I will be once you move this fucking thing,' Conor replied succinctly.

Tom turned to Rosie, grinning. 'He's all right then...'

Between them the three men manoeuvred and shoved with much groaning and growling till the huge slab of masonry was tipped over. It fell back with an almighty thud that sent a cloud of particles into the dusty air. The moment Conor was free Rosie rushed at him, hugging him so violently and tenaciously that he had to lift her with him to stand up. He kissed her gently on the forehead and sat down on the filthy mattress with her beside John.

Conor delved inside his crumpled jacket for a packet of cigarettes while Rosie ran her hands over him checking for injuries. She dabbed dirt off the bloody cut on his cheek with her hanky. 'That might leave a scar,' she said but with relief in her voice that the damage didn't seem to be any worse than that.

'Got a fag mate?' Conor asked Tom, throwing the badly mangled pack of Weights onto the bed.

Tom handed his cigarettes round and they all

took one, cleaning him out.

'I remember you from the other night. Hazel, isn't it? Remember me, do you, Hazel?' The fireman asked, puffing away on his cigarette.

Hazel cocked her head eyeing him through the smoke drifting between them while continuing to patch John up. 'Yeah, I remember you. And who might you be? Gonna introduce yourself then?'

'Phil Redwood, and pleased to meet you again, Hazel.'

Rosie and Conor exchanged a humorous look.

'Well, I feel like a gooseberry,' Tom said in a highly camp voice.

Everyone guffawed, even John, and Rosie felt tears of relief on her lashes. She turned to Conor, kissing him on the cheek, tasting the copper of his blood. 'You should go to hospital for a check-over,' she said as he winced when she cuddled him.

He shook his head. 'No need.'

'Right, done here, but not out there.' Phil pointed to the street sucking deeply on his cigarette. He ground out the stub and strode towards the stairs.

'Same goes for me...' Tom followed the fireman.

Hazel stood up. 'You'll be up 'n' running again in no time, Mr Gardiner.'

'Many casualties?' Rosie asked.

'Not sure yet ... won't know till the fires are under control.' Hazel gazed at her colleague enquiringly then set off after the men with a parting wave.

'Another pair of hands would be useful, I expect,' Rosie called. She looked at Conor and he took the cigarette from his mouth and stroked her face. It was all the approval she needed; she knew he'd care for her father and get him to safety.

'Lou Rawlings is minding Hope. Will you come and fetch her and look after her till I come home?'

He nodded, standing up and for a moment Rosie's throat closed with the love she felt for him. She briefly touched together their lips, conscious of her father watching them, but she murmured the words, closing her eyes as another fingertip caress rewarded her.

Then she was running up the cellar stairs calling, 'Wait for me Hazel ... I'm coming too.'

EPILOGUE

8th May 1945

'Stella and Thora...' Rosie shouted a toast, lifting her gin and orange.

Glasses were raised and swigged from as the ambulance auxiliaries in the pub remembered their colleagues who'd perished on duty.

'Won't ever forget those two,' Rosie said.

'Won't ever forget anybody I met here, even if I reach a hundred,' Hazel slurred, leaning an elbow on the bar and looking dreamy. 'But ... new life opening up at last, and won't be sorry about that.' She proudly polished her engagement ring with a thumb. 'Meeting Phil later in Trafalgar Square and we're gonna dance till dawn then set off to Essex to see Mum about the wedding arrangements.'

'Conor's home today,' Rosie said, a gleam of excitement in her eyes. 'Hope he gets back early so we can go out and celebrate for a couple of hours.'

'You grabbed yourself a hunk there, Mrs Flint. So why did you call yourself Mrs Deane?' she sounded mystified.

'Deane's my mum's maiden name,' Rosie answered quite truthfully.

'I'd've called myself Mrs Flint from the off,' Hazel said. 'You'd have cornered him sooner that way.' Her heavy black lashes drooped in a tipsy wink. 'Can tell he thinks the sun rises in you.'

All of Rosie's colleagues now knew about Hope, believing her daughter to be Conor's. They also thought that following a rocky start they had fallen in love all over again and got married. Apart from the few people who were aware that Lenny Purves had raped her, nobody was any the wiser. Rosie realised that at some time there would be the dilemma of whether Hope should know who'd fathered her but time enough when her daughter was older to cross that bridge...

Jim was standing with his wife and as he saluted her Rosie raised her glass, remembering his kindness on her first ever call-out when the row of corpses had nauseated her. Then her gaze travelled on over her boisterous colleagues: Tom, Clarice and Janet ... just a few of the ambulance auxiliaries who today, on the glorious 8th May,

404

were finally getting the sack as were she and Hazel and Jim.

Peace had come, at a terrible price for some families, but nobody wanted to reflect on that just yet. In a week or two when the euphoria had died down Rosie knew that her family, in common with everybody else, must turn their thoughts to the new problems that faced them as they pieced their lives back together. But nothing would fit as it had, or ever be the same.

'Top up anybody?' Tom called, weaving drunkenly through the revellers with a bottle of gin he'd purloined from behind the bar. The landlord simply grinned, and wagged a finger on realising what he'd done.

'Not for me; off home now. Got to get my husband's tea,' Rosie joked, to much cat-calling.

'That's what it's called now, is it?' Tom chuckled. 'Mind you ... I'd do anything for him. Conor's a sweetheart.'

Rosie hugged all her colleagues, giving Hazel a kiss as well as an embrace. Amidst the good lucks and good wishes were promises to write and telephone, and Rosie stuffed into her pockets all the slips of paper with addresses on that were thrust at her. And she knew she would keep in touch. Like Hazel she'd keep close to her heart until the day she died the memories of the colleagues that she'd laughed and cried with and toiled beside, sometimes until her eyes were dry and her bones ached.

Out in the sunshine she dodged, laughing, past a group of rowdy sailors who tried to make her dance a jig with them. Further on up the road she bumped into Mrs Price and Irene.

'I recognise that pram,' Rosie said chirpily, feeling quite merry now the fresh air had hit her, even though she'd only had a couple of gins.

'Reckon you do know it 'n' all, love,' Peg said with a grin. 'Holding up all right though, ain't it?' She gave the handle a tap. 'Made to last these were. Quality.'

Rosie had donated Hope's old Silver Cross to the Prices as her daughter had grown out of it. 'And how's my godson doing?' Rosie had been invited to be the baby's godmother and Irene had also chosen the name Ross as a tribute to the young woman who, in her mind, had saved her life and her son's.

'He's screaming blue murder all night long,' Irene raised her eyebrows in exasperation. But she gave Ross a fond maternal smile.

'Colic ... or teeth,' Rosie said knowledgeably. 'You'd never believe he weighed in at under four pounds.' Rosie stroked the cheek of the chubby child sitting up in his pram.

'Gonna eat me out of house 'n' home in a few years, know he is,' Peg complained with a proud look at the little chap. 'You off home then?'

Rosie nodded. The Gardiners and the Prices were again neighbours. Following the blast that had destroyed their cellar they'd been rehoused round the corner, next door to Dick's sister where the Price family had decided to all live together.

'Best be off,' Peg said. 'Dick wants a party in our house later. I said I'd get some sandwiches made if I can lay me hands on some bread somewhere. You lot coming round? More 'n' welcome, y'know that.'

'Conor's back this evening...' Rosie started to make an excuse before a dig in the ribs stopped her.

'You'll be busy then, but send John 'n' Doris in,' Peg said lewdly, making her daughter tut disapprovingly. 'Come on, bread'll all be sold out.' Irene pulled her mother on, giving Rosie a smile before they continued up the road.

As she set off Rosie spotted somebody else she recognised, on the opposite pavement. She waved and trotted across and for a moment the two women simply gazed at one another. Although they'd said months ago they'd meet up, they never had until now.

'Well, here we are at last...' Rosie said. 'The day we've been waiting for, Gertie.'

'Been a long time coming ... too long...' the older woman sighed, hoisting Vicky onto her hip as the child started to whine.

'Going out to celebrate with your husband tonight?' Rosie asked amiably.

'Yeah ... going to Piccadilly Circus and taking Vicky with us,' Gertie wiped her daughter's nose with a hanky. 'Joey'll probably bring his sweetheart. Talking of getting engaged the two of 'em, and only just turned fifteen.'

'Grow up quickly, don't they?' Rosie said then wished she'd not. The air was thick with the memory of three little boys who'd never age or talk of getting engaged.

'How about you? Your husband back yet?' Gertie asked brightly.

'Due at the station about seven o'clock. Going

home to get myself out of this...' Rosie pulled at her uniform jacket. 'And put on something pretty. Hope he's not delayed, then we'll all be off out, even Dad with his gammy leg.' Rosie chuckled. Her father had recovered well after the explosion in the cellar, but he did like to play on it, especially since Doris had returned from Gravesend, moaning about what it had cost to stay at her daughter-in-law's.

'Wonder what's in store for us now?' Gertie said, gazing at the blue sky and shaking her head. 'One thing's for sure: there's not going to be much work about for a man with a limp and a damaged hand. Popeye was a nasty sort but he provided for Rufus. So did me brother in his rotten way. Odd, but I miss Michael, and I never thought I'd ever say that.'

Rosie put a comforting hand on Gertie's arm, hearing the tears in her suffocated voice. 'Did the funeral upset your parents?'

'Never buried him ... never found him. Just Popeye got recovered and laid to rest. Me husband went to pay his last respects. Rufus said he owed it to him for the work, if nothing else. Only Rufus and Frank's next-door neighbour was there. Never really found out what happened that night other than the police were chasing the car and it turned sharp and disappeared off the jetty into the water.' Gertie gave a sigh. 'Anyhow, you enjoy yourselves later, Rosie. Take care of yourself.'

'And you do the same.' Rosie gave Gertie's arm a pat and set off, feeling a peculiar certainty that she'd not see Gertie again.

She'd lost touch with much of her past, she mused as she walked on, and more of what was familiar would slip away to be replaced with new. Her childhood home, the very street where she'd been raised, was gone. Only a few of the houses remained occupied by resolute sorts like Lou Rawlings who'd cling on until the bitter end when the demolition men moved in.

Rosie threw back her head, letting the sun warm her face. She was ready for a new start with the man who'd taught her to love and trust and desire him in a way she'd never have believed possible. She opened her eyes and blinked. She stopped, her heart drumming beneath her ribs.

He'd stopped too and had dropped the kitbag he was carrying to the pavement.

She realised he'd been watching her walking towards him, and had waited to savour the expression on her face when she spotted him. Rosie smiled joyfully, allowing him his victory then she drew in a breath and ran, one hand on her heavy skirt holding it away from her flying legs. She launched herself at him and was spun round and round in strong arms, her cheek pressed into his rough uniform.

'You're early!' Rosie wailed. 'I was just on my way home to change into something nice and come and meet you at the station.'

'Couldn't wait. Swapped places with another bloke to get home sooner.'

'Bet it cost you,' Rosie said, stroking his unshaven chin.

'Worth it ... just for this.' Conor gave her a slow thorough kiss. 'How's Hope?'

'Excited. She knows Daddy's coming home today.'

'And John?'

'Yeah ... he's just the same.' Rosie smiled, adoring him with her eyes and caressing fingertips. 'You look tired. We don't have to go out and celebrate this evening.'

'I'd sooner stay home but I'm not tired, promise...' Conor smiled his villain's smile, the one that once would have made Rosie blush and feel nervous. Now it quickened her pulse for a very different reason.

'Dad and Doris have been invited next door to a party later so once our daughter's asleep I want you to keep that promise, and lots more besides...'

The publishers hope that this book has given you enjoyable reading. Large Print Books are especially designed to be as easy to see and hold as possible. If you wish a complete list of our books please ask at your local library or write directly to:

Magna Large Print Books
Magna House, Long Preston,
Skipton, North Yorkshire.
BD23 4ND

This Large Print Book for the partially sighted, who cannot read normal print, is published under the auspices of

THE ULVERSCROFT FOUNDATION

The Evolution of
the American Dream

Also by Bob Skandalaris

Rebuilding the American Dream

The Entrepreneur's Game

The Evolution of
the American Dream

How the Promise of Equal Opportunity
Became a Quest for Equal Results

Thank you for your service —

Bob Skandalaris

with Amber Clark

Pembrook

PUBLISHING

AUBURN HILLS, MICHIGAN

Pembrook Publishing, LLC
1030 Doris Road
Auburn Hills, MI 48326
http://www.pembrookpublishing.com

ISBN: 978-0-9771743-3-1

Written by Bob Skandalaris and Amber Clark
Edited by Sue Knopf at Graffolio
Book interior design by Graffolio
Cover design by John Rios

To the pioneers, inventors,

and entrepreneurs

who made America great.

CONTENTS

◇◇◇◇◇◇◇◇◇◇◇◇◇◇◇◇◇◇◇◇◇◇◇◇◇◇◇◇◇◇◇◇◇◇◇◇

INTRODUCTION

"The American Dream" is one of those phrases we use so often that we assume we know what it means. Yet when you ask people specifically what they mean by the American Dream, you get an astonishing array of definitions.

For many, the concept seems to be centered around the idea of America as the land of opportunity. It is about upward mobility and the chance to better oneself financially, but the question is, to what extent? Is the dream to raise oneself to a middle-class standard of living, whatever that may be, and to maintain and improve on it in successive generations? Or is the dream to achieve extraordinary wealth and prosperity, like John D. Rockefeller or Bill Gates? Is it about pleasure—buying as many toys as one can possibly possess and enjoying as many experiences as life has to offer? Or is it about paying off the mortgage and achieving the satisfaction and security of financial independence?

Then there's the question of how easy the American Dream should be to achieve and how many should reasonably be expected to achieve it. Is the true American Dream about pulling oneself up by one's bootstraps, achieving success by merit of long, hard labor and sacrifice? Or is it about striking it rich quickly and easily, whether by mining gold in California, winning a lottery, speculating in the stock market, or even selling illegal drugs? Is it something that can and should be achieved by a large portion of society, or only by a fortunate few?

Central to our notion of the American Dream is *equal opportunity*, but this is a slippery concept in practice. The opportunity of a new life in a new world offered to the first American colonists often came at the price of years of indentured servitude and a 25 percent mortality rate—not exactly the sort of opportunity most Americans would jump at today, not in a society that offers government-funded public education, Social Security, welfare, unemployment benefits, and health insurance. Yet there are those who would argue that even with these benefits and entitlements, they are disenfranchised and do not have truly equal opportunities. To this, some would reply that the American Dream does not mean equal opportunity in the sense that everyone starts off in roughly the same place, but merely that opportunity is open to everyone and is more plentiful here than in any other nation on Earth.

Dig deeper and you'll find that people's definitions of the American Dream go beyond the purely financial, from broad rights such as freedom of speech and religion to lifestyle matters such as owning one's home, going to college, or enjoying a nice retirement. While the latter have a financial component, they also have to do with security, comfort, and achievement. For others, the dream is not only about fortune but about fame as well—becoming a movie star, an Olympic athlete, or the next American Idol. Finally, there are those who would say, in the words of Thomas Jefferson, that the American Dream really comes down to "life, liberty, and the pursuit of happiness."

This last definition is the slipperiest of all, and it lies at the heart of all the others. We want to be happy, and we assume that fame and fortune—or at the very least a good job that provides us with a nice home, several cars, the latest electronic gadgets, and yearly vacations—will make us happy. Yet surprisingly, an accumulating body of evidence shows that they do not. Consider, for a moment, the standard of living for the average American now, at the start of the twenty-first century, compared to the standard of living one hundred years ago. Thanks to rapid advances in modern medicine, we are much healthier and live far longer than previous generations, and the majority of Americans have health care insurance subsidized by their employer. While unemployment is certainly not unheard of, the government works to keep it as low as possible and buffers its impact with extended benefits.

In addition, today's jobs are, on average, far more secure and offer a broad range of benefits that were rare before World War II. Thanks to government regulation and labor-saving devices, we also work fewer hours and have more leisure time than our grandparents and great-grandparents did, and we certainly have more toys and gadgets with which to fill those leisure hours. The percentage of people who own their own homes has increased dramatically, as has the percentage of Americans who have attended high school and college. Most significantly, a vast, federally mandated safety net now exists to help the poor, the disabled, and the elderly. The standard of living enjoyed by the average middle-class American, and even by those living below the poverty line, far exceeds anything previously experienced in world history. Yet various studies show that a growing number of Americans describe themselves as depressed and are pessimistic about their future. America is the wealthiest, most prosperous nation on Earth, yet all of this wealth and prosperity apparently hasn't made us happy.

So where, one may well ask, did the American Dream go wrong, if pursuing it has made us so depressed and unfulfilled? Have we been chasing a false dream all this time, or is the problem that the dream has become corrupted? Just what is the modern American Dream, anyway?

To answer this, we have to go back to the words of historian James Truslow Adams, the man who first coined the phrase "the American Dream" in his book *The Epic of America*. Published in 1931 during the Great Depression, the book was written during a crucial point in American history when frontier self-reliance—the idea that every man was responsible for his own welfare—was starting to give way to the idea that the federal government had a significant role to play in protecting people from the slings and arrows of economic misfortune. This was a dramatic shift from the rather narrow view of the American Dream as the opportunity for upward mobility to a more expansive one that led to the American Dream of excess and entitlement that we have today. But Adams, writing at the tipping point of this shift, had a more moderate view of the American Dream: he defined it as "that dream of a land in which life should be better and richer and fuller for every man, with opportunity for each according to his ability or achievement."[1]

"Better, richer, and fuller" promises improvement, but it doesn't promise unbridled wealth. What's more, while Adams's definition is based on opportunity, he didn't say that the American Dream promised *equal* opportunity, or at least not as that phrase is understood by many Americans today. Rather, he thought there should be opportunity for each *according to his ability or achievement*, which is a much lower standard, and far more realistic. Life is not fair. We do not all start out on the same rung of the economic ladder, even here in what is arguably the most egalitarian nation in the world. Nor is climbing the ladder meant to be easy; it requires daring, perseverance, and hard work.

Our ancestors recognized that achieving the American Dream involved occasional setbacks and inevitable risks. Success is not guaranteed. By contrast, today we believe that as long as we play by the rules and work hard enough to fulfill expectations, we are entitled to economic stability, job security, and never-ending upward mobility. This is a dramatic shift in our expectations and a corruption of what the true American Dream is all about. Moreover, the lifestyles we have adopted to achieve all of this upward mobility—and the demands we have made on our government to provide us with security—aren't making us happy. On the contrary, they are making us stressed out and depressed. So before we engage in massive social reengineering programs and promise yet more entitlements we can't afford, it's worth asking whether these changes will truly produce a better society and greater happiness, or whether we're simply chasing a flawed version of the American Dream that bears little resemblance to what it was originally.

This book is an attempt to trace the changing shape of the American Dream over the course of our nation's history. And changed it has, because we Americans have a propensity to tinker with things, and each successive generation has reinvented the American Dream to suit the wants and needs of the time. In the colonial era, the dream was about the opportunity to own land and build a better life for one's children. By the time of the Revolutionary War, it was about political and religious freedom. In the nineteenth century, it was about upward mobility, living a life of self-reliance on the frontier, or amassing vast fortunes like Cornelius Vanderbilt and Andrew Carnegie did. By the early twentieth century, it was living the good life, with a car in every driveway and a chicken in every pot. Then the Great Depression came, and the American Dream took a sharp swing toward security and ensuring the comforts of a middle-class lifestyle rather than chasing a better one. As prosperity returned after World War II, the dream morphed into a house in the suburbs and a college education for one's children, and then into a vision of a Great Society where government could cure all social ills—supported by massive government spending programs that produced several economic booms and busts.

This was a long way from where the American Dream started. After the political and social turmoil of the 1960s and '70s, Ronald Reagan tried to revive the nineteenth-century American Dream of upward mobility and self-reliance in the 1980s, but it proved an impossible task. The idea that the federal government could manipulate the economy, provide security, and solve all of our problems had taken hold of both the Democratic and Republican parties. By the start of the new millennium, our expectations and appetite for spending, in both the public sphere and our private lives, had mushroomed out of control, and spending continues to increase. Self-indulgence—the American Dream of security and wealth without diligence, hard work, and risk-taking—has now become the dominant vision.

That version of the American Dream, however, cannot last. When the Berlin Wall came down in 1989, the world economy was redefined and capitalism spread worldwide, ushering in a new age of globalization. The old American Dream of upward mobility through diligent effort and self-sacrifice is now the Chinese Dream, the Indian Dream, and the Brazilian Dream. People in these countries and elsewhere are not only taking "our" jobs, but also appropriating the dream itself, and the question is, what will that do to the American Dream for Americans? Will it force us to reinvent and redefine the dream once more, as we have done so often in the past? Or will the American Dream disappear from our shores entirely? Is the entire concept a figment of our imagination, or is there still an authentic, achievable version of the American Dream today?

These are important questions, because the American Dream has been a driving force in the development and success of our nation and a key motivating factor in all that we have achieved, individually and collectively. It's worth preserving, for as Adams argued in *The Epic of America*:

> The American Dream that has lured tens of millions of all nations to our shores in the past century has not been a dream of merely material plenty, though that has doubtless counted heavily. It has been much more than that. It has been a dream of being able to grow to fullest development as man and woman, unhampered by the barriers which had slowly been erected in older civilizations, unrepressed by social orders which had developed for the benefit of classes rather than for the simple human being of any and every class. And that dream has been realized more fully in actual life here than anywhere else, though very imperfectly even among ourselves. It has been a great epic and a great dream. What, now, of the future?[2]

This question is as relevant now as it was when Adams asked it, and is in even greater need of an answer.

1

THE DREAM OF A NEW LIFE
IN THE LAND OF OPPORTUNITY

◇◇◇

The phrase "the American Dream" may not have been coined until the twentieth century, but the American Dream itself has been in existence far longer, arguably from the moment Christopher Columbus set sail for the East Indies by traveling west. It took a while before Columbus realized that what he'd discovered was not a westward trade route to the Orient but an entirely new continent, one that was quickly rumored to be brimming with gold. In mercantilist Europe, gold was, as Columbus himself wrote, "the most precious of all commodities; it constitutes treasure, and he who possesses it has all he needs in this world."[1] Within a year of his first voyage, Columbus returned to the Americas with seventeen ships and twelve hundred men ready to colonize the New World, convert the natives to Christianity, and, he hoped, become rich in the process.

It was a dream that was taken up a little over a century later by a group of British merchants and financial "adventurers"—venture capitalists in today's vocabulary—who formed the Virginia Company for the purpose of establishing a permanent colony in the New World. Jamestown, the first successful colony in what would eventually become the United States, was chartered by King James I, but it was not founded by the British state. Instead, it was founded by a joint-stock corporation, and like all corporations, its primary purpose was to generate a profit for its investors. From the beginning, the accumulation of wealth through hard work, daring, and luck was a cornerstone of the American Dream.

As with most revolutionary new business ventures, colonization proved to have a very steep learning curve; 39 of the men who left England in the Virginia Company's first three ships died at sea. Those who survived the voyage and founded the Jamestown colony discovered that there was no gold or other precious metals at the chosen site, which was located sixty miles up the James River so as to be protected from Spanish assault. The Spanish left the colonists alone, but the mosquitoes from the nearby swamp did not, and malaria, poor sanitation, and general ignorance about how to found a viable colony took their toll. Nine months after the colony's founding in 1607, only 38 of the original 144 men who had set sail from England were still alive.

Undaunted, the Virginia Company sent additional colonists, who were also lured by promises of the ever-elusive gold. But this was a fatal mistake on the company's part, because it attracted people with a get-rich-quick mentality. They were unwilling to do the back-breaking labor, such as farming in virgin soil, necessary to scratch out a settlement in the wilderness, and a significant portion of them died from starvation every winter. No gold having been found, the company's investors searched for an export that could yield a profit, and tried lumber, sand, iron, pitch, tar, and sassafras to no avail. By 1616, the Virginia Company had transported more than seventeen hundred people to Jamestown, at a cost of more than £50,000, but had still failed to generate a return on its invested capital.[2]

Yet after a decade of missteps and mistakes, 1616 proved to be a turning point for the Jamestown colony for two reasons. First, it had discovered a crop that could be grown and shipped to England profitably, namely tobacco. But equally important, it changed the primary incentive it offered to potential colonists. Rather than holding out the promise of gold, the company changed its land policy so that colonists could actually own land rather than just work it for the benefit of the investors. Every man who could afford to pay his own passage was awarded fifty acres and an additional fifty for every relative he brought with him. Those who could not afford their own passage were given the opportunity to work as indentured servants for a set period of time, generally four to seven years, at which point they also were entitled to fifty acres, free and clear.

The opportunity to own land proved to be a powerful incentive—one capable of attracting the hard-working men with knowledge of farming that the company needed. At the best of times, land in Europe was hard to come by, concentrated as it was in the hands of the nobility and the aristocracy. Most peasants worked the land as tenant farmers, renting the land they worked from wealthy landlords and paying heavy taxes on what they managed to produce. In the early seventeenth century, however, the English system of tenant farming was undergoing tremendous upheaval. The landowners had discovered that it was more profitable to use their lands to graze sheep and cattle than to farm it, and as a result were enclosing their estates and dispossessing their tenants, most of whose families had been farming those lands for generations. With the lands enclosed, the former tenants had no place to go and few marketable skills. For most of them, farming for the benefit of the Virginia Company's investors wasn't enough of an inducement to undertake the perilous voyage to the New World, but the chance to own fifty acres of land was. That chance, open to any who were willing, gave birth to the American Dream.

Unlike the pipe dream of gold in the hills, the dream of owning land had staying power—first because land was so abundant in America, and second because in an agrarian society, land equals wealth. Once tobacco farming proved economically viable, Jamestown and other Virginia settlements attracted an ever-growing stream of colonists, all chasing the American Dream of free land and prosperity. In 1618, Virginia farmers produced and exported twenty thousand pounds of tobacco; a decade later, that number had grown to half a million pounds, sold back in England at a tidy profit.[3] That profit, however, came too late for the investors in the Virginia Company, whose American Dream died when an Indian attack on Jamestown sent the company into bankruptcy. The learning curve had proved too steep, and in 1624 King James revoked the company's charter and made Virginia a crown colony.

Life for the colonists wasn't exactly a cakewalk, either. At least a quarter of those who came to Virginia as indentured servants in the early years didn't survive long enough to receive their fifty acres. Those who did faced years of back-breaking toil, first working someone else's land, then their own, before their hard work paid off and their dream was realized. But for those who survived and persevered, profits and financial independence did come, and working one's own land instead of someone else's was deeply satisfying. Moreover, their success fed the American Dream for their friends and relatives back in the Old World, and that dream has exerted a powerful pull ever since.

• • • • •

If the colony at Jamestown planted the seed of the American Dream by proving America to be a fertile land of financial opportunity, then the colonies at Plymouth and Massachusetts Bay are where it flowered into a dream that was somewhat more complex. Unlike the displaced tenant farmers who settled at Jamestown, the Separatist Pilgrims were of a higher social class. They were well-educated and, while generally not wealthy, certainly not impoverished either. So while the people who sailed to Jamestown had often been in desperate financial straits in their native England and had nothing to lose (except their lives) by coming to America, the Pilgrims most certainly did. Materially, their lives would have been more comfortable, or at least more secure, back in England.

The Pilgrims, however, were not concerned with comfort but rather with realizing their utopian vision of a faith-based community, untainted by heretical doctrines or corrupt church leadership. Religious freedom and purity was the core of their dream, although freedom to them did not mean the freedom to simply do as one pleased. After all, these were people who believed in discipline, self-sacrifice, and submission to authority. To the Pilgrims, freedom didn't mean being free *from* authority; it meant having the freedom to choose the authority to whom they submitted. They reserved the right to judge who was fit to lead them and who was not, in both spiritual and secular matters. When it became clear to them that the dream they were envisioning would be impossible to realize in England or even Holland, where they first exiled themselves, the vast, relatively uninhabited shores of America beckoned instead.

This is not to say that the Pilgrims were averse to financial gain. Quite the contrary—they saw economic prosperity as a sign of God's favor. Even the Plymouth Colony's governor, William Bradford, admitted that he came to America partially because in England, for various political and economic reasons, he could not maintain the standard of living to which he was accustomed. But farming in what would come to be called New England was not the path to wealth, for unlike the fertile lands of Virginia, the soil was thin and rocky, and the growing season was short. Thus, the Plymouth Colony came to depend on trade rather than agriculture, and the colonists would commonly write, "in the name of God and profit" at the head of their business ledgers—evidence of their faith in the value of hard work and industriousness.

The Pilgrims wove several additional threads into the American Dream that have become inextricably linked with the premise of upward mobility and financial opportunity. The first new thread was the idea that, instead of putting up with life the way it was, with all of its unfairness, injustice, and corruption, you could start over in

America and build a new life. On the shores of this distant continent, you could create a better world—or at least a better community—for yourself and for your children. Indeed, the role of family was essential to the Pilgrims' version of the American Dream. It was years before the all-male colonists at Jamestown got around to building a church, whereas the Pilgrims came with their families and built not only a church but also a school right from the start. For the Pilgrims, the dream was about more than just fifty free acres. It was about a way of life and about taking action to create the life you wanted.

Second, the Pilgrims deserve credit for introducing the twin concepts of freedom and self-governance to the American Dream. Granted, the House of Burgesses at Jamestown was the first instance of representative government in the colonies, but like the church, it was an afterthought, dictated by the Virginia Company's directors rather than the colonists themselves. The Mayflower Compact, on the other hand, was signed before the Pilgrims ever left their boats. Voting rights, admittedly, were restricted to white males who were members of the church. (In their minds, religious freedom didn't necessarily equate with religious tolerance. There was only one true religion, and it was theirs.) Still, despite the restrictions, the Pilgrims provided the prototype of a community based on freedom of religion and self-governance, and their example inspired other immigrants to follow it.

Finally, the Pilgrims were a shining example of what is often referred to as the Protestant work ethic, a cardinal virtue in American society and a prerequisite to attaining the American Dream. The indentured servants at Jamestown were certainly no strangers to hard work, but the Pilgrims and Puritans who colonized early New England elevated it to an art form, believing that idle hands were the devil's playground. This work ethic, which they applied not only to their religion but to their secular lives as well, contributed in no small part to the success of the colonies in general and of New England in particular.

Yet while the Pilgrims contributed much to the foundation of the American Dream, they usually aren't the first people who spring to mind when thinking about it, probably because their dream ended so badly. Plymouth was annexed by the Massachusetts Bay Colony in 1691, which shortly afterwards degenerated into the horror of the Salem witch trials. The Plymouth Pilgrims have been inextricably linked to the Massachusetts Bay Puritans ever since, and our most enduring impression of the latter is that they were the people who inspired *The Scarlet Letter* and *The Crucible*, not to mention *Sinners in the Hands of an Angry God*. The Puritans of Massachusetts Bay had many of the same goals as the Pilgrims, and you can admire their pluck and perseverance in building a shining city upon a hill, but you probably wouldn't want to live there. In the end, the Pilgrims added much to the American Dream, but their lives were far from perfect, and like most utopian visions, theirs eventually faded.

• • • • •

While the specific American Dream framed by the Pilgrims may not, in the end, have been a lasting success, the larger dream of American colonization most certainly was. Over the next century, the lure of that dream drew a steady stream of immigrants across the Atlantic, and a hundred years after Jamestown and Plymouth were founded, the population of the American colonies had risen to 750,000. In the North, cities such as Boston, New York, and Philadelphia had sprung up and prospered, spurred by the growth of industries such as banking and shipping. In the South, vast tobacco, rice, and indigo plantations had been founded. Those who managed to buy large tracts of land or found successful businesses became wealthy, but for most colonists, their American Dream was economic self-sufficiency. They aspired to a stable living as small farmers, craftsmen, or merchants, and eventually, perhaps, enough income from their farms or businesses to become learned men of leisure or to enter political life.

No one typified this newfound upward mobility better than Benjamin Franklin, whose life story was in many ways the prototype for the American Dream. Born in Boston in 1706, he was the youngest son of Josiah Franklin, an English tradesman who had immigrated to Massachusetts in search of better economic opportunities and greater religious freedom. The family were devout Congregationalists—ideological descendents of the Puritans, who among other things believed that each village church should run its own affairs. While young Benjamin would eventually reject Congregationalism in favor of deism, his Puritan heritage had a profound impact on his character, particularly his work ethic and his perceptions about the role of industry and public service in relation to leading a virtuous life.

From a very early age, Franklin was filled with a seemingly boundless—almost restless—energy that expressed itself in surprisingly focused activity, allowing him to become a highly successful writer, printer, entrepreneur, inventor, statesman, and philanthropist as an adult. After only a few years of formal schooling, he was apprenticed to his brother James, printer and publisher of the *New England Courant*, the first newspaper in Boston. Steeped in the tradition of the professional trades, whereby one rose from unpaid apprentice to wage-earning journeyman to master of one's own shop, it is hardly surprising that Franklin would aspire to own his own press. What *is* surprising is that he would become the modern equivalent of a millionaire in doing so. Generally remembered as one of our most prominent Founding Fathers, he could equally well be described as the father of American entrepreneurship.

Franklin's rise to fame and fortune did not come easily. As a teenager, he quarreled with his brother, who was jealous of his talent, precipitating Franklin's flight to Philadelphia at the age of seventeen. After working for several years as a journeyman printer, he returned to Boston and asked to borrow money from his father to set up his own press. His father refused, thinking the boy not yet ready to manage his own shop. Undaunted, Franklin returned to Philadelphia, where the governor of Pennsylvania offered to back him in business and encouraged him to go to London to buy printing equipment. Franklin eagerly accepted and undertook the voyage to London, but the promised letters of credit from the governor never arrived, and he was stranded overseas for several years before a friend offered to pay his passage back to America. He employed his time in London wisely, however, continuing to work as a journeyman in the rather more sophisticated London print shops, learning techniques that would provide him with competitive advantages in his later career.

Once back in America, Franklin eventually found a business partner and finally opened his own shop. He also bought the failing *Pennsylvania Gazette*, which due in great part to his own incisive and entertaining writing soon became the most popular newspaper in the city. Having gotten his big break, he expanded in several directions, winning a contract to print paper currency, setting up a stationery shop, and launching his enduringly popular *Poor Richard's Almanac*—the venue for many pithy sayings that have been handed down to us through generations. Franklin was also a pioneer of the franchise system, helping several former employees to set up presses in other cities in exchange for a percentage of their profits. He was so industrious and successful that he was able to retire at the age of forty-two, a mere two decades after first going into business for himself. Through talent, hard work, and great perseverance, he had risen from a penniless apprentice to a leading citizen of Philadelphia.

The first half of Franklin's life can easily be stereotyped as that of an energetic and spirited young man, one determined to succeed and rise to wealth and prominence. Indeed, many historians and biographers have characterized him during this phase of his life as opportunistic and even ruthless in business. This latter characterization is perhaps unfair, but there is no doubt, based on Franklin's writings, that he considered the building of wealth to be an important goal— at least to the point of financial independence. His autobiography, as he himself noted, talks little about his life as an inventor or statesman, and was intended primarily to be of use to young people in "exemplifying the effect of prudent and imprudent conduct in the commencement of a life in business."[4] In it he emphasizes the virtues of productivity and economy, as do many of his more memorable sayings from *Poor Richard's Almanac*, such as "A penny saved is a penny earned." Indeed, the final issue of *Poor Richard's Almanac* featured an essay by Franklin entitled "The Way to Wealth," in which he encouraged his fellow citizens to forgo foreign luxury goods and save more of their earnings instead.

In his early years, Franklin, on the whole, practiced what he preached. He made it a priority to pay off his business debts and developed a plan to guide the conduct of his life, exhorting himself to "work very hard at whatever business I undertake in the future. I will not distract myself from my business by any foolish scheme for getting rich quickly. Hard work and patience are the most certain ways to wealth."[5] He considered it a duty to be able to sufficiently provide for oneself and one's family, and through prudent reinvestment of his business profits in real estate, he became one of the richest Americans in the colonial era.

Over the course of Franklin's long life—he died at eighty-four in an era when men were lucky to reach their fifties—his wealth and prominence grew, and his habits and tastes understandably altered. The man who penned the maxim "Early to bed and early to rise, makes a man healthy, and wealthy, and wise" was accused by his colleague and fellow Founding Father John Adams of leading a life of "continual dissipation" when they served together as diplomats in Paris.[6] During his years in France, Franklin developed a fondness for good food and fine wine, and in his old age, the man who in his youth had adopted vegetarianism out of thrift built a house with a dining room capable of accommodating twenty-four people and a wine cellar stocked with almost a thousand bottles. Yet to characterize Franklin as obsessed with the accumulation of wealth is to misunderstand the measure of the man. He espoused the rather radical notion that what a person owned beyond what was necessary to keep him fed, clothed, and sheltered ought to be considered the property of his community, writing in a letter to a friend, "I imagine that what we have above what we can use, is not properly ours, tho' we possess it; and that the rich man who must die, was no more worth what he leaves, than the debtor who must pay."[7]

While some of Franklin's words and actions may seem contradictory, his overall dedication to living a life of virtue and giving back to his country and community can clearly be seen in his actions as an inventor and philanthropist. In his later life, he helped to organize the first volunteer fire-fighting organization in the American colonies, followed by a library, a hospital, and a college that eventually became the University of Pennsylvania. His many inventions were widely adopted, and they improved the quality of life for his fellow citizens. Yet Franklin declined to patent any of them, noting in his autobiography, "Every day we benefit from the inventions of other people throughout history. We should therefore be honored to return the favor by freely and generously giving back an invention of our own once in a while."[8]

Thus, to Franklin, living a life of virtue was about much more than simple accumulation of wealth. While he enjoyed the fruits of his labors, particularly in his later years, his life was one of public service as much as private profit. Upwardly mobile, industrious, and civic-minded, he brought together many of the threads that the Pilgrims had contributed to the American Dream and wove them into a far more appealing pattern that is quintessentially American. While the Pilgrims believed that their salvation was predetermined by God, Franklin rejected this notion. He believed in the ability of individuals to effect change, both in themselves and in their communities, and he worked tirelessly throughout his life to do so. He is one of the few Founding Fathers who came from modest origins, and thus it is Franklin who can most legitimately be called the founding father of the American Dream.

• • • • •

Apart from his accomplishments as an inventor, philanthropist, and entrepreneur, it is Franklin's role in the American Revolution that earned him an indelible place in American history, particularly his involvement in the creation of our nation's two most important documents—the Declaration of Independence and the U.S. Constitution. In many ways, these two documents are the Founding Fathers' blueprints for what eventually became their shared version of the American Dream—a free and independent nation. Yet it took them many years to reach the conclusion that a new nation, conceived in liberty, was actually what they wanted. Indeed, most of them began as loyalists and were merely agitating against England's increasing infringement upon rights and freedoms that they had previously enjoyed. As the British parliament laid an increasingly imperialist hand on the American colonies in the wake of the French and Indian War, the Founding Fathers gradually came to the conclusion that American independence was the only way to ensure autonomy in managing their affairs.

While sparked by what on the surface appears to be a series of largely economic complaints, the American Revolution was nonetheless a principled uprising based on philosophical theories that grew out of the Enlightenment, particularly those pertaining to individual rights and the rule of law. Although in general there was comparatively little formal schooling in the colonies, the Founding Fathers were highly educated and well read on a wide variety of subjects, particularly law, history, and philosophy. Indeed, the Founding Fathers' generation was the most philosophically inclined in American history, and while some of the founders were self-taught, a good number attended prestigious colleges and universities, both in the colonies and in Edinburgh. The latter was the heart of the Scottish Enlightenment, to which the Founding Fathers owed many of the ideas that formed the philosophical basis for the American Revolution as expressed in the Declaration of Independence. To a great extent, these ideas drew on classical liberal concepts such as the rights of the individual, rational self-interest, limited government by the consent of the governed, liberty, and equality.

It was this liberal philosophical tradition that Thomas Jefferson drew on when he drafted, with the editorial assistance of Benjamin Franklin and John Adams, the Declaration of Independence. While many of Jefferson's most cherished passages were stripped from the final document, what emerged as the final version was still a masterful work of prose that proclaimed:

> We hold these truths to be self-evident, that all men are created equal, that they are endowed by their Creator with certain unalienable Rights, that among these are Life, Liberty and the pursuit of Happiness.—That to secure these rights, Governments are instituted among Men, deriving their just powers from the consent of the governed,—That whenever any Form of Government becomes destructive of these ends, it is the Right of the People to alter or to abolish it, and to institute new Government, laying its foundation on such principles and organizing its powers in such form, as to them shall seem most likely to effect their Safety and Happiness. Prudence, indeed, will dictate that Governments long established should not be changed for light and transient causes; and accordingly all experience hath shewn, that mankind are more disposed to suffer, while evils are sufferable, than to right themselves by abolishing the forms to which they are accustomed. But when a long train of abuses and usurpations, pursuing invariably the same Object evinces a design to reduce them under absolute despotism, it is their right, it is their duty, to throw off such Government, and to provide new Guards for their future security.[9]

It was a bold vision, elegantly expressed, particularly the part about all men being created equal and having a right to life, liberty, and the pursuit of happiness. Those words have been echoed by countless others in pursuit of their own versions of the American Dream, yet do they really mean what we think they do? After all, the sentiment about equality was penned by a man who owned slaves, so the phrase as originally intended wasn't as inclusive as we might think. Which begs the question, exactly what did Jefferson and the men who signed the Declaration mean by "all men are created equal" and "the pursuit of happiness"?

In order to answer that question, you have to go back to the philosophical sources that informed the ideas of Jefferson and the other Founding Fathers, particularly the works of John Locke. In *Two Treatises on Government*, Locke argues that primitive people in a state of nature without any government are essentially equal. They vary widely in strength, intelligence, beauty, and other qualities, but there are no formal titles, no aristocracy, and no classes that elevate one person above another. Furthermore, they have certain "natural rights," including the right to life, liberty, and estate, which are not granted to them by any governmental authority but are simply inherent in an individual. Everyone shares a capacity for reason, and this leads them to act in their own rational self-interest.

The problem with a state of nature is that some people don't respect others' natural rights and may attempt to deprive them of their life, liberty, or property. Therefore, people, in their own rational self-interest, will band together and consent to give up some of their liberty in order to form a limited governmental authority, one that will agree to protect their natural rights. All who are possessed of reason are fit to understand and be held accountable to the rule of law, and therefore are equal in their capacity to enter into political and social compacts to govern themselves. If, however, the government oversteps its authority and threatens rather than protects the people's natural rights, then the people have the right to revolt and overthrow that government. Ultimately, it is reason, rather than a parliament or a king, that is the highest authority, and the proper role of government is to secure people's rights to life, liberty, and property.

This, then, is the philosophical framework that Jefferson referenced in defending the right of the Thirteen Colonies to break with England and the context in which the basic equality of people and their unalienable rights to life and liberty should be understood. Whether or not these rights extended to slaves was at the time an open question, one that the concept of natural rights actually brought to the forefront. Indeed, the entire abolitionist movement, which first emerged in the eighteenth century, was based on the Enlightenment critique of slavery as violating natural law and the rights of man. Jefferson, in his original draft of the Declaration, included a passage condemning the slave trade and placing the blame for it squarely on King George III, arguing that he had "waged cruel war against human nature itself" by propagating the slave trade in the first place, and charging that he had suppressed "every legislative attempt to prohibit or to restrain this execrable commerce."[10]

This passage seems hypocritical coming from a man who owned slaves himself, and yet it demonstrates Jefferson's perception, or perhaps rationalization, that slavery was an evil institution that the colonies inherited and which they were largely powerless to do anything about. This reflected a pervasive view among the Founding Fathers from Virginia, who provided much of the intellectual leadership for the American Revolution, that the southern economy was so deeply dependent on slave labor that it would be impossible to forcibly eradicate it and would have to be allowed to die out naturally. In the meantime, recognizing that this passage would cause the southern colonies to reject the Declaration entirely, the Continental Congress deleted it from the text.

The issue of slavery also influenced Jefferson's decision to substitute "life, liberty, and the pursuit of happiness" for Locke's more familiar "life, liberty, and property." Property rights were of central importance to the colonists, and Jefferson's echoing of Locke's phrase certainly implied them. Yet declaring a right to property gave Jefferson and the drafting committee pause—it might easily be interpreted by slave owners as proclaiming their right to own slaves. This interpretation would have been contrary to natural law theory, as Locke himself argued, "Though the earth, and all inferior creatures, be common to all men, yet every man has a property in his own person: this no body has any right to but himself. The labour of his body, and the work of his hands, we may say, are properly his."[11] But in order to avoid controversy and opposition, the drafting committee decided to substitute the phrase "the pursuit of happiness" instead. After all, the issue at hand was the right of the American colonies to sever their ties with Britain and to justify their reasons for doing so to the world at large. Any issue that might threaten the fragile alliance among the colonies was a threat to the Founding Fathers' dream of self-government, and thus the less said about slavery, the better.

The vagueness of the meaning of "the pursuit of happiness," however, presented its own problems. The meaning was drawn from Locke's *An Essay Concerning Human Understanding*, in which he wrote, "The necessity of pursuing true happiness [is] the foundation of liberty. As therefore the highest perfection of intellectual nature lies in a careful and constant pursuit of true and solid happiness; so the care of ourselves, that we mistake not imaginary for real happiness, is the necessary foundation of our liberty."[12] In this context, "the pursuit of happiness" should not be equated with either materialistic wealth or hedonistic pleasure. Rather, it draws on the Greek concept of *eudaimonia*, which is closely linked to *aretê*, the Greek word for "virtue" or "excellence." The pursuit of happiness in this sense is better understood as a full and virtuous life lived in pursuit of excellence, one in which there will undoubtedly be unexpected setbacks, but where there is overall progress toward perfection, although it is ultimately never achieved.

The common man, however, could hardly be expected to be sufficiently familiar with natural law theory and philosophy to understand these rather nuanced meanings of equality, liberty, and the pursuit of happiness. They were vague constructs that left a lot open to interpretation, perhaps deliberately so. The signers of the Declaration clearly intended it to be a reasoned argument for their case for independence, to be read and judged by learned men back in Europe with a shared philosophical background. But it was also intended as propaganda to rally their fellow colonists to their cause—which it did most effectively. The soaring rhetoric of the Declaration helped to spark popular support for the revolution, but at the same time, it opened something of a Pandora's box, for once the words *We hold these truths to be self-evident, that all men are created equal* were out, they could not be put back in again. Everyone who read the Declaration of Independence or even just heard those words chose to interpret them in his or her own way. The will of the American people had been unleashed, and the American Dream with it, to be shaped and twisted by events the Founding Fathers could not have foreseen or even imagined.

2

THE DREAM OF SELF-GOVERNMENT
AND MANIFEST DESTINY

◇◇◇

The great irony of fighting a revolution in pursuit of a shared dream is that often, once the dust settles, the participants discover that the dream they were fighting for wasn't so shared after all. So it was with the American Dream of a new nation conceived in liberty, where all men were created equal. In the disordered years during and directly after the Revolutionary War, the great American experiment of self-government very nearly failed. Under the relatively weak Articles of Confederation, the federal government was unable to levy taxes to fund the war effort and instead had to ask for voluntary donations from the states, which only some of them paid. Nor did the central government have the authority to establish a single, national currency or to regulate trade and commerce among the states, which frequently engaged in destructive price wars. With ultimate sovereignty residing with the states, the central government was simply too weak and ineffective to accomplish much of anything.

The result was chaos. Having accumulated massive war debts and unable to establish a stable economy, the country fell into a depression. General business fell off sharply, farm prices plummeted, and creditors were calling in loans. Taxes that had been levied to pay off public debts from the Revolutionary War had fallen most heavily on the poorest citizens, and the economic situation became so dire that it sparked Shay's Rebellion, an armed uprising of seven hundred farmers, most of them war veterans. After being conscripted into the Continental Army, many veterans had been paid no salary and, upon returning to their farms, were locked up in debtors' prisons and had their homes and other assets confiscated. Anger over crushing debts and taxes led to riots that culminated in Shay's Rebellion, as armed protesters attempted to prevent the seizure of property by forcing the closure of several courts in western Massachusetts.

Thomas Jefferson, who was in Paris at the time, shrugged off the seriousness of the rebellion, noting in a letter to a friend that "God forbid we should ever be twenty years without such a rebellion... The tree of liberty must be refreshed from time to time with the blood of patriots and tyrants."[1] George Washington, on the other hand, was appalled, and the incident convinced him and many of the country's other leading statesmen, including James Madison and Alexander Hamilton, that a stronger central government was necessary. So in 1787, in an act of great statesmanship, the Founding Fathers once again met and drafted the Constitution, hammering out the basic structure of a government with a stronger executive branch and greater centralized authority. While we tend to think of the Founding Fathers as speaking with one voice, during both the Constitutional Convention and the debate over ratification that followed, many opinions emerged, and delicate compromises were forged that glossed over the deep divisions within the group. Among the Founding Fathers themselves, as well as the country at large, there were serious disagreements as to just what sort of government would best secure the realization of the dream set out in the Declaration of Independence.

For James Madison, often considered to be the father of the Constitution, the goal was clear: he wanted to create a governmental structure that would stand the test of time. In the days leading up to the convention, he devoted much effort to studying failed republics, and he concluded that one of the primary reasons for the ultimate failure of government by the people was the destructive power of factions. He addressed this issue in the *Federalist Papers*, defining factions as a majority or minority "who are united and actuated by some common impulse of passion, or of interest, adversed [sic] to the rights of other citizens, or to the permanent and aggregate interests of the community." Madison's primary argument in Federalist No. 10 was that the "instability, injustice, and confusion" created by factions were "the mortal diseases under which popular governments have everywhere perished." While factions could form on the basis of all sorts of issues, he noted that "the most common and durable source of factions has been the various and unequal distribution of property. Those who hold and those who are without property have ever formed distinct interests in society."[2]

Minority factions, Madison argued, were not a serious problem, because the majority could always vote them down. The real threat was what Alexis de Tocqueville would later refer to in his seminal work, *Democracy in America*, as the "tyranny of the majority": in a system where the majority rules, the majority will always vote in favor of its own interests, even if this actively oppresses or infringes on the rights of individuals.[3] This had become a pernicious problem in America under the Articles of Confederation, because the depression had led state legislatures to pass laws invalidating business contracts and flooding the market with paper money to make it easier for debtors to pay off their debts. As James Madison explained in a letter to Thomas Jefferson, "The mutability of the laws of the States is found to be a serious evil. The injustice of them has been so frequent and so flagrant as to alarm the most steadfast friends of Republicanism...A reform, therefore, which does not make provision for private rights must be materially defective."[4]

One cannot suppress factions without denying individual liberty, and therefore the only option, Madison reasoned, was to structure government so as to control its harmful effects. As he and Hamilton argued in Federalist No. 10, the best structure to achieve this was a federal republic with separation of powers and checks and balances—not a confederation, and definitely not a democracy:

> A pure democracy can admit of no cure for the mischiefs of faction. A common passion or interest will, in almost every case, be felt by a majority of the whole; a communication and concert result from the form of government itself; and there is nothing to check the inducements to sacrifice the weaker party or an obnoxious individual. Hence it is that such democracies have ever been spectacles of turbulence and contention; have ever been found incompatible with personal security or the rights of property; and have in general been as short in their lives as they have been violent in their deaths.[5]

Madison and Hamilton were certainly not alone in this view. Almost all of the Founding Fathers saw *direct democracy* as dangerous, and thus, to fulfill the dream of American independence and self-government, they created a *representative democracy*—a *republic*. They feared that if power was vested directly in the people, they would be led astray, so they opted for a system of government in which the will of the people was mediated by elected representatives who were presumably wiser and better educated than the common man. Most of the Founding Fathers believed the nation should be governed by what John Adams referred to as a "republican aristocracy"—men of talent and virtue in whose hands wealth and power would naturally accumulate due to their own merits. Even Jefferson, who had great faith in the common man and objected to any idea of a pseudo-aristocratic ruling class, nevertheless conceded to Adams that there was a "natural aristocracy" of men based on talent and virtue, unlike the artificial aristocracies based on heredity and wealth back in England and Europe.

While this viewpoint sounds elitist to the modern ear, the distinction between a naturally occurring aristocracy and one based on hereditary titles was important to the Founding Fathers and central to their idea of equal opportunity. This concept did not mean, as it is so often interpreted today, that American society should be constructed so that everyone has equivalent opportunities and starts off in the same place. Equal opportunity, as conceived at that point in our nation's history, simply meant that the opportunity to advance existed and was open to all. Differences in natural faculties will lead some people to accumulate greater wealth and property, and it was the role of government to defend the rights of those citizens to maintain the property they had accumulated in the face of a less well-off majority that could vote to take it away from them. Redistribution of wealth would have struck the Founding Fathers as contrary to the core principles of the American Revolution. "All men are created equal" did not imply that people should have equality of condition forced upon them by a government that was supposed to protect their individual rights.

While the principle of representative government was widely accepted by the Founding Fathers, creating a federal government with greater central authority was a source of great disagreement and a subject of controversy long after the Constitution was ratified and George Washington inaugurated as the first president of the United States. Madison argued that a more centralized, national government would help to check the power of factions because regional interest groups that might be large enough to gain a majority in the state legislatures would be unlikely to do so on the national stage. "Extend the sphere, and you take in a greater variety of parties and interests; you make it less probable that a majority of the whole will have a common motive to invade the rights of other citizens; or if such a common motive exists, it will be more difficult for all who feel it to discover their own strength, and to act in unison with each other."[6] A republican government with centralized power, in Madison's view, would be more likely to correctly balance the interests of the nation as a whole while still protecting the rights of minority groups.

From Madison's coauthor Hamilton's perspective, the need for a stronger national government was self-evident. As General Washington's senior aide-de-camp during the Revolutionary War, he had witnessed firsthand Washington's desperate and sometimes vain attempts to convince the states to contribute more money to the war effort. This experience convinced Hamilton that a national defense called for a national government with the right to tax its citizens. A functional national economy similarly required a truly national government, for as he argued in Federalist No. 6, "men are ambitious, vindictive and rapacious,"[7] and without a strong national authority, their pursuit of local interests would inevitably lead the separate states to fall into conflict with each other. In fact, for Hamilton, the proposed constitution did not go far enough. At the Constitutional Convention, he argued in favor of electing the president for life and giving him far greater powers than the rest of the delegates were willing to seriously consider. He also argued, in Federalist No. 84, that there was no need to amend the Constitution by adding a bill of rights, noting that there were plenty of provisions in the Constitution already that protected citizens' liberties.

While the *Federalist Papers* in general proved decisive in swaying public opinion in favor of ratification of the Constitution, on this last point Hamilton misread public sentiment. Antifederalists were horrified by the degree to which power would be concentrated under a central authority, confused about what fell under national versus state jurisdiction, and deeply fearful of the potential for tyranny from a strong executive. During the ratification process it soon became apparent that a bill of rights would be critical to adoption, and as soon as enough states had ratified the Constitution to bring it into effect, the first Congress proposed the series of amendments that became the U.S. Bill of Rights. Among other things, they guaranteed the rights to freedom of speech, assembly, and religion that today we consider so central to our heritage that we take them for granted.

At the time, however, they were cherished rights that were hard-won and jealously guarded—the very essence of what that American Dream of independence was all about.

• • • • •

When George Washington was elected as the country's first president and set about the business of actually governing a new nation, the men who had worked so hard drafting the Constitution found that they had wildly different opinions as to what the document really meant. There wasn't just one shared, coherent vision, but many, and as a result, a philosophical divide opened during Washington's presidency that represented two contrasting versions of the American Dream. One vision was championed by Thomas Jefferson, a states' rights advocate who served as Washington's secretary of state, and the other by Alexander Hamilton, an ardent federalist and Washington's secretary of the treasury. Rather than decisively picking one vision over the other, Americans have always tried to balance the two philosophies, with the result that it has blurred our vision of the American Dream.

Hamilton's version of the American Dream was one in which the United States would develop into an economic empire to rival England, and where talented individuals had the opportunity to rise to prominence and wealth, as he had. Like Franklin, he was one of the few Founding Fathers who came from a modest background, having been born into obscurity in the West Indies. Once Hamilton made his way to New York, however, his brilliance was soon recognized. He subsequently learned the financial trade, became a lawyer, made his fortune, and married into a wealthy family. His role in writing the *Federalist Papers* vaulted him to national prominence, and during the course of Washington's administration, he became the *de facto* leader of the emerging Federalist Party.

Hamilton's financial background gave him a better understanding of economics than most of the Founding Fathers had, making him the natural choice to serve as Washington's secretary of the treasury. Adam

Smith's *Wealth of Nations* had been published in 1776, and while Hamilton wouldn't completely embrace free trade, he understood the implications of Smith's treatise and the revolutionary potential of industrialization and capitalism. More than any of the other Founding Fathers, he anticipated the country's future as a manufacturing powerhouse and did all he could to forward its progress toward that goal. Hamilton wanted to build up the banking, shipping, and various domestic manufacturing industries in order to develop a truly national economy, and as such he favored a strong federal government. As secretary of the treasury, he advocated the establishment of a national bank, federal currency, and the assumption of state debts to restore public credit, even though none of these powers were expressly granted by the Constitution.

Thomas Jefferson's vision of the American Dream, and thus his views on the meaning of the Constitution and the role of the federal government, was distinctly different from Hamilton's. Jefferson had missed the Constitutional Convention entirely because he had been serving as an ambassador to France at the time. As Washington's secretary of state, his primary focus was foreign policy, and he well understood the importance of economic stability for the sake of establishing credibility on the world stage. So he initially supported Hamilton's efforts, but over time both he and Madison began to question, and then outright oppose, Hamilton's economic and political agenda. By the end of Washington's administration, Jefferson had become the acknowledged leader of the Federalist Party's rival, the Democratic-Republican Party.

Jefferson's resistance to Hamilton's agenda was based in great part on his vision of America as an agrarian-based society, one with less emphasis on paving the way for upward mobility for a relatively small group of highly talented and motivated individuals in a capitalist society, and more emphasis on securing economic self-sufficiency for as much of the citizenry as possible. A point often glossed over when studying Jefferson is that his faith in the common man was limited to yeoman farmers. His writings show that he had little faith in factory laborers in cities who worked for their wages rather than tilling their own soil. "When we get piled upon one another in large cities, as in Europe," he wrote to Madison in 1787, "we shall become as corrupt as Europe."[8]

Given this view, it is no surprise that once Jefferson realized that Hamilton's ultimate agenda was not merely to put the nation's economic house in order but to push it toward industrialization, he resisted, and the clash between their conflicting views of the country's future came to a head over the issue of creating a national bank. Hamilton had championed the bank as necessary to serve as a repository for federal funds, a source of loans for the federal government and other banks, and as a tool to regulate the money supply. While the Constitution did not expressly give the federal government the power to create a national bank, he argued, the power to do so was implied by a clause in Article I, which read, "The Congress shall have power...to make all Laws which shall be necessary and proper for carrying into Execution the foregoing Powers, and all other Powers vested by this Constitution in the Government of the United States, or in any Department or Officer thereof."[9]

Jefferson objected to a national bank partially as a matter of personal prejudice. In debt for all of his life, he had the typical debtor's loathing for creditors and the financial elite. "I sincerely believe... that banking establishments are more dangerous than standing armies, and that the principle of spending money to be paid by posterity under the name of funding is but swindling futurity on a large scale,"[10] he once wrote to his friend John Taylor. But Jefferson also considered a national bank to be bad public policy, specifically because Hamilton wanted the national bank to be in private hands rather than owned directly by the government, which Jefferson strongly opposed.

> [The] Bank of the United States... is one of the most deadly hostility existing, against the principles and form of our Constitution... An institution like this, penetrating by its

branches every part of the Union, acting by command and in phalanx, may, in a critical moment, upset the government. I deem no government safe which is under the vassalage of any self-constituted authorities, or any other authority than that of the nation, or its regular functionaries. What an obstruction could not this bank of the United States, with all its branch banks, be in time of war! It might dictate to us the peace we should accept, or withdraw its aids. Ought we then to give further growth to an institution so powerful, so hostile?[11]

In addition, Jefferson also opposed the proposed national bank on constitutional grounds, and rejected outright the idea of implied powers. He favored a strict interpretation of the Constitution, one where "necessary and proper" meant "absolutely or indispensably necessary," not simply convenient. To interpret it otherwise would set a precedent allowing the federal government, on the basis of the "necessary and proper" clause, to do anything it wished. This went contrary to the spirit of the as yet unratified Tenth Amendment, which stated that the powers not delegated to the federal government by the Constitution, nor prohibited by it, were reserved to the states.

In the end, Hamilton won the argument. The banking bill narrowly passed in Congress, and Washington, after consulting both Jefferson and Hamilton on the issue of its constitutionality, sided with Hamilton and signed the bill into law. But the essential debate about the scope of federal power remains with us to this day, and underneath it lies an even more fundamental question about the nature of the American Dream. Ultimately, is the dream political or economic? Was the Revolutionary War fought in order to secure a government by the people, one that protects liberty and individual rights? Or was it fought to create an economically prosperous nation in which even people of the most obscure birth can, through hard work and determination, achieve wealth? For most Americans, the answer is that the American Dream encompasses both ideas, and yet they are somewhat contradictory. The former requires a government that stays out of people's affairs as much as possible, only intervening when their rights are threatened, while the latter requires a strong national authority to promote conditions favorable to trade and commerce without stifling them. It is a contradiction that has never been settled, and from that day to this, we have tried to have our cake and eat it too.

• • • • •

While the Federalists and Democratic-Republicans differed in their views on many things, one issue they did agree on was the right of American citizens to expand the westward frontier. In the century leading up to the Revolutionary War, the colonial population in America had grown from a little over 150,000 to 3 million, and there were those who felt that the opportunities for advancement in America were somewhat less than they had been previously. In the early days, the sheer amount of work involved in founding a colony meant that even relatively wealthy men such as the Plymouth colony's governor, William Bradford, worked side by side with indentured servants. By the mid-1700s, that was no longer true. As the early colonies became successful and entrenched, they grew less egalitarian and more hierarchical. Land and wealth had concentrated in the hands of an elite banking and merchant class in the north and an elite planter class in the south, where those who had prospered had bought up large tracts of land and created country estates similar to those back in England. As a result, society, while certainly far more fluid than in Europe at the time, was still more rigid than it had been during the early days.

The great irony of building a better life for one's children is that having been born into that better life from the start, the progeny can never fully appreciate the improvement. By the eighteenth century, the standard of living in the colonies had improved so much that descendents of the original colonists, rather than being thrilled to have their fifty acres, had begun to feel that they were at a distinct economic disadvantage compared to those with larger estates. Resentment and jealousy on the part of the poor and middle classes toward the rich was nothing new, of course. What was different was the feeling among the poorer colonists that they had been promised something—economic opportunity—that they were now being denied.

So strong was the power of the dream, and so widely had it been fulfilled, that a century was sufficient for it to be considered a right or an expectation rather than simply a hope or even a privilege. Thus, when the doors of opportunity seemed to be closing on them in the older, more established areas of the colonies, Americans looked west, to the frontier. By picking up and starting over, they might escape the competition from the big plantations and established businesses and carve out a place for themselves in a new town that, with a little luck, might become the next Boston or Philadelphia. Indeed, pulling up stakes and starting over was a pattern that was endlessly repeated throughout early American history. The frontier became a safety valve of sorts for those who felt that equality of opportunity and upward mobility were being compromised by wealthy, established interests back east.

During the inevitable recession that followed the French and Indian War, the colonists looked eagerly to the lands west of the Appalachians and in Canada that had been gained by England as spoils of that war. They had helped the mother country to win those lands, and now they expected to settle them. England, however, was heavily in debt and not overly inclined to spend the money and dedicate the military resources necessary to police such a vast frontier full of sometimes hostile Native American tribes. Thus, it banned settlement west of the Appalachians, a decision that did not go over well with the colonists. They saw the ban as an infringement on their freedom to pursue the American Dream, and it was one of many factors that led to the writing of the Declaration of Independence just thirteen years later.

After the Revolutionary War ended, however, the new American government had no reservations about opening up land west of the

Appalachians for settlement, whether the Native American tribes of the Ohio Valley liked it or not. In 1785, Congress passed a land ordinance, largely drafted by Jefferson, for the survey and sale of land in the Northwest Territory, which would eventually become the states of Ohio, Indiana, Illinois, Michigan, and Wisconsin. The ordinance provided for the division of the territory into townships six miles square, which were then divided into sections of 640 acres each. While Jefferson hoped the land might be offered at no charge to all who were willing to work it, the cash-strapped government, which under the Articles of Confederation did not have the power to levy direct taxes, decided to sell it for $1 per section—at the time, more than pocket change, but not out of reach of the common man, either.

Another key part of the ordinance was the reservation of a section in each township for the purpose of public education, as education was deemed essential to the functioning of a republican government and the promotion of equality of opportunity. Slavery was prohibited in the territory, and in 1787, Congress passed the Northwest Ordinance, which codified federal supervision and laid out the criteria for statehood. The Northwest Ordinance was the single most important piece of legislation passed by Congress under the Articles of Confederation, and it established the precedent for westward expansion by admitting new states to the union rather than adding territory to the existing states. Together with the Land Ordinance of 1785, it set off a flood of migration, and by 1800, there were over a million Americans settled in the area, nearly a quarter of the total population of the United States.

The frontier mindset did much to shape the American Dream throughout the eighteenth and nineteenth centuries. Life on the frontier involved hard labor, with little in the way of education, culture, or entertainment. The sheer isolation fostered a strong ethic of self-reliance, and it was during this period that raising oneself up by one's bootstraps truly became an acknowledged virtue of the American character. The decision to start life over on the frontier was almost always economically motivated; income disparity in settled areas tended to increase over time, and westward migration was seen as a cure for economic difficulties. Westward expansion was also thought to be inevitable. At the start of the nineteenth century, there was a growing belief that the United States was destined to expand across the North American continent, from the Atlantic seaboard to the Pacific Ocean. It was the country's manifest destiny.

So strong was this belief that when France offered to sell its entire Louisiana Territory to the United States for $15 million, Jefferson, then president, jumped at the chance. It was a radical move for a strict constructionist who believed in limited government, and the action was considered by many—including Jefferson himself—to be unconstitutional. But the purchase furthered Jefferson's vision of an agrarian-based nation, and he justified the act on the grounds that it was a good deal for the country, which it was. With the stroke of a pen, Jefferson doubled the size of the country, secured control of the all-important Mississippi River and the port of New Orleans, and added a million square miles to the western frontier in the bargain. Just a few years into the new century, America's Manifest Destiny of expanding its borders all the way to the Pacific was well under way, and the American west was a boon to all who felt the frontier was their best chance of fulfilling their American Dream.

• • • • •

As westward expansion added to the country's size, America's leaders continued to argue about the nation's future and its economic character. Alexander Hamilton's fiscal policies as secretary of the treasury under Washington, particularly the establishment of a national bank and currency, had resulted in a period of comparative financial stability. Yet due to the Founding Fathers' overwhelming preference for an agrarian vision of the American Dream, the nation lagged behind Britain's industrial transformation by half a century. The Washington administration did make some tentative steps toward encouraging greater innovation by drafting the Patent Act of 1790, but the act merely set up a national register of claims. This was an improvement in that inventors no longer had to win exclusive licenses state by state, but the act didn't require an examination for proof of originality or validity. It wasn't until 1838 that inventors were finally given full protection under a national patent law.

If America's leaders were somewhat reticent in fostering invention, they seemed downright hostile to encouraging the development of American industry. In a report to Congress in 1791, Hamilton had urged the development of American manufacturing and industry through the use of tariffs, immigration policy, and internal improvements. Yet the normally persuasive Hamilton was unable to convince Congress to devote any public funds to the project; early American entrepreneurs had to go it alone. Despite the lack of support, colonial entrepreneurs still managed to develop some of America's earliest industries, such as textiles and woolens, and Eli Whitney's invention of interchangeable parts in 1797 was a significant factor in industrial advancement and a precursor to mass production. In general, however, northern entrepreneurs from this period were traders and merchants rather than industrialists. It was Thomas Jefferson, not Hamilton, who spoke for the majority of Americans when he wrote, "While we have land to labor, let us never wish to see our citizens occupied at a workbench or twirling a distaff. Carpenters, masons, smiths, are wanting in husbandry; but for the general operations of manufacture, let our workshops remain in Europe."[12]

Ironically, it was Jefferson who proved instrumental in setting America on the path to capitalism and industrialization, albeit unintentionally. As president, he declared a trade embargo in 1807 to avoid being drawn into the Napoleonic Wars in Europe. The impact on the northern economy was devastating, because the act essentially forbade American ships from engaging in foreign trade. American exports fell from $108 million in 1807 to $22 million in 1808, and European imports were practically unobtainable. The country plunged into a depression, but the trade embargo and the subsequent War of 1812 with Britain encouraged American entrepreneurs to invest in manufacturing rather than trade. In the wake of the war, a wave of nationalism swept the country, and demand for American-made products increased.

Meanwhile, the ever-expanding West needed a market for its agricultural goods, and the biggest roadblock was lack of transportation. The North and South, located along the Atlantic, had a variety of ports at their disposal; the West's only transportation outlets were the Mississippi River and the port at New Orleans. The country needed a network of roads, canals, and railroads to link the West to the eastern seaboard, allowing it to transport its agricultural goods to markets in New England in exchange for goods made in the North.

This is exactly what Congressman Henry Clay of Kentucky had in mind when, based on the rising tide of nationalism, he started advocating a national economic plan, one which eventually came to be called the American System. Essentially Hamiltonian in nature, it called for the establishment of a second national bank (the charter on the first had been allowed to lapse) as well as protective tariffs that effectively raised prices on European imports in order to build up American manufacturing. While this would primarily benefit manufacturers in the North, Clay argued that the growth of factories and the number of factory workers would also benefit western farmers by creating a market for their agricultural foodstuffs, while the South would benefit by selling its cotton to the northern textile mills. The revenue from the tariffs, meanwhile, would be used to fund transportation improvements such as roads and canals, benefiting everyone.

Clay, the Speaker of the House and a talented orator, was persuasive, at least in Congress. He got his new national bank and, over the years, a series of protective tariffs that outraged southern and western farmers alike. Egalitarian in nature, the frontier settlers, who were perpetually in debt, were deeply suspicious of the financial and political elite back East. The western ethic of self-reliance had led them to establish and administer their own local governments, and they had developed a strong belief in government by the common man and only by consent of the governed. The Founding Fathers' vision of a republican aristocracy was wholly alien to them, and as more states joined the union, they were increasingly in a position to supplant it with their own version of American democracy.

By 1820, the population of the West had swelled to over 2.5 million, a million more than the population of New England, and with this increase came political clout. Up to this period, all of the presidents—Washington, Adams, Jefferson, Madison, and Monroe—had hailed from either Massachusetts or Virginia, the centers of political power for the North and South. But in the election of 1824, the West had not one, but two candidates in the running: Henry Clay and Andrew Jackson. The latter was a Revolutionary War veteran who had made his fortune on the Tennessee frontier by practicing law and speculating in real estate. After serving as Tennessee's first U.S. representative and then briefly as senator, he was appointed commander of the Tennessee militia and made a name for himself fighting Native Americans and also in the War of 1812, winning a decisive victory at the Battle of New Orleans.

While unimportant from a military standpoint (the battle occurred three weeks after peace negotiations had been concluded, news of which had not yet reached New Orleans), the victory nonetheless established Jackson as a war hero. When he ran for the presidency in 1824, he received the most popular votes as well as a plurality of the electoral college votes, but not an outright majority. This threw the decision into the House of Representatives, which voted for John Quincy Adams after Clay, who had finished in fourth place, gave his support to Adams in exchange for being appointed secretary of state. The public, particularly small farmers in the South and West, were outraged by this result, convinced that corrupt pseudo-aristocrats in New England had subverted the will of the people.

This led to a wave of reform in voting laws that had a lasting impact on the American political landscape. In drafting the Constitution, the founders had left the question of voting rights to the states, most of which required that one own property in order to have suffrage.

This had the effect of restricting voting rights to a tiny percentage of the population—less than 5 percent of Americans were eligible to vote in the presidential election of 1800. In the aftermath of the 1824 election, however, there was a mass movement in favor of "universal male suffrage," and in most states all impediments to voting for white men were removed, which greatly expanded the electorate. It also moved the country away from the Founding Fathers' ideal of a republic governed by the virtuous elite and toward a far more democratic society. By the time Jackson ran against Adams again in 1828, he scored a resounding victory, one that would usher in the era of the common man and "Jacksonian democracy."

• • • • •

The first president from the western section of the country, Andrew Jackson was a stark departure from the natural aristocracy of the Founding Fathers. Here, at last, was a man of the people, a president who had actually lived the American Dream of upward mobility. Jackson was a self-made man who embodied the frontier ethic of self-reliance. His version of the American Dream emphasized equality, not just of economic opportunity in the sense of having a chance at upward mobility, but also in the sense of giving the common man an equal voice in political and economic affairs. Closer in philosophy to Jefferson than to Hamilton, he nonetheless rejected the elitism of both, embracing the egalitarianism of the western frontier where citizens had a more direct voice in government rather than being represented by a learned, wealthy elite.

Jackson was also a man who followed his own judgment. As president, his first order of business, admirably enough, was to pay off the national debt. He called it "the national curse" and vowed to eliminate it in order to "prevent a monied aristocracy from growing up around our administration that must bend to its views, and ultimately destroy the liberty of the country."[13] In pursuit of this goal, he was one of the few politicians in American history who was willing to actually cut spending, including spending on vital internal improvements such as roads, which were key to Clay's American System and which would have greatly benefited the West. There would be plenty of money for improvements, Jackson told Clay and his other critics, once the national debt was paid off. By the middle of his second term, Jackson reported to Congress in his State of the Union address that the country was running a balance of $440,000. It was the first time in our nation's history—and the last—that we were debt free.

While he was dedicated to fiscal responsibility, Jackson's western sensibility led him to be deeply suspicious of banks in general, and of the Bank of the United States in particular, which represented what he called "the money power." Most people who pulled up stakes and moved to the western frontier were poor, and even at prices of a few dollars an acre, buying land and the necessary materials to farm it meant going into significant debt, placing them under the thumb of the financial elite back in New England. Worse, speculators routinely bought up vast tracts of land and sold them on credit to settlers at prices significantly higher than the federal government. As a result, the entire West was in debt to the North, and a major panic in 1819 precipitated widespread bank failures and foreclosures, with defaulted payments amounting to over $21 million.[14] The crisis created great resentment towards banks and financial creditors back in New England, as the western farmers perceived that the monied class was using its influence to lobby Congress to adopt policies that favored the North, rather than balancing the interests of both sections.

As a result, people on the frontier began to feel that once again they were being denied the equality of economic opportunity that was the basis of the American Dream. Self-reliance was well and good, but how could they have a decent chance of making a go of life on the frontier when land speculators were driving up prices beyond their reach? Their agitation grew, and in the wake of the financial panic, westerners began demanding free land as a right— their right to equality of opportunity—for any who would settle on and improve it. The federal government responded in 1820 by passing an act that abolished the credit system and reduced the price of land in the western territories to $1.25 an acre.

For Jackson, however, this wasn't enough. He considered the federal bank to be a tool of the corrupt elite and unconstitutional, even though the Supreme Court under Chief Justice John Marshall had ruled otherwise in *McCulloch v. Maryland* in 1819. Marshall, a staunch federalist, had based his decision on the same reasoning as Hamilton had, namely the doctrine of implied powers. But Jackson, a states' rights advocate, favored a stricter interpretation of the Constitution, as did the man he eventually appointed to replace Marshall, his secretary of treasury, Roger Taney. So when Congress voted in 1832 to recharter the bank, Jackson vetoed the bill, issuing a damning statement written by Taney in which he argued that the bank was a monopoly that benefited the private investors in the bank at the expense of ordinary citizens. Unable to obtain the votes necessary to override the veto, the bill died, and the bank, with four years left on its charter, was effectively crippled.

Without a national bank to regulate the money supply and exert discipline on the state banks, however, the American financial system quickly grew even more chaotic and speculative, particularly in the West. The country was experiencing a boom period, and as the number of state and local banks proliferated during Jackson's presidency, the face value of banknotes in circulation tripled, and outstanding loans quadrupled. The increase in circulating paper currency, which Jackson hated on principle, set off a real estate bubble as land sales by the federal government increased from $2.6 million in 1832 to $25 million in 1836. Most of the land, predictably, was bought by speculators back East who had no intention whatsoever of actually settling on the acres they bought, but rather reselling them for a significant profit.

Legitimate frontier settlers were outraged, and Jackson, man of action that he was, resolved to put a stop to it. Waiting until Congress was out of session, he issued an executive order that required payment for federal land to be in gold or silver, with an exception made for buyers who actually intended to settle on the property they bought. This action successfully brought most of the speculation to a halt, but it also created a huge demand for gold and silver specie in the West, which led to hoarding. This set off a series of massive bank failures that spread from the West to the rest of the country, and as Jackson left office in 1837, the country slid into a deep depression that would last for the next six years. Ironically, the self-made man of the people—who had waged war on the financial elite in the name of equal opportunity for the common man—had ushered in a free-banking era of repeated boom and bust cycles that would widen the financial gap even farther.[15]

Jackson's understanding of macroeconomics may have left something to be desired, but his actions were the result of principled stances in favor of individual rights and limited national government. The events leading up to his election extended voting rights—and access to the American Dream—to a much greater portion of the American population than before. He embraced Manifest Destiny and the expansion of the western frontier, and his fight over the bank, and ultimately his appointment of Taney as chief justice of the Supreme Court, turned back the tide of federalism, returning greater power to the states. The Founding Fathers' dream of a republic of virtue, led by a natural aristocracy, was over. The era of Jacksonian Democracy had arrived.

3

THE DREAM OF FREEDOM
AND JUSTICE FOR ALL

◇◇◇

In retrospect, the year 1776 was critical to the formation of the American Dream, not just because it was the year that America declared its independence, but also because of two other crucial developments: the publishing of Adam Smith's *Wealth of Nations* and the introduction of James Watt's first commercial steam engine. In a world that for centuries had been dominated by mercantilist economic policies, Smith's seminal work laid out with clear, impeccable logic the benefits of a system of free trade and free markets, division of labor in manufacturing, and government keeping its nose out of private industry—in a word, capitalism. As Smith himself pointed out, America had yet to develop much of a manufacturing mentality; the lure of uncultivated land and untapped natural resources was simply too strong. Americans, he argued, felt that a manufacturer was "the servant of his customers, from whom he derives his subsistence; but that a planter who cultivates his own land, and derives his necessary substance from the labour of his own family, is really a master, and independent of all the world."[1]

James Watt's condensing steam engine helped to change America's agrarian mentality, at least in the North. The raw power it unleashed dramatically increased productive capacity and was the catalyst that sparked the Industrial Revolution on both sides of the Atlantic. During the colonial period, a grand total of seven manufacturing corporations had been formed in all of British North America. In the last four years of the eighteenth century, however, 355 businesses were incorporated in the United States,[2] and northern manufacturing grew rapidly after the War of 1812 brought an end to American mercantilism. The states had relaxed their restrictions on corporations in order to encourage business development, and the growth of industry was also fueled by a crucial Supreme Court decision. In 1819 the court ruled that corporations possessed private rights and that states could not rewrite corporations' charters at will. This made joint-stock corporations much more attractive, and limited-liability provisions made it far easier to raise capital for large-scale ventures. Corporations started to be used extensively to finance canals and roads, which linked the various sections of the country and became yet another catalyst for American industrialization.

While America had lagged behind Britain in developing the steam engine, it led the way in developing the steamboat. American John Fitch had invented the first workable steamboat in 1787, but several decades passed before Robert Fulton and Robert Livingston made steamboats into a commercial success. America's vast networks of waterways made steamboats eminently useful, and the gross tonnage of steamboats built in the United States rose from 17,000 in 1819 to more than 202,000 by 1840.[3] The ever-increasing demand for them spurred the growth of machine shops and foundries all along the Ohio River, giving rise to future manufacturing hubs like Pittsburgh, Cincinnati, and St. Louis. This linked the Northeast and Midwest both geographically and economically in a way that would have profound implications on the course of American history.

One of the central figures in the story of the American steamboat industry was Cornelius Vanderbilt. Like Benjamin Franklin, Vanderbilt came from modest origins—he was born in 1794 in Staten Island, New York, the son of English and Dutch immigrants—but he grew to be an entirely new breed of entrepreneur the likes of which America had never seen before. Vanderbilt dropped out of school at the age of eleven to work for his father by ferrying passengers around New York Harbor in his father's boat. By his sixteenth birthday, he had earned enough money to buy a barge named the *Swiftsure*, and when the War of 1812 broke out, he won a contract to supply six military garrisons around the harbor. He repeatedly ran the British blockade to do so, earning him the nickname "the Commodore," and in his spare time, he transported food from farms on the Hudson River to the starving people under blockade in New York.

A true businessman, Vanderbilt used his profits to buy an interest in two other barges, and by the age of twenty-three, he had saved $9,000 and owned several boats. Vanderbilt used his little fleet to transport not only passengers, but also oysters, whale oil, cider, and beer, and when he got married at the age of nineteen, he was reportedly back at work the following morning. When steamboats appeared on the scene, Vanderbilt initially dismissed them, but when they started cutting into his business, he realized the tremendous opportunity they represented. So he sold all of his boats and started working as a steamboat captain, negotiating a salary of $60 per month plus half the profits from the bar. Over the next ten years, he learned everything there was to know about the steamship trade. His wife, Sophia, supported their growing family by running an inn, while Vanderbilt saved all of his earnings in anticipation of the day when he would be able to start his own steamboat business.

In the meantime, Vanderbilt occupied himself with building up his employer's business on the Raritan River, part of the transportation network that ran from New York to Philadelphia. Once he had developed this route fully, he set his sights on making passenger runs across New York Bay. It was a profitable route, but there was one catch—it was illegal for him to operate there, because the New York legislature had granted exclusive rights to Fulton and

Livingston. Vanderbilt decided to ignore the prohibition and made the runs anyway, charging $3 less than his competitors and making up the loss by charging more for food and drink. Livingston promptly obtained a restraining order, and Jacob Hays, the high constable of New York City, was sent to serve Vanderbilt with the papers and arrest him. "If you want to arrest me, you'll have to carry me off my boat,"[4] Vanderbilt declared, whereupon Hays seized him under the armpits and threw him over the railing onto the dock.

For the next two months, Vanderbilt played a cat-and-mouse game with the New York monopoly. Every day they sent someone to arrest him, and every day he found a way to evade capture, sometimes even hiding in a secret closet on board the ship. (One day, as he was preparing to pull away from the dock, a constable came on board to arrest him, so Vanderbilt ordered his crew to cast off. Afraid of being carried out of his jurisdiction, where most likely he would have been imprisoned in retaliation, the officer quickly jumped back ashore.) Vanderbilt wasn't the only one waging war against the New York steamboat monopoly, both on the water and in the courts. A tangled web of legal suits was filed and made it all the way to the Supreme Court, which ruled unanimously against the New York monopoly. Within Chief Justice John Marshall's carefully worded opinion was the precedent that states were not entitled to place restrictions on interstate commerce, as this power was reserved for the federal government.

The Supreme Court's decision liberated American business by helping to promote a more national economy, and its immediate effect on the steamboat industry was to open America's waterways equally to all entrepreneurs. Vanderbilt, for his part, seized the opportunity to build his steamboat empire. By the age of thirty-five, he and his wife had saved $30,000, which they used to set up a steamboat route between New York and Philadelphia. Vanderbilt's business model was straightforward and simple: he ran an efficient, low-cost operation, and then undercut the competition on price until they either went bankrupt or paid him to stop operating. After winning a price war on the New York-Philadelphia route, he staged an even more ruthless price war on the Hudson River, offering passage for free. This bled his competitor, the Hudson River Steamboat Association, so badly that they agreed to pay him $100,000 and an additional $5,000 per year to stay off the Hudson River for the next ten years. With this nest egg, he set up steamboat routes around Boston, Hartford, Providence, Washington DC, and Charleston, which became the foundation of his steamboat empire.[5]

While Vanderbilt's tactics drew the ire of some, most notably his competitors, consumers benefited. Every market in which he operated saw a reduction in fares that continued long after the initial price war had ended. Of course, Vanderbilt benefited as well—by his mid-forties, he owned more than one hundred steamboats and had accumulated a fortune of over $10 million. It was the perfect example of Adam Smith's economic theory of rational self-interest in practice; by acting in his own best interests, Vanderbilt had driven down prices and extended steamboat service to a far greater area. This lesson wasn't lost on the country's leaders or the American people at large. By the middle of the 1800s, individual ownership rights, patent law, and capital markets were firmly established in the United States, and inventions and entrepreneurial capital were coming together with an ease that had started a boom of investment in manufacturing. From that time forward, the agrarian way of life extolled by Thomas Jefferson gradually declined, to be supplanted by Alexander Hamilton's vision of a vibrant industrial nation with economic opportunities on an entirely different scale.

● ● ● ● ●

While the North was embracing industrialization, the South had gone in the opposite direction. There was a brief period after the Revolutionary War when the South, dependent on exports to England of indigo, rice, and tobacco, might have pulled back from its traditional dependence on cash crops and developed a more diversified economy. But that was not to be. With the invention of the cotton gin, cotton production suddenly became profitable—as long as there were slaves to provide the labor. The South committed itself to the production of this overwhelmingly profitable crop, and in doing so sealed its fate. While the North and the West modernized, the South remained an almost feudal agrarian economy that required the perpetuation of slavery to be sustainable.

The Founding Fathers, who in drafting the Declaration of Independence had sidestepped the issue of slavery entirely, were forced to deal with it in framing the Constitution, although they avoided using the actual word. Most of the delegates at the Constitutional Convention, including many from Virginia, thought slavery was immoral. In fact, in the years following signing of the Declaration of Independence, there had been a rising tide of abolitionism. In 1777, Vermont became the first state to abolish slavery, followed by Massachusetts in 1780, which granted African American men the right to vote as well. That same year, Pennsylvania adopted a gradual emancipation law, which declared that all children born after November 1 of that year would be free on their 28th birthday (a provision that allowed slave owners to recoup some of their investment). Connecticut and Rhode Island soon followed with their own gradual emancipation laws, and the strength of the gathering movement led Congress to ban slavery entirely in the Northwest Territories in 1787, with the concession that fugitive slaves who escaped to the territories had to be returned to their owners.

The drafting of the Constitution put an abrupt end to such progress. The Founding Fathers' primary concern was to keep their dream of self-government alive, and they needed to craft a document that had a reasonable chance of being accepted not just by the southern delegates, but also by their constituents. Expressly condemning slavery, much less abolishing it, was hopelessly problematic, because the southern states would never ratify the Constitution if it included a prohibition against slavery. Doing so would have dismantled the entire economic system the South had come to depend on, and it was taken for granted that any serious proposal of emancipation would have to include compensation to slaveholders, which most agreed would be prohibitively expensive. Worse, forced emancipation by the government, in the wake of the Revolution and all that had preceded it, would be viewed by many as a tyrannical act on the part of the federal government towards owners of property, and would thus set a dangerous precedent.

Realizing this, the delegates from South Carolina and Georgia pressed their advantage to win several concessions during the drafting of the Constitution. Citizenship was restricted to free persons, yet for purposes of determining proportional representation in the lower house of Congress, all free persons (including women and children) were to be counted, Native Americans excluded, and all others (meaning slaves) were to be counted as three-fifths of a person— the infamous Three-Fifths Compromise. The southern delegates also won the right to have fugitive slaves returned to their owners, but the antislavery delegates from the North did not capitulate entirely on this issue. They knew that slavery was utterly irreconcilable with the core principles laid out in the Declaration of Independence and later the Bill of Rights, so in return for keeping import taxes on slaves below $10 a head, they forced the southern states to agree to a ban on importation of slaves after 1808. Sadly, it turned out that this had the perverse effect of dramatically increasing the rate of importation in the years leading up to the ban, but at the time, it was considered a small but important victory. As James Madison wrote in Federalist No. 42, "It ought to be considered as a great point gained in favor of humanity that a period of twenty years may terminate forever, within these States, a traffic which has so long and so loudly unbraided the barbarism of modern policy."[6]

Madison, like most of the delegates who opposed slavery, believed that the issue would be taken up by the next generation. And indeed, there was a brief moment in 1790 when the Pennsylvania Abolitionist Society submitted a petition to Congress to "take such measures in their wisdom, as the powers with which they are invested will authorize, for promoting the abolition of slavery, and discouraging every species of traffic in slaves."[7] The petition had been signed by none other than Benjamin Franklin, in his last great act of statesmanship before his death. But he alone of the Founding Fathers was willing to risk raising the issue of slavery so directly. Congressmen from the South threatened secession if it were so much as discussed, and those from the North still felt that the new government was too fragile to dare calling their bluff, if indeed it was a bluff. The Pennsylvania Abolitionist Society's petition was sent to committee and allowed to die without being addressed, and the founding generation kept its silence and hoped that slavery would dwindle out naturally once the ban on importation went into effect.

Ironically, slavery might very well have been banned within a few decades had Eli Whitney not invented the cotton gin in 1793 in an attempt to help revive depressed southern agriculture. The profitability of the South's key cash crops—rice, indigo, and tobacco—had been on the wane, and while long-staple cotton grew well in the South's hot, moist climate, particularly in the Mississippi Delta, the painstaking process of manually removing the seeds from the cotton fibers by hand had made it an economically unviable crop. The cotton gin removed that bottleneck from the process and made the production of long-staple cotton profitable. In doing so, it revived the southern economy and renewed its need for slave labor. In the years between the invention of the cotton gin and the start of the Civil War, nearly a million slaves from Virginia, Maryland, and northern states that had adopted gradual emancipation laws were "sold south" to cotton country.

Meanwhile, even in the states where slavery had been outlawed, African Americans were second-class citizens to whom the American Dream was largely denied. At the time the Constitution was ratified, black men could vote in ten of the thirteen states and women in four. As restrictions on owning property were lifted, however, most states adopted laws that specifically denied both African Americans and women the vote. Racism was particularly blatant in New York, where the slave trade had long flourished and where one of the bloodiest slave uprisings in the entire country had taken place. While the state eventually adopted a gradual emancipation law, working-class whites who feared economic competition from freed slaves waged a not-so-subtle campaign of terror against them, and authorities frequently detained free blacks on suspicion of being runaway slaves, holding them in local jails and running advertisements seeking their owners. If someone claimed ownership, generally little attempt at verification was made; if not, formerly free blacks were often sold into slavery to cover the cost of detaining and advertising them. As the emancipation deadline neared, kidnappings rose, and thousands of African Americans lost not only their freedom but also what little property they had.

While racism was rampant in both the North and South, political movements in favor of abolition gained steam as the nineteenth century progressed, and one of the most prominent spokesmen of the movement was Frederick Douglass. A former slave, his primary goal was the abolition of slavery, but he also argued for greater equality in the form of suffrage as well. Douglass based his arguments to some extent on the concept of natural rights, but he took the idea of equality farther than the Founding Fathers had, arguing not only for recognition of African Americans' equal claim to the natural rights of life, liberty, and the pursuit of happiness, but also for equality of social standing. Moreover, he wanted the government to actively intervene and remove the constraints that made it impossible for African Americans to achieve political and social equality.

This was a radical notion, because removing such restraints required actively infringing on the property rights of white men. The rights of liberty and property were at odds, and the federal government's role in adjudicating between the opposing rights was unclear—at least until the Supreme Court's infamous ruling in the Dred Scott decision of 1857. The opinion of the court, as written by Chief Justice Roger Taney, was that people of African descent imported into the United States and held as slaves, as well as their descendents, were not protected by the Constitution and could never be citizens of the United States. Slaves were not citizens, could not be taken from their owners without due process, and could not sue in court. Taney concluded that the framers of the Constitution had viewed all African Americans as "beings of an inferior order, and altogether unfit to associate with the white race, either in social or political relations, and so far inferior that they had no rights which the white man was bound to respect."[8]

With this decision, Taney denied not only the notion of African-American equality, but also the idea of the federal government taking an active part in abolishing slavery. This was perhaps not surprising. Taney was, after all, a firm believer in limited government—the same man who had written Andrew Jackson's statement vetoing the renewal of the national bank. He believed the Dred Scott decision would settle the slavery question once and for all by making it a matter of law, but instead it made the debate more heated. The Dred Scott decision actually strengthened opposition to slavery in the North and divided the Democratic Party on sectional lines, paving the way for the emergence of the Republican Party. In the meantime, however, the African-American dream of both freedom and equality was flatly denied.

• • • • •

The American Civil War can be attributed to a variety of causes, the issue of slavery chief among them. However, the differing lifestyles, economic interests, and attitudes toward government held by various sections of the country played major roles as well. With each passing year, the economic interests of the North and South, and the differing visions of the American Dream they embraced, were increasingly at odds. When their interests clashed in Congress, it fell to the ever more powerful West to break the stalemate.

Clay's American System had done its work in linking the North and West both geographically and economically, but it had been less beneficial to the South, which had plenty of potential markets for its cotton outside of America. The South also dedicated almost all of its economic effort to cotton production, and thus the southern states had to import—and pay heavy tariffs on—everything else they needed. So when Congress passed increasingly high tariffs in 1828 and 1832, the South protested vociferously and expected the West to support it. But the western section of the country had developed a distinctly different character from the plantation-based economy of the South. The West was agrarian, but life there was reduced to its simplest terms; it lacked the refinement and gentility of the older, more established culture and lifestyle of the South, with its aristocratic families and grand houses.

The West had economic interests—and a distinct frontier character—that made it a separate section rather than merely an extension of either the North or South. Southern congressmen expected western representatives and senators to side with them on issues such as the tariff. But although the western frontiersmen still harbored a deep antipathy toward the northern financial elite, the West was forward-looking in a way that the South was not. When it came to tariffs and a host of other economic issues, the West increasingly sided with the North, which provided both a source of manufactured goods and a market for the West's agricultural products.

Southerners in Congress failed to perceive this shift, and when South Carolina responded to the tariffs by passing the Ordinance of Nullification in 1832 and declaring the tariff unconstitutional, the public expected President Jackson, as a westerner and a states-rights advocate, to support the southern position. When a visitor asked the president if he had any message to convey to his friends back in South Carolina, however, Jackson replied, in his typical forthright fashion, "Yes I have. Please give my compliments to my friends in your state and say to them that if a single drop of blood shall be shed there in opposition to the laws of the United States, I will hang the first man I can lay my hand on engaged in such treasonable conduct, upon the first tree I can reach."[9]

Congress was a tad more conciliatory, and it negotiated a new tariff that was more satisfactory to South Carolinians, while at the same time authorizing the president to use military force if they persisted in claiming the right of nullification. South Carolina backed down, and southern secession was temporarily averted, but the incident made the South aware of the West's changing priorities and its growing political importance. By the middle of the century, the West was growing rapidly. Most of the states formed from the Northwest Territories had long ago joined the Union, as had Kentucky, Tennessee, Mississippi, and Alabama. Louisiana, Arkansas, and Missouri soon followed; Texas was annexed in 1845; and Maine, Florida, Wisconsin, and Iowa soon joined the nation as well.

Then, in 1848, Mexico ceded—in exchange for $15 million and the assumption of several million dollars in debt—almost a million square miles of what now constitutes the southwest portion of the United States, including California. By the end of the year, California had more than twelve thousand settlers, one of them a Swiss immigrant named John Sutter, who owned a large ranch near what is now Sacramento. Sutter hired an American named James Marshall to build a sawmill on the south fork of the American River, and one day when Marshall was inspecting the millrace, he caught sight of a gold nugget the size of a pea. He and Sutter tried to keep the discovery to themselves, but the news was soon leaked and made its way back to Washington. When President James K. Polk presented Congress with a twenty-pound nugget worth almost $5,000—enough to sustain a large family in an upper-middle-class lifestyle for over a year—the California gold rush was on.

Unlike most metals, which are extremely difficult and therefore expensive to mine, gold is comparatively easy. It is inert, and therefore is generally found in a pure state, either as small flakes or as dust, but sometimes as large nuggets. It's also quite heavy, so when it erodes out of hillsides and is washed downstream, it tends to settle out and concentrate wherever the current slows. At that point, all one needs is a pan and a few tools to literally pluck it right out of the water. While not exactly easy labor, panning for gold was a faster path to wealth than either farming, land speculation, or starting a business—theoretically at least. The idea that instant wealth could be found at one's feet cast a powerful spell on the American imagination, and this was the foundation of what would later become the American Dream of "the good life."

The California gold rush held out the potential for all the rewards of the American Dream with a fraction of the effort of running a farm or starting a business, although in reality very few people made their fortune in the gold fields. Ironically, even Sutter went bankrupt, and Marshall eventually drank himself to death. Still, the dream beckoned, and over the next two years almost 1 percent of the total American population, as well as many thousands of others from across the world, made their way to California in pursuit of an easy fortune. By 1854, the state's population had reached 300,000, and it would double every twenty years for the next century. In the ever-changing story that is the American Dream, California had added its own unique twist.

● ● ● ● ●

As the West expanded and new states were admitted to the union, the contentious issue of tariffs was replaced by the even more contentious issue of the expansion of slavery into the new territories. Back when abolitionist fervor was high in the years after the Revolutionary War, the Northwest Ordinance had been passed with a provision that outlawed slavery north of the Ohio River, but since then Congress had enacted a series of delicate compromises designed to keep the balance of power between pro-slavery and antislavery states approximately equal. As part of the Dred Scott decision, however, the Supreme Court ruled that Congress did not have the power to ban slavery in the territories, throwing this delicate balance into question and creating an uproar. The Democratic Party split into northern and southern factions, and the Republican Party, which had been formed by antislavery expansion activists in 1854, seized the initiative.

The Republicans had vaulted past Henry Clay's Whig Party to become the primary opposition to the Democrats in the 1856 election, largely by campaigning on a platform of "free soil, free labor, free speech, free men." Realizing that carrying the West would be the key to winning the presidential election in 1860, they forwarded a platform supporting the passage of a bill that would provide free land to settlers in the West, protective tariffs for New Englanders, and an end to the spread of slavery in the territories for abolitionists. The platform united the interests of the North and the West and gave the Republicans enough electoral votes to win the election. True to their word, the Republicans passed the Homestead Act in 1862, which offered 160 free acres to any settler who agreed to work the land for five years. By 1865, nearly 2.5 million acres had been claimed in pursuit of the frontier American Dream.

The Homestead Act wasn't the only carrot the Republican Party offered westerners in the 1860 election. They also nominated a western candidate for president by the name of Abraham Lincoln. Like Jackson, he was a self-made man from the frontier who had, through perseverance and hard work, lived the American Dream of upward mobility. He was born in a log cabin on the Kentucky frontier, and with little formal schooling, he moved to Illinois and as a young man worked as a hired hand, a surveyor, and a postmaster while educating himself. Eventually, he won election to the state legislature and studied law before embarking on a highly successful and lucrative legal career.

Lincoln's rise from humble beginnings had a powerful impact on him, and his dedication to preserving the Union as president was due to his belief in the American Dream, which the American experiment in democracy had made possible. Lincoln defined the American Dream in a way that still resonates with many people today—that given an opportunity, any man can raise himself upward in society through hard work:

> A young man finds himself of an age to be dismissed from
> parental control; he has for his capital nothing but his two
> strong hands that God has given him, a heart willing to

labor, and a freedom to choose the mode of his work and the manner of his employer; he has got no soil nor shop, and he avails himself of the opportunity of hiring himself to some man who has capital to pay him a fair day's wages for a fair day's work. He is benefited by availing himself of that privilege. He works industriously, he behaves soberly, and the result of a year or two's labor is a surplus of capital. Now he buys land on his own hook; he settles, marries, begets sons and daughters, and in course of time he too has enough to hire some new beginner.[10]

Lincoln feared that if the United States fell apart, the unique political and economic environment that made the American Dream possible would disappear along with the dream itself. The possibility that the nation the Founding Fathers had brought forth—conceived in liberty and dedicated to the proposition that all men were created equal—might perish from the earth was unthinkable. So much so, in fact, that he was willing to fight a war to force the South to remain part of a government that it no longer felt represented its best interests. While clearly abhorring the South's "peculiar institution" and opposing its spread into the western territories, he clearly considered preserving the Union to be more important than ending slavery. "My paramount object in this struggle is to save the Union, and is not either to save or to destroy slavery," he wrote in 1862 in response to a critical editorial by Horace Greeley. "If I could save the Union without freeing any slave I would do it, and if I could save it by freeing all the slaves I would do it; and if I could save it by freeing some and leaving others alone I would also do that."[11]

In some ways, Lincoln's reverence for the Union above all else is curious. Surely, if the American colonies had the right to declare their independence from Britain over economic issues such as taxation, then by similar reasoning the South had the right to secede from the United States when faced with an even greater threat to its basic economy. What's more, while southern secession might have been a serious threat to the nation at its founding, it was far less so by

1860. Franklin's famous quip at the signing of the Declaration of Independence—"We must all hang together, or most assuredly, we shall all hang separately,"[12] made sense at the time. The colonies were weak, and it took the combined, united efforts of all thirteen to defeat England. By 1860, however, an industrialized North and rapidly expanding West, now linked by canals and railroads, were fully capable of standing on their own two feet; the South was increasingly being left behind economically and had become largely incidental. Yet Lincoln still feared that secession would set a dangerous precedent, and that if he let the South go, eventually every state would secede when its particular interests went against those of the nation as a whole. For Lincoln, the Civil War was being fought, not to end slavery, but to preserve the American Dream, and that dream required the preservation of the Union.

At the same time, however, Lincoln realized that "a house divided cannot stand."[13] Over the course of his career he began to feel that preserving the Union and ending slavery were inextricably intertwined, and that freedom and equality must be extended to African Americans. They were natural rights, possessed by all, and it was the proper role of government to defend those rights against the encroachment of others. As Lincoln would write in a letter to Boston Republicans in 1859, he thought the southern Democrats, in holding the right to property above all else, had lost their way and turned their backs on the core principles of what was once the party of Thomas Jefferson. Lincoln argued that it was the Republicans who had become the true heirs of Jefferson, because Jefferson held individual liberty above all other natural rights, including property rights. Republicans, he asserted, "are for both the man and the dollar, but in cases of conflict, the man before the dollar."[14] Jefferson's legacy must not be tarnished: "The principles of Jefferson are the definitions and axioms of free society…This is a world of compensations; he who would be no slave, must consent to have no slave. Those who deny freedom to others, deserve it not for themselves; and, under a just God, cannot long retain it."[15]

Slaves, Lincoln was coming to conclude, had a natural right to their freedom, even if it deprived others of their "property" and critically wounded the southern economy. What's more, freedom was not enough; equality was also of paramount importance. To the Founding Fathers, freedom and equality were largely interchangeable. All men were equal in their possession of natural rights. But the institution of slavery demonstrated clearly that all men were not equal in their possession of natural rights, and thus Lincoln began to see equality as a fundamental, inalienable, natural right of its own. Granted, by equality, Lincoln didn't mean true social equality— he considered African Americans to be inferior in intellect, moral development, and social capacity. But he thought they had a right to political equality and to equal economic opportunity as well. As he noted in a speech in Philadelphia shortly before his inauguration:

> I have often inquired of myself, what great principle or idea it was that kept this [nation] together. It was not the mere matter of separation of the colonies from the mother land, but something in that Declaration giving liberty, not alone to the people of this country, but hope to the world for all future time. It was that which gave promise that in due time the weights should be lifted from the shoulders of all men, and that all should have an equal chance.[16]

It was this conviction that finally led Lincoln, under his war powers, to issue the Emancipation Proclamation on January 1, 1863, which freed all of the slaves in the states that had joined the Confederacy. Less noted but equally important, Lincoln proposed at the same time an amendment to the Constitution that would require the compensated emancipation of all slaves in the North. The Emancipation Proclamation wasn't just an empty gesture. Lincoln meant it, as he would make clear in his Gettysburg Address, reminding his listeners, "Our fathers brought forth on this continent a new nation, conceived in liberty, and dedicated to the proposition that all men are created equal."[17] *All men*, not just white men of property.

For Lincoln, the purpose of the war had progressed beyond simply preserving the Union; it had become a quest to fulfill the inherent promises of the Declaration of Independence. The American Dream was for everyone, as he made clear in a speech to the 166th Ohio Regiment in 1864:

> I happen temporarily to occupy this big White House. I am living witness that any one of your children may look to come here as my father's child has. It is in order that each of you may have through this free government which we have enjoyed, an open field and a fair chance for your industry, enterprise, and intelligence; that you may all have equal privileges in the race of life, with all of its desirable human aspirations. It is for this the struggle should be maintained, that we may not lose our birthright—not only for one, but for two or three years. The nation is worth fighting for, to secure such an inestimable jewel.[18]

In the end the war did, finally, bring about the end of slavery. In its wake came amendments to the Constitution that abolished slavery, granted citizenship to all persons born in the United States, and prohibited voting restrictions based on race. But the American Dream as Lincoln perceived it was still denied to African Americans, as in the ensuing decades the Supreme Court chose to interpret those amendments very narrowly. It would take another century before African Americans were granted anything approaching true social and political equality.

In freeing the slaves and fighting to force the South to remain part of the Union, Lincoln had pushed the power of the federal government farther than ever before. Locke had argued that the proper role of government—indeed, the *only* role of government— was to protect the natural rights of individuals. But when those rights had come into conflict, the U.S. government had taken a moral stand and actively sided with one group of individuals over another. This opened a door, one that radical Republicans would walk through after

Lincoln was assassinated in order to forcibly reconstruct the South. This set the precedent for a far more active, interventionist national government, one which would reach into more and more aspects of its citizens' lives. Meanwhile the North, in triumphing over the South, dealt a major blow to the Jeffersonian dream of an agrarian society of yeoman farmers, and paved the way for an increasingly capitalist and economically focused version of the American Dream.

4

THE DREAM OF WEALTH
IN THE GILDED AGE

◇◇

The Civil War was a decisive moment in American history, one that would finally put an end to slavery and the southern way of life, but the South wasn't the only section of the country undergoing radical changes. The period between the Civil War and World War I is often referred to as the Gilded Age, and it saw one of the greatest economic expansions in the history not only of the country, but also of the world. Whereas land had formerly been the primary source of wealth, with industrialization wealth came from the ownership of factories, patents, machinery, and resources. While the country in 1865 was still largely agrarian, manufacturing and urbanization were on the rise and approaching a tipping point, one that would forever alter the nation's character and vastly expand the scope of the American Dream.

The industrial revolution in America had been well under way before the Civil War, and after the war it resumed at an even greater pace, due in no small part to the building of railroads. In 1830, there were only twenty-three miles of railroad track in the entire country; by the time of the Civil War there were over thirty thousand.[1] Most were in the North and Midwest, and the lines were short and generally owned by competing interests. There was much waste and duplication, and numerous transfers were required to travel any significant distance. In 1853, fourteen short lines in New York State were consolidated into the New York Central, creating a single continuous line between Albany and Buffalo—but such consolidation was unusual. It wasn't until the first transcontinental railroad was built and began operating that the transformative potential of railroads began to have a major impact on the American economy.

The story of the building of the first transcontinental railroad is a tale that could fill an entire book in and of itself. The project, begun in 1863 and completed in 1869, was a phenomenal feat of human engineering and perseverance—one that wouldn't have happened without the financial support of the federal government, which authorized the construction of the line with the passage of the Pacific Railroad Act of 1862. The act provided financial support through land grants and the issuance of 30-year government bonds to the Union Pacific and Central Pacific railroads, which laid track westwards from Council Bluffs, Iowa and eastward from Alameda, California. The undertaking was so massive and risky that the Union Pacific wasn't been able to sell a single share of its stock, and Congress was obliged to double the land grants given to both companies before wary investors could be tempted into financing the bold gamble.

The sheer logistics of the endeavor were overwhelming. Laying track required massive amounts of iron, tools, ties, spikes, bolts, and lumber, not to mention food and water for more than ten thousand men and thousands of horses, mules, and oxen. The Great Plains, as yet unsettled, could provide no supplies of any kind. Everything had to be brought via steamboat from St. Louis along a river that was navigable only four months of the year, or on a work train with a forge, carpentry shop, machine shop, and kitchen on board. In the Sierras, workers had to cut their way through walls of solid granite, drilling holes with spikes and eighteen-pound sledgehammers and then filling the holes with black powder to blast away the rock. Upon reaching Cape Horn, near Sacramento, California, workers had to suspend themselves by rope from the top of the thousand-foot cliffs and hack at the rock with hammers and chisels. At a rate of eight inches per day, it took half a year to carve out a trench large enough to accommodate a railway track. The joining of the Central and Union lines at Promontory Summit, Utah, was the crowning of a monumental achievement.

Yet this was only a beginning. Once that first transcontinental railway had been shown to be not only possible, but also profitable, a railroad boom ensued, and by the end of the century there were five intercontinental railroads, all connected with numerous regional lines. Fruit from California, potatoes from Idaho, wheat from Kansas, and meat from Chicago could now be transported across the country in record time. Railroads significantly lowered transportation costs and reduced the cost of producing manufactured goods, which in turn spurred an increase in demand for those goods. These railroads also opened up new markets in the West, and by 1897, there were over 200,000 miles of railroad track in the United States, creating a truly national mass market rather than a series of isolated local ones.[2] This national market made it feasible for a single enterprise to sell more of its products, build larger factories, and take advantage of economies of scale, thereby reducing costs and increasing demand even further.

Thus, in addition to being an important new industry, railroads also started a technological revolution that significantly impacted the way people did business. This new method of transportation cut out the middleman, allowing manufacturers of a huge variety of products to bypass or swallow up networks of jobbers, agents, and merchants. The construction of railroads also helped to spur the development of numerous other industries, as it required large amounts of iron, coal, glass, and rubber, as well as a variety of industrial goods, including locomotives, freight and passenger cars, rails, spikes, and more. A growing number of consumer goods were now within reach of the average American, both geographically and financially, and an army of entrepreneurs emerged to meet the growing demand. The railroad industry enriched not only those who built it, like Edward Henry Harriman and James J. Hill, but also those who used it to transport their goods, such as lumber baron Frederick Weyerhaeuser and catalog retailer Richard Warren Sears. In the course of a few decades, as a result of railroads, the United States was dramatically transformed into a place the Founding Fathers would not have recognized.

Nor was the railroad the only transformative factor at the time. The telegraph, which connected all of the major American cities and spanned the continent by the end of the Civil War, did as much to speed communications as the railroad did to accelerate travel. Andrew Jackson's victory at the Battle of New Orleans took place three weeks after a peace treaty was signed because news of the treaty had not yet reached him from Washington. Similarly, it took him a month to travel by coach from Nashville to the capitol for his inauguration. Three decades later, the same trip typically lasted three days by rail, and news could be wired to any large American city within hours.

The country had effectively become smaller and its people more connected, a trend encouraged by the rise of the modern newspaper. In Benjamin Franklin's day, newspapers were expensive to produce and highly political, generally containing a collection of partisan editorials with a bit of very outdated and suspect news mixed in. The invention of rotary presses powered by steam, however, greatly increased the speed and quantities that could be produced, while lowering the cost of production, and the telegraph allowed news reporting to become timely and relevant. By the 1860s, the nonpartisan *New York Herald* had a national daily circulation of more than 400,000, with foreign correspondents in London, Paris, and Rome supplying its readers with world news.[3]

City life in general became more recognizably modern with the invention and proliferation of gas lamps and streetlights, central heating, running water, and the cast-iron stove. Large, lavishly appointed department stores offered clothing and home furnishings and were elaborately decorated for Christmas, which had become a major secular holiday and an important driver of retail sales. Thanks to mass production and economies of scale, all of these inventions became accessible not merely to the wealthy, but to an increasing portion of the middle class as well, at least in urban centers where high population density made them possible.

The American Dream of upward mobility changed during this era, swinging decisively away from Jefferson's vision of economic self-sufficiency through farming and toward Hamilton's more industrialist version of growth and accumulation of wealth. In Hamilton's day, such wealth was theoretically open to all but was actually achieved by only a few. In the decades following the Civil War, however, it seemed that vast fortunes might be accumulated by anyone with a little luck and pluck. The South, which had adopted a system of sharecropping, admittedly endured many decades of painful reconstruction before it finally industrialized and was capable of joining in the new, more modern American Dream of affluence. But in the North and West, opportunity was everywhere, and the only question was whether one was man enough to seize it.

• • • • •

For those who had expectations of accumulating a vast fortune, the most likely path to success in the Gilded Age was through entrepreneurship. As the country became industrialized, there was an increasing realization that large-scale manufacturing, not agriculture, was the path to wealth, and the number of manufacturing companies in the United States increased 80 percent during the 1860s alone.[4] The government took a hands-off approach to business, and the economy grew rapidly, yielding unprecedented fortunes. Fourteen of the seventy-five richest people in recorded human history (based on a comparison of net worth in current dollars) were Americans born between 1831 and 1840, including well-known figures such as J.P. Morgan, Andrew Carnegie, and John D. Rockefeller.[5] Born well after the Revolutionary Era, they reached adulthood right as the country was industrializing and hit the peak of their careers just in time to take advantage of the resulting economic boom. In the process, these captains of industry created business empires the size of which the world had never seen before.

These empires did not spring up out of nowhere, and the fact that fourteen of the richest men in the history of the world were born during one decade in one country was no coincidence. The confluence of industrialization, laissez-faire capitalism, and the railroad boom made it possible, as the upward trajectory of Cornelius Vanderbilt's fortune demonstrates. Having accumulated a decent fortune after forty-odd years in the steamboat industry, most people would have been content to retire, but not Vanderbilt. Instead, he set his sights on the railroad industry, which turned out to be even more cut-throat and tumultuous than the steamboat business, due in large part to the machinations of one of the most infamous characters in Wall Street's history, Daniel Drew.

While entrepreneurship may have been the surest path to wealth in the America of the nineteenth century, it was by no means the easiest. In the free-for-all business environment of the decades following the Civil War, the vast array of new economic opportunities changed the timeline for success, and in the minds of many, lessened the effort required to achieve it. Making money became a great and exciting game in which many participated, Daniel Drew among them. Unlike Vanderbilt, Drew wasn't content to live a life of frugal self-sacrifice while patiently building up an empire over the course of a lifetime. On the contrary, he was looking for a fast and easy road to wealth, and with the rise of Wall Street, speculation became a favorite method of building a fortune with a minimum of effort. Due in part to the invention of the telegraph, New York had become the financial center of the country at a time when Wall Street had no oversight and the New York legislature was corrupt to the core. (In 1868, it passed a law that effectively legalized bribery.) While no industry at the time was immune to corruption, railroads required so much capital that they were usually financed by selling securities, and thus they were prime targets for speculators.

It was amidst this environment of speculation and corruption that Vanderbilt plunged into both the railroad business and the world of Wall Street investing. His first purchase was the New York and Harlem railroad, an unprofitable line that nevertheless had the advantage of being the only one that went into the city. He talked the aldermen of the common council into granting him a franchise to extend the line so that it ran the entire length of Manhattan, and the company's stock promptly jumped. Always alert to a speculative opportunity, Daniel Drew convinced the aldermen to sell the stock short and then rescind Vanderbilt's franchise. When Vanderbilt heard about the scheme, he responded by cornering the market on New York and Harlem Railroad securities, and much to the aldermen's consternation, the stock rose steadily upwards. They quickly reinstated his franchise, and Vanderbilt extended the line.

Next, he bought the Hudson River Railroad, a line that ran along the Hudson from New York City to Albany, where it connected to the New York Central line. Previously, the Hudson line had run only in winter; during summer the New York Central used steamboats to ferry passengers between the two cities. Vanderbilt would have none of that arrangement and retaliated by stopping his trains two miles short of Albany and refusing to connect with the Central line, stranding its passengers and cutting off those in Albany from New York City. Vanderbilt's competitors soon capitulated to his tactics, and within a year, he was named president of the New York Central Railroad, which he planned to merge with the Hudson to create a line going all the way from New York to Buffalo.

His primary rival on this route was the Erie Railroad, whose stock was a darling of speculators and known as "the scarlet woman of Wall Street." Vanderbilt initially went to Erie's board of directors to propose splitting the traffic, but when they refused, he resolved to gain a controlling interest. The Erie board's treasurer, none other than Daniel Drew, countered by converting bonds into stock and selling shares on the open market. Vanderbilt got a judge to issue an injunction against Drew and told his brokers to buy all of the Erie stock available, but Drew persuaded his own judge to rule that the Erie could continue to convert bonds into stock upon request. Vanderbilt then got *his* judge to issue arrest warrants for the entire Erie board, most of whom fled to New Jersey. The matter went to the courts, and eventually Vanderbilt gave in, although only when the board agreed to buy back his worthless stock and sever all ties with Drew. The fight, however, had wounded the Erie Company's financial position to the extent that it was no longer a major threat. For Vanderbilt, the loss was worth the price. He had earned $11 million from steamships in forty-odd years; he made $90 million from railroads in a decade.

By the time he died in 1877, Vanderbilt's net worth was $105 million, far eclipsing John Jacob Astor's fortune of $20 million and making Vanderbilt the second wealthiest entrepreneur in American history by percent of gross national product.[6] Despite his wealth, Vanderbilt lived relatively modestly, residing in a townhouse in Washington Square that cost only $55,000. Unlike Benjamin Franklin, however, he wasn't much of a philanthropist. Vanderbilt gave $1 million to Central University in Nashville, now called Vanderbilt University, but that was an exception to his usual practices. When he was once asked to give aid to impoverished people standing in line for food, he replied, "Let them do what I have done."[7] In a land and an era of unprecedented opportunities, many echoed his sentiments.

• • • • •

Cornelius Vanderbilt's views on what a successful man owes to society reflected a growing trend toward what would later be called Social Darwinism. Developed by an English journalist and philosopher named Herbert Spencer in his 1861 work, *First Principles*, it applied

Charles Darwin's theories of natural selection and evolution to economics. The basic idea was that life is an economic competition—those who best adapt to their economic environment succeed. Extraordinary individuals drive progress in society by contributing positively to the country through increased productivity, expansion of markets, and job creation. Government should stay out of individual economic competition, because active government intervention limits individuals' freedom and opportunity to succeed. By taking from those who have to give to those that have not, government denies successful individuals their just compensation, and in doing so limits growth and progress.

The most prominent American Social Darwinist during the Gilded Age was William Graham Sumner. A first-generation American, he was for the most part a self-taught and self-made man who attended Yale and then became a professor of political and social science. Sumner used Social Darwinism as a way of defending laissez-faire capitalism against those who argued that the government ought to take a more active role in curing social inequalities. Calls for greater intervention on the part of the federal government had increased after the Civil War, and for a variety of reasons. Many people wanted not only to integrate former slaves into society, but to bring about greater economic equality in general, as income disparity had significantly increased with industrialization.

Sumner saw those who wanted to use government to actively bring about social change as nothing less than enemies of society. In *What Social Classes Owe to Each Other*, published in 1883, he argued against the idea that the well-off had a moral obligation to aid those less fortunate than themselves. For Sumner, life was inherently competitive, and self-reliance was a moral obligation of every individual in a competitive environment. "In a free state every man is held and expected to take care of himself and his family, to make no trouble for his neighbor, and to contribute his full share to public interests and common necessities," he argued. "If he fails in this, he throws burdens on others."[8] Competition implied that there would be winners and losers, and while losers were often unhappy, happiness was not guaranteed. The achievement of happiness was up to the individual, and Sumner believed that people must strive for it at their own risk. It was not the role of government to prop up the losers in the economic competition of life by taking from the winners in order to make the losers happy. Everyone must be responsible for their own happiness.

In Sumner's view, active government intervention was immoral, because it took from the deserving and gave to the undeserving. Redistribution of wealth was simply government-sanctioned robbery that absolved individuals of their responsibility to take care of themselves. He rejected the notion that economic forces create the underclass; he believed one's social level was a function of one's work ethic and capacity for self-denial. By working and refraining from spending, anyone could accumulate capital. Sumner viewed poverty as an individual's fault and responsibility, not some insurmountable constraint. One was not a creature of one's economic environment but rather its creator. Those who actively created their environment would succeed and had a right to enjoy the benefits of that success. They owed others nothing. No one had a claim on anyone else. A man "should be left free to do the most for himself that he can, and should be guaranteed the exclusive enjoyment of all that he does," Sumner argued. "A free man in a free democracy has no duty whatever toward other men of the same rank and standing, except respect, courtesy, and good-will."[9]

Sumner also argued against active government intervention in economic affairs because it impeded economic progress. As he argued in his essay, *Sociological Fallacies*, written in 1884:

> Now, the achievements of the human race have been accomplished by the *élite* of the race…A man is good for something only so far as he thinks, knows, tries, or works. If we put a great many men together, those of them who carry on the society will be those who use reflection and

forethought, and exercise industry and self-control. Hence the dogma that all men are equal is the most flagrant falsehood and the most immoral doctrine which men have ever believed; it means the man who has not done his duty is as good as the one who has done his duty, and it takes away all sense from the teachings of the moralists, when they instruct youth that men who pursue one line of action will go down to loss and shame, and those who pursue another course will go up to honor and success. It is, on the contrary, a doctrine of the first moral and sociological importance that truth, wisdom, and righteousness come only by painstaking, study, and striving. These things are so hard that it is only the few who attain to them. These few carry on human society now as they always have done...Men are very unequal in what they get out of life, but they are still more unequal in what they put into it.[10]

For Sumner, equality meant equality of chance, not equality of results. What really mattered was not equality but the freedom of the individual, which he defined as the liberty to act unimpeded by external government restraint. In a society where freedom and competition are not constrained, those with the most talent and perseverance win, and everyone gets what they deserve. A rising tide lifts all boats, which is the sum of social progress. Winners must be allowed to win, and losers must be allowed to lose. Government's only proper role is to ensure fair competition.

The Social Darwinists' focus on government as the key threat to individual freedom and liberty is often used to trace laissez-faire ideas back to Jefferson and his preference for limited government, but this is not entirely accurate. Liberty, for Jefferson, was a political rather than an economic matter. With his strong preference for an agrarian lifestyle and his inherent distrust of bankers and the financial elite, he could hardly be characterized as a supporter of nineteenth-century industrialization and laissez-faire capitalism. He feared, rather than supported, the aggregation of capital in the hands of a wealthy elite and supported many government policies designed to spread economic opportunity as widely as possible. On the other hand, Jefferson was no friend of the idea of a welfare state and redistribution of wealth, for as he noted in his second inaugural address, "Our wish is that...[there be] maintained that state of property, equal or unequal, which results to every man from his own industry or that of his fathers."[11]

Sumner's philosophy that poverty is one's own fault may sound a bit extreme to modern ears, but it fit well with the prevailing optimism of the post–Civil Wars years. While Reconstruction in the South was certainly an example of overly zealous government intervention and encroachment on individual liberty, it was viewed as necessary to ensure the emancipation of former slaves, a singular solution for a singular problem. Those who felt that government needed to take a more active role in curing economic and social ills more generally were still, while growing in number, a minority. Opportunity beckoned, and as long as there was hope that those who started with nothing might eventually amass great wealth, laissez-faire capitalism would be held as the basic foundation for the achievement of the American Dream.

• • • • •

American citizens weren't the only ones who felt the pull of Sumner's version of the American Dream. On the contrary, the tales of vast fortunes to be made in America continued to lure people from across the world to American shores throughout the nineteenth century. The factories in the North required an increasing supply of cheap labor, labor that native-born Americans had little interest in supplying as long as there was the promise of cheap land out West. Who would consent to be a wage slave in a factory when he could command his own destiny on the frontier?

The answer was people from the lowest rungs of the economic ladder in Europe. As a steady stream of American citizens migrated to the western frontier in the 1800s, they were replaced by a tidal wave of immigrants from Europe in what became known as the Great Atlantic Migration. Some went straight to the gold fields of California or settled on farms in the West, but the majority took jobs in heavy industry, construction, or the garment industry, providing labor for the vast numbers of factories being built in the Northeast. They came in pursuit of the American Dream, and so high were their hopes that some of them expected the streets to be literally paved in gold.

Labor shortages had been a chronic problem in America since the colonial days, because few people were willing to work very long for someone else when it was relatively easy to buy land or start one's own business. This led to a policy of comparatively open immigration, and people from the lower classes in Europe flocked to the New World in pursuit of higher wages and a chance at a better life. In one of the largest migrations in human history, approximately 40 million Europeans came to the United States between 1820 and 1924, the bulk of this migration occurring after the Civil War. The first wave of immigrants before the war were mostly western Europeans, particularly Irish and Germans suffering in the wake of the potato famine and general crop failures. As western Europe became more industrialized, however, more and more immigrants came from the less-developed countries of southern and eastern Europe such as Poland and Italy. Many were migrant workers—single men who intended to build up some capital and eventually return to their home countries. But a significant portion of them liked America so well that they stayed, and letters sent home with money and glowing descriptions of the United States prompted their friends and relatives to join them, fueling further immigration.

Life as a hired laborer in a mid-nineteenth-century factory certainly wasn't easy or pleasant. Factory wages in the increasingly industrialized North were low, and conditions were appalling, but the standard of living was still equal to or better than what immigrants had been used to in Europe. More important, with the lack of legal class distinctions, the opportunity to rise was significantly greater, and few immigrants with any ambition whatsoever intended to remain factory workers for long. Their intent was to live frugally and save as much as possible so that they could go into business for themselves. Unlike those who went to California hoping to strike it rich, the immigrants who got off the boat at Ellis Island didn't necessarily think wealth would come easily, and they were willing to work hard for years and even decades to achieve their dreams. A worker in a textile mill might, within a few years, save enough to start a tailoring business of his own, and who knew what might happen from there. In the rapidly expanding American economy of the late nineteenth century, opening a business was often not so much the end goal as just the start—a rung on a ladder that even the poorest and obscurest of immigrants hoped to climb all the way to the top. This is the essence of the immigrant American Dream, and it persists largely unchanged to this day.

When it came to climbing that ladder and playing in the rough-and-tumble competition of Social Darwinism, none climbed as high or succeeded as well as Andrew Carnegie. Born in Scotland just as the industrial revolution was getting into high gear, his family moved to Pennsylvania when Andrew was twelve years old. His father, a former weaver, went to work in a textile mill, and young Andrew got a job as a bobbin boy at the mill for $1.20 a week. Highly capable and industrious, Carnegie took it upon himself to travel into Pittsburgh several nights a week to learn bookkeeping, and through the friend of an uncle, he obtained a job as a messenger boy in the Pittsburgh telegraph office. His promotion to full-time operator was swift, and by the age of sixteen he was earning $25 a month.

But this was just the beginning. In 1852, the Pennsylvania Railroad opened a line between Philadelphia and Pittsburgh, and Thomas Scott—the newly appointed superintendent for the western division of the line—was constantly in the telegraph office. Carnegie caught his attention, and he soon offered the boy a job as his personal telegraph operator and private secretary. This was a tremendous opportunity, for not only did Carnegie learn a great deal about business by working for a railroad company, but Scott also taught him about investing. He loaned Carnegie the money to buy ten shares of Adams Express Company stock, a valuable blue chip investment that was not available on the open market. Within a month, Carnegie had received a $10 dividend check, which opened his eyes to the power of invested capital. Within two years his investments were producing an annual income of almost $5,000, more than three times his annual salary, and Carnegie was soon on his way to becoming a millionaire.

As a young man, Carnegie was more of an investor than an entrepreneur, but that changed after the end of the Civil War. The railroad industry boomed, and he saw an opportunity in building iron bridges for the railroad lines, as the wooden ones were frequently destroyed by fires or floods. In 1865 he left the railroad company, where he had succeeded Scott as superintendent, to found the Keystone Bridge Company. Keystone was a success from the start, and Carnegie soon developed it into the largest bridge company in the nation. With demand for iron bridges rising rapidly, he decided it would be wise to control his own supply of iron, so he bought an iron works and created the Freedom Iron and Steel Company. Not long afterwards, he began converting the plant so that it could process Bessemer steel, which was much cheaper and stronger than traditional steel. But on a trip to England in 1872, he visited their cutting-edge Bessemer steel plants, and what he saw convinced him that his plans for converting his own iron works were too limited. It was evident that there were tremendous cost savings in economies of scale, and that he could not possibly hope to compete with the British plants unless he matched their size and technology. He resolved to build an entirely new mill dedicated to producing steel with modern equipment, and to do so he formed a new corporation called Carnegie, McCandless & Company.

Carnegie adhered to several business practices that served him well over the course of his career. First, he considered people to be his most important asset, at least at the management level, and took care to surround himself with highly capable and motivated people. (Carnegie once suggested that his epitaph should read, "Here lies a man who was able to surround himself with men far cleverer than himself."[12]) Second, he avoided overcapitalization and preferred to have a private company rather than one traded on the open market, as he had more control that way. Third, he believed in holding back a large portion of profits as a reserve rather than distributing them as dividends, so that he could finance plant expansions even during bad economic times. Finally, he relentlessly pursued efficiency and introduced new inventory and accounting systems in order to keep tight control of costs. By 1876, his plant was able to produce a ton of steel rails for $50.

In 1875, the Bessemer Steel Association was formed, and while initially it was organized as a trade association for the purpose of lobbying in support of favorable tariffs, Carnegie saw that it had the potential to function as an oligopoly to control prices and production. The other members of the association saw Carnegie as an upstart and originally allotted him a mere 9 percent of the rail market, while the top company received 19 percent. Enraged, Carnegie announced that he could produce steel rails for $9 a ton and would undersell the whole lot of them unless he received the greatest share of the market. It was an outrageous bluff, but apparently convincing, for the association capitulated. They had cause for resentment in later years, for whenever Carnegie felt that the market was weak or that he had gained some technological advantage, he would disregard the pricing agreement, run his mill at full capacity, and sell for whatever he could get.

By 1881, he had consolidated most of his various interests into Carnegie Bros. & Company, with himself holding the controlling interest and his brother as chairman of the board. That year, the company made a profit of $2 million, and in 1889, Carnegie Bros. & Company was consolidated with the former Pittsburgh Steel Company into Carnegie Steel, which at its peak produced profits of $4.5 million annually. Over the next decade, he built his steel company into a steel empire through vertical integration, branching into iron ore mining and later into production of finished steel products. When it came to the latter he faced stiff competition from J. P. Morgan, who owned a controlling interest in the Federal Steel Company. Morgan was heavily invested in his steel business and had no wish to cooperate with or yield to Carnegie, so instead he decided to buy him out. Carnegie, who was sixty-five and ready to turn his attention to philanthropic matters, agreed to sell the company for $480 million in 1901. One of the first things he did was to put $5 million of the proceeds into a pension and benefit fund for his employees.

Had Carnegie kept this money and invested it, he might very well have become the richest entrepreneur in American history. Instead, he became one of America's most celebrated philanthropists. Unlike Vanderbilt or Sumner, Carnegie saw it as a rich man's duty to give back to the community, and over the next ten years, he gave away over $350 million as well as establishing an endowment of $125 million. He founded 2,811 public libraries, donated 7,689 organs to churches, and funded both Carnegie Hall in New York City and the Carnegie Institution in Washington. While he was sometimes ruthless in generating his fortune, he was certainly generous in giving it away, and his success was a story of inspiration for every penniless immigrant who came to the United States in hope of a better life.[13]

In general Carnegie was much admired, but not everyone was so impressed with the increasing throng of multimillionaires that seemed to be sprouting up everywhere in the decades after the Civil War. Where some saw perseverance and determination, others saw greed and ruthlessness and they were determined to do something to stop it. The captains of industry did much to further the wealth and prosperity of the country, but there was no doubt that they broke promises, skirted laws, and promoted their own self-interests as well. In addition, many of them flaunted their wealth to a degree that provoked jealousy, and underneath all of the wondrous fortunes and prosperity there were rumblings of discontent. As more miles of railroad track were laid across the country, one had to wonder if the American Dream had become derailed. Was the dream people were chasing the true path to happiness, or was the glitter of the Gilded Age merely fool's gold?

5

REINVENTING THE DREAM
IN THE PROGRESSIVE ERA

◇◇

The nineteenth century was in many ways the zenith of the classic American Dream—a time of great optimism, boundless opportunities, and one of the greatest economic expansions in history. Like all boom periods, however, it had its busts, and the fallout from those busts led people to question the fundamental nature of the American Dream.

The business cycle dictates that every economic expansion has a contraction, but in the closing decades of the nineteenth century, those contractions were made far worse by the lack of a sound financial system. The chaos of the free-banking era had finally come to an end during the Civil War with the passage of the National Banking Act, which created a system of national banks that were required to back up their notes with treasury securities. Although the national banks were better regulated and provided greater stability than the state banks, however, there were still significant problems. When treasury bonds fluctuated in value, the national banks had to recall loans or borrow from other banks, creating liquidity crises.

These crises were exacerbated by the fact that smaller, rural banks kept deposits at the larger national banks and tended to draw on them at the same time, during planting season. When liquidity was insufficient to meet demand, bank panics and failures spread throughout the financial system and repeatedly plunged the country into recessions and depressions.

One of the most severe, the appropriately named Long Depression, started in 1873 and was precipitated by overinvestment in railroads, specifically the Northern Pacific Railway. The largest bank in the country at the time, Jay Cooke & Company, had financed the early stages of this second transcontinental railroad, but Congress's decision to return to the gold standard had caused a contraction in the money supply, and Cooke found himself unable to market several million dollars of Northern Pacific Railway bonds. Rumors began to circulate that the bank's credit was worthless, and the firm suddenly declared bankruptcy after failing to secure a government loan. This set off a panic, leading to a chain reaction of bank failures that marked the beginning of a severe six-year depression—the longest economic downturn in American history. Of the country's 364 railroads, 89 went bankrupt, and over 18,000 businesses failed between 1873 and 1875 alone. Unemployment reached a peak of 14 percent in 1876, and those who managed to keep their jobs saw their wages cut almost in half.[1]

The economy eventually recovered, but another boom of railroad construction from 1879 to 1882 again led to overinvestment and another depression during which business activity declined by nearly a third and more than 10,000 small firms failed. This was followed by two more recessions and then the Panic of 1893, which was precipitated by the failure of the United States Reading Railroad. The financial panic led to a stock market crash and yet another wave of bank failures as well as a run on gold reserves and subsequent withdrawal of European investments. Again, industrial output fell by over a third, 15,000 firms and 500 banks failed, and a fifth of the American workforce became unemployed.[2]

Every one of these panics and depressions had serious consequences for the working class, whose dreams were dashed when they were forced to default on their mortgages or their entire life savings were wiped out by bank failures. During boom times there was optimism and the feeling that the American Dream was open to everyone, but during the ever more frequent and severe busts, that optimism was shattered. As the country became more industrialized, an increasing percentage of the population relied on wages for income and had no way of paying for food, clothing, or shelter when depressions hit and jobs suddenly disappeared. Nor was the West the safety valve it had once been. Manifest destiny had been fulfilled, and the country encompassed all of the land between the east and west coasts. The Great Plains and the Rockies were still only sparsely populated, but by 1890, the Census Bureau had declared that there was no more frontier. With its disappearance went the opportunity for people who had lost everything to easily pull up stakes and start a new life out West.

Instead, people turned to the cities, and as a result of industrialization, a great migration began from rural farms to urban centers. When people arrived in the cities, however, they found increasing competition for jobs not only from fellow Americans who had been forced to abandon their farms, but also from a new wave of European immigrants, who drove down the cost of labor. Between 1860 and 1880, a total of 250,000 eastern and southern European immigrants came to the United States; between 1890 and 1910 that number jumped to more than 8 million, and they were more likely to settle in cities and work in urban factories than their predecessors were.[3] Americans who moved to cities in hopes of new economic opportunities soon felt they were being held back by competition from cheaper foreign labor and the threat of blacklists. (Workers who either quit voluntarily or were let go were often blacklisted and denied employment elsewhere unless they had a signed card from their previous employer.) Many questioned the validity of equal opportunity in an environment where their ability to sell their labor depended on obtaining a release from their previous job.

As the century drew to a close, belief in the American Dream faltered, particularly during the Panic of 1893. Those in the working class increasingly felt that opportunity was closed to them, and they began to resent the fortunes of men like Vanderbilt, Carnegie, and J.P. Morgan, whom the press was starting to label as robber barons. A large gap opened between the haves and the have-nots, both economically and philosophically. There was a pervasive opinion among those who had succeeded and prospered that those who had not were lazy, incompetent, or of flawed character. In a land where one could rise from a penniless immigrant to a multimillionaire, so the thinking went, if a man did not succeed, it must be his own fault. But as banks failed, businesses went bankrupt, and unemployment rose, small farmers and unskilled wage laborers began to rebel against this notion and to fight for a larger slice of the economic pie that the captains of industry were feasting on. Their chosen weapons in this tumultuous era were labor strikes and the formation of unions.

● ● ● ● ●

The American Dream up to this point had always been one of personal agency. Whether your ambition was to own your own farm or to build a business empire, holding your destiny in your own hands was a key part of the dream, and working for someone else was something to be done only temporarily on the way to fulfilling it. In preindustrial America, most wage laborers were highly skilled craftsmen who could command a decent wage, as skilled labor was generally in short supply. Businesses were relatively small, so employees and employers interacted frequently, and if you didn't like your employer, you could always leave. Although they started out as apprentices in the employ of someone else, most craftsmen worked their way up to become masters and eventually opened their own shops.

As the size of business enterprises and the supply of labor grew, however, wage laborers, particularly unskilled ones, were increasingly at a disadvantage. Working in a factory, mine, or for the railroads became a dead end in terms of upward mobility; wages were barely enough to live on, much less to allow for savings. During the Long Depression and the financial panics and recessions that followed, these workers began to question what the promise of the American Dream really was. By resigning themselves to a life as wage laborers, had they given up on the American Dream and renounced all claims to it? Or were they entitled to a version of that dream in exchange for helping to build the business empires and wealth of their employers? The latter was a somewhat radical notion, but people were struggling to make ends meet and in a mood to question the self-reliance of the previous era. When management cut jobs or pay during hard economic times, bitterness and resentment inevitably bubbled up, and sometimes it boiled over.

One of the times when it boiled over was during the Great Railroad Strike of 1877, one of the first major labor strikes in American history. Several years into the Long Depression, at a point when children in poor families had begun dying in large numbers from starvation and disease, a number of eastern railroads suddenly announced a coordinated pay cut of 10 percent for their workers, as well as cutbacks to two or three days of work a week. Management and labor had never enjoyed particularly good relations in the railroad industry, and workers on the Baltimore and Ohio Railroad in Martinsburg, West Virginia—for whom the pay cut was their second in less than a year—reacted by seizing possession of the rail yards. They refused to allow any trains to leave until the pay cut was revoked, and the strike soon spread from Martinsburg to Baltimore, where a sympathetic crowd of 15,000 surrounded the train depot and set it on fire. From there, the strike spread throughout the Northeast and much of the Midwest, inciting spontaneous demonstrations and protests in almost every major city, and setting off general strikes in Pittsburgh, Chicago, and St. Louis.

Initially, as with most strikes over the next several decades, public sympathy was with the strikers. But management during this era refused to negotiate, taking much the same stance toward strikers as we do toward terrorists today. As the standoffs lengthened, desperation on the part of the striking workers inevitably turned to violence perpetrated not only against company property, but against local law enforcement and strike breakers as well. When demonstrations turned into riots that led to casualties, public sentiment would abruptly turn against labor, and federal troops and state militias would be called in to restore order. The Great Railroad Strike followed the same pattern. As the strike spread westward, escalating in violence as it went, a U.S. Court of Appeals judge ruled that strikes and other unlawful interference with the railroads were a violation of United States law. Federal marshals were ordered to protect the railroads, and President Rutherford B. Hayes sent federal troops from city to city to restore order. Eventually, forty-five days after the original strike in West Virginia had started, the violence subsided and the strike was over, leaving millions of dollars in property damage and more than a hundred people dead as a result. The strike had failed, and the pay cuts were not revoked.

The Great Railroad Strike was an extreme, unorganized event precipitated by great suffering during the Long Depression, but it was a harbinger of things to come. Relations between labor and management, particularly in the railroad and mining industries, went from bad to worse during the closing decades of the century, and the Great Railroad Strike was followed by the Haymarket Square bombing in Chicago in 1886, the Homestead Steel Strike near Pittsburgh in 1892, and the nationwide Pullman Strike in 1894. The chaos and violence of these strikes, along with general failure of the strikers to achieve their goals, convinced many that more organized, disciplined action was necessary. On their own, wage laborers, particularly unskilled ones, had little bargaining power, so they began to organize and form unions on both the local and national level.

The country's first national labor organization, appropriately named the National Labor Union, had actually been founded shortly after the Civil War in 1866. However, it lasted a mere six years before being dissolved and supplanted by the more popular Knights of Labor and a number of other unions comprised of skilled workers, unskilled workers, and farmers. The Knights organized several successful strikes, and the group's leader, Terrence Powderly, helped to found the People's Party. Often referred to as the Populist Party, its platform merged the Knights of Labor's urban labor agenda with that of rural farmers. It called for the abolition of national banks, direct election of national senators, government ownership of railroads and telegraphs, a graduated income tax, an eight-hour workday for city laborers, restricted immigration, and free coinage of silver. With populist sentiment running high, James Weaver, the party's presidential candidate in 1892, won four states and received twenty-two electoral votes. The People's Party also captured eleven seats in the House of Representatives, several governorships, and majorities in the state legislatures of Kansas, Nebraska, and North Carolina.

Free coinage of silver turned out to be a key issue for the People's Party that rallied many people to its cause. During the Civil War, the federal government had gone off the gold standard internally and started printing paper money to help finance the war, which led to inflation. Although the government stopped printing greenbacks at the end of the war, it started minting silver dollars from the rapidly expanding silver supply coming out of mines in the West instead, giving the country a bimetallic standard. While farmers and debtors in general liked the inflated silver currency, as it made it repaying loans easier, bankers and merchants back east, who had to use gold for international trade, lobbied for a return to the gold standard. In 1873, Congress voted to demonetarize silver and return to a *de facto* gold standard, creating a sharp contraction in the money supply that contributed to the Long Depression.

The pro-silver farmers and miners, who referred to the demonetarization as the "Crime of '73," pushed hard to reinstate the coinage of silver, and in 1890 Congress capitulated by passing the Sherman Silver Act. Without repealing earlier legislation that embraced the gold standard, Congress required the U.S. Treasury to purchase 4.5 million ounces of silver bullion per month and use it to coin silver dollars. In addition, the act set a fixed ratio of 16:1 for the value of silver to gold, regardless of the actual market price of either metal, and earlier legislation mandated that all silver coins were redeemable in gold on demand. In effect, the gold standard kept the value of the dollar steady, while the increasing number of silver dollars continually inflated the money supply. In an attempt to have it both ways, Congress created an untenable situation that eventually imploded during the Panic of 1893. Confidence in U.S. currency plummeted, and gold reserves quickly drained out of the U.S. Treasury, which had to be bailed out by J.P. Morgan.

The disastrous monetary policy proved fatal for the People's Party, which by 1896 had abandoned most of its platform and endorsed the Democratic nominee for president, William Jennings Bryan, based solely on his pro-silver stance. But their legacy lived on in the idea that the federal government had a primary role to play in the economic prosperity of the country, which by the turn of the century was an idea widely accepted by Republicans and Democrats alike. The debate in the future would no longer be about *whether* the government should intervene in the economy, but rather *in what way* it should do so. That's really what the free silver debate was all about, as Bryan would argue in his famous "Cross of Gold" speech at the Democratic national convention:

> The sympathies of the Democratic Party, as described by the platform, are on the side of the struggling masses, who have ever been the foundation of the Democratic Party. There are two ideas of government. There are those who believe that if you just legislate to make the well-to-do prosperous, their prosperity will leak through on those below. The Democratic idea has been that if you legislate

> to make the masses prosperous their prosperity will find
> its way up and through every class that rests upon it.[4]

Ultimately, Bryan's pro-silver stance lost him the election, because the Republicans successfully blamed the depression on the effects of the Sherman Silver Act, which was quickly repealed. The People's Party soon fell apart, as did the Knights of Labor, whose membership had fallen from a peak of 700,000 members to less than 17,000.[5] It was replaced in popularity by the American Federation of Labor, which achieved greater success by working within the capitalist system to negotiate for better pay and working conditions rather than trying to form a labor party to achieve political goals. Difficult as the panics and depressions had been, there was still too much of an ingrained sense of self-reliance—and too much faith in the fluidity and openness of American society—for a true labor party to gain traction politically. Although union membership reached 10 percent by 1900, it would be several more decades before unions would wield the power necessary to shape the American Dream.

• • • • •

As the twentieth century dawned, the average American was still far too committed to the dream of upward mobility to embrace anything so collectivist as socialism, but there was no denying that the excesses of the Gilded Age had taken their toll on the notion of equal opportunity. With increasingly nationalized industries, depressions and panics were having a more widespread effect. The frontier was no longer a safety valve, so the urban poor had fewer avenues of escape, and reformers urged government to address the problems that resulted. For the first time, the middle class (and 90 percent of Americans counted themselves in that category)[6] began to pull away from the doctrine of self-reliance and to demand greater federal-government intervention in the private sector on behalf of their interests. While average Americans were far from asking for handouts or entitlements at this point, they felt increasingly that equal opportunity was being denied to them. They wanted government to curb the overwhelming power of the capitalist elites who, as a result of muckraking journalism, they had come to believe were thoroughly corrupt.

The rationale for greater intervention on the part of the federal government was provided by a man named Herbert Croly. Author of *The Promise of American Life* and founder of *The New Republic* magazine, Croly argued directly against William Graham Sumner and other proponents of Social Darwinism. His main thesis was that government action is needed to create the conditions of liberty by guaranteeing a sort of rough economic equality among its citizens. He rejected socialists' arguments in favor of equal outcomes, and instead championed the idea of equal starting points, so that everyone could compete fairly. In this, Croly was attempting to use the Hamiltonian means of a strong, active government to achieve the Jeffersonian end of equal opportunity, although his emphasis was on economic equality rather than political equality.

Unlike Sumner, Croly believed that the government owed something more to its people than protection of property rights. In *The Promise of American Life*, he argued:

> The American democracy has confidently believed in the fatal prosperity enjoyed by the people under the American System. In the confidence of that belief it has promised to Americans a substantial satisfaction of their economic needs; and it has made that promise an essential part of the American national idea...
>
> ...What the wage-earner needs, and what it is to the interest of a democratic state he should obtain, is a constantly higher standard of living. The state can help him to conquer a higher standard of living without doing any necessary injury to his employers and with a positive benefit to general economic and social efficiency. If it is to earn the loyalty of the wage-earners, it must recognize

the legitimacy of his demand, and make the satisfaction of it an essential part of public policy…

The American state is dedicated to such a duty, not only by its democratic purpose, but by its national tradition. So far as the former is concerned, it is absurd and fatal to ask a popular majority to respect the rights of a minority, when those rights are interpreted so as to seriously hamper, if not to forbid, the majority from obtaining the essential condition of individual freedom and development—viz. the highest possible standard of living.[7]

It is with Croly that we first hear the assertion that average citizens need—not want, but *need*—an increasingly higher standard of living, and that the government has a responsibility to help satisfy that need. This is the promise of American life. In the early days of the Republic, he argued, the expanding frontier allowed this promise to be kept without active government intervention. There were always economic opportunities for the poor and uneducated as long as the country's resources had not yet been fully developed and appropriated.

Once Manifest Destiny was complete and this safety valve no longer existed, however, economic conditions changed. Wealth accumulated in fewer and fewer hands, encouraged by a legal system that held the rights of property above all else. While Social Darwinists welcomed and championed this inequality, Croly argued that ultimately it was detrimental to both individual and societal interests. Extreme concentration of wealth undermined political and social stability, because as wealth was passed down from one generation to the next, privileges and inequalities persisted and became largely insurmountable for those who were less wealthy, creating permanent social classes. The only way for an individual to succeed under laissez-faire capitalism was to possess capital, special training, or an unusual amount of ability and energy, and the first two were far more likely to be possessed by those who were born into wealth. This unfair advantage was passed on to subsequent generations that in many cases did nothing to deserve it. "Individual freedom is important," Croly acknowledged, "but more important still is the freedom of the whole people to dispose of its own destiny."[8]

Therefore, Croly argued, if equality of opportunity was to be maintained, the government must step in and take a more active role. The American people should adapt their social and political theory—and their expectations of government—in order to meet the needs of changing times. "The truth is that Americans have not readjusted their political ideas to the teaching of their political and economic experience," he observed. "What is good for one generation will often be followed by consequences that spell deprivation for the next."[9] The function of government must adapt to changing circumstances, he argued, for if it does not, it will fail, and that failure will lead to the very sort of revolution that socialists predicted and embraced.

In order to avoid this, Croly thought that Americans should interpret the Constitution differently in the light of changing circumstances and amend it if necessary. "Difficult as it may be to escape from the legal framework defined in the Constitution, that body of law in theory remains merely an instrument which was made for the people and which if necessary can and will be modified,"[10] he asserted. The Constitution was not a static document but rather a living one that could be continuously adapted to modern times. American society in the twentieth century must be organized for the benefit of all, rather than for the benefit only of the individual. Government's proper role was to balance the competing interests of liberty and equality to avoid the formation of persistent social classes that gave permanent privileges to some and permanent deprivation to others. The key to doing this was providing equal rights in the form of equal opportunity:

> American political thinkers have always repudiated the idea that by equality of rights they meant anything like equality of performance or power. The utmost varieties of individual power and ability are bound to exist and are bound to bring about many different levels of individual

achievement. Democracy both recognizes the right of the individual to use his powers to the utmost, and encourages him to do so by offering a fair field and, in case of success, an abundant reward. The democratic principle requires an equal start in the race, while expecting at the same time an unequal finish. But Americans who talk in this way seem wholly blind to the fact that under a legal system which holds private property sacred there may be equal rights, but there cannot possibly be any equal opportunities for exercising such rights. The chance which the individual has to compete with his fellows and take a prize in the race is vitally affected by material conditions over which he has no control. It is as if the competitor in a Marathon cross country run were denied proper nourishment or proper training, and was obliged to toe the mark against rivals who had every benefit of food and discipline. Under such conditions he is not as badly off as if he were entirely excluded from the race. With the aid of exceptional strength and intelligence he may overcome the odds against him and win out. But it would be absurd to claim, because all the rivals toed the same mark, that a man's victory or defeat depended exclusively on his own efforts. Those who have enjoyed the benefits of wealth and thorough education start with an advantage which can be overcome only by very exceptional men, —men so exceptional, in fact, that the average competitor without such benefits feels himself disqualified for the contest.[11]

A society that allows for radically different levels of wealth, Croly argued, simply cannot provide equal opportunity. Liberty and equality can be achieved in the modern world only if government equalizes the starting point by attempting to raise up those who are less prepared. The Jeffersonian notion of limited government worked in the frontier agrarian society of his day but could not possibly be maintained in a modern, industrial world. The national government must therefore use its power to help realize individual merit through constructive and desirable discrimination.

Croly's conception of the proper role of government was quite different from that of either the Founding Fathers or the Social Darwinists, and naturally he was accused of being a socialist. He vigorously denied that charge, however, noting that his focus was still on the individual and the ability of the individual to rise in society. Those who earned wealth through their own merit were free to keep it, but inheritance of wealth ought to be limited, and extreme poverty addressed. Democratic government, he argued, must be employed "for the joint benefit of individual distinction and social improvement."[12] The task of government was to measure, manage, and maintain a just society in order to deliver on the promise of American life, and in forwarding this vision, Croly provided the intellectual underpinnings of the modern welfare state.

• • • • •

Herbert Croly's ideas reflected a fundamental shift in American political thought that became known as Progressivism. A largely middle-class reform movement that was critical of both radical labor movements and big business, it greatly influenced the political philosophies of Theodore Roosevelt, Woodrow Wilson, and Franklin Delano Roosevelt.

By the turn of the century, the Democrats had incorporated much of the populist platform into their own, and a progressive wing of the Republican Party had come to power in Congress. Together, progressive leaders in both parties led the passage of legislation creating the Interstate Commerce Commission to regulate the railroad industry. They also created the Sherman Antitrust Act, the purpose of which was to forbid business combinations and mergers that resulted in monopolies, as well as anticompetitive business practices such as price fixing. When the conservative President McKinley was shot and killed in 1901, he was succeeded by the far more reform-minded Theodore Roosevelt, and the Progressive Era was soon in full swing. For the first time since the presidency of Andrew Jackson, a man who was thoroughly committed to wielding the power of the presidency on behalf of the middle class was holding the reins of executive power.

The three most contentious issues of the day for Progressives were tariffs, taxes, and trusts, and the extent to which Congress and the president were willing to use the federal government to intervene on these issues was an indication of just how much American political philosophy was changing. Public sentiment against monopolies had steadily grown in the years leading up to Roosevelt's presidency. With the American population increasingly concentrating in cities, the influence of the press was on the rise, and journalists and newspaper owners were finding that they had considerable power to change public opinion through investigative reporting. When muckraker Ida Tarbell published a series of articles in *McClure* magazine about the ruthless business tactics used by John D. Rockefeller to ensure the success of Standard Oil, the trust became the most vilified organization in the nation, and people called repeatedly over the next several years for it to be dissolved.

Five months after assuming office, Roosevelt moved decisively on the trust issue by having the Department of Justice file suit against the Northern Securities Company—a holding company that had combined the formerly competing railroad interests of J.P. Morgan, E.H. Harriman, and James J. Hill—for violating the Sherman Antitrust Act. Public sentiment against trusts was running high, and after a century of laissez-faire capitalism, Progressives were now pushing for government regulation of business practices to ensure competition and free enterprise. Although the Sherman Antitrust Act had been passed a decade earlier, the only time it had been invoked was against the American Railway Union during the Pullman strike in 1894. It wasn't until Roosevelt's presidency that the Sherman Act was finally brought to bear against a trust, its intended target.

The case against Northern Securities wound its way through the judicial system all the way to the Supreme Court, which eventually handed Roosevelt a narrow victory of 5-to-4. In the meantime, the reform-minded president convinced Congress to pass additional antitrust legislation and create the Department of Commerce and Labor, whose purpose was to watch over the economic interests of the American people at large. During Roosevelt's presidency, the Justice Department brought cases against and dissolved forty-four trusts, earning him his reputation as a trust-buster. One of the last suits filed was against the behemoth Standard Oil Company of New Jersey, the largest trust in the country, which the Justice Department sued in 1909. Two years later, after a long legal battle, the U.S. Supreme Court announced its decision to dismantle Standard Oil, and the company was ordered to divest itself of its subsidiaries within six months.

Trust-busting was by no means the only item on the Progressive agenda. The redistribution of income through various forms of taxation was an equally contentious issue in the opening decades of the century. Since the days of Alexander Hamilton, the federal government had relied on tariffs as its principle source of revenue. During the Civil War, however, it had for the first time imposed an income tax on all but its poorest citizens. The tax was gradually rolled back and eventually eliminated altogether in 1872, although not without protest. As senator John Sherman of Ohio argued during a congressional debate on the issue:

> Here we have in New York Mr. Astor, with an income of millions derived from real estate…and we have alongside him a poor man receiving a thousand dollars a year. What is the discrimination of the law in that case? It is altogether against the poor man. Everything that he consumes we tax, and yet we are afraid to tax the income of Mr. Astor. Is there any justice in it? Why, sir, the income tax is the only one that tends to equalize these burdens between rich and poor.[13]

It was a sign of the times that Sherman—a Republican—was arguing in favor of keeping the income tax, but his argument failed to persuade his fellow congressmen. The tax was allowed to expire, but when federal revenues dropped sharply after the Panic of 1893, there was increasing pressure to reinstate it. The following year, a Democratic majority in Congress did just that, levying a 2 percent tax on all incomes over $4,000. Unlike the earlier Civil War tax, however, this one impacted only the richest 1 percent of Americans, who understandably cried foul. The constitutionality of the income tax was soon challenged, and in a 5-to-4 decision, the Supreme Court ruled that it was unconstitutional.

Progressives, however, were strongly in favor of an income tax for the wealthy. So was President Roosevelt, who, over the course of his two terms in office, grew increasingly antagonistic toward big business and the financial elite. He had started out as something of a moderate, declaring in a speech in Providence, Rhode Island, during his first year as president, "Probably the greatest harm done by vast wealth is the harm that we of moderate means do ourselves when we let the vices of envy and hatred enter deep into our own hearts."[14] It would not do for the poor and middle class to begrudge the captains of industry their wealth and success—not when they had contributed so much to the prosperity of the nation.

By his second term, however, Roosevelt advocated an estate tax as part of his "Square Deal" domestic program, which was designed to promote the interests of middle-class Americans. His purpose went far beyond simple redistribution of wealth—he was in favor of an estate tax to explicitly prevent the passage of large fortunes from one generation to the next, which he perceived as an unfair advantage. If the children and grandchildren of multimillionaires like Vanderbilt, Carnegie, and Rockefeller wanted to build their own business empires in pursuit of the American Dream, they were free to do so, but as far as Roosevelt was concerned, they should start from square one, just like everyone else.

The conservative base of the Republican Party was horrified by this idea, as were many middle-class Americans whose motivation in pursuing the American Dream was specifically to build a better life for their children. Conferring financial and social advantages to their descendants was part of that dream—they didn't want their children to have to start over. Rather, they wanted every generation to build upon the successes of the last. Those who had spent years making sacrifices to build up a nest egg to ensure the financial future of their families were understandably upset at the idea of the government taking a significant portion of it away. Several states had already instituted an inheritance tax; a federal estate tax would have doubled the injury, and the idea had yet to generate significant support among the public.

An income tax on the wealthy, however, was another matter entirely, one that threatened to split the Republican Party in two. When it looked like Progressives might successfully reinstate the income tax as an amendment to a tariff bill, conservatives appealed to then-President Howard Taft to intervene. Taft, a former lawyer with immense respect for the Supreme Court, was aghast at the idea of reinstating a tax that the court had already declared unconstitutional. He called for an amendment to the Constitution that would specifically give Congress the power to levy income taxes and in the meantime suggested that Congress pass legislation to tax corporate profits instead.

Having gauged the mood of the country, the conservatives in Congress agreed, realizing that public sentiment would insist that the wealthy be taxed one way or another. When the corporate tax was challenged, the Supreme Court concurred with Taft's assessment that it was constitutional and upheld it. A year later the Sixteenth Amendment, which gave Congress the power to levy income taxes, was ratified by state legislatures and took effect on February 3, 1913, in the last month of Taft's presidency. He was succeeded by reform-minded Democrat Woodrow Wilson, who rang a decidedly Progressive note in his first inaugural address:

> We see that in many things that life is very great. It is incomparably great in its material aspects, in its body of wealth, in the diversity and sweep of its energy, in the industries which have been conceived and built up by the

genius of individual men and the limitless enterprise of groups of men...

...We have built up, moreover, a great system of government, which has stood through a long age as in many respects a model for those who seek to set liberty upon foundations that will endure against fortuitous change, against storm and accident. Our life contains every great thing, and contains it in rich abundance.

But the evil has come with the good, and much fine gold has been corroded. With riches has come inexcusable waste. We have squandered a great part of what we might have used, and have not stopped to conserve the exceeding bounty of nature, without which our genius for enterprise would have been worthless and impotent, scorning to be careful, shamefully prodigal as well as admirably efficient. We have been proud of our industrial achievements, but we have not hitherto stopped thoughtfully enough to count the human cost, the cost of lives snuffed out, of energies overtaxed and broken, the fearful physical and spiritual cost to the men and women and children upon whom the dead weight and burden of it all has fallen pitilessly the years through...The great Government we loved has too often been made use of for private and selfish purposes, and those who used it had forgotten the people.[15]

One of Wilson's first acts as president was to sign the Revenue Act of 1913 into law, instating a graduated income tax as well as reducing basic protective tariffs rates from 40 to 25 percent. Wilson did not stop there. A few months later, the Seventeenth Amendment, which provided for the direct election of U.S. senators, was ratified, and the following year he persuaded the Congress to pass the Clayton Antitrust Act, which greatly strengthened the Sherman Antitrust Act. He also established the Federal Trade Commission to promote consumer protection and eliminate anticompetitive business practices. Two years later came the Federal Farm Loan Act, which enabled small farmers to borrow up to 50 percent of the value of their land at competitive interest rates. Perhaps most important, he established the Federal Reserve System to regulate and maintain the stability of the nation's financial system and money supply.

This torrent of legislation angered Social Darwinists and all who believed that the federal government should stay out of economic affairs. To make things worse, Taft's corporate income tax, which he had intended to be a temporary measure to be repealed once personal income tax was legalized, turned out not to be so temporary. Wilson and the Democratic Congress kept both the corporate and personal income tax in place as well as passing an estate tax so that, as the Committee on Ways and Means of the U.S. House of Representatives explained, "a larger portion of our necessary revenues [will be] collected from the incomes and inheritances of those deriving the most benefit and protection from the Government."[16] From that point on, the country's tax system grew increasingly complex, and never again would Americans amass fortunes on the scale of the captains of industry. The American Dream of the twentieth century would evolve into something very different from what it had been in the nineteenth.

6

THE DREAM OF THE GOOD LIFE
IN THE CONSUMER AGE

◇◇◇◇◇◇◇◇◇◇◇◇◇◇◇◇◇◇◇◇◇◇◇◇◇◇◇◇◇◇◇◇◇◇◇◇◇◇

As wars go, World War I was both one of the deadliest and one of the most pointless in history, erupting almost out of nowhere over the assassination of an Austrian archduke most Americans cared nothing about. Whereas World War II would have a clear moral purpose, World War I did not, and Woodrow Wilson won reelection to a second term in office by campaigning not only on the success of his Progressive domestic programs, but also on the mantra "he kept us out of war." Less than a month into his second term, however, a German telegram came to light soliciting Mexican support if war should be declared between Germany and the United States. American public opinion, which had taken a sharp turn in favor of the Allied Powers upon the sinking of the *Lusitania*, was finally galvanized, and Wilson promptly asked Congress for a declaration of war. One of the first casualties was Wilson's domestic agenda, as he understandably spent his second term focused on the war, eventually brokering the peace treaty and fighting to establish the League of Nations.

From an economic standpoint, the war was a boon to American prosperity. At first chaos and panic in the European stock exchanges sent shock waves through the American financial system as well, war being an uncertain business. By 1915, however, neutrality was working to America's advantage as gold and other assets were sent to the United States for safekeeping and exports of agricultural products and manufactures, especially munitions, skyrocketed. Exports of American explosives alone rose from $6 million in 1914 to $467 million in 1916, and exports of steel and iron doubled, as did net farm income. In 1915, the Dow Jones Industrial Average jumped 86 percent, its largest annual percentage gain in history, and over the course of the war, the gross national product increased by 24 percent. By the time the peace treaty was signed, America had emerged as the world's undisputed manufacturing powerhouse and its new financial center. No longer the world's largest debtor nation, we were now its foremost creditor, holding foreign assets worth $12.6 billion.[1]

After a century of isolationism, however, the United States seemed uncomfortable with its new leadership role. Americans wanted nothing more than to forget the war had happened and resume chasing the American Dream. But economic prosperity was sharply curtailed when the Federal Reserve, which had kept interest rates low to help finance the war, raised them dramatically in an effort to control runaway inflation. This overcorrection sent the economy into a brief yet severe recession. Wholesale prices declined by 40 percent, and unemployment jumped to 12 percent.

Even those middle-class Americans who managed to hold onto their jobs felt the sting. The graduated income tax instituted by the federal government in 1913 had exempted those with incomes less than $3,000, and the highest tax bracket was 7 percent, levied on those with annual incomes of $500,000 or more. During the war, however, the exemption was lowered to $1,000 and the highest tax rate raised to an astonishing 77 percent, making income tax rather than tariffs the primary source of federal revenue for the first time in American history. With this shift came the fulfillment of William

Jennings Bryan's prediction from his Cross of Gold speech in 1896 that the primary power struggle in the twentieth century would be between economic classes. The tariff issue in the nineteenth century had led to political power struggles between the various sections of the country, but the income tax now reframed the debate over the American Dream as middle-class interests versus those of the wealthy.

Predictably, the party in power was blamed for the country's economic troubles, and in 1920 the Republican presidential candidate, Warren Harding, promised voters exactly what they wanted: a return to normalcy. In many ways, the battle between Harding and the Democratic candidate, James Cox, was seen as a referendum on whether the country should resume Wilson's prewar Progressive agenda or revert to the laissez-faire policies of the nineteenth century. Harding's platform—which contradictorily promised to reduce both income taxes and the national debt as well as protect farm interests and cut back on immigration—proved immensely popular, and he was elected by a landslide, winning over 60 percent of the popular vote. The Progressive agenda was decisively at an end.

By the time Harding took office, unemployment had reached 20 percent, and excessive immigration was held partially to blame. More than 40 million Europeans had come to America's shores during the Great Atlantic Migration, the numbers increasing with each passing decade. Prior to 1890, the overwhelming majority came from western and northern Europe, but by the 1920s, over 60 percent hailed from southern and eastern Europe, and increasingly xenophobic Americans were less amenable to their assimilation.[2] Starting in 1917, immigrants from Asia had been barred from coming to the United States, and in 1924 Congress passed the American Immigration Act, which limited immigration from "undesirable" countries. Over the next two decades, the restrictions grew, and the massive influx of southern and eastern Europeans that occurred during the first two decades of the century slowed considerably.

Meanwhile, President Harding rolled back income taxes as promised in 1922, the maximum rate being reduced from 73 to

58 percent, with preferential treatment for capital gains at a rate of 12.5 percent. Vice President Coolidge, taking over after Harding died a mere two years into his term, further reduced income taxes on the wealthy to 25 percent in 1925, and the country experienced widespread growth and prosperity. Yet while both presidents were generally considered to be fairly hands-off when it came to the economy, they actually employed greater government intervention than was typical in the previous century, not to mention considerably higher levels of federal spending. Before World War I, the most the federal government had ever spent in one year was $746 million; the first year after the war it spent $2.9 billion, and with each passing year the size of government and the national debt grew substantially.[3]

On the whole, however, America's new position as the world's leading industrial power—as well as a relatively loose monetary policy on the part of the Federal Reserve—kept the economy growing. While there were a few minor recessions, the major bank panics of the nineteenth century were a thing of the past, and the American public's taste for reform seemed to have run its course. Having emerged from a war that historians would later judge largely unnecessary, Americans were in a mood to enjoy themselves and live it up, resulting in the so-called Roaring Twenties. The American Dream during this period was to live "the good life," as defined by an industry that soon began to influence and shape the American Dream as definitively as did the frontier in the previous century.

• • • • •

When it came to living the good life, there was no place better than Hollywood, the center of the new and increasingly influential movie industry. Although today we think of it as quintessentially American, the film industry was founded almost exclusively by the sons of Jewish immigrants, who considered themselves to be perpetual outsiders. Barred from the financial and business power structures of the East Coast, they went to the West Coast and built a new industry from the ground up instead, creating the great movie studios that became not only the purveyors, but also in many ways the creators of American culture in the twentieth century.

Cultures are defined by the stories people tell about themselves—by the myths they create and propagate. In the 1920s and '30s, no one did this better than the movie studios and their moguls, each of whom lived out the story of the American Dream in building his movie empire. But these moguls didn't just live the American Dream; they defined it in the minds of the public through their movies. Each of the studios developed a distinct style and sensibility—influenced greatly by its founder—that had a profound impact on Americans' aspirations and how they saw themselves. In fact, the studios shaped many of our core values, traditions, and archetypes, creating an America "where fathers were strong, families stable, people attractive, resilient, resourceful, and decent."[4]

Metro-Goldwyn-Mayer, the biggest and most prestigious of the studios, arguably had the most influence. It made pictures that depicted a sort of fantasy America where men were strong and courageous, women beautiful and virtuous, children obedient and innocent. MGM went out of its way to portray idealized versions of the American family. Studio favorite Mickey Rooney starred in a series of films as Andy Hardy, an all-American boy with an all-American family, which became a prototype for television's *Leave it to Beaver*. Everything in MGM films was picture perfect and led people to want that perfect lifestyle for themselves.

The movies made by Warner Brothers, by contrast, had a grittier, more urban edge. They were fast-paced stories about outsiders and antiheroes. Warner Brothers created America's love of underdogs, who were featured prominently in their movies and were often slightly unsavory, like nightclub owner Rick Blaine in *Casablanca*. This was the studio of Humphrey Bogart and Bette Davis, movie stars with rough edges rather than the perfect polish of MGM's heroes and heroines. Yet underneath the grit there was always a certain sense of honor—a moral code imposed by the hero himself rather than society at large. Warner Brothers' movies tapped into the American desire to live life on one's own terms that went all the way back to the Puritans and made it into a distinctly American virtue.

Universal Pictures, the oldest of the studios and one that targeted rural audiences, pandered to nostalgia for the fading frontier lifestyle by making westerns its specialty. Its movies elevated the cowboy to the status of an American hero, glorifying the old frontier characteristics of independence, resourcefulness, and self-reliance. In Universal's movies, there were no complex moral waters to navigate. There were white hats and black hats, and in the end the hero always triumphed against the villain and got the girl—this studio would never have made a film as dark or conflicted as *Casablanca*. Quite the contrary, Universal's pictures were straightforward, unpretentious tales about the basic courage and decency of the American people.

Paramount, on the other hand, went out of its way to be sophisticated. Its films emphasized wealth, beauty, and glamour rather than character or virtue. More than any other studio, Paramount imported its stars and directors from Europe and churned out witty, stylish comedies that on the surface had little to do with the "traditional" American values as depicted by the other studios. But what Paramount's movies contributed to American culture was a tangible vision of what it was like to have attained the American Dream. If MGM represented mainstream suburban America, Warner Brothers urban grit, and Universal the rural frontier, then Paramount was all about Millionaires' Row. Its movies gave working- and middle-class Americans a taste of what it was like to be wealthy, and once they had a taste, people inevitably wanted more.

Influenced by what they saw on the big screen, Americans became fascinated not just by the movies but also by the movie stars themselves, a fascination that created modern celebrity culture. Among the era's most prominent stars were the swashbuckling Douglas Fairbanks and America's sweetheart, Mary Pickford, Hollywood's first power couple. Their two-story colonial mansion, Pickfair—featuring a lavishly decorated interior as well as stables, a tennis court, a golf course, and a swimming pool—was prominently featured in newspapers, magazines, and newsreels, giving middle-class Americans a visual taste of a new, increasingly upscale American Dream. To see was to admire, to admire was to want, and to want was to need. Once upon a time, the promise of fifty free acres was enough of an incentive for potential American colonists to risk starvation and death. Now, thanks in part to the movies, Americans' dreams and expectations had grown considerably.

• • • • •

The movies weren't the only factor shaping Americans' wants and desires in the Roaring Twenties. Urbanization, the rise of radio programming, and increasingly easy access to credit also played their part in the development of America's consumer culture. The 1920 census revealed that for the first time in America's history, more people lived in cities than on farms. This population shift encouraged consumerism by putting people in closer proximity to each other and thus in a position to be more aware of their neighbors' possessions and lifestyles. Out on the frontier of the nineteenth century, life was spartan and people were spread out, so there was less opportunity for comparison. In the far more crowded cities of the 1920s, everyone's possessions were on display, feeding the desire to "keep up with the Joneses."

While the influence of one's neighbors on one's spending was generally unintentional, the influence of radio was quite deliberate. The first radio news program was broadcast in 1920 by a station in Detroit, Michigan, and later that year a series of Thursday night concerts became the first public entertainment broadcast in the United States. The business model adopted for radio entertainment programs, whereby programming was paid for by advertising, helped to introduce and popularize a wide array of new consumer products to urban listening audiences. There were more and more new products and gadgets for Americans to want, and radio advertising explicitly encouraged Americans to buy all of them.

At the top of the list of what Americans wanted most in the 1920s was an automobile. In addition to being eminently useful, owning a car was also a sign that one had achieved the American Dream of middle-class prosperity, and by the twenties, Henry Ford's use of mass production techniques had brought the price of his groundbreaking Model T within reach of the average American. Ford also paid his employees well in order to increase the purchasing power of the working class and create a market for mass-produced goods. It was a brilliant strategy—one that made Ford one of the most influential entrepreneurs of what would come to be called the American Century.

Ford was born in Michigan in 1863, a bit too late to be part of the lucky group of entrepreneurs who transformed the country in the late nineteenth century. But he came of age in plenty of time to capitalize on America's newfound status as the world's leading manufacturer. From an early age, Ford liked to tinker with anything mechanical—he fixed his friends' clocks and watches as a hobby. At seventeen he became an apprentice at a machine shop, and after two years there he was hired by the Westinghouse Company to operate steam engines. Active and industrious, he also worked in the engine shop of a steamboat company, operated his own sawmill during the winter, and took several courses, including bookkeeping and mechanical drawing, at a business college in Detroit.

By his twenties, Ford was already mulling over the idea of creating what he called a *quadricycle*, and realizing that he needed to know more about electricity to do so, he took a job at the Edison Illuminating Company. A born mechanic and inventor, he built his first gasoline engine in the garage of his home in 1893, and three years later, his first quadricycle. It was considerably lighter and faster than most automobiles of the day, and over the next several years he continued to refine it. Contrary to the popular picture of Ford as a loner, he actually had a wide circle of friends who helped him to build his first automobiles and supported him in his early ventures. He was charismatic and a good salesman, and in his early years he surrounded himself with talented people. He made friends with Detroit mayor William Maybury, who in 1899 helped him to raise

$15,000 to start the Detroit Automobile Company, but Ford was only named chief engineer.

The venture was short-lived, as the company's directors inexplicably decided to manufacture a delivery truck rather than Ford's automobile. Angered by this decision, Ford became uncooperative, and the company quickly collapsed. Undaunted, he started to design racing automobiles, and after his cars won several races, he attracted enough financial backing to start the Henry Ford Company in 1901. Once again, however, he was named chief engineer and had no real say in how the company was run, as most of the capital was provided by more powerful investors. Ford disagreed with company management as to what vehicle to produce—he wanted to manufacture a bigger version of his racing car, while the management wanted a more conventional version for the public. Four months into the venture, he quit and vowed never to be put in the position of taking orders again.

Ford went on to build his bigger racing car, the 999, and daredevil racer Barney Oldfield drove it to a resounding victory at the Grosse Pointe racing track in 1902. Yet Ford was also continuing to tinker with and improve his original quadricycle, and by the end of that year he had turned his attention to building a practical car for middle-class Americans. His racing success helped him to attract the financial backing of Alexander Malcomson, a Detroit coal merchant with a great deal of business savvy. Malcomson helped Ford to put together a solid management team, including James Couzens as treasurer and office manager, and on June 15, 1903, the Ford Motor Company was born. This time, Ford shared a controlling interest in the company with Malcomson and was named vice president and general manager.

Couzens and Ford balanced each other perfectly. Ford was continually improving his design in an attempt to match the industry-leading curved-dash Olds, which was priced at $650, and he had the typical inventor's habit of never wanting to freeze the design, so that more improvements could be accommodated. Couzens, by contrast, was a realist. While praising Ford's improvements, he convinced him that they would have to be placed on hold, for the company would go bankrupt if they failed to actually produce cars. The Ford Motor Company soon started manufacturing the Model A, a lightweight car with few parts that sold for a relatively modest $750. After nine months 658 Model As had been sold, and models B, C, F, K, and N soon followed.

Predictably, however, Ford found himself in conflict with Malcomson. While Ford now wanted to focus on manufacturing cheap cars for the masses, Malcomson preferred concentrating on their high-end luxury model K. Consequently, Ford and Couzens started to maneuver behind the scenes. Along with several other shareholders, they founded the Ford Manufacturing Company, which supplied parts to the Ford Motor Company. This allowed them to charge high prices for parts, which significantly reduced the Ford Motor Company's profits. Malcomson rashly started his own Aerocar Company in retaliation, and with much animosity on both sides, he and four other major shareholders sold their shares in the Ford Motor Company. Ford essentially forced out the man who gave him his start, and in the process he became president of the company as well as its major shareholder.

Finally in the driver's seat, Ford was able to focus his attention on building the perfect car for the masses, and in 1908 he announced the Model T. Sold for $850, it could attain a speed of 45 miles per hour, had a three-point suspension system, and was practically indestructible. From the start, demand outstripped supply, and Ford responded by introducing the first automobile plant assembly line in 1913. As a result, the time it took to produce a Model T dropped from more than twelve hours to an hour and thirty-three minutes. The assembly line and the continual stripping away of unnecessary elements allowed the price of the Model T to drop as low as $360 by 1916, the equivalent of a little over $7,000 in today's dollars. Demand soared, and owning a Model T became almost obligatory for every family that could possibly afford it.

In part due to Ford's philosophy of paying his employees well, an increasing number of people *could* afford a Model T. In 1914, the Ford Motor Company paid its line workers $5 per day, double the standard market rate. This attracted the best mechanics to his company and drastically reduced employee turnover, which raised productivity and lowered training costs. It also created a workforce that could afford to buy the products it produced and demonstrated the power of a well-paid middle class to fuel the American economy through consumption. In total, the public bought more than fifteen million Model Ts during the course of its production. The potential of mass markets that had been created by the railroads in the nineteenth century was finally realized by the mass production of automobiles in the twentieth.[5]

● ● ● ● ●

As cheap as the Model T was—by 1926 the price had dropped to $260—a car was still a big-ticket item for most families. In fact, cars were expensive enough that they would have been beyond the reach of many Americans had it not been for the installment plan, a form of credit popularized by Ford Motor Company's primary competitor, General Motors.

GM was the brainchild of William Durant, a born marketer if ever there was one. (In one of his early jobs as a salesman for a cigar manufacturer, he sold 22,000 cigars in his first two days on the job.) Durant had founded a successful carriage company, and when the Buick Motor Car Company ran into financial difficulties in 1904, the investors asked him to take over its management. At that time, the company had sold only forty cars and was unable to pay its creditors. Durant immediately went to an auto show in New York City and sold 1,108 cars, then purchased 220 acres north of Flint, Michigan, and built the largest automobile factory in the country. Over the next several years, he helped to orchestrate a merger with Olds Motor Works; he then bought the Oakland Motor

Car Company and the Cadillac Automobile Company to create the General Motors Company.[6]

While Ford focused on ways to manufacture cars as cheaply as possible, General Motors looked for ways to make it easier for Americans to buy them. The Federal Reserve's generally low interest rates encouraged the use of credit not only to finance businesses and home mortgages, but also to buy consumer goods, and General Motors started pushing the use of installment plans as a way to make automobiles affordable for everyone. For the first time, the material aspects of the American Dream could be enjoyed now and paid for later.

Previously, buying on installment, or using credit in general, had been looked upon very negatively by most Americans. But this attitude changed when, in 1919, General Motors created GMAC, the first automobile finance company. Auto sales were seasonal, tending to spike in the spring and summer, and General Motors used installment plans to even out sales and production runs, with GMAC providing the capital to maintain dealer inventories. The desirability of having a car and the relatively large sticker price finally overcame the average American's reluctance to make purchases using installment plans. People saw cars everywhere—in movies and in their neighbors' driveways—and everyone wanted one. During the 1920s, the percentage of households buying cars on installment more than tripled, from 5 to over 15 percent.[7]

The success of installment buying in the auto industry removed much of the stigma from the practice, and it was rapidly adopted by other durable goods industries. In general, the 1920s were characterized by a dramatic increase in both the average household expenditure for durable goods and the amount of credit issued to help pay for those goods. By the end of the decade, 90 percent of all durable goods sales were financed at least partially with credit, and the average amount of disposable income that Americans spent on major durable goods nearly doubled. Accompanying this rise in purchases was a corresponding drop in the average personal savings rate, from 6 percent of disposable income before the war to 4 percent by the end of the Roaring Twenties.[8] The public had decided there was no reason to be frugal and save when the American Dream was something that could be had right now.

As a result of this increasingly consumer culture, in the presidential election of 1928, people voted with their pocketbooks. Rather than rein in and regulate business in the interest of the middle class, the public now wanted the federal government to take an active part in promoting economic prosperity. As the demand for more money to meet the increasing cost of living the American Dream became incessant, middle-class Americans wanted the value of their stocks to go up in order to finance their new lifestyles. Progressivism was out and Social Darwinism was in, so when President Coolidge left office in 1929, he was succeeded by fellow Republican Herbert Hoover, his secretary of commerce. Hoover campaigned largely on a platform of continuing and expanding on "Coolidge prosperity"—the Republican Party promising not only a chicken in every pot but a car in every driveway. This was just what Americans wanted to hear.

As the decade drew to a close, a sunny optimism reigned, which led hundreds of thousands of Americans to invest heavily in the stock market. During World War I, sales of war bonds had made 65 million Americans the owners of securities, introducing the middle class to the stock market and the rudiments of finance. As the wants and desires of middle-class people increased, they turned to the stock market to enhance their incomes, which led to a great deal of reckless, ill-informed speculation. The phrase "buying on margin" entered the middle-class vocabulary during this time, and by August 1929, brokers were routinely lending small investors more than two-thirds of the face value of the stocks they were buying. As share prices rose, more people invested, creating a cycle that fed upon itself until the average price-to-earnings ratio of stocks in Standard & Poor's composite index was 32.6, well above historical norms. This led economist Irving Fisher to famously proclaim, "Stock prices have reached what looks like a permanently high plateau."[9]

They hadn't, of course, and when the crash finally came in October 1929, it sent the country into a downward spiral from which it would struggle mightily to emerge, and the federal government's role in securing the American Dream would be forever altered in the process. Previously, the government had run deficits during wartime but had always returned to balanced budgets afterward, often to the short-term detriment of the economy. During Hoover's administration, however, real per capita federal expenditures increased by 88 percent as he battled the devastating effects of the Great Depression, from which few Americans would escape. As economist Richard Salsman would later note, "Anyone who bought stocks in mid-1929 and held onto them saw most of his or her adult life pass by before getting back to even."[10]

Henry Ford weathered the storm, and the Ford Motor Company emerged from the depression as one of the "big three" auto companies, along with General Motors and Chrysler. William Durant, however, was not so lucky. He was forced out of GM, lost his entire fortune in the stock market crash of 1929, and filed for bankruptcy in 1936. To support himself, he opened a bowling alley in Flint, but a few years later he suffered a stroke that left him partially paralyzed. In one of the most stunning reversals of the American Dream, Durant and his wife were forced to live off of the charity of friends, and the former multimillionaire died penniless.

7

THE DREAM OF SOCIAL SECURITY
AND FREEDOM FROM WANT

◇◇

The Great Depression was a pivotal moment in the development of the American Dream, one that shook the American psyche and fundamentally altered what the dream meant to the American public. Previously, the American Dream had encompassed concepts such as freedom of religion and freedom of speech, as well as a core belief in equality of economic opportunity. The latter relied on the ability of an individual to come to this country and, through hard work, rise in the world. Whether this meant simply owning one's own farm and being economically self-sufficient, striking it rich through speculation or the gold rush, or rising to great wealth as a captain of industry, the basic premise was always equal opportunity. As long as average citizens had the ability to improve their standing, the government wasn't expected to play any particular role in the economy; its primary financial responsibility was to manage the national debt and balance the budget.

During the Progressive Era, however, the middle class became restless and shifted its expectations of the role of government. With basic freedoms and rights now taken for granted, people focused increasingly on economic matters and began demanding greater intervention to ensure equal opportunity—yet they were still far from insisting on equality of economic condition. It was assumed that some individuals would succeed and some would fail, and while sometimes bad things happened to good people, such was life. It was not the role of government to provide a particular standard of living for everyone.

As the country slid into yet another depression following the stock market crash of 1929, this fundamental attitude, which had started to crack during the boom and bust craziness of the Gilded Age, finally crumbled. The country had come a long way since the early colonial period, when settlers were willing to endure appalling conditions and possibly death in their quest for a new and better life. The standard of living for the majority of Americans, who were now living in cities, had increased dramatically throughout the early twentieth century. As a result, the public demanded more government intervention to maintain the economic prosperity. Now, when bad times hit, there was the possibility of a free fall, and this was one of the reasons the Great Depression became the event that led Americans to embrace big government and entitlements. Life for average Americans had become so good that they now had a lot more to lose.

Historically, Americans had tended to attribute lasting poverty to individual character flaws such as laziness rather than bad luck or external forces. They felt that poverty was best dealt with by help from extended family, churches, and private charities, not government. The Great Depression changed this outlook, mainly because unemployment soared as high as 25 percent and remained around 18 percent on average throughout the 1930s. Even those who managed to keep their jobs had to deal with pay cuts and intermittent part-time work. Without the safety valve of the frontier, there was no escape from relentless unemployment for the wage-dependent working class. As the economy limped along, the length and severity of the Great Depression caused many to question whether the American Dream had died, and public opinion began to sway decisively toward the notion that the federal government had a role to play in regulating the economy in order to secure a reasonable standard of living for all. While understandable at the time, this shift would weaken one of the core principles of the American Dream—our belief in taking personal responsibility for our own destinies.

• • • • •

When the stock market initially crashed in the fall of 1929, it wasn't immediately obvious that the country was headed into the worst depression in its history. Quite the contrary, the crash was seen as yet another natural, albeit severe, market correction in response to frenzied overinvestment. Those with level heads and a modicum of financial savvy clearly saw it coming, as the Dow Jones Industrial Average had increased by 400 percent over the previous decade, while the gross national product had gone up by only 59 percent—not bad, but not nearly good enough to justify the speculative boom on Wall Street. In 1928, the New York Federal Reserve had raised its discount rate from 3.5 to 5 percent in an attempt to rein in speculation, and the eleven other Federal Reserve Banks soon followed suit. By the following spring, the economy had slowed perceptibly, worsening the depression in the agricultural sector that had been under way for several years. Yet on Wall Street, the frenzy of buying on margin continued throughout the summer, at least with the most widely reported blue chip stocks. The speculative bubble had grown to gigantic proportions, needing only the slightest of pricks to burst.

The prick came in the form of a speech given by Roger Babson—a successful entrepreneur and the founder of Babson College—to the Annual National Business Conference in Wellesley, Massachusetts, on September 5, 1929. While the Dow had closed at a new all-time high of 381.17 just two days earlier, Babson, who was no fool, noted in his speech that, "Sooner or later a crash is coming, and it may be terrific,"[1] a prediction he had been making for several years without

Wall Street taking any notice whatsoever. This time, however, Wall Street did notice. When the Dow-Jones News Service ran Babson's comment on its news ticker at 2:00 PM, a massive and unexpected sell-off started, and the Dow closed down almost 3 percent by the end of the afternoon. Over the next six weeks the market slid inexorably downward, with huge plunges on Black Thursday, October 24, and on Black Tuesday, October 29. On the latter date, trading volume reached sixteen million shares in one day, a record that stood for over forty years. The Dow had fallen nearly 40 percent from its high in early September and continued to fall in the early weeks of November.

But then the market stabilized, and by the end of December some market sectors were actually showing gains for the year as a whole. While the crash had been spectacular, it affected relatively few Americans directly—less than 3 percent owned brokerage accounts—and no major banks had failed, thanks to a substantial infusion of liquidity on the part of the New York Federal Reserve. By the following spring, the stock market had regained about 45 percent of what it had lost, and some thought the economic crisis had passed, at least on Wall Street. Even among those who were more pessimistic, few would have predicted that it would take twenty-five years for the market to fully regain its losses from what is now known as the Great Depression. As far as Wall Street was concerned, it was back to business as usual.

Elsewhere in the country, however, things were a bit dicier. The other Federal Reserve banks had not cut interest rates, and after the crash, lending and business activity perceptibly slowed. The previous summer, a special session of Congress called to deal with the ongoing agricultural depression had raised agricultural tariffs to protect American farmers, and in the wake of the economic slowdown, representatives from virtually every industry lobbied their congressmen for similar treatment. The result was the infamous Smoot-Hawley Tariff Act, which imposed the highest protective tariffs in American history. President Hoover, in spite of his own reservations and a petition signed by hundreds of professional economists urging him to veto the bill, signed it into law, undoubtedly his worst mistake as president. As soon as it was signed, investors on Wall Street, who understood that the act would prompt retaliatory tariffs and sharply curtail global trade, began selling. The Dow resumed its downward spiral, and the bank failures started.

While most of the banks that failed were small, the Bank of the United States, with deposits of $268 million and more than 450,000 depositors, most of them working class, was not.[2] When it went bankrupt in December of 1930, a wave of panic spread across the world, as many people understandably thought it was the official bank of the United States government because of its name. It wasn't, but it was the largest bank failure in the country up to that time, and the incident proved to be the critical turning point that transformed an "ordinary" depression into the Great Depression. The unemployment rate as of 1930 was still under 9 percent, but in May 1931, Austria's largest bank, Credit Ansalt, failed, and two months later Germany's largest bank, Danat Bank, suspended operations. By September, the entire European banking system was on the verge of collapse, and when currency traders started selling off British sterling in favor of gold, leading to a run on the Bank of England's gold reserves, the situation became dire. The British Empire, which had pioneered the gold standard in 1821, went off it in 1931, and the ripple effect forced practically every central bank in Europe to do the same.

The United States Federal Reserve, however, decided to remain on the gold standard to defend the value of the dollar. This required raising interest rates and contracting the money supply at a time when greater liquidity was needed to stabilize the banking sector. The effect was disastrous, setting off severe deflation. Prices fell, and more banks failed. To make matters worse, the unintended consequences of the Smoot-Hawley Tariff were manifested as global trade plummeted from $36 billion in 1929 to only $12 billion by 1932, with American exports plunging 78 percent. Unemployment shot up to almost 16 percent, the GNP fell by 20 percent, and the federal deficit ballooned as expenses rose and revenues fell. The American economy was in a death spiral, as was the world economy in general.

Contrary to popular myth, President Hoover did not sit idly by. Hoover was often characterized by the press in his own era, and by historians in later ones, as indifferent to the suffering of the American people during this difficult period. Yet he actually intervened in the economy to a far greater extent than any previous president, with programs that laid the foundation for the New Deal. Hoover established public works programs in the early months of 1930, and by the following summer he was arguing in favor of further government programs to counteract the effects of the bank failures. While he was opposed to the idea of direct government relief to banks, corporations, or individuals, as the depression worsened Hoover made a number of increasingly interventionist proposals. In 1932 he persuaded Congress to pass the Home Loan Bank Act, which created a number of Home Loan banks that could lend money based on the mortgage portfolios of commercial banks, as well as establishing the Reconstruction Finance Corporation (RFC), which provided emergency loans to banks, insurance companies, mortgage associations, and railroads. He followed this up with the Relief and Reconstruction Act, which financed public works to generate jobs, and lent money to states to do the same.

Yet much of this legislation was not well received. The RFC, in particular, was often characterized as the "millionaire's dole," because while it saved banks and other lending institutions from failure, it necessarily saved the investments of the stockholders in those companies as well. The bank bailouts were no more popular in 1932 than they were in 2008, and the fact that the bailouts also helped the employees and depositors of those institutions generally went unappreciated by the general public. Justified or not, all of these interventionist measures cost significant amounts of money at a time when federal deficit spending during peacetime ran contrary to deeply-rooted American political thought—particularly in the South and West—despite gaining favor among professional economists. Hoover, facing sharp criticism for running a deficit during a depression, bowed to political pressure and levied a huge income tax increase, which Congress passed without much debate. Higher taxes reduced consumer spending still further, and by the autumn of 1932, industrial production was less than half of what it had been in 1929. The Dow had fallen 90 percent from its high that same year, and at 41.22 was less than a point above what it had been on the day it was first calculated in 1896.

The press—and the country—blamed Hoover, who had certainly made some serious mistakes. Many of those mistakes, however, were made in response to political pressure and conventional wisdom that was seriously outdated. Nor were the mistakes entirely Hoover's fault, as Congress, Wall Street, and the Federal Reserve had all contributed to the calamity as well. If Hoover failed to act quickly enough or go far enough, it was largely because the American public had historically been averse to government intervention and deficit spending, and because the depression during its onset did not seem particularly severe. By the time of the presidential election in November 1932, however, the situation was dire, and Hoover was the easiest scapegoat. The buoyant, optimistic Franklin Delano Roosevelt, while arguably far less knowledgeable when it came to economics than Hoover, nevertheless had a far better grasp of the collective American psyche. What Hoover had failed to realize, and what FDR instinctively understood, was the toll the worsening economic crisis had taken on the public's faith in the American Dream. The country could not conquer the Great Depression until faith in that dream was restored.

• • • • •

The opening months of 1933 were some of the darkest in all of American history, and a time when the American Dream was struggling to survive. In the presidential election, Hoover was roundly defeated by FDR—he won only six states in the electoral college after having carried forty just four years earlier. During the lame duck period before Roosevelt took office, the economy had continued to deteriorate, and in February a banking panic that started in Michigan, the center of the auto industry, spread rapidly throughout the country. By March, thirty-eight states had ordered all or nearly all of their banks to close, and withdrawals were strictly limited in the remaining states. Then, on March 4, the day of Roosevelt's inauguration, the New York Stock Exchange announced that it would not open and gave no indication of when it would. The country had come to a standstill, and everyone looked to the new president as the only hope to turn the situation around.

FDR did not disappoint. In his inaugural address he told Americans, millions of whom were listening on the radio, "The only thing we have to fear is fear itself—nameless, unreasoning, unjustified terror which paralyzes needed efforts to convert retreat into advance."[3] The next day, he issued an executive order to close all of the nation's banks, called an emergency session of Congress, and four days later presented its members with the Emergency Banking Relief Act. The act removed the United States from the gold standard, allowed the Treasury Department to initiate reserve requirements, and provided federal bailouts to large failing banks.

By this point, the banking system had so clearly ceased to function that the public finally saw the wisdom of bailouts, and the House and Senate passed the bill within four hours, unread and virtually without dissent. Roosevelt signed it into law that same evening, and three days later, he delivered the first of his now-famous fireside chats. In a confident, reassuring voice, he advised the American people that it would be "safer to keep your money in a reopened bank than under the mattress,"[4] and banks that had undergone federal inspection and were deemed to be sound reopened the following day. In a sign of the American people's faith in their new president, deposits came pouring in, ending the panic and stabilizing the system. Psychologically, the country had finally turned the corner, and from then on the economic situation slowly began to improve.

In the first hundred days of his presidency, Roosevelt inundated the overwhelmingly Democratic Congress with a vast array of legislation that historians would later refer to as the New Deal. It included the Economy Act, which cut the salaries and pensions of government workers and veterans, an action deemed necessary to balance the budget, as Roosevelt was initially opposed to deficit spending. (During his long tenure as president, FDR eventually made a distinction between the "regular" federal budget, which he balanced, and the "emergency" federal budget, which he did not.) The New Deal also included many new government agencies and programs, including the Federal Emergency Relief Administration, the Civilian Conservation Corps, the Public Works Administration, and the Tennessee Valley Authority.

In addition, the New Deal included revolutionary new banking legislation that, among other things, strengthened the Federal Reserve, established the Securities Exchange Commission to regulate Wall Street and other securities markets, and created the Federal Deposit Insurance Corporation, which guaranteed deposits in member banks up to $5,000 per depositor. These reforms proved invaluable, as every depression in the country's history had been precipitated by a major bank failure, which then prompted runs on the banking system as a whole. Roosevelt worried about the moral hazard created by guaranteeing deposits, as it allowed banks to act more recklessly, knowing that their depositors' assets were secured. And he was right to worry, as today banks take far more risks than they did in the nineteenth century, when banking was the most conservative of industries. Yet one can argue that the trade-offs have been worth it, as there has never been a serious bank run since the establishment of the FDIC.

Other New Deal measures included legislation to assist people in obtaining and refinancing home and farm mortgages, as well as the National Employment Act, which provided funding to state employment agencies to help the unemployed find jobs. Yet not all of the New Deal legislation enacted in the early days of Roosevelt's presidency was particularly successful or wise. Raising taxes during a depression was certainly a drag on the economy, although the desire to balance the federal budget was admirable. Among the more controversial measures passed was the Agricultural Adjustment Act, which established limits on agricultural production and subsidies to help stabilize prices for farm products, which had fallen by 50 to 60 percent. While eventually declared unconstitutional by the Supreme Court, this legislation led the federal government down the path of central planning in the agricultural sector, a folly from which it has yet to escape. The court also invalidated much of the National Industrial Recovery Act, which attempted to combat deflation by allowing trade associations to cooperate in stabilizing prices and by forming industrial cartels and establishing codes of fair competition.

The extent to which the various pieces of New Deal legislation helped or hindered the economy in its recovery has been a subject of much debate among economists ever since. What is inarguable, however, is that the flurry of activity restored consumer confidence. It gave the American public the sense that the president and Congress were finally taking bold action rather than tinkering at the margins. Yet the underpinnings of the early New Deal legislation actually came from the Hoover administration, a fact that was little appreciated at the time. Much of the language of the legislation passed in the first hundred days of Roosevelt's presidency was drafted by Hoover appointees in the Treasury Department. In terms of who got the credit, it was all a question of timing.

Most of the interventionist measures Hoover proposed in the early years of the Great Depression had been resisted by his advisors and the public. By the depth of the depression in 1933, however, the country was in dire enough straits to embrace massive federal spending, regulation, and programs on a scale that would have horrified Thomas Jefferson and most of the Founding Fathers— but much of it appeared to work. After three and a half years of contraction, the economy finally began to recover. Wall Street experienced one of its best years in history, the Dow rising almost 60 percent by the end of 1933. Prices stabilized, the money supply increased, and business activity began to rebound. Unemployment, however, remained high, which led the general public to pressure Roosevelt and the federal government to do even more to alleviate people's suffering. FDR responded in 1935 by introducing several new programs and agencies, some of which fundamentally altered the economy, the middle class, and the American Dream in ways that long outlived the immediate impact of the Great Depression.

The first of these was the Works Progress Administration (WPA), which was granted a budget of $5 million dollars to provide relief to the unemployed in the form of public works projects such as the construction of buildings and roads. The largest of the New Deal agencies, it nationalized and greatly extended previous public works projects, with the goal of providing employment for all unemployed heads of household in the country who were willing and able to work. During its eight-year existence, the WPA provided more than eight million jobs, making it both the single largest employer in the country and the employer of last resort. Virtually every community in the country benefited from a WPA project during the depression.

Unlike the earlier Civilian Conservation Corps—a much smaller agency that was very popular with the public because it was seen as tackling useful rural conservation projects—the WPA was often criticized for doing unnecessary projects that were undertaken for political reasons. Its employees were perceived as lazy and inefficient, with no particular incentive to do their jobs well, as it was almost impossible to get fired from the WPA. While the program was discontinued with the start of World War II, it was these types of government projects—paid for by the country as a whole yet benefiting only one part of the community and wasteful and inefficient in their spending—that constituted much of what came to be considered "pork" in the federal budget from this period onward.

Roosevelt's next major piece of legislation, the National Labor Relations Act, considerably increased the power of labor unions by guaranteeing their right to collectively bargain with management. Previously, the federal government and the courts had almost always sided with the owners of capital in disputes between management and labor. This preference came not only from the general tendency of those in positions of political power to be drawn from the ranks of the wealthy, but also from a fierce desire to defend the rights of property ownership that can be traced all the way back to the Founding Fathers. Yet the widespread suffering of the American people—and the resulting demands on the part of the wage-earning classes to do something to alleviate it—had shifted the balance of political power very much in favor of catering to the wants and needs of the middle class. As a result, the pendulum of political opinion swung decisively in favor of guaranteeing the rights of labor over management.

The National Labor Relations Act took an explicitly pro-labor stance, encouraging the use of collective bargaining and legally prohibiting certain management activities that might discriminate against union employees or discourage them from forming unions in the first place. While not covering certain types of workers, including railroad, agricultural, and government employees, in general the act greatly enhanced the power of labor by defining many labor practices that management was forbidden to engage in without placing any prohibitions on labor unions themselves. The act also established the National Labor Relations Board to regulate the process of unionization and elections, and the result was an explosion in the growth of labor unions. By 1940, union membership in the United States had doubled, much of the growth coming from unskilled and semiskilled workers. With the stroke of Roosevelt's pen, the National Labor Relations Act did more to raise the standard of living of the working class than any other single piece of legislation that had come before it. But it also made unions so powerful that they eventually went too far and crippled the competitiveness of some American industries.

When it came to securing middle-class prosperity and the American Dream, however, by far the most important and influential New Deal legislation was the Social Security Act. Now practically a synonym for universal retirement pensions, the original act also allocated money to the states for unemployment insurance and welfare programs (specifically aid to dependent children and the handicapped) as well. The latter two programs were controversial from the start, as most Americans, even in the depths of the Great Depression, were deeply uneasy at the thought of their tax dollars being used to pay people not to work or to allow parents to shirk their financial duty to support their children. Roosevelt himself had misgivings about funding unemployment insurance, far preferring to spend federal money on public works programs.

The retirement pensions portion of the Social Security Act, on the other hand, was widely approved. It addressed one of the prime worries of the middle class—how to support themselves in old age, when they were no longer capable of working. This was an especially pressing problem in the 1930s, when the majority of jobs still called for hard manual labor, employers could easily fire elderly employees at will, and more than half of the elderly lived in poverty. Unlike unemployment and welfare programs, which were perceived as taking money from honest, hard-working Americans and giving it to those who were undeserving, Social Security pensions were viewed as a means to pay into a system on one's own behalf and then be paid back later. At Roosevelt's insistence, the program was funded by payroll taxes paid half by employees and half by their employers, a decision he explained by noting, "We put those payroll contributions there so as to give the contributors a legal, moral, and political right to collect their pensions and unemployment benefits. With those taxes in there, no damn politician can ever scrap my social security program."[5]

Roosevelt was quite correct in this assessment, as having paid into the Social Security system over the course of their working lives, Americans quite naturally felt entitled to receive their pension payments upon retirement. Indeed, Social Security pensions have proven to be one of the most popular government programs in American history, so much so that the program has been nearly impossible to reform, other than expanding it to include more people. In its early years, Social Security pensions were limited to those in traditional white male occupations, with farmers, government workers, and most minorities and unmarried women in traditional female occupations excluded. Only half of Americans were eligible, but the program was gradually expanded in the following decades to include almost everyone. In doing so, the government arguably made Americans far happier and far more secure than they had ever been before; prior to Social Security, most families lived in fear of the day when their primary breadwinner would no longer be able to work. But it also made retirement a "right" that Americans felt the government owed them, and it created a financial obligation for the government that as time went on became more and more untenable.

• • • • •

Roosevelt was overwhelmingly reelected president in 1936, and at the start of his second term in office, most economic indicators, with the exception of unemployment and the stock market index, had returned to their 1929 levels. The depression appeared to be over, and Roosevelt cut back on his emergency spending, particularly public works projects, in order to balance the budget. At the same time, the Federal Reserve raised interest rates, and the collection of Social Security payroll taxes began under authority of the Federal Insurance Contributions Act (FICA). The combined result was a sharp economic downturn that shot unemployment back up to 19 percent while manufacturing output fell 37 percent, back to 1934 levels.

This relapse profoundly shook Americans' confidence in the economic recovery and the effectiveness of the New Deal. While Roosevelt moved quickly to ramp up government spending on relief programs, the public's belief that such programs could end the depression, rather than just soften its effects, evaporated. The country had experienced depressions before, but none had lasted as long as this one, and no one in either business or government seemed to have a clear understanding of what had truly caused it, much less how to stop it. Roosevelt's popularity and the overwhelming Democratic majority in Congress gave way to more polarized, fractured politics, and the country became sharply divided in regard to the wisdom of the New Deal. As the economy limped through the closing years of the decade, many began to believe that the depression was permanent and that the vision of America as the land of opportunity was a mirage.

Roosevelt blamed the relapse on the business community, which in turn blamed it on the government—particularly on FICA taxes and the trust fund the U.S. Treasury had built up to fund the Social Security program. This led to a slight retooling of the program so that pensions would be funded by current contributions rather than by a large reserve. In 1940, pension payouts began, and the first monthly Social Security payment of $22.54 was issued to Ida May Fuller on January 31. Having paid a total of $24.75 into the system before retiring at age 65, she broke even by her second payment and proceeded to collect a total of $22,889 in payouts before she died in 1975 at the age of one hundred. Fuller was unusual in her longevity— at the time the average remaining life expectancy of those who lived to 65 was 12.7 years for men and 14.7 years for women.[6] Even so, over the long term, the program was financially unsustainable, although this was not immediately clear to the American public. In the early years, the trust fund always had a substantial surplus, as during the phase-in period there were far more people paying into the system than drawing on it. The deficits would take several decades to appear, and by then Social Security would be firmly entrenched.

With the new recession, Roosevelt began running into greater opposition in Congress, and once it began, he managed to sponsor only one final piece of New Deal legislation, the Fair Labor Standards Act of 1938. It established a minimum wage as well as a *de facto* forty-hour work week by requiring companies engaged in commerce or the production of goods for commerce to pay employees time-and-a-half for hours beyond forty a week. While certain classes of employees were exempt, notably most white-collar professional workers, the restrictions provided an incentive for companies to hire additional people rather than pay overtime, yet guaranteed a reasonable annual income to those who worked a forty-hour week. Severe restrictions were also placed on child labor, which provided the additional benefit of encouraging young people to stay in school longer.

The Fair Labor Standards Act, along with $3.75 billion in additional spending for relief and recovery, put an end to the depression, at least according to the official economic indicators. But the recovery was weak, and unemployment would remain stubbornly high until the start of World War II. At that point the economy finally recovered, due to the demands of war production, which created so much need for labor that even women were drawn into the workforce in unprecedented numbers. Yet the psychological scars the Great Depression left on the collective American psyche would last much longer, and from then on the federal government's first priority was seen as doing whatever was necessary to prevent another Great Depression.

This was a crucial change that would fundamentally alter the role of the federal government in the lives of the American people. Those who had weathered the 1930s wanted nothing so much as security, a desire that Roosevelt, who on the eve of war had been elected to an unprecedented third term in office, instinctively understood and spoke to in his State of the Union Address to Congress on January 6, 1941:

> In the future days, which we seek to make secure, we look forward to a world founded upon four essential human freedoms. The first is freedom of speech and expression—everywhere in the world. The second is freedom of every person to worship God in his own way—everywhere in the world. The third is freedom from want—which, translated into universal terms, means economic understandings which will secure to every nation a healthy peacetime life for its inhabitants—everywhere in the world. The fourth is freedom from fear—which, translated into world terms,

means a worldwide reduction of armaments to such a point and in such a thorough fashion that no nation will be in a position to commit an act of physical aggression against any neighbor—anywhere in the world. That is no vision of a distant millennium. It is a definite basis for a kind of world attainable in our own time and generation. That kind of world is the very antithesis of the so-called new order of tyranny which the dictators seek to create with the crash of a bomb.[7]

These were Roosevelt's justifications for entering World War II, and while freedom of speech and religion were long established in the American political lexicon, freedom from want and fear were entirely new concepts—the direct result of the hardships of the Great Depression. Never before had the American government promised its people so much, and never before had the American people been willing to embrace such promises as a fundamental part of the American Dream. It was a dream that Roosevelt and the United States would now seek to spread to all nations and peoples of the world.

8

THE DREAM OF HOME OWNERSHIP AND A COLLEGE EDUCATION

◇◇◇

When World War II broke out in Europe in September 1939, the overall state of progress and development in the United States, while markedly improved since colonial times, was nevertheless very different from the standard of living most Americans enjoy today. Over a fifth of all Americans still lived on farms, of which only a tenth had flush toilets and less than a third had electric lights. Even among those living in cities, the majority didn't have either a refrigerator or central heating, much less air conditioning, and 56 percent rented rather than owned their homes. Half of the labor force worked in factories or in mining, construction, or agriculture, all of which involved hard physical labor. Despite the growth of unions and the increasingly pro-labor policies of the Roosevelt administration, workers were still routinely laid off due to seasonal shifts in production, illness, injury, or age, and few women or minorities qualified for retirement or unemployment benefits. Medical insurance was almost unheard of, and antibiotics had yet to come into wide use. Almost 15 percent of the workforce was unemployed.[1]

But all of that was about to dramatically change. After Pearl Harbor was attacked on December 7, 1941, the United States declared war on Japan and shortly afterward on Germany and Italy. Within months, the war effort had shifted the American economy into overdrive, as the country's manufacturing base switched to wartime production in what essentially became a planned economy under the direction of the War Production Board. While central planning is almost always a miserable failure when it comes to efficiently producing consumer goods, it worked fairly well in producing war goods. In the process of arming itself, the United States government awarded over $100 billion in military contracts in the first six months of 1942 alone—more than the nation's entire GNP in 1940.[2]

With this massive jump in industrial production, unemployment finally eased. In fact, by 1943 it had dropped to less than 2 percent, and a fifth of America's men were serving overseas. African Americans from the South migrated to northern factories, and women flooded into the workforce, taking on jobs that would previously have been unthinkable for them. Even with stringent wartime wage and price controls, incomes skyrocketed due to massive amounts of overtime. Seventeen million Americans owed income taxes in 1943, up from four million the previous year, and those in the highest bracket were subject to an astonishing 94 percent marginal tax rate to help fund the war effort.[3] Up until then, Americans had paid their income taxes in a lump sum at the end of the year. But in order to help reduce the sting to taxpayers and smooth out the U.S. Treasury's cash flow, the government began withholding estimated income taxes from each paycheck, along with the previously implemented FICA taxes for Social Security.

Thanks to the huge demands of wartime production, however, the increased taxes had little impact on the overall economy, which was booming. Indeed, the demand for raw materials and foodstuffs was so great that the government was forced to ration everything from butter to tires, and thus there was little in the way of consumer and durable goods to buy. As a result, income inequality declined sharply, and saving increased. The American people as a whole had personal savings of a meager $4.2 billion in 1940; by 1945, total savings had increased to an astronomical $137.5 billion, of which a significant portion was held in war bonds.[4] Despite the annoying shortages, most Americans were significantly better off than they had been during the previous decade, at least economically.

On the personal front, the war was a tragedy for the 400,000 young Americans who lost their lives in combat and for their families as well. But for those who survived, and the American public in general, the war reinvigorated faith and confidence in the United States and the American Dream. In marked contrast to the end of World War I, Americans emerged from World War II with the overwhelming conviction that they had fought and won a historic war for a great and noble purpose. They had successfully defended their own nation from attack as well as liberating their European allies from tyranny. Hollywood, which during the war years was relentlessly patriotic, was quick to cast America as a knight in shining armor—the hero and savior of the world. Americans liked the image and the way it made them feel about their country, so rather than return to isolationism, they finally accepted the United States' role as a world power. Henceforth, we would be champions and defenders of freedom, democracy, and the American way of life, purveyors of the American Dream.

• • • • •

In the early years after the war, a humbled Europe looked to America with gratitude, and in many ways there was much to admire. While economists generally predicted that the end of the war would result in a new depression, pent-up demand for consumer and durable goods, easily funded by massive personal savings, set off a boom instead. Contrary to predictions, the postwar period in the United States was characterized by strong growth, prosperity, and continually rising standards of living as American manufacturers moved to fill the vacuum left by Europe's destroyed industries. While there were a couple of minor recessions, unemployment during the postwar period averaged 4.5 percent, growth in productivity rose about 3 percent annually, and median family income rose 38 percent from 1950 to 1960.[5] The Great Depression, although it had certainly left its scars, was truly over.

Nor did the economic boom occur only in America. Fearing that the rising tide of Communism might engulf all of Europe, President Truman's secretary of state, George Marshall, proposed a plan to counteract the widespread hunger, unemployment, and general devastation that faced Europeans in the aftermath of World War II. The physical destruction of the war had severely impacted the infrastructures of many European countries. Raw materials, food, and housing were in short supply, and war-damaged industries needed machinery and capital before production could be resumed. Marshall suggested setting up a program for economic reconstruction, with the United States to provide financial assistance.

In an enlightened act of both statesmanship and self-interest, President Truman proposed and Congress ratified the Marshall Plan, which provided $13.3 billion in foreign aid to sixteen countries in western and central Europe, the greatest part of which went to West Germany, France, and Italy. The plan's major aims were to prevent the spread of communism in Western Europe and to promote the development of political democracy and free markets. The United States, which had learned its lesson from the results of the retaliatory tariffs that had started the Great Depression, finally embraced the concept of free trade and encouraged Europe to do so as well. For the first time in history, a world power sought to enhance its own economic interests by helping to rebuild the economies of its allies, seeing them as trading partners rather than rivals. By the time funding ended in 1952, the GNP of every participant country was at least 35 percent higher than it had been in 1938, before the war.[6]

A secondary goal of the Marshall Plan was to stimulate the American economy, for many were concerned that it would lapse into another depression after wartime production ceased. As Europe recovered, it began to import significant quantities of American foodstuffs and manufactured goods, providing a boost to the U.S. economy in the short term. Over the long term, however, the investments made in rebuilding European manufacturing and infrastructure provided European countries with a competitive advantage, as their new factories were more technologically advanced and efficient than America's aging plants. While the United States strengthened and solidified many of its relationships with Western European nations politically, it paved the way for the growth of the European Union as a powerful economic rival by encouraging greater economic intra-European trade and interdependence.

The United States also had a significant hand in Japan's emergence as an economic power in the latter part of the century, although the role it played was not nearly as benevolent as it has been in Europe. The United States occupied Japan for six years after its surrender in 1945, during which time it engaged in what is probably America's most successful attempt at nation-building. The two main objectives of the military occupation were to dismantle Japan's war capabilities and infrastructure, and to modernize and transform Japan into a western-style, capitalist democracy. Under the Americans' direction, the Japanese adopted a constitution that vested sovereignty in the people, guaranteed fundamental human rights, and in general was modeled very much after the U.S. Constitution, with one significant difference: the Japanese constitution included a "peace clause" that renounced war and prevented the country from maintaining any armed forces.

While the United States' efforts to rebuild Japan transformed it into an economic trading partner, the Soviet Union's development of nuclear weapons and its growing dominance in Eastern Europe turned that former ally into a new and potentially deadly enemy. The rising threat of communism led to ongoing political conflict and military tension between the United States and the Soviet Union which continued for the next several decades. Rather than engaging each other directly, these two superpowers fought proxy wars in countries like Korea and Vietnam, providing weapons, aid, and military support to their preferred ideological side. As the so-called "Cold War" heated up, the constitutional restriction on Japan's armed forces was relaxed at America's request. Yet in the ensuing years, Japan spent on average only 1 percent of its total GNP on military spending, far less than the United States. This allowed Japan to concentrate government spending on modernizing its infrastructure and manufacturing base while relying on the United States for defense. Japan also encouraged industrial development overseas while restricting foreign competition within its borders, and by the 1980s its industrial sector was second only to that of the United States itself. By then, Japan's competitiveness in the electronics and auto industries would present major problems for American manufacturers.

But that was still several decades away. During the early postwar years, free trade and the rebuilding of war-torn economies benefited America greatly. Spurred by the economic recovery in Europe and Japan, world trade had increased sixfold by 1960, creating worldwide economic growth on an unprecedented scale. A huge slice of this economic pie went to the United States, and stable growth, fostered by both government and business, started to create a large, very affluent middle class. So confident had we become that we began to export the American Dream itself, and never before had the promise of that dream been realized by so many, both at home and abroad.

● ● ● ● ●

What World War II bequeathed to the American public, in addition to a renewed confidence that they could do anything when they put their minds to it, was a new model for achieving the American Dream on a national scale. Laissez-faire capitalism with minimal government intervention had proven disastrous at the end of the Roaring Twenties. Likewise, the massive government intervention of the New Deal had proven largely ineffective at ending the depression and restoring economic stability. But the war had showed Americans that collaboration between business and government could produce the sustained economic growth and prosperity they were seeking. Americans' faith in capitalism was now thoroughly restored, and the private sector would forevermore be the driver of the country's economic engine. But the government would no longer be shy about stepping in to tweak that engine, fine-tuning it through regulation, taxation, and redistribution of wealth. Henceforth its primary responsibility would be to keep that engine humming and above all to avoid the negative effects of another depression, particularly high unemployment.

Congress formally acknowledged this new responsibility in 1946 when it passed the Employment Act, which declared that the policy of the federal government was to maximize employment, production, and purchasing power. In the words of President Truman, "[T]he job at hand today is to see to it that America is not ravaged by recurring depressions and long periods of unemployment."[7] Already, Congress had taken steps to blunt the impact caused by the return of war veterans to the workforce by unanimously passing the Servicemen's Readjustment Act. More popularly known as the GI Bill, it provided tuition and housing assistance to veterans who wished to pursue vocational training or a college degree as well as low-interest loans for those who wanted to buy a house or start a business. This proved to be one of the most important factors in creating the large and affluent middle class of the postwar years.

Marketed to the public as a reward to returning veterans for their bravery and sacrifice, the GI Bill was also intended to ward off a spike in unemployment by channeling some of the vets into additional schooling. The tuition assistance portion of the GI Bill sparked something of a social revolution by opening the halls of academia to a much broader array of individuals than had ever been able to afford higher education previously. Although one of the side effects of the Great Depression was an increase in the average number of years spent in school by young Americans due to a scarcity of jobs, only one in twenty Americans had a college degree in 1940. In the years after the GI Bill was enacted, however, veterans accounted for almost half of all college admissions, and by the time the original bill ended in 1956, almost 8 million veterans had taken advantage of a subsidized education program.[8]

College education, an advantage formerly pursued almost exclusively by children of the wealthy, subsequently became something to which middle-class families aspired as a means of upward mobility for the next generation. By 1965, one in ten Americans had a college degree, and by 2000 it was one in four. The GI Bill, which disbursed $14.5 billion in aid to veterans, paid for itself several times over, as every dollar invested generated a $7 return in economic productivity, consumer spending, and increased federal income taxes. To date, the GI Bill has produced 14 Nobel Prize winners, 3 supreme court justices, 3 presidents, 12 senators, and 24 Pulitzer Prize winners, as well as 91,000 scientists, 67,000 doctors, 450,000 engineers, 240,000 accountants, 238,000 teachers, and millions of lawyers, nurses, artists, and entrepreneurs.[9]

In addition to education assistance, the GI Bill also made available low-interest, zero-down-payment home loans, backed by the Veteran's Administration, to 2.4 million veterans. Home ownership had always been a top priority for Americans, particularly among immigrants: a study made in Detroit in 1900 revealed that 55 percent of German, 46 percent of Irish, and 44 percent of Polish families owned their own homes and generally deemed home ownership an even greater priority than a quality education for their children.[10] But the supply of housing had been unable to keep pace with demand throughout the 1920s, and housing construction had slowed considerably during the Great Depression and World War II. By 1945, with millions of American veterans returning home and placing a high priority on starting families, the housing crunch had become severe.

The problem was seen as an opportunity by William Levitt, a navy officer and real estate developer who became one of the many returning veterans who channeled their energy and talents into entrepreneurial ventures. Prior to the war, his company had built mostly upscale housing on Long Island in New York, but with the passage of the GI Bill, Levitt's company began constructing more affordable housing for returning veterans. He purchased seven square miles of land near Hampstead, Long Island, and, using a process he compared to an assembly line in reverse, built a massive complex of 17,500 single-family homes by moving the workers from house to house, having them perform the same task at each, greatly lowering the costs of production. "Levittown" offered a 750-square-foot ranch or Cape Cod–style house with two bedrooms, a living room, kitchen, and bathroom on a 60-by-100-foot lot for as low as $7,990. It was the first suburban housing complex in America.

It was also an immediate hit, and soon planned communities were springing up all across America, financed in large part by Veterans Administration–backed mortgages. Thus, the GI Bill enabled millions of families to move out of urban apartments and into suburban homes, and home ownership became a primary goal of the middle-class. In fact, it was a cornerstone of the new, postwar American Dream. From 1900 to 1940, the percentage of families that owned their own homes had remained steady at around 45 percent. But by 1950 this figure had increased to 55 percent, and by 1955, 4.3 million home loans had been granted, with a total face value of $33 billion.[11] Nor was it just veterans who were buying new homes. Middle-class Americans of all ranks were moving to the suburbs in droves, and while the homes they bought were a far cry from the 4,000-square-foot McMansions of today, it was the start of a trend toward increasingly large and luxurious homes to which Americans in the postwar era would henceforth aspire. The house in the suburbs with the job in the city also made cars far more important. This increased demand for automobiles, particularly as women started joining the workforce in greater numbers, making the auto industry one of the primary drivers of economic growth for the remainder of the century.

The Veterans Administration also guaranteed more than 50,000 business loans in the years following the war, providing a boost to business and entrepreneurship in general. In direct contrast to the malaise and fear that had taken over the country during the Great Depression, the war had made men out of boys, and they returned home with the supreme confidence that they could achieve whatever they set their minds to through sheer hard work and determination. While many who had been scarred by the Great Depression held tenaciously to the safety of their jobs, returning veterans plunged overwhelmingly into entrepreneurship, aided greatly by the innovation of the business franchise, which provided a turnkey operation with a proven business model. Other veterans invested in and greatly expanded family businesses, and in 1953, President Dwight Eisenhower established the U.S. Small Business Administration to provide additional financial and educational support for the thriving small business community.

Meanwhile, those who preferred the security of working a steady job began to experience unprecedented prosperity as the growth and strength of labor unions appropriated a larger slice of the American economic pie for labor than ever before. Hospitalization insurance had first been introduced as a form of nonmonetary compensation during the war years, when wage controls had made it difficult for companies to compete for scarce labor. (By the end of the war, with the maximum marginal tax rate at 94 percent, hospitalization insurance was a way for companies to provide a tax-free benefit to their employees.) It had proven extremely popular, as insurance cushioned families from the potentially staggering costs of a hospital stay, and by 1948 the National Labor Relations Board had ruled that health benefits were subject to collective bargaining. A mere two years later, one in three Americans, some 54.5 million people in total, had employer-paid health plans, and the number continued to grow thereafter.[12] Health insurance had quickly morphed from a rare employee perk into a necessity, and labor unions contributed much to the modern American Dream by establishing it as a basic requirement of any employee compensation package.

While the trend toward widespread health insurance coverage was universally supported by the general public, by the mid-1940s many Americans were beginning to think labor unions had grown a bit too powerful. Over a third of the workforce was unionized, and by the start of 1946, a full 3 percent of it was on strike, battling for a larger share of corporate profits in the form of higher wages, old-age and disability pensions, health care, and other benefits.[13] That same year the newly conservative Congress passed the Taft-Hartley Act, which revised some of the provisions of the National Labor Relations Act and outlawed some of the labor unions' most powerful tactics, such as secondary boycotts and closed shops, in general balancing power more evenly between management and labor. The rebalancing worked, and by the following year the number of strikes was significantly reduced. An era of more amicable and cooperative relations between labor and management began, helped greatly by ongoing economic prosperity. During a decade when the United States accounted for half of the world's combined GNP, management could afford to be generous, although in doing so American companies set precedents that would later become very difficult to sustain.

• • • • •

The millions of veterans who attended college thanks to the GI Bill weren't the only source of human capital fueling the economic prosperity of the postwar period. By the early 1950s, significant numbers of highly educated Europeans—particularly scientists, artists, and intellectuals—were immigrating to the United States, leaving behind the destruction of their war-torn homelands for the greater economic and research opportunities in America. From its earliest days, innovation had been a primary force powering the country's economic engine, and by the 1950s the combined impact of increasing education on the part of veterans and the brain drain from Europe created one of the most innovative periods in American history.

Intellectual migration started in the 1930s as increasing fascism and anti-Semitism led hundreds of scientists in Germany, Austria, Hungary, and Italy (including such luminaries as Albert Einstein, Enrico Fermi, and Niels Bohr) to flee Europe, most of them opting to immigrate to either Britain or the United States. This migration slowed during the war, as Germany and the other Axis powers attempted to hold on to their own intellectual capital, but after the war the brain drain resumed and intensified. In an effort to deny Nazi technology and expertise to the Soviet Union, the U.S. government specifically recruited more than 1,600 key scientists and engineers under the Project Paperclip program and brought them to America for "intellectual reparations." By 1990, these men had produced patents and industrial processes worth over $10 billion for their new home country, including significant advances in rocket science, molecular biology, and the field of electronic processing and computing.[14]

Those bright and talented individuals whom the United States did not manage to spirit away during the early days after the Allied victory often came of their own volition over the next several decades. As the Cold War intensified and the Soviet Union set up communist puppet regimes in Eastern Europe, a so-called Iron Curtain slammed down that split Western and Eastern Europe along ideological lines, and those who were politically opposed to communism and the increasing totalitarianism under the Soviet Union's oppressive influence scrambled to escape. As early as 1922, the Soviet Union imposed severe restrictions on emigration in order to protect its investments in intellectual capital, and by the early 1950s, the Soviet-occupied satellite states (Eastern Germany, Poland, Czechoslovakia, Hungary, Romania, and Bulgaria) had adopted the same types of restrictions. The border between East and West Germany was closed in 1952, but before 1961 it was still possible to escape through East Berlin to West Berlin, and 3.5 million East Germans—approximately 20 percent of the population and most of the young and well-educated—did just that. Even in Western Europe, economic conditions after the war were so poor that a significant portion of the intelligentsia left, never to return.

Europe's loss was America's gain, and the flood of scientific and technical expertise, combined with increased government and corporate spending on research, fueled a boom of innovation. While many of the resulting advances were in the areas of basic research, the practical applications of this research resulted in the invention of a number of important new technologies that several decades later would become the building blocks of modern life, including fiber optics, computers, integrated circuits, microchips, and lasers. The development of a massive interstate highway system, along with the introduction of air travel, revolutionized transportation and mass transit, while a number of inventions from earlier eras, such as antibiotics, air conditioning, central heating, long-distance phone service, television, and a wide variety of consumer products and appliances were refined and widely proliferated.

These products significantly improved Americans' quality of life, but none raised middle-class expectations so greatly as did television. While only 9 percent of American homes had a TV set in 1950, that figure had increased to 87 percent by 1960, making television the dominant form of media. Originally thought of as yet another medium for delivering information and entertainment, much like radio or movies, television had an impact far beyond what anyone expected. Movies were larger than life and good for building myths, but television was normative. Something about the way family life, schools, and workplaces were depicted on television suggested that this was how they should be. The way fictional people acted on television set standards for behavior in real life, and seeing the material trappings of fictional lives shaped people's expectations about what constituted a middle-class standard of living. Television was a subtle, unconscious instructor, significantly impacting consumer tastes both directly through advertising and indirectly through television programming.

While early television programming included a lot of newsreels, sportscasts, and variety shows, the Hollywood studios—notably MGM, Warner Brothers, and Fox—soon moved in to create the dramas and situation comedies that came to dominate the networks' prime time schedules. Just as with the movies, they created programs, such as *The Adventures of Ozzie and Harriet* and *Leave It to Beaver,* which presented an idealized version of America as the studio founders wanted it to be rather than as it really was. The former, which featured the real-life family of Ozzie and Harriet Nelson and their two sons, premiered in 1952 and ran for fourteen seasons, the longest-running sitcom on television prior to *The Simpsons.* The show ostensibly strove for realism, using exterior shots of the Nelsons' actual home and a close replica of its interior built on a soundstage. But the storylines, while written by Ozzie and often based on actual family incidents, nonetheless presented a highly idealized version of wholesome American family life that did not in fact exist. *Leave It to Beaver,* which premiered in 1957 and used a full slate of professional writers and actors, was even more idealized and divorced from reality. Yet it became an iconic representation of middle-class American boyhood and left an indelible impression on the baby boom generation.

Then there were the commercials. While the earliest television programs generally had a single sponsor, the networks soon moved to a business model based on selling small blocks of advertising time to multiple sponsors. This made television advertising more affordable, and it soon became the preferred method for reaching a mass audience. Yet the short blocks of time necessitated getting one's message across quickly, ushering in the so-called "creative revolution" in advertising, whereby the advertising industry became far more sophisticated than it had ever been before, with vast amounts of research and creative effort poured into developing brand image and a unique selling proposition for each product. Some of the most effective consumer-marketing campaigns of all time, including the Coppertone Girl, the Marlboro Man, and Volkswagen's "Think Small" campaign, were launched in the 1950s, and the sheer number of slogans that are still familiar today—De Beers' "A diamond is forever," Maxwell House's "Good to the last drop," and M&Ms' "Melts in your mouth, not in your hand"—are testimony to the enduring impact of modern advertising on the American consciousness.

Television news programs also came to have a significant role in shaping public opinion, particularly in regard to politics. Since the time of Benjamin Franklin, newspapers had been the primary method for engaging in political discourse, although radio had made inroads by providing coverage of important political events in real time. With the introduction of television, however, it was not only the message that was important, but also the appearance and personality of the person conveying that message. While radio news programs had anchors, in the age of television those anchors became far more important, and in those early days men such as Walter Cronkite and Edward R. Murrow set a standard for journalistic integrity that led the public to respect and trust them completely.

It was Murrow who, on March 9, 1954, broadcast one of the most famous programs in journalistic history, *A Report on Senator Joseph McCarthy*. Fear of communist infiltration and espionage had risen in tandem with the Soviet Union's increasing control of Eastern Europe, and in 1947 the House Committee on Un-American Activities had summoned a number of Hollywood actors and directors to appear before the committee. Some refused, citing their First Amendment rights to free speech and assembly, but they were held in contempt of Congress, and proceedings against them began in the full House of Representatives. The "Hollywood Ten" were blacklisted, as were many others in the Hollywood community over the next several years, whether there was any real evidence against them or not. Merely being suspected of being a communist was enough to get one blacklisted, and fear was so rampant that in essence, free speech and assembly were no longer protected.

The Red Scare waxed and waned over the next several years, and then received new life when Senator McCarthy started making claims that there were large numbers of Communists spies and sympathizers inside the United States federal government. His televised addresses whipped up even greater fear and anger among Americans, and it was Murrow who finally stood up to McCarthy by wielding the power of television. His damning report was composed almost entirely of McCarthy's own words and pictures. It painted a portrait of a fanatic, and its rhetorical impact finally called McCarthy's motives into question. Aired shortly before the Senate began a series of televised hearings investigating McCarthy's allegations against the U.S. army, it turned the tide of public opinion against him, and his bombastic performance in the hearings sealed his fate. The combination of Murrow's report and the drama of the publicly televised spectacle broke the senator's hold over the nation. Through the power of television, his credibility was destroyed, and Americans' right to free speech was restored.

McCarthy wasn't the only politician to struggle with the new medium of television. In 1960, the Republican presidential candidate, Richard Nixon, discovered its pitfalls when he debated the handsome and relatively young Democratic candidate, John F. Kennedy. It was the first televised presidential debate, and the potential influence of the medium was unappreciated by most politicians at the time. Nixon had been leading in the polls going into the debate, but he made critical tactical errors by refusing to wear makeup and by wearing a gray suit, which gave him a washed-out appearance made worse by a recent bout with flu. Kennedy, who had been coached on how to sit and to look at Nixon when he wasn't talking, wore a dark suit and makeup, giving him a more vigorous and healthy appearance. In Kennedy's opening statement, he declared, "I don't believe in big government, but I believe in effective government action,"[15] and he took the offensive by addressing his greatest perceived weakness—his lack of experience—by talking about his work in Congress. Those who listened on the radio thought the debate was a draw or that

Nixon had a slight advantage, but those who saw it on television thought Kennedy was the clear winner. He rode that television-enhanced perception all the way to the White House, winning an election in which his margin of victory in the popular vote was less than one-tenth of a percent, although he took the electoral college with 303 votes to Nixon's 219.

The television era had arrived, and it was a powerful tool—for politicians and celebrities, for the news media and the television networks, and for the advertising industry and corporations—for shaping the American Dream. In the waning years of the Great Depression, FDR had promised Americans freedom from want. Now families who gathered around their television sets in the new American paradise of suburbia were increasingly promised the freedom *to* want, and to want on an unprecedented scale. The ongoing postwar boom gave Americans a new faith and confidence in the ability of government and business to foster economic growth and prosperity, and their expectations of what it meant to achieve the American Dream significantly expanded. The dream wasn't fifty free acres anymore, or even a chicken in every pot and a car in every driveway. It was a house in the suburbs with a television, an automatic washer and dryer, central heat and air conditioning; a steady job with health insurance and pension benefits; children who thrived thanks to vaccines and antibiotics and attended college; family vacations and a golden retirement. While most of this was good, the problem was that it still wasn't good enough. Aided and abetted by television, the former self-reliance of the American people was slowly forgotten. The Age of Entitlement had begun.

9

THE DREAM OF EQUALITY OF OPPORTUNITY AND EQUALITY OF RESULTS

◇◇◇

During the century following the Civil War, the nature of the American Dream changed and evolved substantially. Decade by decade, the nation's mindset transformed from the self-reliant, frontier attitude of a nation rapidly expanding in size and population to the more entitled, secure outlook of the world's leading military, industrial, and economic superpower. With that transformation, hard-won rights that had been central to the American Dream at its founding—such as the right to vote, to speak and worship freely, and the right to liberty itself—had slowly come to be taken for granted. While Nazism and Communism had reminded Americans that these rights were not guaranteed, there was still a certain complacency regarding them. Short of nuclear war, most people felt that the American way of life was secure within our own borders, and with the prosperity of the postwar era, the focal point of the American Dream became increasingly economic in nature for the majority of Americans.

Yet there were factions—namely African Americans and women—for whom the more basic tenets of the American Dream had yet to be realized, and in the 1950s these groups once again began to push for greater social equality and economic opportunity. For African Americans, much of the progress that had been made after the Civil War and passage of the Reconstruction Acts under the Thirteenth, Fourteenth, and Fifteenth Amendments was undone when the Supreme Court declared the Civil Rights Act of 1875 to be unconstitutional. On the basis of the enforcement clause in the Fourteenth Amendment, the Civil Rights Act attempted to strike down segregation laws by prohibiting racial discrimination in public places. Based on a very narrow interpretation of the Fourteenth Amendment, however, the Supreme Court ruled that this prohibited only states from engaging in discrimination, not individuals. With this decision, all serious attempts at integrating African Americans into the American society at large ceased. By 1896, the Supreme Court determined in *Plessy v. Ferguson* that the Fourteenth Amendment applied only to political rights, while social rights fell under the power of the states. In doing so, it tacitly endorsed the doctrine of "separate but equal" facilities for African Americans, a decision that stood for more than half a century until finally it was overturned in *Brown v. Board of Education.*

During this period, the question of how to fully integrate African Americans into society and help them to achieve the American Dream became the life's work of two influential men—Booker T. Washington and W.E.B. DuBois. While their end goal was the same, their answers to this central question were very different. Washington, a former slave who experienced Reconstruction firsthand, concluded that Reconstruction was a failure because it both alienated whites and tossed blacks unprepared into the world without the skills or training necessary to succeed. Before African Americans could be accepted socially and politically, he argued, they first had to catch up economically. As head of the Tuskegee Institute, he championed vocational education in an address at the Atlanta Exposition in 1895, noting:

> Our greatest danger is that in the great leap from slavery
> to freedom, we may overlook the fact that the masses of
> us are to live by the productions of our hands, and fail to
> keep in mind that we shall prosper in proportion as we
> learn to dignify and glorify common labor, and put brains
> and skill into the common occupations of life; shall prosper
> in proportion as we learn to draw the line between the
> superficial and the substantial. No race can prosper until it
> learns that there is as much dignity in tilling a field as in
> writing a poem. It is at the bottom of life we must begin,
> not at the top. Nor should we permit our grievances to
> overshadow our opportunities.[1]

Vocational education, Washington reasoned, would allow blacks
to prosper economically, and this would further social and political
acceptance. Technical skills would allow African Americans to earn
a respectable living, which was the first step on the path toward
achieving the American Dream. On the basis of this first crucial step,
equality and acceptance would naturally follow:

> The wisest among my race understand that the agitation
> of questions of social equality is the extremest [sic] folly,
> and that progress in the enjoyment of all the privileges
> that will come to us must be the result of severe and
> constant struggle, rather than artificial forcing. No race that
> has anything to contribute to the markets of the world is
> long in any degree ostracized. It is important and right
> that all privileges of the laws be ours, but it is vastly more
> important that we be prepared for the exercises of those
> privileges. The opportunity to earn a dollar in a factory
> just now is worth infinitely more than the opportunity to
> spend a dollar in an opera house.[2]

W.E.B. DuBois, born a free man in Massachusetts in 1868, had a
very different perspective from that of Washington. DuBois believed
that political equality must come first, and that African Americans

had to force a state of equality through the active intervention of the federal government. The slow progress toward equality that Washington endorsed simply gave whites an excuse to treat blacks as second-class citizens. DuBois' goal was full and immediate equality, and he called his fellow African Americans to "seek and seize" the right to vote, social equality, and education according to ability. Having earned a Ph.D. from Harvard, DuBois taught sociology at both Atlanta University and the University of Pennsylvania, which led to his belief in the importance of a collegiate liberal arts education, as opposed to a vocational one. In his article "The Talented Tenth" he argued:

> The Negro race, like all races, is going to be saved by its exceptional men. The problem of education, then, among Negroes must first of all deal with the Talented Tenth; it is the problem of developing the best of this race that they may guide the mass away from the contamination and death of the worst, in their own and other races. Now the training of men is a difficult and intricate task. Its technique is a matter for educational experts, but its object is for the vision of seers. If we make money the object of man-training, we shall develop money-makers but not necessarily men; if we make technical skill the object of education, we may possess artisans but not, in nature, men. Men we shall have only as we make manhood the object of the work of the schools—intelligence, broad sympathy, knowledge of the world that was and is, and of the relation of men to it—this is the curriculum of that higher education which must underlie true life. On this foundation we may build bread winning, skill of hand and quickness of brain, with never a fear lest the child and man mistake the means of living for the object of life.[3]

Dissatisfied with the slow progress of African Americans toward these goals, DuBois helped found the National Association for the Advancement of Colored People (NAACP) in 1909. Organization, he argued, was necessary to pressure the government to deliver on the promises of political equality that blacks were entitled to from the Civil War amendments. It was largely through the NAACP's efforts that the Supreme Court slowly began to strike down discriminatory legislation, ultimately resulting in their ruling in *Brown v. Board of Education* in 1954. While this decision outlawed segregation in public schools, however, it still didn't really define what equality meant in the legal sense, and there was no formal public policy in place to achieve it.

Yet buoyed by this breakthrough, the civil rights movement rapidly gained momentum. The following year, Rosa Parks refused to give up her bus seat to a white man, prompting Martin Luther King Jr. to lead the Montgomery bus boycott and vaulting him to national prominence. King's goal was to extend what he saw as the promise of the American Dream to all African Americans, and like DuBois, he rejected the gradual approach of Booker T. Washington in favor of immediate social equality and justice. King argued that liberty is never freely given by oppressors and must therefore be demanded by those who are oppressed. "Oppressed people," he said, "cannot remain oppressed forever. The yearning for freedom eventually manifests itself."[4]

King's central strategy for achieving this freedom from oppression was civil disobedience, the purpose of which was to draw the attention of white Americans to the continued inequality of African Americans. Through peaceful protest, he wanted to confront American society and make it difficult for whites to continue with their hypocritical double standards. As he explained in "Letter from Birmingham Jail" in April 1963, he saw peaceful, nonviolent protest as a way to foster moral crisis and tension in communities "to so dramatize the issue that it can no longer be ignored," thereby forcing white Americans to confront segregation and inequality. "We who engage in nonviolent direct action are not the creators of tension," King argued. "We merely bring to the surface the hidden tension that is already alive. We bring it out in the open, where it can be seen and dealt with."[5]

If African Americans were not allowed to express themselves through civil disobedience, he warned, their pent-up anger and frustration would ultimately express itself in violence. This was not a threat, King warned, but a simple fact of history. He praised the young students who had courageously staged a sit-in at a Birmingham lunch counter, predicting that they would one day be recognized as "standing up for what is best in the American dream" and "carrying our whole nation back to the great wells of democracy which were dug deep by the founding fathers in their formulation of the Constitution and the Declaration of Independence."[6]

King's peaceful protest movement culminated with the March on Washington later that summer, organized in part to support a new civil rights bill. There, in front of the Lincoln Memorial, King delivered the speech he is most remembered for, which set out his own American Dream of living in a nation with racial equality and harmony. The speech is rarely read or heard in its entirety, as it is copyrighted rather than part of the public domain. Thus, only the most famous of snippets are widely known, such as King's hope that "my four little children will one day live in a nation where they will not be judged by the color of their skin but by the content of their character" and that one day all Americans would "be able to join hands and sing in the words of the old Negro spiritual, 'Free at last! Free at last! Thank God Almighty, we are free at last!'"[7]

King's stirring words went down in history, and the following year Congress passed the Civil Rights Act of 1964, which among other things officially prohibited racial segregation in schools, in the workplace, and at facilities that serve the general public. It then passed the National Voting Rights Act of 1965, which definitively outlawed discriminatory voting practices. The African-American Dream of freedom and political equality had finally been achieved, but the problem of how to translate it into the economic American Dream of upward mobility and acceptance into the middle class was still unsolved.

• • • • •

The Civil Rights Act was landmark legislation not just for African Americans, but for also for women. It prohibited discrimination in education and employment based not only on race, but on gender as well, and in doing so opened up a broad new world of opportunities for women.

Feminist stirrings in America were to some extent present as far back as the colonial period, when women who owned property—usually because they inherited it—were in some cases allowed to vote. Still, women did not have the same rights as men, and in a series of letters exchanged between John Adams and his wife, Abigail, in the months leading up to the signing of the Declaration of Independence, Abigail reminded him to "remember the ladies and be more generous and favorable to them than your ancestors."[8] John, however, did not take her seriously, replying, "We have only the name of masters, and rather than give up this, which would completely subject us to the despotism of the petticoat, I hope General Washington and all our brave heroes would fight."[9]

His teasing response was hardly surprising. Women at the time simply did not participate in the political sphere, and Adams was actually more enlightened than most of the men of his day in his behavior, if not his rhetoric. His letters clearly indicate that he respected and relied upon Abigail's political advice—in many instances a great deal more so than upon the advice of his cabinet. It was Jefferson who truly reflected the general attitude of the Founding Fathers on the subject when he wrote that women "should not mix promiscuously in the public meetings of men."[10]

Thus, while African Americans and the issue of slavery were discussed fairly extensively at the Constitutional Convention, women and their rights were not addressed at all. While the Constitution recognized women and children as citizens, voting rights were left to the states. During the Revolutionary War, women had already lost their right to vote in New York, Massachusetts, and New Hampshire, and in 1787 they lost voting rights in all other states except New Jersey, which denied them the vote in 1807. Thirty years after the Declaration of Independence proclaimed all men to be equal, the disenfranchisement of women was complete.

In tandem with the rise of the abolitionist movement, however, the first stirrings of a true women's movement began to be felt in the early nineteenth century, due in great part to Elizabeth Cady Stanton. Born into a relatively wealthy family in New York, she became involved at an early age in both the abolitionist and temperance movements, through which she met her husband, Henry Stanton. They married and had seven children, but as a signal of her own independence, she refused to be referred to as "Mrs. Henry Stanton," a form of address that was customary at the time. She argued that to refer to her in such a manner took away all of her individuality and was a sign of the subordination of women. Instead, she insisted on being called Elizabeth Cady Stanton.

In 1848, Stanton helped organize the Women's Rights Convention in Seneca Falls, New York, and issued a declaration that was deliberately patterned on the Declaration of Independence, using it to claim equal status with men:

> When, in the course of human events, it becomes necessary for one portion of the family of man to assume among the people of the earth a position different from that which they have hitherto occupied, but one to which the laws of nature and of nature's God entitle them, a decent respect to the opinions of mankind requires that they should declare the causes that impel them to such a course. We hold these truths to be self-evident: that all men and women are created equal.[11]

In the years leading up to the Civil War, the abolitionist and women's movements worked together for universal suffrage, even though to some extent they approached the problem from different viewpoints. For Frederick Douglass and the abolitionists, freedom was the primary goal—a necessary prerequisite to achieving political and social equality. But for Stanton and the other supporters of the women's movement, equal status with men was the prerequisite to achieving greater political and social liberty. For a while the two movements' interests coincided, but after the war Douglass and other abolitionists backed away from women's rights in preference for gaining voting rights for black men. In response, Elizabeth Cady Stanton and Susan B. Anthony founded *The Revolution*—a newsletter dedicated to women's rights—as well as the National Woman Suffrage Association. Not until the ratification of the Nineteenth Amendment in 1920, however, would women finally earn the right to vote.

This critical point gained, the women's movement largely died out until the Civil Rights movement of the 1950s and '60s revived it, this time on the basis of equal economic opportunity. While the "traditional" role of women, as portrayed on television, was viewed as being in the home, in reality women had always worked a wide variety of so-called pink-collar jobs in service industries or as secretaries, teachers, or nurses. But during World War II women were exposed to a wide variety of traditionally male occupations, and little by little, they were gaining greater access to higher education as well. Less than 3 percent of America's 350,000 female World War II veterans attended college via the GI Bill; many of them didn't even know women were eligible for benefits. Yet the tide was shifting, and with a broader range of experiences, their expectations increased. Some women began to feel dissatisfied with the role of the devoted, picture-perfect wife and mother that was imposed on them by the media and society at large.

One of them was Betty Friedan, a journalist who had followed the traditional path for American women in the postwar era by getting married and quitting her job to stay home and raise her five children. Over time, she began to suffer from depression and to question whether being a good wife and mother was all there was to life. At her fifteen-year college reunion, she began to ask her classmates about their experiences and discovered that many of them shared her feelings. She wrote an article about the "problem with no name," but it was rejected by all of the women's magazines, which glorified the role of the traditional stay-at-home mother. So Freidan eventually expanded her findings into a book, *The Feminine Mystique*, in 1963. It quickly became a bestseller, as it put into words the vague sense of dissatisfaction that many American women felt:

> The problem lay buried, unspoken, for many years in the minds of American women. It was a strange stirring, a sense of dissatisfaction, a yearning that women suffered in the middle of the twentieth century in the United States. Each suburban wife struggled with it alone. As she made the beds, shopped for groceries, matched slipcover material, ate peanut butter sandwiches with her children, chauffeured Cub Scouts and Brownies, lay beside her husband at night—she was afraid to ask even of herself the silent question—"Is this all?"[12]

The question had to be asked silently, Friedan argued, because middle-class American women were supposed be the happiest women on earth. They had been "freed by science and labor-saving appliances from the drudgery, the dangers of childbirth, and the illnesses of her grandmother."[13] Unchained from the necessity of work, all the American woman had to do was concentrate on ensuring domestic tranquility. The queen of her home, she was free to choose all that pertained to that sphere—able to buy food, clothes, and appliances that her ancestors would have envied. The modern American housewife "had everything that women ever dreamed of."[14] She was living the feminine version of the American Dream.

Except that she wasn't, according to Friedan. The postwar prosperity that had enabled women to stay home had also taken away their freedom. Trapped in their perfect homes in the suburbs while their husbands drove the family car to work, they were cut off from the broader range of experience in the city and limited to the more prosaic, parochial concerns of the local neighborhood, which revolved around the activities of their children. They had no meaningful intellectual lives of their own. American society denied women the full development of their abilities by imposing a domestic stereotype on them, Friedan argued, a stereotype created by custom, social conventions, and most particularly the media. With this stereotype in place, women couldn't be taken seriously in the workplace, and having the right to vote didn't change that. What was needed was equal opportunity.

The Civil Rights Act of 1964 was a big step toward this goal, but as the feminist movement gained steam, Friedan and her peers argued that it wasn't enough. In 1966, she helped found the National Organization for Women, whose purpose was to "take action to bring women into full participation in the mainstream of American society," for, as Friedan wrote, "the time has come to confront, with concrete action, the conditions that now prevent women from enjoying the equality of opportunity and freedom of choice which is their right, as individual Americans, and as human beings."[15]

With this statement, feminists rejected the American Dream of being perfect wives and mothers, the domestic goddesses of their homes in the suburbs. The new dream was an America where women worked side by side with men as equal and respected partners, able to realize their fullest potential. Yet as with all dreams, this one turned out to have its disappointments and problems as well.

• • • • •

By the mid 1960s, African Americans and women had finally achieved legal protection from discrimination, and they were eager to press forward and realize their political, social, and economic equality. How exactly to go about this, however, set off a debate about the meaning of equal opportunity that went all the way back to Sumner and Croly at the dawn of the twentieth century. Was a law banning discrimination, if enforced, sufficient to provide equal opportunity? Was it enough to simply prevent further discrimination? Or was it necessary for the federal government to take more direct action in order to right past wrongs and to bring those who had long been kept out of the economic race to a point where they legitimately had a chance to compete and win?

The answer to these questions, at least from the perspective of the civil rights and women's movements, was decidedly in favor of government action. With the passage of the Civil Rights Act, African Americans and women now had formal legal rights on paper, but overcoming centuries of racism and sexism and enforcing those rights in the real world was a different matter. In a sense, both movements saw African Americans and women as injured parties, and thus they argued that society at large had an obligation to redress the wrongs that had been done to them. In a court of law, if a man is found to have caused harm against another person, he isn't simply told not to do it again. He has to pay damages of a sufficient amount to make the situation as if the damage had not occurred—this is the basic legal principle behind tort damages.

Using the same reasoning, leaders of the civil rights and women's movements concluded that society had done substantial economic harm to African Americans and women, as evidenced by the fact that the proportion of African Americans and women in high-level jobs and higher education was not representative of society at large. It was therefore incumbent on the government to in some way raise up African Americans and women and make the situation as if discrimination had never occurred. The federal government, they argued, was needed to actively fight individual and societal-level discrimination. From this conviction developed the government's public policy of affirmative action. Designed to overcome both overt and latent discrimination, affirmative action's ultimate goal was to maximize diversity and create truly equal opportunity.

The government's first official affirmative action program, Executive Order 10925, was launched by President John F. Kennedy in 1961. It was directed at government contractors, and it mandated that projects financed with federal funds must "take affirmative action to ensure that applicants are employed, and that employees are treated during employment, without regard to their race, creed, color, or national origin."[16] Kennedy supported affirmative action based on gathering evidence among the social science community that ability was not just the product of nature, but of nurture as well. Individual achievement could be greatly affected by one's socioeconomic environment, particularly one's family and one's neighborhood school. Hundreds of factors in children's environments—more than just their talent, perseverance, or character—could and did influence how they turned out as adults and their relative success in life.

As nurture gained the upper hand in the nature vs. nurture debate of the 1960s, the idea of affirmative action gained greater acceptance, and the major question became how to judge whether or not true equal opportunity existed. The answer was provided by President Lyndon B. Johnson in a 1965 commencement address at the predominantly African-American Howard University:

> In far too many ways American Negroes have been another nation: deprived of freedom, crippled by hatred, the doors of opportunity closed to hope…But freedom is not enough. You do not wipe away the scars of centuries by saying: Now you are free to go where you want, and do as you desire, and choose the leaders you please. You do not take a person who, for years, has been hobbled by chains and liberate him, bring him up to the starting line of a race and then say, "you are free to compete with all the others," and still justly believe that you have been completely fair. Thus it is not enough just to open the gates of opportunity. All our citizens must have the ability to walk through those gates. This is the next and the more profound stage of the battle for civil rights. We seek not just freedom but opportunity. We seek not just legal equity but human ability, not just equality as a right and a theory but equality as a fact and equality as a result.[17]

This speech was a critical turning point in American thought, the moment when equality of result became the yardstick by which one measured the existence of equal opportunity. Only when the proportion of African Americans and women in all public and private institutions, from colleges to boardrooms to the halls of government, reflected that of society would true equality have been definitively achieved. Less than proportional representation was proof of ongoing latent discrimination. Equal opportunity now implied equal results—a leap of logic that was a far cry from the Founding Fathers' original thought and intent on the nature of equality in America.

Under Johnson, the government's affirmative action policy was expanded to include women, its stated goal "to correct the effects of past and present discrimination."[18] Johnson's executive orders went a step beyond Kennedy's in requiring that government contractors and certain other organizations that accepted federal funds have a written affirmative action plan to increase employment of minorities and women. This plan had to include goals and timetables for achieving a proper proportion of women and racial minorities, using quotas based on an analysis of the workforce compared to the availability of women and minorities in the general labor force.

The Nixon administration implemented this policy in the Revised Philadelphia Plan, which required government contractors and also the labor unions they hired from to use quotas and timetables to combat institutionalized discrimination. Nixon also instituted a federal policy that provided technical and management assistance to support minority businesses, and in 1973, Congress passed the Rehabilitation Act, which required all federal agencies to implement affirmative action programs as well. Due in part to the federal government's influence, affirmative action programs in state universities and agencies, as well as in private industry, were common by the end of the 1970s.

As the use of affirmative action programs became more widespread, however, it sparked an angry backlash, particularly over the use of quotas, which were seen by many as carrying affirmative action too far and implementing a system of reverse discrimination. In 1978, the Supreme Court ruled in *Regents of the University of*

California v. Bakke that the medical-school admissions policy at the University of California at Davis violated the equal protection clause of the Fourteenth Amendment by using quotas. Yet at the same time, the court noted that promoting greater diversity at universities was a compelling interest, and that race was an appropriate factor to consider in university admission policies.

It was an inherently contradictory ruling, one that reflected ambivalence on the part of both the Supreme Court and American society at large. While there was general agreement that women and minorities were often at something of a disadvantage through no fault of their own, choosing a comparatively less qualified woman or minority candidate for a job or admittance to a university required passing over a better qualified white male candidate. Affirmative action programs were meant to make it easier for minorities and women to achieve the American Dream, but at the same time, promoting a less qualified candidate over a better qualified one simply went against all that the American Dream stood for—the ability of the best and the brightest to rise. It had been one thing for the federal government to use its authority to free the slaves a century before; it was quite another to implement programs and quotas that ignored individual merit and ability altogether. Yet somehow, that's exactly what had happened. Equal opportunity, the core foundation of the economic American Dream, had become a quest for equal results.

10

THE DREAM OF A GREAT SOCIETY
AND THE AGE OF ENTITLEMENT

◇◇

The civil rights movement of the 1950s, while beneficial in many ways, also opened something of a Pandora's box. The movement's emphasis on equality of results as a measure of success changed our expectations of both the American Dream itself and the federal government's role in helping to secure it. Denied equal status and opportunity for so long, women and minorities began to reject the core American idea that ultimately, every person is responsible for his or her own success. Instead, they began to use social reengineering as a tool to achieve what they believed to be a more fair and just society. In the wake of their success, much of American society at large, particularly the young and idealistic baby boomers, embraced this interventionist approach as well. Led by the charismatic and idealistic John F. Kennedy, they began to set their sights on using the federal government to tackle problems such as war, poverty, and social injustice.

Kennedy may have claimed in his debate with Nixon that he did not believe in big government, but his expansive New Frontier domestic agenda called for an increase in the minimum wage, retraining for workers displaced by new technology, affordable housing for middle- and low-income families, federal funding for education, medical care for the elderly, equal rights for women, an end to racial segregation, the establishment of the Peace Corps, and putting a man on the moon by the end of the decade. Although the American economy had done spectacularly well in the postwar years, it was overly ambitious to think that government could take on such a wide range of domestic issues while winning the Cold War and the space race at the same time. The New Frontier agenda sounded wonderful, but could the federal government deliver on all of its promises, and could the American people afford to pay for them?

The latter question hinged on whether the American economy would continue to grow and prosper as it had during the postwar era. At the beginning of the 1950s, a significant portion of Americans, as well as professional economists, believed that a depression was likely before the end of the decade. This didn't come to pass, and by the start of the 1960s, America's standard of living was vastly different than it had been just fifteen years previously. In the 1950s alone, median family incomes rose an astonishing 38 percent, with the majority of the gains going to those in the bottom half of the income distribution.[1] Better medical care and increasing access to health insurance had reduced mortality rates and led to fewer illnesses in general. A large and affluent middle class had emerged, living the kind of lifestyle and enjoying the sort of leisure and activities that would have been available only to the very wealthy just a few decades earlier. While there had been several minor recessions throughout the decade, the economy's ability to rebound and continue on its rapid growth trajectory convinced many that with moderate government intervention and benevolent business practices, growth could be permanently sustained.

When Kennedy took office in 1961, the country was experiencing a slight recession, due primarily to the Federal Reserve raising interest rates. This recession was minor in comparison to the Great

Depression, with peak unemployment of 7.1 percent, and it lasted only ten months. Nevertheless, the new president was committed to maintaining full employment, and his Council of Economic Advisors thought the economy could be tweaked to do better with the right economic policies. In the wake of the Great Depression, professional economists had advanced many theories to explain what had gone wrong and why, and the explanation that stuck, which was based largely on the theories of John Maynard Keynes, came to be called the "new economics." A British economist, Keynes had come to prominence when, disgusted by the draconian war reparations enacted at the Treaty of Versailles after World War I, he published a highly prescient book, *The Economic Consequences of the Peace*. In it, he correctly predicted the dire consequences those reparations would have on the world economy and gained much credibility in doing so.

Having been proven correct, Keynes went on to address the causes of the worldwide depression that followed in his seminal work, *The General Theory of Employment, Interest and Money*, which made him the most influential economist since Adam Smith. Keynes challenged the prevailing wisdom of classical economics, which argued that free markets would naturally establish full employment equilibrium so long as there was no government interference. The Great Depression had shown that assumption to be patently incorrect, and Keynes's theory argued that active government intervention could be effective in managing national economies. In particular, Keynes challenged the standard wisdom of balanced budgets, advocating deficit spending and tax cuts during economic slowdowns to counteract the negative effects of the business cycle, theoretically to be offset by running a surplus during periods of growth in order to keep inflation in check.

While Franklin Roosevelt had employed some of Keynes's ideas, several decades passed before his theories were widely accepted and adopted, particularly his ideas regarding deficit spending. Since the time of the founding of the nation, maintaining a balanced budget had been considered one of the president's most sacred duties. "It is incumbent on every generation to pay its own debts as it goes," Thomas Jefferson wrote in a letter to a friend. "A principle which if acted on would save one-half the wars of the world."[2] Even Roosevelt had disliked running deficits, and as late as President Eisenhower's administration in the 1950s, balanced budgets, at least during peacetime, were still political gospel. While not all of his budgets were in balance, Eisenhower still resisted demands from Republicans to lower taxes, even though he agreed they were too high, for the sake of trying to exert some fiscal discipline. In his final year in office, he noted in an address to Congress, "This truth we must take to heart: in good times, we must at the very least pay our way."[3]

Eisenhower, born in the nineteenth century, was the last American president to genuinely embrace that view. Starting with Kennedy, our nation's leaders occasionally paid lip service to the notion of balanced budgets, while deliberately using deficit spending as a tool to manage the economy and smooth out the ups and downs of the business cycle. During Eisenhower's administration, growth of the GNP had slowed; and it actually declined during his last year in office, while unemployment had gradually crept up from 3 to 7 percent. Putting Keynesian ideas into practice, Kennedy proposed much-needed tax cuts—when he entered office, the top marginal tax rate was a crippling 91 percent—and also expanded government spending. In 1961, he ran the country's first peacetime, nonrecession deficit, and his second budget, in 1962, was the first to exceed $100 billion.

The economy initially responded well, prospering during Kennedy's administration with an average yearly GNP increase of 5.5 percent. Inflation, somewhat surprisingly, remained steady at 1 percent, while unemployment dropped and industrial production rose. Kennedy's proposed tax cut wasn't enacted by Congress until 1964, three months after his assassination. But once it was enacted, the GNP rose 10 percent in the first year alone and increased an average of 4.5 percent annually until Nixon's election in 1968. Keynesian economic policies appeared to be a great success, and in 1965, *Time* magazine featured Keynes on its cover, noting in the accompanying article that Americans had "come to accept that the government should actively use its Keynesian tools to promote growth and stability."[4]

As burgeoning deficits appeared to have no ill consequences, a dangerous precedent—lowering taxes and increasing spending without balancing the budget—was set. Deficit spending, in the name of promoting the economic stability and growth necessary to fund the American Dream, was no longer an evil to be avoided. Instead, it would provide a justification for increasing government spending without raising taxes to pay for that spending. As a result, the size of the national government grew in tandem with the size of the federal deficit. Our success in World War II and our subsequent emergence as a political and economic superpower led Americans to believe that they could solve most social problems and ensure a high standard of living for all of our citizens via continual economic growth. This national belief led Lyndon Johnson, who in the 1964 presidential election had swept all but six states and won 61 percent of the popular vote, to propose and persuade the Democratic majority in Congress to pass what became known as his Great Society legislative agenda.

Significantly older than Kennedy, Johnson was an ardent admirer of Franklin Roosevelt and the New Deal. He saw the Great Society as a continuation of the New Deal, and his goal was to tap into the vast amount of wealth being created by the postwar boom and use it to fund a sweeping set of government programs that were intended to solve social problems. "We are going to assemble the best thought and broadest knowledge from all over the world to find these answers," Johnson said in a campaign speech given at the University of Michigan in 1964. "I intend to establish working groups to prepare a series of conferences and meetings—on the cities, on natural beauty, on the quality of education, and on other emerging challenges. From these studies, we will begin to set our course toward the Great Society."[5]

A former Speaker of the House of Representatives, President Johnson proved adept at persuading Congress to approve program after program—of the eighty-seven bills he submitted to Congress, eighty-four were eventually signed into law. Among them were two expensive new entitlement programs, Medicare for the elderly and Medicaid for the poor, as well as an expansion of Social Security; $3 billion in appropriations to help fight the "War on Poverty" through education, job training, and community development; federal aid to public schools as well as college scholarships and low-interest loans; various consumer protection laws that addressed child safety, fair packaging and labeling, and truth in lending; environmental protection laws, including air pollution control, land and water conservation, and endangered species protection; the creation of the National Endowment for the Arts and Humanities to support public broadcasting and cultural centers; and last but not least, civil rights legislation banning segregation, job discrimination, voting discrimination, and housing discrimination.

While all of these programs were admirable in their intent, they were costly, requiring a significant expansion of the federal government to administer, as well as a huge increase in the deficit and the national debt to subsidize. As the country's commitments in Vietnam grew, so did defense spending, increasing the deficit even further and making the Great Society programs harder to fund. Some were eliminated or cut back, yet many still exist today, despite the American public's unwillingness to pay for them via higher taxes. In 1929, federal expenditures had equaled 3 percent of the country's total output; by the end of the Johnson administration, that figure had climbed to almost 20 percent, and the federal debt was $368.7 billion. Yet rosy economic predictions on the part of the Congressional Budget Office assured everyone that future tax revenues would be sufficient to pay for the American people's dream of a Great Society.

And so it was that the American Dream expanded far beyond our ability to feasibly achieve and pay for. Many who had lived through the Great Depression continued to be haunted by its memory, but those who were born between 1946 and 1964 as part of the baby boom generation had experienced prosperity for most of their lives, and they quite naturally expected it to continue. They had become the consumer generation, but rather than enjoy the level of unprecedented affluence they had achieved, these young Americans instead became even more ambitious in their dreams and desires. They now expected government to control the business cycle, ensure a rising standard of living, and provide a safety net to address all of the country's social problems. It was a set of expectations that, once established, proved nearly impossible to rescind, no matter how high the federal debt climbed in ensuing years. The logic of using deficit spending during recessions was embraced, but without the necessary discipline of paying down those deficits during times of plenty. The baby boom generation and the consumer culture of the 1950s had begat the entitlement culture of the 1960s.

• • • • •

The national economy wasn't the only thing to be scientifically managed according to new principles with the rise of the Great Society. In the private sector, new theories of business management, based largely on quantitative analytical techniques, had been developed to run America's growing multinational corporations. Successful leadership of these companies was crucial in the attempt to tame the business cycle, and the companies themselves had a vested interest in avoiding a repeat of the Great Depression. The New Deal had forcibly demonstrated just how far the federal government was willing to intervene in business affairs in the name of stable employment, so big business pragmatically decided to take the lead in providing stable jobs, high wages, and good benefits. Median family incomes rose another 37 percent during the 1960s, and by the end of the decade, 52 percent of full-time workers had employer-financed pensions.[6] America's leading companies took on a quasi-paternalistic role during these years, the productivity and profits of the postwar period allowing them to nurture and provide for a growing and increasingly affluent middle class.

The managerial profession grew exponentially during the postwar era, due to the rapid growth of American industry itself and to the increasing pool of college graduates. The number of Americans who had completed four years of college doubled between 1940 and 1965, and they fed the ranks of white-collar management in the corporate world. Before the war, white-collar jobs such as managers, office workers, teachers, and medical professionals accounted for less than 40 percent of the total workforce; by the end of the 1960s, that figure had jumped to 60 percent. And while it had been rare in America in the days before the Great Depression to work for one company one's entire life, by the sixties it was far more common.

This new class of career managers sought to reform the negative image of business that Americans had developed during the Gilded Age and the Great Depression. These were not robber barons, but rather compassionate professionals whose goal was to serve not only the interests of stockholders, but also the interests of their employees, communities, and society at large. This benevolence was financed by gains in productivity from investment in technology, education, and analysis, all yielding greater efficiency and profitability. Good managers viewed their employees as assets to be nurtured and developed rather than interchangeable parts to be whipped into submission and discarded when necessary. Like the fathers portrayed on American television, professional managers were expected to be wise and responsible, firm when necessary, but ultimately good-hearted and committed to keeping their lambs in the fold.

The stable, lifetime employment offered by America's newly reformed managers and corporations soon earned the loyalty of what became known as the "organization man," a term coined by William H. Whyte, an editor for *Fortune* magazine. For Whyte, the type of corporate culture that produced the organization man—characterized over the years as a bland cog in the corporate machine, devoid of personality, incapable of originality or independent thought and slavishly devoted to the company that paid his salary—was something to be scorned. But at the time, organization men themselves were for the most part grateful to the companies that provided the stable, cushy jobs that were necessary to sustain their increasingly affluent lifestyles.

Leading the way among America's "good corporations" was IBM. The Computer-Tabulating-Recording Company (later renamed International Business Machines) was created in 1911 as a conglomerate of various companies that dealt in business information, such as tabulating machines and punchcard time clocks. It had been shepherded by Thomas Watson from a tiny company with revenues of $1.3 million in 1914 to one of the darlings of postwar corporate America with revenues of over $700 million when he retired in 1956.[7] Even in the company's early years, Watson was ahead of his time when it came to employee relations, offering good pay, lifetime job security, ongoing education and training opportunities, and rewards for great performance to white collar employees. (He eventually adopted progressive policies toward blue-collar workers as well.) He was an early adopter of professional management, referring to bosses as managers rather than foremen, and while he was an authoritarian and demanding boss, he was also a relentless promoter of talent and innovation.

Ironically, IBM got its big break during the Great Depression. With the passage of the Social Security Act, the government and corporations needed machines that could not only tabulate payroll taxes, but also compare two sets of records, such as a pension payment and a date of birth. Watson had taken a great risk, both personally and professionally, by building up inventory during the depression and increasing his workforce from several hundred to more than seven thousand employees. He had invested all of his spare capital in IBM stock over the years, and when it fell by over 200 points from 1929 to 1932, he nearly went bankrupt. But the information-processing demands of Social Security saved both him and the company, and within a few years his earnings made him the richest man in America—his salary exceeded even those of the big three auto executives and the Hollywood moguls. Watson shared the wealth, rewarding each of his employees with a $1,000 life insurance policy and announcing a minimum pay increase of 37 percent.

By 1948, IBM had developed, at Watson's insistence, the Selective Sequence Electronic Calculator, one of the first supercomputers. It had 12,500 vacuum tubes and could perform addition or subtraction of a nineteen-digit sequence of numbers in 0.35 seconds. Watson promptly dedicated it on a nonprofit basis to "the use of science throughout the world" and then instructed his engineers to get to work on a "machine of the same type, with reduced capacity, to meet the requirements of the ordinary businesses we serve."[8]

The fulfillment of that vision would be left to his son, Thomas Watson Jr., who succeeded his father as president of the company. Watson Jr. spearheaded the development of the IBM 701, which occupied less than a fourth of the space of the SSEC and operated twenty-five times faster. By 1956, the outcome of the presidential election was forecast, correctly, as a landslide for Eisenhower by an IBM mainframe computer, and by 1965 IBM had an 80 percent share of the mainframe market. When Watson Jr. retired six year later, IBM's revenues had soared to over $7.5 billion, and the company employed 270,000 people—over a quarter of a million workers to which IBM's managers firmly believed they could assure a lifetime of employment.[9]

In the process of growing so large and conquering the mainframe computer market, however, IBM had incurred massive debts. The System/360 mainframe that had given IBM dominance in the industry had cost $5 billion to develop at a time when the company's annual revenue was only $3.2 billion. It was the most expensive privately financed commercial project in history up to that point, a gamble which, if it had gone badly, probably would have bankrupted the company. It didn't, but the size of the venture was indicative of a trend in corporate America toward massive growth and high risk investments. From the late sixties to the mid eighties, the share of

America's corporate cash flow dedicated to servicing debt doubled, due in large part to a sharp increase in the formation of conglomerates.

In 1949, nearly 70 percent of the country's top 200 industrial companies confined their business to one industry. By 1970, only 35 percent of America's top corporations did so, having formed conglomerates that often ran dozens of businesses in varied industries that had little to do with one another.[10] In effect, corporations were investing on behalf of their shareholders rather than returning profits to them in the form of greater dividends. The argument in favor of doing this was that managers, better informed about business matters in general, made superior judgments when it came to investing. Also, as dividends were double-taxed, once as corporate profits and again as individual income, it made sense to retain and reinvest profits within the firm rather than pay out additional dividends. (On the other hand, stock appreciation created capital gains when sold, and the Tax Reform Act of 1969 raised the maximum tax rate on capital gains to 49 percent, the highest level since 1921.)

Tax issues aside, the real reason behind the rush to form conglomerates was constant pressure for growth, both for its own sake and also to provide an increasing number of higher-level management positions into which middle managers could be promoted. Rather than simply giving out yearly bonuses based on performance, corporate America had fallen into the habit of handing out a series of promotions to its middle managers over the course of their careers, with each job requiring greater responsibilities and conferring greater perks and rewards—hence the term "climbing the corporate ladder." But since the hierarchy of a firm is inherently a pyramid, it is impossible for every low-level manager to rise to the level of executive management without greatly increasing the size of the company, which led to a great deal of overexpansion. (One of the worst offenders was General Electric, which by 1968 had grown into a corporate behemoth with 190 departments reporting to 46 divisions, which in turn reported to 10 groups accountable to executive management.)[11] The theory was that a good manager was a good manager, regardless of industry knowledge or experience, so companies bought other companies in completely unrelated industries and expected their own successful managers to make a success of them as well.

Nor were GE and IBM, two of the biggest corporations in America, in any way outliers. "Bigger is better" was an unwritten rule of the postwar economy and one of the main reasons corporate America felt it had successfully tamed the business cycle. The world described by Adam Smith in *The Wealth of Nations* was one where hundreds or thousands of small suppliers produced goods and services for innumerable small buyers, all of whom were subject to the uncontrollable ups and downs of the market. But the business world of the 1960s was a very different place—one where almost every industry had come to be dominated by a handful of large firms, large enough that they exerted a great deal of influence on the market rather than being subject to its whims.

What's more, technology was playing an increasing role in productivity. It had become expensive and complex enough that most research and development could be effectively conducted only by large companies. These companies also had the cash to buy small technology developers and commercialize their products more effectively, ensuring their continued dominance and longevity, at least in theory. In practice, the coming decades showed that even the largest and most well-established firms were subject to a variety of market predators, from foreign competition to small-business entrepreneurs to hostile takeovers conducted by corporate raiders. But that was all in the future, and throughout the 1960s, the supremacy and permanence of America's leading companies was unquestioned, as was their ability to forever finance the American Dream.

• • • • •

The changes wrought by big business and big government on middle-class America's expectations were revolutionary. The American Dream always had a strong economic component, but had the postwar prosperity reduced it to an eternal quest for economic progress and material gain? The Puritans had wanted to build a better life for their children, but what they'd wanted was something simpler and more profound than Barbie dolls and GI Joes, or even a college education and a rising standard of living. They had wanted the freedom to worship as they chose, to govern themselves, and to work for themselves without limits being placed on them because of their faith or lack of hereditary title. The material wealth of the average American family of the 1970s exceeded anything the Puritans might have imagined, and the materialism and degeneration of cultural values that accompanied it would no doubt have disgusted them. Yet materialism and the quest for an ever-rising standard of living—and the role of government, business, and organized labor in helping Americans to achieve it—had become so ingrained in our culture that few seriously questioned it.

By the end of the 1960s, the American Dream was no longer about freedom of speech, freedom of religion, and providing an opportunity to climb from the lowest rung of society to the top. Rather, it was about guaranteeing continual prosperity and growth, raising everyone up to a "middle-class" standard of living, and ensuring that this standard increased with each successive generation. The stable white-collar job with hefty fringe benefits, the house in the suburbs, the best health care available, the golden retirement—these were all things Americans now expected as a matter of course. A half-century before such things were rare—practically unheard of—and certainly not thought of as rights. Now they were the very basics of a middle-class existence that all Americans felt they deserved and expected business and government to provide. This was the new American Dream, and Americans now felt entitled to it.

As the 1960s drew to a close, however, the facade of scientifically managed prosperity started to unravel. The long, hot summer of 1967 saw the emergence not only of hippie counterculture in San Francisco, but the eruption of race riots across the United States as well, as the civil rights movement suddenly turned violent. While the waves of protest surged and ebbed at home, America also became more deeply involved in the Vietnam War abroad as North Vietnam launched the Tet Offensive in January 1968. The nation also suffered two traumatic blows when Martin Luther King Jr. was assassinated in April, followed by the shooting of Robert F. Kennedy in June. The country was still reeling from the assassination several years earlier of President John F. Kennedy, whose promise to put on a man on the moon by the end of the decade was fulfilled with just months to spare. Neil Armstrong's "one small step for man, one giant leap for mankind" was a magical moment that closed out a decade of both tragedy and triumph, but unfortunately there was more of the former than the latter on the horizon.

Just as America was launching the ambitious but costly programs of the Great Society—and embracing the expanding version of the American Dream that it promised—the cracks in the dam of the economic growth and prosperity that were necessary to finance that dream were already beginning to show. The fine-tuning of the economy to achieve full employment that had begun during President Kennedy's administration and continued through President Johnson's administration gradually began to produce the predictable result of inflation, which rose from less than 1 percent in 1961 to 5.6 percent by the time Richard Nixon was elected in 1968. The boom period of the sixties—the longest uninterrupted economic expansion in American history—ended with a relatively mild recession in which unemployment reached 6.1 percent.

Worried about his forthcoming bid for reelection, Nixon decided to combat the growing unemployment and inflation by instituting temporary wage and price controls. It was a remarkable step for a Republican president and an indication of the extent to which the concept of an active, interventionist federal government had been embraced by both political parties. At first the controls appeared to work, and by 1972 the economy had improved just enough to end the recession and help Nixon win his second term in office. An illusion of prosperity was reestablished, and government spending once again increased, while the Federal Reserve unwisely kept interest rates low—despite the fact that there was already too much money chasing too few goods. However, with the outbreak of the Yom Kippur War and the oil crisis of 1973, during which the members of OPEC proclaimed an oil embargo that sent international prices for oil soaring, the system of price and wage controls broke down. This kicked off another, deeper recession, and when Nixon allowed the wage and price controls to lapse in 1974, inflation skyrocketed up to 12.3 percent.

Nor was inflation the only problem ailing the American economy. Corporate profit margins, which had averaged 15.7 percent in the 1960s, fell to 10.7 percent in the 1970s due to a variety of factors.[12] Management at American's leading companies had become bloated and top-heavy, and corporations had formed conglomerates that made little sense and proved inefficient. Increasingly, powerful unions also reduced profitability by pushing relentlessly for higher wage and benefits packages while resisting cost-cutting measures, improvements, and innovations that would have eliminated some jobs in the name of greater productivity. Consequently, by the 1970s, many viewed "big labor" as nothing more than a self-serving special interest group, one that served the interests of the unions themselves more than their members. Highly publicized scandals involving union bosses—whose shenanigans rivaled those of the robber barons of the Gilded Age—certainly didn't help. Dave Beck, president of the Teamsters Union, was prosecuted for embezzlement and labor racketeering, and his successor Jimmy Hoffa was convicted of bribery and fraud.

As unions matured and became part of the establishment, their entrenched bureaucracies mirrored those of big business. Much of this was due to the difference in structure and philosophy of American labor organizations, which were far less political than their European counterparts. As the American Federation of Labor's leader George Meany noted, "We do not seek to recast American society in any particular doctrinaire or ideological image. We seek an ever-rising standard of living."[13] This relentless focus led to a decentralized union strategy in which local unions were organized to collectively bargain with at most a handful of individual firms. As a result, there were more than 70,000 local and 174 national unions in the United States at the time, with nearly 60,000 paid, full-time union officers. These jobs were largely administrative, and the officers' primary goal was negotiating for ever more generous wage and benefits packages on behalf of their workers.[14]

It was a philosophy very much in line with the New Deal American Dream of upward mobility for the working class, but the problem was that employee performance in the 1970s wasn't sufficient to justify what the unions were demanding. Productivity had increased an average of 3 percent annually in the postwar decades, but by the 1970s it had fallen to only 1 percent, a major factor underlying the decline in overall profitability. Meanwhile, Europe's and Japan's industries had finally recovered from World War II, and foreign competition and productivity was on the rise. Free trade and utter dominance of world manufacturing had given the United States a consistently favorable trade balance throughout the postwar era, but in 1971 the trade balance turned negative as inflation made American goods appear more expensive relative to the world market, and foreign goods less expensive. From 1975 onward, the trade balance stayed negative and deteriorated as Americans used increasingly easy access to credit to finance purchases of cheaper foreign imports.

Yet despite all the clear indicators that the postwar boom had passed, the American public refused to accept the reality that the economy was slowing down and that permanent growth and full employment without recessions or inflation was impossible. People had come to rely on big government, big business, and big labor to provide an ever-rising standard of living, and they expected these institutions to deliver on their promises one way or another. Throughout the seventies, many of them did. Workers in the heavily unionized steel and auto industries, among others, successfully negotiated high wage settlements while resisting cost-cutting changes in work practices. Even at nonunion companies, across-the-board salary increases and routine promotions were standard practice, as was the expectation of lifetime employment. As late as 1980, IBM promised its workers, in a short book called *About the Company*, "In nearly 40 years, no person employed on a regular basis by IBM has lost as much as one hour of working time because of a layoff. When recessions come or there is a major production shift, some companies handle the work-force imbalances that result by letting people go. IBM hasn't done that, hopes never to have to. People are a treasured resource."[15]

The federal government was also blindly optimistic, continuing to make promises and expand programs while racking up increasing deficits and debt. In 1972, Congress increased Social Security benefits—which had already been increased seven times since the program's inception—by 20 percent and indexed them to inflation. In fact, during Nixon's tenure in office, direct payments from the federal government to individual American citizens, including benefits such as Social Security and Medicare, rose from 6.3 percent of GNP to 8.9 percent, while defense spending decreased from 9.1 percent to 5.8 percent. Total food aid and public assistance also rose by almost half, and a revenue-sharing program was instituted that channeled $80 billion to state and local governments. The federal deficit averaged $35 billion annually throughout the 1970s, and by the end of the decade, the national debt had grown to two and one-half times what it had been at the start.[16]

Oddly, however, this increase in patronage on the part of business and government didn't appear to inspire much gratitude or confidence on the part of the public. In fact, Americans' faith in big institutions fell precipitously during the late '60s and early '70s. That their confidence in the executive branch should fall during this period isn't really surprising, given the Watergate scandal and Nixon's resignation from office. But Americans' faith in Congress experienced a similar decline of almost 30 percent from 1966 to 1975, and their faith in major companies experienced an even greater one.[17] Ironically, making promises and ensuring a high standard of living had somehow made people more distrustful and unhappy with the very institutions that were providing those benefits—especially when the promises they made were inevitably broken.

New York City was a case in point. For well over a century it had been considered the greatest city in the country—the one most closely associated with the American Dream and a beacon of hope for most immigrants. But as tax revenues declined, quality of life in the city fell precipitously, and by 1975 it was a crime-infested shadow of its former self. Having embraced the Great Society redistributionist model, it provided a degree of social welfare and services beyond that of any other American city, but as the economy stagnated, it found itself in a financial crisis. The city almost declared bankruptcy in October of that year, a disaster that was averted only when several of the city's unions agreed to furnish money from their pension funds to buy municipal bonds. Two years later, a lengthy citywide blackout led to widespread violence, looting, and civil unrest. As a result, middle-class families, who had already been moving out to the suburbs for the past several decades, started leaving in droves. By the end of the seventies, nearly a million people had left, and the growing belief that New York City was in a permanent decline reflected Americans' increasingly pessimistic mood about the country's future in general. The postwar boom was clearly over, and as uncertainty spread, many Americans were wondering if the American Dream of a continuously rising standard of living was coming to an end as well.

11

THE DREAM OF MORNING IN AMERICA AND THE REAGAN REVOLUTION

◇◇◇◇◇◇◇◇◇◇◇◇◇◇◇◇◇◇◇◇◇◇◇◇◇◇◇◇◇◇◇◇◇◇◇◇◇◇◇

A t the start of the 1970s, the American Dream had evolved into something quite different from what it had been just a half-century earlier. In the aftermath of the Great Depression and the New Deal the small, limited government of the Founding Fathers had transformed into a much larger entity—a bureaucratic web of institutions that had more direct impact on Americans' lives. Eighty-five percent of Americans now paid income tax, and almost all working Americans paid payroll taxes, but in turn a social safety net provided far greater security than ever before. Big government and the modern welfare state had come to be accepted as a given by both political parties and by the American people at large, as had our status as a global superpower. In the face of rising Communism and the threat of nuclear war, Americans were now comfortable with the idea of the United States being the leader of the free world and the defender of capitalism and democracy on the world stage. The "American Dream" was no longer just a vague notion. The phrase had definitively entered the American lexicon and was increasingly referred to and marketed by American politicians both to motivate the American people to achieve greater growth and prosperity at home and to promote our way of life around the world.

Pervasive as it was, this version of the American Dream, and particularly the federal government's role in providing it, was not without its critics. While the Democrats had technically been in control of both houses of Congress since 1954, an informal coalition of conservative Republicans and conservative southern Democrats formed in opposition to the New Deal had carried considerable influence up until 1961, when the coattails from John F. Kennedy's election put liberals firmly in charge. Lyndon Johnson had defeated the unabashedly conservative Barry Goldwater in a landslide in the presidential election of 1964, prompting the Republican Party to run the far more moderate Richard Nixon in 1968. But this backfired when the Watergate scandal forced Nixon to resign in disgrace, leaving Americans disenchanted with politicians in general and Republicans in particular.

Nixon's resignation was one of a series of troubling events that plagued the country throughout the 1970s. On the economic front, the country was suffering from the unprecedented phenomenon of simultaneous high inflation and high unemployment. Under Keynesian theory, so-called "stagflation" should have been impossible—increasing demand for goods that spurred rising prices usually encouraged companies to hire more workers, whereas falling demand produced unemployment but also tended to slow or even reverse inflation. The oil shock of 1973, however, had put pressure on prices that had everything to do with supply and nothing to do with demand, raising consumer prices and also cutting into corporate profit margins. When the economy contracted and companies started laying off workers, the government tried to stimulate the economy by spending more and increasing the money supply—the standard Keynesian response to a recession. Yet since the inflation was fueled by commodity shortages and government spending rather than consumer demand, it persisted, with stagflation the result.

It didn't take long for the worsening economic situation to take its toll on Americans' pocketbooks. Median family income, which had doubled during the postwar years, increased a mere 7 percent in real terms during the 1970s.[1] Yet despite the underlying uncertainty in the economy, persistent stagflation only encouraged Americans to spend more, as putting off purchases might make them more expensive. The introduction of credit cards had made it easier than ever before for the average American to access credit, and by the seventies more than half of all families had one. Rather than scaling back on their spending, Americans went on a shopping spree in what would come to be called the "me decade," which saw not only the launch of the appropriately named *Self* magazine, but also the rise of the self-help genre and a rash of books with titles like *Looking Out for Number One* and *How to Be Your Own Best Friend*.

Nor were things any better on the social front. California, ever innovative, had introduced the "no fault" divorce in 1969, and as the practice spread across the country, the divorce rate doubled. Protests and violence were on the rise, volunteerism was on the decline, and societal norms were crumbling. Americans were filling their leisure hours by watching vapid television shows like *Charlie's Angels* and *Dallas*, reading gossipy magazines like *People*, and succumbing to the disco culture of New York's infamous Studio 54. Jaded after the Watergate scandal and increasingly self-absorbed, only 54 percent of Americans bothered to vote in the 1976 presidential election that brought Jimmy Carter to office, and only 38 percent voted in the mid-term elections that followed. By 1978, *Christianity Today* reported that a certain "doomsday chic" had settled upon the nation—a feeling that America was in decline and was increasingly at the mercy of oil-exporting third-world countries.[2]

President James Carter, often seen as one of our most morally trustworthy, if ineffectual, presidents, was deeply troubled by the breakdown of the traditional family and worried that the country was experiencing not only an economic crisis but a spiritual one as well. The situation came to a head in the summer of 1979, when OPEC voted to raise oil prices by 24 percent, creating massive gasoline shortages. Inflation, which had already hit double digits, rose to over 13 percent, and the public's anger bubbled over into violence as increasingly long lines formed at gas stations around the country. When a full-fledged riot broke out in the formerly peaceful suburb of Levittown, Pennsylvania, Carter, whose approval ratings had dipped almost as low as Nixon's at the height of Watergate, knew he needed to speak to the nation and try to assuage its anger and frustration. But he had also come to believe that there was something fundamentally wrong with the country that went deeper than stagflation and energy shortages. So in July, he went before the nation to deliver an address that he explained was "not a message of happiness or reassurance, but it is the truth and it is a warning."

The central theme of the speech was what Carter termed the country's "crisis of confidence." "We've always believed in something called progress. We've always had a faith that the days of our children would be better than our own," he declared, arguing:

> Too many of us now tend to worship self-indulgence and consumption. Human identity is no longer defined by what one does, but by what one owns. But we've discovered that owning things and consuming things does not satisfy our longing for meaning. We've learned that piling up material goods cannot fill the emptiness of lives which have no confidence or purpose...
>
> ...I do not promise a quick way out of our nation's problems, when the truth is that the only way out is an all-out effort...
>
> We can manage the short-term shortages more effectively and we will, but there are no short-term solutions to our long-range problems. There is simply no way to avoid sacrifice.[3]

The initial reaction to Carter's address was surprisingly positive for a nation that social commentators had written off as hopelessly narcissistic; 84 percent of the telephone calls and 85 percent of the letters that came flooding into the White House in response were positive. But the national press dubbed it the "malaise speech," a name that stuck despite the fact that Carter never used the word *malaise* in his address. Although the president received a brief bounce in the polls, his political opponents cast the speech as Carter's attempt to blame the nation for his own failings and inadequacies as the nation's leader. When he asked for the resignations of his entire cabinet just two days after the address, the press moved on to the much juicier story of the controversial firings, and the speech was largely forgotten.

While Carter didn't use the phrase explicitly, his address had asked some very fundamental questions about the nature of the American Dream, questions that no American president had asked for a very long time, if ever. Certainly no president of the modern welfare state had questioned it, at least not until Carter, and he committed political suicide by doing so. As the press and Carter's political opponents ridiculed the so-called malaise speech, his brief increase in approval ratings vanished, and thus one of the few attempts by a sitting president to ask tough questions of the American people was brushed aside. It would fall to another, more inspirational president to lead Americans back to embrace an older, more traditional version of the American Dream.

● ● ● ● ●

When Ronald Reagan defeated Jimmy Carter in the 1980 presidential election, it was more than just a referendum on Carter's tenure in office. The Reagan Revolution was the result of a tidal wave of American conservatism that rose in response to what was seen as the excesses of the modern welfare state. Reagan himself had once been a Democrat and a supporter of the New Deal, but after serving in World War II, his views became increasingly conservative, influenced by the writings of prominent thinkers like Dr. Russell Kirk, author of *The Conservative Mind*. Kirk was one of the primary intellectual leaders in the postwar conservative movement, developing over the course of his career ten basic principles of conservativism that included a belief in an "enduring moral order" as well as adherence to "custom, convention, and continuity." Conservatives, he argued, "sense that modern people are dwarfs on the shoulders of giants, able to see farther than their ancestors only because of the great stature of those who have preceded us in time," and therefore unlikely "to make any brave new discoveries in morals or politics or taste."[4]

Kirk believed that both man and society were by nature imperfect and that liberal attempts to create perfect equality were both dangerous and doomed to failure. "For the preservation of a healthy diversity in any civilization, there must survive orders and classes, differences in material condition, and many sorts of inequality," he wrote. Liberal attempts to erase social and economic inequality were misguided, for "man being imperfect, no perfect social order ever can be created," he argued. "All that we reasonably can expect is a tolerably ordered, just, and free society, in which some evils, maladjustments, and suffering will continue to lurk." Taking a page from John Locke, he further argued that freedom and property were inextricably linked:

> The institution of several property—that is, private property—has been a powerful instrument for teaching men and women responsibility, for providing motives to integrity, for supporting general culture, for raising mankind above the level of mere drudgery, for affording leisure to think and freedom to act. To be able to retain the fruits of one's labor; to be able to see one's work made permanent; to be able to bequeath one's property to one's posterity; to be able to rise from the natural condition of grinding poverty to the security of enduring accomplishment; to have something that is really one's own—these are advantages difficult to deny.[5]

The federal government, therefore, had no business trying to impose involuntary collectivism on its citizens. It was far better if "the decisions most directly affecting the lives of citizens are made locally and voluntarily." In a healthy community, some functions were best carried out by local government, while others were best left to churches and private institutions. The key was that decisions be kept local and thus able to be influenced by those who would be most affected. When local control was ceded to a central, distant authority, communities were put at risk, for "a central administration, or a corps of select managers and civil servants, however well intentioned and well trained, cannot confer justice and prosperity and tranquility upon a mass of men and women deprived of their old responsibilities."[6]

Change was an inevitable part of life, Kirk recognized, but the zealous progressivism of the modern liberal agenda failed to recognize that "when a society is progressing in some respects, usually it is declining in other respects." Change ought to be made gradually, and government measures should be considered and judged based on their probable consequences in the long term rather than cater to public whims and desires. "The conservative, in short, favors reasoned and temperate progress; he is opposed to the cult of Progress, whose votaries believe that everything new necessarily is superior to everything old,"[7] he declared.

Kirk and William F. Buckley Jr., founder of *The National Review*, had a profound influence on Reagan, and by 1961, he was speaking out against the legislation that would become Medicare, telling Americans that it would lead to socialism. A few years later, Reagan officially joined the Republican Party and endorsed Goldwater for president, arguing, "The Founding Fathers knew a government can't control the economy without controlling people. And they knew when a government sets out to do that, it must use force and coercion to achieve its purpose. So we have come to a time for choosing."[8]

Americans weren't quite ready to choose Reagan's brand of conservativism at that moment. A majority of the public was still very much invested in the idea of government as the solution to social problems and an instrument to create a better and more just society. Thus, conservatives were on the defensive throughout the 1960s as the Kennedy and Johnson administrations pursued a decidedly liberal agenda, greatly expanding the federal government in the process. Equally alarming to conservatives, the Supreme Court, under chief justices Earl Warren and Warren Burger, handed down a series of controversial rulings, decisions that upheld liberal stances on issues such as abortion, due process, capital punishment, school prayer, and desegregation of schools through busing. These rulings were unpopular with many, and the activism of the courts as well as the social and economic turmoil of the 1970s slowly drew more and more converts to the conservative cause.

As the decade drew to a close, a growing segment of Americans was appalled by what they saw as the decline of traditional moral values as well as the encroachment on individual rights by the modern welfare state. Conservatives began pushing back hard against the notion of economic leveling, arguing that it violated the central premise of the American Dream—equal opportunity—and instead insisted on equality of results. Many were also troubled by the government's policy of appeasement toward Soviet communists in the aftermath of the Vietnam War and wanted to take a more aggressive stance in defense of the American way of life. It was their goal, and Reagan's, to restore the American Dream to what they saw as a more authentic, realistic version based on modern conservative principles. The best way to do this, they argued, was to reduce the size and scope of government, revert to a more hands-off economic policy, and rebuild the strength of the American military. By 1980, the tide of political thought had once again turned as free-market businessmen in the Northeast, social conservative evangelicals in the South, and limited-government libertarians in the West finally came together under the Reagan banner.

An optimist by nature, Reagan had great faith in the essential strength and character of Americans and a steadfast conviction that they were God's chosen people. In officially announcing his candidacy, he rejected Carter's diagnosis of what ailed America, observing, "For the first time in our memory, many Americans are asking: does history still have a place for America, for her people, for her great ideals? There are some who answer, 'no,' that our energy is spent, our days of greatness at an end, that a great national malaise is upon us." Reagan's response? "I find no national malaise. I find nothing wrong with the American people."[9]

During his campaign, Reagan frequently invoked John Winthrop's vision of America as a shining city upon a hill and promised to "begin the world over again." It was a hopeful message that tapped into Americans' core belief that it was always possible to make a fresh start and that tomorrow would undoubtedly be better than today. While Carter had come to believe that the American people needed to scale back their expectations, to accept a slower rate of growth and progress, and to find happiness with fewer material things, Reagan saw no reason why the American Dream of upward mobility and a rising standard of living could not continue as long as we scaled back government and changed our economic policies. He believed that America's core problems were due to the government, not the people, and he firmly believed that America could return to its former glory, noting in his inaugural address:

> It is no coincidence that our present troubles parallel and are proportionate to the intervention and intrusion in our lives that result from unnecessary and excessive growth of government. It is time for us to realize that we're too great a nation to limit ourselves to small dreams. We're not, as some would have us believe, doomed to an inevitable decline...
>
> ...It does require, however, our best effort and our willingness to believe in ourselves and to believe in our capacity to perform great deeds, to believe that together with God's help we can and will resolve the problems which now confront us. And, after all, why shouldn't we believe that? We are Americans.[10]

While in retrospect Carter's warnings with regard to the dangers of dependency on foreign oil and increasing materialism proved to be prescient, Reagan's reassuring vision of the future was far more in tune with what Americans in general wanted to hear—that far from scaling back their expectations, a return to growth and prosperity not only was possible, but was what Americans deserved. He had scored a landslide in the election, winning all but six states, and commentators hailed his victory as a crucial political realignment. The New Deal and the Great Society, they declared, were dead. The Reagan Revolution had begun.

• • • • •

Ronald Reagan came to the Oval Office with a very different vision of the American Dream than that of Jimmy Carter. The latter may have concluded that the American Dream needed to be rethought in the face of modern challenges, but Reagan believed Americans simply needed to embrace the old ethic of frontier self-reliance and the wisdom of the Founding Fathers. For much of the twentieth century, progressive politicians had been somewhat dismissive of America's early statesmen, finding their notions inadequate to deal with a modern democracy. As Woodrow Wilson had argued in *Constitutional Government*, "As the life of the nation changes, so must the interpretation of the document which contains it change, by a nice adjustment, determined, not by the original intent of those who drew the paper, but by the exigencies and the new aspects of life itself."[11]

Reagan, on the other hand, firmly believed that the core principles and ideals expressed in the Constitution were timeless, and that constitutional issues—and the role of government in general—ought to adhere as closely to the founders' original intent as possible. Reagan referred to the Founding Fathers repeatedly, extolling their vision of small, limited government and the idea that, in the words of Henry David Thoreau, "that government is best which governs least."[12] So in a complete reversal of the New Deal philosophy that had dominated American politics and economic thinking since the 1930s, in his inaugural address Reagan declared, "In this present crisis, government is not the solution to our problem. Government *is* the problem."[13] In order to solve this problem, Reagan repeatedly argued, the government needed to get "off our backs and out of our pockets," by which he meant cutting taxes and regulation.

After a decade of questionable economic policy and persistent stagflation, Americans were quite receptive to Reagan's view, particularly when it came to taxes. In 1980, the top marginal tax rate stood at 70 percent—an unthinkable figure today and one that was crushingly oppressive to business investment. Americans' total tax burden in general had grown throughout the 1970s as inflation had pushed middle-class citizens into increasingly higher tax brackets. Voters in California had finally rebelled in the summer of 1978, passing a proposition that put limits on property taxes and kicking off a grass-roots tax revolt that quickly spread across the country. By November, sixteen states had organized antitax ballot initiatives, twelve of which passed. The tide had started to turn against the notion of big government as the solution to social problems, at least if it involved raising taxes on the middle class.

In such a climate, Reagan's antitax, antiregulation, antigovernment message struck a chord with the American people, and he arrived in Washington determined to put the nation's economic house in order. When he was sworn into office in January of 1981, the country was in the worst economic shape it had experienced since the Great Depression. The unemployment rate had shot up to 7.8 percent the previous summer, and inflation had reached an astounding 13.5 percent. Stagflation was out of control, and Reagan's first priority as president was to stabilize the economy and restore the necessary conditions that would allow the private sector to create growth and prosperity. His economic plan for the country rested on three basic tenets: tightening the money supply, regulatory relief, and tax cuts.

The first two points weren't particularly controversial; Carter had actually endorsed both, although to a lesser degree. Tax cuts, on the other hand, were vociferously opposed by Democrats and moderate Republicans alike, mostly because Keynesian theory predicted that cutting taxes would worsen inflation. But Reagan was an ardent supporter of supply-side economics, a central tenet of which is that excessive taxation and regulation can stifle economic growth. Therefore, growth can be most effectively created by using incentives—such as adjusting income tax and capital gains tax rates—to allow the middle class to retain and spend more of their earnings and to encourage the wealthy to invest in new ventures rather than hide their wealth in economically unproductive tax shelters. The resulting economic growth resulted in additional tax revenue in the future that essentially offset the losses from lowering the tax rates in the first place.

It was this last argument—that tax cuts would pay for themselves—that led Reagan's opponents on both sides of the political aisle and in the press to dismiss his plan as "voodoo economics." It took an intense lobbying effort on his part to convince Congress to pass his tax bill, which cut tax rates for all fifteen tax brackets in effect at the time, lowering the top marginal tax rate from 70 to 50 percent. (He reduced them still further in his second term, lowering the top bracket to an effective rate of 28 percent.) In response, the Federal Reserve, anticipating increased inflation, hiked the federal funds rate up to 20 percent in June 1981, plunging the country into a sharp recession. While the Fed had taken more drastic action than Reagan would have preferred, he nevertheless supported a tighter monetary policy in general, knowing that it was the only way to tame inflation. By the time the recession ended in November 1982, inflation had fallen to 4.6 percent and averaged around 3 percent for the remainder of his presidency.

Tight monetary policy may have been the medicine needed to cure inflation, but the recession that accompanied it—the worst since the Great Depression—was bitter medicine with unpleasant side effects. Unemployment rose to almost 10 percent during the recession, but when the recession ended, the economy began to grow dramatically for the first time in years, at a rate of almost 9 percent annually. Tax cuts on capital gains and incomes, and the sharp reduction of inflation, had finally produced renewed business optimism, and by 1984 business investment had grown 32 percent. Unemployment and interest rates were all falling, while after-tax incomes had risen significantly. With inflation hovering near 2 percent and gasoline priced as low as 89 cents per gallon, Reagan could reasonably claim that it was "Morning in America."

For the first time in over a decade, Americans reported they felt optimistic about the coming year. Reagan's approval rating, which had taken a beating during the recession, rose sharply—a key indicator of just how closely presidential approval ratings had become tied to economic performance. He won the 1984 presidential election in a landslide, his Democratic opponent, Walter Mondale, running on the sort of Great-Society big-government platform that many Americans felt had led to the troubles of the 1970s. Reagan carried every state except Minnesota (Mondale's home state) and 59 percent of the popular vote, the last time a presidential election has been so clearly decisive. Americans might have trouble adjusting their expectations downward, but they adjusted them upward easily enough, and the days of stagflation and gasoline shortages were forgotten. Reagan's economic plan had restored prosperity to the nation, and while the gains from that prosperity were far from evenly distributed, the idea that the American Dream was to be achieved through hard work and individual effort had been at least partially restored.

• • • • •

While Reagan's tax cuts successfully put the American economy back on track, his other goal—restoring a more limited government—was only partially achieved. Federal regulation had ballooned during the previous decade, with more regulatory statutes passed during the 1970s than in the previous four decades combined. Supply-side economists argued that, as with excessive taxation, excessive regulation stifled business productivity and growth. So Reagan created the Presidential Task Force on Regulatory Relief to cut through the red tape that was strangling corporate America, particularly small business. By the end of 1981, the size of the Federal Register, in which all new regulatory activity is published, had fallen by a third and the number of new rules issued by federal agencies had fallen by half as new regulations were subjected to cost-benefit analysis. The Reagan administration also aggressively deregulated transportation and energy-related industries that had long been considered to be natural monopolies, exposing them to the rigors of the free market, while simultaneously cutting back on what it considered to be overly zealous antitrust litigation.

The conservative White House made little headway cutting back on health, safety, and environmental regulation, however, and even less in reducing government spending. The projected federal budget deficit for 1981, the year Reagan took office, was $59 billion, and there were widespread calls to balance the budget by both raising taxes and reducing spending. But Reagan was vehemently opposed to raising taxes since the core of his supply-side economic program rested on lowering them. He was also committed to increasing defense spending, which meant that a balanced budget would have to be achieved purely by cuts in domestic programs—entitlement measures that were at the heart of the New Deal and the Great Society.

Naturally, everyone who believed in these programs—namely, special interest groups, citizens who benefited directly from them, and federal employees who administered them—strongly resisted any cutbacks. The rhetoric on both sides flew, as liberals accused Reagan of dismantling the welfare state, and conservatives complained that he wasn't doing enough. The national news media seized upon the debate, having learned that controversy generated ratings and increased advertising revenue. In the early days of television, the networks had agreed to provide nightly news coverage as a public service in exchange for their broadcasting licenses. By the 1980s, however, television news shows were expected to generate a profit just like any other program. Thus, objective reporting and analysis went by the wayside as the nightly news shows focused more and more on stories that were controversial, shocking, or frightening.

This unfortunate trend in journalism and the inflamed political rhetoric on both sides obscured the fact that most of the cuts the White House managed to achieve during the Reagan era were really just reductions in the *growth* of federal spending, as the baseline budget for most entitlement programs had a built-in annual increase. Total spending on social programs in 1982, for example, was still $53 billion higher than in 1980. Yet the relatively mild cuts that Reagan proposed still set off a firestorm of criticism from those who believed in the basic principles of the Great Society. While there was widespread support among the public for the idea of reducing the size of government in general, cuts in specific programs always generated second thoughts, particularly when the media ran stories about families who had fallen through the increasingly large cracks in the social safety net.

What was often overlooked was that even after the cuts in federal spending, the government still spent an average of $6,500 annually on every poor, elderly, or unemployed person in the country.[14] Reagan didn't want to get rid of the social safety net entirely, but his point was that spending by the federal government wasn't the best way to deal with social problems. He once argued that the need for welfare could be completely eliminated if every church in America were to look after the needs of ten poor families, noting that "the actual help would be greater because it would come from the heart."[15] Assistance offered between people who knew each other also had the advantage of preventing abuses and waste, while ensuring that those who received aid were truly in need of it.

This viewpoint—standard wisdom in the nineteenth century—was no longer taken seriously, and by 1982, the controversy over the budget deficit and cuts in federal spending had reached a fever pitch. In his annual State of the Union address, Reagan once again called for a halt to the growth of federal government, noting that while in 1960 the government had 132 grant programs costing $7 billion, by the time he took office those figures had grown to around 500 programs costing nearly $100 billion.[16] In keeping with the Founding

Fathers' core principle of leaving to the states all duties not explicitly assigned to the federal government, Reagan proposed pushing $47 billion of these programs down to the state and local level—an idea that liberals swiftly rejected. In the Democrats' televised response to Reagan's address, Detroit mayor Coleman Young cited the "pursuit of happiness" clause in the Declaration of Independence as an implicit obligation on the part of the federal government to secure "the right of a job, the right to eat, the right to human dignity"[17] for every American, one that should not be shifted to states or cities.

Thus, while Reagan did manage to achieve some modest cuts, in the larger scheme of things he did little to significantly halt the growth of government or federal spending. A case in point was Social Security, which despite having been "fixed" in 1977 with an increase in FICA taxes, was nevertheless predicted to go broke again within a few years. Reagan had long favored either privatizing Social Security or making it a voluntary program, but by the 1980s the idea of tampering with Social Security retirement benefits in any meaningful way was politically impossible. As Roosevelt had predicted, once people paid into the system, they felt entitled to the benefits, even though what they received was generally far greater than what they paid into the system. So when Reagan approved a proposal to reduce benefits for people who took early retirement (starting to draw Social Security at age 62), the Senate swiftly responded by voting 96–0 in favor of a resolution opposing any attempt to penalize early retirees.

Reagan quickly backed away from the proposal and never made a serious effort to reform Social Security again, which meant that he failed to make any real dent in the deficit. Quite the contrary—thanks to falling tax revenues and increases in defense spending, the deficit and the total federal debt soared during his tenure. Part of this was beyond Reagan's control; Congress controlled the purse strings, and they repeatedly refused his request for a line-item veto, which would have helped the executive branch to keep legislative spending in check. But giving up on a balanced budget was also a deliberate decision on Reagan's part. When he was pushed to raise taxes to counter the increasing deficit, he wrote in his journal, "I told our guys I couldn't go for tax increases. If I have to be criticized, I'd rather be criticized for a deficit than for backing away from our economic program."[18]

This problem has plagued presidents ever since Kennedy embraced peacetime deficit spending in the 1960s. While they support balanced budgets in principle, they all have pet programs—for Reagan it was tax cuts and defense spending—which they perceive as being so urgent and important to the overall well-being of the country that adding to the federal debt by enacting the programs is preferable to reducing it by forgoing them. Reagan, who had been a strong supporter of a balanced budget when he came to office, later downplayed its importance. "I don't worry much about the deficit," he once joked. "It's big enough to take care of itself."[19] Consequently, despite campaign promises to balance the budget and reduce the size of government, the national debt, which was just under $1 trillion when he took office, was almost $3 trillion when he left. While his advocacy of a return to smaller government and frontier self-reliance resonated with many Americans, when it was time to make cuts, most were adamantly opposed to giving up any of their government entitlements. The federal behemoth had grown so large that it had proven impossible to subdue.

● ● ● ● ●

Reagan's last task in restoring the American Dream, to which he devoted much of his second term, was winning the Cold War and returning America to preeminence in military strength and world affairs. In this, he arguably strayed from the original intent of the Founding Fathers. While they clearly intended military matters to be left to the federal government, George Washington had advised against getting entangled in European affairs, and the Monroe Doctrine had clearly drawn a line between the Eastern and Western hemispheres. For much of the nation's history, the American people had been all too happy to ignore what was happening on the other side of the world, but World War II changed that attitude. Having emerged as a superpower with nuclear-weapons capability, America could no longer remain isolated from world affairs, particularly when the Soviet Union joined the nuclear club and announced itself to be the leader of a global communist revolution that was in perpetual war with capitalism. This presented a potential danger to the American people and the American way of life that had to be dealt with, either diplomatically or militarily.

The United States' response to the Soviet threat throughout the Cold War that ensued was containment—a halfway position between appeasement and rollback that was designed to use economic, military, and diplomatic strategies to spread American influence abroad, thereby mitigating Soviet influence. But Americans' will and confidence had been greatly diminished by the failure to contain the spread of communism in Vietnam. This led to Nixon's strategy of détente, which bordered on appeasement, and defense spending had been sharply curtailed after the Vietnam War, weakening the American military. Thus, the country was unable to respond adequately when the Soviet Union invaded Afghanistan and set up a puppet regime or when Americans were taken hostage in various Middle Eastern countries during several incidents in the late 1970s and early 1980s

Reagan's vision of the American Dream, one in which the United States served not only as an example of freedom, democracy, and prosperity to the rest of the world, but also as an active champion in promoting American values, was incompatible with détente or military weakness. He believed that halting the spread of Communism required actively engaging it, and so he began to rebuild the American military, increasing defense spending 7 percent annually during his first term in office. (It was this military buildup, combined with tax cuts during a recession, that led to the massive deficits and acceleration of the national debt during the Reagan era.) During his presidency, the United States deployed intermediate-range nuclear forces in West Germany, Italy, and the United Kingdom; channeled funds and weapons to anticommunist resistance movements in Afghanistan,

Angola, Cambodia, Nicaragua, and other nations; bombed Libya; and took military action in Grenada to reinstate constitutional government following a Marxist coup.

Reagan's foreign policy came to fruition when, after the death of three elderly Soviet leaders during his first term in office, the much younger and more open-minded Mikhail Gorbachev came to power in 1985. Reagan and Gorbachev held a series of four summits during Reagan's second term, covering not only intermediate-range nuclear forces (INF) issues, but also strategic weapons and the militarization of space as well. At the second summit, in Reykjavik, both sides agreed in principle to remove INF systems from Europe, and speaking at the Berlin Wall the following year, Reagan challenged, "General Secretary Gorbachev, if you seek peace, if you seek prosperity for the Soviet Union and Eastern Europe, if you seek liberalization, come here to this gate! Mr. Gorbachev, open this gate! Mr. Gorbachev, tear down this wall!"[20]

A little over two years later, the German people themselves did just that as the ailing Soviet economy—bankrupted in part by trying to keep up with the U.S. in the nuclear weapons race—was no longer able to support or control its satellite states. By 1991, the Soviet Union itself collapsed, and Americans understandably viewed its downfall as validation of the power of the American Dream and the American way of life. As Reagan had promised, we had begun the world over again, and the United States was restored to its rightful place as the shining city upon the hill. In time, Reagan's foreign policy came to be seen as one of the most successful aspects of his presidency. Paying for the military buildup required to achieve it, however, fundamentally undermined his attempts to reduce the size of government and greatly increased the federal debt. In many ways, the Reagan Revolution, and the left's resistance to it, was really an argument about the nature of the American Dream, and Reagan's failure to significantly reduce the welfare state demonstrated just how deep the fault lines over the American Dream had become.

12

THE DREAM OF GLOBAL CAPITALISM
IN THE INFORMATION AGE

◇◇

The fall of the Berlin Wall on November 9, 1989, had implications for the American Dream far beyond what anyone imagined. At the time, it was viewed mainly in geopolitical terms as the death knell for the Soviet Empire, the collapse of which officially brought about an end to the Cold War. It appeared to be a triumphant victory for democracy, capitalism, and the American way of life—the implosion of a threat that had loomed large for nearly half a century. The very existence of the United States was no longer in constant jeopardy from an empire that considered capitalism—the driving force behind the American Dream—to be its enemy. On the contrary, capitalism had been undeniably shown as the only viable way to organize a modern economy, so countries like China and India started moving toward being more open, capitalistic societies as well. This meant that as the century drew to a close, billions of additional people and their governments started participating in the free market and pursuing their unique versions of the American Dream.

The triumph of capitalism and democracy was a stunning ideological victory, but there is always a danger in getting what you wish for, and few Americans grasped the long-term implications of adding all those hungry new capitalists from Russia, Eastern Europe, China, India, and many other second- and third-world countries into an integrated world economy. In 1985, only 2.5 billion people were part of that economy, but by 2000, 6 billion people had access to it, thanks to the proliferation of personal computers, the Internet, and fiber optics. The convergence of information technology—particularly networked computers—and the increasing openness of markets around the world created a truly global economy the likes of which had never been seen before. This convergence kicked off a worldwide economic boom as companies moved into new foreign markets, creating jobs both at home and abroad and leading to the growth of a global middle class.

The rapidity with which all of this happened was stunning. In the course of a single decade, the world was transformed from one dominated by an ideological clash between capitalism and communism to one dominated by a global, integrated, digital knowledge economy. And it happened thanks to technology such as computer software applications, search engines, web browsers, and cellular telephones that made the world faster, more connected, and more egalitarian than ever before. Bright, talented, and ambitious people from across the world no longer needed to come to the United States to chase the American Dream. They could chase it from their laptops from almost anywhere across the globe in places that had standards of living far below what middle-class Americans—even poor Americans—had come to expect. By the turn of the twenty-first century, the American Dream was no longer reserved just for Americans and a few million lucky immigrants. It was the Chinese Dream, the Indian Dream, the Russian Dream, and the World Dream, and people everywhere chased it with far more determination and willingness to sacrifice than most Americans themselves.

• • • • •

The road to globalization was paved by the end of the Cold War, but what made it more than simply the opening of new markets was the proliferation of personal computers and the Internet. The mainframe computers pioneered by Thomas Watson Jr. at IBM had initially relied on vacuum tubes, but as early as 1939, William Shockley, a scientist at Bell Labs, had theorized that an amplifier using semiconductors rather than a vacuum was possible; this was the fundamental insight that created the field of electronics. By the 1970s, Intel had developed the first microprocessor, the brain on a chip that runs all personal computers. It was this tiny chip that, like the steam engine, ushered in a new era and remade the American Dream in the process. Back when the United States had an agrarian economy, the classic American Dream was owning land and building up an estate in the country. When the nation shifted to an industrial economy, the dream became having a good job in the city and a nice house in the suburbs, along with a car and other labor-saving devices. With the transition to a knowledge-based economy, the American Dream shifted once again, primarily because of the personal computer.

The first commercial microcomputer had been introduced as far back as 1974, but even its inventors failed to understand its full potential. Ken Olsen, founder of Digital Equipment Corporation, had pioneered the use of minicomputers for commercial business applications. But when his engineers showed him designs for a personal computer, he asked, "Why should anyone need a computer of their own?"[1] It took Steve Jobs and the Apple II to sell America on the value of the personal computer and turn it into a commercial success. Only then did IBM, which had missed the transition from mainframes to minicomputers, get into the act by developing its own personal computer. Needing an operating system and software, they sought out Bill Gates and Microsoft. The introduction of IBM's PC and Microsoft's MS-DOS operating system coincided perfectly with the more probusiness environment of the 1980s to jump-start the information age, eventually giving rise to the dot-com era and the knowledge economy.

Gates became the most successful of a revolutionary generation of "New Economy" entrepreneurs whose wealth and influence rivaled that of the Gilded Age's captains of industry. The postwar era in American business had been dominated by large corporations, in large part because they had the necessary resources to conduct costly research and development. Entrepreneurs in the 1950s and 60s had gravitated toward turnkey franchises, while inventors and innovators went to work at places like IBM and Bell Labs. High capital gains taxes and high income tax rates led investors to seek tax shelters rather than finance small-time entrepreneurs, leaving innovation to the established blue-chip companies.

But this changed in the late seventies when Congress passed the Tax Reform Act, which retooled tax brackets and lowered the effective capital gains rate to 28 percent. As a result, the venture capital industry, which had raised a paltry $39 million in 1977, raised $1.3 billion in 1981—the same year IBM's PC went on the market.[2] With the introduction of that key technology, readily available venture capital, and the first wave of corporate downsizing, Americans' entrepreneurial spirit was once again unleashed. Inspired by the wild success of Bill Gates, Steve Jobs, and other information-age entrepreneurs, thousands of people pursued the American Dream by founding small companies in Silicon Valley and elsewhere. Like the building of railroads across the continent in the mid-nineteenth century, the proliferation of networked personal computers fundamentally changed the way business was done, eventually impacting almost every industry. The railroad boom of the nineteenth century had created an environment in which it seemed that fortunes were waiting to be made for anyone with pluck and a reasonably good idea; the personal computer revolution held out the same promise to eager young entrepreneurs. If a computer nerd like Bill Gates could become a billionaire, surely anyone could.

Not that everyone was as smart, determined, or just plain lucky as Bill Gates. The son of a successful attorney, Gates grew up in an upper-middle-class neighborhood and met his future business partner, Paul Allen, while attending Lakeside School in Seattle, Washington. Lakeside was one of the first schools in the country with access to a minicomputer, a fortuitous circumstance that allowed the future founders of Microsoft to get an early start in business. At the age of fifteen, Gates and several other Lakeside students were asked to write a payroll program for Information Sciences Inc., in Portland, which netted the boys approximately $10,000 in free computer time and royalties in exchange for their work. Next, Gates and Allen started a company called Traf-O-Data, for which they developed a process that read computer cards from machines that monitored traffic flow for local municipalities. They eventually earned $20,000 in proceeds from the sale of Traf-O-Data, all while Gates was still in high school.

Gates and Allen had already started to discuss starting a software company when the world's first kit microcomputer, the Altair 8080, was introduced by Model Instrumentation and Telemetry Systems in 1974. Gates phoned the company's founder, Ed Roberts, and claimed that he and Allen had developed a BASIC language for the Altair. Roberts, who had heard the same claim from others, told Gates that whoever showed up with a working model first had the deal. So Gates and Allen worked for eight straight weeks to develop a BASIC language for the Altair 8080, quite a feat given that they didn't even have access to one. The first time they were able to test it on the actual Altair 8080 system was when Allen loaded it to show Roberts. Luckily, it worked, and on the basis of this important sale, Gates and Allen went on to found Microsoft the following year. Their BASIC soon became the standard programming language in the personal computer industry, and by 1976 they had landed accounts with General Electric and National Cash Register. Revenues for the first year totaled more than $100,000, and the following January, Allen quit his job and Gates dropped out of Harvard to devote themselves to Microsoft full time.

Just three years later, Microsoft had forty employees and $7 million in annual sales, and in 1980, IBM approached Microsoft about licensing its operating system and developing software for its planned PC. The problem was, Microsoft didn't own the CP/M operating system that was the industry standard at the time; CP/M was owned by Gary Kildall of Galactic Digital Research. Gates referred IBM to Kildall, and what happened next is shrouded in controversy. Urban legend has it that Kildall blew off the meeting to go flying, but in reality negotiations with IBM apparently broke down over objections to IBM's draconian nondisclosure agreement and other issues. Frustrated, IBM apparently went back to Gates, who in a move that would have made the entrepreneurs of the Gilded Age proud, pointed out that Kildall had yet to produce a 16-bit version of his operating system, and that Microsoft could provide IBM with one, even though it didn't actually have an operating system in development.

IBM, apparently feeling more comfortable with Gates than Kildall, agreed, and Gates negotiated and signed a contract whereby Microsoft would retain ownership of its software and receive royalties from licensing fees. When Gates learned that a company called Seattle Computer had already developed a workable 16-bit operating system called QDOS, he offered to buy it for $75,000. The company, strapped for cash and unaware of the deal with IBM (Gates had signed a nondisclosure agreement), took the deal, and Gates renamed it MS-DOS and took it back to IBM. But QDOS had striking similarities to CP/M, enough that Kildall considered it a clone and threatened to sue for copyright infringement. Software development, however, was in its infancy, and copyright law had not yet been extended to cover issues such as the look and feel of software. Digital Research let the issue slide, a critical error that ensured that it would eventually become a mere footnote in history. Microsoft, on the other hand, flourished and soon was earning more than $200 million a year from the sales of MS-DOS alone.

Too late, IBM realized that the real money to be made in the computer industry was in software, not hardware. When it finally made plans to get into the software game by developing a graphical user interface (GUI), Microsoft, which was already developing its own GUI, retaliated by forming alliances with twenty-four of IBM's competitors and formally announcing Windows, even though it was not yet ready. The first version of Windows generated lackluster sales, but by the time the third version was released in 1990, Gates had lined up every major software company to write applications for it. Within four months of its introduction, one million copies of Windows 3.0 had been sold, and Microsoft became the first software company to achieve $1 billion in annual revenues. By then, Microsoft had eclipsed IBM in profitability and influence, and Gates had become the youngest billionaire in American history at the age of thirty-one.[3]

Gates's stunning success inspired thousands of other young entrepreneurs, and soon dozens and then hundreds of venture capital–backed companies were founded in what came to be called "Silicon Valley." Among them was Netscape, a startup that unveiled its first commercial web browser, Netscape Navigator, in 1994. Within a year it had completely dominated the market, and when Netscape went public, its stock closing out the first day of trading at twice its initial offering price, the dot-com era was underway. As former Netscape CEO Jim Barksdale noted, "Netscape going public stimulated a lot of things. The technologists loved the new technology things it could do, and the businesspeople and regular folks got excited about how much money they could make. People saw all those young kids making money out of this and said, 'If those young kids can do this and make all that money, I can too.' Greed can be a bad thing—folks thought they could make a lot of money without a lot of work. It certainly led to a degree of overinvestment, putting it mildly. Every sillier and sillier idea got funded."[4]

Once again, the potential of a transformative technology led to a stock market bubble, one that would inevitably burst. But as Gates pointed out at the 1999 World Economic Forum, all of that investment spurred ever more innovation. Among all the silly ideas that shouldn't have been funded were a number of great ideas as well, like Amazon, eBay, Google, and many other legitimate high-tech companies. All of them provided thousands of new well-paying, white-collar jobs such as network administrators, software developers, technical writers, and graphic designers, along with all the requisite administrative and management positions needed to replace the jobs being lost in the continuing deindustrialization of America. The dot-com craze may have created a bubble, but after the bubble burst, many of the computers, networks, fiber optics, and web sites were still there. Innovation was still accelerating. New technologies were still proliferating. The world was changing before our eyes. The dot-com bubble wasn't an indication that the New Economy was a fluke; it was a hiccup in a transformation of lasting importance.

• • • • •

By 2000, the revolutionary nature of the information-based New Economy was readily apparent to everyone. The new engine of the American Dream had arisen with amazing rapidity, given that a mere fifteen years earlier, computers were just toys that allowed people to do word processing, create spreadsheets, and play Pac-Man. Few people at the time imagined that computers and the digital age would transform the American economy, which had turned in an increasingly strong performance through much of the "go-go eighties." The Dow Jones had surged from a low of 776 all the way to a high of 2722 under Reagan's tenure, and deregulation on Wall Street had lowered the costs of investing and allowed many more Americans access to the stock market than ever before.

These gains, combined with a steady increase in after-tax incomes, made Americans significantly wealthier than they'd been just a few years previously, and as a result, middle-class expectations soared. *Forbes* magazine first printed its iconic list of the "Forbes 400" wealthiest Americans in 1982 and in doing so created hope in the heart of young urban professionals that they too could achieve the American Dream of fame and fortune. There was a desire—even an expectation—that one could accumulate great wealth on the scale of the Carringtons on *Dynasty*, or at least the Huxtables on *The*

Cosby Show, and the massive fortunes to be made on Wall Street merely fed this desire. All told, America achieved enough growth and prosperity during the eighties to feed the increasingly consumer-driven, materialistic version of the American Dream, but it was by no means apparent that the country was on the cusp of an extended economic boom. On the contrary, a spike in the price of oil and rising inflation and unemployment had led to a brief recession as the country headed into the 1992 presidential election.

By then, thoroughly indoctrinated with the idea that the federal government was responsible for the state of the economy, and that all recessions were avoidable, Americans blamed the incumbent, George H. W. Bush, for the recession. Yet the Reagan Revolution had enough of a lasting impact that the people replaced him not with a Great Society-style Democrat but rather with a New Economy, pro–globalization, pro–free trade Democrat by the name of William Jefferson Clinton, whose narrow victory reflected the increasingly schizophrenic nature of the American political psyche. People were disenchanted enough with government in general that Ross Perot, an independent third-party candidate, actually received a significant percentage of the popular vote, but the two-party system was so entrenched that he failed to make a dent in the electoral college. Clinton thus won his first term with a plurality, rather than a majority, of the popular vote and therefore not much of a mandate. From that point forward, politics in America became increasingly polarized, with presidential elections split almost fifty-fifty in the popular vote and little in the way of bipartisanship in Congress.

In some ways this was curious, because Clinton, viewed from the perspective of the twentieth century as a whole, was one of our most moderate, centrist presidents. Declaring the era of big government to be over, he convinced his fellow Democrats to enact welfare reform and pass the North American Free Trade Agreement—both planks of the Republican platform. While he raised the top marginal tax rate to 39.6 percent, this was far below what it had been for much of the postwar era. (Under Eisenhower, a Republican, the top tax rate had been an astonishing 91 percent. It had taken Kennedy, a Democrat, to lower the top rate to 70 percent, and Reagan and Bush to get it all the way down to 31 percent.) In this context, Clinton's tax hike on the top bracket was a fairly mild change, although the new point of contention was the distribution of the tax burden between the middle and upper class, as an increasing number of middle-class Americans were paying no taxes at all. Still, something of a consensus had actually emerged that Reagan had a point, and taxes did impact business investment. Yet the bitter partisan rhetoric over taxes and other issues in the 1990s actually increased, making it appear that Republicans and Democrats were at an impasse that was impossible to breach.

While the public blamed the government for getting nothing done, the stalemate in Congress reflected the fact that Americans didn't fundamentally know what they wanted—smaller government or bigger government, lower taxes or more entitlements. Or rather, they wanted to have it all. By the start of Clinton's presidency in 1993, roughly 70 percent of Americans thought the federal government was too big and wasteful in its spending, despite the cutbacks of the Reagan era. Yet at the same time, four out of ten Americans polled agreed with the statement that the government should "use its power more vigorously to promote the well-being of all segments of the population," while another four out of ten disagreed. Even more telling, when asked about specific issues, 68 percent thought the federal government should spend more on education, 61 percent on aid to the poor, and 66 percent on health care.[5] Americans might want government off their backs and out of their pockets, but by 1992, a majority of families were receiving at least one entitlement benefit, and they weren't willing to give those benefits up. The American Dream in the closing decade of the twentieth century was having your cake and eating it too.

The desire to have it all left many Americans with one foot in both the Democratic and Republican camps—at least when it came to economics—and our inability to commit to one consistent economic philosophy is a key factor in the extreme polarization of American politics. At the birth of our nation, the central political argument was over federalism vs. states' rights. Then the country aligned behind Jefferson and the Democrats, who essentially remained in power until there was another realignment behind Lincoln and the Republicans over slavery and the Civil War. The Republicans mostly held power until there was yet another crucial realignment behind Franklin Roosevelt prompted by the Great Depression and the New Deal, when the primary political debate became one of economics. The Democrats held sway until Reagan was elected, and another realignment seemed at hand based on the idea of returning to smaller government.

But the Reagan realignment didn't hold. Both the Senate and the House went Democratic when Clinton was elected in 1992, showing that the public wasn't all that committed ideologically to the neoconservative platform. A simple recession was enough to sway public opinion back in favor of the Democrats, because the American people saw the federal government's primary duty as ensuring economic growth with no hiccups. While Reaganomics had restored overall prosperity to the American economy, the trickle-down effects of that prosperity were highly uneven. Some people did well and experienced significant upward mobility, but a large number of others saw their real incomes stagnating and found themselves out of a job due to massive corporate downsizing and plant closures. As dependent on consumer credit as Americans had become, the loss of a job for a significant period could soon lead to personal bankruptcy, which was a shock to those who had come to expect lifetime employment. The economy had done well as a whole, but some people were suffering. Clinton wrested power back from the neoconservatives because he assured those on the lower rungs of the economic ladder that he felt their pain and would do something about it.

Fortunately for Clinton, the economy turned in an increasingly healthy performance as the decade progressed, thanks to the New

Economy and expanding global trade opportunities (for which Reagan deserves at least some of the credit). Technological developments brought a wide range of sophisticated new electronic products, and innovations in telecommunications and computer networking spawned a vast computer hardware and software industry and revolutionized the way many industries operated. The U.S. economy grew rapidly, inflation and unemployment once again fell, and rising corporate profits sent the stock market surging, the Dow hitting 11,000 in 1999. While the gains still weren't distributed evenly, under the Democrats they were distributed a tad more evenly than before, and the economy and overall wealth grew so substantially that it really did lift a majority of boats.

This was good news for the federal deficit, which after peaking at $290 billion in 1992, steadily shrank as economic growth led to a marked increased in tax revenues. In 1998, the government posted its first surplus in 30 years, and the consensus was that the computer and Internet-based New Economy was producing and sustaining a faster rate of growth than before. This was exactly what Americans had been hoping for—a renewed era of prosperity capable of creating dot-com millionaires as well as supporting an increasing standard of living and upward mobility. Yet instead of taking advantage of this boom period to pay down the federal debt—which by then stood at $5.6 trillion—the government contented itself with merely balancing the budget. Growth of the economy alone, no matter how rapid, wasn't going to make much of a dent in the debt, and inevitable future downturns would demand greater government stimulus spending anyway. The growth of the federal debt during the 1990s should have made it clear to everyone that the central problem was future liabilities from the big three entitlement programs—Social Security, Medicaid, and Medicare. The debt could not be brought under control until these programs were realistically reformed, yet Americans weren't ready to accept scaling back these crucial entitlements, and no politician was brave enough to seriously suggest it. The programs were too central to what had become the twentieth-century American Dream.

• • • • •

As the New Economy took off with the dot-com craze, it set off renewed consumerism fed both by increasingly easy access to credit and home mortgages, and the creation of a broad array of new consumer products and services for the information age. Some of these, such as DVD players, MP3 players, video game consoles, and digital cameras, were merely expensive toys, albeit highly desirable ones. Others, however, such as cell phones, Internet service, and computers themselves were truly must-have equipment for survival in the knowledge economy, and they were expensive. Personal computers could cost hundreds if not thousands of dollars by the time all the necessary software and peripherals had been purchased. Internet and cellular phone service, meanwhile, required payment of ongoing monthly fees, adding to the stacks of bills for gas, electricity, water, and cable TV service that by the 1990s were standard.

The list of things that Americans both wanted and needed had grown significantly with the introduction of high-tech electronics. Add to this two car payments (which to some extent had been subsidized by the auto manufacturers to reduce payment amounts) and mortgage payments for increasingly large, McMansion-style houses (which were encouraged through various government incentive programs). Given the inducements to spend, it was no wonder that Americans turned to credit cards to pay their bills, a temptation that was encouraged by the fact that it was difficult to get a mortgage or car loan unless you had built up a credit history.

Bank credit cards had been invented nearly half a century earlier in 1946, when the Flatbush National Bank of Brooklyn started issuing plastic charge cards as part of their "Charge It" program. The cards allowed bank customers to shop at various local stores; the merchants then deposited sales slips with the bank, which in turned billed the customer who had used the card. The Charge It program, however, was strictly local, and the concept of credit cards didn't really gain traction until businessman Frank McNamara found himself at a restaurant one night without his wallet. Embarrassed by his predicament, he founded Diner's Club and thereby invented one of the most transformative financial products in all of history.

Initially intended for use by traveling businessmen, the Diner's Club card, which was first issued to two hundred customers who could use it in twenty-seven restaurants, was a near-instant hit. The company soon had twenty thousand customers across the United States as well as a quickly growing list of retailers subscribed as credit providers. Technically, the Diner's Club card was a charge card rather than a credit card, as the customer had to pay the balance in full when billed. The company charged 7 percent for each individual transaction, with card subscribers paying a $3.00 annual fee. The idea of the Diner's Club card was soon copied, and by 1958, American Express had begun issuing true general-purpose credit cards, which allowed customers to carry a balance on which they were charged interest. The Bank of America soon followed suit with its own BankAmericard (later renamed Visa) and MasterCard, which catered to a more middle-class clientele, was created in 1966.

Although credit card usage was still relatively conservative during the 1970s—only 22 percent of cardholders carried a balance from one month's bill to the next—the trend toward spending beyond one's means was clear.[6] Older people who had lived through the trials of the Great Depression and World War II often eschewed the cards completely, at most using them as a convenience and scrupulously paying off the monthly balance in full. The baby boomers, on the other hand, who had only known the wealth and plenty of the postwar boom, embraced credit cards and used them more liberally to finance the sort of lifestyles they saw on television, which had become increasingly upscale. The comparatively modest homes shown on *Ozzie and Harriet* and *Leave It to Beaver* had given way to the more spacious tri-level depicted in *The Brady Bunch* in the

1970s and Monica and Rachel's ridiculously large New York apartment in *Friends* in the 1990s.

As women began working outside the home in greater numbers, their contribution to household income had a profound impact on middle-class lifestyles as well. Dual-income families were far better able to afford the fancy homes, luxury cars, and expensive family vacations featured in the fantasy world of 1990s television. Yet two working parents also entailed greater expenses, such as two cars and childcare, not to mention all of the more frivolous purchases such as designer handbags, high-end golf clubs, and closets full of shoes that families living on the frontier a century earlier would have considered both patently ridiculous and unnecessary. Nevertheless, thanks to the power of television and advertising, Americans now wanted such things, and so they turned to credit cards to finance them. Just as the widespread acceptance of installment plans in the 1920s helped Americans to buy more of the products they heard advertised on the radio, the introduction of the credit card in the postwar era enabled Americans to buy more of the products they saw advertised on television.

Personal spending in the 1990s mirrored that of the federal government. Unwilling to make hard choices when it was temptingly easy to have it all, Americans began to adjust to the idea that they could run up debts and simply pay interest on them indefinitely without the bill ever coming due. Thus consumer debt, which was $5.7 billion in 1945, had risen to $1.5 trillion by the end of 1999. Yet with the economy booming, most Americans felt confident of their ability to pay, and indeed, 95.5% of that consumer debt did get paid in the 1990s, due in part to rising home values.[7] Since the interest on home mortgages was deductible for tax purposes and credit card interest was not, an increasing number of Americans starting tapping into their home equity and taking out second mortgages in order to pay their credit card bills.

Unfortunately, the unexpected loss of a job, a sudden reduction in home values, or a medical crisis, particularly for the uninsured, could cause financial disaster for a household. In the 1950s, when expectations were lower and most families relied on a single income, the loss of a job was less devastating. Families scaled back their discretionary spending, and women often took temporary jobs to provide supplemental income. By the 1990s, most of American families' paychecks went toward fixed monthly payments that couldn't easily be eliminated, and they had scaled their standard of living to rely on two incomes, not one. Those who were flexible, specialized, and good with computers could generally find new jobs in the growing New Economy. Those without college educations or who were at the end of their careers in traditional semiskilled occupations, however, often had difficulty if they were unfortunate enough to have their jobs outsourced, offshored, or simply eliminated. As the decade progressed, the gap between the winners and losers in the new global economy steadily increased.

• • • • •

Overwhelmingly, the losers in the New Economy were blue-collar workers in manufacturing industries, and by the 1990s these industries were shedding workers by the thousands. The labor market during the previous decade had been wracked by a great deal of turmoil, as many of America's leading corporations found themselves struggling to compete. Many industries had, in the wake of the New Deal, come to be dominated by three or four large companies, which throughout the postwar era had the American market largely to themselves. As free trade and the falling value of the dollar opened American markets to imports, however, older American factories in the Midwestern "rust belt" were often unable to compete with the newer, technologically more advanced and efficient factories in Europe and Asia, which were more automated and required fewer workers.

When the recession of the early 1980s hit, American companies responded by abandoning their commitment to lifetime employment, shutting down factories and laying off thousands of employees. Union workers in manufacturing industries were particularly hard hit as companies sought to cut costs by eliminating expensive union labor. The changes were not simply a product of the recession. Prior to the 1980s, layoffs were generally associated with downswings in the business cycle, and when conditions improved, workers were often recalled. But the economic woes of American corporations in the eighties were more fundamental, resulting in downsizing and permanent plant and office closures that the unions were powerless to stop. The long decline in well-paid blue-collar manufacturing jobs had begun, and by the end of the decade two-thirds of all non-government American jobs were in service rather than goods-producing industries.

White-collar workers weren't safe from downsizing either. Many of the conglomerates that had been formed in the postwar era had fallen victim to corporate raiders, who felt the pieces were worth more than the whole, while at the same time new mergers and acquisitions had been formed. By the end of the 1980s, over a third of the top Fortune 500 companies had either been taken over or merged, and even white-collar workers found themselves unemployed as redundant administrative and middle-management positions were eliminated to improve efficiency and profitability. In fact, a majority of the downsized workers were college-educated, salaried employees. The promise of lifetime employment that had given rise to the organization man was no more, and even IBM finally gave in and cut its workforce by 407,000 in 1986.

As the New Economy developed and started to provide a significant number of jobs in the 1990s, most college-educated workers found their way into new companies and careers. The loss of blue-collar manufacturing jobs, however, not only continued but also accelerated as automation, outsourcing, and offshoring came increasingly into play. Hardest hit were the residents of decaying inner cities, which had suffered a double whammy with the closing of major factories and middle-class flight to the suburbs. These cities, which were now populated by a high percentage of low-income minorities and single mothers, had become dinosaurs of the industrial age. While areas with a high concentration of creative people—places like Silicon Valley, Seattle, and university towns like Ann Arbor, Michigan—thrived in the New Economy, industrial rust-belt cities like Detroit, Cleveland, and Newark were unable to provide the essential city services, quality public education, and safe environment necessary to give children from low-income families the sort of start in life that constituted true equal opportunity.

Welfare had not served poverty-stricken single mothers or their children well. Originally designed to provide aid to families with dependent children—a noble goal—it had the perverse effect of both encouraging unwed mothers to have more children in order to receive greater benefits and allowing fathers to shirk their financial duty to support their children, guilt-free. Welfare reform had introduced welfare-to-work programs to transition low-income mothers into jobs, but inevitably they were minimum wage positions that required these women to then pay for childcare while they worked, which was a zero-sum game. Grandparents and schools had to pick up the slack, and the lack of male authority figures had detrimental consequences, particularly for teenage boys.

That this was a problem was evident to most Americans, and there was general agreement that a child from a low-income broken family who had been educated in a failing inner-city school did not have the same opportunity to achieve the American Dream as one who was from a middle-class family in a nice suburban neighborhood with decent schools. Yet no one seemed to have a very good idea what to do about the problem without resorting to measures such as busing and affirmative action, which by the 1990s had become highly unpopular. Most Americans accepted the fact that historical disadvantages still lingered and that something proactive needed to be done to ensure equal opportunity for African Americans and other disadvantaged minority groups, although quotas were generally considered going too far. While the civil rights movement saw affirmative action as a way to guarantee equal opportunity, its opponents saw quotas as an entitlement that guaranteed a particular result for one group and denied equal opportunity to others.

Affirmative action was particularly controversial with regard to college admissions, where instances of highly qualified white candidates being passed over in favor of black candidates with lower grades and test scores created outrage. White students who had attended inner city schools, it was argued, were at just as much of a disadvantage as their black peers. Affirmative action, being race-rather than income-based, was reverse discrimination, and it struck most white Americans as grossly unfair that their children should be denied scholarships or admittance when, based on objective measures, their qualifications were superior. As Reagan's assistant attorney general for civil rights, William Bradford Reynolds, had argued, "The idea of equal opportunity got changed in the minds of some to a concept of equal results, and individual rights were translated into group entitlements."[8] The line between ensuring equality of opportunity and equality of result was not so much a line as a gray, murky swamp, and many Americans were starting to conclude that even if opportunities weren't exactly equal, they were certainly good enough.

As a result, states started amending their constitutions to ban affirmative action programs, and the focus shifted to improving public schools through other methods such as spending more money on education, establishing higher standards for students, and attracting better teachers. While good ideas in theory, they were inadequate to deal with what was in many ways a cultural issue, particularly in failing inner-city schools. Inner-city teens were increasingly joining gangs and turning to drugs and other criminal activities, both for a lack of legitimate economic opportunities and for other reasons. But there were also many for whom the American Dream of clawing one's way from the bottom of the socioeconomic scale to the top was very much alive.

• • • • •

Interestingly, middle-class African Americans, those who appeared to have achieved the American Dream, were significantly less likely than white middle-class Americans in the 1990s to say that they believed in it.[9] Their success had been tempered by enough instances of continued discrimination that they saw the marketing of the American Dream—the idea that even those who come from the most disadvantaged backgrounds can rise to great wealth—as an excuse for white America to ignore the very real problems of the inner city. By contrast, low-income African Americans did believe in the American Dream, but for those who couldn't afford college, their options in the New Economy were limited.

In Vanderbilt's day, anyone could have amassed the knowledge of steamboats necessary to conquer the industry; what set Vanderbilt apart was his work ethic, determination, and drive. A critical factor in Bill Gates's success, on the other hand, was his early exposure in high school to computers—expensive technology that few high schools at the time could afford, much less high schools in the inner cities. As a result, students in low-income neighborhoods were unlikely to come into contact with and develop skills associated with technologies that would provide most of the job and entrepreneurial opportunities in the New Economy. But the American Dream still beckoned, and for inner-city youths the two favored methods of achieving it were to become professional athletes or musicians. Getting athletic scholarships had long been one of the few ways that poor inner-city kids with lackluster grades could access a college education and thereby a better shot at a middle-class lifestyle. When it came to achieving fame and fortune, however, the music industry in the 1990s was rivaling professional sports as the African American Dream of choice, due in large part to hip-hop and rap music, which as the decade progressed spread from music to television, movies, advertising, fashion, and other culture-influencing industries.

A major force behind the rise of hip-hop music and culture was Russell Simmons, the promoter and older brother of Joey Simmons of the breakthrough hip-hop band Run DMC. Raised in a traditional family with a history professor father, the Simmons brothers grew up in a fairly decent part of Queens, New York, and attended an integrated school. Despite this relatively auspicious, middle-class start, by his teens Russell Simmons was selling drugs in order to pay for fancy clothes and other possessions he couldn't have afforded working a legitimate minimum-wage job. But one night, upon hearing hip-hop pioneer Eddie Cheeba, he had an epiphany. "Seeing Eddie spitting them flames on the mike made me feel I'd just witnessed the invention of the wheel," said Simmons. "Just like that I saw how I could turn my life into another, better way. All the street entrepreneurship I'd learned I decided to put into promoting music."[10]

So Simmons stopped selling drugs and instead founded Rush Productions. He began by promoting club parties and then moved on to managing artists—the sort of artists that the mainstream music industry had no interest in at the time, or so Simmons thought. When a group from New Jersey called the Sugarhill Gang broke through with a song called "Rapper's Delight" and sold fourteen million copies, he was stunned. "Someone had just taken our rhymes, our attitude, our culture and made a record," Simmons wrote in his memoir. "And not one of us in the community had anything to do with it."[11]

Determined not to let that happen again, Simmons, like Bill Gates, dropped out of college—in his case just four credits short of earning a degree. But the success of "Rapper's Delight" had opened his eyes to the broader appeal and potential of the hip-hop trend, and he was determined to capitalize on it. In 1983 he formed Run DMC with his brother and Darryl McDaniels. In 1984 he partnered with producer Rick Rubin to start a new label called Def Jam Records for an investment of $4,000 each. Together, they kick-started the careers of LL Cool J, the Fresh Prince (Will Smith), Public Enemy, Slick Rick, and the Beastie Boys. The following year, they signed a distribution deal with CBS for $600,000 and in 1999 sold the label to Universal for $120 million. Within three years of the sale, Def Jam had become the second largest label in the industry, with sales of over $700 million.

By then, hip-hop had become a cultural phenomenon that cut across racial barriers—even white kids embraced it. Simmons, having conquered the music scene, went on to create the highly successful *Russell Simmons' Def Comedy Jam* on HBO, spreading hip-hop culture into television. He also started a hip-hop clothing line called Phat Fashions that he eventually sold for $140 million. After he had pushed the boundaries of hip-hop in every conceivable direction, *Business Week* reported in 2003 that a full quarter of all discretionary spending was influenced in one way or another by hip-hop.[12] In its own way, it had as much influence on the American lifestyle in the 1990s as the personal computer did, and Simmons was as much an example of achieving the American Dream as Bill Gates was.

Yet hip-hop and rap culture had their critics. While supporters argued that wars of words and dance moves were preferable to street battles with guns and knives, the ugly truth was that hip-hop glamorized the defiance and violence of gang culture. And while it provided an alternative to the "street entrepreneurship" of selling drugs, not everyone had the talent or drive necessary to become a hip-hop artist or producer. Hip-hop could produce stars and millionaires, but what it didn't provide was a legitimate path to middle-class success the way the knowledge economy did. Some hip-hop acts, like Public Enemy, used their success to deliver antidrug messages or support the value of education, but far too many fed off of resentment, anger, and jealousy, encouraging materialism and victimization. Hip-hop had in some ways brought America's white and black youths together, but whether its influence would be helpful or harmful in meeting the demands of the knowledge economy and achieving the American Dream in the new millennium was in serious doubt.

13

THE AMERICAN FANTASY
AND THE PURSUIT OF UNHAPPINESS

◇◇

A t the dawn of the new millennium, almost four hundred years after the Virginia Company founded Jamestown, America was experiencing a dramatic transformation. With the rise of the New Economy, increasing standards of living and upward mobility for the middle class had once again become the norm, feeding a new wave of materialism and consumerism. But the gains were uneven; income inequality rose sharply during the 1990s as some benefited substantially from globalization and the transition to a knowledge economy, while others did not. For those in the lower echelons of the middle class, the American Dream at the turn of the century seemed increasingly out of reach. Yet compared to the rest of the world and all of previous history, their standard of living was remarkably high.

By 2000, a full 23 percent of U.S. households earned what was considered an upper-middle-class income of $75,000 or more, as compared to only 1 percent in 1890 who earned an equivalent inflation-adjusted amount. Their jobs were also far more pleasant, as

58 percent of men and 52 percent of women worked in white-collar occupations, as compared to 21 percent of men and 20 percent of women a century earlier. The average work week was about 42 hours, down from 53 hours in 1900, and 86 percent of Americans had health insurance. Most working Americans could expect to receive Social Security and Medicare benefits once they retired, and collectively, U.S. households owned $12 trillion worth of stocks, much of it in employer-sponsored 401k programs.

When their work was done, twenty-first-century Americans got into cars carefully engineered for maximum safety and performance and drove back to homes that were much larger and more luxurious than just a few decades previously. The size of the typical home was 2,250 square feet, twice the size of one in the 1950s, and on average there were two rooms per person, up from one room per person a half-century earlier. Yet despite having substantially larger houses, far fewer hours were spent doing chores and housework than in the past, thanks to numerous labor-saving devices. What's more, over 99 percent of houses now had indoor plumbing, 95 percent had central heating, and 78 percent had air conditioning. Compared with the mud walls, thatched roofs, and open fireplaces of typical family dwellings in the Middle Ages, modern American homes were palaces fit for a king. Two thirds of American families owned their own homes rather than renting, and a third owned three or more cars.

Similar strides had been made in health care. In the early 1900s, approximately 10 percent of American children died before their first birthday; by the early 2000s, this figure had fallen to less than 0.7 percent (7 children in 1000 live births), and overall life expectancy had climbed to 77.7 years. On the educational front, a full 80 percent of Americans were high school graduates, and two-thirds of those graduating in 2000 went on to attend at least some college. When they weren't studying, American kids spent their time watching cable TV, playing video games, listening to their iPods, and surfing the Internet. So did the adults, who could devote more of their time to leisure than ever before. Americans in the new millennium typically treated themselves to dinner out once a week (four times a week if you counted fast food restaurants and coffee houses), compared to once a month in the 1950s. About 70 percent had flown on an airplane at least once, and collectively they took 25 million trips overseas annually. If a Jamestown colonist could have been transported into the future to experience all of these riches, he would have been flabbergasted.[1]

Yet paradoxically, in spite of all this material wealth and the existence of a vast social safety net, Americans of the new millennium apparently weren't any happier than those who had lived in earlier times. The percentage of Americans who reported being "happy" had held steady from the 1950s through the 1990s, despite the rapidly rising living standards of the postwar era. Even more puzzling, the percentage who said they were "very happy" actually decreased over the same period and was trending downward. Thirteen percent of Americans described themselves as "lonely," compared to only 3 percent in the 1950s, and adjusting for population, ten times as many people suffered from depression.[2]

Most telling for the state of the American Dream, 52 percent of those polled in one 1996 survey agreed with the statement that the United States was "worse off than when their parents were growing up," and 60 percent reported that they "expected their children would live in an even worse country."[3] It was a shocking result given that the economy was at the start of the dot-com boom and was doing well. Historically, even in the worst of times, when Gallup polls have asked Americans to predict where the country would be in five years, they have always said it would be doing better. In the opening decade of the new millennium, however, traditionally optimistic Americans had for some reason become unhappy and pessimistic, despite a standard of living that was the envy of the world. An increasing number questioned whether the American Dream of upward mobility and a rising standard of living was going to be possible for their children in the future.

• • • • •

The root causes underlying American's loss of faith in the American Dream are many-faceted and complex, the first and most obvious being that the world at the start of the twenty-first century was one of great uncertainty. The Y2K scare fed into people's fears that we as a country had become too reliant on technology and that something as simple as a programming glitch might bring civilization to a halt. While Y2K turned out to be a tempest in a teapot, the implosion of the dot-com bubble and the aftermath of the 9/11 terror attacks, occurring in quick succession, were real and substantial threats. They not only plunged the country into a recession serious enough to make people question whether the New Economy had been a transient fluke, but also made people wonder whether America itself might be vulnerable to angry terrorists. Not since the Cuban missile crisis had the threat of a serious, large-scale attack on American soil been so frighteningly real, and while Americans initially experienced a brief surge of solidarity and patriotism after the 9/11 attacks, the ongoing quagmire of Iraq and Afghanistan sapped their confidence and led to feelings of helplessness and futility in the new post–Cold War era.

The news media in all of its forms did much to reinforce these fears and anxieties, as well as emphasize political and philosophical differences. When Americans got their news from the big three television networks as a public service, news was far more balanced, thoughtful, and objective. Yet with the proliferation of cable, radio, and online media, the competition for viewers' and readers' attention led to ever more shocking headlines, biased reporting, and pseudo-journalism. Twenty-four-hour news services dwelled on stories of school shootings or child kidnappings for days on end, while bloggers and news anchors became increasingly outrageous, their primary goal to stir up controversy and generate higher ratings and bigger audiences. All of this led to more polarizing politics, as people tuned in to programs that reflected their own biases and presented them with only one side of the story. This created the sense that the world was more controversial and dangerous than it actually was, and that our problems were insurmountable.

Heightening this uncertainty were the ongoing effects of globalization, which in the opening years of the new century were accelerating and making themselves more deeply felt. Free trade, which President Clinton had championed with the passage of the North American Free Trade Agreement (NAFTA) in the 1990s, started to look like it had set off a global race to the bottom rather than a rising tide that lifted all boats, as promised. Outsourcing and offshoring threatened American jobs and wages, leading to a great deal of anxiety about job security and lowered incomes. Loss of manufacturing jobs had continued apace, and even staple high-paying jobs of the New Economy such as computer programming and technical support were outsourced to places like China and India. No job, no matter how specialized or technical, seemed safe. On the contrary, high-tech jobs proved as vulnerable as manufacturing ones, while service jobs that couldn't be automated and required face-to-face interaction generally paid less than was necessary to support America's increasingly expensive middle-class lifestyle.

Globalization and the end of lifetime employment meant that no one could count on a predictable career path, making income over the span of one's life uncertain. The house, cars, and gadgets that were affordable for a hiring manager or customer support worker were suddenly beyond their means when those jobs were outsourced, and sometimes the best laid-off workers could do without taking on more loans and going back to college was to take lower-paying jobs in the service industry. Even a college degree wasn't the sure path to success that it once was, as a quarter of college graduates found themselves in jobs that didn't require a college education, struggling to pay back tens of thousands of dollars in student loans racked up from the huge cost of their higher education. Young adults in their twenties often found themselves moving back in with their parents after college or in between jobs, unable to afford the middle-class lifestyle they had become accustomed to as children.

This uncertainty and unpredictability, particularly with regard to income, was one of the key factors behind Americans' unhappiness. Income and happiness don't correlate well when viewed at a single point in time; in a recent National Opinion Research Center poll, 58 percent of those with incomes below the poverty line rated themselves as "pretty happy," and 21 percent rated themselves as "very happy."[4] What matters is how income changes over time. Psychological studies have shown that animals that experience unpredictable feast-or-famine conditions exhibit considerably more stress than those who receive food in consistent amounts at regular intervals—even if the total amount of food received is less than in the feast-or-famine scenario. This holds for humans as well, especially in a world where so many of our expenses are in the form of regular monthly payments. We need our incomes to be regular in order to tailor our spending to our income; otherwise stress and considerable unhappiness results.

Similarly, we tend to have a strong aversion to loss, and while we adjust to increases in our incomes very easily, it takes far longer and causes us a great deal of anguish to adjust our expectations downward if our income falls. Viewed in this context, upward mobility—which for many is what the American Dream is all about—is something of a double-edged sword: it opens us up to greater uncertainty and the risk of loss. As it turns out, people judge their well-being not by measuring where they stand today, but rather on whether they think their circumstances and income will improve in coming years. Since most of our basic needs are already met, people find it harder to believe that life will keep improving—yet they want it to anyway.

If happiness isn't strongly tied to income, why do we so zealously pursue more money and an ever-increasing standard of living? While lacking money for basic needs such as food, clothing, and shelter certainly creates unhappiness, once those basic needs are met, earning more money with which to buy more things does not make us happier. Millionaires, as a group, have been found to be no happier than people with middle-class incomes, because great wealth creates its own new problems. In general, older people are happier than younger people, as Social Security and Medicare have eliminated much of the uncertainty of retirement and allowed people to enjoy their golden years. Most surprising of all, disabled and chronically ill people report a slightly higher sense of well-being than most Americans, apparently due to a greater appreciation for what is good in their lives.[5]

Many Americans agree with the common wisdom that money can't buy happiness, yet most of us can't manage to live our lives according to this dictum. Our material wants keep increasing with our income, and we are predictably irrational in wanting ever-greater wealth. Partially this is because we make comparisons between ourselves and our friends and peers. We admire what they have—a bigger house, a luxury car, an expensive watch—and we understandably want it for ourselves. These items are known as *positional goods*, and when we first buy one, reward neurons fire in our brains and produce dopamine, making us feel happier. Unfortunately, we quickly adapt and no longer get the dopamine rush from the expensive item, but we've still raised everyone else's expectations, prompting them to copy us. In doing so, they devalue the item in our own eyes because it is no longer special. Thus, upscaling to more and more expensive items can quickly escalate out of control without producing any lasting happiness.

Comparing ourselves to those in our peer group is damaging enough, but the influence of the media makes it worse, both by manipulating us with sophisticated advertising and by continually presenting us with stories and images of celebrity millionaires and their lifestyles. These influences play upon our material aspirations, stoking our desire to be rich and making us feel inadequate by comparison. *Forbes*'s annual list of the 400 wealthiest Americans does us no favors, particularly as the size of their fortunes has grown significantly in recent years. CEO pay increased almost 300 percent between 1990 and 2005, while corporate profits increased a little over 100 percent, but average worker pay only rose 4.3 percent.[6] The earnings of top actors, athletes, and musicians have similarly grown, making us feel like we're falling behind rather than continuing to gain ground with respect to the previous generation, a far more reasonable comparison. It's hard for Americans to appreciate what we have and how blessed we truly are when we are constantly being bombarded by messages that tell us we ought to be doing even better.

• • • • •

Money does not buy happiness, yet the pressure to make sure that we are among the winners rather than the losers in the global economy leads many of us, almost inevitably, to join the rat race. Driven by the American Dream, or what we think of as the American Dream, we go to college, find a decent job, buy a car, and get an apartment. The early years after we land that first job are often tough, particularly when the student loans start coming due. But after a few years and a couple of raises, we start filling the apartment with nice furniture from hip stores, flat-screen television sets, Blu-ray players, and video game consoles, and building up libraries of music and movies. With experience, we get a better job, marry, buy a house, and are saddled with a mortgage, but it's all manageable because two can live more cheaply than one. If times are good, there is money left over for vacations, fancy clothes, expensive dinners, and the latest electronic gadgets. Life seems good. We are upwardly mobile.

It's when we have children that the picture changes and tradeoffs are introduced that feed our unhappiness. For the average middle-class American family, and even for upper-middle-class ones, what ought to be a purely joyous event also forces a difficult choice: Do you put the child in daycare and maintain both incomes, or do you have one parent stay home and somehow scale back expenses to one income in the face of an increasingly long list of must-have baby items? The guilt of leaving a child in daycare makes many new mothers extremely unhappy, yet so does seeing their family income reduced by half. The expense of daycare, particularly for several children, offsets much of the family's second income. Meanwhile, those who leave the workforce for a few years and make raising their children a priority often find that getting back into the workforce later can be extremely difficult, particularly in a world where only those with recent experience need apply. This leads many stay-at-home parents to start their own business or purchase a franchise once their children are in school, making them key drivers of small business entrepreneurship. Unfortunately, for those who don't have the training, personality, or access to startup capital necessary to start their own business, often the only option is to start over in an entry-level position with an entry-level income—one of the many reasons women's career incomes generally lag behind those of men.

Whether to keep working or stay at home with children is a choice that's particularly difficult for highly educated women with multiple degrees, who are more likely to earn higher incomes and be more invested in their careers than most other women. These women have been a key factor in the growth of middle-class incomes, as manufacturing jobs that allowed men to raise a family on a single income are disappearing fast, and most of the increases in family earnings over the past forty years have been due to the increase in dual incomes. Now, in the first part of the new millennium, more women than men are graduating from college, and 28 percent of married women between the ages of 30 and 44 are married to men who are less well educated than they are, while only 19 percent are married to men better educated than they are. Overall, women still earn only 78 percent as much as men and they work fewer hours, but in 22 percent of households, wives now earn more than their husbands, compared with only 4 percent in 1970.[7]

This has led some men to stay home to take care of their children while their wives shoulder the responsibility of providing the family income, a trend that accelerated during the recent recession as 4 out of 5 of the job losses were borne by men. There's nothing wrong with this—as long as both husband and wife are happy with the situation, as some are. But gender roles hardwired into our brains over thousands of years are not easily dispensed with, and in most cases it is women, even highly educated ones devoted to their careers, who would prefer to stay home with their children when they are little, while their husbands would rather work. A recent survey of 2000 married mothers found that only 16 percent would prefer to work full-time if they could choose their ideal work situation, while the rest would rather work part-time or not at all.[8] Although stay-at-home dads often enjoy spending extra time with their kids, dropping out of the workforce entirely frequently makes them desperately unhappy. The social environment is difficult for dads who stay at home, and men's sense of self-worth tends to be closely tied to what they do for a living and how much they earn. That most are better off working is clear, but it does not follow that high-income, high-powered careers add to their overall happiness.

Thus many men, and highly educated women as well, fall into the trap of climbing the corporate ladder. They are pushed by their parents, their families, and their own egos into careers in business, law, or medicine when they might actually be happier as teachers, technical writers, or graphic artists, working fewer hours and spending more time with their families. The dream of upward mobility beckons; especially if one spouse stays home with the children, the pressure on the other to maintain a high income is all the greater—and this assumes that having one spouse at home is even a viable option. Those lower down the economic ladder generally feel that they have no such choice; for them the American Dream is now really possible only with two incomes. Unlike those in the upper middle class, these couples don't overspend on luxury items. The majority of their joint income goes toward housing, education, and health care, and rising costs in all three areas have far exceeded growth in income for the average American family in recent decades.

In the global information age, chasing the American Dream of upward mobility forces a tricky balancing act between work and personal life, a balance people often fail to maintain. While new technologies such as laptops, e-mail, and cell phones initially seemed promising as a way to help people to maintain a better balance by enabling knowledge workers to telecommute, in reality the opposite has happened. These technologies have proven to be intrusive and addictive, keeping us constantly interconnected and making it hard for Americans to take a step back from their jobs, social networks, and the world at large to relax with their families and close friends. Even when they're on vacation, adult Americans are constantly checking their e-mail, while their children make friends in chat rooms with people they've never even met.

The introduction of social media such as Facebook and LinkedIn further increases the demands on our time, but maintaining these networks is crucial, for if our job disappears, it is through these networks that we are most likely to find our next job. One has to wonder whether smart phones and social media have made our lives better or worse. The necessity of dual incomes means that we already have little time to spend with our families; living in a constantly interconnected society often means that we have even less. It's no wonder that running ever faster on a treadmill we can't afford to get off, in a world full of uncertainties, we've become increasingly stressed, unhappy, and anxious about the future. There is a growing fear among Americans that the United States as a whole cannot maintain its current standard of living, and as the financial crisis of 2008 unfolded, it seemed that our worst fears were becoming a reality.

· · · · ·

The immediate causes of what some have called the Great Recession, which began in December of 2007 and is still ongoing as of 2010, are far too technical and complex to provide a meaningful explanation of them here. Suffice it to say that in the worst financial crisis the United States has experienced since the Great Depression, easy credit and irresponsible lending practices in the sub-prime mortgage market ultimately resulted in the failure of several large financial institutions and very nearly brought the entire world financial system to the brink of failure. To some extent, the crisis was fueled by greed on Wall Street, but on a deeper level it was driven by our own rising expectations of what it means to live the American Dream of middle-class prosperity.

The root cause of the banking crisis was a rash of defaults on sub-prime mortgages that had enabled hundreds of thousands of Americans to buy more expensive homes than they could realistically afford. Our home is often one of our most prized possessions, and as the average size of American homes has increased, the temptation to keep up with the Joneses has intensified. Yet because buying a home is such a great expense, usually requiring loans that take decades to repay, extravagance in home buying is particularly hazardous. Too many bad loans led to bank failures, and in the global economy of the twenty-first century, major bank failures in one country can create strong aftershocks throughout the world banking system. Only by restoring liquidity via massive bank bailouts, paid for by American taxpayers, was a worldwide depression avoided.

Still, the economic effects were devastating. Between June 2007 and November 2008, Americans lost more than a quarter of their collective net worth. The U.S. housing market collapsed, resulting in numerous home foreclosures and the loss of a central facet of the American Dream for many families. Millions of others lost so much home equity that they soon owed more on their home than it was worth—total home equity in the United States plummeted from $13 trillion at its peak in 2006 to $8.8 trillion after the crisis. The stock market fared no better, as by early November 2008 the S&P 500 was down 45 percent from its high the previous year. As a result, total retirement assets—Americans' second-largest household asset after their home—lost 22 percent of their value, at a time when the leading edge of the baby boomer generation was just about to retire.[9] Meanwhile, the U.S. real gross domestic product (GDP) fell approximately 6 percent, and the unemployment rate soared to over 10 percent. In the face of falling tax revenues, states like New York and California were struggling just to stay afloat. It wasn't the Great Depression, but it was by far the worst recession that most Americans had ever experienced.

The federal bailout of the financial system, occurring just a month before the 2008 presidential election, was enough to turn what had previously been a close campaign into a decided victory for Barack Obama. In doing so, he fulfilled his own American Dream, and that of many African Americans, by becoming the first biracial president. Yet the country's economic situation was perilous, and with the specter of a worldwide depression a real possibility, the pendulum of American political thought swung back toward government as a provider of economic stability and security. But many Americans were incredibly angry with the government for authorizing the bailouts, arguing that it was unfair for American taxpayers to be forced to reward the banks' bad behavior. Were the banks too big to fail, or should the government have let the market take its course? Was the best remedy to lower taxes and spend money to stimulate the economy, or to tighten our belts? Was the root cause of all our problems big business or big government? There was much anger but little consensus. In fact, almost the only thing Americans could agree on was that the American Dream was in serious jeopardy.

Obama took office at one of the most critical and difficult moments in our nation's history; the country teetered on the edge of depression at a time when we were fighting two wars—in Afghanistan and Iraq. Obama himself noted the extreme challenges facing both himself as president and the nation at large by declaring in his inaugural address:

> Our economy is badly weakened, a consequence of greed and irresponsibility on the part of some, but also our collective failure to make hard choices and prepare the nation for a new age. Homes have been lost, jobs shed, businesses shuttered. Our health care is too costly, our schools fail too many, and each day brings further evidence that the ways we use energy strengthen our adversaries and threaten our planet.
>
> These are the indicators of crisis, subject to data and statistics. Less measurable, but no less profound, is a

> sapping of confidence across our land; a nagging fear
> that America's decline is inevitable, that the next generation
> must lower its sights.
>
> Today I say to you that the challenges we face are
> real. They are serious and they are many. They will not
> be met easily or in a short span of time. But know this
> America: They will be met.[10]

Obama called the financial crisis, with all of its consequences in terms of jobs lost and homes foreclosed, a "disaster for America's working families…the American Dream in reverse."[11] Addressing this crisis and ultimately restoring Americans' faith in their country, their government, and the American Dream would be no easy task. In an attempt to bridge his trademark hopefulness with a call for sacrifice and greater responsibility, he invoked the Declaration of Independence, on which the American Dream is based, while still acknowledging that rebuilding the dream would not come easily:

> The time has come to reaffirm our enduring spirit; to
> choose our better history; to carry forward that precious gift,
> that noble idea passed on from generation to generation:
> the God-given promise that all are equal, all are free, and all
> deserve a chance to pursue their full measure of happiness.
>
> In reaffirming the greatness of our nation, we
> understand that greatness is never a given. It must be
> earned. Our journey has never been one of short-cuts
> or settling for less. It has not been the path for the faint-
> hearted, for those that prefer leisure over work, or seek
> only the pleasures of riches and fame. Rather, it has been
> the risk-takers, the doers, the makers of things—some
> celebrated, but more often men and women obscure in
> their labor—who have carried us up the long rugged path
> towards prosperity and freedom…
>
> This is the journey we continue today. We remain the
> most prosperous, powerful nation on Earth. Our workers
> are no less productive than when this crisis began. Our

minds are no less inventive, our goods and services no less needed than they were last week, or last month, or last year. Our capacity remains undiminished. But our time of standing pat, of protecting narrow interests and putting off unpleasant decisions—that time has surely passed. Starting today, we must pick ourselves up, dust ourselves off, and begin again the work of remaking America.[12]

In Obama's address were many familiar ideas as to what the American Dream is all about—freedom and equality, the chance to pursue our own happiness, the necessity of hard work and self-reliance, and the idea that America is a unique and special country. Yet while most Americans agreed with those basic principles, there were still deep disagreements about the government's proper role in securing the American Dream. The financial crisis had sapped the confidence of many Americans, but it still wasn't severe enough to produce the sort of consensus in favor of big government that had led to the New Deal during the Great Depression.

Nevertheless, Obama's legislative agenda during his first two years in office, while certainly not equaling the sheer volume or impact of the New Deal, proved to be the most ambitious and expansive since the Great Society under Lyndon Johnson. It included an economic stimulus bill that, in addition to rebuilding infrastructure, also set out to both reform and provide additional funding for education and scientific research—although it included a lot of pork as well. The stimulus bill was passed relatively easily by the Democratic-controlled Congress, but debate over a sweeping healthcare reform bill that would mandate insurance coverage for most Americans became a deeply divisive, hard-fought battle. But it eventually passed as well, at an initial cost of $940 billion over ten years, making it the most significant and costly expansion of the social safety net in decades. It was followed by a financial regulatory reform bill—designed to prevent a repetition of the specific circumstances that led to the financial crisis—which imposed new regulations and restrictions on banks and allowed the government to seize collapsing financial firms.

The point of all of this legislation, from Obama's and the Democrats' perspective, was to sustain and expand the American Dream for the middle class by spending on programs that would promote economic growth in the long term. However, it also added greatly to the federal debt, which had soared to over $13 trillion by 2010. While some of this was a short-term spike in spending to combat the effects of the recession, over the long term, federal spending, which was approximately 20 percent of GDP in 2007, was projected to be almost 23 percent in 2019.[13] This growth in federal spending was alarming to many, but equally significant was what the money would be spent on and who was going to pay for it. The primary goal of Obama's domestic agenda was to rebuild the American Dream by fostering future growth, but it was also intended to reduce income inequality, and this ran contrary to most conservatives' views of what the American Dream is all about.

The healthcare reform bill particularly rankled conservatives, as much of the financial burden for the program fell on the wealthiest 2 percent of Americans—couples earning over $250,000 and individuals earning over $200,000—by increasing their tax burden an average of $30,000 annually. While the top marginal tax rate was still less than 40 percent, far lower than after World War II, this legislation continued a trend of reducing taxes on the middle class in the face of burgeoning debts. In the 1960s, approximately 15 percent of Americans paid no income tax. By 2009, that figure had jumped to nearly 47 percent despite the fact that government spending and the federal debt had greatly increased. Most of those who paid no income tax considered themselves part of the middle class and were the beneficiaries of many government programs. Yet the taxes to support these programs were increasingly being paid by the members of our society with the means to provide capital for new ventures, sapping their incentive to create the new businesses and jobs that in the wake of the financial crisis were so desperately needed.

Meanwhile, almost all Americans were still paying payroll FICA taxes, and with the passage of the healthcare reform bill, many felt that those taxes were destined to increase. In 1936, a government pamphlet on Social Security told voters that starting in 1940, they and their employers would pay 1.5 cents into the system for every dollar they earned, up to a cap of $3,000 per year. This rate would slowly increase until 1949, when it would be 3 cents per dollar earned, and, the pamphlet promised, "That is the most you will ever pay."[14] That promise turned out to be false, as Congress has voted to expand Social Security many times since then, necessitating increases in FICA taxes that became higher with the addition of Medicare. At the start of the program in 1966, Medicare cost $3 billion annually, and the government estimated that it would cost $12 billion annually by 1990. In reality, the cost had risen to $107 billion by 1990 and over $420 billion by 2010. Americans now pay 7.65 cents in FICA taxes on every dollar they earn up to $107,000, a maximum of $8,185 per year. With the passage of the healthcare bill, few Americans doubted they would one day have to pay more. The question was, would the benefits be worth it? Only time would tell, but for those who thought the American Dream was best served by getting government off their backs and out of their pockets, the answer was an emphatic no.

As the recession ended and the economy slowly recovered, debate over how to best address our nation's problems grew more vitriolic. Disaster in the short term had been averted, but the future of the American Dream in the long term was still very much in question, since unemployment remained alarmingly high. Polarization in American politics had been on the rise for several decades— President Clinton's impeachment in the late 1990s had left both Democrats and Republicans embittered, as had the controversy about the 2000 presidential election results that brought George W. Bush to office. Disagreements over the handling of the war in Iraq, the existence of global warming, and the aftermath of Hurricane Katrina only made things worse, and while the financial crisis had brought the Democrats back to power, the country was still deeply divided as Republicans' outrage mounted over tax increases, government spending, and the size of the national debt.

As President Obama argued when answering his critics, government spending isn't inherently irresponsible. Spending on scientific research and education, when done wisely, is an investment in our country's future that will lead to future economic growth, and the Obama administration had in some ways taken a plank from the Republican platform by trying to improve education through greater accountability and market competition. In government as well as in business, taking on debt in order to develop assets that may one day generate greater income is often a good decision. On the other hand, borrowing money from Peter simply to improve the quality of Paul's life makes sense only if it will improve Paul's productivity and potentially benefit both.

The real question facing America is this: To what extent is the massive increase in the federal debt, whether it pays for the war on terror or for an expanded healthcare program, a necessary or wise investment that will one day yield a return on investment? And to what extent are we charging a long list of highly desirable or even "necessary" programs to the national credit card and leaving the bill for future generations to pay? As Americans contemplate these questions and their future, we have to start distinguishing between federal spending that is an investment vs. that which is an entitlement and ask whether it is fair—or wise—to keep shifting the tax burden to the wealthiest of Americans. Does it make sense to force those who have achieved success through diligence and hard work to fund the American Dream for the rest of us, particularly if chasing that dream isn't even making us particularly happy? Or are we simply repeating on a national scale the same mistakes we made as individuals: taking on more debt than we can afford to repay by chasing an American fantasy that has grown beyond our ability to reasonably achieve?

14

THE FUTURE
OF THE AMERICAN DREAM

◇◇◇

In this book, we have explored the historic development of the American Dream and why present-day expectations of that dream are dramatically different from those of our ancestors. The concept of the American Dream has always been a part of America's heritage, but its meaning has changed based on shifts in individual values, the political environment, and economic factors. For some, the American Dream is all about freedom—freedom from persecution, the right to worship as one chooses, or the ability to voice a dissenting opinion. To others, it centers on the opportunity to improve one's financial standing, whether by building a business empire or simply going to college and getting a good job. Then there are those for whom the American Dream is about creating a better and more "just" society and even remaking the world in America's image. No matter what version one believes in, the American Dream is a powerful motivator, and to underestimate its importance in the ongoing development of our society is a mistake.

In these opening decades of the twenty-first century, America stands at an important crossroads in our history. Crucial decisions must be made, and in making them there is much we can learn from that history. In many ways, our experiences in recent years have borne a striking resemblance to the early 1900s. The years leading up to World War I were also an era of globalization, one in which the great powers of the world competed for trading dominance. These great powers—the United States, Britain, France, Germany, Russia, and Japan—had been at peace with one another for fifty years. Yet at the same time, they had frequent conflicts with other, less powerful countries over largely economic matters. The new technology of the telephone was transforming the way people communicated, both socially and at work, in much the same way the Internet has done in the new millennium. The emergence of this new technology and other innovations were revolutionizing business, making it more efficient and lowering prices to an extent that created mass markets. This in turn stimulated greater demand that spurred further growth of those markets in what became a self-perpetuating cycle. There was an emphasis on individual achievement, entrepreneurship, and economic growth, which lead to increasing polarization of wealth. Over time, this polarization produced a backlash in which the public called for greater government intervention to equalize incomes and level the economic playing field. Unfortunately, this emphasis on equality over opportunity threatened some of the core principles of our society that made the American Dream possible in the first place.

The challenges we now face are to some extent the repetition of a familiar cycle, and if we respond to them with the same old solutions, we can probably predict their results. Excessive consumer spending and irresponsible banking, without significant government intervention, could have led to another worldwide depression similar to the Great Depression of the 1930s. In the worst case, the fallout may lead countries to focus on greater nationalism and centralization to aid their ailing economies at the expense of international trade, precipitating military conflicts and perhaps even large-scale wars. The latter would probably cause scientific competition that would lead to innovation and technological advancement. But the increasing expense of maintaining a strong military, basic social programs, an educated citizenry, and decent infrastructure would take its toll on world economies as well. It might take decades to recover, and the balance of world power and standards of living across the globe, including here in America, could be altered dramatically.

Yet for all of the similarities, in many ways the problems we face in the twenty-first century are radically different from those of the twentieth. The pace of technological change is accelerating at a much faster rate now than a century ago, particularly since the onset of the information age, and this is forcing people to adjust more quickly to change. China and India are becoming major players in the global economy, and the power of national governments in general is being supplanted to some extent by multinational commercial empires. We are deindustrializing rather than industrializing, and one has only to study the changes that have occurred in our major cities over the past century to see that the United States is a very different place now than it was then. Cities and towns that once prospered around a major manufacturing plant or industry are struggling as the factories they once depended on shut down, and the blue-collar middle class these factories created is now in sharp decline. Given this reality, one has to wonder how the working class will achieve the American Dream in the twenty-first century. Americans are resilient, and the dream will doubtless be reinvented in the face of new challenges, but what exactly the American Dream will mean in the years and decades to come depends on the choices we make now.

If society is shaped by our dreams and aspirations, we must ask ourselves what particular dreams and aspirations will help to create the future we want for our children and their children. We need to appreciate what we already have, set more realistic expectations, and be willing to make the tough choices and sacrifices necessary to preserve a healthy version of the American Dream for future generations. To do that, we must understand the key factors that have driven the development of that dream, and those that will continue to do so in the future. We have identified twelve key issues that will dramatically impact how Americans view their country, their personal lives, and their future opportunities. Understanding and addressing these issues is crucial, for we are now in an economic bubble that has been building for more than fifty years, and how we respond to our current situation and the challenges we face will determine how the American Dream evolves for years to come. Briefly, these issues are as follows:

1. Entrepreneurship and Job Creation

In a society where the overwhelming majority of Americans' only significant source of income is from wages, the availability of well-paying jobs is absolutely essential to maintaining the American Dream. Economists estimate that it will take at least five years to replace the 8.2 million jobs lost during the "Great Recession"—longer than any recovery since World War II. The unemployment rate is still hovering near 10 percent, and as of May 2010, 4.3 percent of America's workforce had been unemployed for over six months, the highest percentage that statistic has reached since it was first tracked in 1948. We must create new jobs, or unemployment will stabilize at unacceptable rates and our standard of living will decline.

In the current global economy, entrepreneurship and innovation are the key drivers of new job creation. The simple truth is that many of the manufacturing, retail, and marketing jobs that have been lost over the past few years will not return to the United States, and service industry jobs and the exportation of knowledge will not be enough to fuel recovery and reduce unemployment. We must take the lead in creating new industries and start building tangible goods here in America again. Only when we can legitimately compete with the rest of the world in all facets of the business development and delivery cycle—from research and development to manufacturing to marketing and distribution—will we have any chance of creating the number of well-paying jobs necessary to restore true prosperity and maintain an acceptable standard of living for the middle class.

Fostering entrepreneurship is an area in which government has a legitimate role to play and one that it must focus on. Innovation is always a challenge, and the availability of money to fund basic research and development, think tanks, loans for new and expanding businesses, and scholarships for scientists and engineers will be critically important. Government tax policies and regulations also have a significant impact on our ability to create new jobs in the United States. Our tax burden is increasingly falling on the members of our society who are most likely to start, manage, and invest in the very businesses that are most likely to produce the job growth we need. Similarly, the regulations and red tape that are meant to keep large, mature businesses in line are often oppressive and unreasonably costly to smaller, newer businesses that could better use that money to hire additional workers. More taxes and greater regulation are not the solutions to our problems.

Instead, we Americans must reconsider our expectations of government in securing the American Dream. If there is a lesson to be learned from the past fifty years of scientifically managing the economy, it is that the federal government cannot guarantee full employment or prevent all recessions, nor should it. Half of today's Fortune 500 companies were started during recent economic slowdowns, and brief recessions exert necessary discipline on the market that helps to ward off larger disasters and shift resources to new, more productive industries. While this creates temporary unemployment, a healthy economy—one in which society has refrained from unnecessary spending while making wise investments in education, research, and infrastructure—will bounce back quickly and create more jobs than it destroys. If job creation is our primary goal, we must invest in activities that produce reasonable, sustainable growth rather than simply redistributing income.

2. Government Policy and Accountability

Since the founding of our nation, Americans have vociferously debated to what extent we want government, particularly the federal government, to intervene in our lives in the interests of helping those less fortunate and protecting us from harm. As government has become larger and more active, its policies have had an increasingly significant impact on the lives of Americans through social spending programs, tax policies, and regulation. This will continue into the future, and the tyranny of the majority that James Madison warned of in *The Federalist Papers* is becoming a dangerous reality, because those who want more government services vote for candidates who make the most promises. Yet an almost equal percentage of Americans are against further expansion of government, with the result that America is as polarized today as it has ever been. For all intents and purposes, we have two equal majorities in American society at large, yet every time one political party or the other gains an advantage, it acts as if it has a mandate and presses its agenda despite clear opposition, and thus half of our population is angry at every president and unhappy with most legislation passed by Congress.

This polarization is not good for our country, as our happiness depends in part on having a government whose elected representatives further the interests of all Americans, not just their party's concerns. We need public servants who respect the will of the people at large, who have integrity, and who value fairness, honesty, and transparency. To promote the American Dream in the future, we must return to policies that assist Americans with their needs rather than their wants. Spending at all levels of government is growing much faster than the tax base that is required to fund that spending. Even without considering future obligations for programs like Social Security, Medicare, and Medicaid, the costs of which are accelerating rapidly, government spending has grown from $870 billion in 1970 to $2.8 trillion in 2008 (adjusted for inflation). This represents an increase of 220 percent, yet household income has grown only 32 percent over the same period (also adjusted for inflation). Not all government spending is bad, but we must distinguish between spending that is an investment in the future that will yield a return on that investment, such as the G.I. Bill, and spending that simply borrows money from future generations to fund the desires of our own. We would be wise to heed the words of Thomas Jefferson, who predicted happiness for Americans "if we can prevent the government from wasting the labors of the people under the pretense of taking care of them."[1]

It is time to put a stop to government spending practices that lead to public outrage and distrust. In a nation that is split on the basic issues of what the government's role is in creating a society that is fair, equal, and just, this will be a challenge. Yet while the goals of the New Deal and the Great Society were in many ways admirable, we simply cannot afford to pay for all of the government programs we would like to have without saddling our children and grandchildren with mountains of debt without their consent. Clearly, we must gain control of governmental spending—if we don't, taxes will have to increase to levels not experienced for over thirty years. The tax burden must also be shouldered by a broader segment of society, and we will have to make many sacrifices in order to reduce the federal deficit and our long-term debts. This will adversely affect many Americans, and our political leaders must be honest with the American people about the magnitude of the problem and not manipulate the numbers to win reelection and satisfy short-term agendas. We have a severe problem just waiting to explode, and the American people need to hear the truth—the growth in tax revenue must exceed government spending for many years to come. Future Congresses and presidents have the responsibility to cut spending and reduce our debt, as unpopular as this may be, because our current course is simply unsustainable.

3. Financial Markets and Regulation

The American financial system is the strongest and most adaptable in the world, and our stock markets, venture capital industry, banking institutions, and brokerage companies have helped many Americans to achieve and sustain the American Dream. American consumerism has been funded by readily available credit, which has enabled people to finance homes, cars, and college educations. Yet in some ways credit has become too easy to access and Americans have used it irresponsibly to purchase larger homes, more cars, and unnecessary luxury goods. The availability of credit is critical to our lifestyle, yet as individuals we must be able to repay our debt; otherwise its burden creates stress that supersedes the happiness we experience from our expensive way of living.

Americans must learn not to borrow so much money that we leverage our future, and people who borrow money must be provided with incentives to repay the debts they accumulate rather than add to them. This is the basis of personal financial responsibility, and financial institutions should not create policies or financially engineered products that tempt those who are already stretched financially to take on greater debt simply to maximize profits. While ultimately individuals are responsible for their own financial choices, the modern financial industry and the products it provides are highly complex and lack transparency. The financial industry contributed substantially to the recent economic crisis by granting mortgages to people who could not even provide proof of income and then repackaging them as AAA bonds with no grounding in solid financial reality. While our financial system does much that is good, it is also prone to emphasizing profit at the expense of corporate responsibility.

A nonpartisan political approach to solving this problem is the only way for us to succeed in fixing it. Everything in our lives has gotten bigger—government, corporations, homes, debts—and our financial institutions are no exception. Friendly community bankers who know their customers personally have been replaced by large institutions and credit committees that view customers as a commodity, and some of our leading banks and financial institutions have become so large that they are considered too big to fail. Yet when they act irresponsibly, they deserve to fail, and we must find ways to let them fail without resorting to government takeovers and bailouts in order to avoid pulling our economy down with them. Corporate culture and accountability grows from the top down, and bank executives who once expected a reasonable salary to protect the bank's assets and serve the community have been replaced by high-income CEOs who take unnecessary risks and don't know their customers. This presents an unacceptable risk to the banking system, which is the very lifeblood of our economy, but increased regulation is not the solution to this problem. Instead, boards of directors, not the government, must be held accountable to shareholders and serve as the true oversight committee for this industry. This will require cultivating more proactive and experienced individuals to serve the public shareholders. Until this is accomplished, little real change will occur.

4. Corporate Competitiveness and Labor Relations

Organized labor has been critical to the development of America's middle class. Thanks in part to unions, Americans receive higher wages and better job security than most of the world's workforce does. They also experience better work environments, receive excellent benefits, and have more say in their future than do workers in many other nations. On the whole, unions in the United States have represented the best interests of their workers and have shied away from acting like management or shareholders. But at the same time, they have been slow to accept the economic realities of globalization and what this means for their workers. It is simply not possible for American companies to continue to burden product cost with the expense of high fixed labor rates, fewer working hours, increased benefit costs, and guaranteed employment.

To better represent the middle class, unions and their members must reinvent themselves and adjust to the current global competitive landscape. Workers who pay dues to their unions must be realistic about what can be negotiated, and union leaders must consider the tradeoffs between short-term gains and long-term competitiveness. All of this requires America's middle class to have greater participation in the companies they work for and the profits that result from their hard work. American workers are as capable of innovation and improvements in productivity as anyone in the world, but they must be provided with incentives to create them. In a global economy, profit participation and wealth creation via stock appreciation must gain acceptance and become a greater part of employee compensation.

American workers cannot continue to expect corporations to provide lifetime employment, generous benefits, and ever-rising incomes and still remain competitive in a global market. Both white-collar and blue-collar employees will have to accept less stability, variable pay based on company performance, and greater responsibility in planning for the future. In exchange, however, companies must trust their workers more and follow technology and employment practices that enable greater autonomy, flexibility, and work-life balance. The companies that succeed in the twenty-first century will be the ones that hire hardworking, talented people and then take the shackles off them, creating jobs that are satisfying and that help to improve the company's bottom line without necessarily costing more money. In a world where people are seeking happiness from something other than material things, the best jobs are the ones that engage people's talents over a full work week and then let them spend time with their families, not the jobs that pay the most money.

America's leading corporations and unions wield considerable political power, and they must use this power in a productive rather than a destructive manner. Sometimes compromise and sacrifice are required to create a stronger America, and in supporting future political candidates, both corporations and unions must support those with a nonpartisan approach to long-term solutions—like plans to reduce our federal deficit and national debt—rather than narrowly focusing on their singular concerns. In the long run, this would be the most meaningful contribution big business and big labor could make to American workers and our society as a whole.

5. Healthcare Reform

An affordable, efficient, effective healthcare system generally isn't something we specifically associate with the American Dream, yet it is a crucial underlying component of the American lifestyle and our overall high standard of living. Americans have more top medical professionals available to them than any other society in the world, a fact we frequently take for granted. Each year, fewer children and mothers die during childbirth, and the development of vaccines and government programs to fight poverty has dramatically reduced the incidence of childhood diseases and overall mortality. Due to the introduction of new drugs, medical diagnostic systems, treatments, and surgical equipment and techniques, we have a greatly increased life expectancy, despite many lifestyle issues that ought to decrease it. We are living longer and better lives than previous generations, and this carries many benefits for American society as a whole.

Because we are living longer, many Americans don't want to retire—at least not completely—as soon as they can draw Social Security. They see themselves as capable, or in many cases obligated, to work into their later years. This is extremely beneficial in that it provides an experienced workforce to mentor America's youth as well as the capital to help develop new industries. On the other hand, Americans are also having fewer children, so the country is aging, and the period of our lives during which we require the most medicines and medical interventions is greatly extended. Unfortunately, the healthcare industry is one of the few in which new innovations often increase costs through availability of more sophisticated and expensive treatment options rather than reduce expenses through greater efficiency. As medical costs increase, employers and individuals alike struggle to afford the increases, and more and more Americans experience gaps in their coverage, denial of coverage because of previous medical conditions, or going without health care completely.

The healthcare reform bill passed by Congress in 2010 addressed some of these issues, but at very great cost, and in a way that places an undue burden on a small segment of American society while being unrealistic about the program's long-term sustainability. We need to continue to work on healthcare reform because as our society ages, we will need a strong healthcare system to meet the growing needs of the population, one that we can afford without compromising the drivers of job creation and economic growth. Health care is a complicated and very misunderstood industry. Drug companies require massive amounts of capital to create and test new drugs and are often vilified for not providing them more cheaply. Universities perform valuable research to identify diseases and cures, which requires the availability of significant amounts of funding for research grants. Hospitals and doctors strive to provide top-quality care, but this is expensive, and the system is under attack from opportunistic patients and lawyers seeking huge damages for every mistake (or perceived mistake) made by the system.

We need to protect our healthcare system and the medical professionals that provide our care, continue to perform cutting-edge research at our major universities, control costs within the system, and find affordable ways to make health care accessible to most Americans. Many jobs are created by the healthcare industry, but its true importance may be the peace of mind Americans have when they know their healthcare needs will be addressed. The debate continues as to the best approach to making affordable health care available to all Americans, but one cannot deny the quality of our healthcare system or its importance to our society.

6. Education Reform

While some might argue otherwise, America's educational system has been an integral part of our evolution as a society and the bedrock of equality of opportunity in our country. The public school system through high school is available to all Americans and, despite its faults, graduates many students who successfully go on to higher-learning institutions that include our country's most prestigious universities. While the education students receive in the inner cities is not always on par with what is available in the suburbs, the public school system is still a great equalizer. Yet there are undeniable problems, and given its importance, our educational system is in need of significant improvement. In a knowledge-based economy, education is not an option—it is a requirement.

Most Americans believe that education is essential to upward mobility and that a higher level of education produces better employment opportunities. But prestige matters as well, and as a result, most parents want their child to go to a top university. This has led parents to pressure not only their children to achieve high grades, but also teachers to lower their standards, leading to rampant grade inflation. There is a pervasive notion among American parents that when it comes to children, everyone deserves to succeed. Junior sports teams give an award to every child so that children don't lose self-esteem. While this impulse is understandable, the result is that it devalues true effort and achievement and erases the incentive to work hard, which is problematic for American competitiveness in the long term. Sheltered by parents and teachers who tell them everything they do is wonderful, young Americans are in for a nasty shock when they grow up, enter the workforce, and find that their knowledge-economy competitors half a world away are more disciplined, better prepared, and willing to work harder for less pay.

We need to teach our young people the value not only of a college degree but of the work ethic necessary to achieve it as well. While other countries value education and pursue knowledge as a means to success, the United States now ranks only tenth among industrialized nations in the proportion of citizens with college degrees, behind Canada, Japan, Korea, and several European countries. China and India graduate more university-trained engineers than the United States does, and these talented foreign students no longer come to our country to learn, hoping to stay here as they once did. As opportunities develop in their native countries, foreign students who study in the United States return home to pursue their careers, taking their knowledge and their work ethic with them. Historically, the United States has been an importer of scientific talent, but more recently, due to the growing global economy and difficulty on the part of foreign workers and students in getting visas, we are rapidly becoming an exporter of knowledge. This trend does not bode well for our future.

We need to address the problems in our educational system and raise it to the current global standard. If we don't, we may lose our ability to continue achieving the American Dream. Lack of accountability, outdated teaching methods and classes, lower standards and expectations, diminishing research grants for universities, and the skyrocketing cost of a college education all cause damage to one of America's strongest assets. Most Americans agree that our public education system needs to be improved, yet it is difficult to do so when teachers and schools have been charged with babysitting our children, feeding them properly, providing discipline, and taking on other responsibilities that were previously considered family obligations. Teachers affect student outcomes more than any other single factor, yet they are underpaid, often unappreciated, and increasingly constricted by the necessity of teaching to a competitive achievement test. At the same time, however, teachers unions have been resistant to attempts to introduce greater accountability and have gone out of their way to protect mediocre teachers as well as good ones. Faced with strong unions, a diminished tax basis, and a get-it-done-now attitude among parents, public school administrators are fighting an uphill battle. As a society, we need to revisit the obligations that families, teachers, unions, communities, government, and students themselves have in the educational process. This will be a difficult task, as there are many conflicting interests and opinions, but improving our educational system is of vital importance to the future of America.

7. Technological Advancement and Innovation

Technology is critical to the American Dream in that it is both a driver and a result of innovation. New technologies create new industries that provide jobs, which America needs, as well as life-saving and life-enhancing devices. In the past, people have been slow to accept new technologies and have taken their time adjusting to most types of change. Television, for example, took decades from its inception to be adopted by most American families. Today, by contrast, the rate of introduction and acceptance of new technologies is growing at an unprecedented pace. New communications technologies in particular are quickly adopted because they enable people to remain constantly connected to one another and quickly share ideas and socialize. Their introduction has created changes that are positive for many of us and enhance our lives in many ways.

Yet these technologies also diminish the quality of our lives. Children play at home by themselves on computers rather than in parks with other neighborhood kids, with the result that obesity, cyber-bullying, and isolation are growing problems. Letters delivered through the postal service have been replaced by faxes, e-mail, and social networks, and every communication seems to require us to immediately respond. We are connected to one another other twenty-four hours a day, taking away our ability to relax and decompress. Our homes, our cars—even our vacation spots—have been turned into hubs of constant activity, creating stress levels we've never experienced before. We text while we drive, we talk on our cell phones while we walk, and we feel out of touch when our e-mail and phones are not available. Ironically, this dependency on technology has made many Americans less satisfied with their lives rather than more satisfied.

Since these new communication technologies are here to stay, Americans will have to adjust to both the constant sense of connectivity and the change it creates, and find ways to preserve traditional values like quality family time. We need to set boundaries and limits for ourselves and our children and learn to make deliberate choices about how, where, and when we want to use these technologies so that they enhance our lives rather than detract from them. Young people in particular are prone to share everything about themselves online without considering what they should or should not keep private, a trend that parents often find alarming. As we become more skeptical about the intrusiveness of communications media, we may find ourselves facing an interesting conundrum: the pace of technological change we seek to slow for cultural reasons is in fact accelerated by our constant push for innovation and the economic growth it stimulates.

From a business perspective, innovation is being made increasingly difficult by insufficient global patent laws, piracy, and the breathtaking speed of worldwide communication. A photo from an iPhone of a new Calloway golf driver can be e-mailed to China the day it is launched, and a knockoff can be produced for sale within a week. The same can be said of the entertainment industry, where piracy has become an art form. These threats to our intellectual property are deeply troubling because with the life expectancy of new products very short, the financial gain associated with innovation is decreasing. If innovative new technologies are to attract significant research and development capital, this problem must be addressed. Doing so will mean that all of our global trading partners must admit to the existence of the problem, adjust their intellectual property laws, and act to consistently enforce them.

8. News and Entertainment Media

For the most part, Americans are remarkably optimistic and resilient. We realize that we live in the best country in the world, yet our optimism is rapidly being eroded by the negative messages we are constantly bombarded with. Television, radio, magazines, and the Internet all help us to form opinions regarding style, success, and normalcy. We strive for happiness—this is a core value associated with the American Dream—yet we are told by the media that we are too fat, too ugly, unsuccessful, and not as fulfilled as we should be. We continually hear stories and see images of wealthy and successful musicians, actors, athletes, and other celebrities and find ourselves and our lives lacking by comparison. The photographs we see are digitally manipulated creations that set an impossible standard of perfection, whether they're of a supermodel's face or a billionaire's mansion, as is the music we listen to. Concerts and political speeches are carefully staged, and even so-called reality television is a carefully concocted fantasy. With all of that to live up to, it's no wonder ordinary Americans feel unhappy and inadequate.

Nor is the entertainment industry entirely at fault. Modern news media thrives on fear and controversy, and this feeds Americans' sense of unhappiness as well. Newspapers, television, and radio were once sources of independent information and opinions, and presenting both sides of an issue fairly was a matter of journalistic integrity, but this is no longer true. Profitability has become the primary concern of the news media, and as a result the industry has become dominated by polarizing personalities who court controversy to increase ratings. The news programs we listen to and the blogs we read directly influence and reinforce our existing opinions, and even movies are often made with political agendas. As these media outlets generally present only one side of an argument, or a heavily biased viewpoint at best, Americans are increasingly polarized on many issues.

If America is to thrive, the idea of an independent, unbiased news media must return, or it will be replaced by bloggers and social media participants who spread their opinions in an even more one-sided, and often less truthful, manner. Our continued enthusiasm is essential in these difficult times, and media companies must take a step back and decide whether they want to be the provider of news or the presenter of toxic opinions. With ratings and profits at risk, this will be a major challenge for an industry already in a state of decline, so we must find a way to reinvent it on new terms. As consumers of news and entertainment culture, Americans must begin to tune out polarizing, pessimistic, and superficial messages in favor of news and entertainment sources that provide us with balanced, realistic, and authentic viewpoints.

9. Globalization and International Events

Since the time America emerged from isolationism and took its place as a leading world power, global economic and political events have had a significant impact on our perception of the American Dream.

We have always viewed our country as an exceptional place—a shining example and beacon of hope, opportunity, and democracy to the rest of the world. Throughout most of the twentieth century, military conflicts promoted the view, both here and abroad, that America is a safe and happy place. Yet the invention of weapons of mass destruction and the rise of terrorism has severely threatened our sense of security, making us feel somewhat powerless and uncertain. In a world where our basic security is always at risk, it is hard to feel confident about the future of the American Dream or the world in general.

Other international issues such as oil cartel pricing, environmental preservation, intellectual property protection, currency valuations, and human rights can have a profound impact on our lives as well. Due to the international scope of these issues, the ordinary American has little influence over them, but we feel the effects of international policy decisions on such matters every day. Nor can the United States simply make unilateral decisions on important global matters and expect the rest of the world to fall in line. We must persuade rather than bully, and as international events occur, work collaboratively and adjust to accommodate new political and economic realities.

A prime example of such an international event was the rise of global capitalism that occurred after the collapse of the Soviet Union, which ushered in a new phase of economic globalization as Russia, India, China, and other countries began to adopt free market policies. The result was a few billion additional people seeking the American Dream, but in their own countries and at lower wage rates. These hard-working people aspire to have everything we have, and they are willing to work hard to achieve their goals. China, in particular, has experienced some spectacular growth. Comparing national changes in GDP as a percentage of the world's GDP from 2003 to 2008, China's share grew by 67 percent while the United States' share fell by 20 percent. The overall size of the world economic pie is growing rapidly, but the United States is receiving a smaller proportion of that pie.

China will, at some point, have the largest economy in the world, followed by India. This is simply reality, and we cannot change it by closing our borders, enacting tariffs, and burying our heads in the sand. Whether we like it or not, the United States is now part of a global economy, one where countries are mutually dependent upon and inextricably linked to each other. In such a world, we cannot survive as a net importer of goods, a net exporter of knowledge, and provider of services. We must start manufacturing again and adopt policies that enable American businesses to compete in the new global marketplace. We must adapt the American Dream to global realities.

10. Military Conflict and Spending

America has been involved in military conflicts almost every twenty years since the start of the twentieth century, and these conflicts have significantly impacted our society in many ways. While it would be unwise to promote war as a good policy for America, it does have some positive side effects. During times of conflict, governments push for, and invest in, new technologies as a means of gaining a strategic advantage. These military technologies often lead to peacetime applications in areas such as communications, medicine, transportation, and electronics. In addition, military spending creates jobs in research and development, engineering and technical support, and manufacturing and distribution. Employment is typically higher during periods of military conflict, and immigration often increases as scientists and other highly educated citizens flee countries in areas of conflict in search of a more stable environment. Following World War I and World War II, America benefited significantly from the "brain drain" from Europe and Asia as scholars and scientists looked for a safe place to perform research and create new products. When considering where to make cuts in the federal budget, we must remember to consider the benefits a strong military provides not just in providing security but also in generating jobs and advancing technology.

At the same time, we must be careful to not overly rely on the strength and superiority of our military to influence international events, for doing so often has unfortunate and unanticipated consequences. America is a superpower, one that many militarily weaker countries find threatening, and thus they have united together to oppose our power. As a result, global conflicts have created some unusual partnerships that would have been unthinkable during the Cold War and earlier in history. These alliances have been created for political purposes, not because they make sense, and they have created international gridlock. Iran is a case in point. It has developed strong alliances with Russia and China that offset the influence America and its allies might have, which has brought progress on many important issues to a standstill. Today countries across the globe form alliances aimed at avoiding military conflict, which is good, but these alliances are sometimes used in a negative way. To offset this trend, America must concentrate on using its political power to create opportunities and stability at home rather than conflicts abroad.

The American Dream is based upon a stable United States, which today is complicated by many external conflicts and threats. Americans will unite to address a true threat to our security and way of life, but our government must respect this loyalty and use our military power to address genuine threats, not simply to promote economic or political interests. In short, we must choose our battles wisely. No country spends more money on defense than the United States, and that level of military spending places significant strain on our economy. Yet to eliminate military spending would have a negative impact on our economy, safety, employment, and future innovation. Balancing these complex agendas, while managing the federal debt, will be a major challenge for our future presidents and legislators.

11. Religious Freedom and Tolerance

Today most native-born Americans accept religious freedom as a given, yet this was the most important element of the American Dream to many early American settlers. One only has to consider what is happening in other parts of the world, particularly the Middle East, to realize the importance of religious freedom in creating a happy and stable life. As Thomas Jefferson wrote in his *Notes on Virginia*, "It does me no injury for my neighbor to say there are twenty gods or no God. It neither picks my pocket nor breaks my leg."[2] Religious toleration is a core principle of American society, one that we must be careful to preserve and respect.

Since the time of our country's founding, there has been a wall of separation between church and state to prevent the establishment of an official state religion, but this was not meant to keep religion out of our lives entirely. On the contrary, the First Amendment was intended to keep the government separate from religion in the sense of neither promoting nor hindering it. Some Americans are offended by what they perceive as the continued promotion of a Christian-based society, whether this is manifested in schools via the Pledge of Allegiance or school prayer, on our currency that bears the words "In God We Trust," or through the public observance of holidays such as Christmas. Others are upset by the banishment of religion from social life, particularly in schools, and the teaching of secular theories such as evolution that clash with their own beliefs.

We need to find a way to accommodate faith and spirituality in our lives without attacking either secular science or diversity of religious belief. One cannot deny that American society has, from its start, been fundamentally Christian based, and this is an important part of our heritage. We need to allow other religions the same opportunity to practice their traditions without discrimination, but Christians should also be free to openly celebrate their roots and observe the traditions that have supported America's development. Religious freedom is a gold standard in our society. If it is eliminated or diminished, American society as we know it will be weakened. The ability to practice one's chosen religion without discrimination is a source of happiness and contentment to most Americans. With so many other things to consider, religious freedom should be left alone and treated as a non-negotiable societal norm.

12. Personal Expectations and Priorities

America is the wealthiest society in the world, and we enjoy greater freedom than most of the world, yet many of us are not happy. While there are many reasons for this, the root of the problem is that our personal expectations have grown beyond our ability to reasonably satisfy them without compromising and twisting our priorities. We need to understand why this is true, because our unhappiness is having a negative impact on America's traditional optimism and resiliency and warping our perception of the American Dream.

The boom that America experienced after World War II did much to both increase our standard of living and inflate our expectations. We became a consumer culture, with increasingly sophisticated corporate marketing machines playing to our wants and desires while increasingly easy access to consumer credit made it all too tempting to satisfy them. We now accumulate stuff, much more than we actually need, and much of which we simply end up storing in a closet or throwing away. Worse, most of us simply have no concept of how much we're really spending and to what extent the things we buy make us truly happy. We need to become much more aware of why we buy things and whether they're truly worth the cost. In most cases, we would actually feel happier and more secure if we saved more, but our expenses tend to adjust to the level of our income and often to exceed it. To help finance this lifestyle, credit has become ubiquitous, and our debt has grown along with our consumption demands.

The growth in two-income households over the past fifty years has exacerbated this trend and created some significant changes in American society as well. Many women and young girls aspire to better themselves through education and challenging careers and are more financially independent than women were a century ago. Yet along with their increase in income, working women's—especially working mothers'—needs have grown, including a second car for the family, work clothes, and daycare for the children. In some cases these additional expenses eat up much of the additional income working women contribute to a household, begging the question of whether the tradeoffs involved are really worth it. In other cases, increased household income generated by a second working spouse enables the purchase of larger homes or second homes for vacations; multiple television sets, computers, and other electronic gadgets; and expensive travel; all of which have become expectations rather than luxuries. This change has had a significant impact on our perception of success, as many families have adjusted their material expectations to the level of two incomes.

It is one thing for both men and women to enter the workforce to achieve greater independence and personal fulfillment. This is an understandable and laudable goal, and given the high divorce rate in our country, an often necessary one as well. However, when married couples become parents and both spouses stay in the workforce simply to finance a level of material consumption that may not be making them very happy, it is time to reassess our priorities. There are tradeoffs between work and parenthood. Children from families with two full-time working parents are more influenced by their daycare providers, babysitters, or peers than by their parents, and in many cases not for the better. Now, as the availability of jobs declines in the United States, the historic roles of men and women are being challenged. We are at a crossroads: men who were previously the family breadwinners lose their jobs and stay home to care for the children while their wives work to support the family. Both men and women are at risk of losing roles that are core to their identities, and ultimately the two-income trap may detract from our happiness rather than add to it. We must ask ourselves what is more important to us—our families or our material wants—and adjust our expectations accordingly.

• • • • •

If we are to preserve the American Dream, we must create a society that meets the *needs* of its citizens, not their *wants*, while maintaining our core values. We cannot simply continue on our present course without bankrupting our country and denying the promise of the American Dream to future generations. The question becomes, do we try to use government to socially reengineer society and provide more guarantees, entitlements, and stability? Or do we accept that government cannot completely tame the business cycle and guarantee continuous economic growth, full employment, and prosperity? Do we return to the original version of the American Dream, which guaranteed equal opportunity for all without promising that success would be easy or universally attainable? Or do we insist on some greater level of equality, on closing the gap between the wealthy and the middle class—and if we do, will the middle class really be happier and more satisfied?

If we want the American Dream to survive, the answers to these questions are clear. We must learn to live within our means, keeping in mind that de-leveraging the American consumer will take time and have a negative impact on the American economy in the short term, since the economy is driven by consumer spending. The expansion of government entitlements such as health care insurance, which will require either higher taxes or cuts in other government programs in order to meet the promises made, will create additional hardships on many Americans. If the federal government accepts its responsibility to reduce our country's debts, deflationary forces may come into play, and this will further stymie economic growth, at least temporarily. Americans will not accept this without knowing that in the long run we will be better off if we endure some short-term hardships.

Convincing a nation of over 300 million people who are used to living the good life to accept such sacrifices will be a difficult task, although not an impossible one. As we saw in the wake of September 11, Americans are capable of coming together in support of a common goal, but it generally requires a shocking event to jolt us into action, as well as a transformational, charismatic leader to provide direction and purpose. Such leadership requires forthright honesty in explaining the challenges we face while at the same time providing hope and inspiration. Enthusiasm and hard work foster America's greatness. For Americans to feel that they are living in the best country on earth, they must have confidence, and one of the most valuable contributions future presidents and their administrations can provide to the American people is a renewed sense of confidence in the government and its ability to lead. This will require our citizens, politicians, and the media to work together to overcome our skepticism and restore our faith in the American Dream.

What all of this means from a practical perspective is that, both as a society and as individuals, it is perhaps time to consider lowering our material expectations and learning to live with less. We need to revise our vision of the American Dream to focus more on maintaining and appreciating the unprecedented standard of living we have managed to achieve rather than expecting it to rise indefinitely. This mental adjustment will not be easy, but we must learn to make more reasonable choices so that the house of cards we have built does not collapse upon our children and our grandchildren. As a nation, we must start making distinctions between federal spending that is an *investment*—meaning that we can expect a future return in the forms of job creation and economic growth—and *entitlements*, which are simply payments to individuals that, while they provide a better quality of life for the recipients in the short term, are of little collective benefit in the long term. We cannot solve all of the world's problems, and we must refrain from burdening future generations with crushing financial liabilities in the name of creating a better world for them.

The good news is that to some extent we are doing these things already, at least as individuals. Recessions are never pleasant, but they do force us to face up to the tough choices that we put off during better times and to discipline ourselves. This is shown by the fact that Americans' personal savings rate, which had become negative in recent years, jumped significantly during the recession. Now, in the aftermath of that recession, Americans are waking up from the excessive, materialistic version of the American Dream that has dominated us for the past half-century and asking, "Where do we go from here?" Do we continue to pursue ever-greater material wants, or do we start to acknowledge that doing so is futile and instead start to appreciate what we have—the highest standard of living in the history of the world? Can we focus less on upward mobility and instead find a way to live happier, more meaningful lives?

According to pollster John Zogby, there's reason for optimism. He argues in his latest book, *The Way We'll Be*, that even before the 2008 recession, Americans were starting to ask some serious questions about the role of materialism versus meaning in their lives and altering their priorities and expectations. During his research, Zogby found a number of significant trends that he believes are leading to a transformation of the American Dream, such as learning to scale back our material expectations; looking inward to find spiritual comfort; and demanding authenticity from the media, our leaders, and institutions. What all of this adds up to, Zogby notes, is:

> Collectively, the results of all the polling and investigation undertaken for *The Way We'll Be* have been more revealing and uplifting than I could have hoped for or predicted… Beneath the surface, I have found, millions of us live in quiet acceptance of the new boundaries that have been placed on us…The majority of Americans have mellowed in recent years. They've modulated their desire to acquire material things, adopting lifestyles that respect the environment and human rights, and they take a more critical attitude toward progress. Just as Americans rose to the occasion in World War I and World War II, so we have found that they are again willing to sacrifice for the broader public good, so long as—and this is key—they are certain the sacrifice is shared. That's especially true of such hot-button issues as global warming. Our polling consistently shows that people are well ahead of political leaders in their willingness to tone down acquisitiveness in order to reduce greenhouse gas emissions. But it's true more broadly, too. People want better lives, not more things to fill their hours with. Surprisingly, in ratcheting the dream downward, Americans are finding contentment in a land of less plenty.[3]

This shift in attitude is a positive step for our country, and it springs from Americans' core characteristics of self-reliance and optimism, some of our most enduring and appealing traits. Americans are fundamentally a hopeful people, which is the source of both our greatest strength and our greatest weakness. Optimism that comes from viewing the world through rose-colored glasses, from filtering out all of the problems we face in the misguided belief that America will always prosper simply because it is America, is naïve optimism— the sort of optimism that crumbles into despair in the face of a crisis. What we need instead is the sort of optimism that is grounded in reality—the sort that does not wither in the face of challenges or leave them for a later generation to solve. We need to take responsibility for our own lives and our problems and motivate ourselves to solve those problems in realistic ways rather than point fingers and fall into petty bickering. We must raise ourselves up rather than rely on others, including our grandchildren, to do it for us.

While taking personal responsibility as individuals is an important step in the right direction, that alone will not be enough to rebuild the American Dream. We also need to start working together to develop long-term solutions to our problems in ways that use institutions other than government, which is often a blunt and ineffective tool at best. Making government the solution simply condemns us to a never-ending cycle of partisan politics and vitriolic debate that ultimately gets us nowhere. Instead, we need to harness the creativity and talent of ordinary Americans rather than rely on politicians and bureaucratic experts to solve our problems. It is in the hearts and minds of our inventors, entrepreneurs, teachers, students, and yes, our factory workers and stay-at-home moms and dads that the solutions to our problems can be found. The American Dream has always been about seemingly ordinary people achieving extraordinary things, and ultimately, only when average citizens come together and apply themselves to the challenges of our day will we preserve the American Dream for those who come after us.

NOTES

Introduction
1. Adams, *The Epic of America*, p. 317.
2. Adams, *The Epic of America*, p. 318.

Chapter 1
1. Adams, *The Epic of America*, p. 8.
2. Gordon, *An Empire of Wealth*, p. 14.
3. Gordon, *An Empire of Wealth*, p. 15.
4. Franklin, *America's Original Entrepreneur*, p. xvii.
5. Franklin, *America's Original Entrepreneur*, p. 78.
6. Gaustad, *Benjamin Franklin: Inventing America*, p. 110.
7. Franklin, *The Writings of Benjamin Franklin*, vol. 3, p.6.
8. Franklin, *America's Original Entrepreneur*, p. 159.
9. U.S. Declaration of Independence.
10. Jefferson, rough draft of the Declaration of Independence.
11. Locke, *Two Treatises of Civil Government: Second Treatise*, ch. 5, sec. 27.
12. Locke, *An Essay Concerning Human Understanding*, ch. 21, sec. 52.

Chapter 2
1. Thomas Jefferson to William S. Smith, 13 November 1787 in *The Writings of Thomas Jefferson*, vol. 6, p. 373.
2. Publius, "The Utility of the Union," (Federalist Paper No.10).
3. De Tocqueville, *Democracy in America*, vol. 1, ch. 16, p. 252.
4. James Madison to Thomas Jefferson, 24 October 1787 in "Madison Explains the Constitution."
5. Publius, "The Utility of the Union," (Federalist Paper No.10).
6. Publius, "The Utility of the Union," (Federalist Paper No.10).
7. Publius, "Concerning Dangers from Dissensions," (Federalist Paper No.6).

8. Thomas Jefferson to James Madison, 20 December 1787 in *The Writings of Thomas Jefferson*, vol. 6. p. 392.
9. U.S. Constitution, art.1, sec. 8.
10. Thomas Jefferson to John Taylor, 28 May 1816 in *The Writings of Thomas Jefferson*, vol. 15, p. 23.
11. Thomas Jefferson to Albert Gallatin, 13 December 1803 in *The Writings of Thomas Jefferson*, vol. 10, p. 437.
12. Jefferson, *Notes on Virginia*, 1782 in *The Writings of Thomas Jefferson*, vol. 2, p. 230.
13. Gordon, *An Empire of Wealth*, p. 125.
14. Adams, *The Epic of America*, p. 115.
15. Section on Jackson summarized from Remini, *The Life Of Andrew Jackson*.

Chapter 3

1. Smith, *The Wealth of Nations*, vol. 2, p. 72.
2. Gordon, *An Empire of Wealth*, p. 228.
3. Evans, *They Made America*, p. 19.
4. Asbury, *All Around the Town*, p. 119.
5. Section on Vanderbilt summarized from Renehan, *Commodore*.
6. Publius, "The Powers Conferred," (Federalist Paper No. 42).
7. Ellis, *Founding Brothers*, p. 83.
8 *Dred Scott v. Sandford*.
9. Remini, *The Life Of Andrew Jackson*, p. 197.
10. Cullen, *The American Dream*, p. 84.
11. Cullen, *The American Dream*, p. 95.
12. Franklin, *The Writings of Benjamin Franklin*, vol. 10, p. 297.
13. Cullen, *The American Dream*, p. 95.
14. Hofstadter, "Abraham Lincoln and the Self-Made Myth," p. 11.
15. Abraham Lincoln to the Republicans of Boston, 6 April 1859 in Nichols, *Life of Abraham Lincoln*, p. 207.
16. Cullen, *The American Dream*, p. 94.
17. Lincoln, *The Gettysburg Address*, 19 November 1863 in Nichols, *Life of Abraham Lincoln*, p. 171.
18. Cullen, *The American Dream*, p. 74.

Chapter 4

1. Gordon, *An Empire of Wealth*, p. 148.
2. Evans, *They Made America*, p. 148.
3. Gordon, *An Empire of Wealth*, p. 160.
4. Micklethwait, *The Company*, p. 64.

5. Gladwell, *Outliers*, loc. 769-787.
6. Klepper, *The Wealthy 100*, p. 9.
7. Section on Vanderbilt summarized from Renehan, *Commodore*. Quote from p. xii.
8. Sumner, *What Social Classes Owe to Each Other*, p. 40.
9. Sumner, *What Social Classes Owe to Each Other*, p. 39.
10. Sumner, "Sociological Fallacies," p. 362.
11. Jefferson, Second Inaugural Address, 4 March 1805 in *The Writings of Thomas Jefferson*, vol. 3, p. 382.
12. Krass, *Carnegie*, p. 131.
13. Section on Carnegie summarized from Krass, *Carnegie*.

Chapter 5
1. Rezneck, "Distress, Relief, and Discontent," pp. 497.
2. Hoffman, *The Depression of the Nineties*, p. 109.
3. Adams, *The Epic of America*, p. 245.
4. Bryan, "A Cross of Gold."
5. Gordon, *An Empire of Wealth*, p. 250.
6. Gordon, *An Empire of Wealth*, p. 251.
7. Croly, *The Promise of American Life*, p. 205.
8. Croly, *The Promise of American Life*, p. 178.
9. Croly, *The Promise of American Life*, p. 185.
10. Croly, *The Promise of American Life*, p. 178.
11. Croly, *The Promise of American Life*, p. 181.
12. Croly, *The Promise of American Life*, p. 207.
13. Gordon, *An Empire of Wealth*, p. 273.
14. Morris, *Theodore Rex*, p. 138.
15. Wilson, First Inaugural Address.
16. United States Department of the Treasury, "FAQ: Taxes; History of Taxes."

Chapter 6
1. Adams, *The Epic of America*, p. 294. Gordon, *An Empire of Wealth*, pp. 288-289, 293.
2. Adams, *The Epic of America*, p. 245.
3. Gordon, *An Empire of Wealth*, p. 292.
4. Section on Hollywood movie studios summarized from Gabler, *An Empire of Their Own*. Quote from p. 6.
5. Section on Ford summarized from Watts, *The People's Tycoon*.
6. Section on Durant summarized from Madsen, *The Deal Maker*.
7. Murphy, "The Advertising of Installment Plans."

8. Murphy, "The Advertising of Installment Plans."
9. New World Encyclopedia contributors, "Wall Street Crash of 1929."
10. New World Encyclopedia contributors, "Wall Street Crash of 1929."

Chapter 7

1. New World Encyclopedia contributors, "Wall Street Crash of 1929."
2. Gordon, *An Empire of Wealth*, p. 321.
3. F.D. Roosevelt, First Inaugural Address, 4 March 1933 in Black, *Franklin Delano Roosevelt*, p. 270.
4. F. D. Roosevelt, Fireside Chat, 8 March 1933 in Black, *Franklin Delano Roosevelt*, p. 277.
5. Gulick, "Memorandum on Conference with FDR."
6. "Life Expectancy for Social Security."
7. F. D. Roosevelt, State of the Union Address to Congress, 6 January 1941 in Black, *Franklin Delano Roosevelt*, p. 609.

Chapter 8

1. Statistics in this paragraph summarized from Samuelson, *The Good Life and Its Discontents*, pp. 7-16.
2. Gordon, *An Empire of Wealth*, p. 353.
3. Gordon, *An Empire of Wealth*, p. 359.
4. Gordon, *An Empire of Wealth*, p. 359.
5. Samuelson, *The Good Life and Its Discontents*, p. 70.
6. Eichengreen, *The European Economy since 1945*, p. 57.
7. Samuelson, *The Good Life and Its Discontents*, p. 31.
8. Samuelson, *The Good Life and Its Discontents*, p. 174.
9. American Council on Education, "GI Bill Facts."
10. Easterbrook, *The Progress Paradox*, p. 21.
11. Kamp, "Rethinking the American Dream."
12. Gordon, *An Empire of Wealth*, p. 361.
13. Gordon, *An Empire of Wealth*, p. 371.
14. Gimbel, *Science Technology and Reparations*, p. 206.
15. Freedman, *John F. Kennedy in His Own Words*, p.127.

Chapter 9

1. Washington, *The Booker T. Washington Papers*, vol. 4, p. 10.
2. Washington, *The Booker T. Washington Papers*, vol 4. p. 508.
3. DuBois, *DuBois on Education*, p. 76.
4. King, *A Testament of Hope*, p. 619.
5. King, *A Testament of Hope*, p. 295.

6.   King, *A Testament of Hope*, p. 286.

7.   King, *A Testament of Hope*, p. 220.

8.   Abigail Adams to John Adams, 31 March 1776 in Rossi, *The Feminist Papers*, p. 10.

9.   John Adams to Abigail Adams, 14 April 1776 in Rossi, *The Feminist Papers*, p. 10.

10. Thomas Jefferson to Samuel Kercheval, 5 September 1816 in *The Writings of Thomas Jefferson*, vol. 15, p. 71.

11. Rossi, *The Feminist Papers*, p. 416.

12. Friedan, *The Feminine Mystique*, p. 11.

13. Friedan, *The Feminine Mystique*, p. 13.

14. Friedan, *The Feminine Mystique*, p. 13.

15. Friedan, "The National Organization for Women's 1966 Statement of Purpose."

16. Kennedy, "Executive Order 10925."

17. Johnson, "To Fulfill These Rights."

18. Johnson, "Executive Order 11375."

Chapter 10

1.   Samuelson, *The Good Life and its Discontents*, p. 70.

2.   Thomas Jefferson to A. L. C. Destutt de Tracy, 26 December 1820 in *The Writings of Thomas Jefferson*, vol. 10, p. 175.

3.   Eisenhower, Special Message to the Congress Upon Its Reconvening, 8 August 1960.

4.   Samuelson, *The Good Life and its Discontents*, p. 74. Quote from *Time*, December 31, 1965, p. 67B.

5.   Johnson, Remarks at the University of Michigan, 22 May 1964.

6.   Samuelson, *The Good Life and its Discontents*, p. 70.

7.   Section on Thomas Watson, Sr. summarized from Evans, *They Made America*, pp.356-365.

8.   Evans, *They Made America*, p. 365.

9.   Section on Thomas Watson, Jr. summarized from Evans, *They Made America*, pp. 367-375.

10. Samuelson, *The Good Life and its Discontents*, p. 111.

11. Samuelson, *The Good Life and its Discontents*, p. 116.

12. Samuelson, *The Good Life and its Discontents*, p. 114.

13. Lichtenstein, *State of the Union*, p. 147.

14. Lichtenstein, *State of the Union*, p. 142.

15. Samuelson, *The Good Life and its Discontents*, p. 119.

16. Samuelson, *The Good Life and its Discontents*, pp. 158-160.

17. Samuelson, *The Good Life and its Discontents*, p. 51.

Chapter 11

1. Samuelson, *The Good Life and its Discontents*, p. 70.
2. Samuelson, *The Good Life and its Discontents*, p. 198. Boyer, *When Time Shall Be No More*, p. 11.
3. Carter, "Crisis of Confidence."
4. Kirk, "Ten Conservative Principles."
5. Kirk, "Ten Conservative Principles."
6. Kirk, "Ten Conservative Principles."
7. Kirk, "Ten Conservative Principles."
8. Reagan, "A Time for Choosing."
9. Reagan, "A Vision for America."
10. Reagan, First Inaugural Address.
11. Wilson, *Constitutional Government*, p. 192.
12. Thoreau, "Civil Disobedience," p. 7.
13. Reagan, First Inaugural Address.
14. Heyward, *The Age of Reagan*, p. 203.
15. Heyward, *The Age of Reagan*, p. 204.
16. Heyward, *The Age of Reagan*, p. 201.
17. Heyward, *The Age of Reagan*, p. 202.
18. Heyward, *The Age of Reagan*, p. 206.
19. Heyward, *The Age of Reagan*, p. 191.
20. Heyward, *The Age of Reagan*, p. 593.

Chapter 12

1. Evans, *They Made America*, p. 377.
2. Gordon, *An Empire of Wealth*, p. 395.
3. Section on Gates and Kildall summarized from Evans, *They Made America*, pp. 410-414.
4. Friedman, *The World Is Flat*, p. 70.
5. Samuelson, *The Good Life and its Discontents*, p. 142. Poll results are from *American Enterprise*, March/April 1993, pp. 87-90.
6. Kamp, "Rethinking the American Dream."
7. Calder, *Financing the American Dream*, p. 302.
8. Hayward, *The Age of Reagan*, p. 223.
9. Hochschild, *Facing up to the American Dream*, p. 83.
10. Section on Russell Simmons summarized from Evans, *They Made America*. Quote from p. 454.
11. Evans, *They Made America*, p. 454.
12. Evans, *They Made America*, p. 455.

Chapter 13

1. Statistics in this section summarized from Easterbrook, *The Progress Paradox*, pp. 3-34.
2. Easterbrook, *The Progress Paradox*, pp. 163-165, p. 180.
3. Easterbrook, *The Progress Paradox*, p. 32.
4. Samuelson, *The Good Life and its Discontents*, p. 56.
5. Easterbrook, *The Progress Paradox*, p. 168, based on research by Edward Diener at the University of Illinois.
6. Pizzigati, *Executive Excess 2006*, p.31.
7. Crary, "More Men Get Economic Boost from Marriage."
8. Erickson, *The Motherhood Study*, p. 4.
9. Altman, "The Great Crash," p.2.
10. Obama, "What Is Required: The Price and Promise of Citizenship."
11. Kamp, "Rethinking the American Dream."
12. Obama, "What Is Required: The Price and Promise of Citizenship."
13. Carrol, "Bush Deficit vs. Obama Deficit in Pictures."
14. Social Security Board, "Security in Your Old Age."

Chapter 14

1. Thomas Jefferson to Thomas Cooper, 1802 in *The Writings of Thomas Jefferson*, vol. 10, p. 342.
2. Jefferson, *Notes on Virginia*, 1782 in *The Writings of Thomas Jefferson*, vol. 2, p. 221
3. Zogby, *The Way We'll Be*, p. 24.

BIBLIOGRAPHY

Adams, James Truslow. *The Epic of America*. Garden City, NY: Garden City Books, 1931.

Altman, Roger C. "The Great Crash, 2008: A Geopolitical Setback for the West." *Foreign Affairs*, January/February 2009, http://www. foreignaffairs.org/20090101faessay88101/roger-c-altman/the-great-crash-2008.html.

American Council on Education, "GI Bill Facts," *Today's GI Bill*, http:// www.todaysgibill.org/todays-gi-bill/gi-bill-facts.

Ariely, Dan. *Predictably Irrational: The Hidden Forces That Shape Our Decisions*. New York: HarperCollins, 2008.

Asbury, Herbert. *All Around the Town*. New York: Thunder's Mouth Press, 2003.

Black, Conrad. *Franklin Delano Roosevelt: Champion of Freedom*. New York: Perseus Books, 2003.

Boyer, Paul S. *When Time Shall Be No More: Prophesy Belief in Modern American Culture*. Cambridge, MA: Harvard University Press, 1994.

Bryan, William Jennings. "A Cross of Gold." Address to the Democratic National Convention, Chicago, 9 July 1896. Reprinted in American Rhetoric, http://www.americanrhetoric.com/speeches/ williamjenningsbryan1896dnc.htm.

Calder, Lendol. *Financing the American Dream: A Cultural History of Consumer Credit*. Princeton, NJ: Princeton University Press, 2001.

Cannon, Lou. *Governor Reagan: His Rise to Power*. Cambridge, MA: Perseus Books, 2003.

Carrol, Conn. "Bush Deficit vs. Obama Deficit in Pictures," *The Foundry*, 24 March 2009. The Heritage Foundation, http://blog.heritage. org/?p=4210, accessed October 1, 2010.

Carter, James E. "Crisis of Confidence." Televised address, Washington D.C., 15 July 1979. Reprinted in The Carter Center, http://www. cartercenter.org/news/editorials_speeches/crisis_of_confidence.html.

Crary, David. "More Men Get Economic Boost from Marriage," *ABC News*, 19 January 2010, http://abcnews.go.com/Business/wireStory?id=9598134.

Croly, Herbert. *The Promise of American Life*. New York: MacMillan, 1909.

Cullen, Jim. *The American Dream: A Short History of an Idea That Shaped a Nation*. Oxford: Oxford University Press, 2003.

DeTocqueville, Alexis. *Democracy in America*. New York: George Dearborn & Co., 1838.

Dred Scott v. Sandford, 60 U.S. 393 (1857). Reprinted in Digital History, http://www.digitalhistory.uh.edu/documents/documents_p2.cfm?doc=23.

Dubois, W.E.B. *DuBois on Education*. Edited by Eugene F. Provenzo. Walnut Creek, CA: AltaMira Press, 2002.

Easterbrook, Gregg. *The Progress Paradox: How Life Gets Better While People Feel Worse*. New York: Random House, 2004.

Eichengreen, Barry. *The European Economy since 1945: Coordinated Capitalism and Beyond*. Princeton, NJ: Princeton University Press, 2008.

Eisenhower, Dwight D. Special Message to the Congress Upon Its Reconvening, 8 August 1960, http://www.presidency.ucsb.edu/ws/index.php?pid=11901.

Ellis, Joseph. *Founding Brothers: The Revolutionary Generation*. New York: Alfred Knopf, 2001.

Erickson, Martha F. "The Motherhood Study: Fresh Insights on Mothers' Attitudes and Concerns." Report by the Institute for American Values, New York, 2005, http://www.americanvalues.org/pdfs/motherhoodexsumm.pdf.

Evans, Harold, Gail Buckland and David Lefer. *They Made America: From the Steam Engine to the Search Engine: Two Centuries of Innovators*. New York: Little, Brown, and Company, 2004.

Franklin, Benjamin. *Ben Franklin: America's Original Entrepreneur: Franklin's Autobiography Updated for Modern Times*. Edited by Blaine McCormick. New York: Entrepreneur Press, 2005.

Franklin, Benjamin. *The Writings of Benjamin Franklin*. Edited by Albert Henry Smyth. New York: MacMillan, 1905.

Freedman, Eric and Edward Hoffman. *John F. Kennedy: In His Own Words*. New York: Citadel Press, 2005.

Friedan, Betty. *The Feminine Mystique*. New York: Dell Publishing, 1973.

Friedan, Betty. "The National Organization for Women's 1966 Statement of Purpose," The National Organization for Women, http://www.now.org/history/purpos66.html.

Friedman, Thomas L. *The World Is Flat: A Brief History of the Twenty-First Century*. New York: Farrar, Straus and Giroux, 2005.

Gabler, Neal. *An Empire of Their Own: How the Jews Invented Hollywood*. New York: Crown Publishers, 1988.

Gaustad, Edwin S. *Benjamin Franklin: Inventing America*. Oxford: Oxford University Press, 2004.

Gimbel, John. *Science Technology and Reparations: Exploitation and Plunder in Postwar Germany*. Stanford: Stanford University Press, 1990.

Gladwell, Malcolm. *Outliers: The Story of Success*, New York: Little, Brown, and Company, 2008. Kindle e-book.

Gordon, John Steele. *An Empire of Wealth: The Epic History of American Economic Power*. New York: HarperCollins, 2004.

Gulick, Luther. "Memorandum on Conference with FDR Concerning Social Security Taxation," summer 1941. Reprinted in "Research Note #23 Luther Gulick Memorandum re: Famous FDR Quote," Social Security Online, http://www.ssa.gov/history/Gulick.html.

Hayward, Steven F. *The Age of Reagan: The Conservative Counterrevolution*. New York: Random House, 2009.

Hochschild, Jennifer L. *Facing up to the American Dream: Race, Class, and the Soul of the Nation*. Princeton, NJ: Princeton University Press, 1995.

Hoffman, Charles. *The Depression of the Nineties: An Economic History*. Westport, CT: Greenwood Publishing, 1970.

Hofstadter, Richard. "Abraham Lincoln and the Self-Made Myth," in *The Best American History Essays on Lincoln*, edited by Sean Wilentz. New York: Palgrave MacMillan, 2009.

Jefferson, Thomas. Rough draft of the Declaration of Independence, as presented to Benjamin Franklin and John Adams for correction, prior to submission to committee. As reprinted in "The Declaration of Independence: Rough Draft," Independence Hall Association, http://www.ushistory.org/declaration/document/compare.htm.

Jefferson, Thomas. *The Writings of Thomas Jefferson*, Memorial Edition (Lipscomb and Bergh, editors), 20 vols., Washington, D.C., 1903-04. University of Virginia Library, http://guides.lib.virginia.edu/TJ.

Johnson, Lyndon B. "Executive Order 11375," 13 October 1967. Reprinted in the National Archives online, http://www.archives.gov/federal-register/executive-orders/1967.html.

Johnson, Lyndon B. Remarks at the University of Michigan, Ann Arbor, MI, 22 May 1964, http://www.lbjlib.utexas.edu/johnson/archives.hom/speeches.hom/640522.asp.

Johnson, Lyndon B. "To Fulfill These Rights." Commencement Address at Howard University, Washington D.C., 4 June 1965, http://www.lbjlib. utexas.edu/johnson/archives.hom/speeches.hom/650604.asp.

Kamp, David. "Rethinking the American Dream." *Vanity Fair*, April 2009, http://www.vanityfair.com/culture/features/2009/04/american-dream200904.

Kennedy, John F. "Executive Order 10925," 6 March 1961. Reprinted in the National Archives online, http://www.archives.gov/federal-register/executive-orders/1961-kennedy.html.

King, Martin Luther. *A Testament of Hope: The Essential Writings and Speeches of Martin Luther King, Jr.* Edited by James M. Washington. New York: HarperCollins, 1990.

Kirk, Russell. "Ten Conservative Principles," adapted from *The Politics of Prudence*, ISI Books, 1993. Reprinted in The Russell Kirk Center for Cultural Renewal, http://www.kirkcenter.org/index.php/detail/ten-conservative-principles.

Klepper, Michael and Robert Guenther. *The Wealthy 100: From Benjamin Franklin to Bill Gates—A Ranking of the Richest Americans, Past and Present.* Secaucus, NJ: Carol Publishing Group, 1996.

Krass, Peter. *Carnegie.* New York: John Wiley & Sons, 2002.

Lichtenstein, Nelson. *State of the Union: A Century of American Labor.* Princeton, NJ: Princeton University Press, 2002.

"Life Expectancy for Social Security," Social Security Online, http://www. ssa.gov/history/lifeexpect.html.

Locke, John. *An Essay Concerning Human Understanding.* Kitchener, ON: Batoche, 2001. University of Virginia Library, http://etext.lib.virginia. edu/toc/modeng/public/LocHuma.html.

Locke, John. *Two Treatises of Civil Government.* Charlottesville, VA: InteLex Corporation, 1990. University of Virginia Library, http://etext. lib.virginia.edu/toc/modeng/undone/LocTrea.html.

Madison, James, to Thomas Jefferson, 24 October 1787. Reprinted in "Madison Explains the Constitution to Jefferson," James Madison Center for Liberty and Learning, James Madison University, http:// www.jmu.edu/madison/gpos225-madison2/madexpcontojeff.htm.

Madsen, Axel. *The Deal Maker: How William C. Durant Made General Motors.* New York: Wiley & Sons, 1999.

Mattson, Kevin. *"What the Heck Are You Up to, Mr. President?": Jimmy Carter, America's 'Malaise,' and the Speech That Should Have Changed the Country.* New York: Bloomsbury USA, 2009.

Micklethwait, John, and Adrian Wooldridge. *The Company: A Short History of a Revolutionary Idea.* New York: Random House, 2005.

Morris, Edmund. *Theodore Rex.* New York: Random House, 2001.

Murphy, Sharon. "The Advertising of Installment Plans," *Essays in History*, vol. 37. (Corcoran Department of History at the University of Virginia, 1995.)

New World Encyclopedia contributors, "Wall Street Crash of 1929," *New World Encyclopedia,* http://www.newworldencyclopedia.org/entry/ Wall_Street_Crash_of_1929?oldid=938422 (accessed October 1, 2010).

Nichols, Clifton Melvin. *Life of Abraham Lincoln*. New York: Crowell & Kirkpatrick, 1896.

Obama, Barack. *The Audacity of Hope: Thoughts on Reclaiming the American Dream*. New York: Crown Publishers, 2006.

Obama, Barack. "What Is Required: The Price and Promise of Citizenship." Inaugural address, Washington D.C., 20 January 2009, http://www.americanrhetoric.com/speeches/barackobama/ barackobamainauguraladdress.htm.

Pizzigati, Sam, ed. *Executive Excess 2006: Defense and Oil Executives Cash in on Conflict*, the 13th Annual CEO Compensation Survey from the Institute for Policy Studies and United for a Fair Economy, www.ips -dc.org/files/155/ExecutiveExcess2006.pdf.

Publius. "Concerning Dangers from Dissensions Between the States." *Independent Journal*, 14 November 1787. Reprinted in "Federalist Paper No.6," Constitution Society, http://www.constitution.org/fed/ federa06.htm.

Publius. "The Utility of the Union as a Safeguard Against Domestic Faction and Insurrection." *Daily Advertiser*, 22 November 1787. Reprinted in "Federalist Paper No.10," Constitution Society, http://www. constitution.org/fed/federa10.htm.

Publius, "The Powers Conferred by the Constitution Further Considered." New York Packet, 22 January 1788. Reprinted in "Federalist Paper No.42," Constitution Society, http://www.constitution.org/fed/ federa42.htm.

Reagan, Ronald. "A Time for Choosing." Television address, Los Angeles, 27 October 1964, http://www.nationalcenter.org/ReaganChoosing1964. html.

Reagan, Ronald. "A Vision for America." Election eve address, 3 November 1980, http://www.presidency.ucsb.edu/ws/index. php?pid=85199.

Reagan, Ronald. First Inaugural Address, Washington D.C., 20 January 1981, http://www.presidency.ucsb.edu/ws/index.php?pid=43130.

Remini, Robert V. *The Life Of Andrew Jackson*. New York: Perennial Classics, 2001.

Renehan, Edward. *Commodore: The Life of Cornelius Vanderbilt*. New York: Basic Books, 2007.

Rezneck, Samuel. "Distress, Relief, and Discontent in the United States During the Depression of 1873–78," *Journal of Political Economy,* vol. 58, no. 6, (December 1950): pp. 494–512

Rossi, Alice S., ed. *The Feminist Papers: From Adams to de Beauvoir.* Lebanon, NH: Northeastern University Press, 1973.

Samuelson, Robert L. *The Good Life and its Discontents: The American Dream in the Age of Entitlement.* New York: Time Books, 2008.

Social Security Board, "Security in Your Old Age." Washington D.C., 1936. Reprinted in "Social Security Numbers: 1936 Pamphlet on Social Security," Social Security Online, http://www.ssa.gov/history/ssn/ssb36.html.

Smith, Adam. *The Wealth of Nations.* New York: P.F. Collier & Son, 1902.

Smith, Anthony, ed. *Television: An International History.* Oxford: Oxford University Press, 1995.

Sumner, William Graham. "Sociological Fallacies," *Earth-Hunger and Other Essays.* New Haven, CT: Yale University Press, 1913.

Sumner, William Graham. *What Social Classes Owe Each Other.* New York: Harper & Brothers, 1883.

Thoreau, Henry David. *On the Duty of Civil Disobedience.* Radford, VA: Wilder Publications, 2008.

U.S Constitution, as reprinted in "Constitution of the United States", The National Archives online, http://www.archives.gov/exhibits/charters/constitution.html.

U.S. Declaration of Independence, as reprinted in "Declaration of Independence," The National Archives online, http://www.archives.gov/exhibits/charters/declaration_transcript.html.

United States Department of the Treasury, "FAQ: Taxes; History of Taxes," http://www.ustreas.gov/education/faq/taxes/history.shtml#q2.

Van Dulken, Stephen. *Inventing the 20th Century: 100 Inventions That Shaped the World.* New York: Barnes & Noble, 2007.

Washington, Booker T. *The Booker T. Washington Papers.* Edited by Louis R Harlan. Chicago: University of Illinois Press, 1975.

Watts, Steven. *The People's Tycoon: Henry Ford and the American Century.* New York: Random House, 2006.

Wilson, Woodrow. *Constitutional Government in the United States.* New York: Columbia University Press, 1917.

Wilson, Woodrow. First Inaugural Address, Washington D.C., 4 March 1913, http://usinfo.org/PUBS/LivingDoc_e/wwilson1.htm.

Zogby, John. *The Way We'll Be: The Zogby Report on the Transformation of the American Dream.* New York: Random House, 2008.

INDEX